THE TAGGER HERD COLLECTION TWO

From Book One
The phone call that changed their lives forever

The phone was still ringing, so she hit the answer button and raised it to her ear.

"The Stables," she answered.

There was hesitation before the person spoke. When she did, Dru could tell it was an older woman. "Can I speak with the owner please?" She said quietly.

"I am one of the owners, Dru Tagger."

There was more hesitation. "Oh…good. I'm so sorry to bother you."

She hesitated long enough that Dru could add, "No bother at all, how can I help?"

"Well," another hesitation. Even over the phone Dru could tell she was upset.

"I'm not really sure how to start," the woman paused. "My name is Cora Smith and my husband, Wes, passed away a little over three weeks ago."

Well that was a start, Dru frowned. "I'm so sorry."

"Yes, well, thank you. I received a phone call a few minutes ago," she hesitated again, "I'm a bit confused about the call."

"Was it from someone here at The Stables?"

"No, I got your number from a card my husband had in his wallet."

"Do you have horses? Was your husband looking for somewhere to board them?"

"No horses. We sold all our horses a couple years ago."

"OK…" Dru walked away from the arena and the excited chatter from the two teenagers talking about the last day of school.

"That's what's so strange about the phone call I received. The man who called said he would be delivering the hay in the morning."

"Did they call from Tagger Enterprises for the hay?"

"No."

Dru quietly exhaled in rising confusion. "Hay for what?"

"I don't know; we don't have any animals. I canceled the hay order from the man, but now I'm worried," The woman's voice trembled as she continued. "My husband was being very secretive before he died. He even shipped me to Seattle to spend time with my sister for a couple weeks."

Dru still wasn't sure what this had to do with The Stables.

The woman on the phone continued, "We live in Lenore, but I haven't been there since a week before he died."

"Mrs. Smith," Dru leaned against the back of the building. "I'm a bit confused. How can The Stables help?"

The voice let out a frustrated sigh, "I am afraid my husband bought some animals without telling me and they have been at our home in Lenore, unattended, for over three weeks."

Dru slowly stood away from the building, "Horses, sheep, cattle, chickens…a lot of animals can forage for themselves for three weeks."

"Yes," The woman's voice was a little stronger since she had finally voiced her concern. "After my husband died, we had him brought to Seattle and buried here, with family. I haven't been to our home now for over a month. I have no one there to call to go check the property. With your card here… well, I thought maybe he had talked to you about this."

"No, not with me," Dru frowned. "I'll talk to the manager here to see if he spoke with your husband. If not, then we'll take a drive and check." This could be a total waste of time… she HOPED it was a total waste of time. "You have no idea what kind of animals he may have bought?"

"No," she sighed, "I'm just so worried. The man with the hay was so adamant that my husband had bought the hay AND that it was scheduled to be delivered in the morning."

"Did he say how much hay he was delivering?" It was coming on summer when most large animals would be grazing in pastures and not be dependent on hay. The first hay crop was coming off the fields. He could have been stocking up for winter.

"He didn't say."

"OK, I'll go check it out," Her parents and grandparents had taught her to have respect for animals. Something in her gut told her to make the drive. She wouldn't be able to forgive herself if there were animals suffering because she didn't have time to take a drive 30 miles up the river.

www.thetaggerherd.com

ISBN: 978-1-7339528-4-2

THE TAGGER HERD

Collection Two

A Series by

Gini Roberge

The two men below were the first to know the book existed
and were the first to read it. Through their encouragement I
continued with the series.
Our 'courier' Emily is Ben's wife and now a good friend of
mine as well as their daughter Kenzie.

SPECIAL THANKS TO

BEN SMITH, DVM

For Your Input and Editing Expertise

And the courier Emily!

AND

STEVE ROBERGE, BRO
My sounding board, encouraging voice, and special editor

THE TAGGER HERD SERIES

BOOK SIX

Matt Tagger

Gini Roberge

CHAPTER ONE

Matt stepped into his mother's bedroom to see her peeking through the curtains to the front pasture. She was stunning in her sleeveless lace wedding dress that was just long enough to touch the tops of her new white cowboy boots. There was no hat or veil covering her beautiful blonde hair that flowed in large curls down her back.

She turned and smiled; blue eyes shining with happiness and love.

"Drusilla Anne Tagger, you are the most beautiful bride I have ever seen." He walked to his mother and leaned in to kiss her on the cheek; she sighed in contentment.

"Thanks, my handsome son."

He was wearing the same clothes that Grayson, Scott, Jack and Reilly were wearing for the wedding; black denim jeans and a short sleeve white western dress shirt.

"I'm glad you insisted on everyone being comfortable and no suits or tuxes," He glanced out the window at the growing crowd. The seats were filling quickly.

"I don't know. You would have been quite striking in a tux," She teased.

They stood quietly for a moment, looking at the south pasture where the wedding would take place under the two oak trees that were planted in memory of his grandparents. The reception would be in the north pasture under the trees planted in memory of his great-grandparents.

Grace, Sadie, and Nora were waiting at the pasture gate and wore blue dresses which matched Nikki's, the maid of honor. The day before the wedding, his mother had treated all the women with a day at the spa. The girls were still ecstatic over their manicures and pedicures. They all wore their hair in high ponytails.

Matt and his mother watched as the last guests were seated. Every chair was filled. The music changed and Jack, with Reilly at his side, started walking up the aisle.

"It's time," Matt turned to his mother; the happiness radiating from her warmed his heart. He proudly held out an arm and she slid hers through his. They headed out the door, then down the hallway and steps. Music from the front yard made its way into the house.

As they walked through the front doors, Matt looked out at the pasture and chuckled. "I can't believe you insisted the herd be allowed in the pasture during the ceremony."

His mom laughed softly. "In a way, they are responsible for this day happening. They're a part of the family."

"Well, hopefully they'll have a little respect and not relieve themselves during the ceremony."

"Matt!" She laughed. "Besides, look at Grayson, he couldn't be happier having Eli to occupy his attention away from the wedding."

Grayson was sitting at the end of the first row; Eli standing next to him.

"That horse..." Matt laughed.

They made their way down the steps of the porch and across the green grass to the open gate that led to the pasture.

Nikki and the girls were waiting for them at the gate and Matt's eyes went to his sister. She looked as stunning as his mother in her light blue dress. Nikki leaned in and kissed him on the cheek then did the same to their mother. The girls giggled excitedly seeing the bride for the first time.

"Aunt Dru, you're beautiful!" Grace's eyes shined.

"You are!" Sadie and Nora chimed in.

His mom kissed each one of them on the cheek.

"Now, head out," She said to all the girls. "Let's get this over with."

They all giggled again and Sadie turned to walk down the aisle, followed by Nora, then Grace. Nikki kissed her mother's cheek again then turned and walked slowly down the aisle to take her place to their left, opposite a smiling Jack and Reilly.

"Look at the grin on Reilly's face," Matt whispered.

"I think he's happy," She laughed and Matt thought it sounded like wind chimes in a summer breeze.

He started to step forward, but his mother didn't move. He turned to see her staring up at the large oak trees with tears in her eyes. He understood; it was her moment with her parents and grandparents. She sighed and turned glistening eyes to him, a tear slowly made its way down her cheek.

Matt gently wiped the tear away. "They would have loved Jack," he said softly.

"Yes, they would have." She nodded and took a step forward.

Just as they approached the first row of chairs, Matt stopped. She glanced up in surprise.

He was looking down the aisle at Reilly; the teenager was staring at his 'soon to be mother' with a look of absolute joy.

Matt turned to his mother, "There are times I forget that not everyone has had the privilege of having a caring, loving mother like I have." His voice cracked so he swallowed hard and cleared his throat softly. "I wish everyone had a mother like you." Her eyes welled up with tears again. "Thank you, Mom, for everything." He leaned down and kissed her cheek again.

"Matt!" She leaned into him. "I love you and Nikki with all my heart and soul."

"And now we welcome Reilly in that fold."

"I grew to love Reilly a long time ago."

"We all did…and Jack."

"Oh, yeah," She giggled softly. "Him too…"

They started walking slowly down the aisle. Eli was standing by Grayson, but Harvey, Buttercup and Rufio had made their way over to see about the commotion. Cooper was standing behind the archway, his head held high watching them.

"That's such a bizarre sight," Matt chuckled. "We should have put veils on all the mares." They both chuckled at the image.

The gathered guests smiled at the mother and son as they walked slowly down the aisle.

When they stopped in front of the minister, Grayson and Scott stood and joined them. Nikki and Grayson stood to the left of his mom and Scott stood with him to her right. They faced the minister, a beaming Jack, and a grinning Reilly, who was bouncing with excitement.

The minister spoke; "Who gives this woman to be wed?"

Matt looked down at his mom, over to his sister, and then to his uncles. Finally he looked across at Jack and spoke. "We won't give her away… but we'll share her."

Matt felt his mom's arm squeeze his, as the wedding guests laughed.

"I'm fine with that," Jack grinned at him.

"Me too!" Reilly nearly yelled, which made everyone laugh again.

Matt leaned down and kissed her cheek for a third time, took her hand and very happily placed it in Jack's outstretched hand. As his mother stepped away from him and toward Jack, he realized that he was as happy to have Jack as a step-father, as Reilly was to have her as a step-mother.

Matt took his place next to his sister and their hands instinctively grasped together.

As the ceremony progressed, Matt looked at the first couple rows of guests. Jessup, Cora, and Andy, with his sons and grandkids, were up front and smiling proudly. His wife, Clara, had passed away a few years before.

Nick, the bride's ex-husband, had offered to take care of the ranch so Jessup could attend the wedding weekend. Reilly's girlfriend Kelly, Nora, Grace and Sadie were giggling as they watched Reilly; who was still bouncing. Wade sat at the end of the row with his lariat over his knees. He was slowly circling the coils with his fingers.

Matt looked over at his uncles, who were holding their wives' hands and proudly watching their sister marry the love of her life. He felt the tears well in his eyes when Grayson and Scott both turned at the same time. His love of those two men, as his dads, was almost overwhelming to him at that moment. They both understood and nodded to him.

Nikki squeezed his hand and he turned in time to see his mother and Jack kiss for the first time as husband and wife. Reilly yelled. The guests laughed again.

As Jack and his mother started their walk back down the aisle, Reilly raced over to Nikki and Matt and threw his arms around their necks; the teenager's whole body was shaking in excitement. Once he broke the embrace, Nikki put an arm through Matt's and one through Reilly's. The new brothers and sister walked down the aisle beaming in happiness.

Nikki opened the gate between the two pastures and greeted the guests as they moved to the reception. Reilly and Matt were stopping the horses from walking through. The last ones through were the bride and groom who had taken a moment in The Homestead, just the two of them. The five of them stopped next to the gate to have a family moment together. Hugs and kisses were shared then they walked, as a new family, to the reception.

***

Matt slowly climbed the five steps up onto the back porch and into the kitchen. He had smiled so much his face muscles were hurting. He walked to the large front window of the living room and glanced out at the crowd. As much as he loved everyone, he enjoyed the quiet in the building. He looked for his mother. Reilly had finally left her side but was constantly looking over at his new mom. Matt smiled; he was a good kid, with such a weird bouncing addiction.

Jack walked behind his new wife and slid his hands around her waist; she leaned back into him as he bent down and kissed her neck. A wide grin spread across her face. Matt sighed at her happiness.

He heard the sound of someone opening the backdoor so he made his way to the library. Before stepping into the room he looked at the matching elk horns that decorated each side of the entry door. Good memories, Reilly had told him with a contented smile. "They were meant to be together."

The library was one of Matt's favorite places. Whether reading, playing on the computer or just hanging out at the long table or two large couches, it was the one place that all the kids 'hung out'. Matt made his way to the framed college degrees on the wall. The middle degree was from the University of Idaho and awarded to Grayson Mathew Tagger. There were two other degrees, one on each side of Grayson's. They were formatted and framed the same and were presented to Drusilla Anne Tagger and Scott Anderson Tagger and they were signed by Grayson and Andy, the neighboring ranch owner and mentor to the Trio.

As if on cue, Andy walked into the room.

"So, this is where you disappeared to," Andy laughed. Matt smiled at the elderly farmer. Both his knees were crippled and he had to walk with two canes, but he wouldn't let that stop him. His sons had taken over the ranch but let Andy do whatever he could to help. Matt turned and pulled out a chair for Andy and helped lower him into the chair.

"Just a little break," Matt said then leaned against the wall. He saw Andy's eyes make their way up to the college certificates. The older man sighed, but beamed a proud smile.

"Those were some rough times for your mother and uncles," Andy nodded at the memories. "After the accident, Grayson tried to quit college but Dru talked him into staying. She convinced him that the knowledge he would learn would be worth the extra time she had to work at the ranch." Andy looked up at Matt. "She is one of the hardest workers I've ever met; man or woman. She was pretty close to the same age as Nikki is now. Imagine Nikki handling the ranch, basically by herself," He sighed. "Scott was there every minute after he graduated from high school which Grayson and Dru insisted he finish." Andy glanced back up at the degrees. "Scott and Dru poured over Grayson's books when he came home. He'd record every lecture and they would sit together listening carefully. What I couldn't teach them they learned from the college and by asking questions from anyone and everyone that would help."

Andy adjusted his legs on the chair. "It was a proud day when I got to watch Grayson receive his diploma," He chuckled at Matt. "Grayson and my boys designed the others and gave them to Dru and Scott later that night. They deserved them."

Andy was silent a moment, then looked up at Matt. "The day their parents and grandparents died was devastating to them…understandably. I honestly didn't think they were going to make it at first, but after the first branding…seeing their determination, I knew they would."

The elderly neighbor glanced out the window at the lively crowd. Music had started playing and everyone had started dancing.

"You should be out there," Andy told him.

Matt nodded and helped him stand.

Andy looked up at him. "When are you going to tell her?"

"After they get back from the honeymoon," Matt answered without thinking; then looked down at Andy in surprise. He hadn't told anyone. "How did you know?"

"You don't get this old and not learn a thing about reading people. I know the last thing you'd want to do is hurt her, but you have a sadness that comes with knowing you're going to." They made their way out of the library. "Good plan though; let her have her day…she deserves it. Never seen two people so happy together…except maybe Grayson and Leah." He chuckled again. "Better say me and the Misses were too or she'll have my hide when I meet up with her again!"

Matt helped him out the front door and down the steps. He walked next to the elderly man as he thought about his decision. Knowing how hard his mother and uncles had worked for their education made his decision that much worse. She was not going to be happy he was dropping out of college.

CHAPTER TWO

"Reilly! Make sure it goes in my truck and not Mom's." Matt shouted from the back door and saw the teenager turn and grin at the word 'mom'.

"I will. I can't wait!" Reilly continued running to the trucks and threw the bag in the back of Matt's truck.

"Dru, hurry up." Scott yelled from behind him.

"I'm coming!" She laughed and skipped down the stairs. She was dressed in a tank top and shorts...which she very rarely wore. "Just had to grab the tube of sunscreen you gave us."

"Can you believe her?" Scott asked him as he walked out the back door.

"I have too, I'm her son," Matt laughed and kissed his excited mother on the cheek when she stopped next to him. Jack walked up behind her and, with hands at her waist, playfully pushed her the rest of the way out the door.

Matt helped Jack with the last of the bags they were loading into her truck. They were all packed for the rafting trip Scott had given them for Christmas. It had turned into a honeymoon for the newlyweds.

Cora was taking care of Wade, Sadie, and Nora. Having said goodbye to their parents, they had already left to ride at The Stables. Grayson, Leah and Jordan were already in the truck and waved goodbye. Scott crawled into the backseat next to his wife. All that was left was for his mom and Jack to get in so they could leave.

Matt hugged her again and watched as she embraced Reilly. Grace, who was standing next to Reilly, was also pulled into the hug.

Matt laughed, "Mom, they're going to leave you behind."

She stepped back and looked at the three of them with concern in her eyes.

"You three be VERY careful out there," she said seriously.

"Mom, we're just going up there for a couple of days. I've ridden there before with Jessup," Matt assured her. "I mapped out all the trails that we're taking for Jessup. He knows the area and he agreed they were fine for us and the horses…nothing's going to happen."

"Yeah, but you're there camping for a couple of nights." There was genuine concern in her eyes.

"Mom, it's going to be OK," Reilly assured her. He grinned again because he used the word 'mom'.

She placed her hands on each side of Reilly's face and kissed his forehead, "I love that." She smiled at his use of the word, too.

Jack walked up next to her. "You guys be safe. We'll be out of phone service until Thursday." He looked at his new wife then back up at his sons, "You know she'll be on the phone the second we get back to the trucks. The guides estimated it will be in the afternoon around 3:00."

"We'll be fine," Matt repeated as his mother pulled him and Reilly into another embrace. "Jack, do something!" Matt laughed.

And he did…Jack quickly turned his new wife, grabbed her around the waist and threw her over his shoulder. She screamed and her long legs kicked out in mid-air. A round of laughter and cheers could be heard from the truck.

"I love you kids, be careful!" She shouted as Jack placed her in the truck.

"You, too!" Matt laughed.

"Don't drown!" Reilly yelled.

Grace, Reilly, and Matt stood in the driveway and watched the truck turn onto the road and drive of sight.

Matt turned and looked at the two fifteen-year-olds he was taking for a two night horseback trip to the mountains. It was a brother's bonding trip and training for the younger horses. They looked up at him excitedly.

"I think we have everything packed," Grace smiled. "All we need are the horses!"

Matt turned to the barn. "Which ones did you decide to take?"

"Buttercup for me," Grace answered. "Dad rode Eli all week at the ranch."

"Cooper or Rufio?" Matt asked Reilly.

"I think Cooper," He answered. "So we'll have Trooper, Cooper, and Buttercup can be the pooper." They all laughed…it was going to be a fun couple days.

***

They passed Spalding Bridge as they drove up Highway 12. The road took them by Orofino, Kamiah, and up to their destination; The Weitas wilderness area in the Clearwater National Forest.

"What do you think the horses would do around the river?" Reilly asked.

Matt shrugged, "We haven't really worked them around water yet."

"Is there a place we can stop?" Graced asked excitedly.

He thought about the river ahead. There were many pullouts, but most were high above the river and the embankment was too steep to reach the water. There was one beach that would probably work. "I think Gibbs Eddy will work."

"Can we get the horse trailer down and back up?"

Matt nodded. "No problem."

There was only one car at the beach when they arrived, so Matt had plenty of room to maneuver the truck and trailer. There were two exits from the parking lot so he wouldn't have to turn the trailer around.

Grace and Reilly were already climbing out of the truck before he turned the engine off. Matt chuckled at their exuberance, but he was just as excited to see how Trooper reacted to the flowing water.

The ground was more large rock than sand so they kept next to the boat launch. Matt called out to the eager teenagers, "Watch for holes in the sand where kids played."

"OK," A reply in unison came back to him.

They walked the brown, black, and cream colored horses right up to the water, none of them flinched until they were turned and were expected to put a hoof in. Cooper was not impressed and continued to back-up when Reilly tried to move him forward. It was the same reaction Cooper had when Jack had stepped into the saddle the first time. Reilly quietly calmed the horse with his voice and stroked the black horse's long arched neck.

Grace patiently encouraged her cream-colored Buttercup to walk into the water; the horse put a hoof in then quickly took it out.

"Well, at least she didn't back up like Cooper," Reilly told Grace with a laugh.

Grace tried again and Buttercup took two steps in then stopped. Her nose dropped to the water and she took a drink. They could see the horse's body relax. When Buttercup was done drinking, her head went up alertly looking at the group of people playing just down river.

"Hold her tight in case she gets spooked," Matt told her.

Her grip tightened on the lead rope, but Buttercup just stood quietly.

"Well, she likes water better than she likes cows," Reilly laughed.

Matt nodded in agreement. Buttercups first frantic meeting with the cows at the ranch was panicked. She had stood spread legged and looked for Eli for help.

"Your turn, Matt," Grace turned to him in anticipation.

"OK, Trooper," Matt said turning to his big brown horse. "Let's show them how it's done."

Matt walked next to the water and turned Trooper so the horse would have to step in the water to stay beside him. Trooper stepped in without hesitation and they walked as much of the river as they could without going into the large rocks. At one point, Trooper stopped and drank while pawing and splashing the water.

"Wow, he really is a trooper," Reilly said in amazement.

"Trooper the trooper," Grace laughed, and her laugh was so infectious, Reilly and Matt started laughing too.

"Let's use him to train the others," Matt suggested. "Reilly, bring Cooper up right behind him, Buttercup in the back. Maybe that will encourage him not to backup, but Grace keep an eye on him and BE CAREFUL." Matt instructed then started walking in circles so only a small portion of the circle was in the water.

Trooper walked in and out of the water without a problem, but Cooper scooted to the side since he didn't want to back into Buttercup. Reilly held him firmly and talked to him patiently. Buttercup walked at the water's edge but not into it.

They circled again, then again, then again….Matt just kept them going. Pretty soon, Cooper had stopped side stepping and would allow a little water to touch his hoof, and Buttercup was walking in past her hocks without flinching.

"Good enough for the first time," Matt told his companions.

"They got much better!" Grace grinned.

As they walked towards the trailer, they heard someone yelling from behind. He turned to see the woman from the other car walking up to them. She was waving to get them to stop.

"Hi, I'm sorry for interrupting your day," The woman called out.

"No problem, Ma'am," Matt smiled.

"I was wondering if you would mind if my kids could come pet your horses?" she asked.

"Of course!" Grace answered.

"They are so beautiful," The woman said before turning and waving at her family. She turned back and looked at Matt. "I couldn't help myself; I took a few pictures with my phone of the three of you walking in the water with them."

"...or trying to." Reilly laughed.

Matt gave the woman his phone number so she could send the pictures. She worked on her phone while her husband, daughter, and two sons were entertained by the horses. Grace retrieved some of the mint horse treats and showed the family how to feed it to the horses. The three kids were all younger than Sadie and each took turns giving the treats and petting the animals.

"That was fun," Grace smiled as they loaded the horses back in the trailer.

"I think we made their day," Reilly added.

Matt looked at his phone and downloaded the pictures the woman sent him. He forwarded them to his mother so they would be the first thing she saw when they reached cell phone service on Thursday.

He drove the truck and horse trailer out of the beach parking lot and waved at the family. The kids were so happy, they were jumping and waving with both hands. He could hear them calling the horses by name and telling them goodbye.

Matt grinned and headed down the highway, it was a great start for their adventure.

***

"Let's stop at the store," Reilly turned to Matt as they drove into Kamiah, the last town they would drive through before reaching their campground.

Matt chuckled, "Don't you think you have enough food already?" They had raided Cora's pantry, took nearly everything they could see that would fit in the saddle bags, plus there were all the meals she had prepared and were stored in coolers.

"I can never have enough food!" Reilly laughed.

Matt pulled into the parking lot of the grocery store. He agreed with Reilly, you can never have enough food.

They wandered down the aisle of the store not really in need of anything. Grace had picked up another bottle of vitamin water, Reilly picked up more cookies, and Matt spotted a clearance sale on energy bars. They didn't take up much room in the saddle bags so he grabbed the whole box.

Finally, with more food loaded in the truck, they turned back down the highway.

"What's that town?" Grace said pointing to the right.

"Kooskia," Matt smiled. The highway skirted the outside of the town so most traveler's didn't stop and check out the historic town. "You ever been there?"

"No." Came the answer in unison again.

"Have you?" Grace asked.

"Yeah, one of my ex-girlfriends made me go to a play there."
Matt grinned remembering the pretty blonde.

"Was it any good?" Grace asked.

"What was she like?" Reilly asked.

Matt laughed at their two totally different questions, "Yeah the play ended up being really good and I enjoyed myself and Reilly…the girl? Well…" He raised a brow at the teenage boy.

Reilly smiled and nodded.

"Oh, you two!" Grace laughed, which made all three of them laugh.

CHAPTER THREE

They turned off the highway and followed a narrow dirt road for, what Grace called, "forever!" before Matt saw the road he was looking for.

"Are you going to get the trailer stuck?" Grace asked him worriedly.

"Not intentionally," Matt laughed.

"The trees are so thick that there's no way we can ride through them!" Grace turned wide eyes to him. "Are we just riding on the road?"

"It opens up in a little bit and has a large field we'll camp by tomorrow night. I can use it to turn the trailer."

"How did you find this place?" Reilly asked.

"Jessup," Matt answered. "He used to bring me and Nikki here for a weekend or two each summer. Two years ago we spent a week up here and rode the whole time, it was a blast. We had planned for last year, too, but we cancelled to take care of the horses."

These mountains and the mountains at home were the reason for Matt choosing Forest Management in college. He wanted to work with Trooper in different mountains and streams; areas the horses hadn't seen before. He was hoping that bringing the three horses here for training would help change his mind in leaving school. The classes were boring and sitting in the lecture halls had started to get on his nerves by the last days of school. Even with the future classes being outside, he just wasn't sure he could tough it out.

This trip needed to be the wild card that kept him from telling his mother he wanted to quit college.

The weather in July had been a mixture of rain and sunshine. The days leading up to the wedding were rainy, which had caused a bit of turmoil with the wedding plans, but Matt was thinking ahead to campfires at night in the wilderness. Without the rain, the area would be too dry for fires. The last thing they needed was to cause a huge forest fire.

They followed a long dirt road that had a thick wall of trees on both sides. It then opened to a beautiful meadow filled with tall grass and colorful wild flowers in yellow and purple. The sky was light blue with just a few tufts of clouds. The mountains seemed to go on forever behind the horizon full of flowers.

Both the teenagers sat up in their seats.

"Oh, Wow!" Grace cried out. "I'm glad I brought a camera!"

"The horses are going to love this place!" Reilly said.

Matt smiled and kept driving. He knew that they would be impressed; it was the same reaction he and Nikki had when Jessup brought them the first time.

They followed the dirt road to the left next to the trees. Small camp sites had already been developed but Matt was looking for the site that Jessup had taken them to. It already had poles strung between the trees as a makeshift corral for the horses. He found it, and backed the horse trailer into the space already cleared for campers.

Reilly had jumped out of the truck and was assisting Matt back the trailer so he didn't hit anything. Grace excitedly looked out into the meadow.

"It's so beautiful," she whispered. "I can't wait to ride Buttercup through the flowers."

"Let's make sure to get a picture of you doing it, too," Matt suggested. "Leah would love that."

"Oh yes! Good idea." Graced smiled at him.

Matt adored his beautiful cousin. He was three when she was born and he would place her in his wagon and pull her around the ranch everywhere he went. When he was six and she was three, he decided Grace needed to see the fall branding corrals. He loaded her in the wagon, with cookies and water for both of them, and walked all the way by himself.

It wasn't until years later that he was told that Grayson and Leah had walked just inside the trees and followed them the whole way to the corrals and back. They watched him pick Grace up and walk her around the corrals and through them, telling her about the branding and how it worked.

Matt was excited that he could be the first one to show Grace these beautiful mountains that he had fallen in love with.

"Out you go," He told her as the truck finally stopped.

He didn't have to tell her twice as she jumped out of the truck to join Reilly. They ran across the road and out into the meadow. Reilly stared at the beautiful mountains and Grace spun circles in the wildflowers.

As quick as he could, Matt grabbed Grace's camera and took pictures of the unrelated twins as they walked through the meadow together. That will be a great surprise for her.

Normally the two would be responsible for unloading their own horses, but today he decided to give them time together in the meadow and unloaded all three excited horses. He placed hay and the water bucket into their makeshift corral. They were only going to be in this camp until after lunch, then they would ride out for a sleepover in the mountains. The plan was to come back the next night, Monday; then do a couple day-trips out of this base camp.

Matt pulled out all the coolers and saddle bags. Going through the different food, he loaded the saddle bags. He first placed bottles of water in all the bags, then took all his energy bars and stuffed around the bottles. If they had any bars left after this trip, they could always use them at the ranch. On top, he placed granola bars, Reilly's cookies, cheese, crackers, more cookies, Cora's special trail mix, and sandwiches.

Matt looked inside the cooler at what remained; the best thing was Cora's homemade apple pie. They would save that for tomorrow; an incentive for the ride back.

He lifted all the saddle bags to make sure they weren't too heavy and check that they were balanced correctly. He didn't want to create soars on the horses from too heavy or unbalanced loads rubbing on them.

His horn bag was filled with a camp saw, map, and a GPS. Reilly's contained the flashlight, emergency lite sticks, and binoculars. Grace had a foldable camp frying pan, trail marking tape, matches, and small first aid kit.

The bed rolls were attached behind the saddles. The evenings were pretty warm, so they may not need them to sleep in while they lay next to the campfire, but they make a good ground cover.

All three of them carried a rifle in a gun scabbard. As beautiful as the mountains were, they were dangerous too; mainly bear, mountain lions and wolves. Lariats were also in their normal place on the saddles.

Matt glanced up in time to see Reilly and Grace headed his way. They couldn't have looked any happier or relaxed. They quickly ate a large lunch, so they could get on the trail.

The horses were saddled, truck secured, and riders mounted.

They rode across the meadow and, as promised, Matt took Grace and Buttercup's photo while they galloped through the mountain flowers with the far reaching mountain ranges behind them. The blue sky highlighted her perfectly. It was a beautiful sight. They made their way across the meadow of green grass and purple and white flowers. The more Grace laughed, the more Buttercup pranced.

Matt rode behind the two teenagers so he could watch their reactions to the new discoveries. The same thing Jessup had done when it was Matt and Nikki's first visit. At the top of one ridge, they stopped and watched a doe and fawn make their way across another flowered meadow. Another ridge, in the distance was a small herd of elk...mostly cows and a few little bulls. Reilly was anxious to see the big bulls.

"What is it about elk and deer here that make them different from the ones we see at the ranch?" Grace laughed.

"I know!" Reilly agreed. "I just can't get enough of 'em."

Matt took them along a game trail that led to a clearing that had a perfect view of a crystal blue lake. While they stopped to take in the beauty of the scene, Reilly found little frogs to catch and toss at Grace. Not being the typical girl, she tried to catch them and toss them back. All little frogs were released back to their peaceful life and the riders moved on.

They rode a couple more hours along the ridge of a mountain overlooking the North Fork river below. The wind seemed stronger near the edge. Reilly and Matt pulled their cowboy hats down tighter to keep them from flying off. Grace took hers off altogether so the wind could play in her hair.

Reilly pulled out the binoculars and spotted rafters making their way down a large section of rapids in the river.

"That's what Mom's doing!" Reilly grinned at Matt.

Matt laughed, "And, so is your Dad."

"Yeah, him too," Reilly chuckled.

Matt and Grace took their turns with the binoculars; looking at the river, rafters, hillsides, and finding any animal they could. Next time…they would have to bring more than one pair of binoculars.

The sun began to reach too far west making Matt start scouting camp sites. He found the perfect site tucked into a wall of lodge pole pine trees.

It didn't take long before the saddles were pulled from the horses and camp set up for the night. The horses were tied to a rope high-line between the trees. Dry tree limbs, blown to the ground by the wind, were gathered for the campfire.

Their bed rolls were placed around the campfire and they were tucked in for the night before the last light of day disappeared. They laughed and joked all evening while they prepared dinner and set up camp.

"So," Matt looked between the two campers, "How does it work with both of you dating the same girl?"

Grace snorted and Reilly laughed.

"I'm not dating her," Grace finally giggled.

"I don't know," Matt teased. "Every time I see you, it's all three of you together."

"Just friends," Grace told him. "I like her, but wish she had a brother just like her."

"Gracie and I are together all the time anyway." Reilly rolled onto is back and looked up at the stars. "We're just lucky that Kelly likes both of us and Grace likes her, too."

"So, there is no third wheel in your relationship. The problem will be when Grace finds a boyfriend and he becomes the fourth wheel." Matt nodded as he stared into the fire. There was something hypnotic about watching the fire dance in the darkness of the night.

"We're hoping to find a brother and sister combo that get along as well as we do, so Reilly and I can still hang out," Grace chuckled.

"So, what is her story?" Matt asked.

"She's in the middle of a custody battle between her mother and her grandparents; her late dad's parents," Reilly explained. "If her mother wins she has to move back to Bellingham, if her grandparents win, then she stays in Clarkston."

"Wow, that's got to be tough," Matt shook his head.

"She focuses on the horses and work...it helps her," Reilly explained. "They are trying to get it settled before school starts; so, she should know in the next month."

"Well, it's good that the two of you can be friends for her now," Matt told them. "But, promise me something."

"What?" They said in unison...again.

"You two are still pretty young and you'll have lots of boyfriends and girlfriends in the future. Don't let them tear your friendship apart." He glanced over at each of them; they were both staring at the stars. "If the boy or girl is coming between the two of you, then they aren't the right person. There will always be another boyfriend or girlfriend around the corner, but it's only once in a lifetime, if that, when you find a friendship like yours."

"OK, Matt," Grace said sleepily.

"Sometimes it's hard to see that we're doing it when we're in the middle of it all," Reilly said while he yawned. "Let us know if you see it happening."

"I will," Matt said as he closed his eyes.

CHAPTER FOUR

"Let's get going! We're burning daylight!" Matt hollered at the two lazy teenagers who were putting out the fire. They had slept most of the morning while he fixed them breakfast and brushed out the horses.

"OK, Mr. Anderson." Reilly laughed as he referred to the quote from John Wayne's character in Wade's favorite movie 'The Cowboys.'

"We've been up pretty high and skirted most of the creeks," Matt said as he stepped into the saddle. "I thought we're ride about two hours out to a really nice bluff, then down the mountain a ways to a few streams. There are a lot here, and they'll give us a good opportunity to work on Buttercup and Cooper going through moving water."

"That's a great idea," Reilly nodded.

"The smaller ones they'll probably jump over, but I know a really good one that should be calm and wide enough to train them...without scaring them," Matt added as they rode out. He turned to make sure nothing was left behind at the camp. Other than the small doused fire pit, no one would be able to tell they were there.

They rode at an easy pace towards the bluff he wanted them to see. It was a peak, about half way across the mountain top and looked down into a wide valley with beautiful meadows. Whenever he came with Jessup, they had always seen elk or moose in the meadow.

"Matt, look!" Grace turned excitedly and pointed down the mountainside. Her camera was up and quickly taking pictures.

There were at least thirty elk grazing and sleeping in the green grass. A few elk saw them and stood at attention but didn't leave.

The three riders dismounted and sat on rocks to watch the herd graze. A large bull sauntered out of the trees to their right and wandered over to a smaller bull to push at him with his nose and threaten him with his antlers. The bigger bull grazed peacefully as the sunshine highlighted his tan hide and lit the ivory colored areas of his massive horns.

"This is almost as relaxing as watching the Tagger herd out in the pasture," Reilly whispered.

"What's that?" Grace whispered and pointed down the mountain. "It looks like a squatty bear."

Matt turned to see a wolverine making his way across the meadow. He told the pair what it was and warned them to stay away from the mean little critters. They looked cuddly but they were wicked with long claws and sharp teeth.

They watched the wolverine until he reached the trees then casually mounted the horses and headed on. He led then along the mountain top until they reached sheer drop-offs and moved away from the ledge. When they moved back, there were rock slides that reached all the way down to the river.

In the far distance, Matt could see their destination. He called out to Grace, and as she turned he heard an odd noise behind him. Her eyes lifted over his head and shock registered across her face.

Matt turned in time to see a small airplane headed right at them. The noise he had heard was a sputtering engine. The horses spooked and jumped sideways as the plane flew just thirty feet above their heads.

"Hold on!" Matt yelled as they tried to get Buttercup and Cooper in control. Trooper had jumped, but didn't run.

The plane was gliding down towards the bluff that he had been headed for.

"Come on!" Matt yelled and kicked Trooper into a gallop. He wanted to get to the bluff and see where the plane was going.

They ran across the mountain top. The plane turned left and gained height then it turned right, completing a 180 degree turn so it was heading back at them. Then it dipped down to his left. It was heading towards the meadows he knew was there, but couldn't yet see.

Matt reached the bluff top just as the plane touched down into the meadow. Grace and Reilly pulled the horses to a stop next to him. All three watched as the plane skidded across the meadow towards a wall of trees. It's engine silent.

"They're going to crash!" Grace cried in horror.

The plane skidded across the meadow, hit something that caused it to jump about twenty feet in the air, then it hit the ground again. It slid into the trees enough they couldn't see anything but the tail sticking out. There was no loud crash sound, no fire, or explosion.

"What do we do?" Reilly turned to Matt with anxious eyes.

Matt stared at the plane, then turned and looked back at the trail they had just ridden. He calculated the amount of time it would take to get back. After their afternoon ride the day before, their morning ride, and the run they just completed they were a long distance from the truck. They couldn't run the young horses all the way back, and he wasn't sure they could get there before dark. By the time they got to town to call for help, it would be well after dark. Which meant search and rescue wouldn't arrive to the plane until morning.

He turned back and looked at the plane and calculated they could make it down in a couple of hours, dependent on the obstacles they ran into; other than the steep mountainside. If someone was going to need help, it would be within the first couple of hours.

Matt looked up at Grace and Reilly who were watching him intently.

"We go to the plane crash," Matt decided.

"Do you want me to go back for help?" Reilly offered nervously.

"No," Matt shook his head. "We stay together."

Matt rode to the edge of the mountainside to plan their trail. Everything looked good up to a row of trees about half way across. They stood between them and the plane. He couldn't see what was on the other side; it could be cliffs, rock slides, bluffs, or open range. He hoped for open range, so they could get down faster.

"Grace, you have the trail marker tape. I'm going to take the lead and you come up behind and mark our trail. You should always be able to see one marker from the other."

"Got it!" She said and opened her horn bag. The tape was neon yellow and they should be able to see it at a good distance to make their way back.

"We'll ride at an angle down this mountain and into the trees," Matt told them. He programmed their location into the GPS, then started Trooper down the mountain.

Halfway down, Matt realized they were going to lose sight of the plane as they drew closer to the trees. He turned to Reilly, "Check to see if there is any movement down there."

Reilly pulled the binoculars from the saddle bag, then shook his head.

They pushed on and reached the trees. Matt sighed in dread. The trees were so thick they could barely see through them.

"We're going to have to walk through." Matt turned to his companions and they dismounted. "Keep your head low and let the cowboy hat take the assault of the tree limbs."

The horses still had halters on under the bridles, so they attached the lead ropes and walked into the tangled mess.

It took forever to push through the tree limbs and brush.

"You guys, OK?" He yelled back to the teenagers.

"Glad I have a long sleeve shirt on," Grace answered.

"Tired of trees, but good," Reilly answered.

If only the horses could speak. All three horses had followed their rider without a problem. Trooper's head was tucked into Matt's back. It made Matt grin; the clever horse was using him as a shield.

"Well, at least the horses are getting some different training than normal," Matt yelled. He glanced up to see how far they had left to go; only about ten feet.

When Matt stepped out of the trees and looked up, his heart sunk; rock slide.

They stared at the rock slide while Matt struggled with the next decision. About forty feet across the mountain it dropped off and out of sight, so they didn't really know how wide the rock slide was or what to expect when they got there.

Going up would be near impossible. Going down led them to the river where they couldn't cross without risking their own lives and those of the young horses.

"At least it's not extremely steep," Reilly said encouragingly.

"We have to keep moving," Matt told them. "If I had Monty, or one of the ranch horses, I'd ride across. But these three don't have enough experience going across rocks like this and we don't want to risk our own lives."

"So we walk it, too?" Grace asked.

Matt nodded and started walking forward.

"It's going to be tough footing for them, so don't walk too fast. Take it slow; we don't need twisted knees and ankles from horse or human." He took a few steps out. "Get some distance between you and your horse so he can see the ground."

"She," Grace giggled nervously.

Matt started walking while looking in front and mapped out their best trail across the rocks. Occasionally he looked back and watched Trooper pick and choose his footing before moving. The horse was going along better than expected. Matt's appreciation of the horse grew.

He was nervous as they approached the rise in the mountain. The best case scenario was the ground turning to grass and dirt open range. The worse was more landslide…impassable landslide.

When he crested the hill he stopped and sighed.

"What's it look like?" Reilly asked from behind.

"About sixty feet of landslide, then open range." Matt told him.

"That's not bad." Reilly called back.

"Most of it is shale, though." Shale was flat and slick, making it hard to walk on. At an angle, it was just plain dangerous.

"Dang…" Grace muttered.

Matt stared at the other side of the rock slide, wishing he was already there.

"Matt?" Grace asked.

"What?"

"What are you doing?" She asked.

"Trying to figure out the best way to tackle this," He stepped up the hill so he could see around Trooper and back to his companions.

They stood quietly looking at him.

"We can do this," Grace smiled encouragingly.

"We can do this," Matt nodded at his confident cousin. "But, one at a time."

He stepped in front of Trooper and slowly made his way across the slick shale. The sound of the horse's metal shoes hitting and sliding on the rock started to grind on his nerves making his back muscles tighten. There was one spot that dipped to a cliff's edge. He held his breath going over. Matt made sure that he was far enough away from Trooper so the horse could see the dip and prepare for it or step around. The horse did, with no problem; Matt let out a huge sigh of relief.

Matt slipped twice, but landed on his butt rather than a knee. At least it was padded, he chuckled to himself. The worst part about the sliding of both him and Trooper was knowing when he got to the other side, he would have to watch Grace and Reilly come over with Buttercup and Cooper.

He nearly jumped like a kid on a playground when he finally stepped onto the grass. Trooper instantly put his head down and started grazing.

"OK, Reilly," Matt called out. "There is one spot about three quarters of the way you need to watch for. Hopefully, Cooper won't freak out and back up; if he does, you have to let go."

Reilly nodded grimly and slowly started walking across the slick shale. The tension in Matt's back and the pressure behind his eyes grew with each step of horse and rider.

Reilly was nearly at the dip in the slide when he tripped and fell forward; his boots slid on the shale. Just when Matt thought he was going to land on his butt, he slipped and went down on his side…the rock gave way…Reilly's eyes looked to him in panic as he slid down the mountain and out of Matt's sight.

Matt's heart raced as he let go of Trooper and started running across the shale as fast as he could; slipping the whole way.

"Reilly!" Both he and Grace called out in terror.

The lead rope attached to Cooper was pulled to its tightest, the horse's head low with his nose pointed towards the unseen rider; his legs bracing from being pulled forward.

"Back!" Reilly yelled.

"What?" Matt called out only half way to his new brother. His pulse was racing, heart nearly pounding wildly.

"Cooper! Backup!" The unseen Reilly yelled again. The horse took a tentative, strained step backwards.

Matt stopped, not wanting to startle or distract the horse.

"Back up, Cooper," Reilly repeated. The horse took another couple steps.

"Keep going, Boy," Matt whispered under his breath.

Grace and Buttercup stood like statues.

"Backup, boy, backup, Cooper…" Reilly kept talking to the big black horse and the horse took a tentative step with each command. Cooper was still stretched out, head low, and grunting against the weight on his rope.

Finally, Reilly's hands could be seen gripping the rope so tightly that all of his fingers were white from the strain. Then his head appeared as he swung a boot up onto the rock and pulled himself onto the trail and into a sitting position…his face was pale.

"Dang!" Reilly sighed, looking between his best friend and his brother as he stroked the nose of the black horse. "I love, Nora."

"What?" Matt asked with a very relieved and confused chuckle.

"We have a competition in the arena with backing up the horses," He explained. "She won so many times, we finally made her teach us how to train our horses to back up as good; with leg and voice commands."

"I love, Nora," Grace agreed.

"Me, too," Matt exhaled. "Now, get over here," He smiled at his brother.

Reilly made it the rest of the way without incident and rubbed down his horse.

"Well, this is one time that I was glad Cooper backed up," Reilly laughed nervously.

They both turned to watch Grace and Buttercup.

Grace walked at the end of the lead rope giving Buttercup as much room to see the ground as possible. She watched every place she put her foot, making sure she didn't trip, too. She looked like a ballerina walking across a stage.

Buttercup's back left hoof would ping on the rock then scrape and slide off the side and into midair causing Matt to hold his breath until they were both across safely.

Everyone sighed in relief when they made it across.

"That was GRACE-full," Reilly joked.

Matt chuckle nervously, then turned and looked across the mountainside, down to the plane. If he didn't know exactly where it was, he probably wouldn't have noticed it. He could just barely see it over the rise of the next slope.

"Reilly, can I see the binos?" He asked.

"Matt?" Reilly answered. "My horn bag is gone."

Matt looked over at Cooper's saddle. Saddlebag, rifle, lariat, and bed roll were there, but no horn bag. It must have gotten caught when they went through the trees.

"Grace, you still have all your stuff?" Matt asked while double checking his.

"Yeah, I'm good," she answered.

"The lights were in my bag," Reilly sighed.

Matt nodded. Both the flashlight and emergency lite sticks were in Reilly's bag with the binos. The nights in the mountains were pitch-black, and without lights it could be dangerous.

"Well, lesson learned," Matt sighed. "Next time we split them between all the saddle bags, not just one."

"I'm sorry, Matt," Reilly said.

"Not your fault, Reilly," Matt said, as he stepped onto the saddle. "I packed the saddle bags." No time to stress over it, they needed to get moving.

Matt turned and looked down at the plane. "I can't see anything moving from here."

"Me, either." The other two answered in unison…again.

There was open range of grass, flowers, and a final stand of trees between them and the plane. They should make good time now. Once they were all on their horses and they started the ride down the mountain.

"Matt?" Grace was riding between him and Reilly.

"What?" He pulled his eyes from the plane crash and looked at her.

"What if they're drug runners?" She smiled tentatively.

"Dang, Grace!" Matt rolled his eyes.

"I can't help it," she giggled.

"There are hundreds of possibilities, and you come up with that one?" Reilly laughed.

"This is the first time I've thought about who is in the plane," She explained with a shrug.

"It went over so fast," Matt tried to remember everything he could. "It was not a two person plane, that's for sure."

"Had to be four or six…" Reilly guessed.

"Could be anybody from a single pilot, to a band, to corporate executives, to drug runners…" Matt smiled at Grace. "We could guess all day and probably still be wrong."

They rode quietly threw a thicket of trees and came out in a clearing only fifty yards from the plane…there was no movement.

CHAPTER FIVE

They slid off the horses and started walking towards the plane; there was no sound. Matt looked around to see if there was anyone lying on the ground, maybe they were thrown or crawled out. What condition would the people be in with such a violent crash?

"Stop," Matt told them, almost at a whisper. His heart was racing and hands shaking.

"What?" They asked in unison.

Matt stepped in front of Trooper and handed Reilly his reins.

"Stay here," Matt told them.

"No, Matt, we should go too," Grace whispered in concern.

Matt turned to the two of them, "We don't know what we're going to find down there." They glanced at each other, then back to him. "It could be bad and whatever it is, I don't want the two of you walking away with that memory."

"What about you?" Reilly asked and looked between Matt and the plane.

"Somebody has to," Matt sighed. "And I'm choosing me. Hopefully being older I can deal with it better."

They both nodded at him and their hands grasped each other for support.

Matt turned and walked to the plane. There was no way of knowing what he was going to find. The plane looked like it could hold four or six people, but maybe there would only be a pilot. He hoped; but the nose of the plane was buried in the trees. How could a pilot survive something like that?

His hands were moist so he rubbed them nervously against his jeans. He was within one step of looking into the front of the plane.

"One step," He told himself. But when he took the step, his eyes dropped to the ground. His insides were in turmoil. He knew this wasn't going to be good.

"Matt?" He heard Grace from behind.

Matt turned quickly to make sure she wasn't coming forward. She was standing looking nervous. "It's OK." He lied to her then turned back to the plane.

"Man up," Matt muttered before looking into the window of the plane.

There was nothing, but pine trees…he stretched out a shaking hand and grabbed the handle of the door. He opened the door, saw nothing but blood, and quickly shut it. His insides quivered but his spine straightened. "I can do this." He whispered and opened the door again. There was a pool of blood on the floor and he could see a man's bare legs streaked with blood coming out from the bottom of the pine tree limbs. They were straight out, as if bracing themselves against the impact. The shorts the man was wearing were soaked in blood.

Matt took a deep breath and reached out to touch the legs. They were cold and there was no movement or sound. The man was obviously dead. He was surprised at how calm he felt and shut the door. He walked around the front of the plane. He needed to check on the other side to see if anyone was there.

He had to dip under a limb to reach the door and when he rose, his eyes automatically went to the window. He froze and stared at the empty eyes looking back. He was only a foot away with just the glass separating them. It was a woman with long, straight, black hair matted to the side of her head with blood. Part of the tree had impaled her chest, and split the top of her head.

He started to get dizzy, then realized he was holding his breath. A few deep breathes later the dizziness went away, but he was still staring into the empty eyes of the woman. There was no reason to open the door so he backed up and dipped under the limb. Wow, he was glad that he told Grace and Reilly to stay back. That was a vision that didn't need to be in the teenagers' heads.

Matt walked to the side of the plane to check on the pair. They were still in the same place he left them; staring down at him. He shook his head letting them know. Grace took a step into Reilly and he put his arms around her for support.

Just as he was about to take a step, he noticed the back door of the plane was open, but leaning against the jam so it had looked closed. There must be someone else, so taking a deep breath, he walked straight over and yanked the door open. Then, his heart nearly stopped. There wasn't anyone there…but there were two child car-seats. They were empty.

How did the door get open? Maybe the force of the impact caused it to buckle and pop open. He closed the door and looked at it. There was no damage. Matt took another step back and looked at the plane. All the damage was to the front window where the trees had busted through and killed the two adults. The undercarriage of the plane was scraped, but not too bad. The sides and the back of the plane were nearly scratch-free.

Matt opened the door again and took a closer look. There were four seats in the back of the plane, two were back to back with the front seats and faced the back of the plane. The other two faced forward. There were a couple bags sitting on the floor. Matt reached in and grabbed one of the bags. Hoping it only had adult clothes, he unzipped it. There were clothes…kid's clothes and kid's toys. His stomach started to hurt. He reached over and grabbed the other bag; more kid's clothes and toys. The first bag was full of boy clothes and the second was pink and yellow.

"Dang." Matt muttered and stepped back out of the plane.

He quickly looked around at the area and didn't see any kids. Could they be hurt? He stepped back and looked in the plane again. There was no blood; that was a good sign.

Backing out again, he glanced around the clearing. He couldn't see anything…until he looked at the ground.

His whole body trembled when he saw the tiny footprints on the ground. Heart racing and pulse pounding, he followed them for about twenty-feet until they disappeared into the grass. The larger foot prints were from a pair of shoes but the littlest ones were obviously barefoot.

"Matt?" Reilly spoke this time.

Matt looked up and saw they had moved to the other side of the plane, but were at the same distance. He turned quickly to see if the dead woman was visible. She wasn't.

"Stay there," Matt called out to them and looked back down at the ground and then up in the direction the footprints were headed.

"What did you find? Why are you out looking at the ground?" Grace called out.

Matt turned and quickly walked to them. They needed to help.

When he reached them, he looked at them solemnly and they stared at him in concern.

"There are two people dead in the front, a man and a woman," Matt said calmly. They nodded; a bit glazed in the eyes. "But worse…"

"There's worse than dead people?" Grace's eyes opened wide in surprise.

Matt nodded. "There were two kids in the crash."

"What?" They cried out in unison. "Are they dead too?"

"They were, OK," Matt quickly added. Grace looked like she was in shock. "Grace, you need to take a breath, I can't have you passing out on me. There are two kids out here somewhere."

"What?" The both cried out in unison.

Matt sighed, he didn't handle that well.

"I was tracking their footprints until I got to the grass. We need to go," He reached for Trooper's reins.

Matt walked between the plane and the pair so they wouldn't accidently look into the windows. When they reached the location where he had lost the footprints, Matt pointed out the tracks.

"Spread out and walk slowly," Matt instructed and they did as told. He glanced up at Grace to make sure she was alright. She had tears in her eyes, but they hadn't fallen down her pale face yet. Her eyes were frantically searching the ground.

He looked across the clearing they were searching. There was grass for another hundred feet then it went into trees. But, what he didn't expect was to see the sky growing darker. He'd lost track of the time.

The GPS was in the saddle bag so he quickly retrieved it and programmed in their location. Just in case.

"You guys look through the grass for anything you can find, just walk slow." Matt stepped into the stirrup and slung a leg over Trooper. "I'm going up ahead into the trees to see if they came out there."

Matt pushed Trooper into a trot but the horse didn't want to leave the other two horses and started sidestepping. "Come on, Trooper, I need you now."

He had to kick him harder than he ever had to get the horse to move forward. Trooper jumped, then moved forward without hesitation. Matt sighed in relief and reached down to stroke the horse's neck. He had already exceeded any expectations Matt could have, and hated to kick him to push him harder.

He kept eyes to the ground but paid attention to Troopers actions. The horse moved out without further pressure.

They made it to the trees and walked slowly so he could look for any dirt that would show footprints.

"How far could two little kids walk in just a couple of hours?" His eyes darted back and forth as he searched the ground. He looked up to see how much daylight was left, not much, they only had about a half-hour. Without the flashlight and emergency lights, it would be pitch black out.

He turned to Grace and Reilly; they were walking about ten feet apart, staring at the ground and moving slowly. There was no way they could continue in the darkness. There was no choice; they were going to have to find somewhere to camp for the night whether they found the kids or not. It was too dangerous for them and the horses to continue to walk blindly in the wilderness searching for tracks…that they wouldn't be able to see anyway.

Matt looked back at the plane. All the doors were shut and the trees were jammed tight in the front, but the blood was going to attract bear, cougar and wolves. They had to get as far away from the plane as possible, and get a fire built for protection.

"Matt?" Grace called out to him. When he turned she asked; "What if we tried calling out to them?"

Matt shrugged, "It can't hurt. Call twice then be quiet and listen."

They all three yelled out.

"Kids, where are you?" Matt yelled as loud as he could. Trooper jumped under him.

They were quiet and listened intently…nothing.

Matt nodded and they yelled again.…still nothing.

With dread in his heart, he made the decision to stop for the evening. He looked back at the easily-visible plane.

"Reilly, Grace, mount up," Matt told them and they looked up in dismay. "We need to get away from the plane." He didn't need to say more, they understood.

There were a couple small trees where they were standing, so Grace used the trail marking tape to mark the spot.

The sun had already gone down, and the light was diminishing faster than Matt expected.

"Let's head that way. If the kids went in a straight line then that's where they would be. Hopefully we'll find some good wood for a fire." Matt pointed and they took off in a slow gallop. The horses were only three-years-old, had spent the last year recovering from near starvation, and they were tired. He didn't want to push them any harder.

Matt stopped and looked back. He couldn't see the plane, but wasn't sure if it was because of the distance or quality of light.

"OK," Matt said and they dismounted. "Tie the horses up; we can take care of them once the fire is built. Collect as much dried wood as you can. I'll work on the fire."

He worked as fast as he could to collect dried pine needles and twigs to start the fire. Reilly and Grace were running and piling dried tree limbs as fast as they could.

"We're better with too much than not enough," Matt called out to them just as the fire blazed to life. He quickly added more needles and limbs; careful not to smother it. Within minutes the dried wood had turned into a decent fire. He continued to add wood until they were surrounded in darkness but a good area was lit.

He turned and looked at the pile of wood the teenagers had managed to collect. It was a huge pile.

"Great job," He told them solemnly. It was hard to be excited knowing there were two little kids out in the darkness. They nodded somberly.

They took their bed rolls off the saddles and placed them close to the fire. After removing the saddle bags and rifles before they took the saddles off the horses. Everything was moved as close to the fire as possible, even the horses.

Matt stood next to the fire and looked around. There wasn't anything more he could do except get them fed and protected for the night.

They sat together on their bed rolls with their saddle bags spread out in front of them.

"I don't think we ate anywhere near what we expected we would today." Grace said.

Reilly and Matt nodded as they all ate a small portion of food.

"We're a lot farther than we were supposed to go," Matt told them. "Which means, it's going to take us longer to get back tomorrow to the rest of the food."

"Matt?" Grace's voice was low. He looked over at her. Tears were glistening in her eyes. "We're going to be OK, right?"

Matt held out his arms and she leaned into his embrace. He hugged her tightly and tried to remain calm himself. This wasn't anything he ever thought would happen, let alone HIM being the person responsible for these two and the two little ones lost in the wilderness. He would never tell either one of them how scared he was too. Right now he had to be strong for them.

"We'll be OK," He told her. "I know where we are, plus we have the map, and we have the GPS. We have lots of water and food."

"Especially energy bars," Reilly added with a slight laugh.
Grace half chuckled.

"We'll find the kids in the morning and head out. We should be back before dark." Matt told them. "We didn't call in tonight to Nikki and Cora. If we don't call in the morning they'll have the National Guard out looking for us…besides, there should be search and rescue people out tomorrow looking for the plane."

"Oh, I forgot about that!" Her body relaxed in his arms.

Matt continued to hold her and keep her warm, wanting her relaxed enough to go to sleep. When he felt her body go limp in his arms, he laid her carefully down onto her bed roll.

Reilly placed more wood on the fire and picked up his rifle. He checked to see if it was loaded and ready to go. Matt nodded and did the same thing.

"I'm glad Mom doesn't know what's going on," Reilly looked over at him. It was the first time he didn't grin when he said the word 'mom'.

"Me, too," Matt nodded.

Matt looked out into the darkness. He was worried about the little kids.

"Do you think they're OK?" Reilly asked.

Matt shrugged, "I don't know. They were out there a couple of hours before we got there. At least it's warm out tonight and they won't be freezing."

"How bad was the plane crash?"

"Bad… I'm glad you and Grace didn't go down," Matt answered. His mind flashed back to the stretched out legs of the man and the empty eyes of the woman.

"Are you, OK?" Reilly asked hesitantly.

Matt looked at his new brother and tried to smile, "I will be; it was nerve wracking…I didn't want to look…but…it wasn't as bad to see as I thought it would be. I think the parents would have made it if the plane hadn't crashed into the trees, they needed just a little longer meadow."

"You're tougher than I would have been," Reilly admitted and sounded proud of Matt.

The only thing Matt felt…was tired.

"It's been a long day, Reilly," Matt said. "I'll take the first watch and wake you up in a couple of hours."

"OK." Reilly said and curled up next to Grace.

Matt threw more sticks on the fire and estimated they had more than enough wood to last the night. In the middle of summer, sunrise should be around 5:00. It was well after 10:00 now, so he had seven hours.

It would be seven of the worst hours of his life.

CHAPTER SIX

The first howl sent shivers down Matt's spine. He heard the horses moving for the first time since they had taken the saddles off. Then another howl, another shiver, and Matt picked up his rifle and set it across his lap. He glanced around their small camp site and saw no open food containers that might attract the wolves or a bear. If they were to be attracted to a smell it would be the airplane not them.

More howling, it was getting closer, but not close enough to scare him yet.

He threw more wood on the fire and it lit the night enough he could see the horses. All except for Cooper, who was so black, he looked invisible. Matt stood and walked to the horses, calmly talking to them and trying to make them relax. The horses seemed to calm down, which helped Matt's nerves. If the wolves were close, the horses would be scared; heads up, ears alert, and too nervous to stand still.

He returned to the seat next to the fire; his eyes scanned constantly to watch for glowing eyes that would indicate the wolves were there.

Then, another sound penetrated the darkness. It was low at first, but slowly gained strength. Matt turned and looked for the source even though he knew he wouldn't be able to see it in the darkness.

A wolf howled, then the other sound echoed into the darkness.

"Matt?" Reilly said from behind, but Matt's eyes continued to look into the darkness.

"Yeah?"

"Is that what I think it is?"

"Yeah," Matt sighed heavily and there wasn't anything they could do but listen. "It's the kids crying."

Every muscle in Matt's body was tense. He gripped the rifle so tight his fingers hurt. His eyes had started to burn from staring into the darkness. The worry for Reilly and Grace had changed to the terror for the kids. They were alive...for now.

Matt turned, threw more wood on the fire, then glanced up at the horses. They remained quiet, even with the wolves howling. Their heads were low as they slept. Buttercup's cream colored hair stood out in the night in contrast to Cooper's invisible blackness.

More cries echoed in the night making Matt's neck tense. He shrugged his shoulders and rolled his head to get it to relax. It didn't. He took a deep breath and let it out slowly...that didn't help either. He tried to think of something warm and happy but every howl and cry made him come back to reality.

"If they don't stop crying..."

"I know," Matt whispered. He had thought of nothing else since the cries had started. All predators were attracted to cries of the helpless or injured.

"This is one heck of a bonding moment."

"That's an understatement," Matt sighed.

After a half hour of listening to the intermittent howls and the kids' cries, Matt looked down at Reilly and Grace. She was still sleeping; Reilly was staring at the stars. More wood on the fire and he could see the horses still sleeping.

The cries turned to whimpers.

"If we can still hear them, they have to be pretty close," Reilly finally spoke.

"I was thinking the same thing," Matt nodded into the darkness. "Sound echoes out here, but I don't think we're very far away."

Finally, the whimpers stopped.

"I hope they're asleep." Reilly whispered.

"So do I."

"I just want to grab them and run," Reilly admitted.

"I've been thinking the same thing but, we have one problem."

"What?"

"The shale mountainside..."

"We can't take them over that!"

"I don't want to take young, exhausted horses over it again either. Let alone have you slide over a cliff again."

"What are we going to do?"

"I just about memorized the map before we came out here," Matt admitted. "Other than unclimbable bluffs and more rock slides, there are places on the mountain that the trees and bushes are so thick we couldn't get through them. We'll have to go up and around."

"How long will it take?"

Matt sighed, "If we get out of here early, then we might make it back in time. If it takes a while, we might end up out here overnight again." He sighed. "Even if Search and Rescue get here tomorrow and take the kids, we still have to ride our horses out."

"We have to be out by Thursday at 3:00," Reilly reminded him.

"Yeah," Matt stared up at the sky. "I've been thinking of her, too."

***

As the sun began to rise, Matt looked down at his cousin and new brother. Reilly had finally fallen asleep after the kids' cries stopped. Grace had barely moved all night.

His mind went to Nikki. He was sure she and Cora were already worried since they hadn't called in for the night. It was the one thing Matt swore he would do…and now he couldn't. What was she going through right now?

They were only two years apart in age and had been close ever since he could remember. Because they lived on the ranch most of his childhood, she was his first and only playmate for years until Grace finally grew up enough to join them. But for most of his early years it was him and Nikki tromping through the trees of the ranch, riding horses everywhere, and building boats to race in the creeks of the ranch.

Matt remembered crying forever her first day of kindergarten…they were separated for hours! It seemed like forever to him.

As they grew up, every fear, doubt, joy, adventure and accomplishment they had shared. Together they had solved their world's problems. It was her idea for him to come to the mountains and see if they could help him decide about college.

Even in the situation they were in, he wished she were there sharing it with him.

He threw more wood on the fire and looked up at the horses. They were standing quietly, Trooper's head was up and alert. The horse was looking over at him and the fire. Matt grinned at him. No horse could have worked harder, in fact, all three worked hard, but he was particularly fond of Trooper. As tired as they both were, he still looked forward to riding the horse all day again.

The wolves had stopped howling and the mountains were quiet as he watched the sun rise over the tree tops. There were more clouds this morning and the sun touched them with yellows and pinks that looked soothing and tranquil over the baby blue of the sky. The sun's light reflected on the distant mountains. As the sun rose, the light started heading their way.

Matt stood and stretched, trying to get the nights tension out of his muscles. He needed aspirin and a soft bed. Maybe if they found the kids quick enough, they could be home and in bed that night. He sure hoped so.

After putting more wood on the fire, he reached for the saddle bags. It would help if they had something warm in their stomachs. He took the small frying pan out of Grace's bag and laid it over the fire. He filled it with water and found the packets of oatmeal and emptied them into the boiling water. The smell of brown sugar and maple made his stomach grumble.

"That smells good." He heard Grace's voice behind him.

"I agree," He turned and tried to smile. The tension in his face made him feel like a statue.

"I thought Reilly was taking the second shift," Grace said looking over at her sleeping friend.

"He was up…."

They let him sleep while they saddled the horses and cleaned up the area. When Reilly woke, he sat straight up and looked around the area in a daze.

"You awake?" Grace smiled at him and handed him the last of the oatmeal front the pan.

"Yeah," Reilly got out, before he started shoveling the food in his mouth.

When he was finished, Grace was at the horses, so he turned to Matt and whispered, "Anymore crying?"

Matt shook his head, "Nothing."

The sun was finally up high enough that the light reached them through the trees and they would be able to see any tracks of the kids.

"Let's get going," He said as they put out the fire.

They made it back to the edge of the meadow where Grace had tied the trail markers. Matt looked over at the plane; nothing had changed. What was he expecting?

He turned his attention back to looking for tracks, "Let's just walk the edge and see if we can see a footprint."

"On foot or horse?" Grace asked.

"On horseback first, it'll be faster," Matt decided. "If we don't see anything we'll come back and do it on foot. Hopefully it's worth the gamble."

The two nodded then headed in the opposite direction.

A half hour later, just as he was getting frustrated and panicked, he found a foot print.

"Reilly! Grace!" He called out and stepped out of the saddle.

"Kids, where are you?!" He yelled as loud as he could. Grace and Reilly galloped their horses to him.

They all three yelled, but there was no answer. On foot, leading the horses, they followed the tracks which led them to an animal trail.

"It's good if they follow the trail," Matt told them. "They should be easier to find." Then he froze; next to the tiny print were wolf tracks. The wolves had to be looking, too. His eyes went to Reilly, who was staring back with fear in his eyes.

When they found the kids…what exactly would they find?

Matt shook off the impending vision and hurried up the trail. "Don't forget to mark the trail, Grace," He called over his shoulder. He needed her to stay in the back of the line.

The trail led them up hill and into the trees. Thick brush lined the left side of the trail and the right side was a steep tree filled mountain side. There was no way the kids would have headed up there. The trail was half dirt and half grass which only gave them occasional kid or wolf prints.

Near the top of the hill, the trail widened. Matt turned back to Grace and Reilly. Grace was watching the ground next to the mountainside and Reilly was next to the brush side. Smart pair, he decided.

Just as Matt turned back he heard Reilly call out. Quickly turning back, he saw Cooper, but no Reilly…his brother had vanished. Only his cowboy hat lay on the ground where he had been standing moments before.

"Reilly?" Both he and Grace called out; their voices confused.

Matt let go of Trooper, having faith the horse wouldn't leave, and walked back to where he last saw his brother.

"Reilly?" He called out again.

"I'm here." A voice came out of nowhere.

"Where?" Grace yelled.

"Watch your step," He called back out.

"Reilly, WHERE are you?" Matt searched the ground and only saw ruffled leaves on the ground. His heart had finally started beating again.

"I slipped down the side of the hill," His voice answered. "I didn't have time to tighten the grip on Cooper's rope this time."

Matt started tentatively stepping on the ground by the ruffled leafs and found a soft spot. He knelt down and started clearing away the brush and leaves; there was a three-foot wide hole that was covered by the brush, it was flimsy but thick so he couldn't see clearly through them.

"Matt?" Reilly yelled again.

"Yeah?"

"I found the kids."

"What?" Matt and Grace called out in shock.

"Are they alright?" Matt yelled down into the brush hole, trying desperately to clear it out.

"Well, since a man just dropped out of nowhere and nearly crushed them…I would say yes."

Matt nervously smiled at Reilly's use of the word *man*. The teenager was certainly turning into one quickly.

"Are they hurt?" Grace asked.

"Just some scratches that I can tell…I'm having a bit of a hard time seeing them," Reilly answered.

"Why?" Matt yelled back, still trying to clear the brush.

"They've attached themselves to my legs." Reilly's voice seemed nervous.

Matt turned to Grace. "Tie up the horses and bring me the camp saw from my bag."

Matt turned back to the brush, "Can you get out of there?"

"NO!" Came an instant firm answer, "Do you remember watching '*The Man From Snowy River*'?"

Matt's heart sunk, he knew what Reilly meant. "You're on a cliff ledge?"

"Yeah…it's not as bad as that one…thankfully. The ledge is about five feet wide and about 20 feet down from you," Reilly described his predicament.

"What is the drop off below you?" Matt asked as he tried to picture the terrain.

Reilly hesitated, "At least 40-feet straight down, then another 20 or so slanted to rocks below…all the way to the river."

Matt sat back on his heels and looked at Grace as she handed him the saw.

"What do we do?" She asked while kneeling down next to the hole.

"Matt?" Reilly said.

"Yeah?" Matt looked at the ground trying to come up with a plan.

"At least we now know why the kids were safe last night." Reilly hollered.

Matt smiled, always looking for the positive, even when he was on the edge of a cliff.

"I'm going to start sawing away the brush up here," Matt yelled down to his brother. "Just don't move."

"Trust me...I won't," Reilly chuckled nervously.

He started sawing away at the brush. There was no way he could leave them on the ledge to go get help...he couldn't leave Grace and go himself...and he couldn't send Grace for help by herself.

They were going to have to come up with a way to get Reilly and the kids off the ledge. It was obvious they couldn't go down, so they had to pull them up. They were 20-feet down. They had a couple lariats and the lead ropes to use. He could lower the ropes down and have Reilly attach the kids to the ropes and he would use Trooper to pull them out. Would the kids let them?

As Grace talked to Reilly, Matt cleared the brush from the hole. Even when it was cleared he still couldn't see his brother, just the cliff which made Matt's pulse race again. He needed more room, so he continued to saw away at the edges of the trail and cliff. It took him an hour to get the cliff cleared to his satisfaction and was covered in sweat from the exertion. He crawled away from the side and stood up with aching arms and shoulders. The tension made his back ache. He desperately wanted that aspirin and a soft bed...and for this to be just a bad dream.

"Now what?" Grace said from behind him.

Nope, it wasn't just a bad dream.

Matt looked up at her tense face, "Stay away from the side." He told her; not wanting her down there ,too.

"Matt?" Reilly called up.

Matt decided he was beginning to hate his own name. "Yeah?"

"Can you send down some water and food for them?"

Matt nodded, he should have thought of that.

"Go get one of the saddle bags and a lariat." Matt looked over at Grace and she ran to the horses.

Matt stood quietly looking out at the mountains and sky. He tried to get his back to relax but it wasn't working. Grace returned and he cleared out everything in the bags except a couple bottles of water, the bag of trail mix, and cookies.

"Reilly?" Matt called out.

"Yeah?"

"I'm going to lower the bag down and use it to gauge how far down you actually are," Matt told him.

"OK."

Matt crawled to the edge, flattened out on his stomach and peered over the edge. He couldn't see anything but about a hundred feet hillside below. Dropping the saddle bag over the side and holding onto the lariat tightly, he lowered it down.

"Get a piece of trail marker tape ready." Matt told Grace without looking at her.

Finally, half way through the rope, Reilly shouted and let him know he had the bags, then called again when they were empty. Matt took the piece of tape from Grace and marked the rope before pulling the bags back up.

Crawling back away from the ledge, Matt sat back on his heels to assess the situation. He was getting really tired, and it was still early.

"Are you OK down there?" He asked Reilly.

"Yeah, they've nearly eaten everything already and both bottles of water are gone too."

"How old are they?" Grace called down.

Matt shook his head. He hadn't even thought about that.

"She said six and three." Reilly answered. "The girl is older."

"Wow, that's young!" Grace's shocked expression looked down at Matt's matching one.

For some reason, knowing more about the kids made the pressure weigh heavier on Matt. He needed to get them and his brother off the ledge!

The tape on the lariat was a little over half way on the 35 foot rope. So Reilly was right, they were twenty feet down.

"I was going to lower the rope down and have you attach to one of the kids and raise it like the saddlebags," Matt yelled down. "I don't think that will work, now."

"It would freak them out," Reilly answered. "The thought freaks me out."

"You don't have a choice," Matt yelled back with a tired half chuckle. "The only choice we have is to lower me down the ledge to grab the kids...one at a time." Matt yelled and looked up at Grace. Her eyes opened wide in disbelief.

Matt looked around at the horses and ropes.

"I have a plan." Matt told them.

"Am I going to like it?" Reilly asked nervously.

"Do you like where you are?" Matt tried to smile, but his face was too tense.

"Point taken..." Reilly answered.

Matt took a moment to look at Grace and make sure she was alright. She nodded confidently.

"What's going on?" Reilly yelled.

"Taking a moment to put the plan in action," Matt yelled back.

"Grace, I'm going to loop the lariat around me and tie the other end around Trooper's saddle. You're going to have to control him. Back him up so I can rappel down and then lead him forward to pull us up." He looked down at her. "We can do this."

Grace nodded and took a deep breath. "We can do this, trust me, Matt."

"I am, Grace. With my life." He kissed her forehead and stood up.

It took them awhile to get Trooper in position. They tied two lariats together and Grace came up with the idea to wrap the rope around a second breast collar and then around Trooper's saddle horn for added stability and strength. The pressure would be on Trooper's chest instead of on the saddle. Matt wrapped the lariat loop under his arms and walked to the ledge. His stomach started to turn, but he put on a brave face for Grace.

"We can do this."

"We can do this," She repeated to him with confidence. She gripped the lead rope attached to Trooper so hard her knuckles were white.

Matt knelt down and slid over the side. Once the rope tightened, the pressure from the rope under his arms was intense. He took a few deep breathes.

"OK," Matt called out to Grace. "Back him up."

Matt concentrated on the hillside and pushed himself away with his feet; gripping the rope tightly with his hands. He tried to mimic the pictures he had seen of mountain climbers rappelling down cliffs.

"I can see your feet." Reilly hollered.

Moments later, Matt's feet landed on a ledge and he turned to see Reilly sitting cross-legged on the ledge with two filthy kids in his lap. Two sets of frightened eyes stared at him. Make that three, as he looked into Reilly's eyes. The girl had shoulder length brown hair and brown scared eyes. The little boy had his arms around Reilly's neck; he looked just like his sister, but with short hair.

"That's good!" Matt called out to Grace. "Scoot over here," He told Reilly. The ropes were killing him and he needed to get this done fast.

Reilly scooted the best he could until he was close enough to Matt to touch.

"Good bonding moment," Reilly chuckled.

"Not one we will ever repeat," Matt smiled nervously and stretched his arms out to the little girl. "Come here, Sweetheart, and I'll get you off here and get you more cookies." The little girl reached out to him and wrapped her arms around his neck. Her legs wrapped around his waist.

"OK, Grace!" He yelled out. They started to slowly move up. The girl started crying, which made the little boy cry. His last glimpse of Reilly was of him talking softly and holding the boy tightly while rocking.

Matt had to hold the girl with one arm, as tight as he could, and the other was used to push them away from the hillside. All of his body weight and that of the small girl was on the rope; the pressure from the rope was around his chest. The rawhide of the rope gripped his skin through his shirt and he had to focus to keep from crying out in pain.

"It's OK, Sweetie, we're almost there," Matt whispered to the crying and shaking little girl. He stared up at the ledge. "Cookies are waiting for you."

The girl smelled terrible. Her clothes were torn and the poor thing had soiled herself. The little boy didn't have shoes on. Just before he got to the top, Matt realized he was going to have to go back to the plane for their bags. The thought was nearly worse than having to lower himself over the ledge again.

Matt turned on his side and placed an elbow on the ledge. He heaved them over the ledge; the rawhide pinching at the skin. Grace was standing in front of Trooper talking and soothing him. The horse was leaning forward bracing against the pressure on his chest. Matt's love of the horse grew ten-fold.

"Stay there," Matt told Grace while crawling away from the ledge. Trooper relaxed his stance when the pressure was released.

Matt gently set the little girl away and looked into her scared face.

"It's OK." He pointed to his cousin. "That's Grace. She's going to get you the cookies. Can you go to her?"

The little girl nodded and let go. She stood up and started walking to Grace then stopped. "That's a horse!" The little girl cried out excitedly.

Matt and Grace looked at each other in disbelief. Everything the child had gone through and she could still get excited about seeing a horse.

Grace reached in the saddle bag and grabbed the cookies. She then set her on the hillside with a bottle of water. The girl stared up at Trooper, then looked down at the other horses and smiled.

Matt nodded and slid over the side again, the rope gripped at the already sore skin. He grimaced through the pain. "OK!" He called up to Grace and he started lowering again.

About half-way down, Grace screamed.

CHAPTER SEVEN

"Grace!" Matt called out. The rope around him hadn't gone up or down so Trooper didn't move, but where was Grace?

"GRACE!" His heart raced, terror started to take over as he imagined a wolf or bear attacking her. Matt tried climbing back up the rope.

"Grace!" Matt heard Reilly scream out too. The little boy's cries were louder.

"It's, OK," She yelled down at them. "I'm, OK."

Matt stopped climbing and slid back down; the tension on his armpits and back was severe, the rope burned into his skin.

"What the hell happened?" Matt yelled, still panicked.

"I was concentrating so hard on the rope that he scared me," She called out.

"He? What? Who?" Matt stared up at the top of the ledge. What was she talking about? They were out in the middle of the Idaho wilderness!

Then, appearing over the ledge…was a cowboy hat and then Nick's face.

Matt nearly cried out. He just stared in shock at the concerned face looking down at him.

"Sorry, didn't realize I was going to scare her," Nick said as he looked past Matt and down the mountain side. His face paled and his lips rolled together in a grimace.

Matt was still too stunned to talk, but the pain under his arms screamed at him.

"We can talk later," Nick continued. "Let's get you out of there."

Matt shook his head. "Reilly and a little boy are on a ledge. I have to go down."

Surprise registered on Nick's face.

"Grace, back him up," Matt called out and stared at his dad's face until he was lowered out of sight.

When his feet hit the ledge, he turned to Reilly.

"What happened?" The scared teenager asked.

"Nick showed up and scared her."

"Nick?" Reilly was as shocked as Matt was.

"Yeah, we'll talk later. Give me the boy."

It took both of their strength, to pull the screaming boy away from Reilly. When the boy finally let loose, he turned and wrapped his arms tight around Matt's neck, but his legs couldn't make their way all the way around his waist.

Reilly wiggled out of his belt and wrapped it around the boy. He then attached it onto Matt's belt to help hold him.

"Smart idea," Matt smiled at his brother. "Once I'm at the top, we'll throw the rope down. Wrap it around yourself like it is around me. Hold tight, let us know when ready, and we'll get you up as fast as possible."

Reilly nodded, "Matt, I just want you to know how much I love having you as a brother." Tears finally glistened in his eyes.

Matt smiled, "Back at ya, brother…be careful." They nodded to each other.

"Grace!" Matt called and watched his brother until he couldn't see him anymore. He turned and looked back up at his father who was watching after him.

The boy's grip was almost tighter than the little girl's.

"It's ok, Kiddo," Matt whispered to the boy. "We'll get you some cookies when we get to the top."

"Cookies…" The little boy muttered into Matt's neck. It made Matt smile.

At the top, after Nick had helped pull him up onto the path, Nick reached down, unbuckled the belt and tried to pick up the boy. After a few attempts of being gentle to get the crying boy to let go, Nick placed his arm around the boy's body and yanked. The boy screamed, which made Nick walk quickly to Grace.

Matt scooted away from the edge and took the rope off. The pain made it hard to lift his arms. He looked back to see Nick holding the crying boy at arm's length in front of him and handing the scared kid off to Grace. They exchanged the child for the lead rope. Nick stroked the horse and spoke softly to Trooper, then backed him up.

Matt coiled the rope, as the horse backed up until he had half of it collected, then tossed it over the ledge to Reilly. He stared out at the mountains as he waited for Reilly to yell.

Nick…what a surprise.

"OK!" Reilly yelled.

Matt turned over onto his stomach and crawled to the edge to watch his brother rise from the ledge. The relief was nearly overwhelming when he saw Reilly's face grinning up at him. He reached out a hand and gripped Reilly's as tight as possible to help him the last couple feet. He yanked and pulled him over the ledge and the teenager fell next to him.

They both lay perfectly still and stared at the sky. Grace came over and peered over the top of the two of them. Her tears dropped between their heads. No one spoke. They both reached up to her and she dropped down over the top of them and they held each other in silence.

***

Nick lifted the boy, Adam, onto the saddle in front of Reilly, then turned to help the girl, Amy, onto the back of Grace's saddle. She would be comfortable sitting on top of the bed roll.

Matt stepped into the stirrup and grimaced as he pulled himself into the saddle.

"You OK?" Nick asked.

"Yeah," Matt smiled at him. "Gonna be a bit bruised tomorrow though."

Once they started back down the mountain, Nick told them how he got there.

Nikki and Cora called Jessup telling him that the group had not called in for the night. Jessup loaded Monty in the horse trailer as Nick prepared his saddle bags. They had taken off in the middle of the night. Jessup found their campsite with no problem and before daylight, Nick had taken off on the trail Jessup had showed him on the map. He had started doubting himself when he saw the trail markers Grace had placed. He followed them as fast as he could.

Nick had seen the plane from the same spot they had, and realized why they deviated from their plan. He didn't go down to the plane; using binoculars, he had seen the trail tape on the two small trees from the night before. Those led him to the base of the hill and straight to them.

"I love trail tape," Grace smiled.

"So, Jessup is at the camp?" Reilly asked.

Nick nodded, "We have walkie-talkies."

Matt shook his head. "In these mountains we'd have to get closer than normal," He sighed. "But the sooner we can get word to them the better." He looked over at Nick. "Did you hear anything about the plane crash before you left Jessup?"

Nick shook his head.

"We were hoping Search and Rescue would be out looking for it," Matt said.

"They still could be," Nick nodded. "I'd be surprised if they weren't, but it also depends a lot on if the pilot deviated from his flight plan or not...if he did, then they could be searching in the wrong area."

They arrived the bottom of the mountain and walked to the trees with the trail markers.

Matt looked over at the plane. Nothing had changed and he saw no movement from animals.

"You want me to go?" Nick asked with a look of concern.

Matt smiled in appreciation, but shook his head. "I know what's there, saw it yesterday. No reason for you to have that memory in your head, too." He looked at Grace and Reilly who were talking and entertaining the kids. "Just take care of them and I'll be back as soon as I can."

Nick nodded with rifle in hand.

Matt and Trooper trotted towards the plane and this time the horse didn't hesitate when he asked him to leave the other horses. Matt stroked the horse's neck. He couldn't have asked for a better horse. After the last year the horse had gone through, he was working like a well experienced healthy horse...just amazing.

He slowed down to a walk as they approached the plane. There were wolf tracks everywhere, so he pulled his rifle out of the gun scabbard and checked to make sure it was ready. He placed it across his lap and watched the area closely.

Stepping out of the saddle, his eyes continually searched for any movement. The front of the plane had the most concentration of wolf tracks. It looked like the wolves had tried to get into the front of the plane but the trees had prevented them. Matt knew they would be back to try again, so he quickly led Trooper to the plane and opened the back door to get the bags. The smell of the dead bodies was intense and instantly overwhelming; he started gagging.

Matt grabbed the bags and threw them out, then pulled out his knife and quickly cut the seat cushion off one of the empty seats. He shut the door and started jogging away from the plane as fast as he could pull the horse, then stopped fifty-feet from the plane. He tossed out all the toys and put all the clothes into one bag. There was a pair of shoes for Adam. As he stood, he looked at the pile of toys and picked one up for each kid. They needed something familiar, it was going to be a long ride back.

The group had dismounted while they waited for him to return. The kids were excited to see the toys. He gave Reilly the seat cushion to make a pillow for Adam that would rest above the saddle horn.

Matt pulled out the map so he and Nick could review their path.

"We can't go down…we're blocked by the river," Matt pointed on the map. "We can't go back because of the rock slide. We have no choice but to ride to the base of this mountain and go up. "What time is it?" Matt asked.

"Two o'clock," Nick answered.

Matt sighed. "It took us that long?"

Nick smiled in understanding. "You saved two kid's lives, no matter how long it took, it was worth it."

Matt leaned against Trooper. The lack of sleep and the exhausting, stressful morning was beginning to take its toll on him.

"You're right," Matt smiled wearily. "We just need to be back by Thursday at three and it may take us two days to get there."

"Everyone turns into pumpkins at three o'clock on Thursday?" Nick looked confused.

"Sort of," Matt chuckled. "Mom reaches cell service."

"Understood…" Nick looked over at Reilly. "After his disappearance last month, the last thing she needs is to go through it again with both…all three of you."

"If Search and Rescue gets out here, then we can send a message home." Matt looked up at the sky expecting to see a plane or helicopter. "They have no idea to look for US unless Nikki or Jessup called them."

"We have until tomorrow morning at nine to get within walkie-talkie range before they call out the National Guard," Nick chuckled.

"Well, that gives us seven and a half hours today and about three in the morning. We have three," He looked over at Monty, "…make that four exhausted horses, two little kids, and a tired group of people, so we can't move as fast as I'd like. Plus, there is a long steep climb up the mountain that might take all day. We won't be able to make it in time to stop them from calling for help; not even close."

Matt traced the trail on the map. "We're about a half hour from this creek; we'll stop and bathe the kids. We should be able to get to this meadow to camp for the night along this creek. Then, we can head up this side of the mountain. To miss more rock slides and impassable ravines, we have to go at least an hour or two more into the wilderness and away from any chance of running into a road, before we can hit the base of the mountain. Then, we turn back towards the campground. It'll be a long haul up that mountainside; hopefully we'll find a good game trail to follow. Then, we can just head across the top. If we can get to this butte, we may get high enough to contact Jessup."

Nick patted him on the shoulder; "You have a great handle on this, Matt."

Matt looked over at him and smiled. That little bit of support really helped regain his energy.

"How is the food situation?" Nick asked.

"We're basically down to energy bars," Matt sighed. "We weren't prepared for more mouths to feed and we'll be out two days longer than expected."

"Well, I brought water, lots of it," Nick told him. "But not much food; I figured we could hunt if we needed food."

"And there are berries," Matt added. "We're in huckleberry season. We just have to watch for the bears."

"Bears and wolves," Reilly added as he walked up to them.

Matt nodded. "Let's get going."

CHAPTER EIGHT

When they arrived at the creek, Grace and Reilly helped bathe the kids with the supplies in the bag Matt had retrieved from the plane. Both kids had bruises across their chests from their car seat harnesses.

Matt and Nick loosened the saddles on the horses to give them a break, then found a log to sit and rest.

"Do you have any aspirin?" Matt asked.

Nick dug into his saddle bags and handed Matt the bottle. "After years of bull riding, I don't leave home without it."

"Oh, you're a life saver." Matt quickly took the aspirin.

"How are the arm pits?"

Matt lifted his shirt and showed him the rope burns.

"Well, that answers that…keep the bottle," Nick grimaced. "There isn't anything in the little first aid kit for rope burns."

Matt nodded.

They were far enough from the creek that Matt took the opportunity to tell Nick about the night before; listening to the wolves howling and the kids crying, expecting the worse at any moment.

"Worst night of my life," Matt shook his head and sighed.

"Worse than New Year's?" Nick chuckled, trying to lighten the conversation.

Matt turned and looked at Nick. They had never talked about that night. But now, he realized it would be fair to let Nick know how he felt.

"I don't consider that a bad night for me," Matt told him honestly. He could see the surprise in Nick's eyes. "I know that may be hard to believe, considering..." Matt flashed back to the angry punch he threw at Nick that night, knocking him off his feet. "But after the initial shock of seeing you, then hearing your story..." Matt shrugged. "It worked out in the end." He smiled at his father and hoped he didn't need any further explanation.

Nick took a deep breath and let it out slowly. "I'm glad you feel that way...I've enjoyed the time with you and Nikki."

"I'm glad the Tagger Herd came into our life's and led you back to us," Matt said and slowly stood and looked over at Trooper. The horse was obviously tired, but they had to keep going with hours ahead of them. "We may have to stop earlier than we want to give the horses a good night's rest before another full day of riding. It will be uphill, a steep uphill, for a good portion of it."

"You need a night's rest, too," Nick said as they walked to the kids and horses.

Matt nodded; that was an understatement.

***

They took a couple more breaks before they finally setup camp for the night. The kids helped Reilly and Grace collect dried wood while Matt built the fire. Adam wouldn't let go of Reilly. Nick took care of all the horses.

Once the sun went down, there was complete darkness surrounding them. Nick had a flashlight but they decided not to use it in case there was an emergency. The warmth and soothing glow from the campfire put the kids to sleep. Grace curled up next to the girl, with the boy curled up in front of his sister. Reilly took his place next to the boy, so the two kids were sandwiched and protected from the night between the teenagers. Within minutes of lying down, all four were sound asleep.

Watching them sleep, made Matt's body relax and his eye's start to fall.

"Why don't you turn in and get some sleep?" Nick asked. "I've got the first watch."

Matt nodded and slipped into his bed roll, but lay staring at the sky.

"Do you always sleep with your eyes open?" Nick chuckled.

Matt smiled, but kept staring up into the stars. "I'm waiting for the howls to start."

"Any in this area are probably back at the plane."

"They couldn't get in. I closed all the doors and the trees plugged the front."

"They'll keep trying as long as the scent of blood is in the air."

Matt thought of the horrendous smell when he opened the plane door. His stomach turned.

"Was it bad?" Nick asked.

Matt nodded and glanced over to make sure the kids were still sleeping. They were all breathing deeply. Then, he told Nick about the man's legs and the woman's eyes.

"I thought it would bother me more than it has," Matt told him.

"It could be you're still in shock. Once you get out of here and your system slows down, it may hit you."

"I don't know. I seem to be compartmentalizing it. I think of them more scientifically. It's more like I watched it in a movie, than saw it in real life. What happened with Reilly on the mountainside…both of them…that will come back to haunt me."

"It's personal. If it had happened to someone you didn't know; it probably wouldn't bother you as much."

Matt nodded. That made sense to him.

Nick continued; "I have to admit, seeing you dangling off that cliff was a bit…terrifying."

Matt chuckled. "If it wasn't so painful…or life threatening for Reilly and the kids…or having to trust Grace and Trooper with my life…I think I would have enjoyed it." He looked over at Nick with a grin.

Nick smiled back, "Have you ever been mountain climbing before?"

Matt shook his head, his pulse quickening just at the thought of rappelling again. "Not before today…but I will after. It was exhilarating."

"Dru's going to love that."

"She'll probably want to join me."

"To join in the fun or protect you?"

"Both."

They grinned at each other knowing it was true.

"Have you ever rock climbed?" Matt asked.

"Once in Australia. I understand how you feel. It was exhilarating; you'll enjoy it when there isn't so much on the line."

"Is that why you kept bull riding?"

"At first it was escaping New Mexico. Once I had the money in the bank, and I could do whatever I wanted, I did it for fun and the thrill of the ride. It's the excitement of danger that keeps you getting on bull after bull after bull.…or rappelling over cliff after cliff after cliff."

"…or jumping out of a plane again and again and again." Matt added, understanding what Nick was saying.

"How long did you ride in Australia?" Matt asked with a yawn.

"Just a couple of years, we have two days of riding to catch up. Sleep while you can."

Matt nodded and tried to roll over but his sides screamed out and he grimaced.

"Did you take some aspirin?" Nick asked him. Matt shook his head. "In your saddle bag?" Nick asked and Matt nodded.

Nick retrieved the aspirin then handed the pills and a bottle of water to him.

Matt was sure, that when he closed his eyes, he fell asleep instantly.

***

Nick and Reilly left to hunt for a deer for food. The kids were still sleeping, curled up peacefully in each other's arms. Matt hoped Adam didn't wake up before Reilly got back. Grace placed another bed roll on top of them to keep them warm in the cool morning air. Then she walked up to Matt.

He opened his arms for a hug and she gladly walked into them but kept her arms low so she didn't hit the rope burn. They squeezed tightly and enjoyed the warmth and the love from each other.

"I'm so proud of you, Grace," Matt told her. His chin rested on top her head.

"I didn't do much," She sighed.

"You had my life in your hands. The way you handled Trooper was perfect to get him to lower me and lift us."

She snuggled in closer. "You were the hero of the day. Those kids wouldn't be alive if you didn't decide to go to the plane instead of going for help."

"Have they asked or said anything about their parents?"

"Amy said she woke up and they were in the airplane. She helped Adam get out of his seat and they went looking for their parents. I don't think they realized they were in the front seat."

"The trees filled the front seat, so they probably couldn't see them."

"They asked where they were. I didn't know what to say, so I told them we would ride the horses and take them back home."

"That was perfect."

A gunshot rang out, then a second.

"Someone missed..." Grace said.

"I know Reilly's a good shot, I don't know about Nick."

"He scared the heck out of me yesterday. I was so entranced in talking to Trooper and listening for you that I didn't even hear Monty trotting up the trail. Nick said that Monty and Buttercup even whinnied at each other." She giggled. "I didn't hear it."

"I'm glad you were so focused."

"Except a bear or a wolf could have snuck up on me, too!"

"They didn't."

"It was such a surprise to see Nick."

"Yeah it was...a nice surprise though."

"Yeah, I like him."

"Me, too."

"He avoids the kids."

"He hasn't been around kids at all, ever."

"Huh, I don't think I've ever known anyone that hasn't been around kids."

"Adam will probably ride with Reilly all day. Adam sees Reilly as security."

"I don't blame him; Reilly's the savior that fell from the sky."

They both chuckled at the vision.

"I keep thinking of the family at Gibbs Eddy," Grace sighed. "I picture Amy and Adam with their parents playing on the river in the sand. It seems so sad...they'll never have anything like that."

"They will," He assured her. "Amy may remember things...Adam probably not about their parents, but someone will be there for them and give them memories like that."

"I guess...look at Reilly losing his mother when he was five...now he has Aunt Dru."

"That's a good way to think of it." He smiled at her compassion. "But, today, if you need me to take Amy, just let me know, it gets tiring riding double all the time, and we've got about a day and a half to get out of here."

"Are we going to make the 3:00 deadline?"

"Unless something happens, we should."

"Well, nothing's going to happen," She declared and stepped back out of his arms. "We'll make it."

"We can do this."

"We can do this." She smiled up at him.

Reilly and Nick appeared over the mountain. Reilly was carrying a heavy bag.

"Looks like you need to get your fry pan out," Matt told her and she walked over to her saddle bags.

They cooked all the meat from the deer that Reilly had shot. The smell of the venison made all their stomachs rumble and woke both kids. There would be enough for the entire day. And, once they found a huckleberry bush, they would stop and pick as much as they could.

Nick saddled Trooper for Matt. The hour of sawing brush away from the ledge had made his shoulders and arms sore. The rope burns were incredibly tender and the aspirin wasn't quite keeping all the pain away. Lifting the saddle was nearly impossible.

After a short ride on level ground, the mountain climb started. They zig-zagged the mountain so the climb wasn't too steep and stopped numerous times to rest the horses.

On the last stop, they sat on the mountain taking in the beauty before them. Rolling tree covered mountains, blue sky, and billowy clouds gliding across the horizon.

Grace and Reilly were walking through the wild flowers with the kids. They had split an energy bar for the kids in an attempt to keep them as satisfied as possible.

Nick was checking all the horse's shoes, talking softly to them as he worked. The climb was quite strenuous for them and they were covered in sweat most of the day.

Matt sat quietly on a fallen tree and took it all in; trying to remember this one peaceful moment of such a turbulent trip.

He took the lead with Amy sitting behind him on Trooper. She was excited to ride a different horse. Matt decided to see if he could get some information out of the six-year-old, in his and Nikki's quick fire method.

"How are you today?" he asked her.

"I'm fine," she declared loudly.

"Your name is Amy."

"Yep."

"Do you know my name?"

"Matt."

"That's right. What is your brother's name?"

"Adam."

"Do you have a sister?"

"No."

"What town do you live in?"

"Portland."

"Do you go to football games?"

"No."

"Do you go to baseball games?"

"No."

"Do you go to the zoo?"

"Yes, it's big. I go there with my mommy."

"What about Daddy?"

"Nope, he doesn't go with us."

"What is Mommy's name?"

"Mommy," She said and Matt smiled.

"What does Mommy call Daddy?"

"Roger."

"And what does Daddy call Mommy?"

"Sweetheart!" She giggled and Matt frowned. His mind flashed to the woman in the front seat of the plane, the empty eyes.

"What's your last name?"

"What's that?"

"Do you practice writing your name in school?"

"I do kindergarten. I spell Amy Walters."

"That's a nice name Amy Walters." He got her father's name and hometown, time to just keep her entertained. "Do you like animals?"

"Horses now! I like Buttercup, she's pretty."

Matt smiled and looked over at the pretty cream-colored horse with his pretty cousin riding her. Then, he realized he hadn't heard her laugh since their morning of the plane crash; just before the airplane passed over their heads. He couldn't remember the last time she had gone this long without laughing. Maybe yesterday's events were more traumatic on her than she was showing.

Matt slowed Trooper down so Reilly could ride next to him. Adam was propped on his makeshift pillow in front of the teenager and he was sound asleep.

"What's up?" Reilly asked and looked over at him.

"Buttercup!" Amy said loudly. "I like Buttercup!"

Reilly and Matt smiled at her.

Matt looked over at Reilly. "Have you had a chance to talk with Grace? Is she alright?"

Reilly shook his head, "We've been with the kids."

"Have you noticed?" Matt asked hoping he would understand.

"Yeah," Reilly frowned. "Not since the first morning."

"We'll need to work on that," Matt told him.

"Work on what?" Grace trotted up beside them.

"Work on taking a break at the top," Matt said quickly. "We should be there in a couple of minutes."

They all three looked up to the top of the mountain and rode in silence the rest of the way.

Matt felt a huge sense of relief when they crested the top of the mountain. The rest of the ride should be fairly flat, with a slight decent into the campground. But it was still going to take until the next day to reach it.

He turned to make sure everyone had made it over the hill, when Amy pointed to their left. "What's that?" She asked.

Matt turned and looked the direction she pointed.

Fear shot through him; it was a bear...the worse kind...a grizzly bear...and it was watching them.

CHAPTER NINE

Matt pulled his rifle out of the scabbard. He turned back and saw Reilly, Grace, and Nick were also removing their rifles.

"Come up closer," He called back to the trio. The bear was to their left about seventy-five yards. "Reilly come up on my right. Amy hold me as tight as you can."

"Grace! Can you shoot?" Nick trotted up next to her, his voice calm.

"Yes, I've shot a couple black bear on the ranch," She said without moving her eyes away from the bear.

"Move up between Matt and the bear," Nick told her. "I'll come up behind you, if he charges we'll both shoot."

"OK," Grace said calmly. The butt of the rifle was resting on her right leg, the barrel pointed to the sky.

"Have you ever shot around your horse?" Nick asked.

"No. I don't know what she'll do." Grace was still calm.

The bear took a couple tentative steps toward them.

"Your horse is going to jump after the first shot," Nick told her. His voice was composed. "Not knowing what happened, she may freeze. If she does, shoot again, because she may not give you another chance."

"OK," Grace agreed. "Uncle Scott has shot off the top of Monty a number of times."

"Good to know," Nick said.

The bear took another couple steps.

Matt was leading them forward and to the right, so the bear would know they were leaving, but the bear started walking toward them faster.

All the horse's heads were up and alert…their ears twisting and turning in nervousness.

"Uncle Scott taps him on the right shoulder to let him know what's happening." Grace continued.

"OK," Nick answered.

"If he charges, Reilly and I have to take off and get these kids out of here." Matt was staring at the bear.

"Agreed," Nick answered. "Grace, you good?"

The bear started walking toward them more confidently.

"Yes," She said firmly.

She lifted the rifle over her arm so she was more prepared.

"You're right handed," Nick said talking to Grace but watching the bear. "Put your reins in your left hand so if something happens you can pull her back with your left hand and hold the gun in the right."

"OK." Grace switched the reins to her left hand, leaving enough slack the horse couldn't jerk and move the rifle.

Matt turned and looked at Nick. He was in the same position as Grace.

The bear was getting closer, its pace was faster than the tired horses.

"Matt?" Nick said without turning away from the bear.

"Yeah?" Matt's heart was racing, his eyes hurting from staring so hard.

"You and Reilly start trotting and get some distance from us. We'll give you a couple of minutes then start trotting too, unless he gets too close. If the bear doesn't stop or he charges, we'll shoot and take off at a gallop. If you hear us shoot, take off. We'll meet you at the butte you pointed on the map last night."

"OK," Matt told him. He was barely breathing; he turned quickly and looked at Reilly. His face was pale from the fear. The little boy was still sleeping in his arms.

"Amy, grab my belt with both your hands and hold on as tight as you can." Matt whispered to the little girl and felt her do as he asked. She had gone quiet as soon as the rifles were drawn. The poor girl was going to be traumatized for life after the last couple of days.

Matt turned and looked at the bear. He was closer now. Nick and Grace were ready.

"Good luck," Matt whispered and kicked Trooper into a trot. His heart was pounding, pulse racing, and his back and neck hurt from the tension. Reilly kept up with him on the right. One arm gripping the boy who was now awake, and the other arm held the reins; he was staring straight ahead. They were both waiting to hear either a gun shot or hoof beats.

It was gunshots. The first two were simultaneous, then one after another.

Matt and Reilly took off in a gallop; counting the gunshots. There were seven in all and then all went quiet.

Matt had one arm behind him, trying to hold onto Amy. His shoulder was screaming in pain but he ignored it. She felt pretty sturdy in her seat.

He turned and looked behind and saw Grace and Nick in a dead run coming towards them. No bear following.

"Reilly, hold up!" He pulled Trooper to a stop and turned to watch his niece and dad approach on a run.

Reilly walked up next to him. Adam was smiling. He had enjoyed the run. Reilly was near tears from the fear.

"Amy, you ok?" Matt asked.

"Yes, I liked running, but I don't like bears," She shouted.

Matt chuckled nervously. "I'm with you there."

Matt kept his eyes on the horizon behind the two riders. No bear appeared.

As they approached, he could see the look of excitement on Grace's flushed face. Her hair and Buttercups mane were flying in the air; bouncing with each stride of the horse. The gun was resting on her thigh, barrel in the air. She looked like Annie Oakley riding in.

They galloped right up and reined to a stop; both of them grinning.

Matt felt the tension start to ease in his muscles.

"What happened?" Reilly asked too loudly.

"Just a sec," Grace said and jumped down from a prancing Buttercup. She walked to the front of the horse and rubbed her down excitedly.

Matt looked up at Nick.

"He's down, won't be moving again." Nick smiled at Grace and stepped off of Monty.

Matt slid Amy off the horse and stepped down, turning to Reilly to help with Adam. Adam turned away from him and grabbed ahold of Reilly.

"No!" Adam cried out and buried his face into Reilly shirt.

Matt smiled and shook his head. "I'll hold Cooper. See if you can get down." There was no way he was going to force Adam to let go. The boy could have whatever he wanted to help get through the trauma.

Reilly awkwardly stepped down off the horse with the boy wrapped around his neck. They walked to Nick and Grace and waited for the story.

Grace's breathing was starting to return to normal, but the grin on her face was still there.

Nick was watching her, the elation showing in his expression.

"OK, spill," Reilly said impatiently.

"The bear charged us," Grace said excitedly.

Matt couldn't tell whether she was really excited or if it was her nerves making it sound like she was excited. His own stomach turned at the image of a grizzly charging them.

"We both shot, then shot again, then again." Grace turned back to Buttercup and stroked the horse's neck as she spoke. "When I shot the first time, Buttercup jumped a little then stood perfectly still, for all four shots! She was awesome!"

"Both horses stood like statues while we shot," Nick added; he had his arm wrapped under Monty's nose and stroked the horses face as he spoke. "I tapped Monty on the shoulder like Grace said and he didn't flinch."

"Once we shot, and knew the bear was down, we turned and ran to catch up with you." Grace walked over to Nick and threw her arms around his neck.

Shock registered on Nick's face and an arm slowly wrap around her back to embrace her. He nervously glanced over at Matt, so he smiled to let his dad know it was fine. Nick finally relaxed and she stepped back.

"Sorry, I was just so excited." Grace grinned at him and walked up to Reilly, who had Adam resting on his hip.

She wrapped arms around her best friend and hugged tightly. Matt saw the look of relief on Reilly's face.

Adam must have thought Grace was going to try and take him from Reilly because he turned and wrapped his arm around the teenager's neck, buried his face and screamed "No!".

Grace quickly jumped back and threw her arms in the air. "OK!" She laughed, her 'life is good' laugh.

Reilly and Matt glanced at each other and smiled; their Grace was back.

They decided to have lunch where they were. It took Grace a few minutes to relax enough to take a seat on a fallen tree next to Nick. She couldn't get close to Reilly without Adam yelling.

Matt smiled at Nick and Grace as they talked about the bear coming at them. They had started to trot away when the bear charged. They quickly turned and shot as fast as they could. After three shots each, they stopped shooting, the bear was down. Grace thought the bear moved again so she took aim and shot the bear again. Then they turned and ran.

The more the pair talked, the more Matt's stomach ached. He grabbed his rifle and walked over to the brush next to the clearing. He found a huckleberry bush and started picking as fast as he could while watching the area around him. After cutting off the top of a water bottle he used it as a container for the berries.

He was having a hard time relaxing. The fear for both Grace and Nick was deep and he was having a hard time letting it go.

Nick walked up and started picking too.

"Well," Matt chuckled. "The last thing I ever thought we'd do together is go berry picking."

Nick laughed then looked at him, "Are you OK?"

Matt nodded, he felt his stomach start to ache; maybe he was just hungry.

"Matt?"

He looked up at Nick.

"You've gone white." Nick looked concerned.

Matt glanced over at the small group and moved behind a tree so they couldn't see him. His heart began to ache along with his stomach and he felt his hands start to shake.

"Matt!" Nick quickly walked up to him, glancing out at the teenagers and kids.

Matt turned and started dry heaving. There wasn't anything in his stomach to vomit.

Once the heaves stopped, he stood up and looked back at the small group. They were fine. He glanced up at Nick who was handing him a bottle of water.

Matt swished the water around his mouth and spit, then drank the rest of the bottle.

Without saying anything, he cut the top off of the bottle and walked back to the berry bush. They picked in silence. Once both bottles were full, they walked back to the small group and watched the kids devour the berries.

Matt took a few tentative bites of the venison and was relieved that it made him feel better, so he ate enough to fill his empty stomach.

All four horses were lying down and eating any grass within reach. They had a long morning; from the mountain climb to the run from the bear.

Matt watched Grace picking flowers with Amy and smiled. He remembered doing the same thing with Grace when she was Amy's age. Amy took the flowers and placed them in Buttercup's mane. The little girl was in love with the horse.

"What's up?" Matt asked Amy.

"Buttercup!" Amy yelled and laughed with shining eyes.

Grace looked between the two of them and started laughing.

Her laugh soothes the soul, Matt decided.

"It's almost three," Nick walked up next to him.

Matt nodded; another twenty-four hours and his mom would be in range of cell service.

They remounted the tired horses and headed for the butte. Hopefully, they could reach Jessup tonight so he could let Cora and Nikki know they were OK.

"I'm surprised that we haven't seen any Search and Rescue planes," Matt said as he rode next to Nick. Reilly and Grace rode with the kids in front. They could see the butte and were riding to it.

"Nikki would have called them at nine o'clock this morning," Nick commented. "I would think they would be here by now since Jessup knew your exact plans."

"One thing after another…" Matt sighed and looked over at a confused Nick. "We're way off the original trail." He pointed over Nick's head. "If they are looking, they are over the other side of that mountain."

"We haven't been putting out trail markers since we didn't plan on coming back," Nick nodded.

"We should get to the butte before dark to make the call to Jessup."

"One way or another, we'll be out here another night with the horses."

"If Search and Rescue show up they'll just take the kids." Matt glanced over at his dad. "Reilly needs to go with Adam if they do. Adam's been traumatized enough. Until someone he knows and is connected to shows up, Reilly needs to stay with him."

"I agree."

Matt sighed. "I really want the kids off this mountain and out of danger."

"I wholehearted agree with you on that, too."

"Then we need to get to the butte and get the call out to Jessup."

CHAPTER TEN

As much as Matt wanted to run the horses to the butte, to let the family know they were OK, he knew the young horses couldn't give much more than they had already.

He looked over at Buttercup carrying the two girls. The horse could have freaked out, throwing Grace and leaving her for the bear. But she didn't...the horse had remained calm for Grace. These horses never cease to amaze him. His eyes went to Cooper; who had saved Reilly on the rock slide. Then there was Trooper, who remained calm on the cliff side yesterday. The three-year-old horses were giving them everything they had.

Monty was walking calmly under Nick. The grey horse's head was just at Trooper's hip so Matt could see the scars on his chest. The scars were created when he had rammed the fence and saved Wade the year before. Monty had run all morning yesterday, carrying Nick to find them.

Matt reached down and stroked Trooper's neck. The horse lifted his head and turned back to look at him, the big brown eye looking alert and ready for anything.

"You're good, Boy." Matt smiled at the horse. Trooper relaxed and continued on his way.

Matt looked up into the sky and wished the planes were there. Search and Rescue should be looking for them, but were probably on the other side of the mountain. He looked to the butte. They were only a half-hour away. Pulling the GPS out, he turned it on to check their location compared to camp. They were making good progress, but were still a ways out. According to his calculations, they should be back to the campground and Jessup around ten o'clock the next day. They were going to need to take more frequent breaks the next day; both horses and humans were getting stressed. His calculations didn't take into account any more incidents in the wilderness.

Matt scratched his chin through the whiskers that he wasn't used to. The aspirin was helping keeping the pain from the rope burns at ease. He was tired and just wanted to be home and in bed sleeping…after a long hot shower…or a soak in his mom's Jacuzzi tub.

It was seven o'clock when they heard the first plane in the distance. They could barely see it flying over the area of the wreckage.

Just before dark, the tired group of riders reached the butte and they waited at the base as Monty and Nick rode towards the top. Nick had the walkie-talkie on and was trying to contact Jessup.

"What's up?" Matt called out, as he watched Nick climb the hillside.

"Buttercup!" Amy and Adam answered with giggles.

Their energy was amazing.

Matt saw Nick stop and his hand reaching to his mouth.

"It looks like he reached Jessup," Reilly said.

They all stared at Nick as he spoke with the foreman. Ten minutes later, Nick turned and made his way back down the butte.

"I don't think I've ever heard anyone so happy to hear my voice," Nick grinned as he approached the small band of riders.

The search and rescue team had setup camp with Jessup. The ground team had just arrived at the crash site. Their airplane would be flying over soon and drop a care package of food, water, and a first-aid kit. Nick told them not to risk anyone trying to get to them in the dark. They were all healthy, just tired.

Nick had given them the names and condition of the kids. Jessup would call Nikki and Cora to let them know they were fine.

Just knowing that the family knew they were okay, was a relief that flooded through Matt and left him even more tired than he was before. Even if they couldn't get to his phone by 3:00 the next afternoon to catch the call from his mom, she would at least know they were alright.

The tired group continued on the trail until they arrived at a small clearing in the trees where the plane could drop the care package. It was already eight-thirty, so Matt declared they would stop for the night and give the horses a break.

Monty was tethered to a tree to graze and the other three horses were let loose. There was no fear that the young horses would leave Monty or the riders. They all wandered the meadow, eating ferociously at the grass. A small creek was nearby for their water.

Matt sat on a log watching Grace and Reilly bathe the kids in the creek. Their bruising was a little darker but didn't seem to hurt. He slowly ran his hand over the rifle that rested across his lap.

He had noticed that if Adam wasn't in Reilly's arms, then he had ahold of the teenager's leg. Amy was better; she kept a close eye on Grace all the time, but didn't insist on being held.

Nick was gathering wood for the evening, his rifle in hand at all times.

They heard the plane approaching and gathered together to watch for it. It was low and the pilot tipped the wings up and down to let them know he had seen them. They all waved excitedly. The plane passed by them twice before they saw a package drop from the back. The pilot passed low, tipped his wings again, and flew off into the distance.

The package wasn't too far away, so Matt and Grace, rifles in hand, headed out on foot to get it. Trooper and Buttercup followed closely behind. The horse's connection to their riders was stronger than ever.

While they made their way back to the camp, Grace told Matt about the bear incident again…his stomach started to hurt.

**

With stomachs full and the darkness covering them, the kids, Reilly, and Grace fell asleep next to the fire.

Matt and Nick sat on a fallen log across from the bed rolls.

"I'll take first watch," Matt offered.

Nick nodded then glanced over at him, "You, OK?"

Matt nodded, "I don't know what happened; all the sudden my stomach just lost it."

Nick stretched his legs out in front of him. The rifle was resting next to him. "You weren't in control."

"What?"

"Every step of the way this week, you were in control, until that bear showed up and you had Amy on your horse," Nick explained. "From that point, you had to keep her safe and the control of the situation went to me and Grace."

Matt nodded; it made his stomach turn just thinking about it.

"It was easier for me and Grace because we were in control of our situation and your protection. All you and Reilly could do was run and wait…that's hard to do." Nick looked at him. "I can't imagine how hard it was to worry about Grace, knowing she was facing a grizzly."

Matt shuttered at the image, then looked over at Nick. "It wasn't just worry for her."

Nick nodded and smiled in understanding, "I know…it was for Buttercup, too." He grinned.

Matt laughed. Why couldn't he just tell Nick how he felt? Then, looking into Nick's eyes…he realized he just did.

Nick turned and looked down at the sleeping crew.

"You should have seen her," Nick nodded towards Grace. "I didn't see the first three shots…but the fourth? She was a statue and literally standing in the stirrups, leaned towards the bear, and calmly pulled the trigger." He shook his head and glanced back up at Matt. "I was truly impressed."

Matt nodded, and without realizing it placed his hand over his turning stomach.

"Matt, you have to accept it, be proud of her, and let it go."

Matt nodded. "I know, but I just keep seeing it in my mind…and it has different results," He rolled his eyes. "Can you imagine what Grayson and Leah are going to say? They'll never forgive me for this." He could feel the ache in his heart, the turning of his stomach, and the exhaustion of his entire body. The weight of world was pressing him down.

"Matt, look at me," Nick said. Matt reluctantly turned. "They don't have anything to forgive; you did not put that bear there, it is not your fault."

"I put her in these mountains."

"Because you wanted to spend time with her and Reilly…not that you were trying to put them in danger."

"I let my guard down. I shouldn't have had Amy with me. She should have been with Grace the whole time." Matt shook his head.

"Look at those two little ones there," Nick pointed to Amy and Adam. "Do you think that Grace would choose to be home, rather than have those two kids saved?"

The air went out of Matt, he hadn't thought of it that way. He shook his head and looked up at his father. "No, she wouldn't, Reilly wouldn't, I wouldn't and neither would Grayson and Leah." He felt the weight lift; it brought tears to his eyes.

"Accept it, be proud of her, and let it go," Nick repeated with a soft reassuring voice.

Matt nodded, with more energy than he'd had since the bear appeared. He reached out and gripped his dad's wrist. "Thank you...you have no idea..."

Nick placed his other hand over the top of Matt's and squeezed but didn't say anything.

"Turn in," Matt grinned at his dad with renewed energy, "We have another day ahead of us to catch up."

Nick grinned and stood up. "Wake me at two-thirty."

Nick laid down next to the fire, he was head to head with the small group, and his rifle lay next to him.

One more day and they would be home, Matt thought with a smile. He just wanted this trip over with.

Matt threw more wood on the fire so the light would show him the horses. They had tied the three young horses next to Monty before dark. All four horses stood quietly; heads were low as they slept.

Nick's chest was rising and lowering as he had fallen into a deep sleep. That was fast, Matt smiled. He stared at the sleeping man as he thought back to New Year's Eve...how shocked he was to see him at the party. His first instinct was to get his mother out of the room; he knew Nikki would drag her along as they left.

When they reached the hotel, he had no idea that the man would have any affect in his life...until he saw him. The tension from his mother and sister was intense and Matt's protective mode took over and had no idea he was going to hit Nick, until it happened. He didn't regret it then and, even now, after months of getting to know each other, he still didn't regret it. The man had hurt his mother and sister, Matt wasn't going to let that go.

Listening to Nick's story he began to sympathize with him. He didn't have anything to forgive him for; Matt agreed that Nick did the right thing by bringing Nikki to Dru and leaving. They both had a good life because of his decision.

Another shock that night was realizing that his mother and Jack had a personal relationship. Once Nick had pointed out there were three men supporting him, Matt had put together the pieces and watched the two of them. He was overjoyed because he loved Jack and Reilly.

But he didn't like Nikki's birth mother, Elena, from the moment he met her at The Stables, to the night at the hotel while Nick told his story. There was something wrong with the way the woman was acting. She should have been more excited to meet her daughter after twenty years apart. He was proud how Nikki handled the situation.

The call to invite Nick to help build the arena was a tough one. In his mind, he had told himself that the man had come to Lewiston for them; him and Nikki…there was no other reason for Nick to have been there. If he didn't care, then no matter what Elena was up to…he wouldn't be there. Even though he was sure Nick would accept the invitation to help build the arena, it was still a hard call to make…there was a little hint of fear that Nick would say no and break Nikki's heart.

But he said yes, and the day had gone surprisingly well. He'd enjoyed working with Nick, and could tell Scott and Grayson did, too. The three men's friendship quickly rekindled. Nikki had been happy…which was the most important thing.

Matt stood and tried to stretch, but the pain from the rope burns nearly made him cry out. He took off his shirt and stepped closer to the fire to see what his skin looked like. The portion he could see under his arms was blazing red and the there was a wide band of black and blue bruising on each side. The rope had not broken the skin enough to raise any blood.

"That's nasty," He whispered out loud and slipped his shirt back on.

A twig snapped in the darkness behind him.

CHAPTER ELEVEN

Matt spun around, bringing the rifle up to fire. His heart was pounding, pulse racing, and he held his breath; he could see movement but couldn't quite make out what it was…bear, wolf, mountain lion, deer, elk,….what now? The figure finally walked up close enough to tell… it was the invisible black horse walking towards him. Cooper! He'd nearly shot the horse! Matt lowered the rifle, his breathing shaky, and he started nervously laughing at himself.

Taking a few steps forward, he met the horse before it got into camp. The lead rope was dragging on the ground; he'd gotten loose. Lead rope in hand, he threw wood on the fire to lighten up the horses. He could see grey, cream, and just the hint of brown…three sets of eyes looking at him.

Matt took a few minutes to give the horse his attention. Face, neck, back, and hips; he ran his hand over the horse. Slinging the rifle over his shoulder, he reached up with both hands and massaged the back of the horse. Coopers whole body shivered. Matt understood, they were all getting sore and exhausted.

"Only half a day left, Big Boy," Matt whispered to him and led him back to the other horses.

Matt gave each horse a rub down and a back massage. They all shivered and groaned.

"I think I'm headed to the fitness center for a massage when I get back," He whispered to the horses. "…after I heal."

He sat on the log and looked over at the four kids sleeping. They had barely moved. Nick had rolled over onto his side with his back to him.

Matt realized he had no way of knowing when it was time to wake Nick. His phone was his clock and it was sitting in his truck. Nick had a watch on, but there was no way he was going to try to see it. The night was still pitch black…he'd wake Nick as soon as the sky started to lighten. Tonight he'd be in his own bed, so he only needed a few hours of sleep in the morning to make it through.

Matt scratched his whiskered chin and realized that he hadn't shaved since before the wedding…which suddenly felt like weeks ago, not just five days. He grinned at the memory of his mother standing next to her window looking out at the crowd. She was a vision! Some day he hoped to find a woman like her to marry; strong, determined, beautiful, funny, and compassionate…who loved horses, too.

The blonde, he had told Reilly and Grace about, didn't like horses, another girl had no sense of humor, another thought it was funny when one of the students fell down the steps at school…she just laughed, instead of helping the embarrassed and hurt kid. Matt broke up with her on the spot and helped the boy to the school nurse.

Two girls had gone out with him because of his family name; that was after the Tagger Herd had come into their lives. Both girls had practically stalked him on Facebook before they dated. One date was enough with the first girl, but it took two dates with the second before he realized why she was dating him.

The last semester of school he had stayed away from dating and concentrated on his classes; it was tough, but he had to do it to keep his grades up. Maybe that was why he didn't like college. No social life…too much studying…and really boring classes.

He and Nikki were living in a small apartment within walking distance of the campus. Nikki's new boyfriend had lasted more than a month, but she still didn't tell any family members about him, except for Matt. She didn't even ask him to attend the wedding. The guy was tall, good looking, and always had a smile on his face. He was of mixed ethnicity, but Matt wasn't quite sure what…it really didn't matter, as long as the guy treated Nikki right.

Matt stood and tried to stretch again to wake his tired body. He thought of the lariat digging into the skin as Trooper raised him and the kids. It was scary, but exciting at the same time. Not once did he look down; his eyes had stayed on the cliff edge the first trip, then Nick and Reilly on the second. He was definitely going to have to rock climb and rappel again when the conditions were better…like proper equipment and no one's life depending on him.

The U of I student recreation center had a 55-foot rock climbing pillar he was going to have to try out. Matt chuckled to himself…he was already thinking about going back to college in the fall…if only for the rec center. He turned and looked out past the darkness, remembering what the mountains looked like. Forest Management became his major in school because of the ranch and these mountains and his trips here with Jessup.

Even after the last few days he still loved these mountains and would return again…but was it enough? Was this truly what he wanted or needed to do? Maybe he wasn't mature enough yet to make such a huge life decision. He sighed out into the night and shook his head.

"I just don't know," He whispered into the night.

Matt waited until he could see the outline of the treetops and then woke Nick. Nick stood, stretched, and looked at his watch then over to Matt. "It's 4:00."

Matt shrugged; he was supposed to wake him at 2:30. "I don't have a watch and my cell phone is in the truck."

Nick shook his head, "Get some sleep."

As Matt settled under the bed roll he whispered to Nick; "Don't shoot Cooper if he wanders again. Reilly would kill you." Then everything went black.

***

Matt turned and looked at their final camp as they rode towards Jessup and home. The campfire was out and there was no other trace that they had been there. The supplies and the dismantled box had been separated into all the empty saddle bags.

"Search and Rescue is probably headed our way," Matt told the trail weary group. "They'll be faster than us, since they'll have fairly fresh horses or 4-wheelers depending on the terrain. If they have 4-wheelers they will get stopped about half way."

"Why?" Grace asked; she and Amy were riding to his right. Nick was on his left. Reilly and Adam were on the other side of Grace, with Adam happily singing a song to himself; it lightened Matt's mood.

"We reviewed the map this morning, and we have one more obstacle between us and the campsite." Matt looked over at Reilly. "A creek."

Reilly's eye's widened. "How big?"

Cooper's reaction to their river experiment had them all worried.

Matt shook his head, "Don't know…this time of year it could be two-feet to twenty-feet wide, or dried up to six-feet deep. We're not going to know until we get there."

They entered a thicket of trees that only allowed them to ride 2 by 2. Grace and Reilly moved to the front so Nick and Matt could watch over them.

Buttercup was prancing today.

"You ever notice that Buttercup matches Grace's mood?" Matt asked Nick. "When she's calm the horse walks calmly, when she's happy and laughing the horse prances."

"And when she was facing the bear yesterday… and was a statue…so was the horse." Nick nodded with a knowing smile.

"When Reilly fell on the rock slide, Grace froze…and so did Buttercup." Matt remembered.

They rode quietly watching Grace laugh and Buttercup join her by prancing.

"I need to talk to you about something." Matt glanced over at Nick; his whiskers were thicker than his and he looked as rugged as Matt felt.

"Shoot."

Matt hesitated then looked over at Nick. After their experiences the day before, and the talk last night, there was a new ease between them. They had moved to a more relaxed and open relationship.

"I'm considering dropping out of college." Matt 'spit it out' as his mother would say, and saw the look of surprise cross the older man's face, then a look of concern.

"Have you told Dru?"

"No, I was waiting until after the wedding and river trip. I'm going to talk to her when we all get back."

"You said considering…you're not sure yet?"

"No, that's why I wanted to talk to you," Matt looked over at him with a smile. "I have two surrogate fathers, a new step father, and a father. That's four…I'm going to get fathered to death."

The men looked at each other and started laughing. It felt good to laugh after all the stress the last couple of days.

"Your point is?" Nick finally asked.

"I need you more as a friend right now, than a father." Matt told him honestly.

Nick chuckled, "Well, I think we both know that will be a lot easier for me…but for future reference, what would a father say to you right now."

"Stay in school, you'll regret it for the rest of your life. You can make better money in the future with a college education. First year's always tough. Stick it out…." Matt smiled.

Nick nodded. "Noted…for the next time," He grinned. "So friend to friend, are you dropping out because it's too hard?"

"No, it's boring."

"Are you studying the right thing?"

"I was wondering that last night. I don't know."

"What made you go into Forest Management?"

"The ranch…these mountains…the trips here with Jessup."

"Nikki switched mid-steam from Resort Management to Equine Nutrition," Nick reminded him. "She's very happy with that decision. Have you thought of anything else?"

Matt shrugged. "Agricultural stuff…"

"Think out of the box Matt," Nick looked over at him. "Don't tell Dru I said this, but don't base your future on just what you should do for Tagger Enterprises. Dru, Scott, Grayson, and now Jack are still pretty young; they have the business taken care of for years."

Matt nodded, he agreed with that.

Nick continued; "Again, think out of the box. What do you like to do or want to do… not what you should do."

One thing instantly flashed in Matt's memory and he grinned. "What I want to do is rappel off a cliff with all the right gear and nobody's life at stake."

Nick laughed. When he grew quiet Matt looked over at him; he could tell he was deep in thought.

"What?" Matt asked.

"Have you had any issues with what you saw in the plane?"

"Wow...that was out of the blue," Matt chuckled then thought about his question. "No, not at all; I think about it every once in a while but it isn't bothering me."

"You've handled the last couple days pretty well. You've made difficult decisions, risked your life to save others, kept everyone fed and protected, and stayed calm in hard times..."

"Except one," Matt interrupted as he thought of Grace and the bear.

"But you learned from that one hiccup."

"Yeah, I did," Matt looked back over at Nick. "What are you getting at?"

"Have you ever thought of Search and Rescue?"

Matt's jaw dropped in surprise. He had never even considered it; not even when they discussed Search and Rescue coming for them the last two days.

"I'll take that as a no," Nick smiled. "Watch them when we meet up...you'll see them in action and see if it's something to consider. If it's not, then move on...just think out of the box before you make a decision."

"Good advice." Matt nodded.

They rode quietly awhile, Matt's mind going over the events of the last couple days, how he handled them and what he would have done differently...other than separating all the emergency lights into separate saddle bags and keeping Amy with Grace.

When they took a break, Matt checked the map for their location and tried to estimate their arrival home. It was nine o'clock now, with another hour of riding before they met up with Search and Rescue. He estimated their arrival at the campground at ten, then an hour to share information with Search and Rescue, the Sheriff's office, or anyone else that was waiting for them. If all went well, they could be out of the mountains and nearly home before his mom was due to call. They could be home before the rafting crew arrived home.

Cooper and the creek were the only obstacles he could see right now.

Obstacle was an understatement, he sighed as they approached the creek. With the rain from the week before, it was flowing faster and deeper than he hoped. The young horses were in for another training session.

CHAPTER TWELVE

The creek was twenty-feet wide, and the depth averaged around two feet but could potentially be more depending on where they crossed. It wasn't too bad for an experienced horse; Monty would have no problem and Matt didn't think Trooper would have an issue either.

They dismounted and developed a plan.

Nick rode Monty into the creek and found the shallowest spot to cross that also had a good exit point on the other side. The deepest section was up to the horse's knees.

Matt turned to Reilly. "Get on Monty and take Adam across. I'll follow on Trooper then lead Monty back. We'll repeat the crossing using Monty to get Grace and Amy across. I'll leave Trooper with you two and bring Monty back. Hopefully, Buttercup and Cooper can use Monty as encouragement to cross without too much of a fight."

All were in agreement and the first portion went without a problem. Reilly and Adam were safely on the other side. Pretty quickly, Grace and Amy were sitting with them. Trooper pranced anxiously as Matt rode Monty away from him. He whinnied causing Cooper and Buttercup to do the same.

"OK, Miss Buttercup," Matt slid onto her and Nick mounted Monty, "Let's see how this goes."

Matt nodded at his dad, and they made it a foot in before Buttercup refused to move. Cooper, tied to brush behind them, danced excitedly as he saw everyone leaving.

Matt took a deep breath and let the nerves and anxiety out of his body. "Any ideas?" He asked Nick.

"Let me see if she'll lead in...you'll probably have to kick her pretty hard to get her to move."

Matt untied the lead rope from the saddle and tossed it to Nick. It was already attached to the halter.

Nick put Monty in motion and Matt started kicking. He started lightly and she took a few steps, then started to backup pulling Monty and Nick sideways. Nick turned and started pulling again, Matt kicked harder. They were half-way through when Buttercup decided she'd had enough. She reared in the air. Matt leaned forward and tried to balance in the stirrups but she went too far up, lost her balance and started falling backwards...they were going down.

Matt's eyes went to Buttercups legs, worried she'd hurt them when they landed. It wasn't until the water splash around him that he decided to pay attention to himself rather than the horse. Nick would watch out for Buttercup.

He looked up and saw the horse's back and saddle coming towards him and tried to jump out of the way. She landed on the back of his legs, smashing them into the water and rocks. Pain shot through his legs and up his back. She hit him again as she tried to stand up. This time it was an unintentional kick to the rib, just under the rope burn.

Matt yelled, but his head was in water and it just came out as bubbles, he gasped taking in water. He pushed hard with his arms to get out of the water and his head finally found air. He sucked in as much as he could while coughing out the water.

He heard screaming from the side…sounded like Grace. Crying pierced through her screaming…that was Amy and Adam. Swear words flying in the air…was definitely Nick, with a little Reilly thrown in. Splashing and panicked whinnying…that was Buttercup.

Matt looked over at Nick and Buttercup as they made it to the other side of the creek and Grace ran for the horse. Nick turned Monty and they splashed into the water coming back for him.

Matt pushed himself over so he was sitting in the creek with the cool water rushing by. Stretching his legs in front of him, he then bent them making sure they were OK. A little painful, but OK, Matt sighed in relief and was standing when Nick reached him.

"Are you OK?" Nick grabbed him by the arm causing pain across his back from the rope burns.

Matt grimaced and Nick let him go.

"Yeah," Matt exhaled. "Just give me a second."

"Cooper!" Reilly yelled.

Matt turned quickly to see the black horse pull away from the brush and freeing himself. Then, at a dead run, the horse made his way across the creek to his friends.

They all stared in stunned silence.

Matt started laughing, laughing so hard he nearly fell over in the creek again. He grabbed onto Monty to steady himself.

When the laughter stopped, he looked up at Nick, who was looking at him like Matt had lost his mind.

Matt chuckled, "I'm sorry, but that was the best thing I have seen all week!"

Nick chuckled, then nodded at something behind Matt. Matt turned and saw two large jagged rocks sticking out of the water. He and Buttercup had missed them by inches. If he had landed on them and Buttercup on him…

Matt leaned his head back and looked at the sky. "Dang..."

Then they heard the 4-wheelers.

Nick kicked a foot out of one of the stirrups and Matt used it as a brace to walk the rest of the way out of the creek. Two 4-wheelers pulled in behind the horses.

"Are you alright?" A rider with thick blonde hair in a red jacket asked him. "We saw you go over."

Matt grinned and nodded. "It'll hurt in the morning, besides…I needed a bath." He reached out a hand to greet the two men.

Handshakes and names were exchanged and a quick call to base camp to let them know everyone was safe. The red jacket rider was Steve; Matt guessed his age in the late twenties. The other rider was Kevin and looked in his mid-thirties. They had left base camp at daylight and calculated they would meet up with the riders at the creek.

Nick turned to Matt and smiled. Matt had estimated the same thing. Matt smiled back.

Steve looked over at the two kids; Adam in Reilly's arms and Amy in Grace's embrace. "How are they doing?"

"Physically they are fine," Matt answered even though Steve had looked over at Nick when he asked the question. "They have bruising across their chests from the carseat harness."

"That's typical," Kevin responded looking at Matt. "We were at the crash site yesterday on horseback. Do they know about the parents?"

Matt shook his head. "No, Grace told them we were riding horses and taking them home. She kept them pretty calm once we found them."

"They were out of the plane?" Steve asked in surprise.

"Yeah…long story…away from them." Matt hoped they understood.

They both nodded.

"We're both EMT's, so we'd like to do a quick check on the kids," Kevin looked at Matt. "And you...that was a hell of a crash."

Matt shook his head, "I'm fine."

Matt nodded towards Reilly and Adam. "Little one's name is Adam, and there's Amy." He told the two men. "Adam stays in Reilly's arms while you check him out...you may still have issues if he thinks you're taking him away."

Kevin nodded. "He's psychologically attached himself to Reilly?"

Matt smiled and nodded, thank goodness they understood.

"Can Reilly stay with him until we get some family here? We don't want to traumatize the little guy anymore," Kevin continued.

Again, Nick looked at Matt and smiled. Matt had said the same thing. Matt smiled back.

"How is Amy's connection with Grace?" Steve asked.

"Not as close, she just doesn't get too far away from her," Matt answered.

"Food supplies good?" Steve asked and before anyone could answer he grinned. "Jessup sent you down something, said you might appreciate it." He turned to the box on the back of his 4-wheeler.

He lifted out Cora's apple pie.

***

Apple pie devoured; they checked the horse's legs for injuries. When satisfied the horses were good, they mounted, and started on the last leg of the trip.

Matt had never been so glad to see Jessup and the feeling was mutual. He carefully hugged his friend and raced to his truck to retrieve his phone. There was no service. He'd have to wait, but he had guessed the time right. It was ten o'clock; Nick grinned and Matt smiled.

After the horses were placed in the corral with food and water, the coolers of food were pulled out of Matt's truck. They ate while talking with the sheriff's deputies and waited for news on the family.

Matt glanced at his phone…noon.

"Can we take the kids with us to Lewiston?" Matt asked the sheriff. "We need to be in cell service by 3:00." Steve and Kevin had brought back the car seats from the crash site.

"Just got word the aunt and uncle will be arriving in Lewiston in about two hours," The lead officer answered. "Timing will be fine, we'll have one car lead and another follow." He started to turn away then stopped. "The Tribune wants to interview all of you."

Matt, Nick, Reilly and Grace looked at each other in surprise. They hadn't thought of that part.

"Can you tell them we want privacy until tomorrow?" Nick asked.

The officer agreed and they loaded in the trucks. Reilly was in the back behind Matt with Adam next to him. The boy fought like crazy until Reilly crawled in the seat next to him and they closed the door. Adam realized Reilly was staying and relaxed, but wouldn't let go of his hand. Amy was fine riding behind Grace. They were both asleep before they were a mile down the road.

As they approached Kooskia, their cell phones started chiming as they reached cell service. Matt pulled over so he could check his messages.

"I have 15 from Cora and 5 from Jessup," Grace announced.

"15 from Cora and 5 from Jessup," Reilly grinned.

"31 from Nikki, 20 from Cora, 11 from Jessup and 23 from Nick," Matt laughed. "I win!"

None from Mom, "We made it guys!" Matt looked around at his brother and cousin. "We could be home, showered, and changed by the time they arrive at The Homestead." They quietly cheered so the kids could sleep.

Matt got the call they were to meet the kid's family at the Red Lion Hotel. Matt laughed out loud which Reilly and Grace didn't understand but he wasn't going to tell them that was where he had first met Nick at New Year's.

Matt quickly called Nick to let him know, and got them both laughing.

When he hung up the phone, Matt continued to grin. If nothing else, this weekend brought him closer to his fourth dad.

***

The aunt and uncle ran to the truck as soon as they saw them pull into the hotel parking lot. Amy was excited when she saw them running to the truck. Adam was too small to be able to see them until the door was opened. Reilly had unhooked their harnesses, but Adam wouldn't let go of his hand.

Matt held his breath waiting for Adam's reaction to his relatives.

Amy hugged the crying aunt and uncle. They had been told the kids didn't know their parents were deceased. Amy's enthusiasm must have been painful for them to see.

His leg muscles had stiffened from Buttercup landing on him; Matt wasn't sure he could get out of the truck and back in. He was still in the truck when Adam turned and looked to see why his sister was so happy. His face registered surprise...then he smiled sweetly.

"Aunt Wendy," Adam said looking up at Reilly with big brown eyes.

"Yeah, it is," Reilly smiled encouragingly.

"Uncle Pete!" He said to Reilly after seeing the man.

"Do you want to go see them?" Reilly asked.

Adam looked out the door at the hopeful couple, then over to Reilly. His eyes shined; "Yes." And then he let go of Reilly's hand and crawled out of his car seat and into the arms of his distraught Aunt Wendy.

Matt looked at Reilly, there were tears in his eyes. He didn't want to embarrass his brother by consoling him in public, so when Reilly looked up at him, he nodded his understanding.

Matt looked down at his phone for the time. It was 1:30.

They made arrangements to come back in the evening and visit the kids and tell the story to the family. Grace and Reilly loaded back in the truck up front with Matt.

Matt turned the truck to drive to The Homestead when his phone rang.

"It's Mom." Matt showed them the phone. They all smiled and rolled their eyes in relief.

He stopped the truck and Reilly jumped out to go tell Nick and Jessup.

"Mom!" Matt answered making his voice sound normal. He was so relieved they made it in time.

"Matt! It's so good to hear your voice!" She shouted back, her voice was resonating with happiness.

Matt laughed. Her laugh filled his soul and he closed his eyes as they filled with tears. He was suddenly exhausted.

"How was your trip?" Matt asked. "Everyone safe and no one drown?"

"I can't wait to tell you!" She said excitedly. "Did you guys have fun? How was your trip? Did Grace and Reilly love the mountains like you? I saw the pictures from the river; you looked like you were having fun!"

Matt laughed…she was going to have so many more questions.

"Yes, good, and you'll have to ask them…when you get home."

"Oh great!" Her voice was so happy. "We should be there in about an hour and a half. I can't wait to see everyone!"

Matt saw Jessup climb out of the truck and head to him. "OK, Mom, can't wait to see you and hear your stories."

"You too, love you, Son!"

"You too, Mom." And he ended the call as Jessup reached his window.

"We have an hour and a half before they get home," Matt told him. "We'll stop at The Homestead and drop off the horses, Grace and Reilly. Then, Nick can jump in with me and we'll go to my house to shower, then head back."

"You be there before they arrive." Jessup ordered with a frown.

"I will, but it will be close," Matt said as he put the truck in drive.

CHAPTER THIRTEEN

Matt and Nick arrived, showered and shaven, ten minutes before the rafting crew arrived. The long drive back had made Matt's sides and legs stiffen. Nick had to help him out of the truck and to get his shirt off, then on again. They both laughed nervously at his feebleness.

Matt's heart was racing. He had no idea what to expect. They had setup a plan on how to tell their parents...hopefully all went well.

"You know she's going to hug the hell out of you," Cora said, as they stood at the end of the driveway and watched the truck arrive.

Nikki was at his side, holding his hand tightly.

"I know." Matt nearly grimaced at the thought. "Once she does, you have to distract her so I can get to the chair without her noticing...or any of them."

"Well, that's a challenge," Cora chuckled.

The truck stopped, and the rafters exploded out the doors. They all looked tan, relaxed, and happy; grins were from ear to ear. Sadie, Nora, and Wade, who had no idea what was going on, reached the parents first. Then Grace ran into her parent's arms with so much enthusiasm she nearly knocked them over. Reilly had both his new mom and his dad wrapped in a strong embrace; both their faces grinned first, then started showing their confusion.

"Reilly, it hasn't been that long, let them loose." Matt stood in one place with Nick on one side and Nikki on the other.

Reilly let go and turned back to him; tears were in his eyes. He was as relieved to be home as Matt. Nikki quickly greeted their mother and Jack and then returned to Matt's side.

"Well, that was quite a greeting from one of my son's." She looked at Reilly and they both grinned, Reilly was near tears and dove to give her another hug.

Jack walked up to Matt and stepped in for an embrace. Matt grimaced and lifted his arms to return the greeting. Jack's arms were around his shoulders so it wasn't too bad but hers were going to be around his ribs.

"You're pretty tan," Matt laughed.

Grayson walked by and slapped Matt on the back. It took all his energy not to cry out.

"Nick!" Grayson shook his hand, "We weren't expecting to see you here."

"Just thought I'd spend some time with the Matt and Nikki," Nick smiled and glanced at Matt.

"Matt, are you going to greet your mother or not?" She was standing in front of him with hands on hips. Her beautiful blue eyes were shining with happiness.

Matt slid his arms around her waist so she would have to go to his neck or around his shoulders; he hugged her tightly.

He leaned back, lifting his mom off her feet, and yelled to cover the pain. She laughed and slapped him to put her back down. He did and kissed her cheek. "You're beautiful, Mom." He grinned, "Married life agrees with you."

"Yes, it does!" She laughed and they were interrupted by Cora suggesting they take their bags upstairs.

Nick was watching him closely. "You OK?" He whispered.

"Sort of..." Matt turned to see where the parents were. "You may have to help me up the steps; that nearly took it out of me."

Reilly and Grace placed themselves between Matt and the house. The parents had all gone inside as Cora suggested.

"Go." Grace yelled excitedly at their covert mission.

Matt walked as fast as his stiff legs would let him. Each step up the deck stairs sent streaks of pain up his back and stiffened his shoulders. Nick tried to lift as he pushed up.

Matt had broken into a sweat from the pain by the time they reached the top.

They walked right to the side of the deck table that faced the house so when the parents came out they would have to sit opposite. Matt sat in the middle with Grace then Nick on his right and Reilly, then Jessup on his left. Nikki was next to Nick.

Cora stepped out first and looked at Matt.

"I need pain killers," He told her. She nodded and stepped back in the house.

Cora made it out with aspirin and water before the parents made it down from their bedrooms. She took a seat next to Jessup.

Grayson was out the door first, holding hands with his wife.

"Well, look at you guys," Leah laughed with a confused look on her face.

"We're anxious to hear your story," Grace smiled innocently.

Matt knew she was being honest; they all wanted to hear their rafting stories. Although they were anxious to tell of their last few days in the mountains, they were also worried about the reactions.

Grayson and Leah sat across from Grace and Nick, his mom across from him, Jack across from Reilly, and Scott and Jordan across from Jessup and Cora. Wade, Sadie, and Nora were at the end by Cora.

Matt smiled at the light in his mom's eyes…he hated to see it go away, but he had no choice. He had just learned that Amy and

Adam would be on the plane home first thing in the morning. They wanted to go into town and say goodbye.

"You first," Reilly told the rafters.

Grayson and Jordan had fallen out of the raft and had to ride-out a long rapid in the water. Both were fine and excited about the experience. While sleeping on the beach they had heard elk bugling on Monday night. Tuesday night they were sure they heard a wolf howling.

The days were full of sleeping on the raft in the middle of the day, feet dangling in the water, sun shining down, water warm and soothing. They laughed, played, and on occasion…had a beer or two, wink wink.

They all looked happy and rested.

Grayson looked over at his daughter and smiled. "Did you enjoy the mountains?"

Grace glanced up at Matt, which made Grayson look at him. "Yeah, we did," She smiled.

"What's going on?" Scott asked looking between Matt, Grace, and Reilly.

No one spoke; Matt wasn't sure how to start.

Reilly finally looked up at Matt. "Talk."

Matt nodded down at his brother and smiled nervously, then turned and looked at Grace.

"Talk," She encouraged.

"What happened?" Jack asked, glancing between the two new brothers.

"You're all alright," Scott pointed out. "So what happened?"

Matt spoke fast and as matter-of-fact as he could:

"We headed up and stopped at Gibb's Eddy to test the horses and water. Trooper was a trooper, Buttercup touched but didn't like, Cooper hated. We got to the mountains and had a great afternoon ride. We saw elk and deer all over the place. Slept under the stars, laughed around the campfire, and slept like babies; good times." Matt smiled, all their faces were smiling but a little confused. "The next morning we went out to a mountain bluff to look over my favorite spot. Just before we got there, a plane flew really low over our heads and we watched it crash land in a meadow so we took off and tried to get there to help. It took us a couple hours because Reilly nearly slid down a shale rockslide, but Cooper saved him from falling hundreds of feet and into the river. When we finally arrived, there were two people dead in the front seat, only I saw, Reilly and Grace didn't." Matt looked at Jack and Grayson who were just staring...no expression. Once he got started the words spilled out without a pause. "Then I noticed little footprints in the dirt, but we ran out of daylight so had to camp before we could search for them. Grace fell asleep and Reilly and I listened to wolves howl all night. We also heard the kids cry, so we knew they were close. We got up at dawn and started searching...that's when Reilly fell down a hole and onto a ledge where he found a three-year-old boy named Adam and a six-year-old girl named Amy. I had to dangle off the edge of a 100 foot cliff with a lariat around me, tied to Trooper, who lowered me down and pulled us up one at a time. Grace screamed, Nick had shown up, after Nikki and Cora called to say we hadn't checked in...Grace screamed because Nick scared her, we got both kids and Reilly up then headed out." He paused and met their expressionless stares. So he continued...

"Went back to the plane to get the kids clothes, headed down to a creek for the kids to bathe, couldn't go back the same way we came because of the dangerous mountainside, so we had to go into the wilderness farther to get to the base of the mountain and head back to the camp. Slept in the wilderness again with Nick and I sharing watch. Then in the morning we headed up the mountain side which took us forever…nearly the whole day. Once we got to the top we ran into a grizzly bear, Adam was on the front of Reilly's saddle, where he rode the whole time. He attached himself to Reilly…anyway, Amy was on the back of my horse so when we ran into the bear, Nick and Grace ended up shooting it when it charged, while Reilly and I got the kids to safety. Buttercup was perfect and allowed her to shoot four times." He paused again….still no expressions except for the narrowing of Grayson's eyes.

"OK, well then, we finally got to the butte we were riding to, so Nick could ride up and contact Jessup and let Nikki and Cora know we were OK. Search and Rescue had been called out, but they were over at the plane wreckage and didn't know we were on the other mountain. They couldn't get to us in time before dark, so they dropped a care package. So this morning we got up and headed in but had a creek to pass. Monty and Trooper did great but Buttercup didn't especially like it. Nick was leading her while I was riding and she got tired of me kicking and pushing so she reared up, lost her balance, fell backwards on top of me, pushing me under and then got even with me for kicking her by kicking me in the side." He paused again…no expressions.

"Well, that's when Search and Rescue showed up, with Cora's apple pie, that was more than awesome. We were tired of venison, which Reilly had shot the deer, and energy bars that I had bought on clearance at the store in Kamiah…anyway, we made it out. Amy and Adam's aunt and uncle met us at Red Lion, of all places, and Adam finally let loose of Reilly for the first time in three days. Then we raced up here and put the very tired, wonderful, awesome horses in their stalls, showered, and got here about five minutes before you pulled up the drive."

He stopped and took a drink of water while glancing at the six rafters.

His mom's eyes flickered between him, Reilly, Grace, and Nick then back to him.

"Is that a joke?" She finally asked.

"Not a funny one," Jordan frowned.

"What did you do? Sit on the mountain side and come up with this lame idea?" Grayson looked at him with a frown.

They sat quietly a minute.

"You'll have to show them, Matt," Nick said.

Matt looked at his mom who was glaring at Nick. He turned his gaze to Nick. "I've stiffened even more, you'll have to help."

"What?" His mom whispered with a shaky voice.

Nick and Reilly stood and helped him stand. Every muscle in his body screamed at him. The aspirin from Cora hadn't kicked in yet.

Matt watched his mom closely as they helped him lift his arms up as high as possible. Nick and Reilly lifted his shirt.

Her eyes widened in horror when she saw the deep red rope burn and the bruising that had spread out and created a wide band around his back and chest. Buttercup's hoof print was clearly visible on his side.

Matt heard a sob from Nikki and glanced down at her. Tears were streaming down her face as she tried to hide behind her balled up fists. Their mom looked between the three of them and slowly rose.

"Everything?" She whispered in disbelief. "Everything you just said was true?"

"What the…" Grayson had leaned forward and was staring at his injuries.

Jordan, Leah, and Scott sat motionless and speechless.

"I need to sit," Matt said. Nick and Reilly helped lower him again then returned to their chairs.

Matt looked up at his mom after he was back down. She was still staring. He looked at the six parents who now had expressions of horror and disbelief. His eyes stopped on Grayson; waiting for him to realize the grizzly bear part was true.

It didn't take long…he sat straight up and looked at Grace then to Matt. "A grizzly bear?" He nearly yelled the words.

"Yes," Grace answered and told the story from the moment they saw the bear to the moment she and Nick caught back up.

Matt watched Grayson's body stiffen and his eyes start to burn, he looked at Matt then at Nick who were on each side of his daughter.

"Everything you said was true?" Jordan asked again.

"Yes," Reilly looked at her. "Everything, and actually a little more, but we figured a fast condensed version would help you understand the whole week before we went over each day."

Matt looked at his phone.

"You have somewhere to go?" Grayson asked gruffly.

Matt's eyes shot up to him, Nick's back stiffened and Matt knew he was ready to defend him.

"Yes," Matt answered trying to keep his voice calm. "Amy and Adam are on a flight first thing in the morning. Our only chance to see them again is tonight. We're going in to meet them at 6:00. I was…"

"No, you're not," His mom interrupted.

"But, Adam…" Reilly started to say nervously, but Matt put his hand over his brother's.

"Yes, we are." He looked firmly into her scared eyes. "We were in such a hurry we didn't get to say a proper goodbye to the kids."

"You're not going anywhere except into the couch or Nikki's old bed," She informed him. "They can come out here."

"They could see the horses again," Grace said softly to Matt.

Matt lowered his gaze from his mother to his phone and called the number the aunt had given him. He spoke to her briefly, she happily agreed.

Matt nodded as he ended the call. "They'll be here in an hour."

His mom surprised him by grabbing the table between them and yanked it towards her hard. Jack and Grayson had to jump back to keep from being hit it. They helped her move the table out of the way so she could get to him.

"I cannot believe that you let me hug you," Tears glistened in her eyes. "We'll get you laying on something comfortable, first, then you can tell us everything…every detail."

Nick quickly stood and came to his side and Matt's parents helped walk him towards the house. As they reached the doorway, Matt expected Nick to stop, but he walked into the huge house for the first time ever.

Matt stopped and looked over at him, knowing it was a big step. "Thanks."

Nick just nodded.

***

They heard the car coming down the driveway and the kids ran out of the house with their parents close behind. Nick and his mom helped him slowly rise from the couch and head for the backdoor. The aspirin had finally started to help.

By the time he made it down the steps of the back deck, he saw Adam in Reilly's arms and Amy gripping Grace's hand as Nora, Sadie, and Wade talked excitedly to them.

"What's up?" Matt yelled out.

"Buttercup!" The two faces turned and yelled back at him with happy grins.

CHAPTER FOURTEEN

Matt stared at the ceiling of the guest bedroom at The Homestead and thought of Adam and Amy. He was going to miss them. It was great seeing them playing and having fun with the kids and horses in a natural environment. It took Adam a while to relax, but he finally let go of Reilly and played with the other kids. They had a large barbeque for dinner with the family.

He had a few minutes alone with the aunt and uncle who couldn't have been nicer or more thankful. He learned that the father was an executive at a bank in Portland and a weekend pilot. The mother was a stay-at-home mom. They were flying to Missoula, Montana to surprise his parents. No one was looking for them, because no one knew they were coming. There was no report of trouble from the plane before it went down.

Matt decided fate was responsible for putting the three of them on top the mountain so they could see exactly where the plane had crashed. If he had made the decision to go back for help, he was sure the kids would have died. There are no two kids in the universe as lucky or blessed as them. It was tough to say goodbye.

Wade pointed out that if it wasn't for Matt wanting to train the horses in his favorite mountains and bond with his new brother the kids would have died…it all started with the Tagger Herd coming into their lives.

The business cards Steve and Kevin gave him were sitting on the end table. Once everyone had finally left him alone the night before, he had stared at them, wondering if that was a direction he should go with his life. He was meeting them Monday night for dinner.

He sighed; Grayson had avoided him all night. Knowing your fifteen-year-old daughter had faced down a charging grizzly had to be hard. Considering it had made Matt physically sick, he could understand what Grayson was going through.

Matt's cell phone alerted him of a message. Nick would be there in thirty minutes. He and Nikki had gone back to the house by The Stables the night before.

With a groan, Matt sat up, but he didn't even attempt a stretch. His whole chest and back hurt with every breath. There were bruises up and down his legs from Buttercup landing on him in the water. It was going to be difficult just to move around. He stood and stiffly, painfully walked to the bathroom.

He didn't even try to change clothes by himself, and left the t-shirt and sweat pants on. He looked out the window to see if the horses were in the pasture. He wanted to go check on Trooper and the other three before the onslaught of questions and people hit him for the day.

Stepping out the bedroom door, he didn't see anyone down the long hallway so he took the side door out to the deck and down into the lawn. The horses were in the north pasture, which meant he had to pass the living and dining room windows.

Matt slowly made it to the pasture fence and used it to brace himself as he walked. Every muscle in his body hurt and pain shot up and down his back. He reached the far pasture without anyone calling out to him. Trooper was grazing peacefully by the north pasture island and raised his head alertly when Matt walked through the gate. The same gate he, Nikki, Reilly and their new parents had walked through together as a new family, just the Saturday before. It felt like months.

He became alarmed when all the horses started walking towards him. The thought of them bumping into him right now sent a shiver of panic down his spine so he angled for the island to put the fence between himself and the horses. Trooper followed and he knew their connection would always be strong.

Tucked safely behind the fence, he lifted his aching arms to rub the horse down as best he could, talking quietly and thanking the horse for all he did. Trooper had lost weight on the trip. He glanced over at the Buttercup and Cooper; they had lost weight too. Monty was still there and had lost weight but not as much as the other three.

Buttercup butted in for some attention, so Matt happily gave her a quick rub down and playful twisting of the ears. He could still vividly see her flying backwards and her back and the saddle landing on him in the water. Matt had to bend both stiff legs to make sure they were OK. The rocks Nick had pointed out behind them would haunt his dreams…it was so close…

By the time he had played with each horse, he could hear Nick turning into the property so he turned to make sure his dad saw him. Nick pulled to a stop by the gate, made his way out to the pasture, and walked straight to Monty to give the horse a thorough rub down. Monty stood quietly and took in all the attention.

"They lost some weight," Matt pointed out.

"Not bad…considering. They'll put it back on quickly." Nick smiled over at his son. "Nikki will make sure of that."

Matt nodded and moved away from the horses and onto a bench. Nick sat on the opposite bench.

"You really should go see a doctor," Nick frowned.

"Fathering…" Matt teased as he twisted his torso trying to stretch his back muscles.

"Oh, hey, finally!" Nick grinned.

Matt chuckled then saw, past all the horses, his other three fathers walking out to them.

"We're about to have company," He warned Nick. "But at least it looks like Scott and Jack are bringing us coffee."

"Has Grayson talked to you yet?"

"No, he avoided me all night."

"Well, I imagine this is his meeting." Nick stood, walked to the fence, and took the extra coffee cups and handed one to Matt.

Matt closed his eyes and breathed in the fresh coffee smell before taking the first sip. The pungent odor seemed to help wake all his senses.

"Feeling better?" Jack asked as he sat down next to Matt. Grayson sat next to Nick and Scott leaned against the fence.

"No," Matt chuckled. "Little stiffer actually, but the pains not as bad, I'm staying up on the aspirin."

"That long hot soak in the tub Dru forced you to take last night had to help." Scott smirked.

"One of the best things ever," Matt admitted.

They sat quietly drinking their coffee. Matt waited for Grayson to speak. When his uncle didn't start, he decided to do it himself; taking the bull by the horns and getting it out.

"Grayson," Matt looked directly at him. Grayson's eyes turned from the horses to him. "When they reached us…after shooting the bear…I went over into the brush and dry heaved for ten minutes. The idea of her having to do that…of her just being there in that position…made me ill." His stomach began to ache just thinking of it.

Grayson didn't speak; he just looked at Matt with an unreadable expression.

"I made the decision to go to the plane instead of going for help," Matt stated firmly. "It was my fault she was put in that predicament." He turned to Jack. "And I put Reilly in danger, too."

There was silence again until Nick spoke.

"Matt was sick for hours, every time Grace talked about it, he turned whiter and whiter. And considering how excited she was about shooting the bear, and how Buttercup handled it, she talked about it a lot."

Grayson nodded, but didn't say anything.

"I'll tell you men what I told Matt to help him through the guilt." Nick looked between Jack and Grayson. "If it was a choice between Adam and Amy's lives or facing and shooting the bear, Grace would have chosen to face the bear. And Grayson, you should be proud of her for that."

Matt heard Grayson exhale, it was the same thing he had done when he realized the truth of the statement.

Nick turned to Jack; "And Reilly would have sat on that ledge for days if it meant saving those two kids."

Jack nodded.

Matt looked out at the horses and waited for Jack or Grayson to speak.

It was Jack first, "You made the right decision, Matt."

Then Scott added, "You made the right decision."

When Grayson didn't say anything, Matt turned and looked at him. If he had to do it over again...he would. So Matt would face anything Grayson had to say.

Grayson's eyes were a mixture of understanding and pride. "You made the right decision; I would have done the same."

Matt exhaled in relief.

"And, I have to agree with you about Grace," Grayson smirked. "She couldn't stop talking about it and it was making me ill every time she did."

Matt nodded in relief and looked around at his four fathers; thankful they were there.

"You seem to be forgetting something, Matt," Scott said; which made all the other men look at him. "How many times did you put your life at risk to save all four of them? Grace, Reilly, and the two kids were running around here last night with barely a scratch on them and you can barely move. You need help just to stand."

Matt didn't know what to say.

"And then there is the man that stole my horse..." Scott grinned when it turned to Nick.

Nick threw his hands in the air. "That was all Jessup, I had no idea what horse was in the back of the trailer until Jessup walked Monty out. But ,I was extremely relieved to see him."

"He is an outstanding horse, Scott," Matt added.

"Grace said you talked her through the bear shooting, keeping her calm and telling her what to do," Grayson said looking at Nick. "I can't, ever, thank you enough." Grayson shook Nick's hand.

"She was a rock and so was Buttercup," Nick smiled at him. "She's a hell of a young lady."

"OK, it's my turn." They heard his mom's voice behind them. The men had been so focused on their conversation they didn't notice her approaching.

Scott quickly opened the gate for her and she stepped through. Grayson, Jack, and Nick stood to let her sit in their place. Matt would have, but he hurt too much.

What she did first shocked everyone in the group. She walked straight to Nick and threw her arms around her ex-husband and hugged him firmly. Nick was visibly shaken and it took him a few seconds to return her hug by lightly placing a hand on her back. She stepped back with a grin.

"Thank you for bringing my boys home," she smiled. "…and the rest of them, too."

"It was really Matt, he…" Nick stuttered.

"Nikki and Jessup told me you dropped everything when you heard."

"I'd do it for any of you and the kids, but…" Nick said hesitantly. "Dru…he's my son."

Matt watched her expression change from appreciation to humor. "Yes, he is."

She handed him a picture.

"We uploaded all of Grace's pictures…mostly scenery and the kids, but this one stood out." She smiled.

Nick looked at the picture and started to chuckle. "Dang, we look rough." He turned amused eyes to Matt and handed him the picture.

The picture was of Matt and Nick riding along the trail side by side. They were dirty, whiskered, and looked so rugged that Matt grinned and…they looked identical. Matt stared at the picture a little harder trying to decide when Grace took it. He started laughing because he and Nick were laughing in the picture.

"What's so funny?" His mom asked with a confused smile.

Matt handed it back to Nick. "Know when it was taken?"

Nick looked at the picture closer, then, he too started laughing. Grayson swiped the picture from him, looked at it, smiled then handed it to Jack and Scott.

"It's a great picture." Scott handed it to Nick. "But what's so funny?"

"I had just told Nick that I had two surrogate fathers, a new step-father, and a father…so I felt like I was going to be fathered to death." Matt smiled at his one mother and four fathers. "And just so you all know...I truly couldn't be happier about it. I feel very lucky."

CHAPTER FIFTEEN

The men walked away as his mom sat on the bench across from him.

"Spit it out," She said with a knowing smile.

"I feel like I've been doing that for a week," he sighed.

"Then go back a week and tell me what's on your mind." She leaned back on the arm of the bench and stretched her legs out across the length of it.

"I should have known you knew." He smiled sheepishly.

"Of course, I knew," She chuckled. "I just didn't want to know before the wedding and raft trip; it wasn't going to be good."

"Alright…spitting it out…from a week ago…" He watched her face as he said it. "I'm dropping out of college."

Her eyes slightly widened…she wasn't expecting that.

"I don't understand, I thought you liked college. Your grades are great."

Matt shrugged. "They are only good because I gave up everything else up there to force myself to get the grades."

"Is it too hard?"

"Too, boring."

"The first couple years are more required classes, aren't they?"

Matt nodded. "Yes… and the next couple years I would be doing more on the outside, but the in-class stuff is just killing me with boredom."

"You said that was from a week ago," She frowned. "Has it changed after this week?"

Matt sighed and told her about the conversation with Nick...except the part Nick had asked him not to say.

"You need to disregard Tagger Enterprises in pursuit of your goal...we have that covered...do what you want to do."

Matt smiled, and that was what Nick didn't want her to know he said.

"I've got a meeting setup Monday night with the two search and rescue men I met yesterday to look in that direction."

"I think that's a great idea," She looked proudly at him. "From everything I've heard, you made excellent decisions and got everyone out safely. I am extremely proud of you."

She paused and leaned forward wrapping her arms around her knees.

"I didn't go to college right after school; I didn't know what I wanted to do. Besides..." She said with a mischievous smile. "I wanted to rodeo and play."

"Andy told me how you and Scott used to read everything that Grayson brought home from college and how Grayson would teach you everything he learned. You and Scott worked hard on getting an education, even if you didn't get official credit for it."

"That was after the accident, and I had to take care of the ranch without my parents experience and help," She told him. "Before that, I was fortunate to have the parents that understood my desire to barrel race...then I met Nick." She shrugged. "I don't regret the time with Nick; we had fun and enjoyed life, even if it was only for a couple months. Before we got married...they were literally, some of the best months of my life. Neither one of us had a worry in the world; we weren't tied down to anything. Between my parents and the money we earned, we could go to the rodeos we wanted and play during the week. Scott and Grayson joined in a lot of those weekends and Nick became like another brother to them during those months. I was in heaven!"

"Until you got married," Matt added.

"Exactly," She sighed. "That was the reason I made the huge mistake of turning Jack down when he proposed. Marriage changes things...with Nick it went bad and I was terrified it would do the same with Jack...and there was Reilly, who I adore. I couldn't take the chance of losing them." She sighed. "After Reilly disappeared, and that horrible night, I realized it was me that was causing the problem. Nick's past caused our breakup and his leaving...I was letting my past do the same thing with Jack."

Matt thought back to the night of Reilly's disappearance. All he wanted to do was go look for Reilly, but Scott and Grayson wisely told him to find his mother, keep her calm, and not let her leave The Homestead until they called. He hid all the keys to the vehicles before she arrived home and then had to physically restrain her from leaving. They sat on the living room couch as he held her. Until this past week, they were the worst hours of his life; listening, understanding, and feeling his mother's pain. When the call came in that Reilly was safe, she nearly passed out from the relief and he drove her to Jack's house to wait.

Matt looked up at his mother. "About Nick..."

She turned to him and smiled. "There is a change between the two of you."

He shook his head in disbelief. "Geez mom." She always seemed to know.

She giggled. "I could see it last night. He didn't leave your side and you didn't mind his attention, actually asked for it. He went into the house for you!" She laughed. "When I saw the picture this morning…the two of you laughing, the ease…it just clicked…you two connected."

"I don't feel like I missed out on having a father growing up, because of Scott and Grayson." Matt told her. "And I think our life would have been so much different if Nick had stayed, but probably not in a good way." He tried hard to come up with the right words to tell her how he felt. "I believe he did the right thing by Nikki and I, and that helps me appreciate what he went through…and who he is now…especially when he came back to protect us."

She just nodded while watching him with compassionate eyes.

"Over the last six months, getting to know him…I respect him and like the man he is today."

"I do, too."

"Over the last couple days…the only time he touched Amy and Adam were to help lift them on the horses," Matt chuckled. "But he has improved a lot since the first time helping with the arena. He even talks to Wade, Nora, and Sadie all the time now."

"He has…and the kids like him, which says a lot."

"What I'm trying to say is…" Matt sighed, he didn't want to hurt her and didn't know if he was going to, but he needed to say it. "He has faced his fear of kids to be with Nikki and me. Knowing the trail he rode over with Monty, and how fast he got to us, and facing the grizzly bear, he risked his life for us. The time we spent together and the help he gave me in dealing with the guilt of putting Grace in the line of the bear…" Matt looked directly at his mom so she would understand what he was saying, and hopefully be able to read his eyes…like she had so many times before. "There is a difference in *needing* someone in your life and *wanting* someone in your life."

She nodded.

"I haven't needed him in my life…but I want him in my life and he has proven that he wants to be here with us. But, I don't want you to think it takes away anything that you, Scott, or Grayson have ever done for me. It's because of you guys, that I CAN accept him into my life."

"And I think that's wonderful, Son. Scott and Grayson would agree," She smiled. "Wonderful for both of you. Like I said, I like who Nick is today and will never be able to express my appreciation enough for the last couple days." She smiled mischievously, "I think I shocked him a little while ago."

"You should have seen the look on his face," Matt laughed.

"Matt, you're still young; if you're not ready for college, then wait until you are and you know what you want in life." She swung her legs off the bench and sat up. "Go experiment with different things and jobs...don't get stuck in one because it's right in front of you. The last thing I want is for you NOT to want to get out of bed in the morning because you hate what the day will bring. Find something you love...something that drives you."

Matt smiled at his mother...he couldn't love her any more than he already did, but she kept pushing it farther.

"Well, there is one thing."

"What?"

"Rock climbing and rappelling," He grinned.

"I want to go."

"To join the fun or protect me?" He asked with a chuckle.

"Both!"

***

"You know what the best thing about tonight is?" Reilly asked.

They were at the Wednesday night barrel racing competition. From his perch on the top of the bleachers of the 4-H club arena,

Matt looked around at all the barrel racers preparing their horses. There were females of all ages.

Matt turned to Reilly and chuckled, "Do I really have to answer that?"

"Besides that!" Reilly laughed.

"What?"

"The whole family is here."

"Nobody wants to miss Sadie and Grace's first race," Matt nodded as he looked around at all the family seated in the bleachers around them; everyone but Sadie and Grace who were on Scarecrow and Buttercup just outside the arena gate.

"It's only five minutes from home," Grayson said from beside him. "The girls threatened us with our lives if we didn't show up for the first one."

"You think they'll notice the mass exodus of Taggers once the girls are done?" Scott teased.

"We'll just tell them we're headed down to congratulate the girls." Jack laughed.

Matt grinned at the light hearted banter. As much as they had grumbled about having to go, they were all excited to see the two teams run. Both girls had been practicing every night and all weekend and were extremely excited about their first competition.

Matt stretched his back and sides. Sitting on the hard bleacher with no back support was a bit tough.

"Not good?" Reilly asked.

"It's getting better." He answered.

"It's only been two weeks." Leah said.

"Yeah, I know." Matt nodded. "But I want it to be faster. I start rock climbing with Kevin as soon as I can move without pain."

"That's gonna be cool. After you learn, you'll have to teach me so I can go with you." Reilly grinned.

"Funny…that's what Mom said," Matt laughed.

"It's exactly what I said!" She turned with bright shining blue eyes. "And I have every intention of making him follow through!"

The announcer started welcoming the contestants and family to the evening's event.

Grace's contagious laughter reached them and they turned to look at the excited fifteen-year-old. Buttercup was prancing underneath her…feeding off the energy of the rider. Grace's hair was held back by the Tagger Enterprises baseball cap she was wearing and there was no doubt she was having fun.

Matt turned to look at Sadie. Other than her normal long blonde braid hanging down her back, she was wearing a bright blue short-sleeve western shirt and a wide brimmed straw cowboy hat pulled low over her eyes. The hat blocked her eyes, but the grin across her face was wide and shining through.

"I think she's excited," Grayson grinned.

"Admit it…you are too," Matt teased.

Leah, who was sitting on the other side of her husband, leaned around him. "Are you kidding? This day took forever to get over!"

They all laughed.

"Scarecrow and Buttercup have come a long way this last year." Jordan pointed out.

"Yes they have…they all have…" Cora nodded. "It's amazing to see the two of them out there…after last summer."

The announcer informed them there were five pee wee riders, then six riders in Sadie's youth division. Then Grace would run in the open division.

"OK! Just get it started!" Nora grumbled impatiently.

The pee wee riders quickly entered, raced, made everyone smile, then rode out.

"Those are always fun to watch." Jordan chuckled.

"When does Sadie run?" Jack asked.

"Last!" Nora and Wade said in unison then looked at each other and laughed.

They watched the first five youth riders patiently, then all sighed impatiently when they had to wait for the ground to be raked around the barrels. It was standard practice after every five riders.

The four-wheeler drove out of the arena by the side gate then all eyes turned to the gate opening at the end where Sadie was waiting to come through.

"Here we go…" Leah exhaled excitedly.

Scarecrow calmly walked through the gate until Sadie nudged her into a trot and they completed three circles with Sadie staring at the first barrel. As she came out of the third circle, Scarecrow bolted.

The palomino stretched out with each stride and dug into the arena floor to propel her into the next. Sadie leaned forward over her neck, one hand firmly attached to the saddle horn and the other high over the horse's neck.

"She looks like a racehorse," Matt whispered in awe.

They leaned and turned the first barrel…

"A little wide…" Nora whispered.

They seemed to fly to the second barrel then leaned and turned; both horse and rider already looking for the third barrel.

"Look at Scarecrow bend around the barrel, she's looking at the third!" Matt heard his mother whisper excitedly.

As they raced to the third barrel, Wade was the first to yell, "Come on, Sadie!"

"Go Sadie!" Nora joined him.

The whole Tagger family and extended family started yelling for the blonde team.

Horse and rider felt the energy, Scarecrow's stride widened and Sadie leaned forward more and kicked harder. The turn was good, but the run to the finish was blazing fast.

"Way to go, Sadie! It's a 18.3!" The announcer yelled. "That time is as fast as some of the older and more experienced teams."

Sadie pumped her fist in the air as she trotted out of the arena. When she made it to the stands she grinned up at her family.

They all yelled and applauded for her...except for Jordan who had pulled her phone out of her pocket and was typing feverishly.

"What are you doing?" Leah asked her.

"Checking the rodeo dates for NWYRA, and all the others," She answered. "We were just going to start with local barrels this year, but after that! We're branching out!"

Matt chuckled at his aunt's enthusiasm. She took her job of managing the kids and their rodeos, shows, and events very seriously. The previous fall, she had signed them all up for every club and rodeo organization they were qualified for.

Grace and Buttercup pranced into the arena. Buttercup's turns were as good as Scarecrow's but she wasn't as fast...her time was 18.9. The smile on Grace's face let them all know she was happy with their first ride.

After the last year of bonding while the horses healed, Matt couldn't imagine the horses and their riders could become any closer...but they were. Whether in the mountains, on the ranch, or in the arena, the bond between them became stronger every day.

THE TAGGER HERD

BOOK SEVEN

GRACE TAGGER

CHAPTER ONE

"I can't believe Aunt Dru talked you into this, Dad." Grace handed him the stack of lariats from the cart.

"Talked me into?" He chuckled. "Have you met your Aunt Dru? She didn't really give me a choice," He walked along the fence and threw the lariats on the ground about three feet apart. "She had the announcement posted on the internet, the flyers printed and already sent out when she told me I had to be here this weekend."

Grace laughed, "That does sound like her."

They walked between the office building and the first horse stable to his silver truck to retrieve the rest of the supplies for the roping clinic. Even at fifteen she loved spending time with her parents.

"How much notice did she give you?" Grace crawled into the back and handed her dad the bag of plastic calf heads. He threw them in the cart.

"She told me on Monday," He grinned up at her.

"Well, at least she gave you a couple days to prepare," she laughed.

Grace turned when she heard the tractor moving between the buildings. Jack was hauling bales of straw into the arena to place the practice calf heads in.

"At least it doesn't take much more than straw, lariats, and calf heads."

He held her hand to brace her as she jumped off the tailgate of the truck and down to the ground.

"Well, if you think it's going to be that easy…then you can just stick around and help kids that haven't ever touched a lariat before try to twirl it around their heads and throw without hitting someone else."

They started walking back to the arena.

"OK," Grace grinned with a twinkle in her eyes. "I'll stick around while a dozen teenage cowboys throw ropes at a bale of straw."

Her dad stopped and looked down at her with narrowed blue eyes, "Changed my mind; you're going back to The Homestead."

Grace giggled at his half serious expression and pulled his arm to get him moving again, "I don't think so. I'm sure you need my help for something."

"No, nope, don't think so, you just head home now," He chuckled as they met up with Jack and Reilly.

"Grayson…are you finally coming to your senses?" Jack laughed.

"You thought of that before?" He looked surprised.

"Of course I did," Jack just shook his head. "I can't believe you didn't!"

"Think of what?" Reilly asked.

"That I'll be spending the day with a bunch of teenage cowboys," Grace grinned as she and Reilly grabbed the bag of calf heads and carried them towards the arena.

"Oh that," Reilly winked at her. "That's why you brought that little tank top to wear."

"WHAT?" Her dad asked a little too loudly.

She and Reilly turned to look at the glare on her dad's face and burst out laughing.

"Not funny, Reilly," He literally kicked Reilly's butt when he realized the teenager was teasing.

"Abusing your help already, Grayson?" Uncle Scott walked up behind them.

"And did you think of it too?" Her dad asked a little gruffly.

"Think of what?" Uncle Scott asked.

Grace repeated herself again.

Her uncle looked between her dad, then Jack, then Reilly, and back to her. "Get your stuff, I'm taking you home." He took a step towards her.

"No, you're not," She giggled and backed away from him.

He took a fast step and reached out, so Grace turned and ran from her uncle.

"No…" She ran as fast as she could and, over the laughter, heard him running behind her.

Grace tried to make her legs run faster but her uncle's legs were just way too much longer. He caught up with her and wrapped an arm around her waist lifting her off the ground.

She screamed in laughter as he turned her around and threw her over his shoulder, her long dark blonde hair flew over her head. She had to grab his belt to keep from falling backwards too far as her legs went up into the air.

"Grayson, get the truck and I'll throw her in," Uncle Scott yelled as he carried her back to the group.

"No! I wanna stay!" She kicked harder.

"What's going on out here?" Grace could hear her aunt.

"Help me, Aunt Dru!" Grace yelled in mock fear.

They made it back to the group and her uncle placed her feet on the ground.

Grace ran to her aunt and wrapped her arms around her. "They want to take me home and away from all the cute cowboys."

Aunt Dru hugged her tightly as she joined in the laughter, "Did you finally figure it out, Grayson?"

"You thought of that?" He shook his head at his sister.

"Maybe you forget, brother dear…" Aunt Dru's arms tightened around Grace. "I was a fifteen-year-old girl once too."

Everyone laughed but her dad and uncle.

***

Grace stood next to the fence watching her dad talk to all the clinic attendees. There were seven girls and ten boys; all ranging from ten to eighteen. It was the five teenage boys that were causing Grace the misery. Every time she tried to help or talk to them, either her dad or uncle interrupted. She was banished to the girl's side.

Two of the boys were brave enough to walk up to her during a water break.

"Your name's Grace?" The red shirt cowboy asked with a smile. He was just a little taller than her.

Grace smiled up at him and nervously looked for her dad and uncle. They had their backs to her, so she relaxed. "Grace Tagger," She nodded at his brown eyes under his straw cowboy hat.

"You're related to the owners?" The blue shirt cowboy asked.

"My dad, aunt, and uncle own it," Grace smiled at him. "Where are you guys from?"

"I'm from Weippe," Red shirt answered.

"We're cousins, I'm from Kooskia," Blue shirt answered. His blue eyes were shaded from the sun with his cowboy hat.

"We drove near Kooskia last month," Grace looked behind them. Aunt Dru was smiling and obviously trying to keep her brothers distracted.

"Were you headed to Montana?" Blue shirt asked.

"No, we went to the Weitas for a camping trip and rode the horses for a couple days," Grace answered. She didn't add the rescue of the kid's part.

"We go hunting in that area," Red shirt added.

Grace looked between the two, her heart skipped a beat they were so cute!

"We saw a lot of elk, deer, a moose, and a wolverine," She told them, desperately trying to think of something to say that would interest them.

"I've never seen a wolverine….that's pretty cool," Blue shirt took a step closer to her.

Grace grinned, then looked back at her dad and uncle. Aunt Dru had a hold of Uncle Scott's arm and was trying to keep him from turning. He looked at her confused then quickly turned and looked at Grace. He figured out what his sister was trying to do!

Grace giggled, which caused the two cowboys in front of her to smile wider.

"Do you have these clinics very often?" Blue shirt asked. "I'm definitely interested in coming back for more."

Grace could feel the warmth rise to her face, even when she saw her uncle pull away from her aunt and start walking towards her. He was shaking his head with a 'not gonna happen' look on his face.

"You can keep track online," She said quickly; her uncle was half way to her. "We have a Facebook page for The Stables and The Tagger Herd."

"My name's Alan," Red shirt told her and reached out to shake her hand. She quickly shook his hand and then turned to blue shirt and extended a hand.

"I'm Levi," Blue shirt with the blue eyes smiled and took her hand and shook it. He held her hand a few seconds too long which made her giggle nervously to herself.

"OK, Cowboys," Uncle Scott reached them. "Time to line back up again."

Grace giggled as her uncle stepped in between the two cowboys and her. Both boys looked around her uncle and grinned before they turned and headed back to the clinic.

Uncle Scott turned with a frown, "That was a very flirty little giggle, young lady."

"I know," Grace laughed and walked back to all the cowgirls.

The first throw from all seventeen kids had missed. The last throw from all seventeen kids hit their mark and all the plastic calf heads were caught.

Neither Alan nor Levi were given a chance to approach Grace when the clinic ended. Both her dad and uncle placed themselves in protective positions around her and to her surprise, Jack joined them.

"Traitor," She whispered to him which made him chuckle, his blue eyes sparkling and dimples deepening.

Reilly walked the cousins to their truck.

When he returned, he leaned in and whispered, "You have two Facebook friend requests waiting for a response."

Grace looked up at him and giggled. "Thanks." She could feel her face turning red again.

They walked back into the arena to collect the plastic calf dummies and placed them back in the bag.

"Where's Kelly? I thought she was supposed to be here today," She had been so busy and pre-occupied with teenage cowboys, she didn't realize their red-headed friend wasn't working in the stables.

"I don't know," Reilly shook his head. "I know they had a big court hearing yesterday on her custody battle and I haven't heard from her since."

Grace stopped and looked at him, "You don't think she's gone do you?" The thought worried her, for Kelly's sake. The girl's happy nature had been dwindling over the last two weeks. Kelly had grown quite moody in the last couple of days.

Reilly sighed, "I hope not…I couldn't imagine they wouldn't let her say goodbye to us."

"Maybe Aunt Dru or Jack know," Grace turned to look for the pair. They were standing by the office building in an intense conversation.

"Wow…that doesn't happen very often," Grace looked concerned.

"The only time I've seen it was after Dru turned down Dad's proposal," Reilly turned worried eyes to her.

"Well, they're married now and can't keep from holding hands so we know that's not it." Grace smiled in an attempt to put her soul-mate at ease.

"Do you think it has to do with Kelly and the custody hearing?" He whispered as they walked the full bag to the cart.

They turned to retrieve all the ropes.

Her dad was operating the tractor while her uncle placed the bales of straw on the small trailer behind it.

"I know Aunt Dru and the grandparents met the other day. She looked a little stressed when they left," Grace told him as they placed all the ropes on top the bag in the cart.

Reilly took control of the cart and they walked towards her dad's truck.

"Let's see how they react when we walk by," Reilly whispered. "Happy face."

They turned and looked at each other and smiled, showing each other their happy face.

As they approached her aunt and Jack they turned and smiled at the teenagers.

"Great clinic," Aunt Dru smiled. "You guys were awesome out there."

"Thanks," They answered in unison as they walked by.

Grace looked at Reilly, happy faces disappeared and she shrugged. "I don't know...I couldn't tell, and my phones at home."

"My phones in my truck, Dad doesn't let me carry it when we do clinics."

They put the bag and ropes in the back of the truck and Reilly ran over to his. When he returned he was shaking his head.

"Nothing from Kelly, but I did get one from an odd number I don't recognize it."

"What's it say?" Grace stood next to him and looked over his shoulder as they read it together.

TEXT TO REILLY: GPs took phone, mom won, I am crushed.

Grace felt the tears spring to her eyes and looked at Reilly. There were tears in his eyes, too.

"She's leaving..." Reilly exhaled in disbelief.

Grace wrapped her arms around his arm and leaned her head on his shoulder. "I am so sorry, Reilly."

"Me too," He sounded depressed and rightfully so.

"We have to get back," She pulled his arm to make him move.

As they rounded the corner to the office building, all four adults were standing by the door looking concerned.

"They know," Grace whispered.

As they approached the adults it was Reilly's dad that spoke. "From the look on your faces, you guys know."

They both nodded.

"Her grandparents didn't want to tell you until after the clinic," Jack continued. "They are on their way over."

"How long before she has to leave?" Grace asked.

Jack shrugged, "It sounds like the next week or so."

"But we're at the ranch pushing cows next week." Reilly sounded heart broken.

Grace wanted to cry, Kelly may be here, but they wouldn't be.

"I know, Son." Jack frowned. "Let's just wait until they get here."

Reilly nodded.

"Everything's cleaned up and put back to normal," Uncle Scott said. "I think it went pretty good."

Everyone nodded.

"From the looks of some of them, they could give you two a challenge at the rodeos someday," Aunt Dru teased her and Reilly.

Grace laughed, "Well, the way I look at it," She looked up at her dad. "Dad, was here *today* showing them how to rope and what they were doing right. He's with me *every day* to tell me what I'm doing wrong."

They all laughed...even Reilly.

The discussions centered on the clinic until they saw Kelly's grandparents pull into the parking lot. When the car stopped, the grandparents stepped out of the car but Kelly didn't. The grandfather opened up the back door and spoke to Kelly, but she still didn't get out.

"She's terribly upset," The grandmother spoke as she walked up to them. Grace could tell she had been crying, too.

Grace turned and walked over to the car; her friend was hurting and knew she needed support. As she approached the car, Kelly looked up and saw her. The redhead slid out of the car and jumped into a consoling hug with Grace.

Grace held her friend tightly as the girl cried, tears rolled down her own face. Reilly was quickly beside them and the two girls brought him into the sad hug. After a moment, Grace stepped out of the embrace and let Reilly comfort his unofficial girlfriend.

She turned quickly and headed for the adults to learn what was happening.

Her dad held out an arm as she approached and she stepped in for the supporting hug.

"The judge decided Kelly would go to her mother under a probationary period," The grandfather told them. "She believed that it was important that Kelly be with her mother as long as the guidelines were followed. The courts will be watching closely."

"Did they take into consideration Kelly's request to stay here?" Aunt Dru asked.

The grandfather nodded, "It was argued that Kelly's plea wasn't just based on the future, it was based on her friendship with Grace, Reilly, The Stables, and all the horses."

"But that's so important to Kelly," Grace pointed out sadly.

"I know, Sweetheart." The older man nodded, "That's why the judge stipulated, and her mother agreed, that Kelly would be given a horse and kept in the horse industry unless Kelly wants out of it. Kelly would have to appeal to the judge directly."

Grace sighed and looked across to the parking lot at Kelly and Reilly as they leaned against the car and talked. "At least she'll still have horses."

"Not just any horse," Aunt Dru smiled at her.

"What do you mean?" Grace asked.

"Jack contacted a friend of his in the Seattle area that has a solid barrel horse. They are going to lease the horse to Kelly and put her to work in their stable and help her get in with a few rodeo and show people up there." Aunt Dru answered with a smile. "You'll still be able to see each other when you attend the same rodeos."

Grace smiled, that was great! They weren't losing her forever. "Does she know?"

The grandparents shook their heads. The grandfather spoke, "We wanted Dru and Jack to tell her themselves...they went well above what they needed to do for Kelly and should see her reaction." He looked out to Kelly with sad eyes. "That's why we rushed over as soon as the clinic was done."

Grace looked out to Reilly, he looked up. She waved him over; he nodded and took Kelly's hand to join the group.

As Kelly approached, she looked between Aunt Dru and Jack, tears started falling again. She was so upset she couldn't speak.

Aunt Dru took a picture out of her pocket and handed it to Kelly. The girl's hands shook as she took the picture. Grace leaned over to see a red and white paint horse standing in an arena.

Kelly's tears stopped and a slight smile crossed her face as she was told about the horse, job at the stables, and the possibility of seeing all of them at a future rodeo.

"The horse has been running barrels for a couple of years now, so she'll be a great start for you," Jack added with a smile.

Kelly let go of Reilly's hand and threw herself into Jack's arms and then to Aunt Dru. "Thank you so much. I'm going to miss you."

CHAPTER TWO

Grace stood next to her dad's silver Ford and stared at the dark blue T3E logo. This had to be one of the scariest things she's ever done…besides the grizzly bear. All the horses they were using for the fall roundup were at the ranch except the ones Aunt Jordan and her mom had with Sadie, Nora, and Wade at the show and rodeo. So there were no horses to pull to the ranch. Jack and Aunt Dru were staying at The Homestead with Reilly for another day so he would have more time with Kelly. So it was just Grace, her dad, and Uncle Scott driving to the ranch today.

"Get in, Grace," Her dad said from inside the truck. She could hear the amusement in his voice.

Taking a deep breath…she opened the door and looked up at her dad in the middle seat and her uncle on the passenger side…Grace was driving them!

They both looked highly amused.

"It's not going to be that bad," Her dad laughed at her.

"You can face a charging grizzly with no problem, but you can't face driving us to the ranch?" Uncle Scott chuckled.

Grace saw the quick flash of discomfort in her dad's eyes when the grizzly was mentioned. Matt had told her how much it bothered the two of them so she had quit talking about it. That conversation took place as Matt gave her a picture of the bear that Fish and Game had taken when they retrieved the animal. It was huge…one of the biggest ever seen in Idaho, they estimated the weight at 700 pounds and if it were to stand on its hind feet it would be just under seven feet tall. The picture was in her bag that she slowly placed behind her seat.

Bart and Mavis were lying on the floor in the back. They were nestled in and ready for the ride. Grace scratched each dog behind the ears and they looked at her contently.

"Get in Grace," Her dad repeated.

She gripped the steering wheel and pulled herself up and into the driver's seat. Automatically, she adjusted the seat so she could reach the pedals, buckled her seatbelt and checked the mirrors. Then she sat frozen.

"You have to turn the key..." Her dad chuckled. "...then it starts...we've been over that simple little procedure."

She reached for the key and turned on the truck with a smile. This trip would give her the final amount of accompanied driving time to go from her learner's permit to her official driver's license. Then she hoped her parents would buy her a little truck, too. She and Reilly already had it picked out; a red Tacoma that matched his blue one.

"No yelling," She told them without looking.

"I can guarantee if you go in the ditch or off the grade, there's going to be yelling." Uncle Scott informed her with a chuckle.

Grace made it half way down the long driveway of the Homestead then stopped. She turned and looked at the two men sitting next to her.

"What's wrong?" Her dad asked.

"This is just so freaking bizarre," She laughed. "I have to take a second to let it all sink in."

"You think it's bizarre to you?" Her dad joined her laughter. "I still think of you as a baby."

"I'm still surprised you've grown enough to look over the steering wheel." Uncle Scott added.

Grace slowly pushed down on the accelerator to get the truck moving; thank goodness it was an automatic!

She made it all the way down the driveway, down the long stretch of road, and down the Webb Road short grade that led to the highway without a problem. But no one had spoken.

"You guys have to talk or I'm just gonna go nuts," She told them as she pulled out onto the two lane highway. There were still two hours to go.

"What do you want to talk about?" Uncle Scott asked.

"I don't know…what do you usually talk about?" She asked gripping the steering wheel too tightly.

"The three of us have been together for the last two days…I think we're a bit talked out." Her dad said.

"Then tell me a story about the three of you growing up," She loved to listen to their stories.

"I feel like we've been telling stories since Leah came into the family," Uncle Scott chuckled. "Haven't you heard them all?"

Grace smiled; she knew what story she wanted. "Mom told us the romantic tragedy about how you two met," She said to her dad. "How did you and Aunt Jordan meet?" She asked her uncle.

"I bought a pair of boots from her…" Her uncle started.

"A pair?" Her dad chuckled.

"OK, three pair," Uncle Scott admitted with a smirk. "I found out she was working on commission for the boots, so I bought a couple extra to help her out."

"Well, that was very 'knight in shining armor' of you." Grace smiled.

"And he still wears a couple of them." Her dad added.

Grace heard her uncle actually giggle, "The pair I have on were bought that day."

They all laughed.

"Did you ask her out?" Grace asked.

"Not then," Uncle Scott answered. "You know mine and Jordan's birthdays are only a day apart?"

Grace nodded.

"I saw her at the steakhouse the next night and her friends had brought out a small cake for her. I turned 21 the night before so I sent her a drink, as a happy birthday gift…and she sent it back since she was only twenty."

"Aww…" Grace frowned.

"I sent her another one without alcohol." He added.

"Persistence…" Her dad chuckled.

"When the waitress told Jordan that we were there celebrating my birthday…she sent me a piece of the cake her friends had brought her." Her uncle was smiling; eyes twinkling.

"That was sweet of her." Grace sighed.

"It was." Uncle Scott nodded.

"But it still didn't give him courage enough to ask her out," Her dad teased.

"Really?" Grace laughed.

"I went back into the ranch store a couple of days later and she was working in the feed section…" He started to explain.

"Or he would have had even more boots," Her dad chuckled. "Instead we ended up with a couple of bags of grain."

"Grain?" Grace was surprised. Tagger Enterprises harvested their own grain.

Both men laughed.

"Yeah," Uncle Scott chuckled. "I was being nice, helping her with commission again and it was the only thing I could come up with at the time."

"What did she say when she found out?" Grace giggled.

"The manager went to her as I was checking out, wondering why she sold me the grain and explained who I was and that I didn't need it," Uncle Scott continued. "She came out to the truck while I was loading it and asked why I bought it."

"What did you tell her?" Grace asked, enthralled with his story.

"The truth...that I was trying to help with her commission," He answered.

"But..." Her dad grinned.

"She informed me she only earned commission on boots and clothing," Uncle Scott smiled.

"Oh, dang," Grace smiled too. "So did you take the grain back?"

"No way...that would have made her look bad," Her uncle answered.

"And he didn't ask her out either," Her dad shook his head.

"You didn't? Why not?" Grace said surprised.

"She was too cute! She's over a foot shorter than me, was light as a feather and had real short hair then. She looked like a little pixie girl, like the Tinkerbell dolls that Nikki had all over the house... just too adorable."

"You didn't ask her out because she was too good looking?" Grace couldn't believe it.

"You'll find out that guys don't ask you out because of your looks too," Her uncle warned her. Grace thought it was funny because she thought she was just average looking.

"When did you finally ask her out?" She asked, not responding to his comment.

"He didn't," Her dad chuckled.

Grace wanted to turn and look at him but thought it best to keep her eyes on the road and not have them yell at her.

"She asked me out," Uncle Scott laughed. "When she realized that I was willing to buy something I didn't need to help her out, she figured it was only because I liked her, so she asked me out. After that, every free minute she had, we were together. We got married the following New Year's day and just a couple of days before our birthdays."

"Great way to start a new year," Grace smiled.

She had just crested the top of Winchester grade, they still had a little over an hour to go but neither man seemed stressed by her driving. She rolled her lips together trying to relax and wished she had her chap stick.

Her dad's arm reached over the back of her and grabbed her bag. He must have noticed. "Where is it?" He asked.

"Side pocket…" She answered then immediately regretted it, "Never mind…I don't need it," She said quickly…too quickly.

She could see him glance at her with a frown and flip open the side pocket. He hesitated and then pulled out the bear picture.

Grace caught her breath, gripped the steering wheel tightly, and stared intently at the road.

He just stared at the picture then handed it to Uncle Scott.

"Fish and Game gave it to Matt…he gave it to me." She explained before her dad asked.

"This is the bear you shot?" Uncle Scott asked as he handed the picture back to her dad.

"Yes," She answered. "Matt told me how much it bothers Dad and him when I talk about the bear so I decided not to show it to you."

Her dad stared at the picture. "Look at those claws," He tipped the picture back to his brother.

"Dang…" Uncle Scott muttered. "How big?"

"Just under seven feet and around 700 pounds," She said softly not knowing how much she should say without upsetting her dad. "One of the largest they've seen in Idaho."

"They are pretty rare in Idaho, except by the Montana or Wyoming borders," Her dad whispered.

They were silent while her dad stared at the picture.

"It actually helps seeing the picture," He finally spoke and Grace relaxed. "In my head, I still see him charging you, but seeing this, he's no longer a danger to you."

Grace sighed in relief.

"Do you have nightmares?" Uncle Scott asked.

Grace shook her head, "Not nightmares…just intense dreams," She admitted, hoping it didn't bother her dad. "If I start to get nervous, I hear Nick's voice talking to me, calmly and matter-of-fact and it relaxes me and the bear disappears."

"Did you have problems at the time?" Her dad asked.

It was the first time he had asked her a question about the attack, "No, I thought of it just as a bear…not a grizzly. I think shooting the black bear on the ranch helped me focus that way."

Her dad nodded, "Glad we took you out on those, then."

"Well, we'll have to get you some martial arts training or something to keep the two legged predators away from you too." Uncle Scott teased.

Grace laughed and when she did, she saw her dad's shoulders relax. Reilly told her that her laugh helped his soul, lifted it when he would start to disappear into his 'dark place'. That was before the Tagger Herd, especially Rufio and Cooper, came into his life.

"Actually, Reilly and I have gotten into some pretty good wrestling matches," She admitted and they both looked at her confused. "He and Jack wrestle a lot, so Reilly showed me some of the moves his dad showed him."

"You need protection before you get to that point," Her dad pointed out in concern.

Grace nodded. "Well....I do have my rifle," She grinned. Then thinking of the roping clinic she added: "And with the two of you around, no guy is going to get within six feet of me!"

"I'm fine with that." The two men said in unison which made them all laugh.

***

Grace pulled off the highway and into Cottonwood's small gas station that was their usual pit stop. Restrooms visited and drinks purchased, they made their way back to the truck. This time Grace didn't hesitate climbing into the driver's seat.

"Little more confident this time?" Her uncle teased.

"Yeah, you two aren't as bad as I thought," She laughed. "I think the stories have helped...but it's still bizarre."

They talked about the roping clinic and the second clinic that Aunt Dru had setup where the kids brought their horses.

When she reached the pink house, that indicated the grade was close, Grace took a deep breath and exhaled slowly. There was a long steep drop off to one side of the hill and the corners were tight, narrow, and scary. Reilly had told her about his nerve-racking trip by himself the first time he drove it.

"You want me to drive?" Her dad asked.

"Heck, no!" Grace said, a little insulted he asked. "I can do it myself."

Both men chuckled.

As she approached the first large turn she added: "But you can talk me through."

Her dad calmly talked her around each turn, which ones she could take a little faster than the others and which to go slow around. There was a big hair-pin turn towards the middle that she held her breath through and exhaled loudly when it was in her review mirror. Neither man made a sound; they knew how scary the drive was the first couple of times a person drove it.

"When we get to the ranch, back up to the stock trailer and we'll load Buttercup, Eli and Monty and you can drive to the bull pasture. We'll get the bulls moved today," Her dad said.

"Really?" Grace was surprised; she'd never helped with the bulls before.

"Yeah, we won't let them within six feet of you either," Uncle Scott promised with a deep chuckle.

CHAPTER THREE

It took her ten tries to get the truck backed up to the stock trailer, even with them directing her. She just couldn't get the hitch on the trailer lined up over the top of the ball on the truck and kept having to pull forward and back up…over and over again. They patiently instructed her on how far to turn the wheels on the truck so she didn't over correct and go sideways again. With great relief, she finally did it.

The horses were quickly loaded. As she drove, her dad instructed her how to drive with the trailer attached and when there were horses inside. Sudden stops and turns would endanger the animals but she made it to the pasture with no problems.

"Great job, Gracie." Her dad smiled proudly at her. She only allowed her dad and Reilly to call her Gracie. "If it's still daylight when we get back, we'll practice on backing the horse trailer while we're in the open field and not in a hurry."

"Thanks, Dad," She grinned. "It wasn't as bad as I thought it would be."

They saddled the horses and she rode between her dad and uncle as they made their way to the pasture to gather the bulls. Mavis and Bart trotted next to them. They were constantly looking around for cows.

"There are twelve bulls," Her dad told her. "They range from two years to eight. Right now, we're at 7 red and 5 black Angus. We choose more on confirmation, attitude, and the calves they throw more than the color; although we will keep a good mix of the two.

"During non-breeding season, we keep them away from the cows and let them live their own bachelor life over on that mountain." He pointed to her right, which was south. "We'll move them today from here, where they've grazed it down and it's dried up from the sun, down to the valley. There are a lot of creeks, above and below ground…it keeps it greener. They should be down here for the next couple of months; then we'll move them closer when the weather gets bad so we can feed them easier."

Grace took it all in; she listened to every word he said. It was exciting being out here with just the two of them and learning things she didn't know before.

"Bulls number twenty-five and eighteen are direct descendants from bulls your grandparents used," Uncle Scott told her. "We'll always keep a string of them in the herd."

"The original brand was TE for Tagger Enterprises," Her dad reminded her. "When we purchased stock or bred stock on our own, we changed the brand to T3E so we could tell the difference. That way we knew if our program was working."

"How do you know which ones are the dads so you know what their babies are like?" She asked.

"We separate the cows into different pastures during breeding season," Uncle Scott answered. "The younger cows will be in a pasture with one or two of the bulls that throw small calves to make sure their first calves are smaller. A good bull will throw a medium-sized calf that has a strong growing season before we sell them off. If the calves don't gain weight well, then we'll use a different bull the next year."

"That's why you keep records of the cows and babies…and number their tags? So you can track what type of babies the cows give birth to each year?" She asked.

"That and make sure they are getting pregnant. We had one go three years without having a baby…waste of money to keep her," Her dad answered.

"How old does a cow get before you breed her or when she's done breeding?" Grace asked totally caught up in the ride and conversation.

"We'll start breeding them when they're one so they birth at two…actually a little older than two," Uncle Scott answered. "Then we'll breed them for about twelve years…we've had some up to twenty. There are actually a couple old girls left that were born the last season or two when our parents were alive."

"So when Sadie found Dusty, she could have saved about fifteen future cows and all their babies…hundreds…" Grace calculated.

"Exactly," Her dad nodded. "That's why we take care of our cows, and why predators, like cougar and bear are thinned out so they don't kill our future stock and profits. They can run a ranch into the ground."

"So what's the difference between the red and black angus?" She asked.

"Twenty-five and eighteen are black, that's what your grandparents ran," Uncle Scott answered. "When we; me, Grayson, and Dru, decided to increase the herd, we decided to add red. They are more heat tolerant than the black cows. We'd also heard they were more docile… which is really a bit of a toss-up…it really depends on the cow itself."

"More important is the profit you can make out of a cow, bull or combination," Her dad added. "For us, we found that one color isn't more profitable than the other, it's more the bull or cow line."

They rode over the top of the mountain and the bulls came into view. All twelve were visible, which is always good.

They stopped the horses and her dad pointed to a few bulls. "That's twenty-five, that's eighteen, and that one over there, the red one, is forty-four, our most profitable bull."

Grace looked at the bulls her dad pointed to. She wanted to remember twenty-five and eighteen, they were family history. But they looked so much like the other black bulls she would have to use their ear tags in the future instead of just looking at them like her dad and uncle did.

"Do the bulls know the path as well as the cows do when herding them?" She asked.

"Most of them do," Uncle Scott answered. "That's one of the reasons we run the old and young together, so the old can teach the young the trail. Doesn't mean the young will want to follow the trail. Bulls like to do what bulls want to do."

"That's why they become dangerous and why we don't let the kids ride when we're pushing the bulls." Her dad added.

"But they've been in the spring cattle drive," Grace pointed out.

"They're a little more tired from all their…exercise." Uncle Scott chuckled.

"Breeding," Grace smiled at his attempt to be sensitive. "And they are following all their ladies, not so much being…just pushed."

"Exactly," Her dad said proudly.

"How young were you guys and Aunt Dru when you learned all this?" She asked.

Neither spoke right away which caused Grace to look between the two of them. They were just staring at the bulls.

It was her dad that finally spoke. "We were too busy with rodeo and school to really learn any of it…the business end of it anyway. We always thought we had years and years to learn from our parents and grandparents." He sounded melancholy.

"That's what Dru took over while Grayson and I finished school," Uncle Scott added. "She and Andy went through all the books, back about twenty-years, to see where the ranch was and how it grew and what it needed to keep growing…not just exist."

"She not only had to learn the business end of it, while we were in school, but she had to do the work, too." Her dad added. "Fencing, feeding, ordering supplies, doctoring…everything and anything that was needed, even learning the Federal regulations and the selling end of the raising. Scott and I were help on the weekends…and some evenings."

"From September to June, until I graduated from high school…then she had the chore of teaching me." Her uncle said.

"But it wasn't just the cows and the horses needed to run the ranch, but it was the farm ground we had at the time." Her dad said. "We didn't have as much then as we do now, but it was still a lot of work."

"And she wasn't very much older than what Nikki is now…22 or 23." Uncle Scott pointed out.

Grace was amazed. It gave her a whole new perspective on her aunt and what she accomplished. Since the Stables was built just after Grace was born, most of her memories of Aunt Dru where based from The Stables instead of the business portion of the ranch.

"On top of all that," Uncle Scott added. "She was dealing with the insurance and legal battles over the accident."

"…and the loss of her parents and grandparents plus raising Matt and Nikki." Grace added, truly stunned by her aunt.

"Exactly," They said in unison. She could feel the respect the two men had in their sister.

"Once I graduated from college, we were able to increase the acreage we farmed, so we grow our own feed which saves us money and are able to sell a good portion, plus donate to some equine charities." Her dad said.

"And finally build The Stables for her to run…then came Jessup to help at the ranch…then Jack to help at The Stables so she could divide her time between the two and run Tagger Enterprises." Uncle Scott said.

The three of them sat quietly on their horses and watched the bulls graze; all lost in their own thoughts. Bart and Mavis had lain down in front of the riders.

It was peaceful looking out at the grazing bulls, expanse of mountains, and the deep blue sky dotted with an occasional cloud. The slight breeze perfected the moment.

"OK, let's get moving before we talk ourselves right into the evening and it gets too dark," Her dad said. "Grace you follow me, we'll get the older bulls moving since we have the younger horses. Scott and Monty can take the young bulls sitting up there." He pointed up the hillside.

Uncle Scott called Bart and trotted up the hill. Mavis would stay with them. Grace and her dad waited until the rider and dog pushed the young bulls over to the older bulls, then they started down the hill to push the bulls along the trail.

"If you get uncomfortable around a bull, just back off him," Her dad called over his shoulder. "Buttercup still doesn't like cows and these bulls can be a whole new world for her. They can get aggressive."

"OK," She answered. This was even scarier than getting behind the wheel of the truck this morning.

"That red one over there," He pointed to her right. "...is pretty docile. Go up behind him and get him moving down towards that trail down there."

"OK," She nodded and pushed Buttercup into a trot to move up and around the bull.

The red bull watched her but continued to eat. As she got closer she could see his number was forty-one. Buttercup was still pretty calm so she untied her lariat to use as a flag to push the bull.

"Move out!" She yelled at the bull and lifted the coiled lariat in the air.

Forty-one just stood and looked at her.

She moved a little closer, Buttercup was still calm, so she waved again, "Move out!" She yelled.

Forty-One bounced his head and took a couple steps.

"Move it, I said!" She yelled at the stubborn bull.

And he finally did. The bull slowly meandered down to the trail and met up with three or four other bulls.

"Keep going," She yelled and looked up at her dad and uncle as they moved their bulls down to meet up with hers.

"Grace!" Her dad yelled down. "That big black in the middle looks docile but he's aggressive, stay at least ten feet away from him so Buttercup has time to react."

"OK!" She yelled back, her heart racing and waited for him to join her.

Forty-One decided to wander again so she yelled at him; he turned and looked at her then stepped back with the other bulls. "I wish you were all that easy," She mumbled to the bull.

Bart barked which made her turn in time to see one of the young black bulls charge at Uncle Scott and Monty. She held her breath as the big grey horse shifted quickly to the side so the bull missed him. Then he shot a hoof out and hit the bull in the side.

"You show him, Monty," Grace smiled. "That had to hurt."

The bull turned quickly to see what got him. It snorted a couple of time but didn't move. Her uncle waved his lariat and yelled at the bull. The bull lowered his head and pawed at the ground. Monty spun his backend at the bull and shot out a hoof again, just barely missing the bull's nose. Bart ran up behind the bull and bit at its back leg which made the bull give up the battle and move down the hill.

Grace watched that bull and the bull her dad pointed to, closely as they made their way down the trail with Forty-One taking the lead.

They followed the bulls down the trail for another hour. Bart and Mavis occasionally ran to the side to encourage a bull from straying.

"Grace, there's a fork in the road ahead," Her dad called out to her.

Grace nodded.

"Ride down about thirty-feet to the right of the bulls and head to that fork. Sit in the middle of the road that goes sideways along the mountain. It'll be to your left. We want them to go down the road which leads to the right. If you're in the middle of the road they should naturally go down the easy unobstructed road."

Grace nodded and moved out to the side of the bulls. She kept her eyes on the bulls as she made her way.

Buttercup decided she didn't want to leave Eli and started backing up across the uneven ground then suddenly swung sideways. Grace had to grab the saddle horn to keep from tipping off and landing in the dirt. Her heart skipped a beat, but she focused on the horse.

"Come on, girl," Grace pleaded under her breath and kicked the horse harder to get her to move. She moved…but she just went backwards. Her front hooves lifted to rear up and Grace leaned forward and pushed on the horse's neck to encourage her to stay down. Her mind flashed back to Buttercup rearing up on Matt and slamming him into the creek.

Grace turned quickly to see what the ground looked like behind her; rocks and a little gully. She had to keep Buttercup from tripping on the rocks.

Reaching one hand down even with her knee, Grace pulled the left rein tight to her thigh and kicked with only her left foot. It made the horse turn tight in a circle instead of going backwards. Grace stopped kicking and Buttercup stopped moving. She loosened the rein and leaned down to pat her on the shoulder to let her know it was OK.

The horse relaxed under her, so she instantly moved her forward and in the direction she had requested. Buttercup took a couple steps forward, saw they were moving away from Eli again and started walking sideways. Grace turned her to the left in a circle again and when she stopped kicking...Buttercup stopped circling. When the horse relaxed a little, she nudged the horse into a walk in the direction she was supposed to be moving. This time Buttercup walked correctly and in the right direction.

Grace relaxed and felt the horse's body relax as they moved down the trail.

In the distance behind her she heard her dad yell, "Good job, Gracie."

She smiled as she kicked Buttercup into a trot...down into a ditch...out of the ditch...up a hillside...down the other side and finally saw the road divide. She took her position in the middle of the road and bounced her lariat on her leg anxiously waiting.

It was a couple of minutes before she saw Forty-One leading the line of bulls on the trail. The bull watched her as he made his way down the trail. When he got close enough, she pointed down the road he needed to go. The big red bull walked just where she pointed, which made her laugh out loud, which made Buttercup start prancing.

Grace loved bouncing on top of a prancing Buttercup. It was one of the best feelings in the world. She felt like she was part of the dun horse and the two were dancing.

The rest of the bulls followed Forty-One. Her dad and uncle arrived behind them and waved her to join them so she trotted up between the two men.

"This trail narrows for a little ways," Her dad said. "Then it opens up into the valley we want them in, but we have to push them all the way to the other side where the creek is or they'll come back this way looking for water. They won't like us pushing them. They'll want to stay and just eat."

"Watch yourself," Uncle Scott added.

Grace nodded, inhaled deeply, exhaled slowly and built her determination.

The bulls walked in a straight line until they came to the valley then they started to separate.

Her dad and uncle trotted off to the sides and started hollering and pushing the bulls along. Bart and Mavis worked along next to them. Grace stayed in the back and hollered hoping to keep the majority of them moving. They made it half way across the valley before the first small bull took off to the side. Her dad and Eli went after it.

Grace grinned at Eli, he was so beautiful. Even when he was nothing more than a skeleton the summer before she knew the buckskin would be spectacular. Never in her dreams did she think that Eli would choose her dad to be his human. But the connection was there, the horse loved her dad and she knew the feeling was mutual.

Forty-One had stopped and Grace yelled at him to keep moving. The bull didn't move.

"Come on, you did it before," She whined at him and laughed at herself for doing it…and Buttercup pranced. The bull's head went up and he watched the prancing horse a moment before he turned and walked away from her.

"Just laugh your way across, Gracie!" Her dad shouted out to her with a grin.

She turned and waved at him, then laughed… her horse pranced…the bulls walked forward.

Grace and Buttercup danced across the valley.

Now and then a bull would take off but her dad, uncle, Bart and Mavis pushed them back in line. When they made it across the valley her dad and uncle came to her side; both grinning ear to ear.

"Wouldn't have believed it…if I didn't see it for myself," Uncle Scott laughed.

They turned around and trotted back to the truck.

******

"Sadie and Scarecrow killed it again today," Her dad grinned up at her from his phone. "Leah said they won by a half second."

"Good for her," Uncle Scott smiled. "Nora ended up with three 1st place and two 2nd."

Grace looked between the two men and the proud smiles on their faces. This was the part she never saw…that the kids didn't realize…how proud their dads were of them even if they couldn't be at the show or rodeo.

Nora was showing Isaiah and riding Libby. Sadie was running barrels and poles on Scarecrow. They had entered the first barrel race as training for Scarecrow; so she could get used to the crowd of people and horses. They were all surprised when the horse fed off the energy of the crowd and won her first race ever. Sadie, Cora, and the whole family were thrilled.

"With Scarecrow only being ridden for a couple of months and still only three…dang they are going to be good." Her dad shook his head and smiled. "I can just see them in another three, four years…add Scarecrow's strength as she grows and the experience growth between the two of them…unstoppable."

Grace grinned at the pride shining in his eyes.

He turned to Uncle Scott. "Our girls, down the road…." They grinned at each other and shook their heads.

"Hey…me, too!" Grace's giggle was more of a whine.

They both laughed at her.

"We'll be seeing you in Vegas someday, Gracie…" Her dad shut the door on the horse trailer. "…even if it kills me."

"Hey!" She playfully slapped his arm.

He chuckled and walked towards the passenger side of the truck, "Drive us home, Gracie girl."

CHAPTER FOUR

Grace double checked her water and food in the saddle bags then slung it over the back of Buttercup. She laced the leather straps through the holes and tied the bag securely to the saddle. Turning, she looked around at the horses saddled and ready for the day. Nearly the entire Tagger herd was being ridden today as part of their training. There were only a few areas that would be difficult and would be handled by the more experienced horses. Nick would be riding Trooper and Jack was on Cooper. They had proven themselves in the mountains when rescuing the two kids after the airplane crashed. Her dad was on Eli, who he had ridden exclusively at the ranch for the last month. Then there was the tried and true Monty being ridden by Uncle Scott.

Sadie had ridden Scarecrow all weekend so she wanted to ride Little Ghost, their mom was riding Scarecrow. Nora was on Arcturus, the only horse she rode when not having to prepare for a show. Aunt Dru on Harvey, Reilly on Rufio, and Aunt Jordan on Kit. Wade had talked his dad into letting him ride Rooster since they were on fairly flat land and they would only be walking. Wade beamed with pride when Jessup asked to ride Dollar.

The only horses not being ridden were Nora's show horses; Libby and Isaiah. Nikki and Matt had just started college again and couldn't come up for the cattle drive.

Grace felt the excitement run through her. She loved watching the horses get saddled and bridled, kids laughing, parents helping, and this time, the excitement in the Tagger herd, too. Mavis and Bart trotted around excitedly.

Cora was walking through the group making sure everyone had enough water and snacks. She wasn't riding this time, but had ridden on a couple of smaller cattle drives.

Grace heard Jack and Nick laughing and turned to see her aunt walking away from them while shaking her head. Aunt Dru looked up at her with a wide grin. "Just imagine…I married both of them!"

Jessup and Wade laughed so Grace turned to them. They were quite the pair. She turned to Sadie and Nora; the two had been arguing all morning. Aunt Jordan and Uncle Scott were starting to load the horses into the trailers. Grace looked for her parents. She grinned when she saw her dad giving her mother a piggy-back-ride from the house to the gathered herd. They were both laughing.

"Ready to go, Gracie?" Reilly said from behind her.

"Yep," she nodded without turning away from the happy group. Her dad set her mom on the ground then turned and gave his wife a quick movie kiss, nearly dipping her down to the ground. When he lifted her back up, she pushed him away with a wicked gleam in her eyes and a hearty laugh.

"It's going to be a great day!" Reilly walked past her towards the trucks. "I just feel it."

***

Grace led Buttercup out of the horse trailer and quickly tightened the cinch and stepped into the saddle. It was always fun to be the first in the saddle and watch as everyone else mounted. The only reason she beat Sadie into the saddle was because her sister had to wait for her dad to check Little Ghost's cinch. In the next year,

Sadie would become strong enough to tighten the saddle herself…to their father's satisfaction.

Grace watched as Reilly mounted, then Aunt Dru, Sadie, Nora, Wade, her mother, Jack, Nick, Jessup, and then Aunt Jordan. Once everyone else was mounted and everything ready, her dad and Uncle Scott mounted Eli and Monty. Grace realized that had all worn their Tagger T3E denim jackets to ward off the morning chill…even Nick. They looked like a great team…family together. Her heart warmed at the sight.

After they arrived at the cows to be pushed, Grace stayed close to her Aunt Dru as they moved away from the trailers and towards the cows.

"So, I heard you and Buttercup danced in the meadow yesterday," Her aunt smiled at her.

Grace giggled, "That sounds so pretty."

"Well, I envisioned the pictures Matt took of you and Buttercup running through the wild flowers in the mountains last month."

"That was so awesome!" Grace grinned. "But there was only grass and no wild flowers yesterday."

"But it isn't the flowers that made the picture, Grace," Aunt Dru smiled. "It was the girl, the horse, the laughter, the dance…that's what added the magic. Your dad and uncle enjoyed it."

Grace laughed and Buttercup pranced, "I don't think the bulls liked it."

Her aunt's pretty blue eyes were lit with humor, "Well, let's see if the cows do," She pointed to their right so they trotted towards the small clearing where a dozen pair of cows and calves were grazing.

The cow's heads sprang up and the calves ran around excitedly when they saw them approach.

"Go to the left so we let them know we want them to the right," Aunt Dru called out to her. "But you already knew that didn't you!"

Grace nodded excitedly. Maybe someday she would get tired of rounding up cows, but she couldn't see that day would come anytime soon.

She looked up at the sky. The clear blue had turned grey and she noticed a few dark and menacing clouds on the horizon. Could be rain…then realized she didn't have a rain slicker with her. The denim jackets and cowboy hat would have to be enough today if it rained.

She rode with her aunt most of the day, gathering and pushing cows out of gullies and trees. They would drop down over mountains and push them up to the top so the cows could make their way across the top of the mountain range. Buttercup only had a few moments of concern; going through a small creek, which she jumped, and having to step through a brushy patch of ground. She also didn't want to get out of sight of Harvey and Aunt Dru.

"I think that's the last of them," Her aunt turned and smiled as they made it to the top of the ridge. "Now it's just simply walking them down the road. We just have to watch Windy Gap."

"Why?" Grace rode up next to her and calmed down so Buttercup would walk smoothly.

"Because the cows see the hillside of tall gorgeous grass and bale off the side of the road to get to it. Then we have to push them up the mountainside again. We missed it once and lost the whole herd," Aunt Dru rolled her eyes. "Took us another half day to get them out of the grass and up to the road."

"So how do you keep them from going down?"

"It takes three riders paroling the gap and discouraging them from baling. If you get the front of the herd distracted and moving down the road, most the time the rest follow and ignore the gap...as long as there is a rider blocking them."

"Uncle Grayson!" They heard a female voice yelling.

They turned to see Nora yelling and waving. She pointed down toward the cows in front of her.

Trees blocked their view, so Grace and her aunt turned the horses and trotted in her direction to see why she was yelling.

Her dad was galloping in the direction Nora was pointing so they kicked Harvey and Buttercup into a gallop, too. Mavis was running excitedly next to Eli.

As they crossed the herd, they could see him running towards Sadie and Little Ghost. He pulled Eli up abruptly, stopped, and called Mavis over and told her to stay. The dog quickly trotted to him and sat next to Eli's leg.

Aunt Dru stopped and Grace pulled Buttercup up next to her.

Little Ghost was facing two cows, a black and a red, that were trying to dart into the trees. Every time the cows moved, Little Ghost would block their path by trotting in front of them or jumping his front end from left to right to stop them. Sadie had settled down in the saddle with one hand gripping the saddle horn and the other holding the reins in front of the saddle, low to the horse's neck. Her eyes concentrated on the cows.

The red cow darted to the left and Little Ghost took off on a run to cut her off. When the cow stopped, Little Ghost saw the black cow try to head for the trees and took off at a run to that cow and came to a sliding stop in front of the cow, blocking its forward movement. Sadie sat back then started to slide to the left, her long braid flying in the air. She quickly pulled herself back straight, keeping her eyes on the cow the whole time.

The horse jumped around and faced the cow, lowered his head and laid his ears back. The black cow turned and ran back to the moving herd.

Little Ghost stood upright and the horse and rider looked down at the red cow. It was trotting towards the trees. The horse took off at a run until it was in front of the cow; he turned so fast he nearly slid on his side; Sadie slid forward, but she again pulled herself upright. The red cow stopped within inches of running into Sadie and Little Ghost. Sadie reached down and slapped the cow on the head then quickly grabbed the saddle horn again.

Grace's eyes were transfixed on her sister but she heard Aunt Dru chuckle.

The red cow took a few steps back from the grey horse and blonde girl then turned and trotted back to the moving herd.

Sadie sat up in the saddle and pulled up on Little Ghost reins. She leaned down and started rubbing the horse's neck and laughed. Excited eyes turned to her dad as he trotted up to her.

"Did you see, Dad!?" They heard Sadie yell.

"Dang, that girl can ride," Aunt Dru mumbled and shook her head in amazement.

Grace was grinning at her sister as their dad reached Sadie, wrapped his arms around her and pulled the squealing girl off the grey horse and into a big hug. They were both laughing. As he sat her back down on the horse, their mom reached them and pulled Scarecrow up next to Little Ghost. She leaned over and hugged Sadie.

Sadie turned and saw Grace and their aunt and waved excitedly. They both waved back.

"Let's get back to our post," Aunt Dru smiled over at Grace.

They trotted through the cows and to the mountain ridge. The road the cows were following turned to the left and it followed along the ridge edge. Grace turned away from the cows and looked down the long sloping beige mountainside. The grass was eaten down and dry so there wasn't much worry the cows would bale off the side as long as the riders didn't push too hard. The river was at the bottom.

A flash of bright light nearly blinded Grace and an instant crack of thunder rang throughout the mountains. Grace and Buttercup both jumped, it felt like her whole body vibrated. The hair on the back of her neck was standing up as she turned startled eyes towards her aunt as she tried to stop Buttercup and calm her down.

"Lightening?" Grace's eyes were wide.

"You OK?" Aunt Dru nodded and looked around at the cows and other riders. Other than Aunt Dru, the only one ahead of them now was Nora, who was on the other side of the herd. Sadie and her parents had dropped back on the other side of the herd, too.

Buttercup came to a stop and Grace tried kicking her to keep her moving a long side the cows. The horse didn't move. Grace turned and saw Aunt Dru sitting on Harvey right in front of her blocking their path.

Her aunt had turned towards the steep mountainside and was staring down towards the river. Aunt Dru's eyes narrowed, teeth clenched and her jaw muscles twitched. Grace followed her aunt's gaze and saw someone riding across the middle of the mountain at a dead run. Something no one ever did!

It was Uncle Scott on Monty! Grace had never seen him run so fast…especially across a rocky, steep hillside. Her stomach clenched in fear.

She turned to her aunt who was watching her brother running; her hand was holding the reins so tight her knuckles were white. Tension screamed from her.

Grace turned back to find her parents. They were also watching the rider and horse. She heard a sharp intake of breath from that made her swing back to Aunt Dru. Grace followed her gaze…there was a white puff cloud on the other side of the ridge. That's what Uncle Scott was racing to!

"Grace, that's smoke. The lightening must have hit the ground." Her aunt turned to her. Grace's eyes opened wide in shock as her aunt handed her the rifle from her scabbard. "Grace!"

"What?" Grace reached a shaky hand out to take the rifle.

"Look at me," Aunt Dru ordered and Grace looked into her concerned eyes. "I've got to go down and help Scott. Do you understand?"

"Yes, of course." Grace shook off the shock.

"You are in charge. Get the kids together and watch. On the other side of the ridge is a gully filled with trees and brush. If the fire reaches that gully it's going to spread to other trees and brush quickly and come right up here to the top." Grace looked down where she was pointing then back at her and nodded.

"If it hits that gully, get the kids out of here as fast as possible. Understand?" Aunt Dru kicked Harvey into a trot and over the edge of the mountain.

"What about you guys?" Grace yelled.

"If it gets out of control, we'll run to the river. Get back to the trucks and call for help." She kicked Harvey down the hill faster.

Grace looked back down and saw her uncle had disappeared over the hill. She turned back to see Jessup, Nick, Jack, her parents, and Aunt Jordan all riding down the hill and galloping over the ridge.

"What's going on?" Sadie rode up next to her.

Grace turned and looked for all the other kids. Nora had disappeared ahead of them.

"Fire, Sadie," Grace turned to her sister, her eyes widened in fear. "Go get Nora and bring her back here."

Sadie turned and kicked Little Ghost into a gallop.

Grace turned, she couldn't see Reilly or Wade yet so she kicked Buttercup into a trot and followed the top of the mountain ridge until she could see over the ridge Uncle Scott had disappeared over and where the white smoke was wafting up from.

She turned again…still no sign of Wade and Reilly.

Thundering hoof beats echoed across the pasture, Sadie and Nora were running towards her.

Continuing down the ridge, she finally saw the source of the smoke and her uncle. He had jumped off Monty and was beating something on the ground against the flames spreading through the dry grass…it was his denim jacket. The cows had been on the mountainside for months making the grass short so the flicks of flames weren't high, but they were advancing quickly. There was a small ring of black in front of him and the blaze was fast moving and spreading out in a circle. There was no way he could do it himself.

"What do we do?" Nora asked from next to her.

Grace repeated her aunt's instruction then turned back to see Reilly and Wade making their way to them.

Grace's heart sunk. She forgot Wade was on Rooster…who couldn't run.

CHAPTER FIVE

Grace stared at Reilly's nervous expression then at Wade, then Rooster.

She turned worried eyes back down at the fire. Everyone had reached the fire and dismounted from the horses. They were all using their denim jackets to beat at the fire.

Grace turned back to Reilly and Wade. If they had to take off fast, they could injure Rooster…possibly fatally.

"Reilly," Grace turned Buttercup to him. "Take the rifle." She handed it to him.

"Why?" Reilly asked.

"You never know what's going to be running from the fire," Grace told him firmly. "You have to take Wade and Rooster and head out now."

"But Grace…" Reilly looked down at their family fighting the fire.

"Reilly, don't argue," Grace ordered and he looked at her in surprise. She repeated her aunt's instructions. "If we have to run it could hurt Rooster."

"I'm leaving," Wade looked at each of them then down at his parents. "Good luck," He said nearly in tears and turned Rooster back down the road towards the trucks and trailers.

"Reilly!" Grace pointed down at the back of Wade. "Take the dogs so we don't have to worry about them, too. He shouldn't be alone."

"I'm gone." He turned Rufio and trotted after Wade and called Mavis and Bart…the dogs trotted happily next to the two.

Grace turned back to her sister and cousin, "It's just us."

They nodded and the three stared down at the adults fighting the fire.

"Where did the horses go?" Nora whispered.

Grace looked around, but the horses weren't in sight. Still watching the parents beating the ground and fire with their coats, she turned Buttercup and walked back to where they started. The horses were standing at the bottom of the hill, over the ridge from the fire. She turned back to Sadie and Nora.

"They're on the other side," Grace said quietly.

They watched silently as a gust of wind blew through the ravine and across their faces. The wind fanned the fire and more flames could be seen, spreading quickly and the circle enlarging. There were two trees in the middle of the mountainside. If the fire reached those, it would be like lighting a match. The fire would become extremely dangerous and deadly to the adults trying to fight the fire.

Grace felt Nora's hand over her own and she squeezed her cousin's hand. Grace reached over for Sadie's and they sat quietly on their horses, holding hands, and staring down the mountain at their family battling the fire.

Grace turned and looked down the road, Reilly and Wade were in the far distance, but she could still see them which made her nervous. Her eyes went back down the mountain.

The fire moved quickly up to their right and they saw Nick run up the hill as fast as he could to get ahead of it. He started beating the ground again and stopped its rise up the hill but the fire had reached the two small trees. The blaze quickly rose from the base of the trees and engulfed the dry limbs quickly. The trees went up in flames; the tip of a match was struck.

"Grace..." Sadie turned scared eyes to her.

"It's OK," Grace told her with a firmer, stronger voice than what she felt on the inside. "The ground around the trees is already burnt so it shouldn't spread." As she said the words a few embers from the flaming trees were caught in the breeze and carried up the hill, to the non-burned grass.

Her mother saw the embers and quickly made her way to them and beat them out with her coat. Aunt Jordan saw more embers fly and land. She ran to put them out.

Grace looked to the left of them. The fire was slowly making its way up the hill towards the gully. As fast as the two trees in the middle had became inflamed, if it reached the gully it would make it up to the top within minutes.

With her eyes, Grace followed the gully up to the top of the mountain. There were at least a dozen trees that the fire could spread to before it reached the top. At the top, it would spread to dozens and hundreds of trees. It would endanger the trees, livestock, and with nothing stopping it, could go all the way to the ranch house and buildings.

Grace took in a deep breath and let it out slowly. Both girls squeezed her hands tighter.

Aunt Jordan was running up the hill towards an offshoot of the fire then suddenly she tripped and fell backwards landing hard on the ground. She rolled towards the fire. Turning sideways she tried to stop herself but it made her flip and fly into the air and landing into a blaze of the fire.

They could hear her scream echoing through the mountains.

"Mom!" Nora cried out and stood in the saddle, her voice shaking. Tears started rolling down her cheeks.

Jessup ran to her side and quickly pulled her out of the ring of fire. Her jacket had landed under her arm and waist but her legs were smoking. He wrapped his coat around her legs to smother any possibility of fire. Aunt Jordan glanced over at her husband who had started running towards her. She put a hand up to stop him and yelled that she was OK. He hesitated, then turned his attention back to the fire. With every third or fourth strike to the ground, his eyes glanced over at his wife. She had returned to beating her jacket at the fire.

"She's OK," Sadie whispered, trying to console her cousin. She had ridden to the other side of Nora so their young cousin was between them as they held hands. No matter how much the two fought, they always came together when one needed the other.

Jack ran up the hill to the right, passed Nick and caught another offshoot of the fire. Aunt Dru had stopped the spread at the bottom and was making her way up the right side. The fire was halfway to the gully. There was a chance they could get it out before it reached the top.

They would need the horses once they got the fire out. Grace let go of the girls' hands. "I'll be right back," She told them and headed back to where she could see the horses. They were still standing and grazing towards the bottom.

"Sadie?" Grace yelled.

"What?" Her sister turned to her.

"Can you call Scarecrow like you can Little Ghost?" Grace asked. She wanted to get the horses to the top.

"No. I've never worked with her." Sadie took a few steps towards her then they heard a yell.

Grace trotted back to the tip of the ridge so she could see the horses on the left side and the fire on the right.

Uncle Scott was yelling at Jessup and her mother and pointing to the top. Both started trying to run. The blaze had started moving up the hill again.

Grace could tell they were slowing down and tiring. They couldn't hold on much longer.

"Sadie, Nora…." Grace turned to them. "Both of you go over the ridge a little, not too far, and see if you can get the horses attention. See if they will start moving up."

Both girls nodded.

Grace watched the fire, the adults, and now the girls making their way over the edge of the mountain. Reilly and Wade were no longer in sight.

"Not too far," She whispered to the girls.

To her relief, the horses at the bottom saw the girls and their heads raised from grazing. Trooper took a few steps up the hill then stopped…then Harvey decided to move up a little and stopped. Eli took a few steps. Finally, it was Kit that started a steady walk up the hill, the rest followed slowly.

"I love you Kit Kit," Grace whispered to the horse.

Grace felt a sudden swift breeze against her face that lifted her hair…there was another yell and she looked back at the fire. The pungent odor of the smoke bit at her eyes and in her nostrils. The gust of wind had caused the fire to increase in strength and head to her left…where they didn't want it to go. It was moving quickly and her dad was trying to run up the mountain to cut off the blaze but the fire was moving faster than he could run.

Grace's heart pounded in her chest. The girls were too far away for her comfort. If they needed to run…

There was no way her dad could beat the fire up the hill…but if he was on Eli! Grace turned quickly, excitement and energy flowing through her.

She saw the horses had made it half way up. Eli was nearly even with her dad on the other side but they couldn't see each other. Her dad was still trying to run up the mountain towards Grace to get ahead of the fire. He needed to run up the ravine to her left to see the horses.

Eli would go to her dad…she just knew it.

Grace stood and started waving her hands at her dad. If she could let him know that Eli was there, so close… then maybe they could get ahead of the blaze.

She waved and waved, Buttercup started prancing under her…matching her energy.

"If I had the rifle I could fire in the air!" She screamed out.

Then she screamed again. Waving, prancing, screaming….

Finally, he stopped and looked up at her. She pointed frantically over the hill to the horses. Please understand me! Her heart was racing, her throat starting to hurt from the screams and the acid odor from the fire.

She pointed down at Buttercup then over the hill.

"Eli!" She screamed. "Eli!"

He turned and looked up the mountain then back at her. She pointed at her horse again and then over the hill.

He started running up the hill in the direction of the horses. He understood!

Grace turned and looked at the horse. Eli had to see her dad!

She watched as her dad stumbled and tripped on the rocks and uneven ground as he tried desperately to climb the hill. Grace was holding her breath and turned Buttercup to face the horses.

Only Sadie calling Little Ghost could match Eli going to her dad…it was their only chance.

Her dad finally crested the hill and looked down at the horses. She heard him yell, and Eli's head shot up in his direction. Without hesitation, Eli started running across the hill towards her dad. The horse must have understood the desperation in his voice.

"Yes!" Grace could feel the tears of relief welling up in her eyes, her heart beating so strong her veins were going to split.

She watched the beautiful buckskin run towards her dad; his body heaving forward up the hill. Her dad was waving at the horse. She held her breath as they finally met and he barely let the horse stop before swinging into the saddle and they ran up and over the ridge. At a full gallop, they ran across the mountain to the base of the gully where her dad jumped off the horse and started beating the fire. Eli took a few quick strides away from the fire then stopped.

"Did you see that?" Sadie said excitedly as the girls returned.

Grace nodded and stared at her dad as he frantically beat at the ring of fire and tried to stop the flames from reaching the gully...and possibly the whole ranch.

She quickly flicked her eyes back to her left and saw the other horses come up behind them and quickly lowering their heads to the green grass. She turned farther and saw the cows had spread out across the field and into the trees; they didn't seem too concerned about the fire.

Her eyes went back to the adults. They had all slowed down.

Grace blinked her eyes trying to remoisten them from staring so hard and the smoke that was stinging them.

Nick and Jack were making their way across the top and heading to meet up with her dad on the right. Aunt Jordan and Jessup where coming up to him on the left. Her mother was just below them and watching for embers from the two trees that were still blazing in the middle of the burnt mountain. Aunt Dru was making her way up the right and putting out the last bit of fire along the rim of the black circle. Once she was satisfied, she would continue her climb up to the top.

Their arms didn't rise as high as they once did; the power of the thrust to the ground had diminished. If a gust of wind rose, Grace didn't think they would have the strength to battle much longer, they may lose the battle. The adults would have to run to the bottom as the girls ran the horses to the trailers.

Finally, Nick reached her dad's side and they started putting out the last of the fire that threatened the gully and the ranch.

Her body trembled in relief. Then she felt a raindrop, she looked down at her arm and saw the precious water. Looking up, the sky was dark. The rain was desperately needed but the wind that could accompany it would be disastrous.

Aunt Jordan reached Grace's dad to his left and with Nick to his right, the three beat on the ground for another ten minutes then stopped. Their arms hung low at their sides.

Her dad reached over and pulled his sister-in-law into a firm embrace. He must have witnessed her fall. Grace wished she could hug her right now too.

CHAPTER SIX

"Let's gather the horses." Grace told the girls and they quickly trotted over to the grazing herd. More rain drops.

Grace had a desperate need to see her mother so she raced over to grab Scarecrow and Kit and led them back to the top of the mountain overlooking the fire. All the adults were sitting down, watching the blackened ring, making sure no blaze started back up. The two trees in the middle were only smoking…the blaze had died.

The mountainside was too steep for the younger girls and horses.

"Stay here and I'll start taking the horses down," Grace turned to the girls.

"OK," They answered in unison. There were relieved smiles on their faces.

Grace led the first two horses down to her left and towards her parents, aunt and uncle. They all looked up at her but didn't move. Eli was standing behind her sitting father.

Grace took Kit to Aunt Jordan and Uncle Scott first. "Reilly left with Wade and Rooster right after the fire broke out. They should be back at the trucks by now." She told them and pulled the bottles of water out of Kit's saddle bags and handed them down to outstretched hands.

"Thanks, Grace," Aunt Jordan smiled tiredly as she dropped the lead rope into her aunt's hand. Her face was marked with black ash.

Uncle Scott was sitting next to her, his arm resting over her legs. Her jeans were burnt black.

"I'll be right back with Monty." Grace smiled at him, he just nodded back. As she led Scarecrow over to her mom, she saw Aunt Jordan lean on her husband's shoulder and nuzzle into his neck, her face hidden under his hat. His arms tightly wrapped around her. Her aunt's shoulders were moving and she realized she was crying. Grace quickly turned away.

The rain was still just a drip here and there.

When she reached her mother, she leaned down with the lead rope so she could touch her mother's hand.

"Are you OK?" Grace looked at her worriedly; her mother's face was streaked in black ash from the fire. The few rain drops hit her face and made it look like she was crying.

"I am, Sweetheart," She looked up and reassured her. "Just tired, and really glad I don't have to climb up the rest of this mountain…never been so glad to see a horse."

Grace smiled and looked over at her dad; he was about twenty feet away. They both had water; her dad must have retrieved them from Eli's saddle bags. She handed her mother another bottle.

"Good call, Gracie." He was leaning back on Eli's front legs. The horse's head hovered low over her dad. "He saved the day."

Tears stung in Grace's eyes as she nodded. She turned up the hill to get the next set of horses.

She brought down Monty and Dollar next.

Uncle Scott had moved Aunt Jordan onto his lap and was cradling her. There was concern and relief on his face. His fingers gently caressed his wife's jaw; the rest of her face was blocked by his hat.

As she approached Jessup, he looked up with tired eyes…his face was also streaked with black ash.

"Thanks," He grinned up at her and winked as she handed down a couple bottles.

She made her way back to the top and grabbed the lead ropes for Harvey and Cooper.

Cooper and water were quickly left with Jack as Grace made her way to Aunt Dru, who was the farthest down the hill. She was sitting just above the ring of black, watching smoke drift up from the trees in the middle. The rain started falling just a little harder.

Her aunt looked up as she approached with Harvey.

"I need the first aid kit," Aunt Dru whispered.

Grace stepped out of the saddle and reached into the saddle bags for the kit. Every rider carried a small kit in their saddle bag.

When she stepped around Buttercup, her aunt turned her arm to her. There was an ugly red burn up the side of her arm from her wrist to half way up her bicep.

"It stings like a son-of-a-gun," Her aunt grimaced as Grace opened the small tube of burn ointment. Grace squeezed the white gel over the red area but let her aunt spread it over the burn.

"Are you sure you're ,OK?" Grace frowned.

Aunt Dru nodded. "No blisters," She smiled and grimaced as she spread the ointment across the red streak. Her blue eyes shot across the mountain and over to her brother and his wife.

"What happened?"

Grace retrieved water for her aunt while she told her of the fall into the fire and Jessup saving Aunt Jordan.

"Dang...that had to scare the heck out of both of them." Aunt Dru whispered.

"All three of them," Grace looked across at the group. "Uncle Scott tried to run to her but Aunt Jordan motioned for him to stay and fight the fire."

"Scott saw it?" Aunt Dru exhaled loudly. "Nothing worse than seeing someone you love in jeopardy and there isn't anything you can do to help." She tucked the tube of ointment into her shirt pocket.

Grace's mind went to Buttercup rearing backwards and flying on top of Matt in the creek. All she could do was watch and scream as her horse landed on her cousin.

"I agree," Grace nodded and remounted the horse.

The only horse left was Trooper. She quickly retrieved the horse and made her way to Nick. He was watching the edges of the black hillside.

"Glad to see this rain," Nick smiled at her.

Grace glanced up at Sadie and Nora. They were sitting quietly at the top of the ridge but looking behind them. She hesitated, deciding whether to ride up to them to see what they were looking at when Reilly and Wade appeared. They were riding double on the back of Rufio. Rooster must be having a fit being left behind alone.

She stepped out of the saddle.

"You OK?" Nick asked Grace.

"I'm supposed to be asking YOU that." She smiled.

"Well, we both know what it's like to be on the outside looking in and vice versa." He accepted the bottle of water she handed him. He drank the whole thing and reached for a second. She pulled two more bottles out and watched him down another one then set the third on the ground next to him.

She turned and looked out at the black burnt ground. A shiver went down her back.

"How long do we wait?"

"See where the rain drops are hitting the edges?" He pointed down to their left.

She nodded.

"When it hits a hot spot, a little puff of steam rises."

She looked closely and saw a few puffs.

"Once those are done, we know it won't restart if the wind comes back up." He looked over at the trees still steaming in the middle. "Unless the rain really pours, the trees will internally burn for quite a while."

"Like a log in a fire pit?"

He nodded.

As they were talking, the raindrops grew more frequent and bigger. Soon they were both drenched.

She looked over at the rest of the adults…no one had moved except Uncle Scott who had moved his wife down onto the ground between his bent legs, his arms firmly wrapped around her and he was leaned over to protect her from the rain with his hat.

"I just about had a heart attack when I saw her go down," Nick looked up at Grace. "I couldn't imagine what Scott was going through."

Grace nodded and stood quietly next to him. Buttercup brought her head in and tucked it under Grace's arm. She didn't seem too fond of the rain.

They waited another ten minutes; the rain became a down pour.

Grace looked at the kids on top. Her cowboy hat protected her eyes from the rain so she could see they were still on horseback.

"Let's go." Nick stood.

Grace turned and saw her dad stepping up onto Eli.

They gathered together at the top of the mountain and looked back down at the rain hitting the black mountain side. Steam still rose from the trees in the middle.

"Wade, come here." Uncle Scott called out.

Reilly gave Wade an arm to swing the younger boy onto the ground. Wade ran up to his dad expecting to climb up with him.

Instead, Uncle Scott slid himself behind the back of his saddle and reached over for his wife who was sitting on Kit. He easily lifted her up and placed her in front of him.

"I'm OK, Scott." Aunt Jordan smiled up at him but with a tense face.

"Well," He said in a low gruff voice. "I'm not."

Grace smiled and watched her aunt lean back against her husband, his arms wrapped around her and pulled her tighter. She looked so tiny in his arms.

Wade climbed up onto Kit and the group, after one last look down the hillside, walked quietly in the rain down the road toward the trucks and trailers.

***

Grace rode at the back of the line of riders and horses. She wanted to keep her eye on everyone, she suddenly felt overly protective of her whole family. The rain danced on her cowboy hat causing a continual muffled ticking.

Her parents were riding up front with Sadie between them. They each had ahold of their daughter's hands so her arms were spread out and she was riding Little Ghost with no reins.

Uncle Scott and Aunt Jordan were riding between Wade and Nora. Jessup rode next to Wade.

Jack and Aunt Dru were holding hands, of course, but were talking to Nick who was on the right of his ex-wife. She had her burned arm out showing the two men. The rain drops had to help cool it down.

Reilly slowed down and rode next to Grace.

"I hope you're not going to apologize," He grinned over at her. She looked at him in confusion, "For what?"

"For yelling at me and telling me to leave."

A smile spread across her face, "The thought never crossed my mind."

He chuckled. "Good, because you made the right decision."

Grace nodded and sighed. She thought back over everything that happened the last couple hours. She wouldn't change anything that she did. Matt had told her that he did the same thing after the ride in the mountains and the rescue of Adam and Amy.

"That was the longest, most agonizing, slowest ride I have ever taken," Reilly looked over at Wade. "Don't tell him I said it," She shook her head, "but he didn't talk the whole way...I'm not sure if he was crying or not...but he wouldn't speak...he was scared for Rooster and terrified for his parents."

"I'm glad he didn't see Aunt Jordan fall," Grace sighed. "It frightened everyone that saw it. Nora will probably have nightmares."

"After we waited for what seemed like forever, and didn't see anyone, we decided to ride back. Rooster was having a fit when we left. I put him inside the horse trailer so he couldn't move around too much."

"Good move."

They could hear the horse whinny from the horse trailer as they approached.

"Leave everything on and just loosen the cinches," Her dad yelled over the rain as they dismounted.

Grace stayed in the saddle and watched over the group as everyone else dismounted. Once they were all on the ground, she stepped down from the horse and gave her cream color horse some attention. She stroked the horse's wet nose and up to her ears and playfully twisted them. She patted the large neck and the water splattered back at her, which made Grace giggle; Buttercup's head went up alertly at the sound.

"I love you, Buttercup." Grace sighed as she loosened the cinch and stepped towards the back of the trailers.

***

All the kids insisted the parents take the first round of showers while the kids took responsibility of all the horses and made the parents leave the barn.

During the ride in the trucks, they realized how strong the fire odor was in their hair and on their clothes. All the clothes were gathered into a plastic garbage sack and placed in the back of Aunt Dru's truck.

Reilly built a fire in the stove of the ranch house and the one in the bunk house. The temperature wasn't cold but the heat from the fire helped warm them after the long ride in the rain.

Cora had cooked a large dinner and a selection of pies. It didn't take long for the group of thirteen to eat everything and they were sitting around the living room of the ranch house telling Cora about the cattle drive and fire. They were all dressed in sweat pants or pajama bottoms and t-shirts.

Her dad told the story of Sadie, Little Ghost and the cows. Reilly told about Uncle Scott running Monty across the mountain and towards the fire. Nora recanted the scary story of watching her mother fall into the fire. Uncle Scott was sitting sideways on the end of the couch with one leg propped up against the back. Aunt Jordan was lying between his legs and resting her head across his chest. His arms were comfortably wrapped around her.

As Nora spoke, Grace watched her uncle's face turn white. It reminded her of her dad and Matt listening to the stories of her facing the bear, their own faces turning white.

Uncle Scott reached down and picked up a long strand of his wife's hair and look at it. "Your hair is singed, Tink." He whispered to her.

She nodded, "I noticed that too. I guess I'll have to cut it short again."

"I like your hair short," He kissed the top of her head while staring at the hair he was twisting between his fingers. He turned whiter.

Grace turned and looked out the window. It wasn't the first time she had heard her uncle call his wife 'Tink'. She just hadn't understood where the name came from. She smiled as she remembered what her uncle said of their first meeting; *"She looked like a little pixie girl, like the Tinkerbell dolls that Nikki had all over the house... just too adorable!"* Aunt Jordan was Uncle Scott's Tinkerbell!

There were times she wondered if her aunt and uncle loved each other as much as her dad and mom. Everyone could see the love between her parents, many had commented. But it wasn't always as obvious to her with her aunt and uncle. Glancing at them now, her aunts face content and eyes shining; her uncle's face white with fear as he thought about what happened, and what could have happened. There was no doubt that they were deeply in love.

One more look at her uncle's face, Grace sat up and interrupted Nora's story.

"You should have seen Eli!" Grace called out and grabbed everyone's attention.

As she told the story of Eli's run, she watched the color come back into her uncle's skin. His eyes shone with laughter as he told of seeing his brother running away from the fire and the relief of him returning on the buckskin, like the hero in a western movie.

The conversations continued as Grace stood, gathered plates, and walked to the kitchen. Her dad walked in behind her and wrapped her into a big hug.

"I'm very proud of you," He whispered and rested his chin on top her head.

"It was a bit scary, even watching Sadie and Little Ghost was scary." Grace whispered back as she leaned into her dad, clasping her hands together behind him.

"Not just out there...but what you just did for Scott...I noticed." He chuckled and tightened the hug a little tighter. It was that little bit tighter that Grace loved...that was the special love.

CHAPTER SEVEN

"Scott! What are you doing?" Grace's mother walked down the center aisle of the bunkhouse and to the kitchen. She had seen her brother-in-law grab scissors out of the drawer and head to his laughing wife who was sitting at the table.

Grace was sitting cross-legged on top of her bunk with Reilly watching everyone make their way through the dark outside and into the building. The rain had finally stopped.

"What?" Uncle Scott laughed innocently as he grabbed the back of Aunt Jordan's black shoulder-length hair and raised the open scissors.

"Drop them…or I'll drop you!" Her mom threatened with a laugh.

"I'm tired enough right now…you probably could." He laughed at his sister-in-law and lowered the scissors. Then, he raised them again and grinned mischievously, "But I know you're just as tired as I am."

Grace giggled as her mother reached her uncle and playfully grabbed the scissors. He relented with a chuckle.

"You seriously want your hair cut?" Her mother turned to Aunt Jordan.

"It's singed in the back." She nodded.

"Well, I'll do it now and you can have it fine-tuned when we get back to Lewiston." She pushed Uncle Scott down into the chair.

When Aunt Jordan looked down the bunkhouse to see who was coming through the door next, Grace saw her mother and uncle exchange a quick glance. His face had turned serious and he mouthed, "Thank you." Her mom nodded her understanding of his need to get rid of the evidence of how close his wife was to the fire.

Aunt Dru walked into the building followed by Jack.

She stopped and looked up at Grace, "Good job, today," She smiled and Grace nodded with a sense of pride warming her spirit.

Jack reached up and squeezed her knee and winked at his son. His look showed his pride in both of them.

Aunt Dru gasped as she saw Grace's mother cut off half the length of Aunt Jordan's hair.

Grace laughed at them and turned to the opening door. It was Nick and her dad. She was surprised to see Nick since he always slept in the third bedroom in the ranch house.

Nora's bed was next to the kitchen and Wade was sitting on the top bunk next to her. They quietly watched the adults in the kitchen laughing and watching the impromptu haircut.

When her mother was done, her aunt's hair was cut just above her ears. Grace agreed with Uncle Scott, her aunt, looking in the mirror and laughing, looked like a pixie.

Wade had crawled back into his own bed and both he and Nora were already asleep. Sadie was tucked into her bed and she had tried to stay awake and watch but her eyes had given up.

Grace and Reilly were still sitting on her bunk and talking about Kelly until they heard the adults start talking about finishing the cattle drive.

They were all yawning and stretching, she was amazed they were still awake. Aspirin was passed around for the sore muscles and Jack was applying more ointment on Aunt Dru's arm.

"No doubt we'll all need to sleep in," She heard her dad say.

"It won't take much longer," Aunt Dru added. "We can go tomorrow afternoon and push across the top of the mountain."

"We can push out a day, too. We don't have to do it tomorrow." Uncle Scott said. Aunt Jordan was sitting on his lap and he was playing with her short hair. The two just couldn't let go of each other tonight!

"I have to be back to work that day," Grace's mom reminded him.

Grace and Reilly looked at each other. She knew he was thinking the same thing she was. Grace pulled out her phone. It was 10:00 now... she set the alarm clock for 3:30 am.

Reilly nodded and moved over to his bed.

They got under the covers, lay on their stomachs and watched the parents talking. Grace could tell they were starting to wind down. Aunt Jordan was nearly asleep in her husband's arms.

As they talked, she put the foundation to her plan together. After her talk with Aunt Dru that morning, she knew the only obstacle in the final section of the cattle drive would be Windy Gap. She would need more experienced riders...she needed Matt and Nikki to join them. It was the only way the kids could finish the cattle drive for the parents.

Grace thought over the horses that would be available. The more experienced out there the better. Nora needed to ride Libby. Isaiah was off limits, if anything happened to him Nora wouldn't be able to show him at halter again this year. All the ranch horses were off limits since none of the kids rode them anymore. Eli had earned a day off, as well as Monty.

Wade would have to ride Dollar. Sadie needed to ride Scarecrow. Little Ghost's habit of cutting the cows needed to be with their dad in charge, not Grace! Harvey, Trooper, and Buttercup were also good for the ride. Reilly would have the choice to ride either Rufio or Cooper.

Nora on Libby and Reilly on his horse could take the points. Wade could push from the back leaving Sadie and Grace in between. All they needed to do was gather the cows and get them moving in the direction they already knew. Matt and Nikki would join them and get them passed Windy Gap.

Grace closed her eyes...she needed the sleep to get up that early!

***

The vibration of her phone woke her...it was 3:35 and it would start to get light at 5:00 with sunrise around 5:30 she guessed. They would have to get moving now.

Grace lifted her head and looked around the room. The moon was shining brightly through the windows so she could see the entire room. On the top bunk across from her was Reilly. She couldn't see him. Below Reilly, on his lower bunk were Jack and Aunt Dru. For all Grace's life her aunt had been in the bunk bed below her, so to see her over with Jack was...just bizarre.

The first night they all spent at the ranch, after the engagement was announced, Aunt Dru had automatically crawled into the bunk bed below Grace. Jack and the other adults had teased her so much that Aunt Dru had actually blushed as she moved. Grace smiled at the memory.

Other than Reilly, all the upper bunk beds on the other side of the room were empty. Her parents were in the lower bunk next to Aunt Dru and Jack. Then Uncle Scott and Aunt Jordan were in the next one. The fourth set of bunk beds on that side of the room was empty.

No one was in her aunt's old bed and Matt and Nikki's beds were empty too and the last bed was empty. Wade was in the upper bed next to Grace then Sadie then Nora. So, right now, all the lower beds on Grace's side of the room were empty, which meant all four of them should be able to get out of bed without waking anyone. Reilly's bed was the only concern. He had to get out without waking his parents.

Grace listened to the room, the parents were all deep breathing or snoring...or both. So she sat up in bed and nearly cried out when Reilly sat up too. She grinned...it was just the way they were. She slid out of bed and walked to the bathroom, he followed. She held her breath as he crawled down the end of the bed. She stared at Jack and Aunt Dru to see if they moved...they didn't, not even a little...they were totally out.

She quickly reviewed her plan with Reilly and she knew without a doubt he would agree with it. He did.

Grace sat on the edge of the tub and sent her text.

TEXT TO MATT: Parents exhausted, not riding We, kids, want to bring in herd for them. All cows on top, Windy Gap is concern, need you and Nikki to pull it off.

Grace looked up at Reilly and crossed her fingers. They waited quietly, hoping Matt would be awake enough to get the message. They didn't have to wait long.

TEXT TO GRACE: Just pulled into Homestead...horses?

"What's he doing up this late...or early?" Reilly whispered as they grinned at each other.

Grace shrugged.

TEXT TO MATT: We will leave Harvey and Trooper at corrals. And walkie-talkie.

TEXT TO GRACE: Will grab Nikki and meet you ASAP

TEXT TO GRACE: We can do this

Grace smiled; just those four words meant the world to her; it was complete trust.

TEXT TO MATT: We can do this

"Now we have to get all the kids out without waking parents." Reilly took a deep breath and opened the door. "I'll start with Wade."

Grace walked as soft as she could down to Nora's bed while watching the adults closely. They were all still in deep sleep. She wondered if they even needed to bother whispering...but she wasn't going to take a chance.

She paused and looked down at Uncle Scott and Aunt Jordan. He was spooning her from the back and was so much larger than his wife that the woman was barely visible tucked against him and under the covers.

She made her way to Nora's bunk. Just as she was about to step on the lower bunk, she saw something move and jumped back. Her heart raced... She stared at the bed and realized it wasn't empty after all. Nick was in it! He always slept in the ranch house. He must have been too tired to even walk that far. Grace hesitated, then moved to the end of the bed. She reached up and touched Nora's head. The girl didn't move so she pushed her a little harder.

"What?" Nora said sleepily without moving.

"Nora, it's Grace," She whispered.

Nora's head lifted and she looked at Grace with a frown, "What?"

"Shhhh...come with me," Grace held her fingers to her lips.

Nora looked around and saw Reilly talking to Wade then looked back at Grace. "What's going on?"

"Come with me...I'll tell you," Grace stepped off the bed rails and motioned for Nora to follow.

Nora stared at her then looked down at Wade and Reilly again. Finally she started to crawl out of bed. When she hit the floor, she looked down at Nick lying on the bunk below her. Her eyebrows shot up in surprise.

Grace went to Sadie next. Her sister's eyes flew open as soon as Grace touched her. Grace held her fingers to her lips and motioned for her to follow. She did, without a word.

Reilly was still talking to Wade so Grace stepped on the bed next to Reilly.

"What's the matter?" She whispered.

"He won't get out of bed," Reilly was frustrated.

"What's the matter?" Grace asked Wade.

"I am not sneaking out of here," Wade said firmly, glaring at her. "I promised Dad that I wouldn't EVER sneak out of the bunkhouse again…I'm NOT breaking that promise."

Grace thought quickly, they had to have everyone to pull this off. "Wade, it's not sneaking out…it's not the same as you did before."

"The lights are off, you're whispering, and you're worried about waking the parents," He said gruffly. "THAT'S sneaking out."

"We're just trying to be considerate and let them sleep." Reilly argued.

"No." Wade answered.

"Wade…" Grace started.

"No, no, no!" Wade whispered harshly.

Grace understood his concern, it was important to Wade not to break his father's trust again, the last time nearly cost him his life.

Then she got an idea…she lifted her phone up and brought up the messages from Matt. Turning the phone to him she let him read the messages.

"Matt and Nikki are meeting us," Grace whispered. "They're close to adults…you know they wouldn't agree if it was sneaking out."

Wade frowned between her and the phone, she knew he was battling his emotions, he wanted to go but he didn't want to break his promise to his dad.

"They are going to be there?" Wade stared at Grace.

"Yes, you just read it…they want to help too," Grace confirmed. "It's OK, Wade, I promise they will be there." She waited, watching his expression.

"Get out of my way." Wade smiled and sat up in the bed.

Grace sighed in relief as she turned and stepped off the lower bunk. Sadie and Nora were standing quietly next to them. She motioned everyone into the bathroom. It was a tight fit but they all made it. She told them her plan and they all smiled and agreed.

"Everyone agree with your horse?" Grace asked.

All nods.

"OK, grab your clothes; we'll change in the barn. Then go get your horse saddled and ready to go. The trucks and trailers are already hitched from yesterday." Grace looked at her four co-conspirators. "Move quietly and quickly."

"What about food and water?" Wade asked.

Grace sighed, she hadn't even thought of that.

"Dad has a case of water in his tool box," Sadie reminded them. "He carries water everywhere during the summer."

Grace smiled at her sister, "He also keeps snacks under the seat."

"So does my dad." Reilly informed them.

"After you get your horses loaded, Nora, Sadie, and Wade raid all the trucks while Reilly and I get Harvey and Trooper," Grace told her team. "Don't slam the truck doors."

They all nodded.

"We should get the dogs out so they don't wake them up too," Nora suggested. "We can put them in the kennels."

"Good thinking, Nora," Grace smiled at her cousin.

She looked around at her happy little band of cowboys and cowgirls.

"OK," Grace took a deep breath. "Here we go."

She opened the door and they each tip-toed for their clothes, grabbed boots, hats, and headed out the door. Grace took one last look and listened to the room. Snoring...deep breathing...no one moving...they were totaling exhausted.

She looked at her parents and smiled at how comfortable they looked together, even in sleep.

As Grace shut the door, she knew they were doing the right thing.

Clothes in hand, she ran for the barn. The air was cool and comfortable to the skin now, so it would be a hot day. The stars were clearly visible, as far as she could see, so there weren't any clouds in the sky. Thank goodness.

She changed clothes quickly and ran for Buttercup. The horse was sleeping along the fence next to the barn but became instantly alert when Grace approached her.

The other four caught their horses then opened the gate to let them pass. Rooster, Rufio, Monty and Eli didn't even attempt to move to follow, but Kit did. She didn't want to be left behind. Grace knew, any second, the horse was going to start whinnying. They needed to take her with them, Grace decided.

She let the horse out the gate, knowing she would just follow the other horses to the trailer and not try to run off.

Grace shut the gate and walked to the trailer. Scarecrow, Dollar, and Libby were already loaded. Without encouragement, Kit leaped into the trailer behind Libby. Grace giggled, the horse was not going to be left behind! Trooper, Harvey, and Cooper would be in the second trailer. Grace walked Buttercup into the trailer and tied her up.

With a pat on the horse's rump she stepped out of the trailer and joined her sister and cousins.

Grace looked back at the house and bunk house...still dark.

She made her way back to the corral and caught Harvey as Reilly caught Trooper; they loaded them quickly and quietly into the trailer.

"How's the food and water?" Grace asked when they returned to the small group.

"Lots of water in the tool box," Sadie smiled. "I left it there until we get to the corrals."

"Dad had some bags of peanuts and granola bars in his truck." Reilly added. "I put them in Grayson's truck."

"Uncle Grayson had granola bars, too." Wade added.

"We'll split them all up when we get to the corrals." Grace told them. "Let's get loaded and get out of here."

Grace took a step towards the trucks but no one else moved; they were staring behind her... their faces fallen and disappointed. That could only mean an adult was behind her.

Grace turned...it was Cora.

CHAPTER EIGHT

Grace stood between her band of co-conspirators and Cora. It was her idea so she would take the heat.

Cora stopped in front of her and looked around at all the kids then back up to Grace.

"I brought food," Cora grinned while holding up a large bag.

It dawned on Grace that Cora was fully dressed with a jacket, boots, and her cowboy hat on.

Grace grinned back at the wonderful woman as the relief ran through her. Giggles and sighs could be heard behind her.

"Well, Trail Boss," Cora grinned at Grace, "Who am I riding?"

Wade ran up to Cora and wrapped his arms around her waist. It was another confirmation that he wasn't breaking his promise to his dad.

"Kit loaded up all by herself," Grace told her, relieved that Cora rode Kit when she came up to the ranch. "There's enough tack in the trailer for her."

"Well, let's get out of here before they wake up and ruin our trail drive," Cora said as she took Wade's hand and walked towards Uncle Scott's truck.

Grace, Nora, and Sadie climbed into the truck and holding her breath, Grace turned the key. Reilly, driving the other truck, pulled out in front of her to lead the way.

Just as Grace started to put the truck in drive Sadie hollered.

"Wait!" Sadie yelled and before Grace could answer, had opened the door and climbed out.

"Dang it, Sadie!" Grace cursed and watched her sister in the side window.

Sadie was going back into the bunk house! They were free and clear and her sister was risking everything to go back in.

"What is she doing?" Nora turned to her.

"I don't know...she's in the bunk house...no, here she comes." Grace answered.

Sadie crawled back into the truck and shut the door quietly.

"What...?" Grace started to reprimand her sister.

"I unplugged the coffee maker!" Sadie explained with a mischievous grin, her eyes sparkling in humor.

Grace laughed. It was an alarm clock to the parents.

"Brilliant, Sadie!" Grace high-fived her then watched as Nora did the same.

Grace put the truck in drive and followed Reilly to the corrals.

***

The food and water was divided between the saddle bags, including Harvey and Trooper's. They weren't sure what Nikki and Matt would be bringing. Grace, Reilly, and Cora took the walk-talkies and left one for Matt.

Cora's bedroom overlooked the barn and corrals. She left her window open at night and had heard the horses moving around. When she looked out to check on them she had seen the kids leading them to the trucks. She knew exactly what was going on and dressed as fast as she could. She stopped in the kitchen long enough to throw whatever portable food she could find into a bag and ran out to make sure she wasn't left behind.

"You're our Mr. Nightlinger." Wade referenced the character in his favorite movie, '*The Cowboys*'. He grinned up at her as they were preparing to mount the horses. It was just getting light out enough to see the mountains in the distance.

"Oohh, I like that." Cora laughed. "But I hope you're not going to tie me up."

"Nah…" Wade grinned, his brown eyes sparkling. "I'm pretty sure we'd get in trouble for that."

They all giggled. Grace waited and watched until everyone was mounted and they were ready to go, then she mounted Buttercup.

She faced her fellow riders. All wore cowboy hats and chaps. Wade had his leather vest on over a cream colored shirt. He looked like he had just stepped out of *"The Cowboys"* and should be standing next to John Wayne.

Just like her dad did with her when they pushed the bulls, she told her group exactly what they were doing. "OK, if we're lucky, the cows didn't go too far onto the other side of the mountain to escape the fire. We're going to ride back to the point we left off and start gathering. Reilly and I will take the lead points, Nora behind me, Cora behind Reilly and Sadie and Wade will push from the back. Once the cows hit the road, they should just follow it straight to the fall pasture."

Everyone nodded.

"We'll ride to the left here," Grace pointed towards the ridge where the fire was. "When Matt and Nikki get here, they will cut across, through those trees, to catch up with us before we hit Windy Gap. Hopefully…"

"What if they don't?" Sadie asked.

Grace exhaled, "Well, we need all the experienced horses at the gap opening, which means Kit and Libby need to be with me across the opening." Grace looked over at Nora and Cora. "You two OK with that."

"Absolutely," Nora nodded confidently. Everyone had faith in Libby knowing what she was doing since Aunt Dru rode her all the time. There was no doubt that Nora could stay on top the horse no matter what move Libby made.

"I'll do my best," Cora nodded. "Kit is pretty darn good, too."

"Once we get the cows to their fall pasture, we're all going to have to ride back here to get the trucks and trailers." Graced concluded.

Grace looked across the mountains and valleys checking on the sunlight. It was time. "Well, cowboys...." She turned to Wade and nodded.

"Slap some bacon on a biscuit, and let's go. We're burning daylight!" Wade yelled with a grin and waved his lariat. John Wayne would have been proud, Grace grinned.

Woo hoo's and yee haw's were called out as they started trotting down the road toward the cows.

The air was cool with just a slight breeze so Grace pulled her cowboy hat down just a little tighter so it didn't fly off. It was still wet from the day before. Her heart was racing from the excitement and nervousness. She had every confidence they could pull off this cattle drive, or she wouldn't have brought them all out here. She looked over at her fellow riders, all riding next to each other instead of a single line.

The entire band of riders was smiling confidently. Nora had to keep slowing Libby down, the horse's confident stride was constantly carrying them ahead of the group. The horse reminded Grace of Aunt Dru whose confident stride led the family. Nora handled the horse perfectly, which was a relief. Libby acted differently out on the range than in the arena. The black mare was stronger and more forceful when working with cows.

Cora had a smile gracing her face and rode primly on top of Kit. She looked twenty years younger, Grace decided and was thankful the woman wanted to join their adventure and not stop it. The older woman didn't like shoving a cowboy hat on her head tightly to keep the wind from blowing it off so she wore a looser hat that had the 'stampede string' that lay under her chin. If the hat blew off, the string held it and she just had to set it upright. As Cora put it, her hair didn't get as messed up that way.

Sadie and Scarecrow trotted along comfortably. Sadie looked so tiny on the big horse but Grace knew that Scarecrow would take care of her sister.

Wade and Reilly were talking to each other excitedly. She heard the occasional word; Charlie…Cimarron…Mr. Anderson…bringing in the herd. It was all about the movie, Grace smiled. Wade had to be in heaven.

They rounded the corner to the ridge and saw a few red cows in the road walking away from them. Perfect! Grace smiled. They were already headed the right way!

The ridge they had ridden the day before was on their left. The pasture they had pushed the cows to was on their right. They needed to get the cows onto the road, following the red cows that were already there.

Grace rode up to the ridge and peered over. The site of the near disaster yesterday was calm today. There was no smoke coming out of the two trees in the middle of the black mass left by the fire. No cows down the side. That was a very good thing.

"Sadie and Wade, stay here until we get the cows over there onto the road. Reilly and Cora, take the ridge on the left. Nora follow me," Grace called out and they all went their different directions.

Buttercup pranced excitedly under her, which made Grace realize how excited she was, the horse always matched her mood.

The first couple cows that saw the riders moved out into the wrong direction and Nora and Libby took off after them and quickly had them going the right way…towards the road.

"Good job, Nora!" Grace yelled.

"All Libby!" Nora yelled back.

They found another dozen cows with calves inside the trees and quickly had them moving towards the road.

Grace looked over at Wade and Sadie who had just started moving on the road…perfect.

Reilly was slightly ahead of Cora. He pushed a couple pair of mother and calf towards the woman and Kit and then headed back into a grove of trees. Cora and Kit pushed the cows out onto the road and into the growing herd. Good team.

Grace turned back to Nora. They were walking towards a few pairs of cows and calves just along the tree line. The cows saw them and started trotting over to the road where the rest of the herd was gathering for the walk down the road. Just as Grace had predicted, the cows knew the way, the riders just had to tell them it was time to go.

The pasture in front of them widened with trees on the left and on the right was open prairie that was dotted with cows and calves.

Reilly and Cora continued their pattern of him flushing the cows out of the trees and Cora making sure they made it to the herd. Nora and Grace moved farther to the right to encourage the cows to join the moving herd. Most of them did with only a glance at the riders. Others needed a little more encouragement.

Grace wondered what it would be like to have Mavis and Bart work for her. She decided that was the next thing she wanted to learn from her dad; how to send commands to the cow dogs.

Sadie and Wade were spread out across the back of the herd, waving their lariats and an occasional cowboy hat. The cows were relatively calm…only releasing a moo here or there…they moved along smoothly.

They were making good time, Grace smiled. The sun was up, the air crisp, the cows moving, the riders working together perfectly.

Then she realized…too perfectly. At this pace, they would hit Windy Gap before Matt and Nikki arrived. Grace would have to make the call to put Cora and Nora across the gap and in front of a possible mass exodus of cows down the ravine. They needed to slow down.

With dread, she realized she had given Reilly and Cora the other handsets; Wade and Sadie didn't have one so she couldn't tell them to stop pushing the herd. Stupid, stupid, stupid, she told herself.

"Reilly," She called out into the walk-talkie. "Cora."

Grace watched them intently, hoping one would answer. Whichever did first was going to have to take their handset back to the ten-year olds.

"Grace," It was Cora.

Grace gave her the instructions and Cora turned and galloped back to Wade and Sadie. Cora spoke to them, handed them the walkie-talkie then galloped back to Reilly.

"Grace," She heard over the handset; it was Wade.

"What?" Grace answered holding the handset closer to her mouth and looking back at him.

"Just checking to make sure it worked," He answered and waved to her.

"I bet Will Anderson wished he had a handset," Grace teased him.

"He mighta lived," Wade chuckled.

"Would have ruined the whole story," Reilly added in.

Grace smiled, all handsets working…just needed to hear from Nikki and Matt.

"But no one wants to see John Wayne die," Matt's voice came over the radio.

Grace sighed in relief….they made it! The stress that had been rising was finally leaving and Buttercup started prancing.

"Nice to see you're in a good mood, Gracie." Reilly said over the handset.

"Buttercup's prancing?" Matt asked.

"Yup," Wade answered.

Grace laughed, which made Buttercup prance even more.

"Grace! Look!" Nora yelled from behind her.

Grace turned and saw Nora pointing to her right. There were a half dozen cows coming out of the trees. To go back or not?

"What do you want to do about them?" Wade asked over the radio.

"Leave them," Grace decided. "We can't afford to lose a rider; we're getting too close to Windy Gap."

"We can get them this afternoon," Reilly added.

They rode peacefully for another fifteen minutes.

"Grace, look behind you," It was Reilly.

Grace turned and saw the cows that had been left behind, trotting to catch up with their friends. Right decision, Grace told herself.

Windy Gap was just coming into sight. They were going to be there in the next ten minutes.

"Matt, what's your ETA?" Grace asked.

"At the bottom, coming up as fast as we can, we can see you."

The stress came back; they wouldn't make it on time.

CHAPTER NINE

"Wade, stop, don't push them," Grace turned to Wade and Sadie and watched the pair come to a complete stop; their lariats still by their sides.

It didn't work; the cows knew their path too well and just kept moving.

"Wade, bring Sadie up the side towards us to keep the herd tight. Nora and I are going up to the front to watch the gap." Grace turned and the ten-year-olds started trotting towards her.

"Let's go," Grace said to Nora and they widened the space from the sea of black and red cows and slowly galloped towards the front.

She looked down and could see Matt and Nikki climbing the hill, they still had a ways to go. As they neared the gap, she judged the distance.

"Reilly, send Cora up and around." Grace turned and watched Reilly motion to Cora. The woman took off at a gallop along the other side of the herd then cut across the front of them. It slowed the herd, for just moment, then they started moving again.

Cora reached them, breathing heavy with exertion and excitement. Her cheeks were red and her grin was wide.

"We'll ride up with the beginning of the herd and slowly walk with them," Grace told the duo. "Aunt Dru said if we can keep the first cows going down the road then we have a chance of keeping all of them out of the gap."

They nodded and trotted behind her as they headed towards the front. Grace looked down…Matt and Nikki were not going to make it in time for the front of the herd.

They arrived at the gap just before the lead cows and spread out in a single line to guide the cows down the dirt road. One or two cows looked down the hillside and the green grass below. Grace yelled at them and they kept moving.

"Pace back and forth here until Matt and Nikki reach us." Grace told the 69-year-old and the 12-year-old. She could feel the pressure from the stress behind her eyes.

They nodded.

Grace turned back toward the beginning of the gap. There were enough fallen trees and brush that it should keep the cows from going down, she hoped.

Once she made it to the beginning of the gap she turned, just in time to see a red cow head towards the gap at a run, her baby running excitedly next to her.

Grace took off at a gallop. The cow looked over at her and started going faster, a black cow behind the red one followed. It was not going to be good.

Buttercup got down below the red cow and stopped her and the black one. The cows headed back up to the top and Cora dropped down the hill to escort them up.

Grace turned back to the beginning in time to see another cow try to make her way down. Buttercup took off again…but the horse didn't see a fallen log. As Buttercup hit the log with her front legs she fell forward, Grace lurched over her neck, fear streaking through her and the saddle horn stabbing into her stomach. She flashed to the sight of Buttercup flying backwards over the top of Matt in the creek and burying him under water. Her breath caught in her throat.

Buttercup caught herself and stood back up, Grace reset in time for the horse to start walking backwards; fast and scared. They tripped over the log again; the horse nearly sitting on her haunches. Grace felt the horse starting to roll so she kicked out of the stirrups and pushed herself away with a boot to the saddle. As they tumbled backwards she saw Matt racing towards her on Trooper. He slid to a stop and jumping off the horse before it had completely stopped.

Then, to her horror, she saw Buttercup's legs in the air next to her as the horse flipped over and down the hill.

"Buttercup!" Grace screamed.

As Grace hit the ground, she rolled and tried to stand up. Matt's arms came under hers and lifted her, then they watched Buttercup tumble once, twice, then three times. They both took off running towards the horse as she finally stopped.

Fear ran through Grace, the horse lay still on her side.

Both she and Matt came to a stop next to the horse's head. Grace held her breath, Buttercup's eyes were closed.

"Buttercup!" Grace cried. Still the horse didn't move.

"She's breathing." Matt told her and knelt in front of the horse. He ran a hand down all four legs. "Nothing's broken."

Grace lowered a shaky hand down to the horse's face and to the nostrils to feel the breath surround her fingers. "Buttercup!" She yelled with a trembling voice.

The mare's eyes fluttered open and a deep exhale released from her lungs.

"Oh, Matt," Grace leaned against her cousin, she felt nauseous.

"She'll be OK, Grace," He said; his voice unsteady too.

The mare groaned and rolled onto her side. Grace's heart soared.

Matt stood and pulled on the horse's reins. "Come on girl, up you go."

Buttercup pulled her front legs under her, braced herself, then pushed up to lift the rest of her body. She stood, all four legs spread out wide and shook her whole body.

Grace quickly ran her hands all over the horse. She had a few cuts on her rump and down one front leg where it had struck the log. Jessup would need to doctor the one down her front leg.

"Let's get her to walk a bit," Matt said.

Grace took the reins and led the horse a few steps forward while Matt watched carefully.

"She's not limping," Matt sighed.

Grace wanted to cry out in relief, but kept her composure, she didn't want to scare Matt or Buttercup.

"Walk her up to the top," Matt said and looked up.

Grace turned, she had forgotten all about the cows who were walking calmly along the road. Nikki, Cora, and Nora were watching the cows and constantly turning and looking down at them. Trooper was standing just below them grazing on the deep grass.

Grace took a few steps up the hill then stopped. Her whole body was shaking and she was nauseous. It happened so fast, the image of Buttercup rolling over and over played in her mind.

Matt's arm came up and around her shoulders. He pulled her into a tight hug. She took a moment to take in his strength, support, and love. Her body stopped shaking.

She nodded and stepped away from him. "Thanks, I needed that," She smiled up at him. "We got a job to do...let's go."

"Atta, girl." Her cousin smiled and made his way back up to his horse while picking up items from Buttercup's saddle bags as he went. He tossed Grace the walkie-talkie that had landed on the ground.

Grace turned to her horse and took a moment to give her dirty cream-colored horse some love. She kissed her nose and rubbed her hands up and around her ears then down her neck. The horse's body started to relax.

Just because she needed to see it for herself, she ran her fingers up and down the horse's legs. She grabbed the small first aid kit out of the saddle bag and took out the gauze. With her knife, she cut off the bottom half of her western shirt; the tank top under would cover her midriff. She wrapped half the gauze around the gash then wrapped the shirt around it to protect the initial layer of gauze with thicker material. Finally, she used the remainder of the gauze to tighten it and hold the material in place.

One more check over the horse, Buttercup was relaxed and eating. Grace stepped up into the saddle and sat for a moment letting the horse set her legs. She pushed her up next to Nora and Cora.

"Are you OK?" Nora asked with wide scared eyes.

"Yes," Grace nodded. She took a deep breath and assessed the situation. It had all happened so fast. The cows were still making their way down the road towards them. Sadie and Wade waved. She waved back...there was no way they knew what happened.

"I'm really tired of watching people fall," Nora smiled nervously.

"I don't blame you," Grace smiled. "Just make sure the next one isn't you."

"What's the plan, Trail Boss?" Matt rode up next to her.

Grace smiled, even though he was older and could easily take control of the cattle drive, he didn't...he had confidence in her...and she was going to use that confidence to complete their mission. "I'll take Nora with me, I'd like to get her away from this gap."

Matt nodded, his expression said he agreed with her.

"We'll run up ahead and check on the front of the herd," Grace continued. "Leave Wade and Sadie in the back, they're doing a good job. Put Nikki on the other side with Reilly when you can, then you and Cora handle this side. Once they get by here we should have an uneventful ride."

"Sounds good," He nodded.

Grace checked her walkie-talkie then called to Reilly and Wade. They both answered with an "all's good".

Grace turned and trotted up the trail next to the cows. She motioned for Nora to follow and they trotted up towards the front of the herd.

The mass of red and black backs covered the field in front of her. They had started to slow down and graze so she and Nora yelled and started moving them again. Reilly appeared on the opposite side and the cows quickly fell back in line and moved steadily down the road.

"Status, Matt?" Grace asked.

"Last have just passed the gap," He answered.

"Status, Wade?" Grace called.

"Tired of cow's butts, but having fun," He answered, they could hear his giggle before he disconnected.

Grace laughed. Buttercup pranced, which brought tears to Grace's eyes when the whole wreck ran through her mind again.

"Status, Reilly?" Grace sighed.

"All's good over here," He answered.

Grace turned to see Wade and Sadie making their way into the open. They were done with the gap. Grace wanted to cheer.

The cows walked perfectly down the road. Every once in a while, one would try to take off and they would holler or push them back in.

Grace placed Nora ahead of her so she could watch her. She continually looked back at Wade and Sadie. After her own fall, Grace was afraid for the three of them. The stress of being responsible for them was tightening her back muscles. Even though Cora, Nikki and

Matt were older, it was Grace's plan and decision to do the cattle drive. That made Grace responsible for all of them.

Glancing down, Grace saw sticks and leaves covered her horse's black mane. She spent a few quiet moments picking out the weeds and trying to straighten out the hair. Reaching back, she ran her hand over the rump without looking and felt moisture. She pulled her hand back and there was blood on her hand. She twisted quickly and saw a few of the scratches had started to bleed.

She cleaned off the blood with water and the gauze pads from the first aid kit.

"Grace?"

Grace turned to see Nora had slowed down. "What's up?"

"Buttercup." Nora smiled.

Grace grinned. She always saw Adam and Amy's smiling faces when they said that.

"That was scary," Nora said nervously.

"It felt scary," Grace admitted. "But it happened so fast that it almost feels like it didn't happen."

"I saw her go over and was sure she was going to land on you," Nora's voice was shaky.

Grace realized she had scared those watching nearly more than how much the fall had scared her. She stretched out her hand to her young cousin. Nora squeezed tightly.

"We've got about twenty minutes left until we reach the fall pasture," Grace told her. "Then we'll cut across to the trucks and trailers."

"How long will that take?" Nora asked, her grip started to ease.

"Hour and a half maybe," Grace answered.

"Other than your crash and Buttercup rolling…it's been really fun." Nora smiled, her brown eyes were bright and happy.

"I agree," Grace laughed and pointed out a couple cows that started to wander.

"Libby will get them," Nora smiled and kicked the horse in motion.

Libby was perfect as usual and the cows were quickly returned to the road.

Grace hung back and met up with Matt.

"How are you doing?" He asked.

"OK," Grace answered then smiled nervously. "I thought she was dead for a minute there…my heart stopped."

He nodded with a nervous chuckle, "I thought she was, too."

"She's moving good, I haven't felt her move differently than normal."

"I've been watching. She's not limping or anything."

Grace nodded as she watched Nora. She felt too far away.

"I need to get back up there."

"Go."

***

The cows finally made it to their fall pasture and the group stopped long enough to eat all the food that Cora had brought. They laughed about their trip and listened to Nora recant the tumbling of Buttercup down the hill. Grace examined her horse and all the other horses to make sure they were ready for the ride back to the corrals.

They rode, side by side, as they made it back across the mountainside and down into Windy Gap. They followed the same path that Matt and Nikki had ridden.

"How is college going?" Cora asked Matt as they walked peacefully through the valley.

"Still tough in a couple classes," He admitted. "It's just so boring."

"And the others?" Grace asked.

"They make it worth sitting through the boring classes." Matt grinned.

"Your mother was surprised you went back." Cora informed him.

"Honestly, so was I," He admitted. "But I'm going to college part-time until I get the boring classes done. I'm working on EMT certification classes the rest of the time. After talking to Steve and Kevin from the rescue team, then going rappelling with them, I decided it was the path I wanted to go."

"I know Aunt Dru loved it when she went with you," Grace informed him.

"I'll have to show you the pictures of her dangling off the side of the cliff," He chuckled. "And the faces of all the college guys staring at her...I needed a fire hose to douse them! They couldn't believe she was my mother."

The crew of cowboys and cowgirls laughed.

"Don't tell, Jack." Grace laughed. "He won't let her go again."

"I don't think he would even try....would be futile once Dru gets her mind set on something." Cora snickered.

"Yeah," Matt smiled and sighed. "She's worked hard enough the last nineteen years. It's time for her to have some fun out of life now."

"Couldn't agree with you more!" Cora nodded.

They started the climb up towards the top of the mountain and trucks.

"Did Jack want to go next time?" Nikki turned to Reilly. "I never heard anything."

"She didn't tell him she was going until she got back," Reilly laughed. "He told her to keep it that way so he didn't have to worry while she was gone."

"Worry about the climbing or the college guys?" Nikki teased.

"I don't think she told him about the college guys." Reilly informed them with a laugh.

Grace turned to her right and watched as Matt, Reilly and Nikki laughed then turned to her left for Cora, Wade, Sadie, and Nora.

"We're a great team!" Grace declared with a grin.

"That we are, Trail Boss!" Sadie agreed loudly.

"One little hiccup," Matt nodded. "But everyone has the day off now."

"I wonder if they are still sleeping." Nora added.

"I don't know...but I need a nap," Nikki laughed. "I think I was asleep maybe an hour when Matt stormed the house."

"Which means, I haven't slept at all," Matt countered.

"I have to admit," Wade nodded. "I think I'll need a nap today too."

They were all agreeing and laughing as they reached the top of the mountainside. All that was left was one final push across an open field, but when they reached it, they stopped and stared. Next to the corrals, trucks, and trailers...were the parents, Jessup and Nick.

CHAPTER TEN

Grace turned to her co-conspirators, "Time to face the music gang. They are either going to appreciate our accomplishment or not…either way…they have the afternoon off."

"I'm 69-years-old," Cora chuckled. "What are they going to do? Ground me?"

They all laughed. Grace's laughter caused Buttercup to prance.

She turned Buttercup and they danced across the range to face the music with her parents.

As they approached, all the parents, plus Nick and Jessup, were leaning against the side of the horse trailer.

Grace couldn't tell whether they were upset or not so she rode straight up to them, waited until everyone else dismounted then stepped out of the saddle and to the front of her horse. She smiled at them. All her co-conspirators did the same.

The adults along the trailer looked at each of the riders then came back to Grace. Somehow they knew she was in charge, Grace thought.

Grace's eyes went to Uncle Scott and Aunt Jordan, they were watching her back. Grace turned and looked down at Wade to make sure he was alright. He was watching his parents with a curious frown. She turned back to her own parents.

"It was my plan; if someone should be grounded then it should be me," She said with a proud smile. "But, we did it so you could sleep-in and would have the day off," She took a deep breath and continued, "But, you should know, Cora thinks she's too old to be grounded."

The whole group chuckled.

"I'm not as old as Cora…but I can't be grounded either," Nikki added with a giggle.

"Me either," Matt laughed.

Grace saw the light in her dad's eyes and knew he wasn't mad.

"Who unplugged the coffee pot?" He asked.

"I did," Sadie grinned proudly.

He looked at her with a raised brow, "Good move."

"What happened to your shirt?" Her mom asked.

Grace rolled her lips and then exhaled. She really didn't want to tell them, but Buttercup needed Jessup. "Buttercup tripped backwards over a log and took a little tumble." She saw the concern cross over all the adult's faces but she turned to Jessup. "She has a bunch of scratches on her rump, but she has a cut on her leg. I cleaned it the best I could then, wrapped it with gauze and strips from my shirt to keep it clean."

"Best to keep it covered until we get back to the ranch." Jessup nodded. "Good job."

"Did all the cows get moved?" Aunt Dru asked.

"Yes, they were all still on top and came together quickly," Grace answered. "The ones that fell back, trotted to catch up."

"I was wondering what that was," Aunt Dru smiled.

Grace looked at her confused. "What 'what' was?"

Jack lifted a walkie-talkie out of his pocket. "We woke to a conversation about John Wayne dying in a movie." He looked over at Reilly.

"I didn't even think about the walkie-talkie in the bunkhouse!" Grace rolled her eyes.

"We weren't paying much attention to what you were saying. We thought you were just playing with the walkie-talkies at the barns. Then we heard your status check and Wade said he was tired of cow's butts." Aunt Jordan smiled at her son.

"Are you mad at me?" Wade asked quickly. "Grace said it wasn't sneaking out since I was going with her and Reilly and meeting Matt and Nikki."

Grace watched his parents closely, hoping they weren't mad.

"Grace was right, this time." Uncle Scott said and Wade dropped Dollars reins and ran up to his parents to wrap them in a very relieved hug.

"Are we in trouble? Are we grounded?" Nora asked.

"Well," Her dad looked at her. "There are eight of you…and we've been told we can't ground three of you…so I don't think it's fair to the other five if we grounded them."

"So we're not grounded?" Sadie asked, looking at her dad. "It's OK if you do, cuz we were willing to be grounded so you could have the afternoon off from riding."

He grinned and shook his head. "No…unless you want to be."

Sadie giggled, eyes wide and shook her head. "No, that's OK, I'll pass."

They all laughed.

"Let's get the horses loaded and try to come up with something to do on our day off." Aunt Dru smiled and walked to the back of the horse trailer.

**

It was only noon when they arrived the ranch house. Wade, Sadie, and Nora were sleeping and were carried into the bunkhouse.

While everyone else took care of the horses, Grace and Jessup walked in the barn to care for Buttercup's injuries.

As she removed the makeshift bandage, Jessup retrieved his medical supplies and dabbed antiseptic on the scratches that covered her body.

Jessup began to clean the wound and Reilly walked in, watched Jessup work for a moment, then looked up at Grace.

"You, OK?" He asked.

She nodded with a sigh. "She's OK...so I'm OK."

He sat on the bench behind Jessup so he could have a good view of the foreman at work. Slowly...all the adults made their way into the barn to watch and chat about the fire and the morning's cattle drive.

Grace looked around the room and would have bet money on three things...Matt and Nikki would sit on each side of Nick, Aunt Dru and Jack would be holding hands, and Aunt Jordan would be sitting on her husband's lap. She was right on all three. Her mom and Cora were sitting on a bale of straw next to the bale her dad was sitting on.

Grace frowned at the look on her dad's face. He was sitting with his elbows on his knees and stared at the gash on Buttercup's leg; then he looked down at the ground, then up to Grace. He returned her frown with a creased brow.

"It's not the same, Dad." Grace said quickly. He had to be comparing her tumble on Buttercup to the tumble at the creek with Matt.

"No, it's not," He agreed firmly.

His tone made the low murmur of conversations in the room stop. There was silence except the sound of the horses moving outside in the corral.

"Then why are you looking like that?" Grace asked, not really wanting to know the answer.

"Because I don't want to hurt you, Gracie," He sighed.

Grace felt a chill, this really wasn't going to be good.

"And why would you be hurting me?" Her voice was calmer than the quiver inside her.

"We need to have a serious talk about Buttercup," He leaned back.

Grace's hand instinctively went to the horse's mane and she twirled the hair with her fingers.

"It was an accident, she didn't see the log," Grace quickly defended the horse. She kept herself from looking at Nikki and Matt, they would confirm her argument, but she didn't want to bring them into the discussion that wasn't going to be good.

"From what Nora said, she tripped over the log going forward," His eye's remained on hers.

"That's what happened," Grace agreed.

"Then she got scared and went backwards, over the log and tumbling you off her back in time to roll down the hill a number of times."

Grace nodded, not moving her eyes from his. She was trying to decide where he was going with the discussion.

"There comes a time, Grace, that you have to decide whether a horse is right for mountain work or not."

Grace took in a deep breath; he called her Grace and not Gracie, which meant he was dead serious.

"She just got scared..." Grace started to defend her horse, but her dad raised his hand to stop her. She frowned even more, she hated when he did that.

"She did the same to Matt in the creek," He reminded her.

"But…" Grace started…again the hand. Her back stiffened and her jaw clenched.

"She also backed up and started to rear up the other day with the bulls," He added.

"I handled that," She said quickly.

"That time you did," He conceded. "But, if you were riding the mountains tomorrow, and you were on Eli…would you put Sadie, Wade, or Nora on Buttercup?" He asked calmly, but firmly.

Grace stared at him. She didn't know how to answer. Buttercup was a handful to control because of her prancing and excitement, not because she was unruly or mean. She knew all three of them could ride her…in the arena.

"Answer me, Grace," Her dad ordered with their eyes still locked.

Grace thought of Buttercup rearing up and going over backwards when Matt was on her…slamming him into the creek…pushing Matt down into the water…mere inches from a pair of large jagged rocks…the horse's fear could have killed him.

"Grace," Her dad was still staring at her.

She stared back.

"Wade, Nora, or Sadie…who are you going to have ride Buttercup?" He repeated.

Grace still didn't break the stare as her stomach trembled. She saw Buttercup flying back towards her, then tumbling down the hill. The motionless horse she thought was dead. Grace didn't think her sister or her cousins could have pushed away from the horse to keep from being rolled on.

"Are you going to answer me?" He asked.

Grace just stared back; she didn't want to say it out loud. She didn't want to admit that she wouldn't put any of them on Buttercup in the mountains.

"Your silence is the answer," He said and leaned forward to rest his elbows on his knees again. "I am relieved that you didn't choose one of them. Even if you didn't say it out loud, you have admitted it to yourself."

She finally broke away from his eyes and looked at the mane as she ran her fingers between the strands. The strength she was trying so hard to hold on to, was starting to dwindle. She could feel her throat start to constrict from the tears.

"Grace, look at me," He said with a soft gentle tone.

The tone didn't help…she knew he felt bad for what he was about to say. No matter what it was she knew he would be right. Slowly, her gaze moved from the horse to her dad.

"You ride Eli for the next month. I will ride Buttercup up here to see if I can help her." He slowly stood and walked to her. Her gaze moved up as he got closer. "I will do whatever I can to make her trustworthy."

Grace nodded, her blue eyes glistened with the tears she refused to let fall. As much as she wanted to jump into a hug to cry, she didn't want to do it in front of everyone. He seemed to understand. He cupped the side of her face and kissed her on the forehead.

"Now I have to talk to Sadie," He sighed.

Grace's eye brows went up in surprise, but not as far as her dad's when Sadie spoke up behind him.

"Talk to me about what?" Sadie said as she sleepily walked up to her dad. She lifted her arms for him to pick her up. Which he did then sat back on the bale, settling Sadie on his knee. He sighed when Sadie gently laid her head on his shoulder.

Grace could see the anguish on his face.

"What did you need to talk to me about, Daddy?" Sadie yawned.

"Well...that just tears at your heart." Uncle Scott said softly of the adorable blonde ten-year-old sitting sweetly on her daddy's lap.

Grace turned to him to see the compassion on her uncle's face. She had nearly forgotten that the room was full of people. They would have had to walk between herself and her dad to leave; they obviously didn't want to interrupt them.

Jessup had finished stitching Buttercup's leg and was carefully wrapping it with gauze.

Sadie sat up straight and looked at her mom then her dad. "What?" Sadie asked.

"We need to talk about Little Ghost," He finally said quickly.

Sadie grinned in pride, "Oh, I just love Little Ghost, I could talk about him all day!"

Grace nearly chuckled at the look on her dad's face as he turned exasperated eyes to her mom.

Her mom just smiled in sympathy and decided to try and handle the conversation with their daughter.

"Sadie," She turned to her youngest and smiled. "We've talked about Little Ghost's habit of cutting cows."

"Isn't he awesome?" Sadie sat up straighter, her eyes glowing. "Yesterday was SO much fun. He is just the greatest to ride. I can't wait to do it again!"

Grace couldn't help it, the look of exasperation her mother's face made her giggle as she leaned against Buttercup. More soft laughter from everyone in the room joined hers.

"Dang, I'm glad my kids are grown," Aunt Dru whispered making more giggles echo in the building.

Jessup finished wrapping the horse's leg and stood to look across Buttercup's back at Grace. He gave her an amused wink.

Grace wanted to help, but she didn't know what her parents were trying to say to her sister.

Her dad looked up at the ceiling so he didn't see his daughter's happy blue innocent eyes. "Sadie, we don't think Little Ghost is right for you as a roping horse," He said quickly.

Sadie looked confused. She turned, looked at her dad and then looked up at the ceiling to see what he was looking at. The whole room started chuckling again.

Sadie reached up and put her hands on each side of his face and pulled his head down so they were eye-to-eye. More chuckles and giggles.

"Why not?" She frowned at her dad. When she saw the worry and concern on his face, she stiffly stood up and took a step away from him. "No one is taking him away from me!" Her internal switch had flipped and she had gone from happy to mad in the blink of an eye. "No one..." She repeated in a low angry tone...glaring at her dad. "...is taking him away from me."

The room was quiet again.

"No one is taking him away from you," Their dad assured her.

"Then why can't he be my roping horse?" Sadie's voice rose, her face turned red. "He is doing fine in practice."

"I know, Sadie," He reached out to her, but Sadie stepped away from him. Her braid swung across her back.

The irritation in his eyes flamed.

"We are not taking him away; we just think his natural talent should be used and not force him to do something else." He tried to explain.

"I'm not forcing him, Dad!" Sadie said angrily. "He loves to ride with me."

"Sadie Anne!" Her dad glared and with a low firm voice spoke. "Change that tone of voice, right now."

Sadie's back stiffened even more, but she continued to stare at her dad. She lowered her voice and tried to speak calmly. "He likes to ride with me. He gets excited when we're in the arena. He is a perfect gentleman. I am not forcing him."

"Of course, he loves to ride with you, Sadie," He said calmly back. "But his natural talent is cutting cows. He should be used and ridden for cutting cows and not just for roping them."

Sadie's back relaxed but she didn't say anything.

"There are a number of cutting associations in Idaho and a lot of competitions in the Northwest. If he's going to be a competition horse then he needs to be cutting too, not just roping." He told her.

Sadie tilted her head and looked up at her dad through narrowed eyes. "You're not taking him away from me?" She asked cautiously.

"No. Never." He confirmed.

"But you didn't say I should ride him in competition." Sadie pointed out.

Grace's eyebrows shot up, she hadn't caught that little detail.

"You're going to be very busy with school. And you and Scarecrow are still in training and learning to run barrels and poles, plus working on roping too." He reminded her. When Sadie nodded he continued, "Little Ghost needs to be trained too and you won't have time to do all of it. I was thinking you should ask your Uncle Scott to train him and start him in competition for you until you're both ready."

"What?!" Uncle Scott cried out. Grace turned to see the shocked look on her uncle's face. "You're bringing me into this? There goes all the sympathy I just had for you." He glared at his brother.

Sadie had turned and looked at him while he spoke.

"You don't like Little Ghost?" Sadie asked with a raised brow and a hurt voice.

Grace giggled along with the rest of the room at the exasperated look was on her uncle's face. Aunt Jordan quickly slid off his lap.

"Going somewhere?" Uncle Scott looked accusingly at his wife.

"I'm not getting in the middle of this," She grinned and slid on the bale next to Cora.

The room was quiet as everyone waited to see who spoke first.

Grace saw the twinkle of humor in her dad's eye as he looked at his brother.

Sadie took a slow step towards her uncle, her blue eyes still showing the confusion and hurt.

Uncle Scott just stared at her in disbelief.

"Do you like Little Ghost?" Sadie asked him in a low voice.

"Of course, I do," He stammered.

"Then why wouldn't you want to ride him?" She tilted her head.

"That's not what I said," He muttered to his adorable sweet niece.

"Then you will train him for me and ride him in competition?" She asked with a smile, the excitement starting to rise.

Grace giggled again as her uncle glared at her dad.

"Please, Uncle Scott?" Sadie said sweetly and excitedly; two dangerous combinations.

"Grayson...!" Uncle Scott just looked in hopeless exasperation.

"I'm busy with training horses and kids...I don't have time," He answered with a grin. "You're just sitting on the outside laughing while I'm doing all the work."

Uncle Scott looked over at Aunt Dru.

"Oh, Brother..." Aunt Dru grinned and shook her head. "You get no help from me."

"She's the one that came up with the idea." Grace's mom informed him with a smile.

The whole room erupted in laughter.

"Well?" Sadie ignored everyone around her and walked over to her uncle, who slowly leaned back away from her. "Will you train and ride Little Ghost for me?" She smiled, her eyes sparkling.

Uncle Scott stared at Sadie then looked up at his brother...over to his sister...to his sister-in-law...and to his wife, who was grinning ear to ear.

He sighed and looked down at his niece. "Fine. I'll do it."

"Thank you, Uncle Scott." Sadie jumped at him and hugged him around the neck.

The room erupted in laughter as Uncle Scott continued to glare at his brother's grin.

"I think it's time for a family baseball game in the back pasture." Aunt Dru declared and received a round of agreement.

CHAPTER ELEVEN

Grace slid into Reilly's little blue truck and quickly buckled up.

"I can't believe this is happening," Reilly sighed.

Grace nodded. "We all knew it could happen, but I always figure things will work out the right way…my way…so I wasn't expecting her mother to win."

He turned the truck down the long driveway; to The Stables. Kelly wanted to spend her last hours with them where they had spent most of their time.

"She's already there talking to Dad."

"Is Nikki going to make it down to say goodbye? She's the reason Kelly was hired."

"I know," He sighed. "I still remember seeing her for the first time when I walked out of the horse trailer." He smiled at the memory. "Nikki was pretty happy with herself. She made me promise not to become a distraction or be a distraction."

"How did that work out for ya?" Grace giggled, knowing the answer.

"Distraction all over," He admitted. "I'm really going to miss her, Gracie."

"I know."

"Dad says people will come and go in our lives, it's up to us whether we make the effort to keep them there when things change."

"Sounds wise."

Reilly grinned. "Most the time he is."

"Who knows? Maybe she is the one."

"The one what?" Reilly glanced at her then quickly back to the road.

"She's the one you'll end up with and have a life with…house, babies, old age…"

"She's not the one," Reilly frowned.

"What?" Grace was surprised. "How do you know?"

"I just know."

"Then what's this all about?"

"She's a great person, Grace. I always want her in my life, but as a friend."

"That surprises me."

"Why?"

"How many make-out sessions have you two had?" Grace giggled.

He grinned. "Lots…but that's just practice."

"Practice?"

"Yeah, practice makes perfect." He glanced at her with a mischievous glint in his eye.

"Practicing for 'the one'?"

Reilly nodded, "We're only fifteen…well she's sixteen, but still, it's way too early to be settling into a final relationship."

"Have you had this conversation with Kelly?"

"Sort of. I didn't tell her she was just practice…that would be rude. I did tell her that we'll always be friends and it wouldn't be anything more…that we are too young."

"How did she take that?"

"She knew…who knows?" He grinned. "Maybe she thinks of me as just practice too."

"How do you know?"

"Know what?"

"How do you really know that she isn't the one?"

"I just know," He frowned at her.

Grace shook her head. "I don't understand that. You want her in your life forever but just as a friend."

"Well, when you met those two guys at the roping clinic," Reilly glanced at her again and saw the smile on her face. "That was funny watching Mom try to keep Scott from seeing you."

Grace giggled, "He accused me of having a flirty giggle."

"You DO have a flirty giggle." Reilly laughed.

"Most the time I don't realize it...but I did that morning." Grace admitted with a guilty grin.

"Gracie!" Reilly laughed and shook his head at her. "Back to the roping clinic...when you met them, did you like one more than the other?"

Grace rolled her lips. "Yeah, I liked Levi better, but it was more on looks than anything else...well maybe not."

"Maybe not?"

"Well, I liked his blue eyes, his shirt really made them stand out. I do that every once in a while..."

"You do it all the time," Reilly rolled his eyes. "You and Kelly always wear clothes that make your eye's look good."

"You don't?"

"Not really...I just grab the shirt that's the closest and hope it matches whatever I'm wearing for pants."

"You wear jeans...only jeans...everything goes with jeans." She laughed.

"Guilty...makes it that much easier to find a shirt."

"Geez...to be a guy."

"Not all guys," Reilly reminded her. "Levi obviously wore that shirt for a reason."

"Or maybe his mom bought it for him because she likes the way it made his eyes shine." Grace countered. "My mom does that, AND I noticed Aunt Dru has done that a couple times for you."

"Really?" Reilly grinned proudly. "Dad never did that."

"Dads are different," Grace smirked. "Can you imagine my dad buying me something that makes me look better to guys?"

Reilly laughed! "No, he'd put you in a burlap bag and leave you on the ranch if he could."

Grace nodded, "That he would."

"How did we get this sidetracked from what we were talking about?" He glanced at her.

"We do that all the time."

"So what were we talking about?"

"How you knew Kelly wasn't the one."

"Oh that, so you like Levi better, but why since it wasn't his eyes?"

"No, it was something I said that made him move in closer...I liked that he wanted to be closer. I liked the touch of his hand when I shook it...more than Alan's."

"So there was a feeling," Reilly nodded.

"Yeah, I guess so. They were both good looking, I liked the *looks* of both of them...just Levi's blue eyes caught my attention."

"But it was the feeling when you touched and when he moved closer, not the blue eyes," He pointed out. "You just knew you liked him more."

"Yeah, I guess you're right."

"So, when I'm with Kelly, I just know I like her an awful lot...but I KNOW she's not the one. There is someone out there I know will be the one."

Grace nodded. They were nearing The Stables and she could see Kelly's car in the parking lot.

"Levi asked me out, even before we got home."

"The power of Facebook?" Reilly grinned.

"Yeah, he private messaged me."

"Did you tell him you couldn't?"

"Reilly…remember when the same thing happened to you when you met Kelly?"

"Oh yeah…how did you answer him?"

"Pretty much the same way you did…I said between school and training horses and practicing for the rodeo I couldn't until next summer when school lets out."

"You used Dad's line?" Reilly nodded with a grin.

"It was a good line!" Grace admitted. "And I'll be sixteen the first of April, in plenty of time."

"Did he respond back?"

"No, I just answered him before we came here."

"Check your messages!"

Grace picked up her phone, a couple buttons later she sighed, "Nope, no response."

"Well, he's probably out practicing his roping so he can impress you at the next clinic."

Grace grinned at him. "You're so funny, Reilly. I think I'll keep you around."

He giggled. "You don't have a choice, I'll sic my mom on you if you try to get rid of me."

Grace laughed. "That's a new one! How long have you been waiting to use that?"

"Quite a while actually," He grinned. "But you haven't been giving me anything I could use it on yet."

He stopped the truck and they reached for the door handles.

"I'll try to be better next time."

"Well, I've been saving them up ever since the wedding…"

The office door opened and Kelly stepped out and waved at them.

They both stopped and looked at her. She was smiling… a happy smile.

"What the heck?" Grace glanced over at Reilly, he was looking confused too.

Kelly ran up to Reilly and threw her arms around his neck. She squeezed.

Grace could see a content smile on her face.

"Your dad is just the greatest," She told him.

"I agree…to the most part." Reilly chuckled as she stepped back from him. "But why exactly would you say that now?"

Reilly leaned back against the front of his truck. Kelly leaned in next to him. So Grace stood in front of them.

"My mom came to visit this morning." Kelly said.

"What?" Reilly and Grace said in unison.

Kelly nodded. "She wanted to meet Jack and know why he went to so much trouble for me."

"I don't understand," Grace frowned. "Is she gone? She didn't want to meet us?"

Kelly shook her head slowly, "She left about 30 minutes ago."

Reilly and Grace just stared in disbelief.

"She was afraid to meet you after meeting Jack." Kelly explained.

"That doesn't make sense to me," Reilly seemed hurt.

"Well, Jack took her for a tour of the place and showed her what I've been doing all summer," Kelly's eyes sparkled. "He was so nice and honest."

"He always is." Grace frowned, she was hurt too.

Kelly nodded, "You know how my dad died."

Reilly nodded.

Grace looked confused, "No, I don't."

Kelly's eyes shot up in surprise and she looked at Reilly with a smile. "You didn't tell her?"

"It wasn't my story to tell," Reilly said looking worriedly at Grace.

Grace was stunned. He kept something like that from her!

"My dad died of a drug overdose," Kelly said quickly.

Grace was stunned again. No wonder he didn't tell her about it. She nodded and smiled at Reilly so he knew she was OK with it.

"My grandparents blamed my mother, my mother blamed them." Kelly explained. "I don't know all of it..."

"You're confusing me more," Reilly admitted with a frown. "Why didn't she want to meet us?"

"When she came to visit, they asked her to come out here and at least see what I've been doing...then they got to talking...and realized than none of them are to blame for my dad's overdose."

"Kelly...I still don't understand." Reilly sighed.

"I'm sorry. I just don't know how to explain it well." She sighed. "But when all was said and done...Mom came out here to visit Jack and see what I've been doing. She felt bad about taking me away from all this and meeting you two would have made the guilt even worse."

"What's this got to do with my dad being nice and honest?" Reilly asked, totally confused.

"When she came here, and met Jack, and he offered to hire me next summer, she said yes."

"What?" Grace and Reilly said in unison.

Kelly grinned. "She said I can come work summers here and visit with my grandparents!"

Kelly hugged both of them. "And, I just had a long talk with Jack about my mom."

"What do you mean?" Reilly asked.

She smiled at Reilly, "He told me that there are a lot of kids that go through life without their moms…and all they want is a mother."

Grace turned to Reilly. He was just staring at Kelly; no emotion showed…that was a first.

"He said that I should appreciate the fact that she fought so hard for me, that it meant she loved me and wanted what's best for me." Kelly continued but seemed confused by Reilly's reaction.

Reilly's gaze lifted from Kelly and he stared at the office door.

"Reilly?" Kelly asked confused. "Aren't you happy about this?"

He looked at her quickly, a bit startled by her question. "Of course, I am." He smiled.

Kelly sighed and her shoulders relaxed. She looked at Grace.

"I'm thrilled," Grace said honestly.

Kelly jumped in for a hug from Grace.

Reilly turned and stared back at the office with no emotion showing.

Grace understood.

"We have all afternoon," Grace reminded them. "Let's go for a last ride."

"Oh, I would love that." Kelly agreed.

"Reilly, we'll go get the horses saddled if you'll go make sure your dad is OK with it."

Reilly turned to Grace with this same blank expression, then he smiled at her and nodded. He headed for the office.

They had the horses saddled and ready to go and waited for Reilly in the back arena. They played follow the leader, which wasn't as much fun with only two people.

Grace was worried. This wasn't like Reilly. There was something wrong.

When he finally showed up he was cheerful and excited with Kelly. When the girl wasn't looking at him, Reilly was clearly upset.

Grace's heart hurt for him. She and Reilly spent the afternoon trying hard to make sure Kelly's last day was fun. They rode and laughed and joked and had a great time. Grace left them alone for a while so Reilly could...practice more.

Grace hugged Kelly tightly and walked back to Reilly's car to wait for him. She heard Kelly's car start and turned and waved. Kelly was smiling as she waved good-bye.

Reilly turned, with tears in his eyes.

"Reilly, what the heck?" Grace felt tears in her eyes.

He nodded to the truck and they crawled in and buckled up but he didn't start the engine.

Grace waited.

"I hurt, Dad." Reilly turned to her.

"What? How?"

"When Kelly told us what Dad said about kids going through life just wanting a mom?"

"Yeah?"

"I realized that when I told Dru that I had wanted a mom, and I knew something was missing in my life...it was a mom...it was Dru...I didn't realize it then...but I did when Kelly said that...I hurt Dad."

"What did you say to Jack?"

"I told him what Kelly said and asked him for the truth...I wanted to know."

"And?"

"He said that he didn't realize until I broke down in Dru's arms that I had felt that way. He thought he was enough...that he had tried really hard to be both mother and father to me...that it did hurt at first but he and Dru had talked about it..."

A tear slid down his cheek and Grace wiped it away.

"I didn't know I hurt him Gracie," Another tear fell.

"How did you leave it with him?" Grace asked as she wiped away his tear.

"I told him I was sorry, that no one could have done more or been more to me than he was…is."

"Is he sad?"

"Yeah…"

"And you're sad?"

"Obviously," He chuckled sadly.

"Then, I think we should show him."

"Show him what?" Reilly looked confused.

"Show him…now and everyday how much you love and appreciate him and everything he's done for you…us."

Reilly nodded, "How would you suggest we do that?"

"Well, first of all, change your aura…get rid of the sadness."

"And I would do that by?" He smiled at her.

"That's a start…." She said and reached for the door handle. "Let's get started."

He stepped out of the truck and looked over at her. "Started with what?"

"Jack is sitting in the office feeling sad," Grace reminded him and grinned.

"You're smiling about that?"

"I'm trying to figure out how we stop him from being sad. I have some ideas but I think he wouldn't appreciate most of them."

"Probably not," Reilly agreed as they walked toward the office door.

"So, I was thinking we'd ask his opinion on my flirty giggle." Grace's grin grew wider.

"Oh, dang!" Reilly laughed.

Grace turned to her laughing friend and smiled, she waited for him to realize that his aura had changed. He stopped laughing and grinned at her.

"Oh, Gracie, you're the best," He laughed again and opened the office door to see his dad sitting behind the desk. "Hey Dad, Grace needs your opinion on something."

`

CHAPTER TWELVE

Grace's eyes flickered open and she looked across her bedroom. She could see Nora still sleeping. She could only hear Sadie's breathing.

She rolled onto her back and looked up at the ceiling; a sadness within her. Kelly was gone and Buttercup was at the ranch, so depressing. Adding that to how tired she was from the emotional and physical last two days, all Grace wanted to do was go back to sleep, but her mind was too awake for that to happen. She slid out of the bed and quickly dressed in the bathroom so she didn't wake her cousin and sister, then walked out the door.

As she stepped out of the room, she heard a noise down the hallway. Jack was stepping out of Aunt Dru's room.

Grace grinned as they walked towards each other and met at the top of the stairs.

"I don't think I will ever get used to that," Grace smiled.

He chuckled, "Don't tell Dru, but it's been tough to get used to."

"Really?" They descended the steps.

"Yeah, I'm used to just Reilly and me in the mornings…really quiet."

As they reached the bottom of the steps, they couldn't see anyone. They were the first two up for the day.

"And…" He continued. "I liked fixing breakfast in the morning."

Grace looked at him in surprise.

He shrugged slightly and smiled. "I don't care much about lunch and dinner. Just like fixing breakfast."

"Want to?" Grace grinned. "I don't think Cora would mind too much if we cooked her breakfast for once."

His answer was to open the refrigerator with a grin and start pulling out eggs, milk, butter, bacon…anything he could find that was breakfast related.

As the smell of bacon made its way throughout the house, the family members slowly made their way into the kitchen and dining room. Along with the bacon, they found French toast, biscuits, sausage, eggs, hash browns, cantaloupe, strawberries with whip cream, and two very happy cooks.

"I tell you what, Mr. Morgan." Cora smiled as she placed another bite of bacon into her mouth. "When you're here…you can take over every Sunday morning."

Jack smiled as he sat down next to her, "I'd really enjoy that, Cora." He turned to Grace. "You in?"

"Absolutely, that was fun." Grace nodded emphatically.

She looked around and everyone was sitting at the table eating except her mother. Grace stepped into the kitchen and could hear someone talking in the library. As she got closer, she could tell her mother was talking on the phone.

"It has to be done today, can that happen?" Grace heard as she walked towards the door.

"Great, they will be delivered first thing this morning, what time should we pick them up?" Her mother smiled at Grace as she walked into the room. "We'll be there. I'll send you all the instructions. OK, thanks." She hung up the phone.

"Good morning, Sweetheart." Her mother hugged her. "I saw you cooking away with Jack and didn't want to interrupt you."

"Who was on the phone? Do you need me to do some errands for you while you're at work?" Grace squeezed into her mom's embrace.

"Oh, dang, work," She sighed. "I forgot to call them."

She lifted her cell phone and pushed a few buttons.

"Good morning, Douglas," She paused. "No, we had a bit of an emergency up at the ranch and I won't be in today," Another pause. "I said I won't be in." Her mother's voice sounded irritated. "And, thanks for asking if anyone in my family was hurt." She added sarcastically.

Grace had never heard anything like that from her mom.

"Then tell him I quit," She said firmly and hugged her daughter tighter.

Grace turned surprised eyes at her mother but she was looking out the window towards the pasture. Grace looked out and saw the Tagger herd, less Buttercup, grazing peacefully.

"No, Douglas, I'm serious, I quit. I'll be in tomorrow to pick up my personal items." Her mother pressed the button to end the call.

"Really, Mom?" Grace turned to her in surprise.

"For about 30 seconds," She answered as she moved to the couch in front of the window. They sat together with Grace tucked in next to her mom.

"I've quit a thousand times," Her mom giggled. "They'll call any second and ask me to reconsider."

The phone rang and her mother looked to see who it was, then declined the call.

"I don't think Dad would mind if you quit," Grace told her.

"I know he wouldn't," She was staring out the window, her eyes distant. "We've talked about it."

"Really?" Grace was shocked.

"Yes, I'm a bit jealous of Jordan having all the time this summer to take the kids around to the shows, and Monday's off to herself...days off with Scott..."

"Next year, Reilly and I will be competing too," Grace leaned on her mother's shoulder. "And now Uncle Scott's going to compete with Little Ghost."

"Jordan's been tortured having to choose between Nora and Wade every weekend."

"She still would."

"Yes, but with Sadie and Wade competing in rodeo and only Nora in horse shows, then Nora loses...every time, the poor girl."

"It'll be worse next year with four of us in rodeo."

"At least if I could help out more, Nora wouldn't lose so often."

The phone rang again. Her mother declined the call, silenced the ringer, and then tossed it across to the other couch.

"It's not just the rodeos and shows," Her mother sighed. "You're fifteen, in just three short years, you're off to college."

"I'll be home like Nikki and Matt."

"Not enough, Hon. I miss them way too much now, so how am I going to feel when it's you, then Sadie?" She leaned her head down on Grace's. "I don't feel I had enough time with Matt and Nikki before they left."

"So what's stopping you?"

"I'm the type of person that needs something to do," Her mother explained. "Grayson, Scott, and Jessup have the ranch handled for the day to day. Jack and Dru have The Stables. Jordan works Tuesday through Thursday which keeps her busy, and she loves it, but she has the family Friday through Monday."

"I have an idea," Aunt Dru walked into the room. "Sorry...didn't mean to eavesdrop." She picked up the phone and placed it on the end table then stretched out on the couch. She was wearing jeans, a white tank top, her hair was down, and she was barefoot. The red burn down her arm was clearly visible in the sleeveless shirt and really looked sore.

"And what would that be?" Her mom asked.

"The Tagger Barn and Breakfast," Aunt Dru answered.

Her mom was silent long enough Grace looked up at her. She was staring at her aunt.

"No one's brought that up since Nikki switched majors at school," Her mom said.

"Would you consider it?" Aunt Dru asked, she had on her 'poker face' so Grace couldn't tell how serious she was.

"It would be very time consuming," Her mom answered.

"But you would be around family since we want it near The Stables and it would be cross-marketed."

"The busy time would be over the weekends when I want to be out with the kids at the shows," Her mom countered.

Aunt Dru shrugged, "Get yourself a Jack." Then she grinned. "Maybe not a Jack, he's a one and only. But you could hire a weekend manager or a full-time manager, set your own time…do what you want to do…or don't want to do."

Grace moved away from her mother and turned to see if she was considering the offer. By the look on her face, she was!

Aunt Dru leaned forward, "It just has to be successful and it would be on your shoulders to make it that way."

Grace watched her dad walking towards the library.

"What's going on in here?" He asked looking between his sister and his wife.

Her aunt leaned back and relaxed against the couch.

"Don't you need to vote on it?" Her mom asked Aunt Dru with her eye's flicking towards her husband.

"Vote on what?" He frowned.

"We did a long time ago," Aunt Dru informed her. "We just thought Nikki would be in charge."

"The barn and breakfast?" Her dad looked at his wife in surprise. "You'll do it?"

Her mom sat up straight and looked at him in surprise. "You want me to?"

He chuckled, "Of course, I do." He leaned on the arm of the couch next to his sister.

"You never said anything," She tilted her head.

"Of course, I didn't," He smiled. "What you do for work is your decision."

Uncle Scott walked in behind him. "Who's deciding what?" He looked around the group. Arms appeared around his waist then Aunt Jordan's head peeked from the side of him.

"What decision?" She smiled.

"Do you want us to vote again?" Aunt Dru smiled and quickly did. "I vote yes."

"I vote yes," Her dad grinned.

Uncle Scott shrugged. "I guess I do too, but to what?"

"The Tagger Barn and Breakfast," Aunt Dru said.

"That's up again?" Aunt Jordan asked excitedly. "Leah, you should quit your job and take it over, you'd be awesome at it."

Grace saw a smile cross her mother's face as her dad and Aunt Dru grinned.

"That's what the vote was? Leah? You'll do it? I'd vote yes to that a dozen times." Uncle Scott seemed excited.

"Leah?" Aunt Jordan asked excitedly.

"Don't feel like you're being pressured or anything…" Aunt Dru giggled.

"How much control would I have?" Her mother asked.

"Dru has to be a big part of it," Her dad frowned in concern. "It's her job to make sure Tagger Enterprises grows…it'll be incorporated pretty tightly with The Stables."

"Just Dru and I?"

"Scott and Grayson are involved if a decision is made that involves any other portion of Tagger Enterprises." Aunt Dru answered.

Her mom nodded. "I understand completely."

"Is that a yes?" Aunt Dru asked, the 'poker face' was gone and there was hope in her eyes.

"Yes, I accept!" Her mom said excitedly.

***

Grace stood at the stall door and stared at the buckskin. It had been almost six weeks since she had ridden him. Her eyes moved over to the empty stall next to Eli's. Buttercup's home; her shoulders slumped.

"It'll be OK, Gracie." Reilly walked up behind her and rested his chin on her shoulder and looked in at the horse.

"I think that's literally looking over someone's shoulder." Grace smiled.

"Are you going to just stare or ride?" He asked. She could feel his cheek moving against hers.

"You'd think we would be tired of riding." Grace stepped away from him and into the buckskin's stall.

"I can't imagine a day I would be tired of riding," Reilly chuckled. "I take that back. I needed a couple days off after last month's trip to the mountains."

Grace giggled, "So did I."

As Eli ate his hay, Grace ran her hands over his back, rump, belly, then back up to his chest and underneath his thick mane. Using just the pads of her fingers she massaged the horse's neck. Eli stopped and leaned into the massage. Grace smiled. Last year when they rescued the horses, his neck was the only part of him that she wasn't afraid to touch.

Grace reached out a finger to the horse's muzzle and touched the velvety end. She could feel his warm breath surround her finger and hand. The finger moved up his face to just under one eye. His soft gentle brown eyes closed as she caressed.

"Ride him, Grace." Reilly said from the stall door. "See how different he is then the last time you rode him. Your dad is an amazing trainer."

She looked over at Reilly. "I know, but I miss her so much."

"Well, it's time to reintroduce yourself to Eli," He smiled. "Ride?"

Grace nodded. It wasn't Eli's fault she missed Buttercup.

"He's been roping with Dad," Grace grinned. "Let's do a full on roping practice."

"Awesome!" Reilly ran for Cooper.

***

"Grace, Reilly…" Her dad yelled out. "Just come down along the fence then just kick him into a run and race to the dummy in the middle."

"You're not talking about me are you, Uncle Grayson?" Wade turned with a grin.

Wade was sitting on top of the mechanical calf watching Reilly and Grace practice leg work and control.

"Not this time," Her dad laughed.

They jogged down the side of the arena to the end then completed a roll back followed by a run toward Wade. Eli beat Reilly and Cooper by half a horse length.

"You didn't get turned quick enough, Reilly." Grace turned to him. "We already had a step on him before he took off."

"I know. We need practice." Reilly sighed.

"Then go back and do it again," Wade yelled out.

"Where's my rope?" Reilly looked around. "The dummy's talking!"

They were all laughing when her dad's phone started ringing. He walked away as he answered it.

Grace leaned forward in the saddle and rubbed Eli's neck.

"Well?" Reilly trotted up next to her.

Grace grinned. Eli was fantastic. He listened to her movements more than any other horse had. Just a slight flick of her boot would make the horse respond. A lean forward or back made him react.

"Amazing, no wonder Dad likes riding him." Grace smiled.

"Can I?"

Grace nodded and they moved the horses next to each other and slid into the others saddle. Because her legs were so long, she didn't need to adjust the length of the stirrups.

They trotted down the opposite sides of the arena.

Grace watched Reilly so they stayed even and turned at the same time. Wade called out and they jogged to the designated spot and completed the rollback, coming out at a run. Cooper twisted into the roll and then dug in with his back hooves. She leaned forward and pushed on his neck moving with his motion. The power of each stride pounded through her body as each hoof hit the dirt.

The horse thrust forward, up she went and rocked back as he started another stride. Cooper was faster than any of the horses she'd ridden so far. They beat Reilly and Eli by a full horse length.

"Holy cow!" Wade screamed as she ran by him.

"Gracie!" Reilly yelled out as he pulled Eli to a stop.

She continued to run the horse to the end of the arena then turned left and kicked the horse to move faster. The power of him was tremendous, each hoof beat vibrated through her. She wasn't wearing a hat and her hair was flying behind her, she could feel its movement with each stride of the horse.

As she made the turn back to the beginning, she saw her dad. He was still on the phone but watching her as he climbed the fence to get out of her way. He was smiling…she grinned at him as she and the powerful black horse flew by him. When she reached the beginning she turned him sharply and ran down the side of the arena.

She moved him left for a couple strides, then right, back to left…they weaved down the length of the panels and turned back to repeat the pattern. In her mind, she visualized poles jutting out of the ground and she weaved the horse between them.

"Grace!" She heard her dad yell.

She leaned back to slow the horses forward motion. He listened and came into a slow gallop for another round of the arena. Then she slowed him into a jog.

Her heart was racing and could feel Cooper's sides puffing for air. She shouldn't have ridden him so hard for so long. He needed to be conditioned for that kind of running. She reached down to stroke the horse's sweating neck and could feel his energy. He was ready to go for more. Her dad would shoot her if she took him around again!

He was sitting on the top rail of the fence so she trotted up next to him.

"That was surprising," He looked down at the horse. "Looks like he enjoyed it and could go another round."

"Grace!" Wade had crawled onto the back of Eli, behind Reilly. They trotted up next to her. "I want to do that!"

"No!" Reilly, Grace and her dad called out.

"Aw, come on." Wade frowned at them.

"What were you doing when you were weaving?" Reilly asked.

"Running poles," She laughed.

"Oh! That would be awesome!" Reilly nodded excitedly. "You might as well do more than just one event."

"We can't pull the whole herd to every rodeo," Her dad rolled his eyes. "Walk him around to cool him off then hit the barn."

He waited for Wade to slide off Eli, onto the fence, then to the ground. The two walked towards the barn together.

"I've never even tried to get him to move that fast," Reilly shook his head. "I didn't know he had it in him."

They stepped out of the saddle and walked through the gate towards the barn.

"Isn't it weird that I've never even been on him before?" Grace commented.

"Next time, we should all ride each other's horse." Reilly joked.

"I think they have to do that in some of the competitions Nora's headed to when she's older."

"She'll have plenty of different ones to practice on." He pointed out as they made it to the front of the barn.

"But does it count if they've all been trained by da…"

Grace stopped so fast, Eli bumped into her back.

Reilly's truck was in front of her…but right next to it was a matching white one…with running horse decals on the side of it. She could just see the back window. There were vinyl letters that spelled out, "TRAIL BOSS".

Her parents and Sadie were standing next to it, smiling at her. Everyone else was standing on the deck of the house watching.

Nick appeared next to her, "I'll take Eli."

Grace turned her eyes away from the truck and looked up at his amused grin. She slowly lifted the reins and placed them in his hand.

"Go." He nodded to the truck.

She took off running towards her new white Trail Boss truck!

***

"I don't think I've seen a grin like that since Reilly got his truck." Jack smiled at her.

"I thought I wanted the red one," She admitted to him. They were the only two on the back deck, waiting to be served dinner since they had made breakfast. "But the white one is so much better! We didn't see it when we were looking."

"Well, this has definitely been an eventful week," Jack leaned back. "It was sad to see Kelly go but at least she's not gone forever...you'll still see her next summer."

Grace nodded.

"Grace?" Jack said in a low voice.

She turned to his concerned eyes.

"I know Reilly's pretty upset."

She nodded.

"Is he OK?"

Grace rolled her lips. She didn't talk to anyone about her and Reilly's conversations but Jack seemed genuinely concerned.

"Yes, he is." She finally nodded.

"Would you tell me if he wasn't?" He raised a brow.

"Yes," She answered quickly and firmly. She would do what was best for Reilly, even if that meant breaking his trust and going to his dad for help. No one would want what's best for Reilly more than herself and Jack. She was just going to have to balance what she could share and couldn't in the future.

"Thank you, Grace," He smiled then turned back to her truck. "You and Reilly will have to take turns driving to school when it starts."

"Me first though! Everyone got to see his last year."

Grace leaned her elbows on the table, her chin in her hands and stared at her little white truck.

"Dinner's ready!" Wade called out and carried the first bowl of many out to the table.

Stomach full, still looking at her truck and dreaming of Cooper's run around the arena, Grace decided she couldn't be any happier. Even her mom was going to be around more. She was very content. Then her dad carried a big box out of the house and set it on the table.

"To commemorate such a great day, Leah had these made for each of you." Uncle Scott announced as he pulled a gray T-shirt out of the box. On the front of the shirt, it had black silhouettes of horse riders pushing a herd of cows. Under the picture it read, "Tagger Drive Team". Their names were also written on the front of the shirt. Cora quickly slid her shirt over her tank top. She beamed proudly.

Grace grinned, across the shoulders of her shirt it spelled Trail Boss.

THE TAGGER HERD SERIES

NORA Tagger

Gini Roberge

CHAPTER ONE

Perfect, perfect, perfect...practice to perfection.

Nora held the leather lead perfectly in front of her, the perfect distance from Isaiah and with a perfect smile on her face. She watched the halter class judges intently. The judge pointed to her and she stepped forward. Following the pattern she had memorized, she walked Isaiah towards the judge, then trotted him, then stopped and made Isaiah turn and pivot on his back leg. He did perfect.

Next was backing him up. Piece of cake, Nora thought, as she smiled perfectly at the judge. They moved forward again to finish the pattern. The judge thanked her and Nora nodded then returned to her spot in the line of eight competitors. Still watching the judge she stopped Isaiah in his spot. The horse took two steps to get his hooves squarely set under him.

Nora was wearing crisp black jeans, boots, and her burgundy and black sparkling shirt that matched Isaiah perfectly. Her mother had coiled Nora's hair perfectly which allowed the black cowboy hat she wore to sit perfectly on her head.

Everything went perfectly, Nora thought as she kept her stance perfect and her smile perfect and when the judge announced she had won she smiled and reacted perfectly.

She had spent every night and weekend trying to make sure everything was perfect...every step she took and every step the horse took. Hours of taking classes, watching videos and reading books on how she should move and how Isaiah should move. Libby was already trained when Nora started showing her when she was ten, but Isaiah was just learning…and it was Nora that was teaching him…as she was teaching herself. It had been four months since Cora said she could show the horse. During that time, they had spent hours and hours in the arena and walking in the pasture.

She searched the stands for her mother and found her clapping with a happy smile. It warmed Nora's heart to see her mother and she proudly walked Isaiah out of the arena. These were the moments that made all the hours of practice worthwhile.

"You only won because of your horse."

Nora heard the girl's voice behind her and turned to look. It was Candace Avery. The blonde girl's brown eyes were glaring at her.

Nora had won and Candace had placed second. Not knowing what to say, Nora didn't say anything.

"He's a horse, so I'll admit he's beautiful," Candace said as they walked out of the arena. "But you're still ugly."

Nora felt like she was slapped. Her eyes shot up to the girl but she remained quiet. The blonde glared at her, waiting for a response…Nora didn't give her one.

Candace shook her head and kept walking with her red horse calmly walking behind her.

Nora's excitement of winning was totally drained from her, all she wanted to do was cry, but she kept the perfect smile on her face. She learned a long time before that smiling was a good way to cover-up when you were sad, lonely, or upset.

That was her last class of the weekend and all she wanted to do was go home. Nora looked up in time to see her mom headed for her, she made her smile wider so her mom would think she was happy.

"Nora! That was great!" She said and gave her a strong hug.

"Thanks, Mom," Nora smiled brightly and made sure her voice sounded happy.

"I'm so proud of you," Another hug before they walked towards the trailers. "Natalie's mom wanted to know if we would like to go get dinner before we head back home."

They reached the horse stalls where Libby was waiting for them. Nora had won three competitions with Libby that day…with Candace walking away with a second and two third places.

"I don't know, Mom," Nora sighed. "I'm getting kind of tired…don't we have a long trip home?"

Nora tied Isaiah to the horse trailer.

"It's only a two hour drive, Nora. We've had much longer drives this summer and still stopped for dinner…are you sure? We should be celebrating your wins tonight."

Nora shrugged. "I'm just tired, I guess."

"You were full of all kinds of energy before this class, then you won…now you don't want to celebrate…so what happened?"

There was no way she was telling her mother what Candace said, so she didn't answer.

"Nora," Her mother said and Nora turned to her, trying very hard to keep her expression happy and calm. "Dinner or not?"

Nora sighed and shook her head.

"OK, I'll go let them know. Go ahead and get all the equipment loaded, I'll help with the horses when I get back."

Nora watched as her mother walked away then turned and stared at Isaiah. She had been so happy when Sadie suggested she show him…but now? Not so much.

***

"You can go up to bed, Sweetheart," Her mother said as they stepped out of the truck at The Homestead. "I'll take care of the horses. We'll leave the trailer for tomorrow."

"No, that's OK, Mom. I should help." Nora had slept the entire way home. Normally, she would have been too excited.

She took Libby's lead rope from her mom and walked the horse to the barn. The horses were so used to the late night arrivals that they didn't even whinny at each other. When she walked into the barn and turned on the light, there were twelve horses leaned over stall doors watching her. Nora smiled; it was a sight that she would love forever. It helped put energy back into her body. Horses don't care if you're ugly...they would all love her anyway.

She put Libby into her stall with hay and water. When she walked out, her parents were at the large double door entry way. Isaiah stood patiently behind her parents as they kissed. Since the fire in the mountains, they were happier than ever and were always smiling and kissing.

Nora watched them for a moment...her shoulders slumped...they didn't care if she was ugly...they would love her anyway.

"You want me to get Isaiah out of your way?" Nora called out to them with a soft giggle. She loved to see the two of them happy. When they weren't happy...it was awful.

They both looked up at her with grins. Then her dad took the horse's lead rope and walked him into the barn.

"So, I hear we have more wins for the wall," He stopped long enough to kiss her on top of the head then put Isaiah in his stall.

Nora stopped briefly to greet Arcturus, she had missed him, like she did every weekend. She placed her hand on his star and felt the warmth from his body enter her palm. Taking a deep breath she inhaled his scent...his essence. He didn't care if she was ugly...he loved her anyway. She kissed him gently on the nose, told him good night and turned to leave the barn.

"Where are you going?" Her dad called out to her.

She stopped and look back at him...she knew what he wanted.

Her mom waved her white competitor's number and ribbons from the weekend in the air and her parents walked to the door and opened it.

Nora walked back and stopped just inside the door as he turned on the light.

When they added the extension of more stalls to the barn after Christmas, a large memory room was added for all the ribbons, awards and achievements of the Tagger Herd.

The room was large and pretty much empty, but they all knew there would be a day it would be packed with memories.

Nora stepped in and her eyes instantly rested on the room center piece. It was a large burned tree stump and came from the two trees in the center of the black circle the fire had created on the mountain. It still had a bit of an odor to it, even after a coating was put on it to protect the amber and black wood. It was there in honor of Eli's triumphant run to Uncle Grayson so they could save the mountain and ranch from the fire. Every time she looked at it, the memory of Eli running...heaving himself up the mountainside played in her mind.

On the wall to her left, was a large picture of Amy and Adam sitting on Buttercup and Cooper. Monty and Trooper were standing next to them. Nora loved looking into the faces of the smiling kids knowing if it wasn't for the horses and her family, the brother and sister wouldn't be alive.

Nora looked at the competitor numbers and awards she had contributed to the room. As happy as she was winning, the picture and tree stump kept her humble.

Sadie and Scarecrow were also adding to the room. It was Scarecrow's first year barrel racing but the horse was amazing and already winning first and seconds. She had also started running poles and other games.

Wade was competing in breakaway roping but hadn't won yet. This year was getting Dollar used to the rodeo's and Wade used to competing. He considered this his practice summer and was determined to win next season.

Grace and Reilly were competing at local shows but hadn't won yet. They were fine with that…they were just competing for fun.

Nora took the white competitor's number from her mom and quickly wrote on the back what she and the horses had accomplished while her mother hung the ribbons. Nora glanced around at the summer's awards; looking at them all together made her tired.

"Can I go to bed now?" Nora turned to her parents.

They both looked at her concerned.

"Sure, Hon, it's late." Her mother said.

Nora quickly hugged them then slowly walked to the house. It was late, but Uncle Grayson and Aunt Dru were still sitting at the small kitchen table. They turned and smiled warmly at her. She smiled in return…they didn't care if she was ugly…they loved her anyway.

Nora walked up to her uncle and wrapped her arms around his neck.

"Thank you," She whispered in his ear. He squeezed her hand and leaned his head to her.

"Good show?" He asked.

Nora nodded and gave her Aunt Dru a big hug.

"You look tired, Nora," Her aunt said. "Are you feeling well?"

"Just tired," Nora answered as she walked towards the steps. Her feet felt like there were rocks in her boots as she made her way up the stairs. Each step was harder to get up.

When she finally made it to her room, she climbed on the bed, fully clothed. Just before her eyes closed and the first tear fell, she whispered to herself: "I am not ugly."

CHAPTER TWO

Her arms crossed and resting on the table, Nora watched her parents discuss the horse show versus the rodeo. She knew she was going to lose. It was 2 riders against 1 rider, end of story…just like always. She leaned down and placed her chin on her crossed arms and watched them with her eyes, not moving her head.

They were sitting at the small kitchen table trying to decide what to do when Nora heard laughter echo down the hallway. Matt and Nikki walked into the living room. Nora's eyes went back to her parents, wondering why they were even trying to discuss it, they already knew.

Her cousins walked out of the living room and into the kitchen; Matt's arms were full of clothes.

"Hey, Scott…Jordan…I thought you'd be at the ranch. Miss Nora," Matt smiled at her while juggling the pile of folded clothes in his arms, "Why so sad?"

Nora gave him a half-hearted attempt at a smile.

"We're trying to figure out how to get her to Ellensburg for a show and Sadie and Wade to Philomath for a rodeo on the same weekend. All our friends already have full trailers going over." Scott sighed and smiled at Nora. "I think she's feeling she's going to be on the losing end again."

"When is it?" Nikki asked.

"Two weeks," Her mom answered with a roll of the eyes.

"Ooohhh, bad timing," Matt frowned.

"Harvest..." Nikki nodded with a grimace.

"The only adult that can escape is Jordan." Her dad explained.

"Jordan, you need to clone yourself." Nikki teased.

"Wish I could, for more than this reason," her mom smiled. "We booked both, hoping the fields would be done by then, but with late harvest it looks like everything's going to be ready at this same time. It's going to be very busy for the next month."

Nora's eyes turned to each person as they spoke, she didn't even have the energy to move her head.

Matt adjusted the clothes in his arms and looked at Nikki. "Isn't Nick in Yakima in two weeks?"

"Yeah, he is, Bull Bash, Extreme Bulls...or something bull that weekend, that's why he can't make it for harvest." Nikki said. "Call him, he'd probably do it, it's only a half hour apart."

Nora's eyes widened in surprise...Nick? They were suggesting Nick?

Matt and Nikki headed for the back door.

"Scott, call him." Matt said over his shoulder and a shocked Nora watched the two of them walk out the door.

Her eyes moved quickly back to her parents. They stared at the door then looked down to her then back at each other.

"I'd be OK with that," Her mom said with a surprised expression.

Her dad smiled and nodded his head, "I'd be OK with it, too."

They turned back to Nora, who still hadn't moved.

"How would you feel about Nick taking you?" Her mom asked.

Nora looked at them closely, making sure they were serious...they were. She liked Nick, he was quiet when the kids were around but he always laughed at jokes and he was really great with Nikki and Matt. They had suggested it, so they think it's OK. Besides...he did help save Matt, Reilly, and Grace's lives. And she

REALLY wanted to go to the horse show rather than go watch Sadie and Wade ride.

"If you're not OK with it, we won't even make the call." Her dad said in concern.

Nora's eyes moved between the two of them again. What's the worst that could happen? He would be silent the whole time? Besides…he's probably going to say no anyway.

Nora nodded. "I'd be OK with that." She repeated their words.

"OK, then," Her dad looked at her mom and reached for the phone.

Nora watched him closely…he looked nervous. She moved her eyes to her mom; she looked hopeful. That made Nora smile. Maybe they really were trying to get her to the show…maybe they did really care. Sometimes she wondered…

"Nick? Yeah, it's Scott." Her dad's head nodded as if Nick could see him, Nora smiled at that.

"Well, Matt and Nikki suggested I call…yeah just a couple minutes ago…I think he's bribing Cora into doing his laundry….yeah, typical college student…" He laughed. "We have a problem we're hoping you can help with…yeah…thanks, but let me ask first…" He laughed again with a glance at her mother.

Nora listened as he told Nick about the shows. Her eyes rolled from her mother to her father. She sighed, if they would call Nick for help…that meant they really did care. The thought seemed to make her more sad than happy.

"What?" Her dad turned and looked at her mom anxiously. "OK…yeah…no problem…will do…thanks…yeah…OK…" He ended the call and looked between Nora and his wife.

"He didn't even hesitate…" He grinned. "…just said yes."

Nora's head shot up and her eyes widen…she didn't really think he would do it.

They both turned to her with smiles.

"You get to go!" Her mom said excitedly.

"Are you still OK with Nick taking you?" Her dad asked in concern.

Nora nodded and smiled. She got to go to the horse show!

She jumped up and gave both of them a hug and ran out to the barn to tell Libby and Isaiah.

Wade and Sadie were probably up at the arena so she'd be alone in the barn, which she always liked. She started singing as she skipped out to the barn. *"Nick's taking me to the horse show…I'm going to the horse show…"* She repeated her little tune as she skipped into the barn. *"Nick's taking me to the horse show…"*

"What?" Sadie and Wade asked her at the same time.

She came to an abrupt halt. Dang!

"What did you say?" Wade asked again, looking at her with a raised brow.

"Nick's taking me to the horse show!" She smiled excitedly.

"Yeah, right." Wade shook his head and walked by her, leading Dollar. "Like that's something Nick would do."

"Geez, Nora." Sadie walked past her leading Scarecrow.

Nora's good mood plummeted. She turned and watched them walk away with tears filling her eyes. They thought she was lying…she looked down at the ground then back up again just as they disappeared around the barn. They would know soon enough.

As she turned back to the barn, she wondered if they would ever realize that every time they did that, it felt like they were punching her heart.

Instead of going to Libby or Isaiah, she went to Arcturus. He was her strength. The large black horse with the star greeted her when she entered his stall. She ran her hand down his neck then up the side of his face. She placed her hand on the star on his forehead;

her own personal energy source. The horse's skin warmed her hand...she closed her eyes. Nora imagined the warmth running from his star to her hand, up through her arm and to her heart. She breathed in...taking in his scent. Her eyes opened...her heart was full again. She smiled into his big beautiful brown eyes.

Nora slid her hand from the star and down Arcturus' nose, then back up to gently rub the spot under the eyes that always made him tip his head and close them. That always made her smile. Slowly she moved to his round jaw, then underneath, back up over and then to his ears. She gently massaged each one between her fingertips and thumbs then flattening her hand slowly moved down his big arching neck. This side didn't have his long black mane, so she continued down his side running her hand over the now flat back.

She remembered how bad he looked the first time she had seen him; in the stalls at Cora's property. She had fallen in love with him the moment she touched that star...her energy source. After they found the horses the year before, she would place her hand on the star and will her warmth and energy from her arm into him to help him survive. At that time, she could have gripped his backbone, but now it was covered in muscle and fat. His hair was ink black and shiny.

She walked around the back of him, picked up the length of his tail in her arm and let the hair drop like a waterfall. It was kept meticulously brushed so there weren't any knots or tangles. When he ran... it flowed behind him like a feather.

As Nora continued her walk around him, instead of going across his back again, she ran her hand down under his belly and scratched as she moved forward. Arcturus' head bobbed...it did every time she scratched his belly. Then the horse swung his head back towards her. She giggled and touched the end of his nose, the velvety part that tickled her fingers. She slid her hand up his nose then slowly down the side of his nostril, his warm breath filling the palm of her hand...she sighed contently.

When the horse lowered his head, she turned her attention to his mane. It was long, black, and tangle free as she ran her fingers through the strands. She placed both hands flat against his skin and under the mane then rubbed him with her fingertips until his head started bobbing again making her giggle.

Finally, she stepped in front of his chest, tucking her shoulder just under his jaw and wrapped her arms around the big black horse's neck. She felt him lower his head onto her back...a special horse hug. Arcturus' love and warmth filled her soul as she smiled, then reluctantly stepped away from him.

"I have to work with Isaiah this morning," Nora whispered to Arcturus. "We have a show in two weeks." She kissed him on the black nose. "Don't be jealous, you'll always be my favorite." One last touch, fingertips to star, and she walked away with a contented sigh.

Into the tack room to fetch a halter, then back out to Isaiah, who bobbed his head in excitement to see her. She smiled as he dipped his head into the halter. He liked their walks as much as she did. When they walked out of the barn she stopped, and he stopped perfectly at her side. Where to walk to? Definitely not to the arena where Wade and Sadie were...so down the driveway she headed.

Practice, practice, practice....they walked all the way down the driveway and back. They practiced stopping, backing, trotting, turning...over and over again. By the time they walked the driveway four times she and the horse were bored. The front north pasture was empty of horses so she took Isaiah out there. They practiced different walking patterns that she had completed at all the summer's shows so far. They practiced even more...practice to perfection.

As Nora started walking up to the barn through the pasture, she heard someone turning off the road and up the driveway. She knew without turning that it was Reilly's cute little blue truck. When she did turn, his arm was stretched out the window waving at her. She smiled and waved back. Isaiah stood at attention watching him pull into the parking area and stop.

She continued to the barn, tying the horse to the outside hitching post so she could give him some love and attention for all his hard work. She retrieved the grooming box from the barn and was just starting to brush the horse when she heard Reilly.

"Nora!"

She peered over the horse and smiled. She liked Reilly and loved having him living at the house. He was always in such a great mood now. Before the Tagger herd came into their lives he would get moody and a bit gloomy at times but Grace always made him laugh. After the herd, he was always happy and smiling. But since his dad married Aunt Dru, and they moved into The Homestead, he was rarely without a skip in his step and a grin on his face.

"Are you riding?" She asked him when he walked up next to her and stroked the length of Isaiah's back.

"Yeah, was thinking I'd work on Rufio's stops and turns," He answered. "You riding?"

Nora shook her head. "Wade and Sadie are up there."

"So?"

"Just not in the mood for them," She didn't want to go over the earlier encounter and get depressed again.

"Nora, don't let their immaturity stop you from riding." Reilly said.

She smiled slightly; he didn't take their side like everyone else did. Maybe he would be excited for her about the horse show.

"Mom and Dad figured out a way for me to go to the show in Ellensburg." She smiled.

"Really? How is Jordan going to be in two places at once, hundreds of miles apart?"

"She isn't. Matt and Nikki suggested they call Nick...and he said he would take me cuz he has a rodeo or something that weekend up there."

Reilly's eyes widened in surprise, but he had a grin on his face which made his dimples deepen. "That's awesome, Nora!"

He believed her...not like Wade, who thought she was lying.

"I'm kinda nervous," she admitted.

"Don't be...you'll have a great time...Nick's awesome." Reilly leaned his arms on Isaiah's hindquarters. "I think it's a Bull Bash...you'll get to go to that at night."

Nora's eyes widened, "I hadn't thought of that...it could be fun."

Reilly started to take a step back but she stopped him.

"Reilly?"

"Yeah?"

"Can I ask you something weird?" She asked nervously.

"Sure, weird questions can be interesting," He leaned back onto the horse.

Nora looked at him with a serious expression. "When I told Wade and Sadie earlier that Nick was taking me...they thought I was lying."

"Really?" Reilly looked confused. "Why would you lie about something like that?"

Nora exhaled impatiently, why would he think she would lie at all?

"I wouldn't lie," She frowned. "But he instantly thought I did, but you didn't."

"I don't know that you've ever lied to me, Nora." Reilly said, which irritated her. "So why would I think you were lying to me now…on something that was going to be so painfully obvious later?"

Nora looked at the ground not wanting him to see the tears that formed. "I've never lied to you or anyone else, Reilly."

"Nora, when you say it with your head down it doesn't seem honest." He said softly.

She took a deep breath and lifted her head; the motion made a tear slide down her cheek so she quickly wiped it away and turned her glistening eyes to him. "I don't lie." She repeated.

"Nora…" His eyes were soft and apologetic. "I'm sorry."

She nodded and went back to brushing the horse.

"Maybe they thought you did because…" He paused until she looked up at him. "Because they think you're mean to them, and they get angry at you, so they accuse you of lying."

Nora nodded sullenly. This conversation was getting worse…now they thought she was a liar and a bully.

"You and Grace tell each other everything…and even when you think it might be bad." Nora stopped brushing and looked into his blue eyes.

"Yeah."

"Will you do the same for me?"

"If you want…sometimes I'd rather her lie to me than tell me the truth." He chuckled.

Nora paused, thinking back to the horse show. "Last weekend at the horse show, as we were leaving the arena…" She paused and took a deep breath because she hadn't told anyone about the conversation and it was so hard to say it out loud. "Candace Avery said I was ugly." She could feel the tears pushing their way back up and she didn't look at him.

"You beat her in every competition," Reilly said quickly. "She was jealous, Nora."

Nora looked up at him anxiously...he was smiling.

"I'm not ugly?" Her voice was shaky. Everyone always said things about Sadie and her blue eyes and blonde hair but...

"Absolutely not," Reilly laughed. "You're the prettiest girl in the arena...which makes her jealous, too."

Nora sighed in relief then looked up at him warily. "You're not just saying that because you're my cousin now?"

He laughed again. "You just said you wanted me to be honest with you, like Grace and I are honest...right?"

Nora nodded.

"Then I'm saying it because it's true." He grinned.

Nora smiled. "So I'm pretty?" She asked nervously just to confirm.

"Yes, Nora," He leaned back from the horse. "There are going to be jealous girls that call you names because of your looks. Just remember...it's because they are jealous."

He started to walk away then turned back. "It's not your outside you need to work on, it's the inside." He started into the barn and yelled over his shoulder. "Saddle up and let's ride."

Nora stared at his back in wonder...did he really just say that? Then act like it wouldn't hurt her? The tears were gone, her eyes dry...in shock.

Her hand started moving again as she tried to figure out what just happened. She was a liar and a bully...she was pretty on the outside but ugly on the inside? Was that what he was saying? Her head leaned forward onto the horse as her mind tried to figure it out. Finally, she just gave up and walked Isaiah back into the barn.

She needed Arcturus again. Twice in one day...

CHAPTER THREE

"Why is it OK for you to wear my jeans but I can't wear yours?" Sadie asked with a pout.

"You can't wear my show jeans, Sadie." Nora frowned at her cousin.

"What difference does it make?"

"Because you can rip them or stain them." Nora sighed, they've had this argument ever since Sadie grew enough to fit into the same size pants. They were long on Nora and almost too short for Sadie.

Nora shared the big bedroom with Grace and Sadie. The bedroom was also attached to their own large bathroom; which they fought over all the time.

Their mom's had put three large area rugs on the floor that designated the girls own space. There were white decorative room dividers between the girls area's so they could have some privacy. Grace's area had reds, blues and yellows with horse stuff everywhere. Sadie's area was pink and light blue with horse stuff everywhere. Nora's own area, which was right next to the door was white and dark blue, with horse stuff everywhere.

"I'm just gonna wear them to the store with Cora." Sadie said not moving to take the jeans off. "I told her I'd help and I want to wear my boots, so I need jeans."

"I'm taking them this weekend, which means that have to be clean." Nora said a little firmer. "If you wear them, they'll have to be washed."

"So?"

"They're black so they'll fade with each wash." Nora was getting tired of this argument. "They have to be crisp black for the shows."

"You put too much thought into your show clothes." Sadie said starting to walk to the door without taking Nora's jeans off.

Nora stepped in front of her. "Take off my jeans and put your shorts or something else on."

"NO!" Sadie tried to step around her.

Nora made the move to block her again. "Take my jeans off!"

"NO!" Sadie yelled again.

"Yes!" Nora yelled just as loud.

"Girls!" Aunt Leah yelled from behind Nora which made her jump. "What is going on?"

"I'm going to the store to help Cora and wanted to wear jeans." Sadie said quickly. "Mine are dirty so I borrowed a pair from Nora and she said I can't wear them."

Aunt Leah was home most of the time since she quit her job and was working on the development of The Tagger Barn and Breakfast.

Nora remained quiet.

"Why can't she wear them?" Aunt Leah turned and asked her. Her blonde hair was pulled back into a pony tail, her blue eyes looking irritated.

Nora didn't answer…she just looked between Sadie and her aunt. Aunt Leah NEVER took her side so she knew it would be useless to say anything.

"If you're not going to say anything, then you don't have a good reason." She exhaled and turned to Sadie. "Go help Cora."

Sadie ran out the door without looking at Nora.

"Nora," Aunt Leah sat on the bed. "Talk to me. I hate it when you kids shut down and won't talk to us." She sighed when Nora remained quiet. "You know…we're not the enemy."

Nora looked at her and was about to answer when Sadie sulked back into the room. Cora walked in behind her.

"What's wrong?" Aunt Leah stood.

"Those are Nora's show jeans." Cora pointed towards Sadie as her cousin stepped out of the jeans in question.

Aunt Leah gasped and turned to Nora; "Why didn't you just say that?" She seemed more irritated.

Nora watched Sadie glare at her and put on a pair of shorts. Then she walked out of the room without a word.

"Nora," Aunt Leah said again. "Talk to me right now."

Nora looked up at her, rolled her lips together tightly then exhaled. She had to answer, there was no choice. "I figured you would let her wear them anyway."

"Why?" Aunt Leah asked surprised.

Nora didn't know how to answer without being rude so she just stared at her.

"Why Nora?" She repeated. "Why would you think I would let her wear your show jeans?"

Nora felt the pressure on the back of her head. Her mom had explained it was stress from being scared or worried. She wasn't sure which it was this time. If she didn't explain, she was scared Aunt Leah would get madder. She was also worried that if she answered truthfully, they would say she was rude and disrespectful and not let her go to the show.

So she rolled her lips tightly together and looked down at the ground.

"Chin up." Aunt Leah ordered sternly.

Slowly Nora did as she was told and she lifted her head back up but stared at the "Grace" sign above Grace's bed.

"Cora, could you please give us a minute?" Aunt Leah said as she sat on the bed.

Nora's heart raced. Why did she want them to be alone?

"I'll just take Sadie and Wade and head to the store. We'll be back in an hour or so." Cora said and Nora watched her leave.

"Please sit down, Nora." Aunt Leah said softly.

Knowing she didn't have a choice, she sat down next to her aunt.

"Please look at me." Again with the soft voice.

Nora raised her eyes to her aunts. She didn't LOOK angry.

"I am not the enemy." Aunt Leah smiled down at her.

Nora didn't know what to say…Aunt Leah had never talked to her like this before. She was beginning to wonder if her aunt quitting her job was a good thing.

"No matter what you say right now, I will not get mad and prevent you from going to the show this weekend." Aunt Leah smiled. "Is that what you're worried about?"

Nora nodded.

Aunt Leah exhaled patiently. "Good…communication! Now we're getting somewhere." She giggled.

Nora smiled nervously.

"You and Sadie are at the age that you're not going to get along all the time."

Nora nodded and stopped herself from rolling her eyes.

"When you argue and we have to break in, to referee, we have to know what's going on to make the right call on how to fix the problem." She paused. "Do you understand that?"

Nora nodded. She was starting to get tired of this whole thing and forced herself to look interested.

"Next time I ask you, will you just tell me the reason instead of freezing up?"

Nora looked at her, she seemed sincere, her eyes soft and concerned at the same time.

"OK," Nora answered. "I just didn't think you would care."

To Nora's surprise, her aunt laughed.

"Clothes are expensive, Nora, and you're coming to the end of show season. We don't want to have to buy another pair then have you grow out of them by next season."

Nora smiled, she hadn't thought of that.

"Nora?"

"What?"

"I was in the room when your mother gave birth to you."

Nora looked at her like she was crazy. What did that have to do with her jeans?

"I know," Nora said cautiously.

Aunt Leah giggled. "That means I've been there since you were born...literally."

Nora nodded, still confused.

"Which means, that I have had twelve years to love you." She smiled gently.

Nora's shoulders relaxed. Her aunt cupped Nora's face in her hands and kissed her forehead.

She looked into her aunt's blue eyes and saw the love, so she smiled.

"There," Aunt Leah sighed. "I love your smile."

Nora's smile grew.

"Yea! An even bigger one!" She teased which made Nora giggle. "And a giggle!" Aunt Leah's arms wrapped around Nora in a playful hug.

"You know what?" Aunt Leah said and stood quickly.

"What?"

"We are the only two people in this huge house." She smiled mischievously.

Nora smiled and stood. "Really?"

"I like sprinkles and chocolate on my ice cream." She walked to the door.

"I like caramel." Nora quickly followed her.

"OK, but we have to have a contest to see who fixes whose bowl of ice cream." Aunt Leah grinned.

"What kind of contest?"

They stepped into the real long wood floor hallway.

"Who can slide the closest to the banister?" Aunt Leah grinned.

"Oh yes!" Nora laughed.

Five minutes later, Nora was scooping ice cream into a bowl for her aunt as their laughter echoed throughout the house.

***

"I hate you, Nora."

"I don't care, Sadie."

"You don't care that I hate you?"

"Why should I care about someone who hates me?"

"You should care if your cousin hates you."

"Would you care about me if I hated you?"

Silence. Nora flipped the page of riding patterns she had printed out for the coming horse show. She was memorizing them as she laid on her bed.

"I think you're just jealous," Sadie finally said...but Nora had no idea what she was talking about.

"What am I jealous about now?" She flipped another page...finding it hard to concentrate.

"That I'm two years younger but taller."

Nora frowned. She did hate that fact, but she didn't know if she was jealous about it.

"I saw you roll your eyes the other day when that lady at the store said I had pretty blonde hair." Sadie said.

Nora couldn't see her cousin, she was sitting on her bed doing...whatever. The screen between their sections of the room blocked their vision of each other.

"So?" Nora laid the pattern pages down and slid off the bed.

"So? So that probably means that you're jealous of my blonde ….."

Nora had walked out of the room. She could still hear Sadie talking but her cousin's voice was fading as she walked down the hall. She trotted down the steps and wondered if Sadie was still talking. She giggled to herself.

There wasn't anyone in the kitchen so she turned and walked down the hallway between the kitchen and laundry room stopping long enough in the open closet to slide her riding boots on. It was time to practice again...to be alone. As she shut the back door she heard Sadie yelling down the steps.

"That's rude, Nora!"

Nora giggled and shook her head. And it wasn't rude of Sadie to tell her she hated her and imply she was jealous of her blonde hair?

"Nora!" Sadie yelled from the back door.

Nora stopped halfway to the barn and turned to look at her cousin. Sadie had on the Tagger T3E hat on over her precious blonde hair. She was dressed to ride, too.

"That was mean." Sadie frowned at her.

Nora thought of Reilly's comment about Sadie and Wade thinking she was a bully. This must have been one of those times...but Sadie had just said she hated her and said Nora was jealous about her hair. Seriously! How can she be the bully this time!?!

Sadie walked past her without another word and walked into the barn. Now Nora didn't want to go in there. She sighed then heard footsteps behind her.

Turning she saw her dad walking from his truck to the house.

"What are you doing my beautiful daughter?" Her dad smiled, his blue eyes crinkled on the edges.

"Just going to ride," Nora answered smiling back at him. "Getting ready for this weekend."

He walked over and, since he was way over a foot taller than her, knelt down next to her so his head was lower than hers. She surprised him by wrapping her arms around his neck and rested her head on his shoulder.

"I love you, Daddy." She whispered. Sometimes you just needed a hug when you felt bad.

His arms came around her and he twisted her around so she was sitting on his knee but he was still hugging her.

"I love you too, my little Nora Bug." He squeezed her tight…then just a little tighter…it always warmed her heart to feel that little bit extra.

Then they heard a yell from the barn. "Come on, Nora!" It was Wade.

Nora smiled. She didn't know he was there; he must have come home with her dad.

"Wade was with you?"

"Yep, all morning. He was helping us get all the combines and trucks ready."

"So…you're ready?"

"Wheels moving at 8:00 in the morning."

"Can I come tomorrow, too? We don't leave until Friday morning."

"You want to spend the day in the combine with me?" He asked.

"Well of course I do." Nora rolled her eyes and smiled. "What field are we starting on?"

"Spring wheat for the next two days then we'll move on to canola."

"Sounds like fun." She said excitedly. "I love the bright yellow canola fields."

"Nora!" Wade yelled from the barn.

Her dad lifted her off his knee, stood up, and kissed her on top the head. "Go ride, Nora Bug."

"Bye, Dad." Nora smiled and headed for the barn a whole lot happier.

***

As they walked out of the barn, Nora purposely put Wade in between her and Sadie. Sadie was leading Scarecrow, Wade had Dollar, and Nora was leading Libby. As they rounded the corner from the barn to the arena, they all three stopped.

Uncle Grayson was in the arena with Eli.

"I feel bad," Sadie whispered. "I didn't even notice Eli wasn't in his stall."

"Shhhh" Wade whispered back.

Kids and horses quietly watched the pair in the arena gallop in a large circle. Slowly, the circle got smaller and smaller then, they suddenly stopped, backed up a few steps, then the buckskin would pivot on a back leg, turn around and start galloping in the opposite direction.

After a few circles they moved into the figure eight pattern. Eli was completing his flying lead changes as if he'd been doing them for years…instead of just months. At just the right time, he would switch to his left front leg leading then his front end would bounce and his right leg would lead.

Eli trotted to the end of the arena. In a straight line, the horse started a slow gallop, every fourth step he would bounce and change leads. With every bounce, Eli's long black mane flew into the air. Uncle Grayson barely moved on the horse, they looked as one.

The horse turned and sidestepped a dozen times at an angle across the arena, then turned and sidestepped in the opposite direction.

Eli reached the fence at the end of the arena, closest to his silent audience, and pivoted to face the open arena. Suddenly, Eli was in a fast run, tail and mane flying into the air. Just as they looked like they were going to run into the fence panel, Eli lowered his hind quarters, dug into the arena dirt with his back hooves, and slid to a stop, dirt flying.

"Wow..." Came a quiet whisper. Nora realized it had escaped from her as she stood in awe of her uncle and the beautiful horse.

Eli pivoted, completing a roll back, and ran towards them, repeated the sliding stop, dirt flying as he dug in. He pivoted again and slowly loped to the side of the arena angling to make a large circle. The circles became smaller and smaller. When the horse reached the center and couldn't move into a tighter circle, he started spinning!

Eli planted his left back hoof into the ground, leaned left with his front half and turned faster and faster, mane and tail flying, the man on top looking like a statue. Then the horse stopped, planted his right back hoof into the ground, leaned to the right and spun around the other way.

Nora was holding her breath as they came to a stop again.

Uncle Grayson leaned forward and patted the horse on the neck. Eli's head bounced as if answering the praise the man was giving him.

"That was awesome," Wade whispered. "I love watching him work the horses."

"Me, too." Sadie answered.

Nora didn't speak, her thoughts went back a few years earlier when, for the first time ever, she had sat and watched her uncle working with a young horse on the ranch. They had accomplished many of the things that he and Eli had just completed.

Nora had watched her uncle and not the horse. She watched every flick of the hand, bend of a boot tip, nearly invisible squeeze of a calf or thigh. The slight movement of his body in the saddle would cause the horse to move forward, slow down or come to a halt.

As soon as he was done working the horse, he had her crawl up on the horse in front of him and told her everything he was doing to make the horse move, turn, or stop.

Then they saddled Libby. The horse knew all the cues, and her uncle walked Nora through every movement and turn. Libby responded and Nora couldn't stop grinning. It seemed magical to her as she and the horse would dance. It was that day, working with her uncle, when Nora had decided to show Libby. She had never told anyone about their day and after every time she and Libby competed, she always thanked him...every time.

"You look like that when you work with Libby." Wade whispered to Nora.

Nora smiled....no one could ever give her a better compliment than that.

Uncle Grayson walked the horse to the corner of the arena and stepped out of the saddle. He slid off his riding gloves and stuffed them in his back pocket. As he turned to lead the horse out of the arena, Eli swung over, and with just his lips, pulled the gloves out of the pocket. They dropped to the ground.

Sadie, Wade, and Nora started laughing which caused the grinning man to look up at them in surprise. He laughed with the kids as he retrieved his gloves and kept them in his hand as he and Eli walked out the gate.

Sadie and Wade walked towards the arena but Nora held back. Her uncle looked down at her with a smile.

"Where's your head at?" His blue eyes were…content.

Nora looked up at him and sighed. He did look like a western movie star.

"Will you help me with Isaiah and Arcturus during the off season? I want to be ready for spring shows with them." She stared with hopeful eyes.

"Of course, I will." He answered with a chuckle.

"Thanks." She smiled and walked into the arena to put Libby through the course that he and Eli just finished.

CHAPTER FOUR

"You drive me nuts, Nora," Sadie glared from the library doorway.

"You drive me nuts, Sadie," Nora didn't move her eyes from the computer screen.

Her cousin disappeared and Nora sighed heavily. Two more days until her trip with Nick; at least Sadie wouldn't be there and it would be quiet. She sighed again and continued to watch the videos of the professionals showing their horses. If she wasn't in the arena, she was watching other people in the arena.

Her mom's head appeared around the doorway. "The cow cutting flag came in today. Your dad's headed out to saddle Little Ghost. They want to play with it at least once before harvest starts. "

"Oh! Let's go watch!" Nora ran past her mother and ran down the hallway. She didn't care that Little Ghost was Sadie's horse. It was her dad that was riding him!

He was already on the grey horse and loping circles at the far end of the arena. Nora and her mother, hand in hand, joined up with the group watching on the sidelines.

"I think we're going to have to move The Stables portable bleachers here." Aunt Dru smiled at them.

"That would be cool!" Nora nodded excitedly as she stared at her dad and uncle. "I didn't know Uncle Grayson was back." She looked at Grace. He was bringing Buttercup back from the ranch. After the numerous accidents the horse had in the mountains, injuring Matt and almost Grace...twice, he was trying to get the horse to relax...or she wouldn't be able to be ridden in the mountains anymore.

Nora couldn't tell by the expression on Grace's face what the decision was.

"Grace?" Nora said quietly...just in case it was bad.

Grace turned and shrugged, "He said we would talk after we're done here."

Nora nodded...that didn't sound good.

"How does that thing work?" Reilly asked as he walked up next to Nora.

Nora leaned over and saw Aunt Leah standing on the other side of Grace. Sadie was with Uncle Grayson and Jack. They were working with the new wire contraption that had a black fake calf attached to it.

"The wire is stretched across the arena." Aunt Dru answered from behind Reilly. "When they start the machine the black calf will move back and forth, controlled by either Grayson or Jack. Scott could do it himself too, if he wants too, but this time he wants to concentrate on the horse. The black figure is the "dummy" that Little Ghost will focus on and try to "cut" back and forth."

"Like a remote control calf?" Reilly asked.

"Just like one," Aunt Dru chuckled.

"It's still weird to see him on Little Ghost," Nora said to her mom.

"Funny isn't it, since he's always on Monty who is grey too?" Her mom answered.

"Little Ghost has a blacker mane and tail," Nora told her. "He's not as broad as Monty is."

"It's the same...but different," Her mom nodded.

Nora nodded at her and reached out to take her hand. She was going to miss her mom. What was it going to be like not having her mom in the stands cheering her on?

Her dad trotted Little Ghost towards the line.

"You may want to hold on tight the first time I move it," Uncle Grayson warned him with a laugh.

He nodded with a grin. "I'm just going to walk him up to it and introduce them."

Which he did and Little Ghost's ears were high and twisting; his eyes alert to the figure. He sidestepped a few times then walked up within a foot, stretched his nose out and sniffed then snorted at it. Her dad turned and walked the horse away. He repeated it three more times before Little Ghost started ignoring the figure.

"Stop about 30 feet out and I'll move it a couple feet." Uncle Grayson called out.

Her dad moved the grey horse out and stopped, facing the figure.

"Here we go," Uncle Grayson warned.

As soon as the figure moved, Little Grey's body rose to full alert, head up, eye's staring, neck arched, ears pointed forward toward the movement. He didn't move.

"He looks like he just grew six inches taller," Aunt Dru whispered.

The calf moved a few feet to the left. Little Ghost watched it closely.

Back the other direction and the horse lifted a hoof and stomped the ground.

"Interesting," Reilly whispered. "I wonder what he just told the black calf."

"Get out of my arena!" Nora giggled softly.

The calf flipped around and moved the other direction…Little Ghost lowered his head and pawed at the ground.

The other way…Little Ghost went high on full alert and took a step forward.

As the calf moved the full length, Little Ghost slowly walked towards it. Nora wasn't sure if it was her dad moving the horse or if Little Ghost was walking towards it on his own.

She looked up at her dad; he was staring intently at the fake calf. His boots were deep in the stirrup. He held a rein in each hand, more of a training hold instead of a cutting hold. She had already started reading and watching videos to learn about cutting.

The horse continued forward as the calf moved the other direction.

It stopped in the middle and the horse stopped about ten feet away.

The fake calf quickly moved two feet to the left and the horse's front end jumped towards it and trotted to get ahead of it.

A grin spread across her dad's face.

The calf moved to the right and the horse lifted its front end again and jumped the other way and followed the figure until it stopped and headed the other way. The horse leaned back on his haunches and shifted his body to follow at a trot; his eyes and ears alert to the shadow.

They followed the same pattern for another five minutes then her dad turned and walked away about 20 feet then turned back. He held Little Ghost in place as the horse stared at the black calf. Once the horse relaxed, her dad nodded with a grin. He then turned and walked to the other end of the arena and trotted the horse in circles while the men removed the training system.

"Is that it?" Wade looked up at Aunt Dru.

"For the first time," She nodded. "Little Ghost is pretty young still and needs to get used to the movements. He's using tendons and muscle's that he's not used to working. We don't want to injure them."

Wade nodded and watched his dad trotting the horse in circles at the end.

"Dad looked like he really enjoyed it," Nora looked to her mom.

She grinned, her eyes sparkling, "That he did."

***

Reilly, Nora, Wade and Sadie waited on the back porch and stared at the barn where Uncle Grayson and Grace were discussing Buttercup.

"My guess is no more mountains." Wade's voice was just above a whisper.

Nora and Sadie nodded.

"But she's a really good roping horse in the arena." Reilly added.

"That's what matters…" Nora nodded. "She'll have Eli for the mountains."

"If Dad can't get her to be a mountain horse…then no one can." Sadie said just as her sister and dad appeared from the barn.

From the look on Grace's face and the comforting arm her dad had around her shoulders…the kids were right.

They all sighed but put on brave faces for Grace.

***

"Climb on up here," Her dad smiled at her from his seat in the combine.

Nora happily did what he said. Her old boots hit the green jagged edge of the ladder and she pulled herself up into the small seat next to him. She wore her old jeans and a blue checkered shirt that looked as close to her dad's as she could find. Her long black hair was pulled back into two low ponytails. Then she added the straw cowboy hat like his.

"You're looking like a little farmer's daughter today." He teased as he reached around her and pulled the door closed. His blue eyes shined with love and they crinkled a little on the sides.

"You're looking like a handsome farmer daddy today." Nora laughed and her insides warmed at the proud look on his face.

Her feet dangled in midair so he moved his small cooler so she could rest her feet on the top. Then he started pressing the screen on the small computer.

"What are you doing?" She asked.

"Making sure the calculations and settings for the field are set so we can track our progress today."

He started the machine and slowly moved down the road and onto the field they would be harvesting. The long header lowered and the machine started moving.

Nora quickly became mesmerized as she watched the fingers of the header reach out and grab the tall wheat only to be cut by the teeth near the ground. She had learned years before how the big machine worked but was always fascinated to watch it in action. The wheat was pulled into the auger and moved under them on a conveyer belt to a threshing drum which separated the grain from the rest of the wheat stem. The grain fell through a screen while the rest of the plant, called trash, was transported out the back of the machine. Air was blown at the grain to clean off any small bits of material remaining then the cleaned grain is dumped into a collection tank.

She turned to see the grain begin to pile in the tank. When it was full, a large pipe called an unloading auger would shoot it into a bank out wagon that was pulled by a tractor. The combine never stopped. The tractor would just pull up alongside of it and follow the combine until the grain was off loaded. The tractor pulled the grain filled wagon to a large semi-truck and emptied the grain into it. The big truck would then haul it to Tagger Enterprise's silos.

"Who's doing our off-loading?" Nora asked when she saw the tractor and trailer waiting for them. The large grain truck was down by the main road.

"Leah," He answered. "And Matt is driving the truck she will be loading into."

They slowly made it to the top of the small hill and the wide expanse of wheat fields came into view. Rolling hills of field after field after field of amber grain ready and waiting to be harvested. A deep blue sky over the fields stretched to the mountains in the far distance.

"It's just beautiful out here." Nora whispered.

"I agree." He said with a wistful tone.

Three other combines were moving across the fields. "Who's in those?"

"Nikki is driving the combine over there." He pointed to the field to the right. "Leah will be off-loading for her too." He pointed straight ahead of them. "Reilly is driving that one," He pointed to the left. "And Grayson is in that combine; Dru is off loading for them. Grace is driving truck. Jack and Jordan are also driving but they are with Jessup right now at the silos."

"Where are Wade and Sadie?"

"Wade's with Grayson and Sadie is in with Dru, learning the tractor."

"I can help drive next year," Nora turned to him with wide eyes. "And I learned that tractor with Aunt Dru last year. I can do more training this year."

He nodded with a grin. "We have lots of driving these fields over the next year…we'll get you ready. You can ride with Leah this afternoon and she'll work with you until your mom is ready to head home."

Nora nodded excitedly.

"With you, Wade, and Sadie getting old enough…we might just have to buy another combine." He grinned.

"That would be awesome." Nora laughed.

She leaned her head against his arm and watched the wheat being pulled into the header and listening to the hum of the machine. It was so peaceful.

"Isn't this one of the original fields?" Nora asked.

"It is," He smiled proudly. "This was part of the original farm that your great-great-grandfather plowed. We've never sold farm ground since he bought the place but when we had the opportunity, we would purchase more."

"But you're the only one that works this field."

He nodded with a deep sigh, "I rode on my grandfather's lap at times, depending on what he was doing; sometimes I rode with Dad. Wade has a couple pictures in his room of me on their laps riding with them. But when I finally got old enough to drive, this is the field I started on. I've worked it every fall since."

"Wade has pictures of him riding with you too; pictures for every year." Nora reminded him.

"There's pictures somewhere of you riding with me too when you were little." He grinned at her. "You just didn't have the patients to ride as long as Wade did. He still does; farming is in his blood like it was with me, Dad and his dad…and so on. Wade will be back from the rodeo on Sunday, then Monday morning he'll come back with me to work all week up here."

"How come I didn't get that?"

He shrugged a shoulder, "You got the love of the horse, like Grayson. He's got a special touch with them. Best horseman I've ever seen. You'll be the same, Nora Bug." He grinned down at her. "We can all see it in you, you and your horses. I'll do whatever it takes for you to go as far as you can with Isaiah and Arcturus."

Nora grinned proudly at him. The love in his eyes matched the love she had in her heart for him. She wrapped her arms around his and they continued down the field.

She was watching the grain pour out of the pipe from the combine into the unloading wagon when Cora's car appeared on the road behind it.

"Looks like lunch." Nora said to her dad.

"We'll head down once we're empty." He answered then lifted the header as Aunt Leah drove the tractor away and to the semi-truck.

They were the first to shut down next to all the unused equipment and trucks. Cora was pulling covered dishes out of coolers and placing them on a big table she had setup.

Nora opened the door and stood at the top of the combine's ladder. Her dad stepped out behind her; his hands came to rest on her shoulders.

"Do you hear that, Dad?" She whispered while watching the large green combines moving across the rolling amber hills with the blue sky backdrop.

"Yeah...one of the best sounds ever." He whispered back.

They stood and listened to the other machines working the fields; the chugging of the headers, the roar of the engines...the harvest hum.

CHAPTER FIVE

Nora laid all her show clothes on the bed and her boots across the floor in front of them. Two days of showing…she should take four outfits…just in case.

A half hour later she finally chose the perfect four; pink, deep purple, red, and a dark blue one with white trim. They were all covered with rhinestones making her bed sparkle. She absolutely loved the show shirts and could spend hours on the computer shopping for new ones.

Her attention turned to the matching cowboy hats. On the ground she wore a cowboy hat, she chose the black one…it matched all the shirts. On the horse she wore a riding helmet; she put both hats in their carriers. She wanted one for the rodeo…so she grabbed the straw hat too. Three hat carriers…she giggled to herself.

Next came the outfits for the rodeo…or bull bash…whatever it was that Nick was working. She placed two short sleeve western shirts on the bed…then grabbed a third…just in case.

Then there was all the hair stuff. Nick would be useless for help, so she would have to style her own hair. She brought lots of clips then a couple more…just in case.

All her clothes, hats, boots, and hair stuff were picked out and she waited for her mom to come in and help pack so the shirts wouldn't get wrinkled. She didn't like ironing and she didn't think Nick would be helpful in that either.

What to do when she was bored…because Nick didn't talk. She pulled a couple of books from her shelf and placed them next to the pile of clothes.

Nora looked at her bed, it was covered.

"You're only gone for three days." Her mother teased her from the doorway.

Nora grinned at her. "But I have to make sure…just in case."

"Are you excited?" Her mom asked.

Nora nodded. "Yes, I found out Candace Avery is going to be there, too."

"I didn't think you liked Candace."

Nora shrugged. "Yeah, she wasn't very nice to me last time…" She frowned. "I usually just try to do better than I did the show before…but this time I want to beat her."

Her mom smiled and shook her head. "Well, I guess that's one reason to want to win."

Nora giggled. "I want to beat HER, doesn't mean I have to win."

"Nora, Darling, you're a treasure," She laughed and looked again at the bed. "That's a lot of stuff."

"Yep, but you never know." Nora nodded.

"Just in case…" Her mom teased. "Well, it's a good thing Nick has a big truck. You're still OK with going with him?"

"Yeah, Reilly said I would have fun at the bull thing at night and I have lots of books to read going there and back."

"I know sometimes, it can be scary going on an adventure with someone new."

"He's not new, Mom. Just quiet."

"He'll make sure you're taken care of." Her mom assured her and picked up the garment bag for the dress shirts. "Did you have fun with your dad today?"

"Always," Nora handed her the shirts. "I like farming with Dad and it's so beautiful there."

"He loves having you there, too."

*****

Nora stood at her bedroom window looking out towards the road. Nick should be there any minute. It was six o'clock in the morning and all of her luggage was downstairs. She didn't see him the night before; he had taken Matt and Nikki out to dinner before her cousins drove to the ranch for harvest. Nick was staying at their house by The Stables for the night.

She was still nervous, but before they left for the ranch Reilly, Grace, and Matt all assured her that she would have a good time.

"Sadie, Mom said to get up." Nora said for the fourth time. She could see a black truck coming down the road.

"I will."

"You're leaving in 30 minutes. You can sleep when you get in the truck," The blinker turned on, it had to be Nick.

"Don't tell me what to do, Nora."

"That wasn't telling you what to do, that was telling you what you COULD do."

"Same thing."

"It isn't either," Nora turned from the window. "Nick's here, I'm leaving. You could at least appreciate the fact that MY mom is taking you instead of me. So get UP."

"You're just jealous again."

"You always say that, Sadie." Nora felt the little twinge that said she was a little jealous. "She's going with you because of Wade."

Sadie sat up in bed and looked at her; her blue eyes looking hurt. "So you don't think she would take me if Wade wasn't there?"

Nora sighed because she didn't really know the answer, which made her sad and mad at the same time, so she walked out of the room without answering.

When she reached the kitchen her mother and Wade were there.

Her mom embraced her but Sadie's question really bothered her, so she only half hugged back.

"What's the matter?" Her mom frowned at her. "Are you changing your mind about riding with Nick?"

Nora just shook her head sadly and picked up the hat boxes to carry out to Nick's truck.

He was just stepping out of his tall truck when Nora walked down the deck steps. He was dressed in a tan short sleeve western shirt, jeans, and a straw cowboy hat. His dark hair was just long enough to touch his shirt collar. Sometimes it surprised her how much he looked like Matt; both were quite handsome. Nora decided that he could have joined her dad and Uncle Grayson as western movie stars.

"Good morning, Nora," He smiled, his brownish green eyes were soft.

"Good morning," She answered politely. Now that she saw him, her stomach did cartwheels, she was more nervous than she thought.

"Do you have more bags for the weekend?" He opened the back door of his truck for her and took the hat cases.

She giggled nervously, "Lots, these are just my hats and helmet."

"Well, it's a big truck so we can fit whatever you need."

He followed her back into the house, but her mom wasn't there.

Nick and Wade exchanged greetings and Nick wished Wade good luck on his roping.

When he saw the big suitcase, the little suitcase, the garment bag, and her two boot bags he turned back to her with a smile. "You weren't kidding."

Nora just shook her head and smiled while grabbing the boot bag to carry out. He picked up everything else and they headed for the door.

"I'll back up to the horse trailer," He told her after placing the luggage in the truck's back seat.

"I'll go get the horses," She said and walked toward the barn. All of her show tack and gear was already loaded into the horse trailer. In the front of the trailer was living quarters with two beds, a shower, and a restroom so they could stay at the show.

She walked Libby out of the barn and handed Nick the lead rope, then turned to get Isaiah. Arcturus leaned his head out of the stall, waiting for attention, or his halter too so he could go.

Nora glanced over at her black horse as she hurried to get Isaiah. A twinge of guilt and remorse ran through her. She couldn't wait for the days she would be haltering him for shows too.

As she handed Nick the lead rope, she heard a whinny echo from the barn…and then another. She turned her head back to the barn and sighed…she should have taken the time to go see him this morning before she left so she could say good bye.

When they walked back to the house and through the door, there was another whinny, and another look back.

Her mom was waiting for them.

Sadie and Wade were eating at the small kitchen table.

Nora walked up and gave her brother a big hug but ignored Sadie. "Good luck, have Mom send me pictures of you and Dollar."

"I will," Wade answered and looked between her and Sadie, concluding that they weren't getting along again.

Sadie was glaring at her so Nora turned away just in time to see a shock looked on Nick's face.

"I don't want that!" He took a step back away from her mother, who was holding an envelope.

Nora's heart started racing. Was he changing his mind?

Her mother laughed, "You have to take it."

"No, I don't."

Nora froze, he WAS changing his mind.

"If something happens, you need this medical release to get her help." Her mom's tone changed from laughter to concern.

Nick stared at her mom with a frown then looked over at Nora. He must have noticed how upset she was because his expression changed from shock and horror to helplessness.

"I will only be a phone call away at all times," Her mom continued. "If she needs help, I will tell you what to tell them, but you'll have to sign the paperwork."

Nick shifted from one foot to the other, like a trapped little kid.

"None of the kids have gotten hurt this summer and we've done a lot of shows." Her mother still held the paperwork out to him.

Nick looked at the paperwork then at Nora. She was still frozen, waiting…her eyes wide in alarm.

Slowly, his hand reached out for the envelope. Nora breathed a sigh of relief.

"It's OK, Nick," Her mom smiled. "She'll be just fine."

Nora didn't know what to say, she was afraid if she said anything he'd bolt for the door and leave her behind.

"Nora," Her mom walked up to her. "Do you have everything?"

Nora nodded nervously as her mother hugged her again.

"We're going to load up and go as soon as you're down the driveway," She continued as Nora stared at Nick…who was staring at the envelope. "Here's some money in case you need anything."

Nick's head shot back up to her mother. "I can handle anything she needs."

Her mom chuckled, "Except for medical help?"

A smile slowly crossed his face.

That was all Nora needed to hug her quickly and head for the door. She wanted out before he changed his mind.

Nick was right behind her as she nearly ran for the truck, but she was staring at the barn.

"Go ahead," He said from behind her.

Nora stopped and looked up at him. He was smiling down at her. "What?"

"Go ahead and say good bye," He motioned to the barn.

She quickly ran to Arcturus…she needed her energy source.

***

"Are you hungry?" Nick asked as he turned out of the driveway and onto the main road.

"Yes, I didn't eat." Nora looked at him nervously.

"Let's swing into town and pick something up. What's your favorite breakfast place?"

As soon as she told him, his cell phone rang. He answered it and she listened to him talk to someone about bulls until they got into Lewiston and pulled into the fast food restaurant.

"Just a second," He said into the phone as he pulled out money from his pocket. He handed her a twenty dollar bill. "Coffee for me and anything else you think I might like."

"I don't know what you like." Nora frowned at him as she opened the truck door.

"I'm not really that picky as long as it's edible." Nick smiled.

Nora nodded and shut the door. The horse trailer wouldn't fit into a drive-in so he had parked off to the side.

She had two bags of food and drink carrier as she walked across the parking lot. She had spent all twenty dollars.

Nick jumped out of the truck, took the food and drink carrier and opened her door. He was still on the phone.

"That's a lot of food," He whispered to her with raised brows.

Nora nodded. "I didn't know how hungry you were."

"Good thing I didn't give you a fifty," He chuckled then closed her door and started talking on the phone again.

Nora smiled at his joke. If he stayed on the phone the whole time, she wouldn't have to worry about what to say to him.

Then he hung up the phone.

CHAPTER SIX

"So, here we are…" He said as they drove over the big blue bridge that indicated they moved from Lewiston to Clarkston. Just a few more minutes they would be out of Clarkston and would drive along the river before making their way up a long steep grade; she knew this route by heart.

"Yep," She nodded nervously.

"I've never hung out with a kid before, so you'll have to help with the conversation."

She turned at looked at him in surprise, "Never?"

"Other than Adam and Amy in the mountains? A four day old baby…for two days. That's it."

"Who was the baby?"

"Nikki."

"That's all the time you spent with her?" Nora was shocked and her tone was a bit judgmental.

Nick glanced down at her then back out the window. "Well, this conversation went downhill fast. It's going to be a long weekend."

Nora looked out the side window of the truck at the stores passing by. She had to agree. Maybe it wasn't too late to call Mom and go with them.

"Having second thoughts?" He asked.

She looked up at him. How did he know?

"I would be if I were you," he smiled.

"Are you having second thoughts?" She asked nervously.

"Yes, but for your sake not mine."

"Why?"

"Because I'm the adult and I can do what I want to do or not do…you pretty much don't have a choice," he chuckled.

"Well, that's something."

"What?"

"You told me the truth."

"What was I supposed to do?"

"No adult, I know, would have said that to me."

"Not even your parents?"

"No, they would have tried to make it sound nicer than that."

"Well," He glanced back down at her. "I guess that's where we start this weekend."

"Where?"

"By telling the honest truth, I won't say things to make it sound nicer and you don't say things to make it sound nicer."

She stared out the window trying to decide if he was calling her a liar. He didn't word it that way…maybe that's what he did, just worded things different to make it sound better…that was confusing. He was honest about only spending two days with Nikki…

She sighed, confused, they hadn't even made it out of town yet and she was already wanting to be home…this was going to be a long weekend.

"What's up?" He asked.

"Buttercup," She said automatically then looked up quickly at him.

He chuckled.

She shrugged and smiled.

"Do you think of Grace every time you say it?" He asked.

"Yep, her laughing and Buttercup prancing."

He was quiet then smiled. "You're right. They do make a great pair."

"Buttercup prancing is like her laughing. Grace's laugh always makes you want to smile."

He nodded, "It's good to have someone like that in your life."

Nora smiled, it was cool he said that. She looked out the window and saw the river; at least they made it out of town.

"So why did you go quiet?"

"Truth?" She looked up at him nervously.

"That's what I suggested. I don't think we should start this friendship with anything but the truth."

This time, she stared at him.

"What?" He asked with a nervous voice.

"You said a friendship."

"Yeah, is that a bad thing?"

"I've never heard of a kid and an adult having a friendship."

"What do they have? I'm new at this so I don't know."

She could tell he was telling her the truth.

"Usually dads, uncles, cousins…stuff like that."

"Well, we're not related, so none of those work." He glanced at her. "I'm your aunt's ex-husband…so…what are we supposed to have besides a friendship?"

"Well, you are my cousin's dad…" She reminded him. "So that could be like an uncle."

He frowned in thought, "If we had to explain this to someone else this weekend we can say I'm your ex-uncle…less confusion for them."

"OK."

"But between us, I'm not your uncle, so I think a friendship would be the only thing we can go with."

Nora couldn't think of anything else either. "OK, a friendship." She agreed.

"So, no sugar coating, always the plain truth."

Nora turned again to look out the window...there it was again...just when she thought it was all going good...was he calling her a liar or not? They were part way up the long steep grade.

"Nora."

She turned and looked up at him.

"What?" He asked. "Why do you keep doing that?"

She didn't know how to answer so she didn't say anything.

He sighed heavily. "No sugar coating it Nora, just say it. That's what this is all about."

Nora didn't know what to do, she had to say something or it would be a REALLY long weekend. Finally she turned to him and, like her Aunt Dru always says...she spit it out...

"I don't know if you're calling me a liar or not."

He stared straight ahead, without saying a word. A few minutes later, she heard the blinker turn on and he started slowing down. She looked ahead of them and saw they were approaching the top of the long grade and the rest stop at the top.

They weren't that far away from home. She sat back in the seat and turned away from him again. He must have decided to take her back. She was surprised when she felt tears sting the back of her eyes. Squeezing them as tight as she could, she tried to make them go away.

The truck came to a stop, but he didn't get out.

"What are you doing?" He asked her since he couldn't see her face.

"Trying to stop crying." She answered honestly.

"Why are you crying?!" His voice sounded scared and she had to turn and look. His expression was even scared. He took one look at her and the tears in her eyes, and he opened the door and got out of the truck.

She watched as he took a couple steps towards the horse trailer then stopped. He leaned his back on the truck.

Now she really didn't know what to do. The tears started falling, but she quickly wiped them away just in case he looked at her again. Then a nervous giggle escaped when she realized he couldn't even look at her because of the tears. She looked back at him. He was just standing there.

When he got out of the truck, he didn't shut the door, so he would be able to hear her if she spoke. But, what was she supposed to say?

"Nick?" She finally got the nerve to speak.

"Did you stop crying?"

She giggled nervously again. "Yes."

He walked back up to the door and looked across the seat at her. "Why did you cry?"

"I don't want to go back home."

"Why are you going back home?" He looked confused.

"I thought you stopped to take me back home."

"You're with me for the weekend, kid. I promised I would take you to your horse show and that's what I'm going to do." He was looking directly into her eyes. "But if you keep crying...it's going to take us a long time to get there." He tried to smile through very tense facial muscles.

Nora smiled back at him which made his face relax.

"Why did you stop?" She asked.

"So we could talk; eye to eye. Why did you think I was calling you a liar?" His hands were on his hips and he was staring right at her...it made her a bit nervous. "Have you ever lied to me?"

She quickly shook her head no.

"They why would you think I'd call you a liar?"

"Because of the way you said we would only tell the truth."

"I said I won't say things to make it sound nicer, I'd just tell you the truth, straight out and you promise the same thing to me." His head tipped to the side. "How is that calling you a liar?"

"I've never heard it that way...I got confused." Her shoulders slumped. "Other people said I lied to them...but I didn't. If I don't want to tell the truth...then I just don't say anything."

"A lot of people do that Nora, even adults. It doesn't make you a liar."

Her jaw dropped in surprise. He just defended her...didn't he?

"You've never lied to me, I've never had the feeling you did, and you told me you didn't."

"I haven't lied to anyone."

"Then you're not a liar," He declared. "And from now on we tell each other the flat out truth."

"OK, deal." She said quickly.

"We have a friendship now?" He asked.

"Yes." She smiled, which created a slight smile on his face.

"You're not going to cry anymore?"

She hesitated, "I can't promise that, sometimes I can't control it."

"And that's the truth, with no sugar coating it for me." He grinned at her across the truck seat.

Nora grinned back. She understood now.

"Well, we better get back on the road. We'll never get there at this pace." He stepped back into the truck then pulled back down the road.

"So, now what do we talk about?" He smiled at her, the tension of the last few minutes gone.

Nora laughed. It was a relaxing laugh she decided. There wasn't any stress with him now. She felt like she could talk to him about anything and he wouldn't judge her.

"Wow," He smiled. "I sure like that laugh better than those scary tears."

And she laughed even harder.

She told him about her school and how excited she was for it to start back up the next week. He seemed interested and asked her lots of questions. Most adults didn't do that.

"When you were a kid…what did you do during the summer?" She asked.

"I spent a lot of time at the library."

Nora looked at him in surprise, "Really?"

He nodded with a grin, "It was free and air conditioned."

Nora nodded with an understanding smile.

"I still read a lot," He continued. "I have a room in Australia that must have hundreds of books in it."

"What do you read about?"

"When I was younger, and in school, I read adventure stories…anything to escape my life. Then, when I was on the road I switched to detective books…I like trying to figure out the mystery before the end of the book. Then, I switched to books about business…then psychology…then psychology in business."

"That sounds boring." She chuckled.

He laughed, "Sometimes it is…other times it's interesting to learn about real stories…what worked right in a business and what went wrong if the business failed."

"That sounds like Nikki," Nora tilted her head to him. "She likes business stuff like that too."

A smile spread across his face as he looked out the front window of the truck to the road. That must have pleased him.

***

They stopped a couple of times and let the horses out.

"I've been thinking," He had just closed the latch on the back gate of the horse trailer.

"It's always good to do that now and then," She teased and looked at him to see if he was going to get mad or think it was funny. Much to her delight, he laughed.

As they pulled back onto the road, with only two hours left to drive, he said; "I think it would be best if we left the trailer at the horse show but stayed in a hotel closer to the bull bash."

"Really?" That sounded like fun.

He nodded and smiled at her enthusiasm, "We won't get done until late both nights and there is a hotel close by the rodeo grounds. I'll get two hotel rooms with connecting doors so we each have our own room."

"I can get ready for the show better in my own hotel room instead of the bathroom in the horse trailer." She agreed.

He handed her his cell phone. "Call your mother and get her approval. Let her know I will be paying for both rooms."

Nora did as he asked and her mother said yes. She agreed they would be happier in two rooms instead of one trailer.

Her own hotel room! That was awesome. Nora sat back in the seat and watched the scenery go by again. Maybe the weekend wasn't going to be that bad after all.

CHAPTER SEVEN

"You what?" Nick asked her with a frown.

"I asked Reilly if I was pretty."

"Why would you do that...you're not supposed to be pretty..."

Nora looked at him in confusion. "What am I supposed to be?"

"Ten." He answered firmly.

"Ten?"

"You're ten...you're supposed to be ten...not pretty."

"I'm not ten," She said tartly. "Sadie is ten...I'm twelve."

He looked at her in frustration.

"So," She tilted her head and looked up at him. "Can I be pretty and twelve?"

He shook his head, "No...just be twelve..."

She giggled...knowing he was flustered.

"So...what did he say?" Nick finally asked.

She sighed remembering Reilly's words and looked up at her weekend guardian. "He said that I didn't need to work on the outside...I need to work on the inside."

Nick looked at her with eyes wide, "He actually said that to you?"

Nora nodded. "I told him to be honest...like he is with Grace."

"He says rude things like that to Grace, too?"

"Is it rude if it's true? Isn't that what we talked about before? Not sugar coating the truth?" She asked...really wanting to know if he felt the same way Reilly did.

Nick glanced down at her; he seemed to understand what she was asking.

"Do you think it's true?" He asked.

Nora stared out the window watching the scenery go by. Finally; she answered. "I am a good person, Nick."

"I have no doubt about that." He answered without hesitation; that made her feel better.

"Then why would you ask me if I thought it was true?" She looked back over at him.

It was his turn to stare out the front window as he drove. "Well," He started. "I haven't really seen a lot of things…but, I did hear of one thing that made me wonder."

"What?" She looked at him; an uneasy feeling run through her.

He hesitated, glancing down at her quickly then back to the road. "Milo."

He didn't have to say anything else; she knew what he was talking about. The whole terrible day haunted her. She sadly remembered the look of shock and horror on Sadie's face when Nora had inadvertently given away her first horse, Milo, to Andy's grandson.

It had shocked Nora…she didn't realize right away what she had done but when she looked up at Andy and her parents…and the look on their faces…she began to understand what she did. Then, Uncle Grayson and Aunt Leah made her feel better when they thought it was a great idea…until they looked at their daughter…then it was all bad. She had worked hard to keep the perfect smile on her face to hide her own horror.

No one was happy about it, but they didn't realize how awful Nora had felt about it, they were too concerned with Sadie at the time.

"You going to talk?" He asked her.

"I don't know what to say…" She admitted.

"Did you do it to be mean?" His tone was low but not accusing.

She felt the tears sting the back of her eyes. It hurt that he thought that of her, so she didn't answer him.

"I can't know the truth, if you don't explain it to me," He told her.

She realized how true the statement was…no one had really asked her how she felt about what happened, not even her parents.

She looked up at him. "I told Mom and Dad that I watched Sadie play with Andy's grandson and Milo all day. Sadie was too big for Milo and the only person shorter was Wade."

"He had his own pony."

Nora nodded. "I was excited about telling everyone that I came up with the idea for Milo going to Andy's son. I thought it was a really good idea."

"So you wanted to be the hero?"

Nora looked at him in surprise. She hadn't thought of it that way but it did make sense. "Yeah, I guess so."

"But, you didn't realize that you were going to hurt Sadie by trying to be the hero yourself."

He did understand! She turned as much as she could in her seat to look at him. "I hadn't even thought about her before I said it…until I saw the look on her face…and Andy's…then Mom and Dad's."

"Then how did you feel?" His tone was normal conversation…not accusing or judging her.

"I felt horrible! I remember when I had to give up my first horse…I cried every time I saw him…for months!" She shook her head. "I didn't mean to hurt Sadie."

"Did being the person to come up with the idea make up for hurting Sadie?" He asked.

Nora stared at him. She had never thought of it that way. Geez, he was good. She turned and looked out the front window. At no time, did she think of herself as a hero once it happened…in fact she thought of herself as the villain…like everyone else did. Sadie had finally blown up and yelled at her in the horse meeting, which made her mad at Sadie so Nora had fought for Scarecrow even though she actually wanted Arcturus.

Nora loved Arcturus, adored Arcturus…she remembered the first time she had seen him in the stalls at Cora's property. She had been so worried about touching him and hurting him. Aunt Dru had encouraged her to touch him and give him love. And Nora had…from the first time she had touched the star on his head to the moment she said goodbye to him earlier. Every moment she could, she loved the horse and told him.

"Earth to Nora…"

She turned her eyes to him and giggled at him.

"Where did you go?" He asked her.

"To Arcturus." She said truthfully.

"How did you get there?" He looked at her confused.

She told him the truth.

"So you really didn't want Scarecrow?" He asked surprised.

"I want all horses," she smiled. "But, she belonged to Sadie…even before Mom gave Scarecrow to her."

"Then why didn't you just suggest it yourself?"

"Because I want all horses…" She repeated with a smile.

"Didn't you think you could have been the hero in giving Scarecrow to Sadie before someone else did?"

She shook her head. "I hadn't thought of that."

"So, always being the hero isn't what is most important to you." He concluded.

"No, I guess not." She agreed hesitantly. "But I don't know what is." She added honestly.

"If you had it to do over again, how would you change what happened with Milo?"

"I would have waited and talked to Mom and Dad before I said anything in front of Andy's grandson." She answered quickly. "I tried to make it up to her by having her help me name Isaiah...I named Scarecrow so I thought it would be fair...I thought she would like that...but it didn't seem to help at first." Nora sighed, remembering back to the look on Sadie's face as she lay in her bed. "She did finally help me choose though."

They were quiet for a few minutes before Nick glanced at her and spoke. "Then I agree with you."

She looked at him in confusion.

"You are a good person, Nora Tagger." He smiled.

Nora smiled back. That made her feel good... then she frowned. "I think you're the only one that agrees with me."

He surprised her by laughing and shaking his head.

"What's so funny?"

"Do you think that all those people that live in that huge house with you, would love you and care about you if they didn't think you were a good person?"

Nora didn't answer him; she just thought of all the people in the house.

"Do you think, I would agree to take you for a whole weekend...?" He glanced at her again with a serious look. "Me? Of all people...who doesn't like kids...would agree to take you for a road trip and horse show if I didn't think you were a good person?"

She looked at him in surprise. "You don't like kids?" She asked in shock.

He hesitated before he spoke. "Not that I don't like them…I'm just not used to being around them…you guys scare me."

"We're just kids…how can we scare you?" She giggled.

"Because you're kids!" He chuckled back at her. "But, back to the question…"

She shook her head. "I guess not," She remembered what Reilly had told her. "How do I work on the inside?"

"You hungry?" He asked.

"What?" She asked in surprise.

"Are you hungry?" He repeated.

"That's not what I meant by working on the inside." She frowned.

He started laughing again.

"What's so funny this time?"

"That's not why I asked if you were hungry," He continued to laugh. "One of my favorite restaurants is up ahead and I'm hungry…so I wanted to know if you were hungry."

Nora laughed with him; that was funny.

He pulled into the parking lot and parked off to the side where the truck and trailer could be seen from inside the restaurant.

As he stepped out and she slid out, she heard him say her name. "Nora."

She looked up.

"You don't have to work on the inside; it's good." He looked at her seriously. "You just have to think before you speak, so what you're trying to say is taken the right way."

She smiled at him across the seat of the truck.

"And…" He said as he started to close the door. "Just be twelve."

"Well, at least you finally got the age right." She teased as they closed the doors.

CHAPTER EIGHT

"Wow," Nick muttered as he pulled into the parking area behind the horse park.

"What?" Nora looked around at the horse grounds and thought it looked the same as the one from last week.

"For some reason, I wasn't expecting this many trailers, horses, and people." He pulled up next to a parking attendant. The lady smiled at him. A little too big.

The lady stepped right up to the truck and nearly leaned into the window to hand Nick the map of the grounds. She pointed on the paper, then pointed in the direction of their reserved parking area. He smiled politely at her. The lady placed a hand on his arm and told him to let her know if he has any problems finding the space; she would be more than happy to show him personally.

Nick thanked her with a nod and a smile that made the woman giggle as they pulled away.

Nora stared up at him.

"What?" He smiled in false innocence.

"Do women do that to you all the time?" She smiled innocently. He chuckled, "Now and then…yeah."

"Do you ever take them up on their offer to help?" Nora gave him a concerned looked but was giggling inside.

Nick shook his head and glanced down at her in obvious discomfort, "You're really asking me that question?"

She started laughing, and then laughed even harder when she saw the look of relief and exasperation on his face.

"Nora, Nora, Nora…" He shook his head while looking out the window trying to find their parking space.

"Want me to go back and tell her you need help?" Nora giggled.

He glanced down at her again with an amused look, "No."

"But she said she would be happy to help." She couldn't stop giggling.

"It's right there, funny girl." He chuckled and pointed.

Nora turned and looked at their spot. It was one of the closest ones to the horse stalls and arena. That was always good.

"We'll get the horses unloaded and taken care of then back the trailer into the space. That way we can come and go easily." Nick told her.

They passed their space and drove back towards the stalls and parked.

Nick was opening the back of the horse trailer when they heard a horse approaching them. It was sorrel horse being led by a girl Nora's age. She glanced at Nora then looked away. But the mom was staring and smiling at Nick. He nodded then turned back to the horse trailer.

Nora grinned up at him.

"Not a word, Young Lady," He smiled down at her then stepped into the horse trailer.

"I'll take Libby; she's easier to walk with out here." Nora smiled. "If you will take Isaiah please, he's always excited when we first get to new places."

"That sounds like a good plan." He turned Isaiah and walked him out of the horse trailer.

Nora stepped out of the way and noticed the people around them stop and look at the horse.

Isaiah was magnificent and always drew a crowd when he stepped out of the trailer. His head was held high; eyes and ears alert to the people and horses around him. The dark red horse pranced a little left then a little right. When he stopped, his hoof placement was perfect under him.

Nora just shook her head and sighed. The horse's natural ability was years ahead of her experience.

"What's the matter?" Nick looked down at her.

"Nothing," She muttered and stepped into the trailer to get Libby.

After the horses were groomed and settled in their stalls, they walked around the equine park.

Nora pointed out some of the horses that she had competed against that summer. She noticed he wasn't walking as fast as usual. Considering he was a lot taller than her, it allowed her to walk casually beside him. It was thoughtful of him.

They slowly made their way back to his truck. It was about time to head to the rodeo grounds for the Bull Bash.

"What are you going to do while I'm showing?" Nora asked.

"What?" He asked in surprise.

"What are you going to do while I'm showing?" She repeated, confused.

He stopped and looked down at her, "I'm going to be sitting in those stands over there, not too close to the other parents, to cheer you on...quietly."

Nora's eyes opened in surprise, "Really?"

"What did you expect me to do?" He looked amused.

She shrugged. "I don't know, I really hadn't thought about it until just now."

He chuckled and they started walking again, only to be stopped by a line of horses walking to the stalls.

"That one looks like my first horse," Nora pointed to a black and white pony walking by. She looked up at Nick. "What was your first horse?"

Nick shook his head. "I've never had one."

Nora was stunned, "What? Never?"

He smiled at her surprise and shook his head. "I was a bull rider. First, I couldn't afford one, and then I didn't need one. I always used one from the ranch I worked on."

They finally arrived at the truck and drove back to their parking space.

"Never?" Nora asked again.

"Never," He chuckled. "I didn't ride a horse until I met Dru. She made me ride her barrel horse a couple times."

"You got to ride Jet?" Nora was impressed and jealous.

"Nice horse; scared me a bit to start."

Nora couldn't believe it. He'd never owned a horse, yet he got to ride Jet.

"What's that look for?" He chuckled as he was unhooking the trailer.

"I'm shocked and jealous at the same time."

"We'll let that soak in while we get in the truck and slowly make it out of here." He chuckled again and opened the door for her.

As he walked around the front of the truck a woman stopped him.

Nora watched as the woman smiled up at him, touched his arm, and laughed at something he said. He didn't seem to be as amused. Nick pointed in the direction of the stalls and she nodded. One more touch of Nick's arm and she walked away with a little wave.

Nick walked to the side of the truck, but hesitated at the door while looking at the ground. He slowly lifted his gaze so he was looking through the window at Nora. Then he shook his head at her grin.

Finally opening the door, he spoke before she had a chance. "No comments, Young Lady, she just needed directions to the stalls."

Nora laughed.

"What's so funny?"

"She was here last year!"

***

Nora looked up at the hotel as they drove into the parking lot. This was so exciting! They had stayed at hotels before but none this fancy. And she was going to have her own room!

She opened the truck door, slid down to the ground, and walked around to meet Nick to get the bags. He gave her the small rolling bag and carried the rest; one medium bag for him and all of her bags.

"How can such a little girl have so much luggage for two days?" He shook his head.

"Show clothes and non-show clothes for the bull thing, plus my boots, show hats and helmets." She explained as they walked to the hotel doors.

There was a man in a red uniform that opened the door for them. "Welcome to our hotel, Madam." He said and bowed to her, Nora looked at him in delighted surprise.

The man pulled a big gold cart over to them and Nick set the bags on the bottom. He added Nora's to the top and the man pushed the cart over to the desk where Nick was headed.

She was excited but nervous and desperately wanted to grab Nick's hand for support, but wasn't sure how he would react.

As Nick talked to the man behind the counter, Nora looked around the big hotel. It was a big open lobby and on the other side were a coffee shop and a gift store. She really wanted to see in the store!

A wide hallway led to the back of the hotel and four elevator doors. Riding up elevators, too!

The man in the red uniform was standing next to them, he smiled politely at her. She turned back to Nick, really wanting to grab his hand to help calm her nerves.

"Are you ready, Nora?" Nick was looking down at her.

"Yes!" She said a little too loudly which made them both chuckle.

They walked towards the elevators.

"Can I push the buttons?" She ran ahead of him and pushed the top button.

When the doors opened, she jumped in followed by the man with the cart and Nick.

"What number?" She said excitedly, her hand hovering over all the numbers.

"Four." Nick smiled.

Nora pushed the button then stepped back next to him and she looked up at the man in the red uniform. He smiled at her again which made her step a little closer to Nick. Every fiber in her wanted to grab his hand! Then, to her surprise, Nick slowly moved his arm up and across her back, one hand rested on her shoulder. It was a protective move that her dad did a lot...she felt instantly safer.

The elevator doors opened and she ran out quickly and turned to look up to her companion. "What number?"

Nick pointed to the left. "Four twenty-one and three," He said which sent her running down the hallway. She found the numbers and started jumping excitedly; like Wade and Reilly did.

"Which one's mine?" She asked eagerly.

"You can choose the one you want." Nick answered and unlocked the door to the first one then, as she pushed through the door, he opened the other.

"There is a door in between, open it up." He instructed.

Nora was looking around the big room, the huge bed, couch, a small chair, and a huge TV. She turned back and saw the bathroom door next to the door she had entered. This was the biggest hotel room she had ever been in!

She heard a knocking next to her and looked at the door. She forgot he said to open it.

"Open the door, Nora," She heard Nick on the other side.

When the door opened, he was smiling at her.

"This is awesome!" She started jumping again as she made her way into the second room. It looked identical to the first room. The luggage was in the room but the man in the red uniform was gone.

"He scared you?" Nick asked as he walked to the luggage and picked hers up off the floor. "Which room do you want?"

"This one," She said, and turned back into the first room.

"They're identical, why this one?"

"Because it was the first one I walked in to."

Nick put her luggage on the couch and walked back to the dividing doors. He leaned against the door jam and watched her as she looked out the huge windows at all the lights of town. They twinkled like multi-colored stars. And that made her think of Arcturus, and she sighed.

"Wow," Nick said. "That was a huge change of mood."

"The lights made me think of stars…that made me think of Arcturus." She explained.

"Miss him already?"

Nora nodded.

"Well, let's go over to the arena and let you think of something else."

"Can I change first?" She asked; she couldn't wait to get there.

"What's wrong with what you have on?"

"These are traveling clothes; I want to wear my rodeo clothes tonight."

Nick shrugged, "No wonder why you have so much luggage," He walked over to her door to the hallway and attached the chain lock and twisted the lock on the door. "Don't unlock them; you leave with me in and out the other door." He turned to make sure she heard him.

"OK."

"I'll leave the door open on my side so when you're ready just open your door." He said and she nodded. "You have fifteen minutes; then we need to head out."

"Do we have time to stop at that little store in the lobby?" She asked hopefully.

"Yeah...I guess so." He chuckled.

"Thanks, Nick!" She said excitedly as he shut the door.

CHAPTER NINE

There were too many people, Nora thought, as she walked as close behind Nick as she could. Glancing up at his back she figured he had forgotten she was there. Another group of people walked by and her heart raced as one of them bumped into her which made her fall farther behind him.

"Nick!" She yelled but was sure he didn't hear her over the crowd. He was at least three people deep ahead of her.

She looked up trying to see where they were. Her mom had always told them that if they got lost to go to the last place she had seen them and wait. There was a beer sign and a Ford truck sign. She let out a nervous giggle when she realized that both signs were all over the rodeo grounds.

She could see the back of his head still; it was a good thing he wore a dark brown cowboy hat instead of the straw or black hats that were everywhere.

"Nick!" She yelled hopelessly again.

Another group of people walked by her and pushed her even farther back away from him. She froze because she couldn't see him. Fear rose in her; she was shorter than everyone around her. She turned and looked for something to hold onto so the crowd didn't push her back even further.

A round of laughter erupted next to her and she had to jump back to keep a glass of beer from landing on her.

"Nora!" She heard his voice yell out for her.

She jumped in the air twice before they saw each other. His expression changed from fear to exasperation. He quickly made his way back to her.

"What happened?" He yelled over a burst of laughter from behind them.

"I tried to keep up with you but everyone kept bumping into me." She yelled trying to smile and hide her fear.

Nick stared at her for a minute then he reached out for her hand. She looked at him in surprise.

"My nerves can't take losing you out here," He said curtly. "It's the only way to make sure you don't disappear."

She smiled sympathetically, knowing how difficult it was for him, and reached up to grab his hand.

Nick turned without another word and pulled her behind him. She was glad the crowds were thick and he couldn't move so fast that she had to run to keep up.

She saw a group of people coming; knowing they were going to bump into her she squeezed his hand tighter. He did the same and squished her fingers but she wasn't going to complain.

He turned off the main path towards a door that said "approved personnel only." She hoped that was them. He opened the door and pulled her through in front of him then stopped.

To her left, down a long ally she saw the rodeo arena. To her right, only ten feet away was a HUGE black bull and it was staring at her. Nora nearly climbed up Nick's side to get away from it when she finally saw the black tube fencing between them. She stopped and slowly looked up at Nick; her face heating up from embarrassment. He was grinning down at her.

"Sorry," She said loudly.

"It's OK," He smiled, "I should have warned you."

Still holding her hand, he walked back towards the bull. She stepped behind Nick as they passed the black one, then the black and white speckled one, a cream one, and a red one....she had to stop looking because her heart was beating too fast.

"We'll get you up behind the chutes." He called back to her. Nora looked up and realized they were walking under the main walkway where all the audience was sitting. "I bought a couple seats so you'll have room around you. I hate getting jammed into a small seat."

Nora smiled at his thoughtfulness. Then they burst through the door on the other side of the pens and back into the crowd. He walked her up the steps and through the crowd. They were in the reserved seating section. The people weren't as loud.

She followed him to the bottom row which was right behind the bull chutes. Wow, she was close!

"You're here in 5 and 6." He pointed to the seats.

"Hey, Nick!" They both looked up at a cowboy in a striped shirt standing on the metal walk-way just down the row of chutes. "Who's your date? Going a little young aren't you?" The striped shirt cowboy laughed; the other cowboys around him didn't...they just stared at the cowboy like he had lost his mind.

Nick's hand tightened around hers then released her altogether, she glanced up at him. His expression, as he looked at the striped shirt cowboy, scared her. She watched him take a deep breathe, his shoulders went up, he twisted his neck around then he relaxed.

"Stay here," He smiled stiffly down at her. "I'll get you something to drink and eat pretty soon."

She nodded and he stepped over the rail in front of her and onto the metal walkway. He started walking down to the chutes towards the striped shirt cowboy. The cowboy's expression changed as he started to get more nervous the closer Nick got to him. All the other cowboys had disappeared.

"One more remark about her..." Nick's voice lowered as he whispered to the now scared cowboy. The striped shirt cowboy glanced at her with wide eyes then he started nodding...fast.

When Nick walked past him, the cowboy jumped down from the chutes and followed.

Nora shivered; that was scary, she felt the goose bumps on her arms. Then she quickly looked around her. It wasn't the biggest arena she had seen but the energy made her heart beat faster.

In front of her was the only row of bucking chutes... she counted eight of them. Nick told her they would load the chutes, run the eight bulls, the rodeo clown or entertainers would come out while the chutes were loaded again, then run the next eight bulls. She wasn't sure how many times they would refill the chutes but she knew Nick was going to have a busy night, and she had the best seats in the place to watch!

The seats to her left filled with an older couple who were dressed in western clothes. They smiled politely at her then looked around. She knew they were looking for her parents. She just giggled; it would be her secret tonight.

The seats to her right were a couple young girls. Nora giggled again, she knew they were there for the cowboys by the way they were dressed and how they were watching the cowboys climbing in and out of the chutes.

Nora turned and looked up the bleachers behind her, they were filling up fast. There were very few kids in this section.

Nora bounced between both of her seats as she watched the people. She decided she was totally excited about the night.

She heard a couple of big bangs and looked down to see the first bull enter into the chutes. A number of men made their way over the top of the chutes and helped push the bulls forward so they could fill each pen. Nora leaned forward to see if she could see Nick. No sign of him.

"Excuse me," Nora heard behind her and turned to see the striped shirt cowboy standing next to her. She frowned, her heart raced, and she leaned back away from him.

"It's OK," He smiled politely. "Nick sent me."

Her eyebrows shot up in surprise, then she noticed the food and beverage cup in his hands. He held them out to her.

"This is from Nick. He said if it wasn't enough or what you wanted, to let me know." He smiled nervously and glanced over at the chutes.

Nora turned but still didn't see Nick, so she took the tray of food and cup from him. He had nachos, three types of chips, a hotdog, two hamburgers, a huge stack of curly fries, and a big flat doughnut looking thing that had cinnamon and sugar on it. She laughed. "That's an awful lot of food." She smiled up at him and placed the food on her extra chair.

"I wasn't sure what you wanted, so I just got everything they had." He smiled politely.

Another loud bang and she turned to see more bulls coming in.

"It's OK," He told her. "I've been here a lot, and they've never escaped the chutes this way."

Nora's eyes widened at the thought and she gasped out loud.

"No! Really!" He realized what he had done. "Seriously, you're OK here." He looked down at the chutes again then back to her. "Nick would never have put you here if he thought there was a chance you would get hurt."

She sat back and relaxed, he was right. "Thanks." She smiled.

"They call me Dude," He laughed. "I'll be working out front until I ride, so if you need anything, you let me know."

She nodded. Another bang made her jump and she turned back to the bulls. Nick appeared next to the last one. He was pointing at one of the bulls and the men behind the chute. They all nodded as he spoke directions to them.

He quickly glanced up at her, nodded, then went back to work.

Nora climbed up on the seat on her knees. She turned quickly to make sure she wasn't blocking anyone's view. It was one of the few times she was glad she was so short. There wasn't anyone in the seat yet so she turned back around and started eating her fries.

The arena went black...she froze...all the lights were out! She tried to look around but could only see the people right next to her. Just as she was getting nervous, a fire started in the arena and ran across the dirt in a straight line...then LOUD music started playing and the announcer yelled.

"Are you ready for some bulls...tonight!" The announcer said excitedly trying to get the audience to holler...and they did!

A spotlight turned on and showed a long line of cowboys standing in the arena. They were the cowboys that were going to ride the bulls! She could see Dude standing toward the middle. The spotlight moved around and the music got louder. Her heart pounded! Some of the cowboys started dancing to the music making Nora and the crowd laugh.

The lights went on and the announcer started talking and the crowd erupted in cheers again as the cowboys walked behind the chutes. The bull in front of her was black with long horns and a number of cowboys surrounded him. He was going to be the first! She was so excited. Nick appeared next to them and watched everything the cowboys were doing.

Nora sat as far back on her seat as she could and waited. The announcer yelled, the crowd yelled, the cowboy on the bull nodded his head and the gate was pulled open. Nora stood to see over the group of cowboys.

The bull erupted from the gate and twisted high in the air, then went down, then up, and kicked his back legs out high and far. Then again and again as the cowboy held on then he went flying through the air and landed on the ground. She didn't hear him land because the crowd was screaming. He jumped up quickly and ran for the gates as the bull trotted by.

The cowboy had ridden the full required 8 seconds. Nora looked up at the score board and saw the cowboy earned an 83 for the ride. He jumped up and pumped his fist. He was happy with that one.

Nora's heart was racing and she climbed back on her chair waiting for the next bull. She glanced down for Nick and he was helping the next rider get set. He was leaning around the front of the cowboy; his arm was stretched out in front of the man's chest. The bull bucked and the cowboy went flying forward. If Nick hadn't held him back, the cowboy would have hit the metal chute in front of him.

"Wow," Nora whispered as she watched Nick work.

The next bull exploded from the chute and the cowboy went sailing in the air. He didn't even last a second on the bull! Nora glanced at Nick who watched the cowboy land with a thud. He grinned, shook his head, then looked back at Nora. She grinned back. He nodded, then went back to work.

Once the first set of bulls were ridden, the announcer started talking.

Nora ignored him and started looking at the crowd again. Her neighbors, the older couple, kept glancing over at her. She just smiled back.

A loud bang let her know the bulls were being loaded again. She watched one, two, three…all eight get loaded while the clown in the arena was busy entertaining the crowd. She turned in time to see

Nick walking over the top of the chutes towards her. He grinned at her and took a seat between the rails and the bull. He didn't even look at the girls in the seats next to her.

"Having fun?" He smiled at her.

"Oh, yes!"

He glanced down at her seat full of food. "Hungry?"

She nodded. "I can't eat it all, do you want some?" He nodded so she handed him the hamburger. He ate it in only two bites. She laughed and handed him the drink so he could make sure it would go down. He took the lid off, drank half of it, and replaced the lid before he handed it back.

"I'll get you another one."

She shook her head as the crowd erupted in cheers. The clown must have done something.

"Was that score of 83 good?" She asked.

He looked at her in surprise. "You watch riding on TV?"

"Yeah, just for the flying parts." She grinned.

He nodded, "There are four judges." He pointed to four men in black hats and black shirts. "Each one scores the bull up to 25 points and the rider up to 25 points; then they add them together and cut it in half." Nora nodded her understanding so far. "So the top score from each judge is 50, so a perfect score is 100." She nodded again. "So the rider not only has to ride his best, to get the highest score he can, but he also wants a bull that will buck hard and get a good score, too."

He pointed down at a man with a dark green shirt on that matched Nick's. "He manages the bucking stock, bulls and horses, for rodeos for the stock contractor. The better the bulls perform, the more rodeos and bull events want his bulls at their events. Plus, the cowboys will want to ride his bulls and horses."

Nora nodded just as a large bang rang out from one of the bulls fighting in the chute. She jumped then grinned up at him. "Thank you! It's OK, go to work."

The cowboys started to fill up the chutes again. She thought of him holding back the cowboy so he didn't hit the metal chute.

"Nick!" She yelled as he started to turn. His head tilted in curiosity. "Be careful, I don't have a medical release for you." She grinned and he was laughing as he turned back to the bulls.

CHAPTER TEN

Each time the bulls were reloaded, Nick came over and sat in front of her. He helped her eat all the food. Not once, did she see him look at the girls that were sitting next to her. When he went back to load the next run of bulls, Dude showed up with more food and another drink. Nora just shook her head and laughed.

"When do you ride?" She asked him. She had been watching both him and Nick all night as they helped the cowboys and worked the bulls.

"Second to last," He smiled. He had finally started to relax around her and didn't continually look for Nick. "Then hopefully in the final ten…for the money."

"OK, good luck." She told him as he climbed over the rails to the chutes.

Nora looked around and saw the older couple looking at her again.

"Are one of those your father?" The older woman asked.

Nora smiled and shook her head. She wondered how Nick would react if he knew they thought he was her dad. It made her giggle again.

She turned away from them and the announcer started talking to get the crowd going again. She sat on her knees and looked back to make sure she wasn't blocking the persons view. No one was there.

She looked down the row of bulls and saw Nick bracing the next cowboy in the chute. He had to be getting tired. The announcer started yelling, the crowd exploded, the cowboy nodded and the gate was opened. The cowboy flew forward then back then forward then back, then the bull spun to the left then turned to the right. The rider's arm was high in the air and before she knew it the buzzer sounded and the cowboy was jumping off the back of the bull. He landed on his feet, threw his hat in the air, and shook the hands of the men around him.

The score was 91! With only 100 points possible, it was a great ride! The rider turned and looked towards the chute and ran over to shake Nick's hand.

Turning back to the chutes, Nora saw Dude standing in front of her. He had on a black vest with a bunch of colorful patches on it. He also wore a black helmet with a wire guard across the front of it. He was going to ride the bull directly in front of her! Cool! She climbed back up in the seat on her knees. Before he slid onto the bull, he glanced up at her and grinned.

"Good luck!" She yelled, excited she had made a bull rider friend. Wade and Reilly were going to be so jealous!

Dude's eyes went to the girls sitting next to her and she heard the girls giggling.

Nora shook her head; he shouldn't have looked at them!

Nick appeared in the chute to her right.

The announcer yelled again, and the crowd erupted again, and Dude nodded his head. The gate flew open. Nora had to stand to see his ride over the mass of cowboys in front of her.

Dude held on as the bull spun to the right, over and over again. He had to be dizzy! Nora laughed to herself as she jumped and yelled for him.

The buzzer went off indicating the end of the ride and Dude jumped off and hit the ground but rolled up and stood. He let the crowd know he was OK by waving his hat in the air. Nora turned and looked; he had a score of 85! She turned back and saw Dude watch the bull trotting calmly by him then, Dude turned to head to the chutes. At the last second, the bull kicked out and a hoof connected with Dude's butt and sent him flying forward into the dirt, face first.

The crowd erupted in laughter as Dude stood up again and waved sheepishly.

Nora was laughing with them when Nick took his seat in front of her.

"That's what it's like hanging out with you." He grinned at her.

"What?"

"Everything seems to be going great, then, all the sudden, it's a real kick in the butt."

Their laughter was lost in the laughter of the crowd.

***

He opened the truck door for her and made sure she had her seat belt connected then shut the door and walked around to the driver's side.

She looked at the clock on the dash of the truck as the engine was turned on. It was 11:30 at night, she had to be at the arena by 7:00 in the morning. Libby would be first up and she had to make sure she was perfectly groomed and her saddle and gear perfectly clean.

"It's going to be a short night," Nick glanced over at her.

"It was worth it," She smiled, her eyes already starting to close. "That was one of the funnest nights ever."

"And you have one more tomorrow night," She heard him as her eyes closed.

"Thanks, Nick...I'm glad you're my friend." Was the last thing she said and remembered.

Nora's eyes opened as the alarm went off. She sat straight up and looked around the room. It took her a minute to realize she was in the hotel room. He must have carried her into the hotel. The thought made her giggle.

"You're awake," She heard him in the next room. The door between their rooms was blocked open by a chair.

"Yes," She rolled out of bed and saw she still had her jeans and shirt on from the night before but he had taken off her boots.

"You have about thirty minutes before we need to head out."

"I can't even get my hair done in that amount of time." She ran for the bathroom.

Twenty nine minutes later they were walking to his truck.

She'd been able to roll up her hair but had a hard time pinning it in place. Debating what to do, she finally sighed and asked him for help.

"You want me to do what?" He asked in disbelief.

She giggled. "I need it pinned with these so it doesn't come loose during the competition."

Nora watched him in the mirror as he worked the pins into the hair bun. She giggled at his expressions.

"Stop laughing or I'll quit," He warned while looking up at her reflection.

She rolled her lips tight trying to stop giggling.

"Do you think anyone would ever believe us, if we told them about this?" Nick finally chuckled.

Nora burst out laughing. "No!"

***

"What's up?" He asked.

"Buttercup." She giggled.

He glanced over at her with a smile.

"I was just thinking my mom would go in shock right now if she saw me going in the ring without my hair perfect."

"Hey, I did a good job!" He defended his hair styling technique. "Besides, what difference does it make as long as it doesn't fall down?"

"Have you ever been at a horse show?" She asked.

He shook his head. "I stuck with rodeos."

"Well," She grinned. "You're in for a real treat."

The arena was full of activity when they arrived. Nick went to the horses while Nora went to the trailer to put on her sparkling pink shirt over her tank top.

She looked in the mirror as she placed her helmet on her head. The bun was a little high but it would work.

Nora tucked her pant legs into her boots to keep them clean while she got ready for the ring. Once she was at the arena gate she would let them out so they were perfect.

She stepped out of the trailer and headed for the stalls. Rounding the corner she saw Nick brushing Libby, he was on the opposite side of the horse so he was facing her. There was a woman standing with her back to Nora and talking to him.

Nick's eyes looked over at Nora, he was almost pleading.

Nora giggled inside then realized the woman was stopping them from getting ready. She walked up next to the woman and looked up at her. Nora didn't recognize her, which was really good, considering what she was about to say.

"My mother is going to be really pissed if you don't quit talking to him." Nora frowned at the woman.

The woman's expression registered surprise then embarrassment. She glanced up at Nick, excused herself and hurried away.

Nora stepped over to the gear and handed Nick the saddle pad to place on Libby. When she looked up, he was grinning at her.

"I didn't lie," Nora smiled back with her 'perfect' smile. "Mom would be pissed if she didn't stop talking to you so we could get ready."

Nick's brown eyes sparkled in laughter as he took the gear and helped her ready the big black horse for the show.

He boosted her up into the saddle, took her pants out of the top of the boots and smoothed them to get the wrinkles out.

"Do you need to warm her up?" Nick asked looking over at the girls in the grass enclosure warming up their horses.

"Just for a few minutes, I'll be right back." Nora said and turned Libby. "Then I just need to go watch the pattern, then remember it when I ride."

He was in the same spot when she returned and he walked alongside her and through the groups of horses and people to the arena gate. Nora read through the riding pattern over and over as she stepped into the line of waiting riders. She glanced down at him. He looked relaxed as he watched the activity around them.

"It's OK, Nick."

"Are you sure?" He glanced up at her. "It's actually kind of interesting to watch."

"It's going to be a long day," She nodded. "Hopefully you don't get tired of it too quickly."

"I won't," He assured her and patted her leg. "I'll let you concentrate and get the job done. I'll be right over there." He pointed to a small section of bleachers away from the larger one.

"Thank you, Nick." She nodded and watched him walk away.

Nora turned back and watched the riders in front of her ride the western pleasure pattern. She studied their every move.

"That's not your dad."

Nora turned and saw Candace Avery. The girl's last words rang through Nora's memory. *"But you're still ugly."*

Nora took a deep breath and thought of what Reilly said about her being jealous. She thought of her mom and dad's love and pride, she thought of Arcturus' star…her energy, and she looked over at Nick. He believed she was a good person…those are the things that mattered.

She turned to Candace.

"How would you know?" Nora smiled calmly.

Candace's expression registered surprise and she didn't answer.

Nora turned back and worked hard on concentrating on the pattern and not on the rude blonde.

As the gate opened for her to enter, she sat with perfect posture…and did the pattern perfectly. When she came out of the arena, she looked over at Nick. He nodded and smiled. Nora smiled over at Candace, who was next in line to go into the arena.

First competition, Nora was second, Candace was fourth.

In the next competition, Nora was first, Candace was third.

There was only one more competition before they broke for lunch and she would switch to Isaiah. She looked for Nick. He was still watching her from his perch on the stands, but he was on the phone…he waved.

In the last competition of the morning, Nora was first, Candace was fourth.

As Nora walked to the stalls, Candace was standing to the side; head down and obviously crying. Her mother was leaned into the girl's ear and was upset, her arms motioning wildly as she spoke.

Not wanting to embarrass the girl, Nora turned away before Candace saw her. She quietly walked Libby to the stalls.

CHAPTER ELEVEN

Nora shut the stall door after making sure Libby had plenty of food and water. She glanced in at a bored Isaiah then headed back to the trailer. She still hadn't seen Nick since she had come out of the arena. Where was he?

As she rounded the corner to the horse trailer, she saw him setting up their travel table by the tailgate of his truck. He walked to the front of the truck and returned with bags full of food.

"How much do you think I can eat?" She laughed.

He looked up and smiled.

"Not sure what you like…so I just got a bunch of different things."

"Maybe we should discuss food before you go broke or we both get fat." She sat in the chair across the camp table from him.

He chuckled, "Well, we should have leftovers for later."

They sat quietly for a while as they ate.

"That was pretty impressive out there," He told her. "I enjoyed watching it."

She shrugged.

He looked at her with a brow raised in confusion.

"I win or place because of Libby's experience and Isaiah's looks." She explained.

"You seriously think that?" He asked in surprised.

She nodded, "I'm realistic."

"You're delusional."

She looked up at him in surprise and saw he was serious.

"Do you think that any girl or boy out there this morning would have won if they had Libby?"

She scrunched her face and thought about what he said. There were some that wouldn't have won because of their posture. Some of the kids wouldn't have won because they didn't work the patterns correctly. There were some that didn't pay enough attention to the judge.

"I guess not," She finally admitted.

"If you think you win only because of the horses...why do it?"

"I'm only twelve," She reminded him. "I need Isaiah and Libby to help teach me so when I'm older I can win as a team with them and Arcturus."

"What is your goal?"

She shrugged, she really didn't have one. "What was your goal in riding bulls?"

"To get away from my parents and live somewhere besides a dirt house," He answered honestly.

Her eyes shot up in surprise. "I don't want to get away from my parents." She said quickly.

"And you don't live in a dirt house," He leaned back in his chair. "Everyone out there has a reason for being here." He waved out to the arena. "Watching them this morning it was easy to tell who was here because their parents wanted them here and who was here because they loved the horses and the competition."

"I love the horses and the competition." She admitted, then thought of Candace... what was her reason? Why was her mother making her cry?

"And your parents want you here...or they wouldn't have gambled and sent you with me." He grinned.

Gambled...that was funny...she smiled and nodded.

"That's a pretty good combination, Nora." He looked out at the crowd. "Only a handful of kids out there have the drive you do and the parent's full support like you have."

She followed his gaze and looked at the different people milling around the trailers and stalls. Again she thought of Candace crying. When she looked back at Nick, she realized that he truly believed in her.

"Can I borrow your phone?" She asked.

He looked at her in surprise then, without asking her why, he handed her his phone.

She sent a text message then set it back down on the table.

They sat quietly and finished their lunch.

The phone alerted them of a text message.

He looked at her, "You going to look?"

Nora shook her head and walked their empty sacks over to the garbage can. When she turned, he was reading his phone. She stopped and watched for his reaction.

His head slowly rose and he stared at her. Without a word she walked back to him, took the phone back and typed in a response. She handed it back to him and stepped into the tack room of the trailer. When she returned with the silver plated leather show halter and leather lead for Isaiah she heard the phone alert.

She started to walk away, but glanced back at him. He was reading the message. He looked up at her in surprise.

Nora turned and walked to Isaiah's stall. She touched up his grooming then checked herself. The bun at her neck was still holding tightly, she smiled, Nick did a good job. She placed her black cowboy hat on her head and smiled. He was right; she did have a great family support team and her own will to win. She straightened her back in pride and belief, then walked to the arena for the next competition.

Isaiah walked calmly next to her. Even at three years old and only a handful of competitions behind him, he was becoming a pro.

Nora walked into the line of girls and horses that were waiting to enter the arena. The showmanship class was one of her favorites, because it depended on her experience to win, not the horses.

As she waited, she looked for Nick. He was sitting off to the side of the bleachers, not too close to the parents.

A woman with long blond hair and too tight jeans walked in front of him. Nora was surprised when he didn't watch her walk by; he was watching the riders in the arena start moving to the gate. Then she smiled...he had turned his head and glanced at the blond. He turned back to the exiting horses, then his head turned and looked at the blond again; he didn't just glance...he LOOKED.

Nora started laughing. She remembered telling him he was in for a treat, but she hadn't meant that!

There was a grin on her face as she entered into the arena. It must have been the shine in her eyes that made the judge keep looking at her. She waited patiently and in her mind she critiqued each competitor and horse as they completed their presentation to the judge. It was finally her turn.

Nora nodded to the judge and presented the horse; moving Isaiah back and forth, trotting and walking. Every move Nora watched the judge, her eyes still laughing at Nick, and she was finally having fun showing Isaiah, the beautiful big gelding.

Nora won. She grinned even wider.

After announcing the win, one of the judges approached her as she was leaving the arena.

"Your horse is spectacular." The judge smiled. Nora's smile began to fade. "But you won because of the shine and joy on your face and your showing ability. I could tell you really enjoy what you're doing."

Nora couldn't have grinned any more than she was and her whole body shook with pride. "Thank you," She shook the judge's hand and walked proudly behind the line of girls and horses.

Nick was waiting for her outside the arena gate. Nora couldn't help herself and she wrapped her arms around his waist and hugged. His body stiffened, then relaxed and she felt one of his hands rest across her back.

As they walked back to the stalls to put Isaiah away for the night, she spotted Candace walking with her head down and leading her horse. She hadn't even placed.

"Nick?"

"Yes?"

"Can you take Isaiah for a minute?" She handed him the lead without looking and walked toward the girl.

"Candace?" Nora said as she approached.

The girl's head rose and she quickly wiped away the tears, she was too embarrassed to say anything.

Nora took a deep breath. "Your hands are too high on the horse's neck when you ride and it makes your horse's head too arched."

Candace's eyes widened in surprise.

"When you show, your steps are too loose and you look clumsy. Stiffen up your back and practice a more precise move." Nora smiled, hoping the girl understood she was trying to help.

Candace nodded so Nora turned to walk away.

"Nora?" The girl's voice was shaky.

She turned and smiled into the girl's sad eyes.

"I'm very sorry for what I said," She looked at the ground then back up. "I was upset because every time I lost, my mom yelled at me, and kept comparing me to you. She wondered why I couldn't be more like you."

Nora's jaw dropped in shock.

Candace looked in the direction that Nick had walked. "I knew he wasn't your dad because I follow the Tagger herd on Facebook and I saw your family picture." Candace smiled and let out a nervous breath.

Nora nodded and returned the smile. "He's like my uncle." Nora looked back and saw he had moved on to the stalls.

Candace nodded; eyes sad but they had a glint of light from their talk.

"I have to get back," Nora waved a hand to the stalls. Nick had to get to the rodeo grounds.

"I understand," Candace lowered her gaze again.

"Chin up," Nora said automatically…she was surprised she spoke the words and her eyebrows shot up in shock as Candace raised her gaze back to Nora. "I'm sorry, it's what my parents say when I do that."

"What do they say when you lose?" Candace asked seriously.

Nora looked at the girl in astonishment. "They tell me, not to worry, I'm still young, I'll get there, and to show because I like it and not just to win."

"My mom tells me that if I don't win she's going to sell my horse." Candace said quietly and on the verge of tears again.

Nora was stunned; what a horrible thing to say!

"Well, maybe try my parent's advice next time and see if it works better."

Candace smiled nervously, "You better go."

Nora nodded and turned. When she arrived at the stalls she turned back and watched Candace walking along the fence. Her head was held high and she had a slight smile on her face. Even her horse was walking with more energy.

CHAPTER TWELVE

Nora could barely sit still in the seat of the truck as they drove back to the bull bash. She smiled over at her weekend guardian. He glanced down at her and back out the window.

"You had a good day."

"Yeah, but I can't wait for tonight. It was so much fun last night. I'm glad Dude got third but I hope he wins tonight."

"He's pretty young, but getting better...if he doesn't get hurt he'll have some good years ahead of him."

"I'll have to watch him on TV!" Nora said excitedly.

"Before we get there, do you want to explain the text messages?"

Nora knew the question was coming, but still didn't know how to explain the reason behind her actions.

"I just wanted you to know." She finally answered.

"Everyone knows...they're married now."

"I just wanted you to know that I had known for a long time." She looked over at him. "If I just told you, then you may not have believed me...so having Aunt Dru sort of tell you, you know it's true."

"That's important to you?"

Nora nodded.

TEXT TO DRU: Were you and Jack in the stalls New Year's when you returned back from the party?

TEXT TO NICK(NORA): Yes...why?

TEXT TO DRU: Nora was in stall with Arcturus and heard you two talk about your relationship and Elena.

TEXT TO NICK(NORA): Had NO idea…she never told anyone…that I know of

Nora looked to Nick. "It was important for you to know that I didn't tell anyone I knew they were in a relationship. I know how to keep secrets."

"Why?"

"I don't know…" She answered honestly. "I want you to know I'm a good person."

"Nora…we had that discussion…" He frowned at her.

"I know." She sighed. "But I just needed you to know."

He shook his head. "Like I said last night, everything seems to be going great, then, all the sudden; you're a real kick in the butt."

Nora laughed.

***

She sat in the same seats as the night before. The older couple were there but two seats behind her this time. They smiled and she waved.

Dude showed up with a drink and food again…as much food as the night before.

The first round of bulls came into the chutes…no sign of Nick. He appeared just before the first rider nodded and gates opened. He flew off before the bull was completely out of the chute. Nora shook her head.

She watched as Nick worked with the next bull rider. It was the same rider that scored the 91 the night before. Nick's arm was around the front of the rider when the bull seemed to go crazy bucking while still in the chute. The rider was being thrown around. Another man came around Nick's shoulder so they could both watch out for the rider. It seemed to buck forever!

Once the bull stopped, Nick helped pull the rider off the bull and set him on the rail. Another bull rider was ready and the gate opened and the crowd cheered and the rider flew off in a grand style...flipping through the air and landing on his back. The crowd gasped then cheered when he stood up and waved.

Nick was talking to the 91 rider until the rider looked up at him, nodded and started to slide back onto the bull. The rider seemed to slump over so far that even Nora knew something was wrong. Nick leaned down in front of the rider, then, much to her and everyone else's shock, Nick slapped him a long side the head...twice.

The rider sat back up, looked at Nick, and grinned. Within a minute, the rider nodded, the gate opened, the bull jumped from the chute, its back legs flew into the air then he started spinning. Nora rose to her feet with everyone else and cheered at the top of her lungs. He rode a few seconds after the buzzer went off, then he let loose of the rope and flew off the back of the bucking bull.

The instant he landed on the ground, the rider took off at a run for the chutes with the bull right behind him. Nora held her breath as the bull fighters jumped in between the rider and bull. The bull turned to them but the men were way too fast and the bull missed. The bull ran out into the middle of the arena throwing its head around in anger. It stopped. Nora was still holding her breath as she and the crowd waited to see what the bull was going to do. The exit gate was open so the bull politely walked out without even a swish of a tail. Everyone laughed.

Nora turned back to Nick who was embracing the rider. It was another 91 score!

She waited patiently for Nick to come up and sit in front of her.

"Do you know that 91 rider?" She asked him.

"Nora, he's the reigning world champion bull rider." He laughed.

Nora's eyes opened wide, "Why did you hit him?"

"He was freaking out, closing within his head instead paying attention to the bull."

Nora nodded. "Uncle Grayson slaps the kid's legs with his lariat when they do that during roping practice."

They ate together and he downed her drink again before heading back to work.

Half way through the night, he was sitting in front of her, when he turned around and looked past her with a bright smile on his face.

Nora turned…and saw the most beautiful woman she'd ever seen in her life. And the woman was smiling and waving…at Nick!

Nora stared. The woman had long black hair, curled perfectly around her face and down her back. A white cowboy hat placed on her head with a large silver and gold crown wrapped around the front. She had on black jeans and a white western shirt. A red, white, and blue sash hung from her shoulder that read, Miss Rodeo Idaho.

Nick cleared the food from Nora's extra seat so the woman could sit down. She gave Nick a big hug then she turned and looked at Nora.

Nora was absolutely star struck. She couldn't form a word in her head if she tried.

"Nora, this is Cambria Weber." Nick introduced her with a roguish grin.

The woman smiled the most beautiful smile Nora had ever seen. "It's nice to meet you, Nora." She held out a hand.

Nora's hand slowly moved up to the woman's and she shook it politely.

"I was at a rodeo this afternoon when Nick called and said he had a special friend here that he wanted me to meet." Cambria turned to Nick. "You didn't tell me how precious she was."

Nora forced her mouth closed and her eyes to move to Nick. He was watching Nora with a wicked knowing grin.

"Nick said I was supposed to ask you about your day." Cambria turned back to her. "So…how was your day?"

Nora smiled at Nick then back to the beautiful woman. She spent the next half hour talking as fast as she could and telling Miss Rodeo Idaho about Isaiah and Libby and even Arcturus…the competitions she won and her weekend trip with Nick.

The woman had held her hand the whole time while Nick had gone back to helping the riders and working with the bulls.

"Nora, I have enjoyed this so much." Miss Rodeo Idaho said. She reached in her pocket and handed Nora a card. It had her name and email address on it. "You keep this and send me pictures of your Libby, Arcturus, and Isaiah. Keep me updated on your show wins."

Nora took the card as if it were made of gold. She pressed it between her hands so nothing could happen to it.

"OK," Nora smiled; her heart racing in delight.

"Keep up the good work, and someday you could be wearing this crown and proudly representing Idaho and the PRCA." Cambria Weber stood, waved at Nick then left.

Nora watched her walk away then turned and stared at the card.

"Nora?" It was Nick's voice.

She raised her stunned eyes and looked into his amused ones. Without thinking, she dove over the rail towards him. He had to use both hands to catch her so they both didn't tip backwards toward the bulls. Her arms wrapped tightly around his neck.

Laughing, he pulled her away from him and stepped over the rail to set her back down in her seat.

The crowd roared, and Nora looked up to see one of the bull riders holding on and riding the bull to the left then to the right. He flew off a split second before the buzzer went off, the whole crowd groaned for him.

She looked up at Nick; he was looking down at the chutes and bulls.

"Go." She smiled happily.

He grinned and stepped back over the rail to walk down the chutes.

Nora glanced down at the card in her hand. Her life had just changed forever.

CHAPTER THIRTEEN

Nora watched quietly as Nick helped the rest of the crew feed the bulls and bed them down for the night. The crew, less Nick, would load up the bulls and drive back to their ranch in the morning. Nick would be taking her back to the horse arena to finish out her show.

She anxiously checked her pocket again to make sure the card was still there. She couldn't wait to get home and look on the computer to research Cambria Weber and what it took to become Miss Rodeo Idaho; her new goal.

Nick handed her his phone as he walked past her. "Your mother sent a text."

TEXT FROM MOM TO NICK(NORA): How is it going? Hope all is well, thanks for pictures of Nora! I miss her so much! So proud of her! Wish I was there but Sadie won her race today too…she will be competing for Peewee District Champion barrel racer tomorrow! Wish Nora was here to see her cousin and Scarecrow, amazing team. Give Nora my love…yes I'm asking you to do that. LOL

Nora read the long text over and over again.

***

They arrived back at the hotel by midnight and she lay staring at the ceiling of the hotel room. Between Cambria Weber and her mother's text she couldn't get her eyes to close.

She sat up and looked at the clock…it was 2:00 in the morning.

She hadn't been awake this late, or early, since New Year's when she had sat and listened to Dru and Jack talk about Nick and Elena. She had been amazed when they talked about their relationship; how it had changed since Dru knew why Nick had left her. After they had left, she had snuck back into the house and bed then stared at the ceiling, wondering why they didn't tell anyone. She knew from the beginning that she wouldn't say anything. They had to have a good reason and without knowing what is was, she couldn't take the chance it would be bad. She didn't utter a word about it until she talked with Nick today.

Then she thought of Candace and the girl's mother making her cry. Nora couldn't imagine, in any circumstance, her own mother would say anything to her that would make her cry like that. Or threaten to sell her horse! Even more shocking was the woman comparing Candace to Nora! She wanted Candace to be more like Nora! No wonder why Candace said she was ugly…her mother made her hate her without realizing what she was doing.

Nora lay back down and stared at the ceiling. She had listened to people for years talk about Sadie's blue eyes and long blond hair…how tall she was…already as tall as Nora…going to be tall and beautiful. Had they been conditioning Nora to resent her cousin's looks? Was she being unfair to Sadie because what people were saying? Sadie even used other people's words against Nora…saying she was jealous of her height, hair, and eyes.

Nora thought Sadie was beautiful, but felt like that made her ugly in comparison. That's why Candace's words hurt so much…*because Nora believed them.*

A tear escaped and Nora let it slide down into her hair untouched.

Sadie looked like Aunt Dru, who was really beautiful. But Nora looked like her mother, who was also beautiful.

Nora sat up in bed. Aunt Dru and her mother were both beautiful! They didn't even look alike but that didn't matter. Aunt Dru was tall, blue eyes, and long blonde hair; her mother was barely five foot tall, Native American...the black hair, dark eyes...she looked exotic and beautiful, especially with her new short haircut. Just because one was beautiful didn't mean the other was ugly!

Nora sighed, why hadn't she thought of that before?

She turned on her side and stared out into the dark, the lights twinkled and made her think of Arcturus. Then her mind went to Reilly...telling her she was beautiful. He wouldn't lie. Nick told her she needed to think before she spoke but that she was good on the inside.

Their words and actions began to penetrate the "perfect" façade that Nora had built around herself...she began to believe she wasn't the ugly, bad person she had come to think she was. The darkness inside her began to escape, the light from the belief and love her family gave her pushing it out of her mind and soul, more tears fell.

She turned and stared back at the ceiling...this was one heck of a weekend.

Both nights of bulls, placing in all the competitions, the judge's comments to her, and Miss Rodeo Idaho...she couldn't ask for more....except one thing...

"Nick?" She called out hesitantly.

No answer but his breathing had changed. She didn't dare get up and look into the room but she turned and stared at the opening between the two rooms.

"Nick?" She called out a little louder.

"What?" She heard him yell out and saw his shadow moving in the room.

He appeared at the connecting door in his jeans no shirt.

"Are you OK?" He asked. She could hear the concern in his voice.

"Yeah," She whispered and sat up.

"Then what's up?"

"Buttercup." She quietly whispered with a smile.

He walked back into his room and was sliding a shirt on when he walked back into hers. He grabbed a chair and sat down.

"Talk to me." He said.

"How far is it to Sadie and Mom?" She asked. The light in her room wasn't on but his was…which created a dark shadow across him.

"From the horses…about five hours."

"Is that too far to get to them before Sadie rides?"

He paused. "Are you sure? Don't you have more competitions tomorrow?"

"Yeah, but I really want to see Sadie and Scarecrow ride."

"You're willing to give up your chances of winning?"

"I'll have more competitions…but Sadie only has one chance of winning the Peewee championship...she's in a different level next year."

"OK…"

"I want to be there…can we make it?" She asked. "Would you mind?"

He glanced at the alarm clock. "By the time we go get the horses and head down…it would be pretty close."

"Can we try?"

"It means that much to you?"

"Yes, please."

"Well," He stood, "… you're a real kick in the butt."

She climbed out of bed.

***

Nick sent her mom a text to find out what time Sadie would be riding. They didn't let them know they were coming. She didn't want Sadie to be looking for her or be disappointed if they didn't make it.

"Are we on time?" She asked from the front of the truck. She looked back at the trailer. Isaiah and Libby had loaded quickly and silently. She called and left a message with the arena office and left a note on the outside of the office door. She left them an envelope with note in it for Candace…wishing her good luck and chin up.

"Yeah, it'll still be close."

She turned back and stared into the darkness. It was 3:30. The 10-year-olds would be running first thing in the morning.

"It's going to be a long five hours…" Nick said.

"I know." Nora smiled. "Mom always says something about a watched pot or something like that."

"You're going to have to stay awake to keep me awake."

She turned her head and grinned. "I will, but you may have to talk to me to keep me awake, I don't like coffee." She glanced at the cup in his hand.

"So what would you like to talk about?" He asked. "No more Nora is a good person talk anymore…we both know that already."

"OK," She grinned, he would never know how much that meant to her. "Well…who is Elena?" She asked.

"Really, Nora?" He shook his head. "You are a kick in the butt."

She giggled. "I know she has something to do with you because of the conversation I heard between Jack and Aunt Dru."

"Did you ever see her?"

"She was in Lewiston?" Nora was surprised.

"A couple of times at The Stables and in town."

Nora shook her head.

He didn't speak for a few minutes. "What did you overhear? We'll start from there."

"Just that Jack had been on a date with her, they laughed about that, not sure why…" She glanced at him but his expression didn't change. "Then they said something about her not talking much while you told your story."

"My story…"

"They just said you had been in Australia and that whatever happened between you and Aunt Dru…" Nora stopped, she felt like she was invading their privacy. "Maybe we shouldn't be talking about this."

"I'll give you the very shortened version," He said. "Elena is Nikki's birth mom. I left Nikki with Dru to raise her with Matt, moved to Australia for 18 years, Elena isn't a good person and hopefully won't be around again, and everything worked out for the best with Jack and Dru getting married."

She half giggled, "And with you coming back."

He looked over at her, "Yeah, I think that was good, too."

"That was pretty shortened…" She smiled. "But I don't want to know more."

"Then what would you like to talk about now?"

"Tell me everything there is to know about bull riding."

He smiled, "Oh…I have some good stories that will keep us awake."

For the next couple of hours she listened and laughed at his stories of riding in the States and Australia; the people, the bulls, the equipment.

The text from her mother came just as the sun was coming up.

TEXT TO NICK(NORA): Sadie's division starts at 8:30, will be last to run

Nora read it to Nick and looked at the clock. "Are we going to make it?"

Nick nodded, "It will be close, but we should be good."

Nora's heart was racing. "I never would have thought we would be racing to see Sadie run this weekend."

"Me either." He glanced over at her. "Why?"

"We got in a big argument the day before we left."

"What's changed?"

She smiled and looked up at him. "I guess just getting away from everyone, not being part of a crowd or being lonely."

"Lonely?"

She nodded, "I've never told anyone before."

"That you were lonely?"

"They wouldn't understand."

"I would."

Nora glanced at him, from the look on his face, she believed he would. "Sadie and Wade are like twins…they're always together; same with Reilly and Grace."

"And then there's you."

She nodded. "I just get so lonely sometimes…even when the whole family is together."

"I noticed at branding that you sat off to the side a lot."

"Sadie and Wade came over to talk, but I just felt they were feeling sorry for me so I just walked away."

"They probably had no idea you were lonely."

"I know," She looked out the window at the passing scenery. "Sometimes, when I get really lonely, I do things just to get people to pay attention to me." She said honestly, hoping that when she told him…he would still think she was a good person.

"Like what?"

"Most of the time...it's telling other people's secrets." She talked out to the night instead of to him. "Even though Dad and Uncle Scott knew about Jack and Aunt Dru they said it wasn't their story to tell, so they didn't say anything."

"...you didn't tell anyone."

"I didn't know why it was a secret so that made me nervous." She turned to him. "Did you know about them when it was a secret?"

"I knew New Year's Eve, and was surprised when I realized that they hadn't told anyone. Besides, that's not exactly something they would have talked to me about."

Nora nodded. "I keep forgetting you were married to Aunt Dru." She looked over at him. "Does it bother you? That they're married now?"

"No, I think they're good together. Dru and I are completely different people then when we were married."

"What about Matt? Jack is his step-father now."

Nick shook his head. "Scott, Grayson, and Jack were there for him more than I could have ever been."

"It doesn't bother you though?"

Nick frowned and nodded, "I wish I'd been there for him. I miss what I could have had; seeing the great young man he's turning out to be. I wonder what I missed out on to make him that way." He glanced over at her. "Maybe that's why I'm enjoying hanging out with you this weekend."

"Because of Matt?" She looked confused but was glad he enjoyed hanging out with her.

"No, with Nikki," He chuckled. "I get a little taste of what it would have been like to be around for her when she was your age."

"She did a lot of showing too, just locally though and when they could fit it around the ranch. She used Libby, too."

"But I bet she wasn't as much of a kick in the butt as you are." He smiled at her.

Nora returned his smile then looked at him seriously. "I love my dad."

Nick looked over at her with a frown. "Who said you didn't?"

Nora shook her head. "No one, but when you see me you wonder about Nikki." He nodded so she continued. "When I look at you, I don't wonder about my dad."

"Ok...?"

"After the last couple days...this weekend...I feel like I finally have someone." She could feel the tears sting her eyes so she looked down.

"Chin back up, young lady." He ordered.

She lifted her chin but looked out the front window instead of at him.

"Like Sadie and Wade, Reilly and Grace." He said.
She nodded.

"I feel the same way." He told her and she looked over at him in surprise.

"What?" She was amazed, she hadn't felt lonely all weekend and she realized it was because of him.

"I travel around a lot, by myself. At the bull events and rodeos, I can be in a crowd of ten thousand people and be sitting alone all night. Even going back and forth from Boise to the Tagger ranch is long and by myself." He smiled at her then looked back at the road. "Nora, I haven't felt lonely all weekend."

"Me neither." She felt the tears in her eyes again.

"I'm not looking to replace Scott. He's a great dad for you."

Nora nodded which made the tears fall.

"Stop doing that!" He said in exasperation.

"I'm sorry," She giggled and wiped the tears away.

Nick shook his head at her tears but looked at her seriously; "Any time you need someone to talk to, you call me."

"Will you do the same thing, when you're lonely, you'll call me? Send me pictures of the bulls, Cambria Weber, and Dude?"

He smiled and nodded, then reached down into a small cubby in the dash of the truck. He handed her a business card. "There's my number, call any time, day or night."

She looked down at the card and laughed.

"What's so funny?"

"I've just known you as Nick," She looked at him in amazement. "I've never thought of you having a last name."

CHAPTER FOURTEEN

"Do you know where the rodeo grounds are?" Nora asked as they pulled into town.

"Seriously, Nora?" He laughed.

"Oh, sorry, forgot, rodeos are your job." She grinned.

Nora looked at the clock, 8:25.

TEXT TO MOM: Timing?

TEXT TO NICK (NORA): Ten riders, just getting started.

"Ugh…" Nora cried out. They were so close.

She read the message to Nick.

"We're about ten minutes out," He stopped at a stop light and turned to her. "I'll pull into the rodeo grounds and drop you off by the closest gate." He reached in his pocket and pulled out money and handed it to her. "Do you have any idea where your mom will be?"

Nora nodded excitedly. "She sits right next to the entry gate. I'll find her."

She started bouncing in her seat…it reminded her of Reilly.

They pulled into the parking lot and there was a clear lane to the front gate. Nora was excited to see a trailer parking space right up front and pointed it out to him.

"I'll pay while you park there." Nora said excitedly. "We can go in together."

Nick sighed in relief. She realized he hadn't been too excited about dropping her off by herself.

When she opened the door she heard the announcer; "Well, folks, after a brief delay it's time to get moving with the Pee Wee division. First up we have…."

"We made it!" Nora yelled over her shoulder at him. He jogged up behind her as she was handed the tickets. They took off running.

"She'll be on the left, out of the sun." Nora reached back and grabbed his hand. She didn't want to lose him. His fingers grasped tightly around hers.

She walked along the bottom of the bleachers, pulling Nick and searching desperately for her mom. The third horse was running. She knew that they would take some time and rake ground around the barrels after the fifth horse which would give her some time.

"There." Nick pointed to her mom and Wade right at the end of the bleacher.

Nora turned to Nick and hugged him quickly then started running up the steps.

"Mom!" She yelled as they got closer.

"Nora?" Her mom's shocked expression turned to her. "Heavens, what are you doing here?"

Nora hugged her mom then Wade, she lifted her gaze to the riders waiting to race. "Where's Sadie?" Then she saw her…Sadie was wiping away tears.

Nora turned shocked eyes at her mom. Wade was talking non-stop at Nick.

"What's wrong with Sadie?"

Her mother shook her head. "One of the other riders tripped coming out and pushed her and Scarecrow into the chutes. It ripped her jeans from thigh on down. She's embarrassed and upset to have to ride that way. There's no time to change so they're trying to find some duct tape to at least tape the material up and get her covered."

Nora ran to the edge of the bleachers and looked at her cousin. She was still wiping away tears. Scarecrow turned enough that Nora could see the rip. She looked like she was wearing shorts…very short shorts. Before this weekend, Nora would have left the competition rather than appear less than perfect. Sadie was different…and that wasn't a bad thing. Maybe it's best that they aren't the same…like their hair…and their eyes…it was OK to be different.

How could she help Sadie now, to let her know she was different than she was a couple days ago? Nora knew she had jeans in the trailer but they wouldn't be able to get there and back in time for Sadie to race. Then she took a deep breath.

"Sadie!" She screamed as loud as she could. Her cousin's blonde head looked up in surprise, she waved meekly.

"Sadie!" Nora yelled again and motioned for her cousin to come to her. Sadie turned Scarecrow as Nora reached down to her boots.

"What are you doing?" Wade cried out behind her.

"Giving her my pants, we're the same size." Nora reached up to unbutton her show pants.

"Nora, you can't undress out here." Her mother yelled at her.

"She can't go out like that, Mom." Nora was pulling the pants down under her butt; she hoped her shirt was long enough to cover her underwear. "Her mind would be on her leg and not on the race."

"Dang, Nora." Nick exclaimed. She glanced up in time to see him take off his shirt and quickly take the two steps up to her.

He wrapped his shirt around her as she pulled off her jeans. She trusted he would keep her covered as she turned to Sadie.

Sadie had seen what she was doing and tried to hurry. She carefully trotted Scarecrow towards her.

As soon as Sadie was close enough, Nora threw her jeans as high and far as she could. She watched them fly as if they were in slow motion and felt all the loneliness, anger, jealousy, impatience and frustration at her cousin fly away with them; tears stung at her eyes.

The jeans flew right into Sadie's hands. Her cousin looked up with shocked eyes as Scarecrow sidestepped.

"Good Luck!" Nora blew her a kiss.

Sadie blew Nora a kiss and quickly turned Scarecrow around.

Nora turned and looked up at Nick. She grinned at his shirtless embarrassment.

"How did you get that scar on the back of your arm?" Wade said from behind them.

"Bull horn," Nick answered then turned to Nora.

"As soon as she runs, I'll go get your other jeans," Nick told her. "For now, sit your butt down so I can have my shirt back."

They all laughed with her mother turning to her.

"What has gotten into you and why are you here?" Her mom's arm came around her showing she was happy Nora was there.

"I wanted to see Sadie and Scarecrow run," Nora watched as Sadie jumped off of Scarecrow and a bunch of people created a circle around her so she could change her jeans. There was one rider ahead of Sadie when she climbed back in the saddle. "I can't believe Scarecrow is running this well in her first year."

Her mother looked past her and towards Nick, who had put his shirt back on. He sat close to her trying to block her from the amused crowd.

"Here, Nora," Wade said from behind her, he was taking off his western shirt, he had a t-shirt on underneath.

"Why didn't you do that before?" Nick looked back at him with a smirk.

"You took yours off so fast I barely had a second to even remember that I had two shirts on." Wade grinned.

Nora laughed and wrapped Wade's shirt around her underwear and bare legs as they announced Sadie's name. They all stood to watch.

Sadie and Scarecrow entered the arena at a prance. Sadie looked so perfect on the palomino. The loud speaker announced that if Sadie ran the race in under 17.5 seconds she would be the division champion.

Nora gripped her mother's hand and reached for Nick's. They stood together watching the young team.

Sadie turned Scarecrow and they took off towards the first barrel. It was a little wide but still good. Scarecrow looked like she was flying. Sadie corrected the angle and Scarecrow turned around the second barrel…it was faster and tighter with horse and rider already looking at the third barrel.

Sadie raced to the third barrel and Nora held her breath. The turn, a brush of the barrel, it started to tip, Nora screamed out, the barrel set back up, and Scarecrow dug in and took off. The palomino's long body stretched out and dug in with every stride. Sadie was flying off the saddle, her long braid bouncing behind her. She was leaning forward, patting the horse's neck to encourage her to run. They had never run so fast!

Nora was jumping up and down as Sadie and Scarecrow ran past them and to the end of the arena. Everyone, including Sadie, turned and looked at the timer. They won! 16.7 seconds of holding her breath and her cousin won! She turned back to see Sadie reach down and pet the palomino's neck then ride out the entry gate.

Nora turned to Wade and they hugged, then her mom.

She turned tear filled eyes to Nick.

"Thank you for getting me here on time." She wrapped her arms around his waist and hugged him tightly. "I couldn't imagine having missed this."

She felt his arms tighten around her for one long squeeze then he stepped away. "I'll go get your jeans." He smiled down at her as he backed away. "So you can congratulate Sadie with some pants on."

***

"Where did Nick go?" Nora asked as she sat back down in the restaurant chair. He had offered to buy the celebration lunch before the six hour drive home.

"He'll be back in a minute," Her mother smiled at her. "You have a good time with him this weekend?"

"Oh, yeah!" Nora grinned and proceeded to tell them about the bull bash, Dude, and most of all, Miss Rodeo Idaho.

Nora turned to Sadie, "You should have seen her! She was SO nice! And she had dark hair, not blonde!" She teased her cousin and both girls laughed.

"Girls..." Wade shook his head.

Nora glanced over at her mother, who was still staring at her as if she was an alien.

"What, Mom?" Nora smiled.

"I..." Her mom just shook her head. "I don't know. You're so...happy."

Nora laughed as she looked around the restaurant. "Where is he?"

"I'm right here," Nick said from behind her.

He dropped a small shopping bag over her head and one over Sadie's.

"What's this?" Nora cried out in surprise.

"Jordan approved." Nick told her.

Nora opened the bag and looked in, excitement ran through her. It was their link… the one thing she knew would keep her from being lonely again. Tears sprung to her eyes as she pulled the gift out of the bag.

"A phone!" Wade yelled.

Nora looked up at Nick, the tears glistening.

"Stop that now!" He backed up with the exasperated expression again.

Nora wiped the tears away as they all laughed.

"If Sadie got a phone too, I'm gonna scream." Wade warned them with raised brows.

Sadie looked in her bag and smiled up at Nick. She reached in and pulled out a small silver horse. It was only a couple of inches tall.

"A trophy for your first championship," He smiled at her.

Tears sprung to Sadie's eyes.

"Stop that now!" He left the restaurant.

CHAPTER FIFTEEN

"What time is it?" Nora asked as she watched the river go by. They were just outside of Clarkston, pretty soon they would be driving back over the big blue bridge.

"We'll get there about 8:00." Nick answered.

"Tired of driving yet?" She grinned up at him.

He chuckled. "My butt's tired of sitting in this truck."

Between their drive to rush to Sadie and the drive home, they had been in the truck for eleven of the last thirteen hours.

"Mine too." She giggled.

It was just the two of them still. They were following her mother's truck and horse trailer. Even though Wade wanted to ride with Nick, her mom said no. Nora was glad. She wasn't quite ready for the weekend with Nick to end. And THAT was quite the surprise!

"I don't think I told you…when Mom and Dad asked if I would mind if you took me this weekend, I figured it'd be really quiet and you wouldn't talk." Nora said honestly, then chuckled.

"Well, after the first ten minutes, it was a consideration." He grinned.

"Why did you say yes to taking me?" Nora tipped her head to him. She hadn't even wondered that before.

"Because they trusted me enough to ask," Nick stopped the truck at the first red stop light and turned to her. "I'll take you anytime you need me."

"I'll go with you any time you need company at one of the rodeo's or bull bashes." She offered with a smile.

"I'll take you up on that offer." He smiled. "On one condition."

"What?" She looked at him with concern.

"Who was the crying girl at the show yesterday?"

"Candace Avery," Nora answered in relief; that was an easy condition. "She said some mean things to me at the last show."

"She was mean, but you still approached her yesterday when she was crying?"

Nora didn't tell Nick that Candace called her ugly, but she told him everything else.

"So you helped her so she could win?" He asked in surprise.

"No," Nora shook her head. "I told her so maybe she could do better and her mother would quit making her cry."

He was quiet while he stared out the window and they made their way across the blue bridge. Her mom's truck and trailer turned right just after the bridge, Nick followed. They would travel next to the Snake River and pretty parks. It would go around Lewiston to The Homestead instead of going through town.

"I like you, Nora." He finally said, glancing over at her with a proud shine in his eyes. "You have a good heart."

Nora felt the happiness spread through her; because of what he said…and because she was truly believing it herself.

***

It was still daylight when they arrived at The Homestead. Everyone was by the barn when they arrived and waiting to help the weary travelers with the horses and to congratulate Sadie on her win.

As soon as her mother's truck stopped, Sadie was out the truck and running to her parents for a hug.

Nora smiled as they pulled in next to everyone. Her dad was at her door before she had a chance to reach for the door handle. He lifted her into a big hug.

"Congratulations, Nora Bug." He squeezed. "Thanks, Nick." He said over her shoulder.

"Anytime." Nick answered. "She is a real kick in the butt to travel with."

Nora giggled and turned back to her companion. He had stepped out of the truck and was walking to the trailer.

"I have to help, Dad." She laughed and he put her down.

"I think there are enough people here to help with the horses." He smiled and walked with her to meet up with Nick.

"I know," She smiled. "But I should do it anyway."

Nora turned and saw Matt and Reilly in Nick's truck retrieving her luggage. She felt a twinge of apprehension realizing the weekend was over, and things might go back to the way they were. Her mom walked up to them and took Nora's competition number and ribbons then waved proudly at her.

Nora waved and turned to take Libby's lead rope from Nick.

Uncle Grayson and Jack were leading Dollar and Scarecrow into the barn in front of her and her dad was leading Isaiah behind her. She felt her heart skip a beat that Nick would leave without saying goodbye.

She stepped into the barn and nervously looked back at the truck and trailer. He was standing next to the door talking to Nikki and Matt. They were laughing.

Nora turned and looked towards Arcturus' stall. There he was, head up, ears alert, and nickering at the horses as they came home.

"I'll take Libby." Nora turned to see her mom with her hand out and nodding to Arcturus. "Go say hello."

Nora nearly tossed the rope to her mom and ran for her horse. She had to say hello and give him attention so she could hurry outside before Nick left.

The horse automatically stepped back away from the door as Nora approached. He was bouncing his head excitedly as she stepped into the stall.

"Hello, my boy," Nora whispered. The horse tucked his nose under Nora's arm and pushed into her, making her giggle. She ran her hand over his nose then up to the star. As her fingers touched her energy source, her heart was already full which made tears spring to her eyes. She knew that there would be days she would still need his energy, but today, she was happy.

"It looks like he missed you." She heard behind her.

Nora turned to see a smiling Nick at the stall door.

"I was afraid you'd leave before I had a chance to say goodbye." Nora smiled hesitantly.

He shook his head. "After the last couple days we've had?" He grinned. "I wouldn't leave without saying goodbye. Besides..." He winked. "I'm not in any hurry to climb back in that truck."

Nora's shoulders relaxed.

Her dad appeared at the stall door next to Nick. She smiled happily at the two men.

"Well," Her dad chuckled. "I haven't seen that smile in a long time. You must have had fun."

"I did Dad!" Nora laughed. "I can't wait to tell you about Dude and Cambria Weber."

"What about the show? We have more additions for the memory room." Her dad said.

"Sadie's first!" Nora said and gave Arcturus one last stroke down his neck and headed for the stall door.

The two girls entered the memory room together, hand in hand.

***

"Nora, you have a message on the Tagger Herd Facebook page." Cora called from out the back door.

Nora looked at her in surprise. "I do?"

"Yes, it says to Nora Tagger at the beginning of the message." Cora confirmed with a smile.

Everyone was still sitting around the back deck tables talking about harvest and the shows.

Nora stood tentatively and glanced over at Nick, he was talking to Matt and Jack. He turned and smiled.

"I'm not leaving yet," He assured her.

Nora grinned sheepishly and stepped into the house.

She slid in the chair at the computer in the library.

The message was up already;

"Nora, thank you, I won 2 classes today and got second in another. Mom was happy. I didn't tell her I used your parents advice and enjoyed Lola, my horse, and showing her. I hope to see you at the next show and thank you in person. You are beautiful…chin up."

Tears sprung into her eyes as Nora read the message over and over. One escaped down her cheek.

"Dang! Nora!" Nick had walked through the library door. "You're not supposed to do that!" He started to turn.

"No! Come back!" She giggled, quickly wiping away the tear and pointed at the computer screen.

Nick hesitated then walked in and looked over her shoulder to read the message.

He put a hand on top her head and patted her. "OK, I'll give you that tear…but no more."

Nora laughed as her parents, Matt and Nikki walked into the library through the door from the living room. Sadie entered the room from the hallway and sat down next to Nora.

As the adults moved to sit at the couches by the big window, Nora typed in Cambria Weber into the computer.

"Oh, my GOSH!" Sadie cried out when the picture of Miss Rodeo Idaho appeared on the screen.

Nora turned the screen so everyone in the room could see her picture, her cowboy hat with crown and wonderful colorful western clothes…then there was the sash!

"You got to meet her?" Matt's eyes were wide in surprise and turned to Nick. "You didn't introduce her to me when I went with you!"

Nick grinned. "She wasn't at that rodeo."

"I'm going with you to all the rest of them!" Matt laughed.

Nora glanced around at the laughing group. Her mother was sitting on her dad's lap…again. Nikki and Matt were on each side of Nick. Uncle Grayson walked in and sat on the same couch as her parents.

Nora left the computer for Sadie and crawled up on the couch between her parents and uncle.

She wrapped her arms around Uncle Grayson's neck and leaned in to whisper in his ear, "Thank you."

He turned his head and kissed her forehead. "You had fun," He stated, it wasn't even a question.

"I did." She nodded and leaned back against her dad. She had a hand on her dad's and uncle's shoulders and her feet were tucked under her.

"So what did you think of your first horse show?" Her mother smiled over at Nick.

He nodded. "Wasn't near as bad as I expected."

Nora's giggle was a little devilish which made everyone look at her. Nick leaned his head back, his eyes narrowed.

"What was that laugh?" Her dad chuckled looking between the two.

Nora opened her mouth...

"Nora..." Nick warned with a grin.

"He found out how many single mothers there are at the horse shows." She giggled then laughed at his exasperated expression.

"I am seriously going with you next time!" Matt declared.

***

Nora stood on the back porch and watched as Nick unhooked the horse trailer from his truck. He was driving to Matt's for the night before leaving for Boise in the morning.

She sighed, all the laughter of the last hour was gone. It was Matt that finally declared he was tired and headed home. Nora wasn't happy about it and it didn't seem like Nick was either; their weekend was officially over. The fear of everything returning to normal ran through her, bringing her mood plummeting to the ground. Her stomach was queasy. Sadness started to weigh her down and make her tired. She was just so scared of being lonely again...she just needed him...one more time... to say he'd be there for her.

Her parents walked out of the house behind her and leaned against the rail.

Nick climbed into the truck and pulled it away from the trailer and towards the long driveway. He'd already said goodbye, giving her the pat on the head and a hesitant smile before turning down the steps and walking away.

When he reached the spot in the driveway, equal to where she stood, his truck stopped and he looked down, the light on his phone lit up.

Her phone alerted her to a text message.

TEXT TO NORA: You have your phone?

TEXT TO NICK: Yes, of course

TEXT TO NORA: Don't forget to text me and send pictures

TEXT TO NICK: I won't, you send too

TEXT TO NORA: I had fun

TEXT TO NICK: Me too, miss you already

TEXT TO NORA: Miss you too, long drive tomorrow all by myself

TEXT TO NICK: I am really scared

TEXT TO NORA: It will all be fine, I'll be here if you need me

TEXT TO NICK: I don't want everything to go bad after you leave

TEXT TO NORA: It won't, you are a good person Nora, remember that

TEXT TO NICK: I am really going to miss you

TEXT TO NORA: I don't know about you but…

TEXT TO NICK: What?

TEXT TO NORA: I could really use a hug goodbye

Nora ran down the steps and towards his truck. He barely had a chance to step out by the time she reached him. She jumped into his arms and wrapped hers around his neck. He turned so he was facing the truck and she was facing the house and her astonished parents.

"Thank you so much, Nick." She whispered, her eyes pressed tight to hold in the tears.

"Thank you, Nora." He squeezed, then squeezed a little tighter.

CHAPTER SIXTEEN

Nora watched Nick standing outside the café door talking on his cell phone. Matt and Nikki were sitting across from her. She glanced up at Nikki, who would look up at her father then back down at her plate. She seemed sad. Nikki looked up at her and Nora smiled.

Nora had caught Nikki frowning at her and Nick a couple times during the day while they were talking. She wanted to tell Nikki why her dad liked hanging out with her but thought it would be breaking his trust.

It had been a month since their trip, and as promised, they were in contact every day. When she started back at school, he wouldn't send her anything until he knew she was out for the day. At 3:30 every afternoon he sent her a picture or a text.

The best came in the mail. It was a big envelope, addressed to Nora. It was a picture of Nick, Cambria, and Dude all together, smiling wide at a rodeo. Cambria and Dude both wrote her a message. Nick had written an 85 next to his picture. It was the score that Dude had received when he received the kick in the butt. Nora had laughed all night on that one! Her mom framed the picture and it was now hanging on Nora's bedroom wall.

Nora turned and looked back at him, then around the room. It was a small café attached to the stockyards where the horse and tack auction was held that day. The four of them were there to buy Nick his first horse and decided to have breakfast while other buyers were looking at the horses that were for sale. The tack auction was first and once it started most of the buyers would leave the horses to attend it. That's when they would go look at the horses.

Nick slid back into the booth next to Nora. He started to say something when Nora interrupted him. "You need to tell her," She looked up at him.

He looked down at her in surprise. "Tell who, what?"

Nora glanced over at Nikki then Matt then back up to Nick. "She needs to know."

"Know what?" Nikki asked from across the table.

Nick didn't turn his attention from Nora. "About what?" He asked her again, now knowing who Nora was talking about.

Nora didn't look at Nikki either, she just looked up at Nick. "Why you like hanging out with me."

Nick raised his eyebrows in surprise. "And you say this now so I don't have a choice?"

Nora's face fell in disbelief. She hadn't thought of that. "I'm sorry," She pleaded his forgiveness with her eyes. "I didn't think of that."

"What's going on?" Nikki said with a hint of frustration in her voice.

"Remember, think it through before you talk." Nick said; he still hadn't looked across the table.

"I'm really sorry, I just think she would feel better if she knew and it just popped out before I thought." Nora looked down at her plate gloomily; she had been trying so hard to be good and not hurt anyone and now she hurt Nick.

"Nora, chin up." Nick said so she looked up at him and saw that he was smiling. "I'll give you this one; you were thinking of what is best for Nikki."

Nora sat back up and swore to herself she would do better next time.

"Hello?" Nikki tried to get their attention. Neither of them looked at her.

"You think she needs to know what I told you?" Nick asked Nora.

Nora nodded and thought he would turn to Nikki but he didn't; he just kept looking at her. His eyes were more green today then brown, she decided, and they looked...worried. Maybe he forgot what he said...or maybe he was embarrassed. He wasn't much in talking about himself with anyone else but her. She tried to read the expression on his face but she couldn't.

"Do you want me to tell her?" Nora asked hesitantly.

Nick stared at her a minute then nodded.

Nora looked over at a very confused Nikki and Matt then back up at Nick, "OK," Nora said and turned back to Nikki.

"He misses the time that he didn't have with you," Nora said to Nikki who gasped in surprise. "When he's with me, he feels like he gets a hint of what it would have been like to be with you at my age."

No one spoke. Nora looked around at each of them, hoping this was a good thing...she was sure it would be...but she had been wrong before. Matt looked over at Nikki then to Nick. Nikki was staring at Nick, who was still looking at Nora. Nora smiled up at him.

"And then there is the fact that you are a kick in the butt." Nick teased Nora. When her smile grew, he turned his head and looked at his daughter.

No one spoke.

"It sounds like the tack auction started." Matt said to break the silence. Other than the noise of the auctioneer ringing through the building, many of the customers had left the café.

Nick took a deep breath and sighed. "I do have one more thing to tell the three of you." They all three looked at him in anticipation. "I just closed the deal to purchase Cora's property from her."

"REALLY?" Nora yelled out then covered her mouth because it came out so loud, then she started giggling. The other three started laughing at her as they slid out of the booth and walked to the back horse pens.

***

"How about this one?" Nick asked Nora. They had walked past the first two holding pens with Nora saying no to all the horses that were there.

Nora glanced in and saw a pair of white burros. She laughed. "I don't even think together they could get you up a hill."

"They're pretty tough." Matt laughed.

Nora just kept walking. She glanced back and smiled when she saw Nikki had her arm wrapped around Nick's elbow and she was smiling brightly. Nick's hand was over Nikki's as it rested on his arm. Nick looked relaxed and happy.

Nora stopped at the next pen and started to step in when she felt a pull at the back of her shirt. "Not so fast," Nick said as he prevented her from going in to the horses. "You don't know them."

"OK." She leaned in looking at the horses.

"What do you think?" Nick asked her.

There were four horses tied in the large pen; she started from the left. "Too small, knock kneed, bad hoof, and eyes are scary." She said of the horses and turned to walk to the next stall.

She heard the three of them laugh behind her but just chuckled at them and kept walking. Nora glanced in and walked past four more pens before she stopped and turned. She started to step in then stopped herself with a glance back at Nick, who had started to grab for her again.

When he stopped and looked into the pen she heard him say "Huh." She smiled, that meant he liked the horse. There was only one in the pen and it was a big, beautiful blue roan. The horse had a black mane and tail and his head was so dark blue it looked black too. His body was dark with the light hair over the top. His neck was large and his mane was thick and completely covered one side. He looked so masculine.

"The mane would have to go," Nick commented. "I'm not spending hours brushing it out."

"If you shaved it off, he would look like a big Trojan horse." Nikki commented. "But he's gorgeous."

Nora turned and looked up at Nick. "Go check him out." She encouraged. He did as she said and walked up to the horse.

The horse turned an alert eye at him and his ears twitched forward. He was tied up short but turned its head as far as he could to see the approaching man. When Nick touched the horse's neck, the horse dipped his head to see if there were any treats. He rubbed down the horse and the horse stood quietly and thoroughly enjoyed it. The blue roan lifted each foot easily as Nick picked them up and played with them.

Nora watched Nick give the horse attention for a few minutes then turned to continue her search. She turned the corner and started walking down the next aisle when she saw another horse she liked. It was a big tall bay. She looked at the sign and saw it was a gelding; just like the blue roan. "Perfect." She smiled.

"Now what did you find?" Nick said from behind her.

"Blue's buddy." Nora giggled.

"Blue's buddy?" Nick asked.

Nora nodded. "You should check him out, too." He gave this horse the same treatment as the blue roan. She could see he liked this one. Matt and Nikki walked up behind her.

As Nick walked out, Nikki asked, "Which one?"

Nick looked at Nora.

"Both," She said.

"Both?" They all three asked her.

"If they're going on your new property then you need two."
Nora said and looked seriously at Nick. "So they don't get lonely."

Nick nodded; he understood.

When they entered the building it was full of people. The area
where the horses would be brought in and shown wasn't very large.
There was a lower level of seats that was raised just above the show
area. Matt had gone in earlier and blocked their seats with coats so
they were on the end where the horses entered and right next to the
rail. They would have a good view of all the horses.

The first ones up for auction were the two little white burros.
Nora watched fascinated as an older couple bid on them and won.
They both looked really pleased.

Four more horses came out. Nora didn't recognize them because
they didn't look at all the pens. They stopped after finding the bay
and Blue.

The horses sold quickly and everyone seemed happy.

Nora was sitting between Nikki and Matt, Nick was on the other
side of his daughter.

"Here, Nora," She turned to Nick and he handed her the paddle
that had a number on it. When they wanted to bid, they raised the
paddle.

"Me?" Nora was excited. "I get to do it?"

He nodded with an amused smile.

Nora heard a low murmur go through the crowd and looked
down at the entry door. A large man was walking in a very small, thin,
dirty white foal.

"It can't be five months," Nikki whispered leaning forward.

"It's so skinny," Nora sighed in concern.

The foal walked quietly next to the large man and lifted its head to look at the crowd peering down at him.

"He has blue eyes and he's really alert." Nikki looked down at Nora.

"You could fatten him up." Nora told her cousin.

The bidding started...but no one even raised a paddle.

"Nikki..." Nora whispered as they stared at the foal. "What happens if no one bids on him?"

"He stays with the owner," Nikki sighed.

"But they don't want him," Nora turned her sad, concerned eyes at her cousin.

The auctioneer was talking real hard to try to sell the foal, but no one bid.

Nora felt a hand slide over the top of hers, which was gripping the paddle so hard her fingers started to hurt. She turned to Nikki and they looked at each other and just knew what they had to do. Together they lifted the paddle...and bought the little foal.

Matt started chuckling as he looked at his dad, who was just shaking his head in disbelief. "You may want to take that paddle back."

The two brunette girls turned to Nick and smiled.

The bay was next. Nora had to raise the paddle five times to win him for Nick. There was a man in the showing area that looked for bids, he would point at her each time she bid and yell "Yep". She knew the man was confirming the bids with Nick before he accepted the bids, but it was still fun and exciting.

When Blue entered the arena, there was a man riding him. The rider maneuvered the horse around the best he could, Blue was impressive. Nora couldn't keep her eyes off him. They trotted back and forth, sidestepped across the whole area then started spinning.

Nora grinned and turned to Nick. He was staring at the horse but didn't say anything. The auctioneer started the bidding as the man backed the horse across the length of the area, turned him and backed him up again.

The bidding was so fast Nora didn't know what to do; there were paddles flying up all over.

"Nora," Nick stopped staring at the horse and looked over at her.

"What?" She asked; her heart racing from the excitement of the bidding and the fear of losing the horse.

"Put the paddle up… hold it there until you win the bid." His expression hadn't changed but his voice was firm.

She nodded in exhilaration and raised the paddle as high as she could and held it there. The man pointed at her six times before the bidding slowed down enough she could see who else was bidding. There were two of them; one woman in red and a man in a checkered shirt.

Three more times he pointed at Nora before the man in the checkered shirt stopped. The woman bid again. Nora turned to Nick, he just nodded at Nora so she kept the paddle up. The man in the ring, taking the bids, looked at the woman, waiting for her to bid. The older woman looked at Nora; staring at her with a frown. Nora just smiled at her, which made the woman shake her head and smile back.

The man pointed to Nora and announced her number as the winning bid!

***

They turned into the driveway of The Homestead. Bay and Blue would stay there or at the ranch until Nick moved to Cora's property. Nikki was taking the foal to The Stables.

Nora was excited for everyone to see the horses and could see all the kids and adults walking across the driveway to the small corral. Wade ran ahead of them and opened the gate.

Matt and Nick unloaded the big horses with the Tagger herd running excitedly through the pasture and up to the corral to greet them. Nikki walked with the little foal which made Wade and Sadie cry out but Aunt Dru was first to the foal. She bent down and talk softly to the scared little guy.

Aunt Dru looked up at her daughter and smiled. "Just couldn't help yourself?"

Nikki giggled and looked at Nora.

"Ahhh, it was a conspiracy." Aunt Dru winked at Nora.

"We only paid $50! And he came with registration papers. He's a creamelo." Nora said excitedly.

Jack walked up to Nick and they watched Aunt Dru with the foal.

Jack finally turned to Nick. "I wouldn't have had a chance either."

Both men chuckled.

They un-haltered the big horses and let them run freely in the corral so they could get used to the other horses and their temporary home.

Sadie walked up to Nikki and whispered in her ear. A smile crossed Nikki's face and she nodded then turned to Matt.

"We have our third." Nikki said excitedly.

Matt looked confused then smiled and nodded. "You're right."

They both looked over at Nick, who looked totally confused.

Nick turned and looked down at Sadie, who was grinning excitedly. "What did you just get me in to?"

"I told her at Christmas that Matt and I wanted to team pen but we didn't have a third rider picked out yet." Nikki informed him with a smile. "And since you just bought a horse…or two, and will be up here now…"

Nick nodded and grinned happily. "I've never done it before, but I would love to."

Nora bounced excitedly. The look on Nick's face, while he looked at Nikki and Matt, was just…heartwarming. It made her think of the energy and love she felt from Arcturus' star. She shivered in excitement for him.

"What's going on over here?" Aunt Leah walked over.

"We're going to do team penning together," Nikki turned excitedly. "Matt, Nick and I!"

"Absolutely NOT!" Aunt Leah shook her head which made everyone stare at her in shock.

"What?" Matt said with a confused chuckle.

"Dru, Jordan, get over here!" Aunt Leah yelled and the two women join them.

"What?" They asked in unison.

"Tell them what you THINK you're doing." Aunt Leah had her hands on her hips.

Nora's eyes widened in surprise and she looked at the rest of the group. They were shocked too.

"Nick, Matt, and I ARE doing team penning this winter," Nikki placed her hands on her hips to match Aunt Leah's.

"NO!" Nora's mom gasped.

"Yes." Matt countered.

Aunt Dru started laughing.

The rest of the adults came over to the group to find out what was happening.

"We were waiting until Jordan got back before we said anything." Aunt Dru chuckled.

"What?" Nora's dad looked at his wife.

"Dru, Leah, and I are doing team penning this winter! Dru signed us up on Friday." Nora's mom informed him.

"Well, that just can't happen." Nora's dad shook his head at her mom. Nora quickly turned to her mom who turned and had her hands on her hips!

"Excuse me?" Her mom said tartly at her husband.

Nora's eyes opened in shock.

"That isn't happening without Grayson, Jack, and I joining in the fun." He grinned at his wife then turned to his brother and brother-in-law.

"Oh, I'm all in!" Uncle Grayson laughed and looked to Jack.

"I'm not missing this for anything. I'm there!" Jack laughed at the look of disbelief on his wife's face. "You think you can beat us?"

"Absolutely." Aunt Dru grinned at him.

Nora watched happily as the adults teased each other. This was going to be a fun winter!

Reilly and Grace walked up to the group.

"So you're not going to work with the stock company anymore?" Reilly asked Nick who shook his head. "What are you going to do?"

"Go back to what I was doing in Australia." Nick answered.

"What's that?" Reilly and Grace asked in unison. Everyone but Nikki, Matt and Nora turned to find out the answer.

Nick turned to Nora. "You didn't tell them?"

Nora shook her head and grinned. Then she said very proudly, "It wasn't my story to tell."

THE TAGGER HERD SERIES

NIKKI TAGGER

Changing Times

Gini Roberge

CHAPTER ONE

Nikki leaned her head back against the truck headrest and stared through the large window of the airport. Where was he? The plane landed twenty minutes ago and it is a pretty small airport! "I just want to get there…hurry up." She whispered to the dark night.

The air was crisp for a May evening, so she turned the heater on full blast. Matt had been training in California all week and wouldn't be used to the cold.

She sat straight up as she saw a flash of him through the windows, seconds later he walked out of the sliding glass doors.

Nikki smiled; he looked tan, and had grown his dark brown hair out longer so he looked even more like Nick. He should have been relaxed and happy, but the frown was deep as he spoke to Kevin; his mentor for search and rescue. Matt turned to her, gave her a quick wave then walked to Kevin's truck and threw his climbing equipment into the back. The two men shook hands with solemn nods of the head and Matt turned to jog to the passenger side door of her truck.

"Hey, Sis." He smiled; a smile that didn't reach his brownish green eyes. He slid onto the truck seat and turned the air vents to blow the warm air directly at him.

"Little chilly?" She teased.

"Yea, it was 90 degrees on the rocks. It's gotta be about 40 here," he answered while buckling his seat belt.

Nikki put the truck in drive and pulled away from the airport.

"Where is she?" He asked.

"At the ranch."

"She OK?"

"Best she can be…Grayson, Scott, and Jack are with her."

"Scott? I thought he and Jordan were in Texas?"

"They were; just finished the cutting clinic with the horses when they got the call."

"How did they get back so fast?"

"Jack's parents knew some people with a private jet and called in a favor. They flew Jordan and Scott back as fast as possible."

"Where are the horses? I know Scott took Little Ghost but who did Jordan take?"

"Cooper…Reilly was thrilled. They're at Jack's parents stable."

"Someone going down to get them?"

She shook her head. "No, his parents had some friends that haul horses, so Jack hired them to bring the horses back."

"Well, I'm glad he's there…the Trio need to be together." Matt turned and looked out the window into the night. "This has got to be hard on Mom."

"I know she's anxiously waiting for us."

"We all knew it was coming…but I just hate that it happened." Matt sighed. "At least it was in his sleep."

"But still…" Nikki felt the tears again.

"Andy was seventy-eight and his ranching life wasn't exactly good on his body."

"The last couple weeks he was confined to a wheel chair…he must have hated that." Nikki wiped away another stream of tears.

"Do you want me to drive?"

"Maybe after we stop at home; I am a bit exhausted," She sighed. "I just finished my last final when they called…they waited until they knew I was done."

"I can't believe you're done with college," He smiled, this time the smile reached his eyes and made them shine with pride. "Congrats, Nikki."

"I can't believe it either…I always thought I would be celebrating on my last day."

"Andy would want you to celebrate, Sis."

"Well," She sighed gloomily. "I just don't feel like it today."

"Maybe you will for your graduation ceremony Friday night or the party on Saturday." He encouraged. "I can't wait to see you in that black robe. It takes a lot of hard work and dedication to get there. I am very proud of you and so is everyone else."

Nikki smiled into the dark as they passed The Stables and turned up the driveway to their house. Neither she nor Matt had been there for over two weeks. The look of the house matched her mood; dark and gloomy.

"I'll wait out here for you." She said as he left the truck and walked into th house to get warmer clothes.

Nikki relaxed against the seat and stared out into the darkness. She had completed college classes while in high school and taken a few classes over the summers so she was graduating college at 21 with degrees in animal science and business. She had focused as much as possible on animal nutrition due to her rehabilitation work with the Tagger herd.

Her plan was to go to work for Dr. Mark, but she had blown that. After talking the veterinarian into publishing his journals and they were such a success, the very deserving man was able to retire and would be leaving his clinic at the end of the month. The new owners of his clinic, a pair of sisters, would be taking over the week before he left.

So now, she didn't have the job she wanted, Dr. Mark was leaving to travel around the world on a book tour with his wife, and Andy was gone.

Nikki's phone alerted her to a new message as they arrived at the top of Parson's Grade.

TEXT FROM CORA: Trio in Barn, Alone, Having private ceremony

Nikki read the text to Matt since he was driving.

"Probably the same stall where they were during their parents and grandparents funeral reception," he sighed.

"Where Andy offered his help…and gave it for years."

They rode the rest of the way in silence.

It was nearly midnight when they arrived. The lights to the ranch house were still on but the bunkhouse was dark indicating the kids sleeping.

"It's cold out here." Matt shivered as they made their way to the front of the house.

"I agree, it has to be one of the coldest months of May we've ever had." Nikki pulled her coat closer around her.

"Nikki! Matt!" It was their mom walking out of the barn.

They altered their destination and Nikki nearly ran into her mother's arms. They embraced tightly, Matt's arms reached around both of them.

"Mom…" Nikki started.

"No words," She whispered. "Just hugs."

The funeral was held in the evening, on the west side of Andy's ranch. His son's wanted everyone to be together for the last sunset on Andy's life. It was a spectacular sunset with rays shooting through the yellow and pinks reflecting in the clouds.

"I haven't recited this poem since Angel died." Matt whispered to Nikki as he waited for his cue to go in front of everyone.

"Want some help?" Nikki offered.

"Yes, I'm honored Andy asked me to recite it but we all should…we do when it's the horses."

"Well, I'll work on that." Nikki turned to Nick who was standing on the other side of her. She whispered in his ear and he turned and looked at her in surprise.

"Please?" She asked. He sighed, nodded then turned and whispered to Grayson who nodded and the whisper continued with all the Tagger family.

On cue, Matt walked up in front of the guests followed by Nick, Nikki, Grayson, Leah, Grace, Sadie, Scott, Jordan, Nora, Wade, Jessup, Cora, Jack, Dru and Reilly.

Together, they recited the poem:

Thundering hoofs
Flying manes
A tail that trails
The love that remains

You leave us now
To fly in the sky
Green pastures to run
Under a warm sun to lie

Carry my heart
In your enchanted spell

Of unconditional love
As we say farewell

Your love we share
Without end
As we saddle up
Fly high my friend

As they made their way back to the group, Andy's sons reached out and hugged each one of them, even Nick, which made Nikki smile.

Chairs and tables were setup at the corral next to the barn. A large fire was blazing to warm the guests from the chilly night. The melancholy group quickly turned to laughter and celebration of Andy…his stories…his life.

Nikki stood peacefully watching the flames but even with a coat and the fire it was cold.

"Are you alright?" Nick asked as he approached her.

"I am," She smiled as he placed an arm around her and squeezed. His extra warmth was very welcome.

Matt slowly made his way to them and took her hand.

Nikki stood quietly between the two of them and looked out at the people that loved Andy. Not only the Tagger family, but there were people who had traveled for hours to attend. Dr. Mark and his whole staff from the veterinary clinic were there. Nikki saw most of the people she had seen at the stockyards throughout the years and at the ranch stores in Lewiston.

Hundreds of people were in attendance and Andy would have been mortified that this many people took time away from the farms and ranches just for him. That's what made Andy such a great man. It was always about what he could do for other people, not about what he needed.

Nikki sighed, it was a sad place to be, but it was heartwarming to see the love of family, friends, and community. She leaned her head on her father's shoulder and squeezed her brother's hand.

"Thanks for reciting it with us," Matt said softly while looking out at the crowd. "I know it couldn't have been easy for you to stand in front of everyone."

"It wasn't hard for me to stand with my son and daughter…in front of anyone." Nick whispered with conviction. Nikki leaned closer to him. "I can't ever make up for the years that I was gone…but I will be here for you, whenever you need me."

"You have…since you came back." Matt whispered. "I'm glad you did."

Nikki felt the warmth inside her, this was a special moment between the three of them, and she knew it. They had come so far in the last 17 months since the night Nick came back in their lives…she couldn't imagine life without him now.

"I think it's time." Nikki whispered.

"Time for what?" They asked in unison.

"Time to admit that you're not just "Nick" anymore…but you're Dad." She sighed, turned, and wrapped her arms around him. She felt his arms embrace her and squeeze tightly.

"I agree." Matt whispered.

Her dad squeezed just a little tighter. It's always that little bit more, that makes the tears rise and the heart warm.

"So, Dad," Matt turned with a smile. "I'd like to introduce you to a few people."

Nick nodded, kissed Nikki on the forehead, and proudly followed Matt.

Nikki looked for her mother to let her know about the change. She spied her off to the side of the corral, just out of the light of the fire, and talking intently to Andy's oldest son, Charles.

Nikki's eyes widened in surprise and she began walking towards them. Grayson appeared in front of her, obviously meaning to stop her.

"What's going on?" Nikki looked up at his concerned blue eyes that were just visible under his black cowboy hat.

"I'm not sure," He admitted.

"Then why are you stopping me? I want to find out."

"Have you met your mother? Her names Dru, and she doesn't like to be interrupted." He chuckled.

Nikki hesitated and looked over at her again. Grayson was right, her mother wouldn't be too happy to be interrupted while she was talking so intently.

"Well heck," She whispered, wanting to kick the ground like a little kid.

"I know," he sighed. "I want to go visit with everyone, but I also want to be here when she's done and find out what's going on."

They didn't have long to wait. Charles turned and walked back to the group but her mom stood quietly looking out into the darkness.

Nikki grabbed her uncle's arm and they made their way to her mother who turned sad, frustrated blue eyes towards them.

"Dru, what's going on?" Grayson asked as they finally reached her.

"They're selling Andy's ranch."

CHAPTER TWO

"Dru, we have to take emotions out of this decision." Grayson leaned back in his chair.

Her mother nodded and brought the coffee pot into the ranch house dining room. "I keep trying to tell myself that."

Nikki looked around at the group; her mother and Jack, Grayson and Leah, Scott and Jordan and herself and Matt. Cora and Jessup were entertaining the kids outside letting them discuss business inside.

"But, this is the only chance we have to increase the Tagger Ranch with consecutive land. All the other privately owned land, surrounding the ranch, won't be sold for years, if ever."

"I never thought Andy's land would go up for sale," Scott added.

"It wouldn't quite double Tagger land, but it would be close." Grayson told the group.

"Taking out the emotions…is it the right thing to do for Tagger Enterprises?" Scott asked.

His sister nodded. "Even in the last couple years with it not being worked full time, it was profitable. If we worked it the way it used to be, when Andy was healthy, it is absolutely profitable…especially working the two ranches together."

"Can Tagger Enterprises afford it?" Jordan asked.

She shrugged, "I'll go over the books in the morning but with the construction of the Barn, Bed and Breakfast; I don't know that we can. I financed that project; I don't think the bank will finance the ranch purchase, too."

"If the new construction wasn't there?" Leah sighed. The new business, that Leah had quit her job to manage, had been in construction all winter.

"We could, without a doubt," her mother nodded.

"Just terrible timing," Matt commented.

"So, what now?" Jordan asked.

"I'll get the paperwork together and head to the bank first thing Monday morning. Then we'll go from there," She answered then turned to Nikki. "In the meantime, Saturday we'll watch my beautiful daughter receive her college diploma and celebrate with a party at The Homestead."

"Dru?" Leah spoke softly.

The two women exchanged a glance then turned to Nikki and Matt.

"Well…we need to discuss your house," Her mother smiled hesitantly.

"The house?" Matt asked.

"Well…we kind of offered it to the new assistant manager of The Stables and his family," Their mother said apologetically.

Matt and Nikki both gasped.

"You're very rarely there…" Leah explained. "And we need someone there that will look over the B&B and The Stables.

Nikki looked stunned at her brother then to her mother and aunt. Unbelievably, she agreed with their reasoning. "So you're saying, I graduate college and I get evicted from my home on the same weekend?" She chuckled softly in disbelief.

"Well…yes." Her mother grinned.

The kitchen door burst open with an extremely excited Sadie running in; her blue eyes wide, long blonde hair flying around her.

"Little Ghost is here! Little Ghost is here!" She yelled and turned to disappear out the door again.

"Well," Grayson smiled. "I guess Little Ghost is here… I sure hope Cooper's with him."

Everyone laughed as they left the kitchen and walked out to greet the horses.

"I haven't seen Reilly bounce like that in a long time." Jack shook his head while watching his son and Sadie jumping at the back of the horse hauler's trailer.

The driver swung open the door of the trailer and backed the black Cooper out the end. Reilly quickly took the lead from the man; his smile wide as he greeted his horse then led it towards the barn.

Sadie grinned happily at the driver as he handed her the lead rope to the grey horse. The horse's head was high in the air checking out his friends that had come to the corral fence to greet them. He then leaned down and nuzzled Sadie's neck. She wrapped her arms around the horse's nose and kissed him happily.

The family made their way to the corral fence to watch the two horses join the rest of the Tagger herd. The horses squealed at each other, ran around the corral, bucked and kicked in excitement.

"We haven't even discussed the clinic," Grayson turned to Scott and Jordan. "How did it go?"

Jordan grinned from the comfort of her husband's arms as they watched the horses. She barely came up to his arm pit and her Indian complexion was a contrast to his blue eyes and blonde hair…they were so different…yet complimented each other perfectly.

"That was so much fun. I couldn't believe how fast Cooper is and how well he took to cutting," Jordan said.

"Fast enough to dump her a couple times," Scott laughed.

"You weren't supposed to tell them that!" Jordan playfully slapped her husband's arm.

"I've never seen you dumped!" Leah commented in surprise.

"He took off so fast and turned on a dime and I wasn't ready." Jordan explained in embarrassment. "I tumbled off his back like a little rag doll."

"He is fast," Grayson nodded. "I watched Grace take him around the arena at a breakneck speed. She was thinking pole bending."

"He was great in team penning last winter." Jack reminded them. "I couldn't have asked for a better partner. Even if we didn't win the family bet." Jack winked at Nikki.

Nikki and Matt grinned at each other, then to their uncles, aunts, step-dad and mother...who, with the help of Nick and his new horse Blue, they beat to win the family bet.

"Well, Jack," Jordan chuckled. "I might have to fight you and Grace for him. He was an absolute joy to ride...after I got used to him."

"And stayed on him," Scott chuckled and kissed his embarrassed wife. "And if you thought Little Ghost was good before we went to the clinic, wait until you see him now." He shook his head in respect. "I'd fight Sadie over him if I thought I could win."

Grayson shook his head grinning. "You wouldn't stand a chance. Just appreciate the time she's allowing you to ride him."

"Between Scarecrow and Little Ghost...that girl ended up with the perfect pair for her." Leah commented. "She's a dynamite rider."

Nikki stood quietly listening to her family banter back and forth until Scott and Grayson broke away from the group and disappeared into the barn. She stared at the door, debating whether to go to them. Her decision was made for her when Matt grabbed her arm and pulled her in through the door.

The two men were tossing hay into the feeders for the horses.

"What's up?" Scott asked when he saw them approach.

"Buttercup," Matt smiled; it had become such an automatic reaction.

"We wanted to talk to you about Nick." Nikki said quickly before she changed her mind.

"I heard you're calling him Dad, now." Grayson said just as he turned so Nikki couldn't see his expression.

"Yeah...that's just it." Nikki nodded.

Her two uncles stopped throwing hay and turned to her and Matt.

"What's the matter?" Grayson frowned.

"I just wanted you two to know...." Nikki felt the tears start to form and her throat constrict.

"Nikki, what's the matter?" Scott asked in concern.

Nikki turned her tear filled eyes to Matt.

"We wanted you to know, that no matter what our relationship is with Nick, it will never replace or take away how we feel about you two." Matt told them.

Nikki nodded her agreement.

Grayson walked over and embraced Nikki, she wrapped her arms around him tightly. "We never for a moment thought it would."

"We're happy for all three of you." Scott assured them. "My love for Nora and Wade doesn't take away anything I feel about you two."

"We were lucky enough to have you when you were kids and watching you grow into the great young adults you are now," Grayson hugged her tighter. "Nick is fortunate to come back into your life's to help share it in the future."

"Besides," Scott chuckled. "With a weird twist of fate, I'm having to share Nora with him. Their friendship has really broken them both out of their shells."

Nikki nodded in agreement and embraced Scott.

"I love you both," Nikki told them.

"It's mutual," They answered in unison.

As Nikki received her diploma, her natural father, step-father, and two surrogate fathers stood proudly together and watched her walk across the stage. Matt and her mother were the first to greet her after the ceremony. It was a long journey to get to this point and she couldn't have done it without her family.

And it was family that gathered for her celebration at The Homestead. Nikki couldn't have been happier as she sat on the back deck of the house and watched her family and friends. The kids were playing volleyball in the yard. The men barbequed and talked cows and ranching. "Typical," Nikki grinned.

The women talked horses and competitions. "Not so typical," Nikki laughed to herself.

"What are you laughing about?" Nick slid into the chair next to her.

"My family," She sighed.

"They are a laughable group," He teased.

Nikki reached out and placed her hand over his. "Thank you."

"For what?"

"For being here," She smiled softly.

"Like I said, I'll be here for you when you need me," He glanced out at the laughing group of people. "I've never attended a graduation before."

"You didn't finish school?" She had never thought of his education before.

Nick shook his head, "Thought about it a number of times…but never did."

"You're still young, only forty-one, you could still go back to school."

Nick chuckled and shook his head, "Desires not there."

Nikki rolled her eyes, "It did take that."

"So, now that the vet clinic is out, what are you going to do with your fancy degree?"

"I thought about opening my own business as an offshoot of The Stables. An equine rehabilitation center," Nikki quickly glanced to him. "But I haven't said anything to anyone…not even Mom or Matt."

"Well," He squeezed her hand. "I'm honored you shared with me and your secret is safe."

"Thanks, Dad."

###

"Have you heard from Dad?" Matt asked late Monday morning.

"Not since the party." Nikki answered as she walked to his truck to greet him and grab the empty boxes out of the back.

"Any word from Mom then?"

"She's at the bank."

"I'll be glad when this gets resolved…one way or another," Matt tossed the boxes into the living room. "And I'll be glad when we figure out where we're going to live."

"We've got the house for another week or two. I guess that should give us time to look. Or, I might just move in with Harvey."

"Wouldn't be the first time," Matt smiled. "We basically lived in the barn the first summer."

TEXT FROM CORA: Dru pulling in driveway

Nikki and Matt ran for his truck.

When they walked through the back door of The Homestead, the Tagger Trio were sitting at the small kitchen table with their spouses. Cora was pouring coffee and handed Matt and Nikki both a full mug.

"Well?" Matt asked.

Her mom sighed, "They are reviewing the paperwork and will call."

"Your gut feeling?" Nikki asked.

Her mom shook her head, "I don't think we should plan on it," Her phone rang and they all turned and stared at it. "Hello?"

There was silence from the rest of the group.

Nikki stared at her mother, trying to read her expression. It was useless of course; her mother had the best poker face ever. She needed to take lessons.

"Thank you," She said into the phone and pushed the end button.

She looked around the group and shook her head. "They would do it next year, after the B&B has been in business for a year to prove itself."

Grayson and Scott leaned back in their chairs in disappointment.

"I'm so sorry, Dru." Leah wiped away a tear. "If I had just stayed at work…"

The two women embraced with her mother looking seriously at her sister-in-law, "It's not your fault. Please don't take this on your shoulders."

"Would Charles and the family wait a year to sell the ranch?" Cora asked.

They all turned to her in surprise. Then her mother reached for her phone and called Charles.

Again, they all remained silent as the phone call was made.

When she ended the call, she sighed. "Charles said he would, but it's up to the rest of the family. He's going to call a family meeting first thing in the morning and see if they will wait."

CHAPTER THREE

The next morning, Nikki leaned against the counter in the kitchen and watched her mother's expressions. As usual, she was unreadable as she listened to Charles talking on the phone. But then her mother broke her usual composure by lowering her head to look at the ground, she squeezed her eyes closed tightly, then raised her head and stared back out the window.

It wasn't good news, Nikki sighed.

The color started to rise in her mother's neck and slowly into her face, her blue eyes narrowed and her jaw clenched. "I understand….yes…no…just one year…yes…alright…fine." She lowered the phone and pushed the end button.

Neither Nikki nor anyone else in the room spoke. They waited as her mother stared at the phone, then looked up and out the window. Her face was still flushed…and getting redder.

"They won't wait one year," She finally said and took a deep breath, turned, and threw her phone down the long hallway causing everyone to jump.

Nikki couldn't see it, but with the force of the throw, she was sure the phone screen was shattered.

No one spoke as her mother walked across the kitchen and up the stairs.

When she disappeared, Grayson sighed while looking up the long stairwell. "Well, along with her looks, we know where Sadie gets her temper."

"That is just so disappointing," Leah sighed. "If only I had stayed working and not taken on the Barn and Breakfast."

Grayson wrapped his arms around his tearful wife. "It's not your fault, Sweetheart. It just wasn't meant to be."

Nikki stood and slowly made her way to Matt; they both looked up the stairs.

"How long do we give her before we head up?" Matt looked at Jack.

Jack shook his head, "No clue... I don't think I've ever seen her this upset."

"I'll text Grace and have her pick up another phone at the store after school," Leah said as she headed down the hall to pick up the remnants of the shattered phone.

"I'll call the store and tell them to have it ready," Jordan walked towards the library.

Nikki turned to her uncles. "I'm sorry, I know you guys really wanted this."

They both nodded with solemn expressions.

"I kept telling Dru to keep the emotion out of it, but I couldn't do it either," Scott answered with a tired sigh. "I just don't want Andy's property sold...it's hard enough that he's gone."

"It almost feels personal," Grayson nodded and looked up the stairs. "The first couple years, she spent more time with Andy than any of us. She needed him for the ranch and to deal with the loss."

Nikki felt the tear fall slowly down her cheek. The sadness on both their faces was heart wrenching, it was like they lost Andy all over again.

She looked up the stairs and imagined her mother, by herself, dealing with the loss again. "I'm not waiting." Nikki said as she trotted up the stairs with Matt behind her.

The door to the large bedroom was open and her mother was sitting on the long sofa with her feet propped on the table in front of her. She was staring at the wall until she saw Nikki and Matt approaching.

"Come on in," She leaned her head back and sighed.

Matt closed the door behind them as Nikki sat next to their mother.

"I'm sorry, Mom." Matt said as he sat in the chair across from them.

"Me, too," She squeezed Nikki's hand. "I just really wanted the property to stay in the family." She chuckled sadly. "I guess, technically, he wasn't family."

"Family is in your heart, Mom, not your blood." Nikki said softly.

"That it is, Hon." Her mother whispered and leaned her head on top of Nikki's. "Did I ever tell you about the time Andy babysat you two?"

"No," They answered in unison.

"It was while The Homestead was being built. Matt, you were three and Nikki, you were five. I was at the ranch with Andy going over the books after branding when I got a call that Leah was in labor with Grace, two weeks early. He offered to watch you even though Clara was out of town. I found Grayson and Scott then headed to the hospital," She smiled warmly. "It was another Tagger...our number seven, it meant a lot for all of us to be together and Andy knew that."

"How long did he watch us?" Nikki asked while cuddling into her mother.

"Overnight. It was a long tough labor. Leah was exhausted and so was Grayson." She sighed from the memory. "When Scott and I finally got home, we had to go to Andy's ranch house to get you. He had let Nikki pick out your clothes…which is a pretty good challenge for a five-year-old…color wise."

"Purples and yellows again?" Matt laughed.

"Yeah…on you…we could have spotted the two of you colorful kids a mile away." She sighed again. "In the amount of time he had you, he taught you to call him Papa Andy."

"Oh, I forgot about that!" Nikki sighed, the sadness of his loss descending again. "We called him that for years."

"He loved you two," She told them and kissed Nikki on top of the head.

"It was mutual." Matt said with his eyes glistening.

Nikki opened her eyes and looked at the ceiling of her room…which had been Jack's room for eight years until he became her stepfather and moved into The Homestead. Her first Wednesday after graduating…and she still hadn't thought about getting a job and now she was going to be homeless. She turned and looked at the pictures on her bedside table. One was of her and her mom throwing leaves on Matt; they were laughing and having fun. The other was the picture Grace took of Matt and Nick looking pretty rough when they were riding in the mountains rescuing the kids from the plane crash.

She wanted to talk to one of them, but her mother was upset, she hadn't heard from her dad, and Matt was sleeping in his room…with a girl he knew from rock climbing.

Her phone alerted her to a text message.

TEXT FROM JACK: Your mother needs you now

TEXT FROM NIKKI: Is she OK

TEXT FROM JACK: Physically yes

TEXT FROM NIKKI: Be there ASAP

Nikki jumped out of the bed and into the shower, quickly applied the little makeup she wore and ran a brush through her long wet dark hair. She pulled on blue jeans and a red button up shirt. When she opened her door, Matt was opening his.

"You got the message too?" He asked as he buttoned his shirt, his wet hair soaking the collar.

"Yes." She answered as they quickly made their way down the stairs and to the back door where their boots were.

"Where's your lady friend?" Nikki asked once they were driving down the road. She drove by and glanced at The Stables then over at the new construction of the Barn and Breakfast. Both seemed fine.

"She left a while ago; headed to Riggins to climb."

"You didn't go?"

"No, I wanted to be here for Mom. I can go another day."

"I wonder what's up...did Jack tell you?"

"No, just said to get there."

"I hate this, Matt." Nikki frowned.

"I'm glad Jack hired an assistant manager so he can spend more time with Mom and at the ranch." Nikki said.

"Your old job?" Matt grinned. "And now you're jobless and they're taking your home."

Nikki chuckled. "Totally ironic isn't it? I graduate college and can't even get a job with my own family's business AND I get kicked out of the house."

Nikki turned onto the main road.

"When's your next training?"

"We're jumping in a couple weeks," He grinned. "Don't tell, Mom, she may want to go with me again."

Nikki laughed. "You mean, don't tell Jack. I thought he was going to have a heart attack when he heard you had her jumping out of a plane."

"It was tandem, and I made sure she was with someone I trusted." Matt chuckled. "But you're right…he wasn't very happy about it."

"She loved it."

"Maybe I should invite her…give her something else to think about."

"Don't tell Jack." Nikki smiled as she turned down the driveway to the house.

"It's 9:30; the kids should all be in school and Cora at her yoga class in town."

"I can't believe I was still in bed at nine o'clock."

"Me either, I need something to do when I'm not training. I'll talk to Scott and Grayson and see what I can do to help."

Nikki parked and they exited the truck and jogged to the house. Jack opened the back door and they saw Grayson, Scott, Leah and Jordan sitting solemnly at the kitchen table.

"What happened?" Matt asked.

"She figured out a way to buy the ranch," Grayson answered.

"Really? So what's the matter?" Nikki asked in surprise.

"They sold the ranch already," Scott shook his head.

"No!" Matt and Nikki gasped in unison.

"She's upstairs… pissed, unhappy, frustrated, mad, and anything else you can imagine." Jack leaned against the kitchen counter. "There wasn't a thing I could say to help her. I feel totally useless."

"Oh, Jack!" Nikki gave him a quick hug.

"I hope you can help," He squeezed. "If you two can't…I don't know who can."

Nikki ran up the steps behind her brother and they turned to find a closed door this time. They walked up to the door and glanced at each other nervously before Nikki knocked.

There was no answer.

She knocked again. "Mom, it's Matt and me."

"Come in."

When she opened the door, her mother was dressed in blue jeans and a navy blue top, but was lying flat out on the bed and staring at the ceiling. Her arms were flung out at her sides. When she looked over at them, it was obvious she had been crying.

Nikki sat on the edge of the bed and took her mother's hand and squeezed tightly. She returned the squeeze then flung the other arm over her eyes to hide the tears. Matt gently sat at the head of the bed by the pillows.

They waited until she spoke.

"I figured out what a monthly payment would be on the ranch and calculated we could make that payment to Andy's family each month; until next year, when we could finance it." Her voice trembled in anger or sadness, Nikki couldn't tell. "When I called, they had already sold it…yesterday, right after I talked to them."

"That fast…I didn't even know it was on the market yet." Matt shook his head.

"It wasn't…it was word of mouth," She moved her hand off her face and stared at the ceiling. "They don't know who bought it; it was done through a lawyer."

"Well, that's scary." Nikki frowned.

"That's not even the worse part," Her mom turned her head to look at her. "It was financed INTERNATIONALLY!"

"No…" Matt sighed.

"I couldn't believe it either," She finally sat up and ran a hand through her loose blonde hair. "It's bad enough he couldn't wait a dang year, but selling it so fast! I was hoping they couldn't get it sold for a year." She chuckled sadly and looked between them. "I was still holding out hope."

"Internationally…." Nikki shook her head. "What do you think that means?"

It was the wrong question to ask as the redness started in her mother's neck again and lifted to her face.

"It means they sold to someone that doesn't even know the area…didn't know Andy…can't even understand the history of the land or appreciate it." She stood quickly and started pacing.

"Mom, you're going to have to relax." Matt stood.

Her hands went to her hips as she tipped her head back to look at the ceiling. "I know. I keep trying; it's been an emotional rollercoaster for the last week. I can't believe Jack hasn't given up on me yet."

"He's pretty upset," Nikki admitted. "But he won't give up, you know that. He just doesn't know how to help."

"He called you, didn't he?" She looked at Nikki.

"Yes," Nikki nodded.

"Then he knew exactly how to help." Her mother tried to smile.

"That's a pathetic smile, Mom." Matt chuckled.

"Like I said…I'm trying," She walked over and sat on the chair. "I just need time, I guess."

There was a knock at the door.

"Who do you think got brave enough to come up?" Her mother leaned back with a frustrated frown.

CHAPTER FOUR

"Dad!" Nikki cried out when she opened the door. The look of surprise registered on his face and then the smile. "Still not used to that are you?" She chuckled, then realized… "You're upstairs!" He'd never been on the second floor of the house before!

He nodded and took a step back, "Your phones are downstairs and your 'dang' uncles wouldn't come up and get you; neither would their 'wonderful' wives." He glanced towards the stairs. "I thought of yelling, but figured that was a little too much." He chuckled and took another step back.

"Dad?" Matt stepped behind her. "Where have you been? You just disappeared."

Nick nodded and looked apologetic, "Sorry about that…it's what I need to talk to you about."

"OK," Nikki said and took a step back.

Nick just shook his head, "With all due respect; this is about as far as it goes."

"It's OK, Nick," Her mom walked up behind them trying to smile through her frustration.

"Uh, no." He took another step back. "It may be all natural for you guys, but, no matter how long it's been, it's still the bedroom of my ex-wife and her husband." He smirked, his eyes sparkling in humor at the situation.

Nikki laughed, she hadn't thought of it that way. Matt and her mother chuckled, too.

"Can we just go down to the library? I need to talk to all of you."
He walked to the top of the steps without waiting for the answer.

"All of us?" Her mom asked in surprise.

"Yeah, your wonderful brothers and their wives are waiting for
us. Jack too, he wouldn't come up and get you either." He chuckled
and disappeared down the stairs.

Nikki turned to Matt and her mom, shrugged in confusion then
followed him.

As she entered the library, Grayson, Scott, and Jack were
grinning devilishly. Leah and Jordan were giggling as they were
pulling chairs up to the table. Nick was shutting the door to the
hallway. That surprised everyone.

Following his lead, Matt closed the door that led to the living
room.

"I can't remember the last time those doors were closed." Leah
stated.

Everyone took a seat around the table. Grayson and Leah sat at
one end of the table with her mother taking a seat next to Jack at the
other end, after giving him a quick kiss. Scott and Jordan sat across
from Matt and then Nick walked around the table across from her
and Matt to take a seat. That really surprised everyone in the room.
He always sat between Nikki and Matt.

He dropped two large folders on the table.

"Nick, what's this about?" Her mom asked. She was leaning
sideways in her chair with her arm resting on the back and her head
resting in her hand. She still looked upset and now, impatient.

Nikki sat quietly but nervously…this was so unlike him.

"Before I say anything," He started and opened the top
envelope. "I have to have each of you sign one of these." He looked
at the top of each and slid one paper to each person.

"Sorry," He frowned as he slid one to Nikki then to Matt. "You'll understand in a minute."

Nikki looked at his pleading eyes then down to the paper. It was a confidentiality agreement.

"Whatever is said in the room, in the next few minutes, can never be discussed once we're done." Nick said firmly and looked around to all the confused and surprised faces.

Everyone in the room signed the papers except her mother, who slid the piece of paper back across the table, unsigned. She stood and made it half way to the door before Nick spoke.

"It involves Matt and Nikki." Was all he had to say to make her stop, turn and glare.

"I've never asked you this before…ever," Nick looked up at her. "But I need you to trust me."

"Dru…" Grayson said. She turned and looked at her brother, then to Scott, who nodded.

She turned and sat back down, but didn't reach for the paper.

"I'm sorry, Dru." Nick sighed. "But it has to be signed before I can tell you what I need to say."

Without a word, she slowly reached across, retrieved the paper, and deliberately, excruciatingly slow, signed the paper. She threw the pen down and it slid nearly the whole way down the long table.

"Well, then." Grayson chuckled.

"Thank you," Nick nodded, trying to keep the smile off his face as he opened the other folder

He took out a stack of papers from the other envelope and slid them across to Nikki and Matt.

They both slowly leaned forward to look at them.

Matt gasped first…then Nikki's jaw dropped in shock and they both looked up at him in stunned silence.

"What is it?" Scott leaned forward.

"It's a copy of the deed to Andy's property." Nikki whispered in amazement.

"WHAT?" Her mother stood in anger. "You BOUGHT Andy's ranch?"

Nick's expression was calm; almost like he knew the anger was coming.

"Yes," Nick answered.

She took a few steps backwards. "You OWN Andy's property?" She spit out in angry disbelief.

"No," He answered calmly.

She glared at him in frustration.

Nikki gazed at her mother in shock then turned to Nick. He was staring at his ex-wife, still unfazed.

"You just said you bought it." Grayson frowned.

"I bought it, but Matt and Nikki own it." He said calmly.

"What?!" Nikki and Matt said in unison and looked back down at the papers. There…in writing…were their names as the property owners.

"You bought the ranch for Nikki and Matt?" Leah gasped in amazement.

He moved his eyes from her mother to Leah. "Yes."

"Why?" Matt whispered.

"Because I wanted you to have it, and…" He looked over at their mother. "…because the deal with Dru fell through."

"What does that mean?" Her mother glared.

"It means the purchase was only to go through if you couldn't match what Andy's family wanted. The second it fell through, my purchase went through."

"Did the family know your offer was there?" Scott asked.

"No, only their attorney; I didn't want it to influence Dru's negotiation." He answered.

Nikki looked at the paperwork in shock, her whole body tingling. She and Matt owned Andy's ranch. Tears sprung to her eyes at the thought of Andy being gone. She took a deep breath and let it out slowly then took a closer look at the papers in front of her.

"Dad?" She said raising her eyes to him.

He tilted his head and smiled. He knew what she was going to say.

"It says the deed would be mailed within 48 hours. The actual deed?" She placed a hand over the stack of papers as if to keep them from flying away. He nodded.

"What?" Her mother asked and walked behind her to look at the papers. Nikki picked them up and handed them to her.

"You only get the real deed when the property is paid in full. How is that possible?" Grayson asked staring at Nick.

Nick leaned forward, resting his arms on the table and looked down at him. "When I left, I had a nineteen-hour flight to Australia. I gave them twelve hours to get everything done, and then a nineteen-hour flight back. I came here as soon as the plane landed." He turned to Scott and Jordan. "Nora had left me a couple concerned texts. I've let her know I was OK, and told her I would take her to lunch to apologize…she insisted it be Zany Graze."

Her parents nodded with confused smiles.

"You're not buying her a ranch too?" Jack smiled as he shook his head slowly.

"If I thought Scott and Jordan would let me…I would." Nick chuckled.

Scott and Jordan stared at him in disbelief.

"Who is 'them'?" Matt asked.

"My financial team and attorneys," Nick leaned back in his chair.

"You have a financial team and attorneys?" Jordan asked in amazement.

Nick nodded, "Yes, I do…I think I should explain a few things."

"Yes, please do," Her mother said tersely and sat back in her chair; tossing the papers down on the table in front of her.

Nick leaned forward again and talked straight to Nikki and Matt.

"I told you I was a developer," He started and they both nodded. "That was the dead honest truth, I just didn't explain to what level." He said firmly, looking them both in the eyes. "I have NOT lied to you, nor will I lie to you at any point during this conversation…or ever. If you have any questions, ask, it's back to the open book policy."

Nikki smiled nervously and looked over at Matt, who was staring at their father.

"OK…" Matt finally sighed.

Nick nodded and spoke only to them, as if no one else was in the room. "When I moved to Australia I continued to hit the rodeos for a couple years. I basically lived out of a truck and with a group of friends. Everything I earned went in the bank. Once I got tired of the bulls, I settled down with a few friends and tried to decide what to do next. I'd never worked before, besides on ranches. The brother of one of those friends had a small ranch store that was failing. My buddy, his name's Cid, and I bought the store from his older brother and within six months we had turned it around and it was making a profit. We were able to hire another half dozen people in the store and still make a profit. So we did it again. We purchased another small business, another ranch store on the other side of Sydney, and within six months had it profitable and were able to put another eight people to work…and more money in the bank."

He took a deep breath. "I wanted to continue but Cid was done. I bought his part of the two stores and still had enough to buy a small paint shop. Within a year it was profitable, more people to work. I hired my first financial consultant. We continued for the next twelve years turning 2 to 3 business around per year."

"How many business' do you own?" Matt asked, showing no emotion.

"The corporation owns about thirty-one, very profitable businesses across Australia. They have each doubled or tripled in size from the time I bought them. One has quadrupled and put over 300 more people to work, just by itself."

"The corporation?" Nikki asked. The information was just mind boggling.

He nodded with a smile. "I know it sounds bizarre, as Grace would say, but yes, I own a corporation, no partners."

"And when you disappeared?" Nikki asked, numb with shock.

"The finance team and attorneys started pulling everything together to get enough cash to buy the ranch." He answered. "I had to be in Australia, personally, to sign the paperwork."

"It didn't take them long…for that much money." Matt commented.

"I don't finance very much, only the amount that I have to. I don't like being in debt, it's a fear of being dirt poor again," He shrugged slightly. "Took me a while to realize that."

"What if they wanted more?" Matt asked.

"In all honesty," Nick looked between them. "I could have gathered enough cash to buy the ranch…three times over."

There were shocked gasps in the room. Nikki's jaw dropped.

"Would it have broke you?" Matt was still calm.

"No, not even close." Nick admitted.

Nikki stared at him. There was no reason to doubt his story; like the time before. The paperwork on the table was sufficient proof.

"Why were you working for the stock contractor when you came back?" Nikki asked. "Why work at all?"

Nick shook his head. "I have to do something. I couldn't stand not working. When I got to Boise from Australia I went to the contractor to see about a job to kill time. They were failing, about to close down...so I bought them."

"You owned the stock contracting company?" Grayson asked in shock.

Nick turned and smiled down the table at him, "Yeah, bought it twenty-four hours after walking in the door. By the end of the first season, I had made a profit. Bought a better quality of bulls and horses and marketed them better. I already have enough events booked this coming season to double the business. I'll put another 15 people to work."

"That's important to you?" Nikki turned; her mother had finally spoken.

"What? Putting people to work?" Nick asked.

Her mother nodded.

"Absolutely; after the first store, and I saw we could put people back to work, it became a driving goal of each purchase." He said firmly, looking her directly in the eyes. "I was dirt poor because my father didn't want to work and because my mother had a hard time finding a good job. My goal was to put as many people that wanted to work into good jobs so their kids didn't have to go for days without food or sleep in the dirt...like I did."

"You started with $50, that you won off riding the first bull in a pasture...won off a bet." Matt said and Nick nodded. "And you grew it to become a millionaire?"

"A couple hundred times over," Nick nodded without emotion.

CHAPTER FIVE

Nikki was stunned again. "You don't exactly live like a millionaire…a couple hundred times over."

"It's not who I am, I couldn't live that way," He shrugged. "The money and corporation are there for all the business' and people…not for me to have more money to spend or waste."

"That sounds pretty noble," Jordan chuckled in amazement.

Nick leaned forward and turned to her. "That's why you had to sign the Confidentiality Agreement. I don't WANT people treating me any different because of the money I have or expect me to give them money just because I have it, or try to steal it and jeopardize what we've done."

"You think we would say this to anyone?" Jack asked in irritated surprise.

"Absolutely not," Nick looked at him seriously. "That was all at the attorney's request. I didn't like it," He looked down at his ex-wife. "And I knew you guys wouldn't like it. I was really hoping you wouldn't hold it against me, but the only way we have been able to accomplish what we have is because we listen to the attorneys." He shrugged. "So when they insist on something, I usually give in."

They sat quietly a moment trying to absorb all the information.

"What about Nikki and Matt?" Grayson asked.

"I thought of them every day," Nick answered with a slight smile as he looked across at her and Matt. "As soon as I could, I created the savings account for them, deposited what I could for their support, but I knew they didn't need the money. You and your family would give them everything they needed. I didn't know about the accident until you took in The Tagger Herd and from what I could tell they still didn't need any money. They are, were, my only beneficiaries. They were going to inherit everything when I died."

"Were?" Her mom asked.

Nick leaned back and sighed, "Yeah." But didn't say more.

"Open book policy," She frowned, "Why 'were'? You said you didn't have any other children."

He sighed again.

"Open book policy," She repeated.

Nick rolled his lips together. "OK…" He sat up in his chair and took a deep breath. "I changed my will last winter, and left a portion to each one of your kids." He looked at Scott, Grayson and Jack.

They all sat in stunned silence.

He looked around and sighed again. "They will inherit it after my death but won't be able to touch it until they are 25, which honestly, I'm hoping it's a whole lot later than that." He smiled, trying to break the tension with a joke.

Still no response from the crowd.

He looked around to each of the adults that he just left speechless.

"I really didn't want any of you to know until I was gone, but open book policy." He smiled at his ex-wife, she just stared back. "Can we just skip this part now? Not ever talk about it again? Just know it's there and worry about it then?"

"You think that much of our kids?" Leah finally asked.

Nick leaned his head back in defeat; he wasn't going to get his request.

"Seriously, I hate talking about myself this much. I just don't do it." He shook his head. "You have no idea. I think I'm going to need some Nora therapy after this."

Everyone in the room chuckled, because they knew it was true.

"You have a lunch date with her," Scott reminded him.

Nick nodded and sat quietly, long enough, Nikki didn't think he was going to answer. "OK, the deep stuff…" He sighed, looked down at the table then back up. "It doesn't matter how much money I have in the bank…" His voice had a slight crack of the emotion he was trying very hard to hide. "In the last year…being around your family and these kids…that is more…" He stopped, took in a deep breath to calm the emotions then exhaled again. "Seeing the kids come in after their cattle drive, knowing they could be punished but did it anyway…because of their love for you…" He smiled softly and shook his head. He glanced up quickly, then after deep breath, he looked straight at Matt. "There is no amount of money in this world that could buy the feeling I had when you called and asked me to help build the arena, it was so unexpected…but so…wanted and needed." His eyes started to glisten. He turned to Nikki, "No amount of money…when you said you didn't want me to disappear…then when you reached out to shake my hand, to let the past be the past and move forward, to let me have…a chance…" He cleared his throat trying to rid the emotion.

Nikki felt the tears build.

"When I saw you over the edge of the cliff in the mountains," He looked at Matt and the first tear fell. "I would have given every dime I had ever earned to get you out of there safely…I was so terrified of losing you after just getting you in my life." He turned to Leah, "Every dime…not to have had Grace face that grizzly." He turned to Jack. "Every dime to make sure Reilly didn't go over the edge of the mountain grade when he disappeared." He turned to

Scott, another tear fell. He took a deep breath and let it out slowly. "Every dime…to take Nora on that road trip again so she could help heal the loneliness I had hidden all my life…to realize what I was staying away from…to realize what I had missed…" He turned to his ex-wife. "…to realize what I had lost when I left Nikki and Matt behind."

Nick lowered his head, inhaled deeply and exhaled slowly. He quickly wiped the remaining moisture from his eyes and sat quietly.

Tears slid down Nikki's face, she turned to her mother and saw the tears in her eyes, same with Leah and Jordan. Her uncles and Jack remained quiet each staring at a different point in the room, respecting Nick's emotions. She turned to Matt, he was leaned back in his chair, looking at the ceiling; a tear ran down into his hair. Nikki reached over and took his hand. He gripped it like he was drowning.

Finally, Nick raised his head and looked around at the group. "Dang, I'm glad the attorney's made you sign those Confidentiality Agreements," He chuckled, trying to hide his embarrassment. "This can't leave the room."

"You may need Nora longer than lunch," Jordan commented through her sniffles.

They all chuckled and nodded in agreement.

Leah stood and left the room returning a few minutes later with water bottles, soda, and a few beers. Nick reached for the beer.

"Next question?" Nick finally asked after half the beer was gone.

"You live a pretty normal life." Jack said. "What do you spend your money on?"

"Always buying and improving, employing people, and giving to charities." He answered.

"Charities?" Nikki sat up straight in her chair, her voice had risen in pitch and she looked at Nick accusingly. He just grinned in return.

"What?" Her mom asked.

"I took care of the charity money that came in for The Tagger Herd." She reminded her mother but grinned at her father.

"Let us in on the secret." Leah told her.

"When the donations started coming in, to help take care of the herd, we received multiple donations from businesses all over Australia. Enough from all the businesses that the herd would be taken care of for the rest of their lives…it even covered Rooster's surgery." She announced with a shake of the head.

Nick shrugged, "I found a way to help."

"You know what these means?" Jack asked.

"What?" Her mother turned to him.

"Elena went after the wrong man," Jack smirked.

Nick's eyes widened and nodded emphatically.

"Could you imagine?!" Her mother shook her head.

"That's why I keep everything so distant from me. No one, here in the States, knows about the corporation besides this family." Nick said and looked around at all of them. "It's because of people like Elena, and there are more out there than you could imagine, that I don't tell people. My attorneys and finance team are at your disposal, 24-hours a day; advice and protection. They'll watch after the kids, too."

"It's best the kids don't know," Grayson said.

"I agree," Nikki's mother stated. "It ALL stays in this room."

"I agree," Jordan, Leah, Jack, and Scott all said in unison.

"One of the attorneys, Lucas, came back with me," Nick announced. "Now that you know, he'll meet with each of you to go over everything. He is Cid's younger brother so he knows everything that happened in Australia but he had no idea about any of you until 18 hours ago. I told him on the plane over here. He's a bit shocked, to say the least."

"Seriously?" Nikki was amazed.

"I don't talk about my past," He said flatly. "After the corporation started growing, I didn't want anyone to know about the two of you or Dru so they couldn't go after you…like Elena would if she knew."

"What happened to Cid?" Leah asked.

"He took the money and bought a station, he raises cattle and horses. I spend a lot of free time there." He chuckled. "What's really funny, is when Nora asked me what my first horse was like and I realized that I had all that money at my disposal and had never bought a horse for myself."

Nikki smiled. "The lady trying to buy Blue didn't stand a chance."

"No, she didn't." Nick grinned.

Nick turned back to her mother.

"Dru, I wasn't going to take a chance that ANYONE else got Andy's property. After talking with Nikki Saturday night, I decided if you couldn't buy it, I wanted her and Matt to own it. I knew there were three other buyers lined up after me." Nick smiled. "I tried to get it done as fast as I could, just in case."

"Well," She chuckled. "I couldn't image a half hour ago that I would be thanking you."

"We're good then?" Nick asked with a raised brow.

"Yeah, but," His ex-wife leaned forward, resting her elbows on the table and staring at him intently. "Are there any more secrets you haven't told us? Are we going to be surprised in another year and a half with another one of these meetings?"

"NO!" Nick laughed and shook his head. "If you want to know anything, ask now! No more of this, I can't take it."

Her mother laughed. "Good. So what do we do about the ranch?"

"Ask them," Nick pointed to Nikki and Matt with a grin. "They're the owners."

Nikki and Matt both sat back at the same time, in amazement. Everyone chuckled.

"How do we explain that they not only own the ranch but they own it free and clear?" Her mother frowned in concern.

"Nobody will know unless we tell them that the ranch is paid off. It was all "financed" internationally." Nick explained. "We tell them Tagger Enterprises and I helped them purchase the property. Their attorney signed a Confidentiality Agreement, he can't say a word. Nobody, here in the States, knows me well enough to say I couldn't help purchase the property."

"When does it turn over?" Grayson asked.

"The property itself, stock, equipment…everything except the ranch house, is immediate." Nick answered seriously. "They figured they needed a couple of weeks to clean out the house. They'll call you when it's ready."

"Inventory?" Scott asked.

Nick reached over to the paperwork and flipped through the papers and handed a section to Scott.

Scott quickly scanned through it, frowned, and looked at Nick. "Did you read this?"

"Of course," Nick nodded. "I read every word before I spend that kind of money; on Lucas' insistence. One of the attorneys, actually Lucas, is a rancher. He noticed it too, pointed it out and wasn't sure we should pay the asking price. It's the reason he came over."

"What?" Grayson and her mother said in unison.

Scott slid the paper to her mother and turned to Grayson. "The cattle herd is pretty much what we expected…at its lowest headcount…ever, but he only has a handful of horses and most of those are over twelve."

"Really?" Nikki was shocked.

Scott glanced at her and nodded. "The farm equipment is also mixed, nothing newer than five years."

Nick turned to Nikki and Matt, "In the paperwork is bank information with enough of a start to get the ranch going again."

"Dad…" Matt frowned.

Nick interrupted, "I'm not going to hand you something that has a chance of failing…the money will insure you have enough to make it successful." He leaned forward and sighed. "Unfortunately, Andy's sons didn't keep it up. It needs work."

"He's right," Her mom said and looked at her and Matt. "With Andy's failing health, he had to leave a lot to his sons to do. They just wanted to push cows and brand. They didn't want to do the upkeep and daily work…for years. We helped when we could."

Scott abruptly sat back in his chair and shook his head.

"What?" Matt asked concerned.

"The actual ranch property is just under Tagger Enterprises acreage. But with the State and BLM leased land …it's bigger." He sighed.

"With no workers," Grayson added looking at Nikki and Matt. "…and it's in worse condition."

"It's a big uphill climb." Leah warned them.

"You'll need every penny that's in that bank account…whatever it is…and you need laborers." Jack nodded.

"Putting more people to work…" Their mom said which made Nikki and Matt look at each other then to Nick.

"We'll be right back," Matt said and pushed his chair back. He took Nikki's hand and they walked into the living room.

Nikki glanced at the clock. "Cora should be back soon."

Matt nodded and sighed. "I can't believe all this."

"Me either," Nikki said and walked to the large window and stared out to the herd grazing peacefully in the south pasture.

Matt came up to stand next to her. "I don't know what Mom's plan was if she was able to purchase the ranch, but I know one thing…" He turned and looked at Nikki.

"…we can't do it without her." Nikki finished for him and he nodded.

"We can't do it without the Trio."

"What about your search and rescue?" She didn't want him to give up his dream.

"I can do both, if we have the right people in place while I'm out." Matt smiled. "After the shock wore off, it's the first thing I thought of."

"My mind went to the business end of it, habit from the years of helping with The Stables books." Nikki admitted. "What if we ask them if we can run the ranches together as one, and we'll hire the extra help to work both?"

"But if a decision is made that affects our ranch…" Matt shook his head. "Our ranch…"

She turned to him and embraced him…a big brother sister bear hug.

"We have to be included in the voting." Matt finished.

"Let's talk to them about it…no final decision needs to be made right away….it's not going anywhere."

"Well…we were just talking about needing something to do." Matt grinned.

"And somewhere to live," Nikki reminded him with a smile.

Together they walked back into the library, shutting the door behind them.

"He's sitting at the airport?" Leah was asking Nick.

"Yeah, he's in a comfortable plane and working on his computer and on his phone, he's worked in worse conditions. Greg, the pilot, is there with him." Nick smiled.

"He's in a plane with the pilot?" Leah asked confused.

"We flew the corporation's plane over." Nick said matter-of-factly.

"You have a plane?" Jordan gasped.

Nick nodded. "We fly all over Australia. We're not going to wait on commercial flights; nor pay their prices. We've saved a lot of money over the years with it." He shrugged. "I wanted to get back here as fast as possible and Lucas wanted to come with…so we brought it."

Nick looked up at Nikki and Matt. "You guys OK?" He asked in concern. "I know this has been a lot."

They both nodded.

"No decision needs to be made now." Grayson told them. "Just let it soak in and give it some time."

Nikki and Matt both shook their heads.

"We just decided two things." Matt told them. "They are pretty obvious."

"We'd like to run the two ranches as one," Nikki said quickly. "We'll pay for all the extra workers to help run them together."

"And the other?" Scott smiled.

"If there is a decision to be made that concerns Andy's ranch then we're included in the vote." Nikki answered.

Nikki looked at her mother.

"Are you sure?" Her mom asked.

"Absolutely," They said in unison.

Nikki was shocked again when everyone in the room grinned.

"What?" Matt asked.

"When you walked out the door," Grayson explained. "Nick said the best move you two could make is exactly what you just said."

Nikki shook her head in amazement. She glanced up at Matt who just smiled.

"Are you going to vote?" Matt asked.

"I vote yes." Grayson said.

"I vote yes." Scott said.

"I vote yes." Their mother grinned proudly.

Silence…

"You guys have to vote too." Jack grinned.

"I vote yes." Matt chuckled.

"I vote yes." Nikki giggled.

CHAPTER SIX

Nikki pulled her boots on and sat back to lean against the open closet wall. The house was quiet since the kids had made it home and everyone was at the barn and arena.

Nick had left to retrieve his attorney from the airport and would be back any minute. He also let them know he was going to have to fly back to Australia right after dropping off the attorney.

The back door opened and Nikki glanced over to see Cora and her mother walk in. They stopped at the closet opening and smiled at her.

"What are you doing?" Cora chuckled.

"Enjoying the peace and quiet," Nikki answered with a smile.

"Want us to leave?" Her mom asked.

"No." Nikki giggled.

Cora turned and looked back out the door. "Nick has returned…" Cora whispered. "That's an attorney?"

"I didn't know attorney's looked like that." Her mother gasped.

It was enough to make Nikki curious and she stood quickly and came up behind the two women.

"Oh, you're killing me." Nikki said and peered between the two.

The man standing next to Nick was tall, as tall as Grayson and Scott. He wore a black, weathered cowboy hat pulled low over amber brown eyes that were lit in amusement…which made Nikki smile. He had a black mustache that slid down the sides of his mouth to join a perfect goatee. His dark sideburns were just low enough. His shoulders were wide and waist narrow. Jeans, a light blue long sleeve shirt and a black vest fit him perfectly.

"Look at Grace's face." Cora whispered.

"Absolutely star struck...I think you could knock her over with a feather." Her mom giggled. "Poor Kooskia boy isn't going to have a chance now."

"Nikki?" Cora said.

"What?" Nikki answered without moving her eyes from the tall, handsome stranger.

"Did you see Grace's face?" Cora asked.

Nikki looked at Grace's flushed face. "Yeah," Nikki whispered.

"You have the same look on your face." Her mother giggled.

Nikki leaned back and blushed.

All three women started laughing and walked out the door, which made the group that had gathered at the front of Nick's truck, turn.

When she felt in control enough to look up, Nikki's eyes connected with the attorney's...she was still grinning...and he grinned in return. Her stomach flipped and her heart skipped a beat. His smile was perfect and his amber brown eyes sparkled.

"Nikki!" Her mother whispered. "Gain control."

Nikki started laughing again. "I can't!" She whispered back.

"I don't blame you!" Cora giggled. "If only I was fifty years younger!"

Sadie and Nora reached the group before the three women.

"Nick!" Nora yelled and ran up to him.

Nick leaned down and gave her a huge hug, lifting and swinging her; her feet flying way in the air.

The attorney finally moved away from her eyes and turned to Nick and Nora. His expression changed from grinning to a look of utter surprise.

"Me too!" Sadie yelled. Nick set Nora down and repeated the greeting with Sadie, her long braid flying up in the air as she screamed in delight.

"You're almost too tall for swinging, Sadie." Nick laughed.

The attorney just stared in shock.

"Who's that and why is he looking at us like that?" Sadie asked once her feet were back on the ground.

"This is my friend, Lucas," Nick started laughing when he saw the look on the Australian's face. "And he's looking at you like that because you're kids."

"Is he afraid of us, too?" Nora asked with a curious tilt to her head.

The whole group laughed.

"No, he has nieces your age, so he's used to kids." Nick answered then glanced up at the barn. "Here comes, Matt."

Nikki made it to the bottom of the steps just as Matt was close enough to the group that Lucas got a good look at him.

"Lucas, this is my son, Matt."

"Da…" The man started to say.

"Dang!" Rang out from all the men.

"What?" Lucas' looked around in surprise.

"Dang, is the only curse word you can say around here." Grayson informed him with a smile.

"Well, DANG!" Lucas smiled in amazement as he stretched a hand to Matt. "I saw you in pictures on Facebook…you looked like Nick, but in person...Dang!" He said in an Australian accent, which caught Nikki by surprise.

Matt grinned as they shook hands. "We get that a lot."

"Matt looks more like Nick then Nick looks like Matt." Sadie informed him loudly.

Lucas' looked at her like she had two heads which made Sadie and Nora start laughing again. Sadie looked proudly at Nick and he started laughing which caused Lucas to stare at Nick in disbelief.

Nikki, her mother, and Cora reached the group and Nick turned and smiled at Nikki.

She grinned at him. He looked so happy.

"Lucas, this is my daughter, Nikki." He said proudly.

Nikki took a deep breath to control her inner trembling as she stretched out her hand.

"Dang..." Lucas whispered as their eyes and hands met. His was warm and squeezed hers tightly.

"I don't look as much like our dad as Matt does." She tilted her head with an amused smile.

"No, you don't, but that's OK...they aren't nearly as good looking as they think...you're definitely the improved rendition." He said softly, his accent making the sentence sound like a ballad.

It made her smile brighter and she gripped his hand tighter...her insides just melting.

"And this is her mother, Dru." Nick continued; seemingly unaware of his daughter's inner condition.

Lucas slowly, very slowly, let go of her hand and moved his eyes from hers.

Nikki turned to watch him meet her mother.

"You married this guy?" Lucas grinned and nodded towards Nick.

"I was young." Her mother laughed and shook his hand.

"I think the saying is young and dumb?" His eyes twinkled in delight.

"Are you calling my wife dumb?" Jack asked with a surprised chuckle.

"No," Lucas smiled at him. "That would be Nick."

"That's an understatement." Nick agreed with a chuckle.

"And this is Cora." Nick introduced the older woman.

"It's an honor," Lucas smiled at her.

Nikki could swear Cora blushed!

"She takes care of the herd that lives in the house." Matt added with a proud grin.

"THAT has to be a challenge." Lucas smiled.

"More of a pleasure," She answered.

"Which brings us to the next matter at hand…" Nick said and turned to Cora. "Do you have a passport?"

"What?" Cora asked, a bit startled at the odd question.

"Do you have a passport?" He repeated.

"Yes," She answered cautiously.

"Well, I have to go back to Australia for a couple of days, on Lucas' plane." He grinned as Cora turned surprised eyes at Lucas. "And I would very much like to take you with me."

"Really?" Sadie yelled from behind Nick.

"Can I go?" Nora started jumping excitedly.

"No!" Came from her parents.

She turned quickly, her long black hair twirling and her dark brown eyes frowning at them. "Why not?"

"Because you have school," Jordan answered. "And he's not taking you unless we get to go, too."

The group laughed.

Nick turned back to Cora. "Private jet all the way there. I have friends that will take you sightseeing while I work, then private jet all the way back."

"You're serious." Cora stated calmly.

"Very. Have you ever been there?" Nick smiled.

Cora shook her head.

"Ever wanted to go?" He asked.

"Of course," She answered.

"Then why are you hesitating?" Nick chuckled.

"I just have to make sure you're for real." Cora said and looked at Lucas. "Is he for real?"

"Most of the time I wonder," Lucas grinned. "But, on this one…he's for real."

Cora turned, "Dru?"

"Want me to help you pack?" She asked with a smile.

"Give me five minutes!" Cora yelled as she headed for the house.

"I'm not in that much of a hurry," Nick called back. "I'll give you fifteen."

Nick sighed as he watched his traveling companion enter the house. Then he turned to Nikki then to Matt.

"Can I talk to you two for a minute?" He asked.

"Of course," Nikki slid her arm through his and they walked down the driveway with Matt alongside.

Nikki glanced quickly at Lucas, he was grinning at her again. She smiled back, feeling the heat rise up her neck and into her face.

"Before I leave, I just want to make sure you two are OK," Nick said when they stopped.

"It'll take a while to sink in," Nikki nodded. "But at least I have a job and somewhere to live now."

"The only advice I can give you…is, just live your life the way you always have." He put his arm around her shoulders and looked at Matt. "Depend on each other and your family."

"I want to make sure we do the right thing," Matt nodded.

"You've already had a great start," He smiled. "Same ranch, same work, just more of it."

"How long will you be gone?" Nikki leaned into him.

"Hopefully just a couple of days," Nick answered. "A couple opportunities came up while they were working on the cash withdraws. I just want to check on them."

"Cora may keep you there for a while," Matt chuckled.

Nick nodded. "I'll make sure she has a good time."

"What about Lucas?" Nikki asked.

"He's got my property to stay at, run of the place." Nick answered. "My truck, horses, anything he needs. He'll meet with everyone about the legal details on the wills and trusts."

"That is so unreal." Nikki smiled, thinking of Lucas' grin.

"He'll probably want to go to the ranch, too." Nick added. "He's been a rancher since the day he was born, and he's smarter than anyone I've ever known. Trust him, he'll do what's best for you."

"Why?" Matt asked.

"Because I asked him to." Nick answered.

CHAPTER SEVEN

Nikki and Matt watched as Nick and Cora drove down the driveway, then turned and looked at each other, then to their guest. Lucas was in front of the barn talking with Jordan and Leah.

"This has been the weirdest day ever." Matt leaned his arms on the top rail of the fence and looked out at the empty pasture. The kids were getting ready to ride so all the horses were at the barn

"I'm exhausted," Nikki leaned her back against the fence and returned his look. "Mom was talking about the emotional rollercoaster…I agree."

"I've been thinking about Andy's ranch," he sighed. "I want to go up and ride it. We've ridden all of it, over the years, but not with an owner's eye."

"Well," Nikki grinned. "It's not like we have anything else to do."

Matt chuckled. "You're right."

"Let's drive up Friday and take the kids, we need their energy right now; some kid therapy."

"I agree. Trooper needs to get back to the mountains. I haven't had him out in a couple of weeks now."

"I've ridden Harvey a little, but she needs a good outing."

They heard footsteps walking down the driveway and Nikki had to look around Matt to see Grayson and Lucas walking towards them.

"It still amazes me that Nick has kids." Lucas smiled as the two men stopped next to them.

Matt turned and leaned against the fence next to Nikki.

"He was full of all kinds of surprises today." Matt nodded.

"It's been a mind blowing twenty hours." Lucas smiled softly at Nikki. She felt her stomach tremble again.

"We've known for about four hours now," She replied. "It's going to take a bit to get used to."

Lucas nodded, not breaking their eye contact. "The kids want to introduce me to their horses, then your mother thought you could show me The Stables and the new barn and breakfast. I can get a little feel for the place before we all sit and talk."

Nikki thought she could listen to his accent all day long. It made her smile at him, which made his eyes sparkle at her.

"I'm about all talked out today," Matt replied, looking between Nikki and Lucas with an amused expression. "Why don't we wait for the talk until the kids go to school in the morning?"

"We can talk tomorrow, then get ready Friday morning." Nikki finally broke eye contact with Lucas to look up at Matt.

"Ready for what?" Grayson asked.

"We were just discussing riding Andy's property this weekend and taking the kids," Matt explained. "Camp out Friday and Saturday night. Get some fresh air after this last week."

"The kids would love that," Grayson nodded. "So would I."

"What if we took a section of the property to check out and you take another?" Nikki suggested trying to concentrate on her uncle and not let her eyes go back to the tall Australian next to him. "Between two groups, we can cover a good portion of the ranch to see what needs to be done."

"Great idea, I know Leah would love to get out, too." Grayson nodded. "We'll meet back up on Monday and compare notes."

Matt turned to Lucas. "You're welcome to ride with me and Nikki, if you'd like."

"I'd love to." Lucas nodded and smiled at Nikki which made her cheeks warm again.

Nikki and Matt stood away from the fence and the small group walked back up the driveway. Nikki made sure to put her uncle between herself and the man that made her heart race.

"But, you know," Grayson said. "You can't keep calling it Andy's property forever."

"The change of the ranch name was part of the sale." Lucas added.

"Really?" Nikki was surprised.

"Evidently, one of the brothers wants to purchase a small ranch and use the brand and name, keep it in the family." Lucas asked. "What was the name?"

"Broken Pine Ranch," Grayson answered. "His mother named it when she was a child."

"Been in the family that long?" Lucas asked.

"Tagger Ranch goes back four generations." Matt told him.

"Are your parents at the ranch?" Lucas asked Grayson.

He received silence as an answer.

"What?" Lucas finally asked with a confused look as they reached the rest of the family.

"They were killed in a car accident." Grayson answered just as the kids approached.

Lucas inhaled sharply, just as Sadie and Nora reached him.

"Are you ready to meet Scarecrow and Little Ghost?" Sadie grinned excitedly.

"And Arcturus and Isaiah!" Nora said and grabbed his hand to pull him to the barn.

Lucas turned and caught Nikki's eye. He was smiling for the girls but his eyes were apologetic. She followed them so she could explain when given the chance. Matt walked along with her while Grayson walked up onto the back porch.

The girls excitedly pulled Nick's friend into the barn. Every time he said more than five words they would giggle at his accent.

"Mom said you saw pictures of the horses on Facebook." Nora said.

"I did," He answered. "I looked at all the pictures."

"Can you guess who this horse is?" Nora giggled and looked into the stall.

"You're testing me?" Lucas looked at her with amused surprise.

"Yep!" Nora laughed, her dark brown eyes shining.

"Well," He chuckled. "Let's see if I can name each horse in the stalls." He turned to Nora, "Ready?"

She nodded excitedly.

"Alright first stall, black horse with no star, must be Cooper." He turned to Nora and she laughed and nodded. "Second stall, red roan, that's Rufio."

"Yes!" The girls cried out in unison.

Nikki was amazed as he named every horse right as they walked through the barn. When he reached Harvey, he looked in and smiled. "Now that's a fine filly." He told the girls then looked up at Nikki with a grin. She had no doubt he knew who the horse belonged to and she was sure her face was as red as her shirt.

Matt laughed.

"That's Nikki's horse!" Sadie said giggling. "Her name is Harvey."

"And how did such a fine filly end up with such a strange name as Harvey?" He asked.

Both the girl's expressions changed, not for the better.

Lucas turned startled eyes to Nikki and Matt for help.

"She was named right after Cora saw the horses for the first time, after we rescued them." Matt explained. "They were in pretty bad condition and Cora was extremely upset. Nikki announced her name as Harvey and all the kids laughed…broke the tension."

Lucas nodded and sighed. "Well, sheilas, why don't you introduce me to the famous Rooster?"

"I am not Sheila." Sadie said tartly.

"Me, either." Nora frowned. "I'm Nora and she's Sadie."

Lucas laughed. "Well, Sadie and Nora…sheila is what we call women in Australia."

The girls laughed with him.

"But we're just girls." Sadie grinned. "Nikki's a woman."

Lucas turned and grinned at Nikki.

The look on his face made Nikki's face turn red again and her pulse quickened…and he didn't even have to say a thing!

Matt laughed again.

"Wade's up riding Rooster right now," Sadie said, her happiness had returned.

"Well, let's check-out the rest of your herd then we can go watch."

"OK." Sadie nodded.

"Have you met Blue?" Nora asked looking up at Lucas.

Lucas turned and looked at Matt and Nikki. "I'm almost afraid to ask."

"It's Nick's horse." Nikki explained with a chuckle.

He looked confused. "Nick has a horse?"

"Yes!" Nora said excitedly. "I won him at the auction for Nick. He's a big blue roan!"

"Nick has a horse." Lucas repeated in surprise.

"He has two," Sadie corrected him. "He has Bay, too."

"Nick has two horses." Lucas chuckled in disbelief.

"Well, kinda three," Nora let out a devilish giggle and looked at Nikki. "When we bought Blue and Bay at the auction, there was a little cremello foal. He was SO tiny, but Nikki came up with a great feeding program for him and now he's beautiful."

Lucas looked at the two girls then to Nikki. "I've known Nick for years, we tried to get him to buy a horse, even tried giving him one, but he refused…just said he'd borrow one."

"He really wanted Blue!" Nora said excitedly. "He told me to hold up the paddle and leave it there until we won! And he did!"

"Well, that's sounds like it was exciting," Lucas smiled. "And where are these horses?"

"Blue and Bay are at his house and Bodi is at The Stables, you can meet him later." Nora answered.

"Blue and Bay…the color of the horses?" Lucas asked amused.

"Yeah," Nora nodded. "I named Blue and Nick named Bay…said it was just easier."

Lucas nodded. "And where did the name Bodi come from?"

"His name is Bodacious, but we call him Bodi for short." Sadie smiled.

"He's named after the famous bull when Nick first started bull riding." Nora explained.

"I remember him, he was pretty good, one of the best, and he was cream color too." Lucas nodded. "Did Nick ride him?"

Nora laughed. "No, he says it was more like just sitting on him then getting flung off…there was no riding involved!"

They all laughed at the image.

"Well, let's go check out Wade and Rooster." Lucas suggested and the girls ran out the barn and towards the arena.

As they followed, Lucas commented. "The little brunette, Nora, talks a lot about Nick."

Nikki nodded. "They are friends."

"Friends?" He asked.

"Yes." Nikki said but didn't elaborate.

"I have never seen Nick with kids…ever." Lucas looked over at Matt and Nikki. "I was shocked when I saw him greet the kids."

Nikki and Matt glanced at each other then over to Lucas.

"What?" Lucas stopped and looked at them.

"It's something he's been working on." Matt answered.

"I don't understand." He looked confused.

"Lucas!" Sadie yelled. "Come on."

Nikki and Matt started walking again without commenting. Nikki wished she had more time with Nick before he left, so she knew what he had told Lucas and what he didn't.

"How can you say no to her?" Lucas shook his head and smiled. "She's got to be one of the cutest girls I've ever seen."

Matt chuckled. "It's not easy, but don't piss her off…she'll turn on you in a flash."

"Really?" Lucas looked at the cute blonde with the sparkling blue eyes, big grin and a long braid down her back. "Her?"

"Oh, yeah," Nikki nodded. "She has a mean temper."

"Like a dingo." Lucas chuckled. "They look all cute and cuddly but will rip your throat out given a chance."

"Yeah, call her that, let's see her start ripping." Matt laughed as they reached the arena.

"Wade!" Nora yelled at the eleven year old riding his red horse and practicing his roping. "Lucas wants to meet Rooster!"

Wade sat quietly then lifted the rope, swinging it around his head then leaned forward on the horse and let the rope fly at the mechanical calf. He grinned when the rope floated perfectly over the calf's head and rested around the neck, he pulled tight.

"Way to go, Mate." Lucas yelled out to him.

Wade smiled, then coiled his lariat and nudged Rooster into a walk towards them. Grace and Reilly were walking Cooper and Buttercup from the barn to the arena to meet them.

Lucas walked through the gate and towards Wade and his horse. "How did you get so good at roping?"

Wade grinned proudly. "Uncle Grayson. He's been training me."

"Well, you've both done a great job," Lucas nodded. "Are you competing?"

"I am in breakaway, but with Dollar." Wade explained. "I did some last year and stunk." He shrugged. "But I'm doing better this year. Haven't won yet, but I caught the calf every time."

"That's a great start for your age." Lucas encouraged him.

"I'm gonna try calf tying, too." Wade informed him.

Nikki watched the Australian newcomer charm the kids as well as he had charmed her.

"Can we go to The Stables too and see Bodi?" Nora ran up to the fence.

"Sure." Nikki answered.

"Yea! She said yes!" Nora turned and ran back to the group in the arena.

Bodi put on a show for the crowd. Nikki led him out of his stall and into the corral where the little colt ran, jumped, kicked out, bucked and jumped in the air.

"What a showman." Matt laughed.

"He's a beaut." Lucas agreed.

Nikki pulled out her phone and found the first picture she had taken of Bodi. It was taken while they were still at the auction yard nine months before and the colt was dirty and skinny. She handed the phone to Lucas.

He looked at the picture then up to the muscular, tall, and proud yearling colt that had finally stopped and trotted to the fence to let the excited kids give him the attention the horse thought he deserved.

"The difference is amazing." Lucas looked at her in surprise.

Nikki nodded. "He's taken to his supplement program quite well." She looked at the cream colored colt with the blue eyes. "Plus he comes out and makes the best of his exercise time."

When she turned back, Lucas was typing into her phone. She was about to ask what he was doing when his own phone rang. He retrieved the phone and pushed end on the incoming call.

"What are you doing?" Nikki asked with a quizzical tilt of the head.

His devilish grin was framed perfectly through his whiskers when he handed back her phone. "I'm taking the opportunity to call myself on your phone so I make sure I have your phone number…and you have mine."

Nikki felt the heat rise in her face again and her pulse race as she shook her head in disbelief and grinned back at him…their eyes sparkling at each other.

"I'm going to have to turn a hose on you two." Matt chuckled softly.

Nikki smiled innocently at her brother.

"It's going to be one heck of a camping trip." Matt declared.

"Camping?" Wade asked, turning quickly. "Can I go?"

"Can we go?" Sadie and Nora chimed in unison.

"Yes!" Matt answered them. "I may need you three around to keep it tame out there." He turned and smiled at Nikki.

She giggled and walked into the corral to catch Bodi.

"Tame?" Sadie looked up at him, her sweet blue eyes confused.

"Are we taking the horses?" Wade asked hopefully.

Matt told the kids about the trip as they walked the short distance to the site of the new Tagger Barn and Breakfast.

"It looks like they are almost done." Lucas looked around the building. They were in the large lobby. To their left were the breakfast dining room, small kitchen, and assistant manager's office. To their right were two long hallways leading to the ten rooms; five on each side. The guest rooms were on the outside of the building so they had windows in each room. Restrooms, supply rooms, and offices ran between the two hallways. At the far end was a large room to be used for conferences or special events. Glass patio doors led from the large room out onto a brick floored outdoor deck.

"Next week is painting and flooring, then bringing in the furniture and technology." Nikki told him. "First guests are scheduled to arrive by the middle of June. We have a huge grand opening just after the fourth of July and we're already fully booked through September. Leah even has a number of weddings already scheduled for this summer and next summer."

Lucas walked to the large front window that overlooked The Stables and out to the river canyons, farmer's fields and distant view of town. "This is just tremendous."

"The sunsets are spectacular out here." Nikki walked up next to him. "It's one of the features we used to market the business. It worked well for marketing The Stables; sunset rides and all." She smiled up at him and was met with a warm smile, his eyes gentle.

"Well, I hope we have a couple of those this weekend." He whispered softly.

Nikki shook her head. "Are you this flirty with all the women you meet?"

He shook his head, their eyes connected. "No, actually…never."

"And why am I so fortunate?" She raised a brow in curiosity.

Lucas looked over her head at the kids running down the empty hall of the building. Matt was on the phone by the newly constructed registration desk.

He turned his attention back to her then leaned down and whispered; "I like your smile…it lights up your eyes. When I flirt with you, I get rewarded with both."

Nikki felt the butterflies in her stomach bouncing off the walls.

CHAPTER EIGHT

Nikki stood looking out the front window of The Homestead and watched the school bus slowly pull away. Matt and Lucas would be arriving soon from Nick's house where they had spent the night. They were bringing the horses in for the weekend camping trip.

As if on cue, she saw the truck and horse trailer approaching the driveway. Nikki turned quickly and sat on the couch. She didn't want to look too eager to see Lucas again…even though she was.

She had spent too much time getting dressed for the day. Yesterday she had showered and ran out of the house within ten minutes. This morning it took her an hour to get ready. Every time she looked in the mirror she thought she looked like she spent too much time getting ready and would start laughing at herself.

She finally walked out with blue jeans, her tan cowboy boots that were decorated with little red stars, and a blue short-sleeve blouse. Her hair was in a high pony tail.

"Good morning," Her mother greeted her and sat in the chair across from her.

"Good morning," Nikki smiled, her mother's hair was in a long braid down her back and she was smiling contentedly. "Mini-me day with Sadie?"

"Yes, it's fun, makes me feel like a kid every once in a while." Her mother beamed.

"This is so much better than yesterday."

Her mom rolled her eyes and leaned back in the large cushioned chair. "Isn't that the truth?"

"What's that?" Jack asked as he entered the room, leaned down to kiss his wife then took the chair next to her, their hands reaching out to each other. Nikki was relieved to see the ease and happiness back between them.

"We were discussing how much better this morning was to yesterday." Nikki chuckled.

"I hope we never…ever…have a morning like that again." Jack agreed.

"Morning, afternoon, or evening." Jordan laughed as she entered the room with Leah right behind her.

"Amen." Scott and Grayson said in unison as they walked in behind their wives and moved to sit on the couch on each side of Nikki. She instantly looped her arms through theirs. They both pulled her arm in tightly making her smile inside…it was the little things…

"Oh hey, Nikki," Grayson looked down at her with a mischievous grin. "I've been wondering, can I borrow fifty bucks, is that just pocket change to you now?"

Nikki raised a brow and leaned on Scott's shoulder so she could look up at him. "Honestly, I don't think I have twenty dollars in my bank account or even ten in my wallet and I just recently got an eviction notice."

They were all laughing when Matt and Lucas walked into the room; the two grinned at the happy group. Lucas' eyes sparkled when he caught her eye.

Nikki felt the flush rise as she remembered Lucas' words the night before and hoped the laughter masked the redness.

"And we're happy about?" Matt asked.

"Our eviction notice," Nikki grinned at him.

"You've been evicted?" Lucas looked between them.

"Yes," Matt chuckled. "We're being evicted by our own mother and aunt."

Lucas looked around the room and shook his head in confusion.

"Alright, maybe we better head in and clear up a few things before we really confuse him." Her mother laughed softly.

Her uncles stood quickly and, squeezing her arms tightly, they lifted her off the ground swinging her legs forward; her pony tail swinging wildly. She cried out in surprise then laughed as her boots slammed onto the ground.

"Much better than yesterday..." Her mother chuckled as they made their way into the library.

Jordan and Leah had placed water and coffee in the room and they all settled around the table in the same seats as the day before with Lucas in Nick's chair, across from Nikki. Lucas had a yellow legal pad in front of him, which reminded Nikki that he was an attorney.

"Before we get started on all the legal details," Lucas started. Nikki inwardly grinned at his accent; it caught her by surprise again.

"I'd like to make sure I have all the individual family's right."

They all nodded.

"Obviously Nora and Wade belong to Jordan and Scott." He said and everyone nodded.

"Reilly has to be Jack and Dru's son." He continued.

"Half right." Jack smiled. "Dru is his step-mother, Reilly's mother died when he was five."

Lucas looked surprised but nodded.

"And adorable Sadie belongs to Dru." He continued and was surprised when everyone shook their heads and smiled. "No? But you look identical?"

"No, but you're not the first to make that mistake," Her mother smiled. "Nikki is my adopted daughter, Matt is my natural child with

Nick and Reilly is my step-son…I kind of ran the gamut on that one."

Lucas frowned and looked between Matt, Nikki and her mother. "Nikki's adopted but Matt and her are both Nick's?"

"Yes, Nikki was two when Matt was born." Her mother answered.

Lucas looked at her for a moment until he realized she wasn't going to expand on the story then wrote on his legal pad.

"Grayson, Leah, Grace, and Sadie are one family; Scott, Jordan, Wade, and Nora are the second family, and Dru, Jack, Matt, Nikki, and Reilly are the third family."

They all nodded.

"Good, I finally got something right." Lucas smiled.

"Jack?" Lucas looked at him. "What is your last name?"

"Morgan." He answered.

"Dru, do you go by Tagger or Morgan on your legal documents?" Lucas asked.

"Tagger-Morgan." She answered. "And just so we know…what's your last name?"

Lucas chuckled at her. "Carlile…Lucas Carlile."

"And are you married and have any kids?" Leah asked innocently with a quick amused glance towards Nikki.

Nikki fought to keep her face calm until Matt chuckled which caused a slight smile to escape.

Lucas grinned and looked at Leah. "Never married, no kids."

"Good to know." Matt snickered.

Nikki forced herself not to look at Lucas and to keep her face calm.

"OK, now that marriages and kids are all clear," Lucas smiled. "Nick asked that I cover the inheritance."

They all nodded.

"I didn't draft his original papers, since I didn't know about any of you, but I reviewed them last night." Lucas began. "But...since you spoke with him yesterday he has changed the inheritance. He decided, since you all knew, he wanted the inheritance to happen while he was living, and not wait."

"What does that mean?" Leah asked.

"On their 25th birthdays, all the kids born as of today and on the list we just went over, will inherit $2 million dollars each."

"What?!" Jordan gasped. "He said small portion...I thought it would be just enough for college."

Everyone one else in the room was too stunned to speak.

Lucas continued, "Everything else goes to Nikki and Matt."

Nikki took a deep breath and let it out slowly, she stared at her clasped hands that were resting on the table in front of her. The blood in her veins seemed to have rushed into her head and through her ears which created a buzzing noise.

Lucas continued in a matter-of-fact manner, "Who is the oldest child?"

"Reilly at sixteen, a couple of months older than Grace." Grayson answered in a low stunned voice.

"The youngest?" Lucas turned to him.

"Sadie at eleven, one month younger than Wade." Grayson answered again.

"Nick said that you all decided not to tell the kids?" Lucas asked him and Grayson nodded. "With only five years difference, when Reilly learns of his inheritance at 25, Sadie will be 20, so it's good that she'll be older and able to handle it better."

Lucas wrote on his legal pad...no one spoke.

"The inheritance is in a trust." Lucas looked around the room.

"What does that mean?" Jordan asked.

"It means that no matter what happens with the corporation, the money is not touched and is guaranteed."

Jordan shook her head and looked at her husband in surprise.

"Matt and Nikki?" Lucas looked over at them.

Nikki glanced up from her clasped hands.

"There is $25 million in a trust for you that cannot be touched and is guaranteed on Nikki's 25th birthday. Everything else depends on what the corporation does. At this point, the corporation, which would immediately turn over to you if something should happen to Nick, has a current value of $275 million, that is less the trusts we just spoke of." He said calmly.

Nikki looked back down at her hands, she felt ill. Shouldn't a person be happy to learn that in four years she would have that kind of money? Nick had said a millionaire a couple hundred times over but the numbers really didn't connect with her. She leaned forward and rested her forehead in palm of her right hand and closed her eyes tightly to stop the tears and nausea.

"Nikki?" Lucas asked softly.

"I'm OK," She answered without looking up. She wished her hair was down so it would flow over her face.

Matt reached over and took her left hand and squeezed. It took all her strength to squeeze back.

She listened as Lucas continued.

"So, now that you know the numbers that are involved," He said. "You need to realize it comes with some changes in your lives now."

"What do you mean?" Nikki heard her mother ask.

"Every precaution will be taken to make sure that Nick's life here is kept separate from his life in Australia; at his request. He said he explained that to you."

"He did." Her mother answered.

"There are very few people, mainly just my family and senior executives, in Australia that know who the owner of Jet Development Group is."

"What?" Nikki lifted her head sharply at the name.

"Nick's corporation is Jet Development Group." Lucas told her then looked around at the group. "Didn't he tell you?"

"No." Nikki answered and looked over at her mother who was staring in amazement at Lucas.

"We've never known where Jet came from." Lucas tilted his head. "Do you?" He asked Nikki.

Nikki nodded. "He never told you?"

"No, he just said it represented facing your fears." Lucas answered.

The Trio started chuckling.

Lucas looked at them then to Nikki.

"Jet was mom's barrel horse when they were married." Nikki told him, still a little stunned that he named his business after the horse…and in a way, her and Matt.

"He was scared to death of that horse." Her mom giggled looking at her brothers. "It took me a week to talk him into riding her."

"Even when she finally got him to get in the saddle, he was white as a ghost." Grayson added, still chuckling.

"I thought for sure he was going to throw up all over the horse." Scott leaned back in his chair laughing. "He kept looking at Dru, pleading with his eyes to let him off." He started laughing even more.

Her mom continued as her giggles turned into laughter. "He could get on a bucking bull because he only had to stay on for 8 seconds, but with Jet, he had to stay on for as long as I asked him too."

Scott was laughing so hard he had tears in his eyes. "Even after all these years, I can still see the look on his face when Dru slapped Jet on the butt and got her to trot off away from her."

Nikki watched as the Trio laughed. The nausea and tension she had felt was slowly diminishing.

Grayson and her mother were wiping the tears from their eyes, too.

"He didn't talk to me for hours after that," She laughed.

Everyone else in the room was smiling at the Trio's laughter. It was just what they needed to break the tension.

"He flew off the horse once Dru said he could get down." Grayson laughed.

"It took me another week to talk him into riding her again." Her mom said through her laughter and she placed her hand across her chest to try to stop. "When he did, I had to be ten feet away from them at all times, so I couldn't slap her again."

"When he got on her, he walked the horse around the arena for an hour before he started to relax." Scott's laughter started to diminish. "He was determined to ride her and get passed the fear."

"He spent another hour trotting her around the arena." Grayson added with an amused sigh.

"It took him three rides before he got the courage to get her into a slow canter." Her mom giggled. "He was afraid she would take off like she did around the barrels...which had to be removed out of the arena before he got on her."

While the three worked to contain their laughter and giggles, Nikki turned to Matt so no one could see her stunned expression.

"Do you know what that means?" Nikki whispered to him. Matt leaned down closer to her so they couldn't be overheard.

Matt nodded and whispered back. "It was the only way he could name the company after us without anyone knowing."

"He wasn't kidding when he said he thought about us every day…every time he said his company's name."

"…or read it or wrote it."

Nikki sat back and let the realization run through her; the confirmation of her father's words.

"Do you two need a break?" Lucas asked her and Matt.

Nikki nodded and quickly made her way back to the back porch. She sat in one of the chairs and stared at the barn…she wanted to go to Harvey.

Although the evenings were still cold, the morning had finally warmed. The sun felt good on her skin so she closed her eyes, leaned back in the chair and let the sun warm her face and relax the tension in her body.

She heard the door open.

"Are you OK?" Matt asked.

"Just taking a moment to feel the sunshine." She smiled.

"I think we need to do that more often." He chuckled and she heard him sit in the chair next to her.

"We can't, didn't you hear? We have a run-down 25,000 acre cattle ranch to run." She giggled.

"Well, like Dad said, 'Same ranch, same work, just more of it.'"

"Live your life the way you always have." Nikki smiled. "I believe that's a direct quote."

"We forget about the money, it's not there and just do our work; make the cattle ranch successful on its own." Matt added and Nikki nodded.

The door opened but Nikki didn't move, she kept her eyes shut and enjoyed the warmth of the sun on her skin.

"Beautiful morning," It was her mother. "Maybe we should move the meeting out here."

"I vote yes." Nikki smiled. "Not so claustrophobic."

"I'm game." Matt nodded.

"You going to sit like that the rest of the meeting?" Leah giggled at her.

Nikki sighed. "I think I might just do that."

When the door closed, indicating everyone had joined her on the deck, she opened her eyes and sat up straight.

"OK," Lucas grinned at her which made her insides as warm as her sun kissed skin. She was really getting to like that grin.

"There are a couple more things I need to discuss with you before I let you carry on with your meeting." Lucas said. "Just because the money is there, doesn't mean you need to change the way you live, but there are a few things that need to be adjusted." Lucas said looking around the group.

"Like what?" Jordan asked.

"Facebook, is the biggest change." He answered.

"Jordan and I usually are the only ones to upload to the web pages." Leah told him.

"Within an hour, I knew just about everything about your kids and where they are going to be in the next month for their rodeos and shows." Lucas said flatly. "That needs to stop. The horse information is fine, but anything to do with the kids should be removed."

"Even their horse shows from the past?" Jordan asked.

He nodded. "If they went to a horse show this year, means they will probably go to the same one next year?"

Jordan nodded.

"Changing that up will help too."

She nodded her understanding. "Some shows we don't have a choice, but I'll work on the others."

"It's just little things like that you need to be aware of but the kids will probably not even notice." Lucas said. "OK, a couple more things," He chuckled softly at the quiet group. "It's my understanding that you'll be running the ranches as one."

"Yes." Nikki and Matt said in unison.

"How is Tagger Enterprises managed?" Lucas asked.

"Dru runs the entire organization, keeps tabs over everything and makes sure we keep moving forward." Scott answered. "Grayson handles ranching and livestock, I run the farming portion, Jack handles The Stables, Leah runs the Barn and Breakfast, and Jordan has the toughest job, she runs the kids and their shows and rodeos."

"Matt will work with Scott and Grayson with the farming and livestock for the new ranch, Nikki will do the business portion for it." Her mother added. "She'll also become my backup for Tagger Enterprises. Not just because of the new ranch…but for the family."

"If there are any major issues that affect Tagger Enterprises," Grayson continued. "Then Dru, myself, and Scott vote." He smiled as he glanced at Nikki and Matt. "Now, if there are any issues that affect the second ranch, then Matt and Nikki are included in the vote."

"That is a great practice." Lucas nodded. "But as an attorney, looking out for my clients, which Matt and Nikki are, I have an issue with the fact that the three of you could easily out vote my two clients and do what you want with their property."

Nikki was stunned, the thought had never crossed her mind.

"We'd never do that." Her mother's back stiffened.

Lucas glanced around the room. "I'm not saying you would, Dru. But I have to recommend to my clients what's best for them."

"What would you suggest?" Jack asked.

"If Nikki and Matt agree on their vote, then their vote counts as three instead of two."

"What happens in the case of a tie?" Leah asked.

"Then the situation has to be reviewed, solution adjusted, until one side swings a vote. That way, Nikki and Matt keep control of their own ranch, but they can't, independently, make a decision about Tagger Enterprises."

"I have no issues with that." Grayson nodded. Everyone else nodded agreement.

"A formal contract needs to be written to protect both ranches." Lucas told them. "It won't make any difference in the way you run it, but if something drastic happens to one ranch, and not the other, then only one ranch is affected and the other is protected. Since you're all family, it just makes sure one of your businesses has the chance of staying afloat if something should happen." He looked around at the group. "You're all OK with that?"

"Yes," Her mother answered. "It makes sense."

"Good," He smiled. "Then, while you discuss the ranches, I'm going to run into town and buy some supplies for this weekend."

"What's this weekend?" Jack asked.

Matt updated the group on the weekend camping trip.

"I want to go," Scott said and looked at his wife, she nodded. "We'll take a third section."

"Me too, we'll take a fourth section." Her mother added. "But, if you don't mind." She turned to Grayson. "Would you take Reilly with Grace so Jack and I can ride alone?" She turned to a surprised and pleased Jack. "I think I need some time with my husband to make up for the last week."

Grayson nodded with a chuckle. "That's an understatement."

"We have to come up with a new name for the ranch and brand." Nikki told the group and the reason why. "We have to come up with a brand so next year's Herefords are branded separate from Andy's inherited herd."

"You don't want to brand with T3E?" Leah asked surprised.

Nikki shook her head. "For the same reason Lucas said we need a contract. If something happens, there has to be a clear distinction of what we consider Tagger cows and what belong to the new ranch."

"I agree." Her mother nodded, which made Nikki feel proud. Matt, Grayson and Scott also agreed.

"So, hopefully, by the end of the weekend, Matt and I will come up with a name and brand." Nikki added.

CHAPTER NINE

Nikki sat on Harvey and looked at the expanse of mountains in front of her; they rolled out as far as she could see. Big white billowy puffs of clouds rolled across the top of the mountains and contrasted with the deep blue sky.

Below her, the mountain was covered in trees and a large meadow of grass and wildflowers. To her right was a small creek that settled into a peaceful pond.

Looking left, was more grass covered mountainside speckled with red and white Hereford cows; the only breed that Andy raised.

She heard the kids laughing and turned to see Lucas entertaining them again. They roared in laughter at something he said.

Matt and Trooper were walking towards her.

The whole day had been perfect. Nora rode Arcturus, Sadie was on Little Ghost and Wade on Dollar. Lucas was riding Bay, Matt on Trooper and Nikki on her beautiful Harvey.

She leaned down and stroked the horse's neck. The first time she had laid eyes on the horse she was brown, the next spring she shed out with a hint of red which made her just that much more beautiful as far as Nikki was concerned.

She loved riding the horse, which was good since they were going to spend the summer together repairing fence and pushing cows. She was going to have to use a second horse to give Harvey a break.

Nikki rested her arm across the saddle horn and watched Lucas. He was wearing jeans, a dark red long sleeve shirt and the black vest and hat she'd first seen him in. The well-worn black cowboy hat was low, so she could barely see the brown amber eyes that suddenly turned to her. The mustache and goatee framed his grin. She returned the grin with a warm blush she couldn't blame on the sunshine.

"Another herd pastured where they shouldn't be." Matt grumbled as he reached her.

Nikki nodded. "Not one herd we've seen is in the right place."

"We're going to have to spend the next week pushing cows."

"Oh! The horror!" Nikki gasped with a laugh. They had helped push cows for years…and loved every minute of it.

Matt chuckled in agreement. "Have you thought about the brand and name?"

"On and off…" Nikki smiled while looking over at the tall Australian. "My mind gets distracted."

Matt chuckled. "I don't think I've seen two people hit it off so fast."

Nikki reluctantly turned her eyes from the man and over to her brother.

"Have you thought of something?" She asked.

"I want to name it after Dad."

"I've thought of that too, but I don't know how without making it obvious."

"When he named his company after Mom's barrel horse, no one but him knew why."

Nikki smiled at the thought. "You have an idea?"

Matt nodded and stepped out of the saddle. He found a stick and a bare spot of ground and drew a circle in the dirt. "The circle symbolizes family."

"Yeah…"

Then he drew a 5 and a 0 in the middle.

"Circle 50?" Nikki asked.

Matt turned and looked up at her. "Everything started with a $50 bet to ride a bull."

"Matt!" Nikki was ecstatic. "That couldn't be more perfect!"

"There are only a handful of people that would know what the 50 stands for." He grinned.

"And no one but those few could connect it to Dad!"

"I don't know that we can get Circle 50…we'll have to check the registered brands in Idaho when we get back, we may have to go Rocking 50, Bar 50, Diamond 50 or something like that."

Nikki nodded emphatically, "As long as it has the 50."

"So we made our first big decision?"

"We did!" Nikki laughed.

The happy group had covered a lot of ground since they stayed on easier trails for the kids. Nikki had made notes about the different fences and stock tanks that needed replaced or repaired. She also noted the cows, approximated their head count, and area where they were grazing.

"How about camping over there?" Matt asked.

Nikki turned to see him pointing towards a small clearing next to a thick row of trees. It looked like a hunter's camp. She nodded and turned Harvey towards the clearing.

She watched and made sure the kids dismounted their horses with no problems before she stepped out of the saddle. Nora, Sadie and Wade all declined help from Lucas in getting their horses ready for the night.

Nikki ran her hand down Harvey's neck and gently down the side of the horse's face. Harvey returned the attention with a dip of the head into Nikki's shoulder.

"What a great group of kids." Lucas led Bay behind him as he approached.

Nikki turned, Matt was stringing a highline between the trees to give them a place to tie the horses for the night. He took the kid's horses and tied them to the line next to Trooper.

Lucas stopped next to her, close to her, so close their arms were touching. He looked down at her and grinned through his whiskers.

"There's a lot of hillside here." She teased.

"Yes, acres and acres," He nodded, looking up and around the mountain. "But this is the part I want to be standing on." The grin widened as he looked back down at her. "It has the most beautiful view I've ever seen."

The warm flush rose up her neck and into her cheeks again as she smiled back at him and shook her head in exasperation. They had one more night together in the mountains. How was she going to get any sleep when he said things like that?!

She giggled contentedly and turned from the handsome man and led Harvey towards the highline rope and other horses. Matt and the kids had wandered to the other side of the clearing to collect firewood. Once the sun went down, the temperature would drop drastically, they would need the fire and their thick sleeping bags to keep warm.

She tied the horse securely to the rope line and heard Lucas and Bay walking towards her.

He walked up next to Nikki; just close enough to brush their arms together again. The touch sent warm tingles up her arm and into her stomach. When she took in a deep breath to calm her nerves, she took in the scent of the fresh air, the horses, and him. The flutter returned to her stomach.

He tied Bay to the rope so the two of them were between the two horses and blocked from the kids. He turned to her and Nikki glanced up and smiled. His eyes were on hers. She took in another deep breath; the fresh air, the horses, and him.

It was then that Harvey made her move. The horse sidestepped into Nikki's back, pushing her into him. His arms came up protectively to her waist to catch her. She grabbed his arms and glanced up, they were just inches away. Again, their eyes met. As he leaned down, she rose on her tip toes to meet him. Moments before their lips touched, she whispered.

"Thank you, Harvey."

When their lips separated, he whispered.

"Did you teach her that move?"

Nikki looked up into his dark amber eyes and smiled. "I wish I could say yes."

He leaned down again, this time wrapping his arms around her waist and back, pulling her closer. She rose on her tip toes and slid her arms around his neck.

"Lucas!" Sadie yelled out.

He lifted an inch away and looked into her eyes. The warmth of him surrounded her; she wasn't ready to let him go. He wasn't ready either, as he lowered back down and kissed her one more time.

As he rose, he whispered, "Next time we go camping…it's just the two of us." He grinned; that wonderful grin and turned away from her.

"Sadie, where are you?" Lucas called out, turning back to Nikki and smiling.

"Over here!" Sadie called out laughing.

###

Nikki fell asleep looking across the flames of the campfire at the smile and sparkling eyes from the other side. The grin and the fire created a warmth that let her sleep soundly.

She was still warm when she woke but the smile and man weren't across the newly revived fire.

"Good morning," The accented voice spoke.

She rolled onto her back and looked up, he was grinning down at her. He held out a hand, that she gladly took and he helped her stand.

Wade and Nora were still sleeping. Sadie was at the horses with Matt.

"Little Dingo sure gets up early," He chuckled.

"You call her that to her face yet?" Nikki smiled as she released her ponytail from the band and ran her fingers through her hair.

"No." He chuckled. "You and Matt scared me out of it."

They fixed breakfast together as Lucas told her about his home in Australia. It didn't take long for Matt and the kids to join them and listen.

It was a perfect morning that led to a perfect afternoon.

"Hey, Wade!" Matt yelled out. "What's that over there?"

Wade ran up next to him and looked in the direction his cousin was pointing. The boy's eyes opened wide as he looked up. "It looks like a beaver dam. Can we go down?"

Matt nodded and Wade turned to the girls who were standing between Nikki and Lucas.

"Come on, Sadie! Nora, come on, this could be cool!" Wade ran down the side of the hill to the creek and small pond.

"Are you coming?" Matt looked back at the girls who shook their heads. "It's spring, they could have babies."

"Baby beavers?" Sadie's eyes widened in excitement. She glanced at Nora and then they both ran towards Matt and headed down the hill.

Matt turned to Nikki, winked, and turned down the hill. "Hey, wait for me!"

Nikki felt the flush run up her neck and into her cheeks when she realized that Matt was taking the kids away so she could spend time alone with Lucas.

The Australian had walked back to the edge of the trees and was tying Bay to the tree next to the other horses. He turned with a knowing look… he knew too.

"Do we have to wait for Harvey to make her move this time?" He asked as she walked closer to him.

"No." She whispered and dropped the horse's reins to the ground, lifted on her tip toes and wrapped her arms around his neck; she pulled his lips to hers. She internally melted when his strong arms wrapped around her back and firmly pulled her to him.

Nikki remained in his arms until she heard a whistle, then another, then another…all from different people.

She giggled and stepped out of his arms.

"What is that?" He sighed and looked behind her.

"Whistle contest," She smiled as she reached up and touched her lips and the tender skin around them where his whiskers touched. "Matt's warning us."

"Have I told you that I really like your brother?" He chuckled and stepped towards the horses.

"He owes me." She giggled and stepped towards the hillside and the approaching kids.

"Really? Why?"

"We went to college together," She grinned. "I've introduced him to a girl or two that I thought he would like."

"Wow…he's got a great sister."

Lucas was at least thirty feet from her when the kids made it to the top of the hill.

"Did you see any beavers?" Nikki asked at their excited faces.

"No, but I think I can whistle as loud as you can!" Wade grinned and placed two fingers in his mouth and blew. It was loud!

"You've been practicing." She teased her very happy cousin.

Nikki grinned, placed two fingers into her mouth and blew even louder. All three kids eye's opened wide and they started laughing.

But then, they heard it…a whistle from behind them…that was louder than Nikki's.

They all turned in amazement! Lucas stopped the whistle and winked at Nikki.

"Lucas' is louder than yours!" Sadie yelled excitedly and ran towards him "Do it again!"

Nora and Wade followed her.

Matt came up, put an arm around his sister's shoulders and they stood together to watch and listen to Lucas whistle. The kids bounced in excitement.

"A man after my own heart." Nikki grinned.

"I think you're right, Sister." Matt looked down at her and she looked at him in confusion.

"About what?"

"He is a man after your heart." He smiled and walked towards Lucas and the kids.

###

It was late in the afternoon before their group reluctantly loaded the horses into the trailers and headed home. When they arrived, Matt, Lucas, and Wade took care of the horses while Nikki, Nora, and Sadie made a late dinner.

As she stepped out of the shower, Nikki received a text from the other groups stating they would be staying at the ranch overnight and would see them Monday night. She quickly dressed in clean jeans and a t-shirt then went to tell her fellow campers.

Matt and Lucas were making their way back down the stairs after carrying a sleeping Sadie and Wade up to bed.

Matt drove to their house to shower, Lucas showered in the guest room and Nora went to her bedroom.

Nikki sat at the corner of the couch, curling her legs and bare feet under her, and watched the lights on Matt's truck slowly make their way down the driveway. Just as he turned onto the long road, Nikki heard footsteps from the hall.

She turned in time for Lucas to appear. His dark hair was still damp and glistened in the light. He wore jeans and a white t-shirt. His bare feet made him look…domestic…

Nikki giggled at his grin.

"What was that giggle for?" He sat next to her and turned to face her, a hand quickly went up to push back a strand of hair that had fallen in front of her eye. So intimate…

Nikki couldn't stop herself, she leaned in, smelling the musky cleanliness, and gently touched her lips to his. As she leaned back, his hand moved quickly and slid to the back of her neck and pulled her into a soft kiss.

In the distance, Nikki could hear running, she waited for it to stop, but it didn't. The running footsteps didn't stop until they reached the top of the stairs.

She pulled back quickly and turned toward the stairwell. "They didn't stop..." She said and pushed him back.

"What?"

"They didn't stop and slide." She whispered and stood quickly. She had only taken a step away from the couch when Nora appeared at the bottom of the steps.

Tears streaked her face; she looked frightened.

"Nikki!" She cried.

CHAPTER TEN

"Nora, what's the matter?" Nikki's pulse raced at the sight of the fear on her cousin's face and the terror in her voice.

"Candace." Nora held up her phone.

"What about her?" Nikki frowned.

"Candace is at the rodeo arena." Nora cried.

Nikki glanced at the clock. "It's nine o'clock at night…why would she be there now?"

"Her parents dropped her off this morning to ride," Nora explained through her tears. "They said they would come back…they didn't…she's been there all day…by herself."

Nikki looked up the stairs, Sadie and Wade had been at the house by themselves before, besides they were sound asleep.

She grabbed Nora's hand and headed for the backdoor only stopping long enough to grab her keys.

"She's scared…and crying." Nora continued as they ran out the back door, Lucas was following.

"Call her back," Lucas told her. "Tell her we're on the way. Stay on the phone until we get there. How far is it?"

"Five minutes," Nikki answered as they jogged to the truck. Thank goodness they hadn't unhooked the horse trailer. Half way across she realized she was barefoot but wasn't turning back for shoes. When he climbed in the truck, she noticed Lucas wasn't wearing shoes either.

Nikki turned the truck and trailer as Nora made the call.

"We're on the way," Nora cried. "No, stay on the phone with me…it's OK….it will take us just a couple minutes…it's OK Candace, we're on our way." Nora cried softly and continued to talk to her friend.

"How old is she?" Lucas whispered.

"Thirteen." Nikki turned onto the straight stretch and gunned the engine. "Nora's age."

"All day…" He whispered and shook his head. "She's got to be freezing and starving."

Nikki hadn't thought of that, she had only thought of her being scared.

"Does she have a coat?" Nikki asked.

Nora asked Candace. "No, just a hoodie."

"Look under your seat," Nikki whispered to Lucas. There should be an emergency blanket there. We always carry them during the winter and spring."

Nora continued to talk to Candace.

"She's at the horse stalls by the indoor arena." Nora yelled from the back seat.

Nikki pushed the accelerator a little more. There were a few sharp corners she slowed down for but gunned the truck after the last corner.

"We're almost there." Nora said quietly. "You should see the lights coming down the road….OK…no, stay there." Nora raised her voice. "She's in one of the stalls, there was a man there earlier that scared her, so she hid Lola and her in the stall…she's really scared."

Nikki didn't need to turn to know tears were streaming down Nora's face. It was all she could do to keep from crying.

"Who's Lola?" Lucas whispered.

"Her horse," Nikki answered and slowed the truck down to turn.

"We're turning in right now. Don't come out of the stalls until we get there." Nora ordered.

"Is she on the side facing the arena or the other side?" Nikki asked.

Nora repeated the question into the phone. "On the other side."

Nikki turned the truck wide so she could pull into the driveway to make the truck's lights shine down the whole side of the stall building.

As Nikki reached for the door handle, they saw a little blonde head stick out of one of the doors over half way down the building.

"We see you!" Nora cried out.

The stall door swung open and the young girl, followed by her red horse, flew out of the stall and ran towards them.

Nikki started running with Lucas at her side.

The scared girl was crying and sobbing so loud it tore at Nikki's heart. Half way, Candace stumbled and fell to the ground on her knees. Her whole body was shaking with the sobs wracking through her.

Nikki ran faster and fell to her knees next to the girl. Lucas quickly wrapped the blanket around her and Nikki pulled her in close. Her skin was ice cold, and she was shivering uncontrollably, her tears quickly soaking Nikki's shirt. Nora came up next to them and hugged the girl from the other side.

Nikki rocked her for a few minutes and glanced at Lucas. He had taken the horse and was jogging her to the horse trailer.

"Come on, Sweetheart." Nikki whispered. "Let's get you into the truck."

"I don't want to go home!" Candace screamed. She wouldn't stand and pulled back away from Nikki.

"You're going to our house." Nora said loudly to be heard over the girl's cries.

"You're coming to our house." Nikki assured the girl when she looked up at her with frightened brown eyes. Candace nodded then let Nikki and Nora help her stand.

Lucas returned and scooped the scared teenager up into his arms and quickly walked her to the truck. Candace turned into his neck and curled up in his arms as Nikki ran ahead of him and opened the back door.

He gracefully stepped into the truck and took a seat with the girl still cradled in his arms. He nodded to Nikki, so she closed the door. Nora was climbing into the truck on the other side.

"It's OK, Little Lass." Lucas whispered. "We've got you."

Nikki turned the heater on high and backed the horse trailer. She looked into the backseat. Lucas lowered the girl in between him and Nora, and quickly stretched the seatbelt around her. Nora grasped her friend's hand tightly.

"They told me to wait…" Candace's sobs had stopped but she was still crying through her shivers as she turned into the arm Lucas had around her. "I didn't want them to come back…I didn't ever want to see them again…but I got so scared, I wanted them to come back."

"I'm sorry I wasn't home." Nora whispered. "We were in the mountains and I didn't have my phone…I looked at it when I went to bed."

Nikki's heart ached for her cousin, knowing the undeserved guilt she was placing on herself.

"It's just a couple more minutes." Nora whispered. "Did you have anything to eat?"

Nikki couldn't hear an answer and looked in the rearview mirror at Lucas. He caught her eye and shook his head.

"What are you hungry for?" Nikki asked.

"I like spaghetti." She sat up. The heater, blanket, and the warmth from Lucas had stopped her shivers. "I like hamburgers, too."

"Well, we have the ingredients for both." Nikki tried to comfort her with her voice. "You want both?"

"Just a little of one, is OK." Candace whispered.

Nikki again looked in the review mirror and saw the same expression on Lucas' face that she knew she had; bewilderment.

"Do you like apple pie?" Lucas asked her.

Candace's head went up and her brown eyes looked up at him. "What?"

"Do you like apple pie?" He asked again with a smile. "We have some left from dinner tonight."

The blonde girl just stared at him, then she turned to look at Nora. "Is my brain frozen or did he just talk in an accent?"

Nikki smiled. She saw his amused eyes in the mirror.

"He's from Australia." Nora giggled.

Candace turned again and looked up at him. "Yes, I like pie." She smiled.

Nikki turned into the driveway. "Well, we'll get you into a warm shower and some clean clothes while we get your dinner ready."

"What about Lola?" Candace asked worriedly.

"I'll take care of her." Lucas smiled at her. "There are a couple empty stalls in the barn, I'm sure one will fit."

"I like your voice." Candace smiled and leaned into him.

"I do, too." Nora agreed.

Nikki agreed but didn't say it out loud. "Nora, we don't want to wake Sadie, so take her into the spare bedroom downstairs and get her in the shower. Get her some sweat pants and shirt from the down stairs laundry room. I'll fix Candace some dinner while Lucas takes care of Lola."

###

Nikki set the plate of spaghetti on the table next to the large piece of apple pie and waited. While the food cooked she had run up and checked on Sadie and Wade, they were still sound asleep.

What to do? Call the police or not? Maybe they were in an accident? Call the hospital? She reached for her phone and was surprised to see a missed call from Matt, and a text that said to call him ASAP.

She pushed his number and glanced down the hall to see if the girls were approaching.

"Nikki." Matt answered on the first ring.

"What's the matter?" She asked with a frown.

"Do you know anything about a horse trailer being left at The Stables?"

"Matt…no…" Nikki closed her eyes in dread.

"What?"

She quickly told him about Candace.

"You don't think…" He exhaled.

"I do, can you go check…just to make sure." She asked.

"How would I know if it's Candace's trailer?"

"I saw it at the Moscow show I took Nora to." Nikki tried to remember back. "It had vinyl letters that spelled Lola on the back door. It's an older two horse trailer."

"White?" Matt asked.

"Yeah."

"Size and color are right. I'll call you back."

Nikki turned as she lowered the phone, the back door opened and Lucas walked through. Their eyes met…then the girls could be heard down the hall.

Nikki smiled at him then turned to the girls. Candace was a little taller than Nora and was wearing purple sweat pants and a dark blue sweat-shirt. She had dark blonde hair that just reached her shoulders and her brown eyes were relaxed and content. She looked like a totally different girl then the one that was sobbing and scared a half hour earlier. Candace wore Nora's big white fluffy slippers and they were holding hands as they walked down the hall.

"I like those slippers," Lucas smiled as they walked into the kitchen.

"Funny, aren't they?" Candace smiled and Nora walked her to the table. The too skinny girl stopped and looked at the plate of food, then slowly turned to Nikki with worried eyes. "I don't need that much."

"Well," Nikki answered. "There is a difference between need and want. Do you WANT that much?"

Candace smiled shyly and nodded.

"Then eat all of it and the pie and if you want more…I'll give you more." Nikki gave her a reassuring smile.

Candace sat up at the table and started eating. When she finished the spaghetti she looked sheepishly at Nikki.

Nikki grinned and added more to the girl's plate.

As she ate, Nikki had whispered to Lucas about the horse trailer. The headlights from Matt's truck flashing into the living room gave her the answer.

She turned to Lucas with bewildered tears in her eyes. Candace wasn't forgotten, she was abandoned.

CHAPTER ELEVEN

Nikki stood at the door to the guest room and smiled at the girls. They were tucked in under the blankets. Candace was already asleep and Nora's eyes were closing slowly. "Thank you, Nikki." Nora whispered and fell to sleep.

She stood a moment longer and looked at Candace. Her face was relaxed now but was thin; in fact her whole body was very thin. The girl had eaten three plates of food and two pieces of pie. She was going to have a major stomach ache in the morning.

How could someone abandon a thirteen-year-old in a town she didn't know, with no one there to help? Thank heavens the girl had a phone; which Nikki was sure they left her so she would call Nora. That was why they left the trailer at The Stables. They left Candace for the Taggers.

Nikki turned and slowly walked down the hallway.

"That's the most heart breaking thing I've ever seen." Matt was saying as she walked into the kitchen.

"What?" Nikki sighed and slid into the chair between the two men.

"I recorded it." Lucas said.

"What?" Nikki frowned.

"When you were turning into the stalls, I turned my phone recorder on and placed it in the window. I recorded it." He explained.

Nikki looked at him in shock, she had no idea. "Why?"

Lucas sighed. "Because I'm an attorney, Nikki," he reminded her. "And I don't want the monsters that did that to her to ever get her back…or ever see her again."

Nikki nodded and lowered her head into her hands and closed her eyes. All she could see was Candace running and then falling to her knees.

"The trailer?" She said without looking up.

"It's hers," Matt answered. "The tack room is full of all her clothes."

"I'll take her shopping and get her new ones. I don't ever want to see them, nor have her see them." Nikki said from behind her hands.

How could someone do that? Nikki sighed, then she remembered…the security system at The Stables.

Her head shot up and she looked at Matt. "The video system." She rose from the table and ran to the library.

"What?" Lucas said from behind her.

Matt explained the security system and closed the library door out to the hallway to make sure the girls couldn't overhear them if they woke. Nikki quickly worked the computer and connected into The Stable's security system. She went back to 10:00 am…the trailer was there, 9:00 am…the trailer was there…8:00 am…the trailer was there….7:00…is wasn't. She slowly forwarded the recording until she saw an old blue truck pulling into the parking area. A man was sitting behind the wheel. A woman opened the truck door and proceeded to unhook the trailer from the truck, and without a glance back, climbed in the truck and they drove off.

"Do you recognize them?" Lucas asked.

Nikki nodded. "That was her mother and, I'm guessing, her father."

"7:25…That girl was there for fourteen hours." Lucas leaned back in the chair.

"Why wouldn't they just leave her at The Stables?" Matt sighed. "At least there would have been someone there to contact us."

"They didn't want her to know." Lucas answered and turned to the other computer and started typing.

Nikki sat quietly and watched him work; she had no idea what he was doing.

"How was Lola?" She sighed.

"Skinny, a few scrapes, and needs her hooves trimmed; other than that she looks OK." Lucas answered without turning away from the computer. "I gave her a bale of grass hay and just a little grain."

"What are you doing?" Matt asked.

"I'm researching Idaho law." Lucas answered; only half paying attention. "Where does she live?"

"Plummer."

"Is that in Idaho?"

"Yes."

"Who's your attorney?"

After she gave him the attorney's name she turned to her brother. "Matt, don't you know a couple of sheriffs from the search and rescue?" Nikki asked.

"Yeah," he answered.

"Can you see if any are on duty that could come over so we can report this?" She turned and watched Lucas. "And see if they can come over in plain clothes so they don't scare her. Get an email address that I can send the recording to, please."

"Good idea." He pulled his phone out of his pocket and walked to the windows.

Nikki watched Lucas for another twenty minutes; read, click, print, click, read, read, print, click….

She stood and walked towards Matt. He was explaining the situation to someone over the phone so she made her way back to the guestroom and opened the door slowly to look at the girls. They were on opposite sides of the bed, well covered, and Candace was sleeping, so deeply she was drooling. Poor girl…

"Nikki."

She turned to see Matt.

She made her way back to the library and he closed the door.

"Officer Wendt will be here in about 20 minutes. He went home to change." Matt smiled. "He liked your idea. They have put an APB out on the pair. I gave them the license plate number from the video and then emailed the video of them dumping the trailer…not the other one."

Nikki glanced over at Lucas…he was still clicking and reading.

At two o'clock in the morning, the officer arrived, he pulled into the drive in his personal vehicle then Matt showed him into the library.

Matt sat him at the table and handed him Lucas' phone with the recording at the arena.

"Put the head phones in." Nikki handed him a pair. "I don't want to hear it."

"Me either." Matt nodded.

"Me either." Lucas agreed, which made all three look at him; they didn't realize he was paying any attention to them. He just continued to read and click.

Matt and Nikki sat back and watched the officer's reaction to the video. Candace was easily visible and the sound was perfectly clear. Nikki had watched it until Candace fell to her knees and turned it off. She hoped to never see it again.

Officer Wendt inhaled sharply and frowned when she fell, then exhaled when she yelled she didn't want to go home. His shoulders tensed and his frown deepened the farther into the video he watched. Once the truck started moving, they could only be heard, as the video showed the road. When finished, he turned it off and slowly took out the ear buds.

"I don't want to hear it again either," He shook his head. "Like you said Matt…heart breaking."

The officer was visibly upset.

"Officer Wendt," Nikki reached for his hand. He took it and she walked him to the back room and slowly opened the door to the sleeping girls.

They had moved together, cuddled closely. Candace's face was relaxed and content, clear of all the anguish, fear, and tear streaks he had just seen.

He walked into the room and pulled the blanket up to their shoulders and tucked the blanket around them. He stared for a moment then turned to Nikki, nodded with a sigh, and walked out of the room.

He was on his phone before they reached the library.

An hour later; Nikki walked to the kitchen and put on a pot of coffee.

"Nikki?" She heard Matt's voice and carried the coffee and cups into the library.

"They found them already, they got a speeding ticket in Boise so they had an idea where they were headed." Matt told her as she walked in. "They were already in Reno."

"Are they in jail?" She asked.

"Yes, thanks to the video." The sheriff answered. "No doubt of child endangerment and a few other charges that Lucas has listed out."

Nikki turned to Lucas, but he was intent on reading something on the computer.

"Even a few against Lola," Matt smiled.

"Lola?" Nikki said in surprise.

"In some places," Lucas said without turning away from the computer. "Cruelty to animals has worse consequences than cruelty to people."

"They'll have every charge thrown at them we can." The sheriff nodded.

"Here, sign these." Lucas handed her a few papers without looking away from the screen; in fact, he was still scrolling as she reached for them.

"What are they?" Nikki asked.

"I'll tell you the same thing I tell Nick." He said while reading. "Read every word on papers I hand you, don't trust me blindly because I'll do what I think is right…doesn't mean you'll agree." He was smiling at the computer.

Nikki sighed. "I miss him." She smiled at her brother.

"Yeah, I miss him too." Matt grinned at her.

Lucas chuckled while reading. "I still can't believe he has a son and a daughter to miss him."

Nikki giggled tiredly and sat down to read the papers. Her head was spinning by the time she got done.

"Are you sure?" She said without looking up from the paper.

"Like I said…" Lucas kept reading the document on the computer screen.

"I know," She sighed and signed the papers then slid them over to the sheriff who witnessed her signature.

Without looking, Lucas reached back and took them from her and placed them in the scanner.

"Child Protective Services will be here in the next hour." Sheriff Wendt told them.

"Will they take her?" Nikki asked sadly.

"Not as long as she's sleeping," He sighed. "Then they will do what they think is best for the child."

"Do you know whose coming?" Nikki asked.

"Rhonda Bachman." The sheriff answered.

"I've worked with her before," Nikki smiled. "Great lady, very caring...I used to babysit her kids."

"What?" Lucas asked without turning from the computer.

"I used to babysit for her. You know, watch her kids while her husband took her out to dinner and a movie." Nikki chuckled.

"Why did you work with her before?" Lucas clarified.

"There were times she had to come with parents to The Stables. The parents had chaperoned visitations with their kids. They would come out and rent a horse." Nikki stretched her tired muscles. "She would also bring some troubled kids out just to pet the horses and walk them around, a bit of equine therapy."

He stopped talking and started typing again. Pretty soon he was printing and clicking and reading again.

Nikki looked over at Matt who had sat on the couch and fallen asleep. It was 4:00 in the morning.

"Nothing can happen for an hour," The Sheriff told her. "Lay down for a bit, I'll wake you when Rhonda gets here."

Nikki nodded but stayed where she was.

Lucas stood, walked to her and wrapped his arms tightly around her. The strength in his embrace was comforting. She rested her head on his shoulder and they stood quietly and just held on to each other. The sheriff walked out of the room.

Rhonda, the CPS worker arrived, and Nikki quietly showed her the sleeping girls. The sheriff showed her the video from the arena then the video from The Stables.

Nikki told the woman all the history about Candace as she could. Most of it was from the horse shows and that Nora had been a friend since the summer before. She told her of the desperate phone call to Nora and how Nora had comforted her friend on the phone then in person.

When Nikki returned from retrieving more coffee, Rhonda was signing papers from Lucas, had the sheriff witness it, then he handed it to Lucas. Lucas scanned the document and returned to his clicking and reading.

At 6:30, Nikki received the first phone call from the family attorney wanting to know what all the paperwork was in his email inbox. He watched the two videos Lucas had sent him and headed for his office.

Reilly and Grace arrived from the ranch and stayed long enough to grab something to eat and leave for school. Rhonda and Officer Wendt became "friends" that were visiting. They had no idea that Candace was sleeping down the hall.

Wade and Sadie were woken with just enough time to change their clothes and get something to eat before Matt drove them to school. They were curious why Nora wasn't going to school, but too excited that Matt was taking them to worry for too long.

Nora and Candace were still sleeping.

By 8:00, the family attorney had reviewed the paperwork Lucas had prepared, and with the recommendation of the responding officer and the child protective services representative, he signed the documents. He then personally walked them all to the courthouse and judge's chambers. At 8:15 in the morning, fifteen minutes after arriving at his office, the judge signed all the documents.

At 8:30, all the signed paperwork was received in the Tagger inbox.

By the time the teenager woke, Nikki Tagger was granted temporary legal guardianship of the thirteen-year-old Candace Avery.

CHAPTER TWELVE

"This is the biggest barn I've ever seen," Candace said as they approached the building. "I can't believe Lola's in there."

"She is," Nikki chuckled and opened the small barn door and glanced in. No one was visible. After the girls had woken, Nikki explained to Candace that the sheriff was there, as well as a lady from child protective services but didn't tell her about the guardianship papers.

Candace didn't want to talk to anyone, but Nikki explained how important it was that they hear her side of the story. Candace refused.

"What if you and I go out to the stalls and talk with Lola?" Nikki asked. "It always helped me when I was growing up to have Kit with me, and I talked to her."

"Will the sheriff and the lady be there?"

"Yes, but I can ask them to be in the next stall so you don't see them." Nikki assured her.

So, as Nikki approached Lola's stall, she checked to make sure no one was visible.

"Where is she?" Candace looked around the large barn.

At the sound of her voice, Lola's head popped over the stall door.

"Oh, Lola!" Candace ran down the barn and to the horse.

It was the first time Nikki had seen the horse and was surprised at the sorrel's condition. She had seen the horse six months earlier and she had been healthy and beautiful. Now she was gaunt with ribs showing. Her hair should have been shiny, yet it was dull.

Nikki gave the girl a few minutes of quiet time with her companion.

"Candace?"

"Yes?"

"Where have you been keeping Lola?" Nikki asked.

Candace frowned and hugged into the horse's shoulder. "They hid her in the backyard of the house. She only had a little yard to move around in." She turned into the horse and closed her eyes. "I would find as much hay as I could get to her. A couple of nights ago, when it was raining so bad, Lola was standing in the mud with no shelter. I pulled a bunch of the stuff out of the garage and we spent the night together in there." A tear ran down her cheek as her anguished eyes opened. "Dad wasn't very happy his stuff got wet."

"Well," Nikki smiled, trying to console her. "She'll have a large pasture here to run in…and friends to run with."

"I let her run in the arena yesterday…she loved it." Candace smiled, her brown eyes under her blonde bangs finally showing a bit of light.

"What did they say when they dropped you off?" Nikki asked as she handed the girl a brush.

Candace slowly started brushing her horse. It was very therapeutic to stand and brush an equine friend.

"When we left the house and they had Lola in the trailer," Candace took a deep breath and sighed as she brushed the horse. "I thought they were taking her somewhere to sell her. Then they just kept driving and didn't really talk. When I saw the sign for Lewiston I thought of Nora and tried to figure out how to go see her…without them." She moved to the opposite side of the horse. Nikki looked quickly around the stall and spotted the recording device in the corner. "When they drove into the arena, I knew Nora wasn't far because of the show I came to last year. She told me she lived close, but I didn't know where. I would have ridden here if I'd known."

"Did you ask them about Nora?" Nikki asked quietly. She couldn't bring herself to call them her parents.

"No," She said firmly. "I was afraid if they knew I wanted to see her, they would make sure I didn't."

"What did they say when they left?"

"They just said to wait there."

"Did they say they would come back?"

She nodded and shrugged. "Kind of, they said I should just wait for them."

"Did you think they were coming back?"

"I hoped they weren't."

"Why?"

"Because all they did was yell at me or ignore me. Lola's been the only friend I've had for a long time. Mom never liked me and the last couple months have been terrible."

"Do you know why?"

"My dad came back," She shrugged. "When he did, Mom just wanted to do whatever he wanted and gave him all the food and her money. I was invisible to them."

"Did they hurt you?" Nikki dreaded the answer.

"No, just ignored me or left me at the house by myself for days," She glanced at Nikki for the first time. "I spent most my time with Lola; even took her for a walk so she could get out of the yard. I would try to find somewhere she could eat the grass."

"Why did they keep Lola?"

Candace's eyes widened. "She is mine! They gave her to me for my ninth birthday. I would have screamed and yelled if they had tried to take her. I told them I would call the police if they stole my horse from me." She relaxed and shrugged. "Mom always wanted me to do good so she could have the money I won."

Nikki smiled. "I would have screamed and yelled too if someone tried to take my horse." She took a deep breath and asked the question she knew the people on the other side of the wall wanted to know. "Did they hurt…or touch you wrong?"

Candace turned and looked at her, eyes wide. "No." She said firmly. "One man tried. I don't know who he was, but I screamed as loud as I could and ran."

Nikki sighed in relief. "You did the perfect thing. Did you tell your mother or father?"

Candace nodded, "I told Mom."

"What did she say?"

"Just told me to hide when strange men came over."

What a horrible mother, Nikki thought, but tried to keep the animosity out of her voice, "Did you?"

"I hid a lot." Candace leaned against the stall wall and ran her hand down the horse's nose. "Can we stop talking about them?"

Nikki nodded with a smile. "Yes, but I do want to ask you, if I can do some tests on Lola. I want to develop a diet plan for her."

"Like what?"

"Blood tests, teeth check, and stuff like that." Nikki answered. "I just graduated from college in equine nutrition. I need the tests to know what vitamins and nutrients she needs."

Candace stood quietly looking at Nikki. "You could just do it…why ask me?"

"Because she belongs to you," Nikki smiled and earned a slight smile in return. "There is one more thing."

"What?" Candace glanced at her from behind Lola's head.

"I would like to do the same for you."

"What do you mean?"

"I'd like to get you to the doctor and do some tests, see what you need. You're too skinny, Hon. I'd also like to take you to the dentist; the same health checks on you and Lola. That way, we can get both of you healthy so you're ready for show season. "

Candace frowned. "I don't think I can do shows anymore. I don't even know where I'm going to be." She looked at Nikki. "Do you know where they are?"

Nikki nodded. "The sheriff took care of all the details and they are in jail now."

Candace's eyes grew. "What happens to me? Do I go to jail too?" Tears welled.

"Of course, not!" Nikki said quickly and held her arms open for the girl. She quickly stepped in and squeezed Nikki's ribs tightly. "Lucas, the sheriff, and Rhonda, the CPS lady, made arrangements for you."

"Where am I going?" Candace looked up at Nikki with worried eyes.

"Nowhere," Nikki smiled.

"What?" Candace asked in surprise.

"You are going to stay here with me and Nora."

She took a step backwards and looked up at Nikki with narrowed eyes. "Are you serious?"

Nikki smiled and nodded.

"I'm staying here?" Candace looked over at her horse. "And Lola?"

"She stays wherever you are." Nikki said firmly. "We have plenty of room for both of you."

"For how long?" Candace stood calmly. Nikki was surprised at her lack of reaction.

"They will try to find some relatives."

"Mom has two sisters and Dad has a sister." Candace said quietly, as if she didn't want them to know.

"Do you know them well?"

"Mom's sister Aunt Paige…I don't know her other sister." Candace sighed. "I haven't seen Aunt Paige for a long time. I think Dad's sister is in jail." She looked up at Nikki. "How long?"

"I can't really answer that." Nikki said honestly. "But the paperwork says that I am responsible for you, and I will make sure you don't leave here unless I know that you will be safe and loved."

"You're responsible for me?" Candace asked in surprise.

Nikki nodded. "Yes."

Candace stood quietly a moment then looked up at her. "Why?"

"Why what?"

"I watch a lot of TV. I know they can't put you in charge unless you agree to it."

Nikki nodded.

"So why did you say you would?"

"For the same reason I got to you as fast as I could last night." Nikki smiled softly. "Because I CARE, Candace…I care about you."

"Nobody's cared about me in a long time." Tears glistened in her eyes.

"That's not entirely true."

Candace looked at her in surprise.

"Nora…Nora, has cared about you for a long time." Nikki smiled. "And I will make sure that you have everything that you need."

"Thank you, Nikki." Candace said and ran into her arms.

###

Nikki watched as Nora walked Candace around the barn and introduced her to each of the horses. She had an hour to get as many phone calls made as possible before the girls expected to head to their shopping trip.

A phone call was made to the school district in Plummer. Nikki was surprised that Candace had good grades and had barely missed a day. They were sending her transcripts to Nora's school and she would finish the school year with her friend.

Doctors and dentists appointments were setup for Candace and the veterinarian appointment was setup for Lola. While they were shopping, Lucas and Matt would trim and shoe the horse using supplies Grayson and Scott kept in the trailers. Candace was thrilled Lola was getting so much attention.

Nikki stood back from the computer and stretched her arms high above her head and closed her eyes. It had been a long time since she had slept at the campfire.

She could feel his warmth behind her, fingers wrapped around her balled up fists and they slowly lowered her arms down and crossed them at her waist, his arms over the top of hers. He squeezed tightly.

"Now, ask me again if I was sure you should be made her guardian." He whispered in her ear. His warm breath caused a shiver and round of goose bumps.

"You have to stop doing that." She giggled and blushed.

"I don't want to," He chuckled softly. "I like that reaction."

Nikki turned into his arms and wrapped one arm up over a shoulder. With the tip of her finger she traced his smooth jaw line from his side burns to his goatee and mustache, she lightly brushed a thumb over his whiskers then looked up into his eyes. His intense stare made her gasp just as he leaned down and kissed her, his arms pulling her closer.

When he broke the kiss, she giggled. "Well, I'm not going to stop doing that...because I like that reaction."

Nikki wrapped her arms around his neck and pulled him down into a playful kiss.

They were both laughing when they heard the back door open.

"Someday...I'm going to kiss you and no one will interrupt us." He grinned and stepped away from her as they heard the girls' footsteps coming down the hall.

Shopping time.

Four stores and one shopping mall later, Nikki and the girls arrived back at The Homestead. Candace had everything from socks, underwear, shirts, pants, boots, shoes, hair supplies, a coat, cowboy hat and anything else the girl wanted. A new saddle blanket, halter, and lead rope for Lola were added into the mix. They had 30 minutes before Grace and Reilly arrived and an hour before Wade and Sadie would arrive by bus.

Nikki received a message that all the parents were coming home and would arrive in time for dinner.

"But Nick took Cora," Nora laughed. "Does that mean we have to cook?"

"Who's Cora?" Candace asked.

"Cora cooks for us and helps with the laundry and does all the computer work for the horses." Nora answered.

"You have a maid?" Candace asked in surprise.

"NO!" Nora, Nikki, and Matt said quickly.

Candace stepped back in surprise.

"Sorry, Candace, we didn't mean to scare you." Matt smiled. "We don't think of her that way. Everyone in the house has chores to do and we clean the house ourselves."

"Are we going to cook?" Candace asked, a hopeful glint in her eyes.

"I'm thinking we should be able to figure out something for dinner." Matt grinned and both girls agreed. The pantry and refrigerator were raided.

Lucas was in the library working, so Nikki sat at the small kitchen table and watched Matt and the girls try to decide what to make for dinner. In twenty four hours, Candace's world had changed forever. She looked happy; no signs of the distraught girl from the night before.

"Nikki," Lucas whispered from behind her.

Nikki turned with a smile that quickly faded when she saw the frown on his handsome face. She quickly stood and walked to him. Her stomach turned when he shut the door behind her. The other door was already closed.

Taking a deep breath and letting it out slowly, she prepared herself for what he was about to say.

"The father wants Lola."

CHAPTER THIRTEEN

"No!" Nikki gasped, her hand went to her stomach. "He can't have her!"

"I know. We're working on it."

Nikki's mind raced, the horse had been the only friend Candace had throughout her ordeal. She thought of Candace and the years of horse shows they had gone to, her and Lola hiding in the garage during the rain storm, going for walks trying to find the horse something to eat, cowering at the arena stall last night. How? How could anyone want to take Lola from Candace?

What if she took the horse to the ranch? No one would find her there.

"No, Nikki." Lucas said firmly.

She tilted her head in confusion. "No, what?"

"No, you can't hide the horse."

Her jaw dropped. "How did you know what I was thinking?"

"Because I thought the same thing." He smiled wryly

"Then why can't I?"

He sighed, "Because, if you purposely hide the horse and go against the court, there is a chance they would take Candace from you."

Nikki slowly lowered herself into a chair. He knelt down next to her.

"Candace comes first," He took her hand and squeezed tightly.

"Of course," she whispered in emotional exhaustion. "Why would he want her?"

"He wants to sell her to pay for bail and his attorney."

"I'd pay anything to keep that horse with Candace, but not to her parents that did this to her."

"I know, I thought that too."

Nikki nodded. "I know Lola is a registered quarter horse; is she under his name?"

"Yes."

"But, if she was a gift to Candace, doesn't that mean something?"

"Yes, and the fact that he abandoned Lola when he abandoned Candace. We're working every angle. It's very doubtful that he will win this battle…but you never know."

"When will we find out?"

"Not until morning."

Nikki leaned down to rest her head on his shoulder, his arm wrapped around her, comforting her which caused the tears to rise. Sleep, she thought, I need sleep.

"Let's not tell anyone." She whispered.

"I won't say anything to anyone but you." He leaned into her more.

Nikki fought off the urge to close her eyes and fall asleep leaning on his shoulder with his warm arm around her.

"Go ahead and sleep, Nikki." He whispered.

She pulled away from him and shook her head. "Too much going on, the Trio will be here soon and I want to tell them what's going on."

"The Trio?" He looked at her in confusion.

Nikki giggled and lifted a hand to trace his jawline again and run her thumb over his whiskers.

"Don't do that," He whispered and leaned in softly kissing her. There was a knock on the door.

"Dang," He sighed, leaning back with a grin.

Nikki giggled again and stood to open the door.

Matt was smiling apologetically. "Kids are here…how do you want to handle telling them about Candace?"

Nikki took a deep breath and shook off the sleep that was trying so hard to overcome her. "I think I need coffee."

"I'm sure you do." Matt grinned.

"Reilly and Grace are here!" Nora announced loudly.

Candace ran into the living room and up to Nikki; her eyes wide in concern.

"What's the matter?" Nikki asked.

"Do they have to know?" She asked shyly. "I don't want everyone to know."

Nikki looked up to see Nora in the hallway. "Secret?" Nikki asked her.

"I won't tell anyone, promise!" Nora nodded, eyes wide.

"I won't say anything." From Matt.

"I won't say anything either." Lucas said from behind her.

"I have to tell my mom and uncles." Nikki sighed. "But we won't say anything to the kids…OK?"

Candace smiled, "OK." Then she ran back into the kitchen with Nora, Matt followed.

"Mother and two uncles…is that The Trio?" Lucas asked as they headed to the kitchen.

"Yes, they do so much together, it's much easier than saying all their names. When it was just the three of them, they were inseparable and earned the nickname."

"Just the three of them?" He stopped and looked back at her.

Nikki suddenly realized how much he didn't know. "When Matt was 9 months and I was three, there was a car accident that killed their parents and grandparents leaving them as the last three in the family."

Lucas stared at her, stunned. "No other grandparents, aunts, uncles?"

Nikki shook her head, "Just them, Matt and I."

Reilly and Grace walked in the back door, laughing as usual. They stopped short when they saw the two girls with Matt in the kitchen.

"Candace?" Grace said in surprise.

Candace's eyes shot over to Nikki, she didn't know what to say.

"Candace's mother is ill, so we volunteered to watch her for the next couple of weeks so she can finish school." Nikki said quickly. It wasn't really a lie…the woman had to be sick to abandon her child.

"That's pretty sick." Reilly frowned.

Nikki nodded. "That's why we're helping."

"Did you bring your horse?" Grace smiled at Candace.

"Yes!" Candace said excitedly. "She's out in that really big barn."

"Wanna ride with us?" Reilly asked.

Candace looked over at Nikki, again not knowing what to say.

"Lola had a big riding day yesterday," Nikki answered, she wanted to give Lola some time to put weight on before adding exercise. Candace turned away with a frown. "But maybe she would like to ride Harvey for me."

Candace's head spun quickly and looked at Nikki in shock. "Really?"

"Absolutely, I'd appreciate you exercising her for me." Nikki grinned.

Candace and Nora looked up at Matt.

"Go riding." He chuckled and barely had the words out of his mouth when the girls took off down the hallway to change their clothes.

###

Nikki glanced out the window and saw the trucks and trailers pulling into the driveway. She wanted to go explain Candace's presence there before they saw her, so she quickly headed for the back door. Matt and Lucas were nowhere to be seen.

She stood on the back deck and waited for the travelers to park and exit the trucks. She grinned when she saw all the men start to get out of one truck and the women the other…usually the wives and husbands rode together. They must have had enough time together camping and riding.

Just as Grayson stepped out of the driver's door and Jack right behind him, from the back seat, Nikki saw a movement to her left. It was Candace. The girl walked around the back of one of the horse trailers towards the house and stopped. She looked up at the two tall men who were looking at her in surprise. Candace gasped in fright, then turned and ran as fast as she could into the barn.

"Oh, dang!" Nikki cried out and quickly made her way down the steps and ran towards the barn.

She glanced over at the shocked men as she ran. "Go ask Matt and Lucas!" She yelled and ran into the barn.

"Candace?" She called out.

Horse heads popped up above doors and stall walls but no sound from Candace.

"Candace, it's OK." Nikki called out. She couldn't see her anywhere and guessed she ran to Lola. "That's my uncle and step-father you saw. They would never hurt you."

Nikki looked in Lola's stall and expected to see her, but she wasn't there.

Turning, confused, she looked and walked to each stall. No sign of her.

"Candace? This is Nikki. They won't hurt you. They are Grace and Reilly's dads, they would never hurt you. Please, Hon, let me know where you are."

"In here," A whisper of a voice reached her.

Nikki tried to follow the voice but couldn't tell where it came from.

"Candace?"

"In the tack room."

Nikki opened the door and turned on the light. She walked into the middle of the room and looked around; she still couldn't see her.

"Where?" Nikki asked.

"Here," Candace said and slid out from under one of the saddle racks and looked around the stirrup at Nikki with embarrassed eyes.

Nikki sat down next to her and took the girls hand.

"I'm sorry," Candace whispered looking down at the floor.

"Chin up." Nikki smiled

Candace raised her eyes up to Nikki's. "Nora told me that once."

"She did?"

Candace nodded. "That's when we became friends."

"Have you met Nora's dad?"

"Yes, but he wasn't one of those men…I didn't know who they were. I got scared so I ran and hid."

Nikki smiled and squeezed her hand. "After the last couple months you've had, I don't blame you."

Candace looked at her in surprise. "I'm not in trouble?"

"Of course not; but, here, you're safe. You don't have to run and hide when you see men you don't know. If you're worried, just come ask me."

Candace nodded; "Now what?"

"Well, let's go in the house and I can introduce you to them."

"Are you sure?"

Nikki smiled to reassure her. "We all live in that house together, which means you'll be seeing a lot of them."

"All of you?"

"Yes, three families living all together in one big house. We travel a lot between the ranch and here, so we share."

Candice nodded and they stood together to walk out of the barn hand-in-hand.

The newly returned family, Matt and Lucas were sitting at the table on the deck.

When they reached the top of the stairs of the deck, Candace looked nervously around at the group of adults looking back at her.

"Jordan!" Candace smiled and let go of Nikki's hand to run to the woman.

"Candace!" Jordan stood and reached out to pull the girl in a hug. There were tears in Jordan's eyes as she looked over the girl's head to Nikki.

Nikki felt a hand slide into her own and turned to see her mother smiling up at her. "Matt and Lucas filled us in. We've decided no ranch talk, only family talk until you three have a good night's sleep. We'll wait until the kids go to school tomorrow."

Nikki nodded.

"Besides, we need kid therapy. We were going to go up and watch the kids ride until dark and do movies and popcorn for the evening."

"That sounds wonderful." Nikki answered.

###

"Thank you for letting me ride Harvey." Candace yawned as she settled in under the covers. She was sleeping in the guest bedroom again.

"You've thanked me a dozen times," Nikki teased.

"I know…I felt guilty for not riding Lola."

"She needs a couple of days of good feed then we'll add in the exercise." Nikki tucked the blanket around the tired girl.

"Where are you going to sleep?"

"Right across the hall in Cora's room, I'll leave both doors open."

"OK." Candace turned onto her side and sank further into the big pillow. Her eyes closed.

Nikki sat quietly watching the young girl sleep and thought about the last twenty-four hours. So much had happened. She sighed, so much had happened in the last week! Her whole life had changed; from finishing college all the way to becoming the guardian to an abandoned thirteen-year-old.

"What next?" Nikki whispered just as a shadow crossed in front of the door.

She looked up to see Lucas leaning against the door watching her.

"I'm headed out with Matt to stay at your place…on your couch." He smiled wryly.

Nikki stood, walked up to him and went in for a quick kiss goodnight before someone showed up to interrupt them again.

"Goodnight," She whispered then ran a thumb lightly across his whiskers.

"Nikki…" Lucas leaned down and kissed her again, "I'll see you first thing in the morning." He said softly then turned quickly and walked down the hall.

Nikki looked back and checked on the sleeping girl one more time before she walked across the hall and lay on Cora's bed.

It was 1:00 in the morning when she heard the first cry. Nikki sat straight up in bed and listened, not sure what the sound was. There was another cry and Nikki slid out of the bed and quickly made her way to Candace.

She sat on the edge of the bed and reached over to the blankets…they were empty.

"Candace?" Nikki called in a loud whisper.

All she heard was muffled crying…the sound was coming from under the bed.

Nikki lay on the floor and lifted the sheet to peer under and barely saw her curled up in the corner.

"Candace, it's me, Nikki."

"I got scared."

"What scared you? Did you have a nightmare?"

"Sort of…"

"What's a sort of nightmare?" Nikki asked.

"I dreamt they came and took Lola."

Nikki felt like she had been slapped. She had tried to forget that it was a possibility that Lola would be taken.

"Well, that would have been a nightmare for me if someone took my horse." Nikki said softly.

"When I woke up, I didn't remember where I was and got scared."

"Why don't you come out and I'll sleep in here with you?"

"You would do that?"

"Yes, Hon." Nikki stretched out a hand to help her out.

They crawled up into the bed together and she cuddled the scared girl in her arms, they both quickly fell back asleep.

CHAPTER FOURTEEN

"You look beautiful when you sleep." Lucas whispered to her as they stood in the kitchen alone.

"Excuse me?" Nikki asked as the warmth of the blush rose up her neck and into her cheeks. She looked up at his amused eyes.

He chuckled softly. "I went back to check on Candace when we got here and saw the two of you cuddled up and sleeping."

"You checked in on Candace?"

"Yeah…and got the bonus of looking at you sleep."

"Lucas…" She blushed again.

He shrugged. "I take every chance I can to look at you."

"Seriously," She giggled. "How am I supposed to concentrate on business today when you say things like that?"

"Well it's only fair," He smiled down at her. "With your hair pulled back like that, I would have easy access to your neck to make you shiver again…so if I can't concentrate, it's only fair that you can't either."

"Are you two going to join us today?" Matt asked from behind them.

"Be right there, Mate." Lucas smiled and grabbed the tray she had prepared with water and coffee for the group in the library.

"You may want to wait a minute, Sis. So your face gets back to its normal color." Matt whispered and turned away with a chuckle.

Lucas smiled, winked, and followed Matt.

It took the full minute and more for the warmth and redness to leave her cheeks then Nikki took a deep breath and walked to the library. They were all gathered around the table with solemn expressions. Nikki's first thought was there was something terribly wrong at the ranch.

"Nikki," Grayson started. "Before we get into the ranch business, we'd like to discuss Candace."

Nikki sighed and nodded. She kept from looking at Lucas and concentrated on Grayson and her mother.

"I don't know how much Matt and Lucas told you." Nikki answered.

"Just that the parents abandoned her and are in jail; that you're now her legal guardian." Her mother explained.

"Did you watch the videos?" Nikki asked.

"What videos?" Scott and Jordan asked in unison.

Nikki turned to Matt then Lucas who was sitting across the table from her. They shook their heads, letting her know they hadn't mentioned them.

"Lucas recorded when we found Candace and we have the video of them dropping off the horse trailer at The Stables." She explained then hesitantly said. "We transferred them to the computer…you can watch…probably should watch them."

"The arena video is terrible, so prepare yourself." Matt said and stood.

Lucas stood and walked around the table as Nikki moved to the computer to pull up the videos.

"Where are you going?" Jack asked as the three of them walked to the door.

"We don't want to watch it again," Matt answered while opening the door.

"Just push play. I have it password protected so the kids can't find it." Nikki frowned and looked over at Jordan. "I hate to have you watch it, but I think you should know."

Jordan nodded and stood as the group in the library gathered around the monitor. Matt closed the door behind them and Nikki walked to the large window in the living room to watch the Tagger Herd with their new friend Lola.

"I still see her falling." Nikki whispered. Both men, standing on each side of her, took her hands and squeezed their support.

"Lola and Rooster seemed to have hit it off." Matt said trying to break the tension.

"They have been together since they were walked out this morning. Candace and Wade thought it was funny." Lucas nodded.

Nikki watched as the two horses grazed next to each other, separating themselves from the rest of the herd. Rooster would lay his ears back and push any of the horses away that tried to approach Lola. He was as protective of the little mare as Nikki was of Candace.

The doors to the library opened and the three at the window turned to see Grayson's grim expression as he nodded to them.

They made their way back into the room as Leah, Jordan and her mother were wiping away tears.

Her mother embraced her as she walked into the library and Jordan hugged Lucas, Leah wrapped her arms around Matt.

The all sat quietly for a moment while Nikki explained Lucas' computer work, Matt contacting the sheriff and Nikki feeding the starving girl.

"Are they still in jail?" Leah asked.

Nikki nodded and glanced at Lucas. "Lucas had a pretty good list of charges lined up for the sheriff and prosecuting attorney by the time the sheriff arrived and watched the videos."

Nikki hesitated then looked at Lucas. He returned her gaze, knowing she was debating what to tell them about Lola.

"What is it?" Her mom asked. "Just spit it out."

Nikki nodded at Lucas.

"The father has filed papers asking for Lola so he can sell her and pay for bail and his attorney fees." Lucas told the stunned group.

"That will never happen." Her mother declared.

"No! How could anyone give her horse to that horrible person?" Leah exclaimed.

"I doubt the judge would allow it…but you never know." Lucas nodded.

"What if we took…" Jordan started.

"No." Both Nikki and Lucas answered.

He glanced over at Nikki, "We both thought the same thing, but if we go against the court then they could take Candace from Nikki."

"Dang…and all the other words." Scott exhaled.

"We should know some time this morning." Nikki informed them.

"What would you think of putting her upstairs with Nora and Sadie and letting Grace have the guest room?" Her mother asked.

Nikki frowned, how would Nora and Sadie handle what happened last night? Would they have heard her?

"Nikki?" Her mother asked with a concerned tone.

"She woke up last night crying and scared after a nightmare of people coming to get Lola." Nikki looked at her mom. "I found her under the bed, backed into the corner, and quite scared."

"Oh, I hate those people!" Jordan leaned back with tears falling again. Scott put his arm around her. "That poor girl."

"I think it could work later, after she adapts, but right now, I'd rather keep her close to me." Nikki decided and received nods of agreement.

"Nikki?" Jordan said.

Nikki turned to her.

"Scott and I discussed it last night; if they can't find family for her, we are offering to foster or adopt Candace…long term."

Nikki's eyes widened. She hadn't even thought long term…but she also didn't want anyone taking Candace from her…family or not, she had gotten extremely protective of the girl. Tears sprung to her eyes.

"Grayson and I discussed it last night too," Leah chuckled. "We are offering the same thing."

"Add Dru and I to that list," Jack smiled. "We discussed it, too."

Nikki looked around at her family, and loved them even more, if that was possible.

"Well, the parents knew what they were doing when they dropped her off for the Tagger family." Lucas shook his head.

Nikki stared at him in surprise.

"What did I say this time?" Lucas looked around at all the solemn and surprised faces that were glancing at Nikki. Then he turned quickly to her, "That's what Nick did? That's how you ended up with Dru?"

Nikki just stared. She knew no one else in the room would answer his question. They would wait for her, but she didn't know what to say? How to tell him without telling Nick's story?

"Nikki…I'm sorry." Lucas said softly with concern in his eyes.

Nikki nodded, "My birth mother gave me up to him and he couldn't take care of me…so he brought me to Dru to be raised with Matt."

"I…" Lucas started.

Nikki shook her head. "It's OK, you didn't know, and it's certainly not the same." She smiled to assure him.

He watched her closely for a minute then nodded with a sigh.

"Well, actually," Nikki frowned. "You should know about Elena."

"And she is...?" Lucas asked and leaned back in the chair.

Nikki hesitated; it was Nick's past that he didn't talk about, if he wanted Lucas to know he would have told him on the plane ride over. How could Nikki explain Elena to him without telling him the whole New Year's fiasco?

She looked up at her mother.

"Your choice," Her mother whispered.

Nikki looked at her uncles. They didn't give any indication what she should do.

"Nikki, I can't help if you don't tell me." Lucas commented, rising frustration in his voice.

She looked at Matt who exhaled and raised his eyebrows. He wasn't sure either.

Lucas leaned forward making her look at him.

"I have come to understand how protective you are of your family." He started, looking only at her. "And you're extremely protective of Nick...I don't know why from the little bit of your history I know."

Nikki was instantly pissed and started to speak when he raised a hand to stop her as if she was a little kid. That...just made her mad.

"I'm sorry, that was out of line, but this is very frustrating." He grumbled.

Nikki rolled her lips together to keep from speaking. The comment made her back stiffen and resolve stronger.

He looked around at all the quiet family members. "You are all very protective of Nick, I see that. But on the other side of the Pacific, I am JUST as protective of him as you are. He's done a lot for my family and paid for my education. I've worked for him throughout my studies and every day since." He paused and turned back to Nikki then to Matt. "I've had nothing but respect for him and everything he's accomplished. But, I can't help all of you, nor him, if I don't know the whole truth."

"I won't tell you the whole truth," Nikki said flatly which caused him to glare at her. "And neither will anyone in this room." She leaned forward. "I will tell you what I think you need to know to protect my family and my father. I will NOT tell you everything of his past, if you want to know that, then go to the man himself and ask him." She paused to let her words set in. "And, good luck with that."

Nikki sat back in her chair, crossed her arms and glared back at him. She watched his eyes narrow and his jaw muscle twitch.

She didn't wait for him to speak. "Elena Pelten is my birth mother. I didn't see her until about a year and a half ago. When she found out who I was, who the Tagger family was, she tried to get me involved in an extortion plan against Jack at The Stables for sexual harassment. It was actually the other way around. I recorded the conversation with my phone and let her know I had it."

"What happened to her?" He asked gruffly.

"Nikki literally threw her out the door and told her not to come back or we would turn the videos and recording over to the police." Jack chuckled.

"Can I hear the recording?" Lucas asked looking at Nikki.

Nikki rolled her lips again and thought quickly about the recording. It detailed everything about Nick's relationship with Elena and as Elena put it "abandoned" not one child but two. There was just too much of Nick's past on the recording to let him listen.

"Nikki," Lucas inhaled sharply. "I'm just trying to help."

"I told you what was on the recording." She frowned at him.

"Obviously not all of it, or you would let me listen to it." He said curtly.

Nikki's back stiffened. "The part you need to know is what I told you. The answer is no."

Lucas raised a hand to cover his eyes and rub his forehead in frustration.

"Who else has listened to it?" He asked.

"Only the family in here," she answered and leaned back to see his reaction.

"And Nick." He stated and lowered his hand to look at her.

Nikki shook her head. "No, he didn't want to listen to it."

"Does he know everything that's on it?" He tilted his head in curiosity.

Nikki sighed, looked at the table, and thought back to the horrible night. She tried to remember what she had told Nick and what she didn't.

She finally shook her head and looked up at Lucas. "No, we told him briefly about the extortion attempt, and told him the part of his past that Elena knew and he didn't."

"Was Nick married to her?" Lucas asked.

Nikki hesitated, then shook her head.

He sighed, "How long were they together?"

Nikki stared at him and didn't answer.

"Do you know how aggravating this is for an attorney trying to protect his client and family?"

Nikki didn't respond, she just looked at him calmly.

He matched her position and stared back.

"Anything else YOU think I should know?" He said a bit sarcastically.

"I have a half-sister named Josey somewhere in Montana."

He shook his head and sighed. "You don't know her?"

"No," Nikki answered. "And I have no clue whether she knows about me or not."

"What's her last name?"

Nikki paused, why would he need it? But then again, what would the harm be to give it to him?

"Nikki," He said curtly. "You seem to forget that your life has completely changed since you became a co-owner in a multi-million dollar cattle ranch, let alone the future inheritance."

She frowned. He didn't need to tell her how much her life had changed!

"If Elena's daughter is anything like Elena, then we have to keep you protected from her."

"And if she's not?" Nikki glared.

"Then nothing is said or done, but we have to have her checked out."

"What does that mean?" Nikki asked.

"I have an investigative team that will check her past and current situation to evaluate whether she is a threat or not." He answered coldly.

Nikki rolled her lips again. She didn't want to give it to him.

"Nikki," He said firmly making her lips tighten even more. "When you first found out about Elena, did you know that she would try to blackmail Jack?"

She slowly shook her head.

"If my team had checked her out, then she wouldn't have been able to get near you."

If he only knew that it was Nikki's fault that Elena knew who she was!

"Are you willing to put anyone in this room in jeopardy from someone that could be a potential threat to them? Or the kids? And you could have stopped it?" His expression and tone were calm but she knew he was upset with her.

No matter how upset she was at him, he made a good point...she needed to think of the kids. "I don't want to know what you find out and I DON'T want her approached." Nikki finally relented.

"I promise both conditions will be met." Lucas nodded.

"Franklin." She said quickly before she changed her mind.

"Thank you." He sighed, "Anything else I should know?"

Nikki looked around at the family she had momentarily forgotten were there; then shook her head. "No."

"Anyone else?" Lucas asked looking around the room.

Everyone shook their head no.

Nikki relaxed enough to realize she had a headache. "Excuse me." She stood and walked through the living room toward the kitchen. Something out the large window caught her attention. She walked towards the window...it was a horse trailer. Why was there a trailer in their driveway stopped by the center gate? Then she saw the man walking through the horse pasture towards the Tagger Herd and Lola. He had a halter and lead rope in his hand.

Candace's nightmare was coming true...someone was trying to take Lola.

CHAPTER FIFTEEN

"No!" Nikki yelled and ran for the front door, down the steps, and across the lawn. By the time she reached the gate, Lucas and Grayson were jumping the fence and running toward the man. She made it through the gate and ran after them, her mother right behind her.

"Eli!" Grayson yelled and the horse lifted his head and started trotting to the running man.

Grayson was trying to get the herd moving, which worked. They started walking towards the house; all of them except Rooster and Lola who had wandered farther away.

The man kept walking, not realizing two angry men were running at him.

Nikki knew that Grayson and Lucas would handle the man so she turned to the horse. Rooster and Lola's heads rose as she ran towards them. The man was only 30 feet away from them.

"Rooster!" Nikki yelled and the horse started walking toward her.

The man finally turned and looked at the group running towards him and he quickened his step towards Lola.

"Rooster!" Nikki yelled again and the horse started walking faster but Lola turned and looked at the approaching man carrying the rope and halter.

Grayson and Lucas finally reached the man and stepped in between him and the horse. Her mother came to a stop next to them.

The man started emphatically waving a handful of papers at them.

Nikki reached the horse, slid off her belt and looped it around the mare's neck and started to walk Lola up the pasture. The man started yelling at her, some pretty nasty words she hadn't heard in a long time, but he suddenly stopped.

She didn't know what happened; she just moved Lola into a trot and headed for the house with Rooster following. Jordan met her half way and she handed over the horse so she could go back.

As she turned, she heard the man's truck start and looked over; Jack was at the wheel and was backing the truck and horse trailer down and out of the driveway.

Scott, Leah, and Matt helped Jordan move all of the horses out of the pasture. Matt was on the phone.

When Nikki reached Grayson, he had an arm outstretched to the man stopping his movement towards the house and retreating horses. Lucas was standing off to the side on the phone talking very intensely to someone. Her mother had her hands on her hips glaring at the man.

"I have orders, right here, to pick up that horse." The man waved the papers again.

"Like I said," Grayson said with a forced calm voice. "I don't care what your papers are unless they are a court order. Get off this property now."

"I'm not leaving without that horse. The registered owner of that horse hired me…" The man said again.

"Yes, you are leaving." Nikki said loudly and firmly.

The man turned angry eyes at her. "Listen lady…"

"I told you not to speak to her," Lucas growled as he stepped between her and the angry man.

The man glared at Lucas then Nikki. He turned and looked at his truck that was now sitting outside the gate. Jack stepped out of the truck, shut the gate, and locked it.

"Get off the property." Grayson repeated.

"I want that horse." The angry man said and swung the halter and rope at Grayson.

Grayson stepped back to avoid being hit, but when he stepped forward he did with a fist flying at the man's head. He connected and sent the man flying backwards.

Screeching sounds from the road reached them just as the man hit the ground.

Through her gasp at the sudden physical assault, Nikki looked up and saw a sheriff's officer running around the front of his car and leaping over the fence.

"Stop!" The officer yelled as he ran towards them.

Grayson's expression was pure fury and his sister stepped in front of him to keep him from moving towards the man as he stood up.

"I'll sue you for that!" The man yelled at Grayson.

"Well, you'll have to do it from a jail cell." The officer reached them and grabbed the man. "You're under arrest for trespassing and assault."

"He assaulted me!" The man yelled and nodded towards Grayson.

"Bad timing for you, since I saw the whole thing," The sheriff shook his head. "You assaulted him with the rope and halter, and someone here called about a man trespassing and trying to steal a horse."

"This is ridiculous!" The man yelled as the officer started pulling him towards the fence and his car. "I have papers showing the legal owner of the horse hired me to haul it."

"It doesn't give you the right to trespass on private property and assault the owner." The officer pushed him forward.

Nikki, heart still racing, turned to Grayson. "Are you OK?"

He nodded as he watched the sheriff help the trespasser over the fence and to his car.

"Actually, my hand hurts." He turned and smiled down at her then to his sister.

"That was awful," Nikki shuddered. Her pulse was finally returning to normal as they heard another car stop at the road.

"It's Officer Wendt," Nikki told him and stepped back away from her uncle and mother. She looked towards Lucas who was watching her intently, but he was still on the phone.

Leah was running across the pasture towards Grayson. He stepped up the pasture to meet her.

Nikki walked down to the fence to talk with Officer Wendt. She was quickly joined by Lucas and the whole family except Scott and Jordan who stayed with the horses who were wandering in the driveway between the house and barn.

"Are you OK?" Leah asked Grayson. He nodded and she turned to Nikki.

"I'm, OK," Nikki smiled nervously. "I thought my heart and lungs were going to explode." She looked over at Lucas who still had the phone to his ear.

He caught her eye and nodded with an impatient expression.

"Do you want to press charges?" Office Wendt asked Grayson.

"Yes." Grayson answered firmly.

"We'll keep him in as long as possible so you have time to clear this up." Officer Wendt nodded and returned to his car.

"When?" Lucas yelled in the phone catching everyone by surprise. "Yes, no, sorry about that, just a lot happening right now.

Alright fine, but if I don't hear from you in the next half-hour, I'm going to drive down and sit in your office until you have the answer."

He ended the call and addressed the curious group. "The clerk says the judge signed the papers but they can't find the papers or the judge to find out what his decision was."

 The officers left and the horses were put in the barn. Leah and Jordan fixed everyone lunch and they sat quietly on the back deck and waited for the phone call. It was twenty-eight minutes after Lucas hung up the phone when his phone rang.

Lucas answered and everyone stared as he listened.

Nikki's stomach turned and her pulse raced. The day was already bad with the confrontation with Lucas, then the man trying to take Lola. She put her head down on the table and closed her eyes. She just knew they were going to take Lola now. How could she possibly tell Candace that Lola was gone? She couldn't do it…somehow, if the judge gave the horse to the father, she would have to get it back…even if it meant buying the horse from the monster of a father.

"Nikki?" She heard Lucas but didn't move.

"Nikki?" He repeated.

She slowly rose and looked up at him with fearful, worried eyes.

"The horse is Candace's with you responsible for Lola's care and upkeep until a final decision is made on Candace's permanent placement." He smiled.

Nikki lowered her head back onto the table and closed her eyes. The relief was overwhelming.

"Oh, Sweetheart." She heard her mother say and felt her arms wrap around her shoulders. Her mother's warmth and strength were just what she needed.

Nikki leaned into her. "I couldn't imagine telling that little girl her horse was gone."

She finally sat up and looked around at the group. They all looked tense and relaxed at the same time. It made her giggle.

"Really, Nikki?" Matt shook his head.

"Well, it's been quite the morning and we still haven't talked about the ranch." She sighed with a smile.

Her mother nodded. "Let's take five and meet back up in the library."

Everyone stood and went in the house. Nikki made her way to the guest room bathroom and took the aspirin she had been in search of when she saw the horse trailer. She stood quietly in the bathroom until she realized she was hiding. Chuckling to herself, she looked in the mirror and saw the same stressed, yet relaxed expression that everyone else had.

Stepping into the library, everyone was back in the same chairs they were for the morning onslaught. She took her seat across from Lucas who was typing on his phone and didn't look at her.

"How is your hand?" Nikki smiled at her uncle.

"It hurts," He chuckled and looked up at Matt. "I can't remember the last time I swung a punch at someone, but I forgot how much it actually hurts."

"That it does." Matt grinned back. "Mine hurt for days."

"Who did you punch?" Lucas asked casually, as he continued to type on his phone.

Matt glanced at Nikki with a wicked smile, she wanted to chuckle but kept silent.

"Nick." Matt answered.

Lucas stopped typing and looked up at Matt then at Nikki with a confused expression. He shook his head, sighed, then went back to typing.

"Let's get this going so we can get done before the kids get here." Her mother said. "It's been a long day and I want to play with them in the arena this afternoon."

"Good plan," Leah smiled.

"Nick and Cora will be back in the morning." Lucas announced and laid the phone on the table. He looked up at Matt. "They wanted to be back for a retirement party."

Nikki looked at Lucas in surprise. He didn't even glance at her!

"For our long time veterinarian," Scott told him. "Nikki helped him publish his journals, which have been pretty successful so he's been on a trip around the world to promote them."

Lucas nodded, "Good for him."

He still didn't look at her! Nikki leaned back in the chair and frowned.

"Well," Grayson started. "We found half the fencing down on our trip."

The next couple of hours, Nikki listened and spoke to all the issues on Andy's property; it was more than expected. Her first thought was putting the plans of a rehabilitation business aside to concentrate on the ranch until it was running smoothly.

As soon as they decided on an action plan to start repairs and moving the cows to the correct summer pastures, Nikki quickly changed clothes. She made her way to the barn to spend the afternoon with Candace, Lola, and Harvey.

"Head to the house and wash up for dinner." Nikki smiled at Candace. The girl grinned back.

"Thanks, Nikki." She giggled then ran out of the barn.

Nikki closed the door to the tack room and looked around at the barn. No horse heads greeted her out their stall doors; they were all too busy eating.

She walked into Harvey's stall. The horse glanced at her then put her head back down to the bucket of grain.

"Well, welcome to you too." Nikki smiled and raised a hand to the horse's neck. Slowly, she ran her bare hand down the long back. She needed the warmth of the touch after such a long strenuous day. Nikki stepped between the wall and the horse to scratch under the horse's belly which made Harvey's head bounce as she ate.

She loved these moments with her horse and the smile that graced her face froze when Lucas appeared at the stall door.

"Hiding out with Harvey?" He rested his arms across the top of the door. His hat still pulled low so she could barely see his eyes.

While she rode with Nora and Candace, he had spent the afternoon roping and riding with Sadie, Reilly, Grace, and Wade.

"Equine therapy." She smiled hesitantly. He had avoided her all afternoon.

Lucas watched her as she ran her hands down the horse's neck and back, massaging the horse.

"Therapy, for you or the horse?" He smiled.

"Both, I hope." She didn't look at him. Instead she watched her hand's massaging the horses muscles.

"Nikki?" He said softly.

She glanced at him then back to the horse.

Her heart raced when he opened the door and stepped in.

"Nikki? I need to tell you something." He walked towards her.

She still didn't say anything or look at him.

"I'm not going to let you ignore me." He walked across the stall making her step back away from the horse, only to be stopped by the wall. "We need to talk. I don't want you to be upset with me."

Nikki frowned and looked into his eyes, she could feel herself flush from the intensity in them. "I'm not upset with you. I thought you were upset with me."

Lucas stepped between her and Harvey. "You're protecting Nick, like I said, I do the same thing."

"It's not my story to tell," She explained, hoping he understood. "If he wanted you to know, he would have already told you."

She saw the flicker of irritation in his eyes just before he sighed and shook his head. "You know he won't…but I need you to help me."

Nikki's back stiffened, "I will do what's needed and tell you what I can."

"Nikki, there's something I need to tell you…"

Harvey side stepped into his back, sending him forcefully at Nikki, who fell against the wall with a gasp and grabbed him for support. His hands landed on the wall on each side of her shoulders to protect her from the force of his body slamming into her. She looked up at him and without hesitation his lips came down to hers, one hand slid behind her head to hold her close. She gripped him tighter as the emotions swirled in her, making her light headed. Slowly her arms made their way around his waist and up his back, she leaned into him, thankful he wasn't too mad to kiss her.

He slowly pulled away breaking the kiss.

"I was afraid you were too mad at me." Nikki held him tight so he couldn't move away.

"Frustrated yes, but not mad. If I ever need someone in my corner, protecting me…I want that person to be you."

"You wouldn't even look at me after lunch, you told Matt, not me, that Dad was coming back."

"I couldn't," He sighed and leaned into her more. "I needed to tell you something, but not in front of everyone…it's bothered me all afternoon how to tell you."

"Tell me what?" She looked up into his brown anguished eyes.

"When Nick told me he was coming home, he also told me that I was going back to Australia…tomorrow."

"No," Nikki whispered and gripped his shirt, as if it would keep him from leaving. "I don't want you to go back."

He smiled sadly at her. "I don't have a choice. I have to close the deals that Nick just put in place. There are more people involved in this than us," He sighed, "With Candace and the ranch, there's no way you can come with me."

Nikki nodded her understanding but she didn't want him to go…they didn't have enough time.

She lifted on her tip toes, wrapped her arms around his neck and pulled him to her. Their kiss was powerful with the frustration and disappointment of his leaving.

And then Nikki heard her.

"Nikki?" It was Candace's voice echoing through the barn.

She lowered down to break their kiss and looked into his exasperated eyes.

"I'll be right there." Nikki called out to Candace as she stared at Lucas. She lowered a hand to caress his jaw and run her thumb gently over his whiskers. She felt his body lean into her as he lowered down for another quick kiss.

"Every dang time…" He whispered as he stood.

Nikki sighed and reluctantly walked around him towards the stall door. She turned back to see him sliding a hand across Harvey's back.

"Are you sure you didn't teach her that move?" He smiled and followed her to the door.

"I didn't before, but I will now." Nikki giggled as she stepped through the door and looked for the young girl. "Candace?"

Her head peaked out from the tack room door. She looked nervous.

"What's the matter?" Nikki asked in concern.

"There's a man out there..." She started to look at the ground then caught herself, "Chin up," She whispered with a shy smile.

"Does he limp?" Nikki asked.

Candace nodded, her eyes went to the barn door then back to Nikki. She smiled nervously at Lucas.

"His name is Jessup," Nikki told her and stretched out a hand, Candace took it quickly and squeezed tightly. "He's our foreman at the ranch. He came in to go to Dr. Mark's retirement reception tomorrow."

"I didn't hide this time." Candace smiled. "I came to ask you first, like you said."

"You did perfect." Nikki returned her smile.

"Do I get to see the ranch some day?" Candace asked as she walked between the two adults and out of the barn.

Candace looked over at Lucas' hand then up to him. She smiled when he stretched it out for her to hold.

"Yes, I believe you'll be seeing a lot of the ranch this summer." Nikki answered.

"Oh! I would like that! So would Lola!" Candace said excitedly.

CHAPTER SIXTEEN

Candace made it until three in the morning before she had her nightmare. Instead of crawling under the bed, she had walked across the hall and woke Nikki, who lifted the blankets and the scared girl climbed into the bed. Nikki held her closely while Candace cried herself back to sleep.

Footsteps walking down the hall caused Nikki's eyes to open. Lucas appeared looking into Candace's room then turned to look in Cora's.

He was dressed in the same blue shirt and black vest he had on when she first saw him. A gentle smile appeared through his whiskers when he saw her cradling the girl.

"Nightmare?" He whispered.

Nikki nodded.

"I'm headed to the airport to pick up Nick."

"What time is it?" She whispered.

"Only six." He smiled, turned and looked down the hall then back to her. "Matt's ready. I'll be right back."

She nodded and listened to his footsteps making their way down the hall.

###

Nikki stepped back from her dad when Nora came running.

"Nick! You're back!" Her young cousin yelled. He scooped her up and lifted her flinging her legs high in the air. She laughed excitedly.

"Me next!" Sadie jumped excitedly and giggled as her legs went flying in the air.

Nikki looked passed the excited girls and saw Candace standing shyly watching from the back deck. She'd met Nick at the horse shows he had attended, so she wasn't scared, just nervous.

Nick turned and looked up at Candace then over to Nikki, who nodded. He turned back to the shy girl.

"Don't I get a greeting from you Candace? I bet your legs fly, too."

Candace's eyes got wide in surprise.

"Come on Candace! It's fun!" Nora yelled at her.

Candace looked at Nikki, who smiled and nodded, so she ran quickly to Nick and let him swing her backwards, her legs flying. She laughed excitedly and when her feet hit the ground she ran back to Nora.

As the girls ran in the house to get their school bags, Nick turned to his Nikki.

"I tried to watch the video." He shook his head. "Couldn't do it…as soon as she came out of the stall…"

"It was awful." Nikki told him as she took his arm and they walked to the house.

"Anything yet on the family search?"

"Not that I've heard."

"I'm very proud of you for stepping up for her." He smiled down at her.

"Thanks, Dad." She leaned proudly into his arm. "But I think you can blame Lucas for that one."

"Credit him…and I've thanked him for watching out for you."

Nikki smiled then realized she hadn't thought of how Nick would react to her and Lucas' attraction.

"Cora looks wonderful." Nikki said to change the subject.

"She had a great time…and has no clue about the things we talked about."

They reached the bottom of the steps as Sadie, Nora, Candace, and Wade walked out the door to catch the bus. They all smiled, waved, and ran down the driveway.

As they entered the kitchen, Nikki casually looked for Lucas. She could hear him talking but couldn't see him.

"I need to talk to Lucas." Nick said, kissed her on top the head and left her standing in the kitchen…alone. She heard the library door close.

Nikki could hear everyone else was down the hall in Cora's room listening to her vacation stories, so she walked back outside to the deck chairs.

As she leaned back in the chair, closed her eyes, and let the sun warm her skin, she thought of Lucas. It had been a whirlwind week with him but it was going to end in just a few hours. She didn't want him to go…he didn't want to go…he HAD to go and they both knew it. He'd mentioned her going there but he never said anything about coming back here.

An uneasy feeling started in her stomach and headed for her heart. Doubt began to spread…

The phone rang interrupting her confusing thoughts. She pulled it from her pocket to see a number she didn't recognize.

"Hello?" She answered.

"Nikki?"

"Yes?"

"This is Rhonda Bachman."

Nikki sat straight up in the chair. "Good morning."

"Good morning. How is Candace?"

"She's doing much better; we've dealt with a few tough nights, but the days are good. She loves spending the time with the horses and kids."

Nikki waited agonizing seconds for the woman to talk.

"I know this is tough, so I'll get right to the point."

"I'd appreciate that." Nikki closed her eyes, her heart constricting at the unknown.

"Both parents have signed releases giving up any rights to Candace so she would have a clear adoption process and not have to wait for a court to remove their parental rights."

Nikki's exhale quivered. "Ok."

"The father has a sister, and like Candace said, she is in jail. The mother has two sisters, Vera and Paige. Vera has three kids and said she would take Candace, if there are no other options. They are having a hard financial time…and she's getting a divorce."

"That's not a good situation for Candace." Nikki opened her eyes, sighed and looked at the barn, wishing she was with Harvey.

"No, it's not." Rhonda agreed.

"And Paige?"

"I talked to her late yesterday."

"And?"

"And, a few years ago she had filed a child protective claim in Washington against her sister."

Nikki inhaled. "She tried to help Candace?"

"Yes, but the mother and Candace disappeared and unbeknownst to her, moved to Idaho. Because of the different State, she looked for her but couldn't find her."

"Where does she live?"

"Moscow."

"Is she able to take care of her? Is she willing to take care of her? Does she have kids? Married?"

"More than willing, part of the papers she was filing was to get custody of Candace from her sister. She is not married and doesn't have kids."

Nikki closed her eyes and sighed. She wasn't sure if she was happy or sad. "What about Lola?"

"She's currently in a house without pasture, so she's looking for a new place. Horse shows will be a concern, she's not sure what it takes, but will do whatever she can to make sure Candace can continue showing."

"Jordan would help."

"That's what I thought, but I didn't offer without talking to her first."

Nikki sighed in relief. "So now what?"

"We'll do a thorough investigation of her and evaluate the situation. In the meantime, you still have guardianship of Candace…and Lola."

"I promised Candace I wouldn't let her go without knowing she was going to someone that would give her the love and attention she deserves and needs."

"And I totally agree with that and will support it."

"Thank you, Rhonda. I hope she's all we hope for."

"So do I, Nikki."

They ended the call.

###

Nikki slid out of the truck and looked at the large veterinarian clinic. The parking lot was full and she could hear the buzz of a large crowd of people. She turned to make sure the kids unloaded safely from the truck.

"Come on, Sadie!" Wade yelled as he ran through the parking lot, Sadie right behind him.

"Seriously, Wade." Nikki frowned. "Be careful!"

All the kids made it into the building safely, Candace the last one, nervously looking back at Nikki.

Lucas and Nick had spent the day in the library, the precious hours ticking away before he left. To keep her mind preoccupied, she offered to pick up all the kids from school and bring them to the retirement celebration.

Dr. Mark's voice called out to her as she walked through the clinic doors. "Nikki!"

She turned and saw the wonderful man grinning through his signature mustache. She laughed when she saw he had a Tagger Enterprises T3E hat on. She had only seen him in a cowboy hat or his own clinic's ball cap.

"I've been waiting all day for you girl!" His voice cracked with the emotion and there were tears in his eyes.

Nikki literally ran into his arms and squeezed into the hug. He was another part of her history disappearing, even if it was for a trip around the world.

They held each other tightly for a few minutes, appreciating each other and their past.

"I'm so happy for you." Her voice shook with emotion.

"And I am so grateful to you." He answered, his voice quivered, too.

He finally broke the hug and stepped away from her while wiping the tears from his eyes.

Nikki giggled while wiping her own tears away.

"I am so sorry about the job though." Dr. Mark frowned.

"Don't worry about it." She sighed. "I've had another opportunity arise." She grinned and led him to the side of the room and informed him of the purchase of Andy's property.

"That is just fantastic," He gasped in surprise.

"I tell you what," Nikki grinned at him. "If you need something to do…I'll hire you the second you get back."

"I'll take you up on that!" He laughed.

Nikki glanced around the crowded room and saw her whole family laughing and enjoying the reception, adult and kids, Jessup and Cora. Then she saw the back of her dad, he was talking to Sadie. A quick glance around, and she still didn't see Lucas. Maybe, he didn't come with him. Maybe, it wasn't as important to him, as it was to her to spend time together before he left.

Nikki shook off the depressing thought and maneuvered around the people and made her way across the room. Her dad's back was still to her and Sadie was talking and nodding.

"And how do you know that?" She heard her dad say.

"When Dad has whiskers and kisses Mom, it makes her cheeks red. Mom says its whisker burns."

Nikki frowned in confusion.

"So?" Nick asked.

"When we got back from trying to find the baby beavers, Nikki had whisker burns." Sadie smiled innocently.

Nikki gasped in shock, just as she felt the warmth behind her and a hand rest on the small of her back. She glanced up to see Lucas smiling at Sadie, who was now walking into the crowd. "Little Dingo notices the details," he chuckled.

Her gasp caused her dad to turn and look at her. She stared in bewilderment. He looked at her then at Lucas in surprise.

"I was only gone for six days." Nick finally stammered.

"It doesn't take six days to know you want to kiss someone, Mate." Lucas laughed and Nikki blushed. "I don't think it took me six seconds to know I wanted to kiss Nikki. As soon as she walked out of the…"

"Lucas…" Nick said firmly. "That's my daughter you're talking about."

Nikki's heart was racing.

"Sorry, Nick." Lucas chuckled. "I keep forgetting you have a daughter…or a son."

"And you're headed back to Australia in two hours." Nick frowned.

Lucas sighed, "Yes…that I am."

Nikki glanced up at him wondering if he was going to mention coming back, but he didn't have a chance.

"Nikki!" It was her mom. Nikki turned reluctantly. "Matt said you heard from Rhonda."

"What?" Lucas and Nick said in unison, looking at her in surprise.

Nikki nodded then quickly glanced around to make sure the kids couldn't hear her.

She told her parents and Lucas about the phone call.

"Why didn't you say anything? Why didn't you come tell us?" Nick looked upset.

"You were working," Nikki answered…feeling a little guilty now. "I didn't want to interrupt."

"Nikki!" Her dad glared in frustration. "I told you I'd be there for you. You need me, don't ever let a door keep us apart. Kick the dang door down if you have to."

Nikki giggled. "I appreciate the offer, but could you imagine what Mom would do to me if I kicked the library door down?"

"I'd kick your butt, young lady!" Her mother laughed then turned away.

"Seriously, Nikki…" Her dad started.

"I know Dad and I appreciate it." She smiled gently at him. "And I look forward to the day that I can actually kick a door down to get to you….unless it's a door at The Homestead."

They grinned at each other in understanding.

"Nikki," Lucas said; his hand at her back increased in pressure. "Are you alright?"

She smiled up at him. "I am, if everything goes well with her aunt. I promised Candice I wouldn't let her go anywhere unless I knew she was going to be OK and loved. I'll make that decision once I hear what Rhonda finds out."

"That's a tough decision," He said concerned. "Especially to make by yourself."

"I'm a grown woman." Nikki tilted her head. "I'll be making all kinds of decisions by myself."

"I know you're a grown woman, Nikki." He said with a devilish grin. "I'm very aware…."

"Lucas!" Nick cut him off. "Again…this is my daughter."

Lucas chuckled again and shook his head. "Someday…I'll remember that."

###

Harvey leaned across the fence for attention, so Nikki turned and stroked the horse's neck as Lucas said goodbye to everyone. She heard the girls laughing and trying to mimic his accent. Wade laughed at their attempts then tried it himself, which made everyone laugh.

She didn't have a chance to spend any time alone with him since they stayed at the retirement party so long and now he was rushed to leave.

It was nothing more than a week of flirtation and a few kisses she told herself, he was flying thousands of miles away where it was easy to disappear and forget. He didn't say he was coming back but he didn't say he wasn't; the confusion rolled through her mind. If only they had a chance to speak. It made her heart ache and she closed her eyes to the doubt.

Nikki leaned into her horse's side and tried to let go of the anxiety, the doubt, and the fear she would never see him again. Australia, where people go to disappear... She forced herself to not think of Australia…of him being gone and not returning. There just hadn't been enough time.

"Nikki," She heard him as he stepped behind her but not touching.

"Just a little equine therapy," She turned with a forced smile and looked into his amber eyes. "Harvey always helps."

"We have a lot to thank Harvey for," He grinned and ran a gentle hand down the horse's nose. Harvey bounced her head. "See, even she knows." He chuckled.

Nikki turned and looked towards the truck, Nick was already behind the wheel, ready to go.

"Nikki, I'll be back," He said and with the tip of a finger moved her chin to make her look up at him. He frowned at the tears glistening in her eyes. "I will."

There he said it, but she didn't feel it. Her stomach was in knots and her throat constricted trying to hold back the emotions. She nodded and tried to smile again.

He leaned forward but instead of a kiss, he moved to her ear and whispered. "I will be back, I promise."

She could feel his warm breath across her cheek and down her neck and closed her eyes to the sensation it caused in her stomach and the ache it caused in her heart.

Nikki nodded again and looked, one last time, into his eyes. "I know." She whispered.

"It won't take long…then I'll be here." He assured her, taking her hand one more time and squeezing tightly.

"I know," She nodded then looked away from his eyes and over to the truck. "You should go, Dad's waiting." Inside she was screaming for him to stay.

"Nikki," He whispered. She could hear the desperation in his voice.

"The faster you go, the faster you can come back." She said and raised a hand to gently touch the side of his face, a light touch over his whiskers…just one last touch. "It's OK, go." She sighed and dropped her hand to her side.

Lucas leaned into her, just touching her then turned and walked away.

He walked quickly to the truck and climbed in without looking back.

She took a deep breath and turned to Harvey. She couldn't watch them drive away. He was gone, leaving…the horse nuzzled into her neck.

"We'll be OK." Nikki whispered to the horse.

She heard a truck door close and glanced over to see Lucas walking towards her. She stepped away from the horse, confusion added to the fear and longing inside her.

"You didn't believe me," He stared at her as he slowly walked to her.

Nikki didn't respond, she couldn't, because it was true.

"I said I'd be back…but your eyes told me you didn't believe me." Lucas said as he grew closer.

A whirlwind of emotions ran through her as he approached, his long legs making the distance quickly. Desire for him to be gone so she could recover…the need for him to stay…

"I need you to believe me," He stopped close enough to her she could feel the warmth of him. "I need you to know, that I will be back."

She looked up into his eyes, and tried. She tried to believe…the ache increased in her heart…

"I want everyone to know how I feel about you Nikki," He stepped closer, not quite touching her. "I need you to know that I will be back."

Lucas leaned forward and wrapped an arm around her waist, the other behind her shoulders, a hand in her hair gripping gently. He leaned down and gently kissed the side of her lips making her gasp from the touch. Then he pulled her closer and kissed her. He twisted and dipped her towards the ground. She wrapped her arms around his. It was the ultimate movie kiss …the kiss she had seen between Grayson and Leah for years.

The fear, the doubt, the confusion, swirled inside her making her arms tremble…her head spin. How could he leave? She wanted more time.

Lucas kissed her long enough that she stopped thinking and started listening…listening to what he was telling her with his kiss…that he was telling her the truth…that he wouldn't disappear…he would be back. She relaxed, leaned to him, gripping his arms tighter and returned his kiss…letting him know she understood. He pulled her closer, his hand in her hair gripping tighter to hold on to her.

Slowly he turned and lifted her. His hands gently moving to each side of her neck, then he broke the kiss but didn't move away.

"You know," He whispered, she could feel his lips move against hers, his whiskers tickling her skin.

"I know," She whispered in return, truly believing this time.

Lucas leaned back just enough he could see into her eyes. His amber eyes glistened as he grinned. She returned his grin which made him sigh.

"You know." He nodded and leaned in for one more brush of the lips then he turned.

Nikki watched him this time. She could, because she knew he would be back.

Lucas stopped as he opened the door of the truck and turned to her…with a grin of promise…then he climbed in the truck and they drove away.

It was Leah that walked to her, put her arm around her shoulders and leaned down to whisper in her ear. "It'll be worth the wait."

THE TAGGER HERD SERIES

WADE TAGGER

ALMOST OR FINALLY

Gini Roberge

CHAPTER ONE

"I'm a dingo," Sadie leaned back in her chair in The Homestead library and looked at Wade.

"You're a what?" He glanced at his cousin then looked back to the breakaway roping video he was watching.

"I'm a dingo," she repeated

"What makes you say that and what's a dingo?"

"Lucas said I reminded him of a dingo," She tilted her head, opened her blue eyes wide and nodded. "I have to agree…I'm a dingo."

"What's a dingo?" Wade repeated.

"Well, on this web site it says they are Australian wild dogs."

"He called you a dog?"

"No," Sadie grinned. "It says they are pretty and cute and when they are small…cuddly. But they are wild and will turn on you in a heartbeat."

Wade nodded with a raised brow, "Sadie…you're a dingo!"

The cousins laughed as they looked at the pictures scrolling by on the computer screen.

"They are cool lookin'", Wade nodded. "Was he being mean when he said it?"

Sadie shook her head, "No, we were laughing."

"Are you mad he said it?"

Sadie giggled, "Wade, I'm a dingo, if I was mad, you would know it."

"But if you know you do that…then why not stop?"

"I can't stop. It just happens."

Wade shook his head. "We're eleven and a half, and you're getting pretty tall…you're going to have to figure out how to control it…you're not going to be cute and cuddly forever."

"Well, people just need to quit pissing me off; then I don't have to get mad."

Wade rolled his eyes at her logic, "What made you get mad at Lucas?"

"He said I was too young to go on the ride with everyone this weekend. So I told him about riding Milo to get Nora's saddle all by myself. I was only ten, so I'm bigger now and should be able to go on the ride." Sadie sighed and glanced at Wade. "He laughed because I used one of my worst angry moments as an example."

"Sadie, Sadie, Sadie…." Wade shook his head with a smirk.

"I know…" She shrugged. "But that's when he said I remind him of a dingo and I should come in and look it up."

"We've got the Winchester rodeo this weekend."

"I know, but I just WANT to go on the horse ride, too!"

"Since Nora is the queen of the Winchester rodeo this year, I don't think you have much of a choice." Wade pushed back his chair and walked to the library door. "I'm going to get Dollar and practice for this weekend. Wanna ride?"

He didn't wait for her answer and made his way out of the house and towards the barn. Hot, dry July days caused the arena to be dusty but Grace and Reilly had gone out earlier to water down the arena. They were now leading Rufio and Buttercup out of the barn to ride.

"It's cool she's queen," Sadie said from behind him. "Where is she?"

"Some 4-H club thing."

"She sure has been busy."

"Yeah, I think Mom's starting to wear out and we've still got months to go."

"Well, at least she has the break next weekend with the Barn and Breakfast grand opening."

Wade nodded as he retrieved the halters and ropes and walked to the pasture. Both of his red horses trotted to the fence when they saw him. Scarecrow and Little Ghost did the same when they saw Sadie.

"Hi, Boy," He stroked the red nose of Rooster with a deep sigh. "Sorry Boy, gotta ride Dollar again."

It had been weeks since he'd ridden Rooster for more than a half hour. Sadie was practicing on him a couple of times a week but she was working with Scarecrow today…which meant Rooster was left behind again.

"How about you come watch? We'll getcha around everyone else at least."

He led the two horses out the pasture gate as Uncle Grayson walked down the steps of the back deck.

"Riding both at once?" His uncle smiled.

"Nah, just wanted to get Rooster up around the arena." Wade handed Rooster's lead rope to his uncle as they made their way to the barn. He quickly saddled Dollar.

"It's your turn to win this weekend," Uncle Grayson encouraged him.

"I agree," Wade answered with an emphatic nod as they walked toward the arena. "At least I've caught them all, just can't quite get it done in time."

"In breakaway, as well as tie-down roping, catching is the most important thing. Now we'll work on getting Dollar to stop faster. I watched your mother's video from last weekend…he was a bit lazy on the stop."

Wade listened carefully as his uncle gave him instructions while they walked to the arena.

Two hours later, he was feeling better about his chances for the weekend. The whole time they practiced all the basics on Dollar, but mostly worked on stops. Grace and Reilly practiced their roping on the mechanical steer and Sadie practiced her slow work on barrels. It was a full arena.

He headed for the gate and walked to Rooster. The horse had stood quietly the whole time and watched the other horses running around the arena.

"You and me now," He said to the excited horse as he moved his saddle from Dollar to him.

Cora's dinner bell echoed throughout the property.

"Twenty minutes," Uncle Grayson called out before turning and walking away.

Wade walked Rooster into the arena as everyone else walked out.

"You coming for dinner?" Reilly asked as they passed.

"Rooster needs some attention," Wade shrugged and climbed the mounting block to slide onto the saddle.

He walked the horse for a few laps then moved him into a slow trot. Wade sighed contentedly as he felt the energy increase as they trotted. As much as he loved riding with everyone else and Dollar, he really liked riding alone in the arena; just him and his Rooster.

The horse's head lifted up…his ears twitching towards the cattle chute. Wade turned to see Aunt Dru crawling on top of the fence and resting her feet on the chute, a plate of food in her hand.

Rooster excitedly trotted over to her, immediately trying to stick his nose in the plate of food she was holding. She laughed and stroked his face and neck.

"Rooster…you are some kind of special horse," Aunt Dru smiled up at Wade, her blue eyes sparkling. Her long blonde hair was pulled back in a ponytail and was mostly hidden under her Tagger Enterprises hat.

"I agree, sometimes he thinks he's a dog, not a horse," Wade smiled happily as he took the plate of food from her. "I just wish I had more time for him."

"You do have a busy schedule through the summer between rodeos and both ranches…plus helping your dad with farming." His aunt nodded. "We'll be pushing cows again this week, before the grand opening next week."

"And rebuilding the Circle 50 lower pasture corrals." Wade added. "Which will lead right into harvest."

They sat quietly as Wade finished his dinner and she played with Rooster's ears.

"What would you think of him spending the summer at The Stables with Bodi?"

Wade looked at her in surprise. "I didn't think of that."

"We can give him some extra time, play with him when we work with Bodi. We can also let some of the little kids pet him so he gets plenty of love."

"I don't want anyone making fun of his legs," Wade frowned.

She tilted her head and lifted a brow at him, "Wade, do you think I would let ANYONE do that?"

He smiled and shook his head. She was as protective of the horse as he was.

"Grayson said you're going to win this weekend."

"I hope so, I am really tired of the almost…."

###

Wade sat quietly on Dollar and looked around at the arena. It wasn't the biggest he'd seen but it had the energy of the crowd like all the others. It was encircled by pine trees which gave it a great outdoor feel; it smelled like the woods…like the ranch. There was a feeling of history in the old fencing and buildings. It had to be one of his favorites.

Grace and Reilly had already run their team roping event and placed second. They were more than happy since they had already won a couple of events through the spring, but Wade wanted first.

The rider in front of him walked his horse into the roping box and lined him up. Rope in hand, he nodded to the chute handler and the steer was released. One, two, three, four…circles above the head and he let the rope fly….it floated over the head of the steer then bounced off and hit the ground. Ahhhs rang out from the crowd.

Wade took a deep breath, reached down and rubbed the imprint of Rooster that Jessup had tooled onto his roping saddle. His eyes glancing at the good luck charm dangling from the bridle. It was the clasp of horse hair that held Rooster, Dollars and Angels' hair; his Christmas gift from Aunt Dru. Between the imprint and the good luck charm, Rooster was always with them.

Nora was on Arcturus at the end of the arena. Her long black hair was curled perfectly and lay down her back over a bright red shirt that sparkled in the hot sun. The white queen sash crossed over the shirt and her crown on the black hat shone brightly. As the queen, her job was to push the steer out of the back gate when the ride was done. She grinned and nodded; encouraging him without words. He tipped his head to her then pushed Dollar towards the box.

The big red gelding with the blaze down his nose pranced excitedly as they made it into the box. Wade moved him to the back, next to the fence so the horse's rump bounced against it. He checked his rope, swung it once to make sure it felt right, then nodded to the chute man.

He heard the familiar sound of metal against metal as the chute gate opened to release the steer inside. He kicked Dollar into action and started swinging the lariat. Once, twice, he was ready and let the rope fly…it was over so fast he barely blinked as the rope came down perfectly over the steer's horns and he pulled the horse into a sliding stop. The steer hit the end of the lariat and the rope broke from his saddle and went flying in the air.

Wade spun around to look at the barrier rope…no penalty. He looked at the announcer's booth and not-so-patiently waited for his time to be announced. He was in first place!

He felt a shiver of excitement run down him as he glanced at Nora. She was headed towards the steer to push him out of the arena, but she was looking at Wade and pumping her fist in the air. Wade kept himself from smiling…keeping his face calm as he trotted to the end of the arena and retrieved his rope. He coiled the lariat and headed for the fence to get out of the way of the next team. There were two more riders…the worst he could do was third place…but he'd have to hear the "almost" again.

He patted Dollar's neck, "Good job, Boy. That was the best stop yet." He glanced down at Rooster's imprint and ran his fingers around it.

He looked up just as the next rider nodded his head and the bay horse bolted out of the chute. Rope circling, steer running, rope flying, steer running faster, rope hitting the ground.

Wade took a deep breath and let it out slowly…he had second place or first place, almost or finally…

He couldn't stop himself, he looked at Nora. She had her arms crossed in front of her. Her way of showing him her fingers were crossed and she was pulling for him.

Another deep breath, the next rider slowly walked into the box and then looked over at Wade. He had faced the other boy in most of the rodeos so far this year. Neither team of horse and rider had won first place yet, so…he knew too…one had first place…the other the almost. Wade nodded and received a slight nod in response…almost or finally was seconds away.

Again, his fingers circled Rooster's imprint and he looked up just as he heard the chute open.

Horse bolted, rope circling, steer running, rope flying, rope settling over the steer's head, horse stopped, rope tightened then went flying.

Wade kept his head down and waited patiently for the time to be announced…a smile slowly creased his face, he turned to Nora who was running Arcturus to him and had forgotten about the steer.

He heard the announcer inform the crowd that the very excited queen was riding up to her brother, Wade Tagger, who had just won the breakaway roping competition.

"You did it!" She screamed and rode in next to him for a high five.

"Finally," He grinned back at her, the goose bumps raising on his arm from her excitement.

"I'm so happy for you, Brother!" She laughed.

"Thanks, Sis."

"Go! Mom's probably freaking out now!" She turned with one last 'yee haw' to him and galloped towards the steer.

Wade tried to remain calm as he walked his big red horse out of the arena, his thoughts went to Rooster…he couldn't wait to get home and tell him. Once through the gate, Wade stepped down out of the saddle, not knowing if his legs would support him they were shaking so much. His hand reached up and flipped the good luck charm.

He tried to remain calm on the outside even though he was jumping and doing cartwheels on the inside… until…he looked up. Tears of joy rose to his eyes…there in front of him, was Uncle Grayson walking toward him with the biggest grin Wade had ever seen. His uncle had never made it to one of his rodeos…and the first one he does…Wade won!

Wade's composure was lost and he dropped Dollar's reins and ran to his uncle and jumped to fly into his arms. If his uncle wasn't so tall and broad, Wade would have knocked him over.

They wrapped their arms around each other, both grinning.

"I knew you would do it!" His uncle said proudly as he set him back on the ground.

"I can't believe you're here! You saw my first win!" Wade bounced excitedly, his heart racing in joy.

"Turn around."

Wade turned quickly, there was EVERYONE! His dad, mom, Aunt Leah, Aunt Dru, Jack, Reilly, Sadie, Grace, Cora, Jessup, Matt, Candace, Nikki, Nick, and Lucas! Nora was off her horse and running up behind them.

Over a year of trying…he finally won…and it couldn't have been better than being with his family.

CHAPTER TWO

Wade slowly strode down the road between The Stable and the new Barn and Breakfast. His hand slowly went to his gold belt buckle…his first place trophy. There was no way it was going in the memory room, it was staying with him. He worked hard for it…evenings, weekends, every chance he could…over a thousand hours of roping and riding practice. Wade wore it proudly.

He walked to the new Tagger business; his Aunt Leah's pride and joy. She was so excited to show off all the work. The bottom third of the big building's exterior was layered river rock then it turned to redwood siding. The doors and window frames were also redwood.

There were multiple sleeping rooms on the inside that were named after different horse's colors; the Palomino Room, Sorrell Room, Buckskin Room… Outside were multiple small corrals with loafing sheds for the horses of the guests.

Wade had to agree, it was a beautiful building and if he wanted to go on vacation, it would the perfect place to be…because he could bring Dollar and Rooster. He chuckled to himself.

He had just spent the last hour brushing both Rooster and the cute little Bodi, the yearling creamelo with blue eyes purchased at the auction the previous fall. They were quite the pair. Bodi, ran circles around Rooster as the red horse would just watch. Aunt Dru had made sure Rooster received a lot of attention. Wade knew she would.

From the day they rescued the horses, she had loved the red horse as much as he did. The moment she called Wade into the stall, where Rooster was stuck in the mud, they knew Rooster was special. It was the only time, that whole terrible day, that his aunt had cried.

Before he walked within sight of the people at the new building, Wade dug in his pocket and pulled out the two aspirin and popped them quickly. He had taken them from The Stables office when no one was around. It kept the bottle at home from depleting so quickly. Cora had noticed how fast she had to replace the bottle. Suspicion was rising.

He saw Nick take them all the time for his aches and pains from the years of bull riding, so Wade tried them. It did help relieve the pain; every joint in his body ached, all the time. After searching the internet for causes, he saw all the terrible things the aches could be and it scared the heck out of him. He relied on the aspirin and ibuprofen to deal with the pain. He didn't want his parents taking him to the doctor. He was afraid they would confirm one of the terrible things he saw on the medical websites. So, he didn't say anything to them.

There were at least fifty people in and around the Barn and Breakfast when Wade reached the building. He found a spot to sit in the shade on the split-rail fence that separated the building from the road and watched everyone. Reilly and Grace were entertaining Levi and Allen, the ropers from Kooski and Weippe that they had met at the roping clinic.

Candace, Sadie and Nora were laughing with Nikki and Lucas, who were standing by Nikki's new Circle 50 truck. It was blue with a silver brand on the door. It was just the opposite of the Tagger Enterprises trucks which were silver with a blue brand.

Lucas had been back for a couple of weeks and Nikki had never looked happier.

He didn't see his parents or aunts and uncles…they were probably in the building giving tours.

Wade recognized most of the people that came and went. He expected to see Dr. Mark but Nikki told him he wouldn't be back in time; he was in London finishing his book tour. He'd known the veterinarian his whole life and found it odd to go to the clinic and him not being there.

Kate and Helen, sisters that were the new owners of the veterinarian clinic, came by for the grand opening of the Barn and Breakfast. Aunt Leah was excited they booked rooms over the holidays for their family that would be in town visiting.

An older, small white car pulled into the large parking lot to his right. It slowly made the circle trying to find a place to park in the very full lot. There was a lady driver and a young boy in the passenger seat. Wade waved to get her attention and when she looked up, he pointed to a free spot hidden in the trees. She waved, smiled, and made her way to the empty space.

He tried not to stare, but glanced over a couple of times as she crawled out of her car and made her way to the passenger side. Wade watched in curiosity. When she opened the door, she reached in and helped the boy out. Once Wade could see him, he realized that he and boy were about the same age.

The boy took a step but it looked awkward. Once the door was closed, the pair started walking towards him. She smiled and waved at Wade as they approached.

The boy had a very significant limp.

"Thank you!" She smiled at Wade.

"You're welcome, ma'am." Wade returned her smile.

"I didn't want Alex to walk too far, so I took a chance of finding a close place," She explained.

Wade nodded. She was wearing jeans, a green flowery button up top, and tennis shoes. Her light brown hair was curly and just touched her shoulders. Wade thought she was pretty.

Alex was nearly the same height as his mother. He was dressed in jeans and a t-shirt. Like his mother, he had light brown hair; it was just long enough to cover his ears and was held back with a plain blue ball cap. His brown eyes made it perfectly clear he didn't want to be there.

"That spot is kind of hard to see, so you lucked out." Wade commented politely.

"Well, thank you for pointing it out," She walked up to him and stuck out her hand. "I'm Tessa Elliot, and this is my son, Alex."

Wade shook her hand then reached out to shake Alex's but the boy hesitated, looked at his mom with a frown, then grasped Wade's hand firmly and shook it.

"I'm Wade," He told them. "I haven't seen you before, are you new to the area?"

Alex turned away as if he was bored, but his mother answered. "We moved here last week; to Lewiston." She looked over at the big building. "We read about the open house, and thought we'd take a chance to see it, probably won't be able to see it again." She smiled.

"How come?" Wade tilted his head in confusion.

She started to respond but Alex looked up at her quickly making her stop.

"It's not something we usually do." She finally answered.

Wade nodded, not really understanding.

"Are you from Lewiston?" She asked.

Wade nodded, "I'm Wade Tagger, my family owns this place and The Stables."

Alex's eyebrows shot up in surprise.

"Well, it's really nice to meet you Wade Tagger," She smiled. "So you must ride all the time...that's a great belt buckle. Do you rodeo?"

"Thanks ma'am, I won it last weekend at the rodeo in Winchester." He smiled proudly.

"Mom..." Alex said in a low voice. His expression turned to concern as he looked at Sadie, Nora, and Candace laughing as they were walking towards the building.

Tessa smiled at her son, then glanced, amused, at Wade. "This wasn't really his idea of fun today. I had to drag him here."

"You can stay here with me if you don't want to go in." Wade offered.

Alex looked at him in surprise; then questioningly to his mother.

"You'd make me go by myself?" She teased her son.

"I can get you someone to go with you," Wade chuckled. When Tessa looked at him curiously, he just grinned.

"Nora! Sadie! Candace!" Wade yelled and the girls stopped, looked at him, then turned his way.

"What?" Nora asked. Her long black pony tail was swinging as she walked.

Sadie's long blonde hair was loose and held back by only a head band. Candace's short blond hair was in curls around her face which highlighted her large brown eyes. They were quite the group; always together since Candace's mother became ill and Nikki became her guardian.

Wade stepped off the low fence, "This is Alex and his mother Tessa. Would you show Tessa around the place so Alex doesn't have to go?"

"Oh, yes!" The girls cried out in unison.

"We love showing this place!" Nora said with a big grin.

Tessa turned to her son, "Are you sure?"

Alex just nodded.

"Wade, you are the gentleman," Tessa smiled at him, her brown eyes twinkling in delight. "Parking attendant and arranging me a personal tour!"

Wade chuckled, "Hopefully you're thanking me when you come back. This is my sister Nora, cousin Sadie, and friend Candace."

"Oh, wow!" Tessa laughed. "I really get a special tour group."

"Yeah...they're special alright." Wade smirked.

"Wade!" Nora rolled her dark brown eyes. "Come on Tessa, we'll give you a great tour."

Wade climbed back on the fence. Once the girls and his mother were in the building, Alex limped over to the fence and leaned against it.

"I guess I should thank you." Alex sighed.

Wade shrugged.

"Why did you do that?"

"Because if this wasn't my family's place, I don't know that I would be too interested in a tour."

Alex chuckled; his body seemed to relax.

They stood quietly and watched the people come and go.

"My left leg didn't grow as fast as my right leg."

Wade frowned in confusion, "Why would you tell me that?"

Alex quickly turned to him, eyes wide in surprise. "That's usually the first thing kids ask me...figured you were just trying to find a way to ask."

"Huh," Wade turned to him with a slight shrug. "Two of my best friends limp, so it's nothing new to me."

"Seriously?" Alex asked, looking at Wade like he didn't believe him.

Wade nodded. He grinned and looked at Alex. "Well, my mom is short. That's why I'm not tall."

Alex started chuckling.

"It's just the way it is." Wade said in his best John Wayne impersonation.

Alex turned to try to get up on the fence. Without a word, or fuss, Wade stuck his arm out for Alex to use as a brace. Without a word, or fuss, his new friend grabbed it and pulled himself up.

They sat quietly watching the people come and go.

"Is Candace your friend or your sister's and cousin's?"

Wade shrugged. "Mainly Nora's…but my other cousin Nikki is her guardian for now."

"Guardian? Where's her parents?"

"Not sure, they said her mom was sick so she was staying with us, but now her Aunt Paige is trying to adopt her."

"That's confusing."

"Yeah, I know." Wade nodded. "I don't think they are telling us the whole story. She stays with Nikki during the week and is with my mom and Nora at shows on the weekends. Her Aunt Paige goes with them most of the time. Her aunt is somewhere in the B&B today too."

"B&B?"

"Short for Barn and Breakfast."

Alex nodded and they sat quietly a few minutes.

"Do you think your mom would let you go to The Stables with me?"

Alex shrugged, "Not without her. It's just her and me…she's pretty protective." He paused. "Kind of goes both ways."

Wade nodded, "Do you have time after she gets done with the tour? I'd like you to meet someone."

"Depends on how long your sister, cousin, and friend keep her in there."

Wade chuckled. "Could be awhile, especially if they meet up with my mom or aunts."

"Are you in a hurry?"

"Nope, we can wait."

An hour later, the girls returned Alex's mom. She looked happy.

"You had fun." Alex smiled at his mom.

"I did," She sighed. "What a beautiful place and such nice people."

Wade nodded; it's always good to hear people like your family.

"Wade wants to know if we can go to The Stables," Alex asked with hope in his eyes. It was the most animated he'd been since they arrived.

"Both places in one day! I'd love to Wade," She grinned. "I've wanted to come out and see the horses."

"Do you ride?" Wade asked her.

She shook her head making her brown curls bounce. "Never, but I love horses, they are so beautiful."

"Can we walk down?" Alex asked Wade.

"Sure...it's not that far." Wade answered as they slid off the fence.

The three new friends walked down to The Stables, letting Alex's limping stride determine how fast they walked.

"Who did you want Alex to meet?" Tessa asked.

"One of my best friends," Wade answered.

As they neared the buildings, Tessa looked around in amazement.

"I've never been to a place like this." She said softly...almost a whisper.

"Most of the horses belong to people that board them here." Wade explained. "Others are ones we lease or rent for riding. We have a couple family ones in here."

He opened the small door into the building and let them walk in first.

"I'll be right back." Wade said and hurried down the wide aisle to the tack room. He grabbed a halter and rope and headed to the stall and stepped in.

They were still wandering through the building when he opened the stall door.

Wade hesitated; they looked up at him in confusion.

"Is something wrong?" Tessa asked in concern.

"This is one of my best friends," Wade explained with earnest. "I don't like people making fun of him."

"Why would we do that?" She asked in surprise.

He led Rooster out of the stall. The horse's odd walk was quite evident.

Alex and Tessa's eyes widened in surprise.

"Have you heard of the Tagger herd?" He asked them.

They shook their heads. Alex's eyes didn't leave Rooster's legs as his mother's went up to Rooster's head.

"We rescued a bunch of horses," Wade explained. "When we found Rooster, he was stuck in the mud half way up his front legs. He's had surgery to help but he still walks funny."

Wade walked Rooster up to the pair. The red gelding's head rose high and his ears twisted toward the mother and son.

Alex's eyes still stared at the horse's legs.

"Is it OK if I pet him?" Tessa asked, her eyes wide in wonder.

"Absolutely…Rooster likes attention." Wade nodded and smiled as she slowly ran her hand from the horse's forehead down to the soft muzzle.

Rooster bobbed his head causing her to jump back and giggle excitedly.

"Aren't you going to pet him?" She turned to her son.

Alex looked up at Wade, his eyes shining. "Can I?"

Wade nodded, "I ride him, practice roping on him."

"You do?" They asked in unison.

"Yeah, the doctors said I could until I get too big." Wade answered. "I've been so busy with Dollar, my roping horse, that Rooster was brought here so he could get some attention."

Wade turned to Alex. "Would you like to ride him?"

"What?" Alex nearly yelled in disbelief and looked at Wade like he was crazy.

"Really?" His mom's jaw dropped.

"Sure," Wade smiled. "Is that a yes?"

Alex nodded, still stunned and looking at the horse.

"Wade…" Tessa hesitated, her eyes concerned.

"He doesn't gallop, only walks and trots." Wade smiled to reassure her, then walked Rooster to the tack room and quickly saddled him.

"There's a mounting block just outside the door." Wade pointed.

"What's that?" Alex asked.

"You climb on it to get on the horse." Wade explained and saw the look of dejection on Alex's face. "We all use it, Alex. Nobody gets on Rooster from the ground. I don't want to put uneven weight on his legs. I use it and so do Nora and Sadie when they ride him."

Alex looked at him and nodded his understanding then took Wade's arm as a brace to climb on the block. His mother stood to the side and watched them with tears in her eyes.

"Can you get your leg over him?" Wade asked.

"Yeah, I think so." Alex stepped into the stirrup, grabbed the saddle horn, pulled himself up, and threw a leg over.

Wade smiled at the grin on Alex's face then led the horse away from the mounting block. He stopped to adjust the stirrups, one up higher than the other.

"Can you stand in the stirrups?" Wade asked

Alex chuckled as he stood. "Yeah, I feel level."

Wade led Rooster out to the small arena and instructed Alex how to tell the horse what he wanted then Alex nudged Rooster to walk away from him.

Wade returned to Tessa's side.

"Wade," She whispered.

"What?"

"I haven't seen that grin on his face in years," She had a tear sliding down her cheek and gently wiped it away. "He never lets anyone help him up and down things, he thinks people are pitying him when they do. I… I don't know how to thank you."

Wade sighed happily but didn't respond…he wasn't sure how.

Kelly appeared next to the larger arena, she had returned to work for the summer to the great pleasure of Reilly and Grace. She was walking a group of riders towards the stalls after a trail ride.

"I'll be right back," He smiled at Tessa.

Minutes later, he led the horse that Kelly had ridden on the trail ride into the arena.

"This is Star." Wade smiled at Tessa when she saw him.

"She's beautiful." Tessa smiled and slowly reached out to stroke the dark horse's neck.

"Actually…it's a he."

"Oh," She said with an embarrassed chuckle.

"Want to ride him?" Wade smiled at her.

"What?" She looked at him in surprise. "I've never ridden before."

"Neither has Alex and look at him."

They both turned and saw her son trotting across the arena, laughing loudly.

Tessa turned and looked at Wade. He could see the excitement rising in her.

He retrieved a mounting block and she repeated what her son had done to get on the horse. Wade adjusted her stirrups.

"Mom!" Alex trotted up to them. "Look at you!"

"I know!" Tessa walked to him with a laugh. "Who would have thought when I forced you to come with me today that we'd be riding horses?"

Wade smiled, it was fun watching people enjoy horses. He lifted his arms, stretched, and leaned back trying to get rid of the ache in his body.

CHAPTER THREE

The mother and son walked happily around the arena. They couldn't stop laughing at each other and their luck at running into the best parking attendant ever.

"Holding your own riding clinic?"

Wade turned to see his dad, Uncle Grayson and Nick approaching the corral.

"Yep," Wade answered his uncle and walked to the fence next to them. "How did you escape?" He teased.

"Just left." Nick smiled as he watched the two riders.

"Waited until Leah's back was turned and ran," His dad joked.

Wade turned and saw the riders coming up to them, worried looks on their faces.

"What's wrong?" Wade asked.

"Is it OK, we're riding?" Tessa asked, her eyes glancing at the three men.

"No problem," Uncle Grayson answered with a nod.

"We can pay…" She started.

"No!" All three men and Wade answered.

Tessa smiled shyly at the men.

"Tessa, this is my dad, Scott Tagger, my uncle, Grayson Tagger, and my…" Wade hesitated, not knowing how to describe the relationship between him and Nick. He looked over at Nick who was grinning at him. "My ex-uncle Nick." He finally concluded with a chuckle.

Wade turned to the men. "This is Alex and Tessa Elliot, they came to see the B&B and somehow I ended up putting them on the horses."

"Well," Wade's dad looked up at Alex. "You know, Wade doesn't let just anyone ride Rooster."

Alex looked at Wade in surprise.

"Only his mother, Sadie, Nora, and Wade have ridden him," Uncle Grayson smiled at the shocked boy.

"Is it OK?" Alex asked hesitantly.

"You bet," Uncle Grayson smiled. "That's Wade's decision. Have you roped before?"

"No…" Alex answered in anticipation.

"Uncle Grayson is my roping coach." Wade told him proudly.

"I'll go get a couple lariats and give you two a roping lesson." Uncle Grayson turned to the barn.

"Me?" Tessa asked in surprise.

"Why not?" Wade smiled at her expression. "My Aunt Dru is the second best roper I know."

"Does that make me first?" His dad asked with a grin…knowing the answer.

Wade shook his head slowly with a mischievous glint in his eyes, knowing his dad would take the answer in good stride. "Nope, that would be Uncle Grayson."

"What a son…" His dad smiled up to a grinning Alex and Tessa.

Uncle Grayson returned carrying a bale of straw with a practice calf head stuck in it and two lariats.

Nick opened the gate and all three men entered the corral.

"I think you're trying to take over my clinic." Wade teased his uncle.

Uncle Grayson laughed. "This way, Leah can't get mad at me for leaving her open house."

"So we're excuses," Tessa teased with a knowing nod.

"The best kind…those that ride horses," Nick answered with a smile.

For the next hour, his dad and uncle taught the riders how to rope while Nick and Wade retrieved the lariat loops when they hit the target.

"You're getting pretty good," Nick grinned at Tessa as he removed her loop from the calf head.

She laughed with a blush. "I never would have dreamed this morning that the two of us would be riding horses and getting roping lessons today…and enjoying it so much."

"Well, we thought we were going to be stuck at the open house all day," Nick smiled. "This turned out better for us, too."

"I agree." Wade laughed.

For another hour, Tessa and Alex roped then had riding lessons from Nick and Uncle Grayson.

Very reluctantly, Tessa told Alex they needed to leave.

Nick showed her how to step off of Star while Alex made his way to the mounting block.

Wade lined up Rooster next to the mounting block then stood on the lower step to help his new friend step out of the saddle. Alex stepped back a little fast, but Wade caught him and gave him an arm to brace himself as he stepped onto the dirt.

"Thanks," Alex nodded at Wade then looked up at his mom. "Boy, I'm glad you drug me out of the house this morning."

"Me, too." She laughed and gave him a big hug.

Wade turned Rooster so the horse's head was next to Alex and the boy thanked the horse for the ride. Tessa did the same with Star.

"Alex?" Wade got his attention. "Would you do me a favor?"

"Anything Wade…just ask." The very thankful boy said earnestly.

"Can you come out a couple times a week and ride Rooster for me?" Wade asked.

The boy's jaw dropped and he stared at Wade then looked up at Tessa. "Mom?"

Tessa gazed at Wade but didn't answer.

"We have a lot of ranch work this year, I'm helping Dad with farming plus I have a lot of rodeos. I practice a lot on Dollar…Rooster really needs exercise. I'd pay you to come out and exercise him." Wade said seriously.

Alex and Tessa stared in disbelief.

"Well?" Wade asked with a nervous chuckle.

"Are you sure?" Tessa asked him, tears in her eyes again.

"Absolutely; Jack, Aunt Dru's husband, is The Stable's manager. He will be here to help get Rooster ready. He loves Rooster, too."

"I'll do it, but you can't pay me." Alex grinned.

"How about we do a trade?" Wade negotiated. "How about you ride Rooster and I'll pay for the rental time for your mom to ride Star at the same time?"

"Deal!" Alex cried out before his mom had a chance to answer and stuck his hand out to shake on it.

"Wade!" Tessa exhaled.

"You can't back out of the deal your son just made." Wade grinned roguishly.

"No way!" She laughed, her eyes wide in disbelief. "I wouldn't dream of it."

"Can we come back tomorrow?" Alex asked hopefully.

"Yeah, but there's one more thing." Wade smiled.

"No way, Wade…this is so much." Alex was shaking his head in wonder.

"Just this…." Wade took off his Tagger Enterprises T3E hat and held it out to his new friend. "You have to wear this, to ride a horse from the Tagger herd."

Wade smiled at the look of astonishment on his face.

"Deal!" Alex quickly took off his own plain hat and excitedly replaced it with Wade's. Then looked up at his mom to show it off.

"Oh…Mom…" He shook his head when he saw her eyes glistening with tears.

Tessa giggled with embarrassment then turned to the three men who were standing and watching the exchange with interest. "Thank you, to all four of you, for giving us the best day ever. You have no idea how much we appreciate this."

"I agree." Alex stuck out his hand and shook the men's hands then Wade's.

Wade smiled happily as he watched the two of them walk away.

He looked up in time to see the shocked expressions of the men that were watching Alex limp away.

"I had no idea." Uncle Grayson glanced down at him.

Wade just shrugged.

"You're a good young man," Nick smiled as he picked up the bale of straw and headed to the barn. "You remind me of your sister…a real kick in the butt."

"So…you're telling me you left the open house to hold an impromptu riding and roping clinic at The Stables?" Aunt Leah's head was tilted to the side, hands were on her hips, and an amused smile crossed her face as she looked at the three men.

Uncle Grayson grinned from his seat at the table in The Homestead kitchen. "We went down to see Bodi, we hadn't seen him in a while, and Rooster was missing. So we figured Wade was riding and went out to talk to him."

"And they took over my riding clinic to hold a roping clinic." Wade added with a grin.

Aunt Leah glanced down at Wade and shook her head. "You're sticking up for them?"

Wade nodded. "We men have to stick together."

"Good answer." His dad chuckled.

"Look at it this way, Aunt Leah." Wade smiled. "Isn't it more important that they made two people extremely happy today rather than hanging around your B&B and being bored?"

His aunt burst out in laughter, along with his mom, Cora, and Aunt Dru.

"I imagine you're right, Wade." Cora smiled.

"So, who were they?" Aunt Dru asked.

The men turned to Wade, who shrugged. "Tessa and Alex Elliot," Wade answered.

"You didn't know them before today?" She frowned.

"No." Wade shook his head. "She wanted to see the B&B and drug him along so he stayed with me, outside, while the girls took her on a tour."

"Pretty lady with curly hair?" His mom asked and Wade nodded, "I remember seeing the girls walking her around."

"But you didn't know the son before today?" Aunt Dru asked. Wade shook his head.

"And you put him on Rooster?" She was surprised. "Why?"

Wade hesitated, there were only adults in the room with him, and they would all meet Alex at some point since he would be at The

Stables. If they knew about the limp, Alex wouldn't have to explain it to them and make things uncomfortable for him.

"Alex has a limp," Wade answered looking at Aunt Dru. "One leg didn't grow as fast as the other is what he said. He was pretty self-conscious about it and seemed depressed, and I thought meeting Rooster would help…and then I just thought he would like to ride."

"When we first saw him, on top of Rooster, you would never have known the boy was depressed or self-conscious or had any physical problem." Nick added. "He was all grins and laughter for a couple hours."

"That's why you hired him?" His mom asked.

Wade nodded, "That and Rooster needs exercise," He looked up at his aunt. "That's OK?"

"Yes." She said proudly.

CHAPTER FOUR

Wade woke up the next morning and stared at the ceiling of his room. "Did that really happen yesterday?" He thought to himself. Did he really allow someone he didn't know to ride Rooster AND hired him for the summer? He chuckled.

Lifting an arm in the air he checked for pain, the joint just ACHED! He rolled and his hips and back ached too. He reached under the mattress and took a couple of the aspirin.

The scent of bacon in the air made his stomach grumble. Cora must be up. He smiled and headed down the stairs. As he reached the bottom, he saw Grace and Jack were laughing while they made breakfast. He sighed; he was looking forward to visiting with Cora but forgot it was Sunday.

Wade turned before the pair saw him and walked to the library. While he had some quiet time he would check out roping videos on the internet. As he walked through the living room, he saw someone out at the pasture island. He stopped and looked to see Cora sitting peacefully on the bench.

"Huh," He couldn't remember a time that she had ever gone out to the island and sat by herself.

Her head went up as she looked at the sky, then down to look at her hands folded in her lap. Those little movements gave him the impression there was something wrong. He quietly left the house and made his way across the yard and into the pasture. The horses were still in the barn, so the pasture was empty. The sun had been up for an hour and the morning was quite warm already for a mid-July Sunday.

"Cora?" He called out as he approached the gate into the small fenced in area.

She turned to him with a gentle smile, "Come on in."

"Are you sure I'm not intruding?"

"I'm sure. Besides, I would never consider you an intruder." Her smile always warmed his heart.

He sat on the bench across from her.

"Is something wrong?"

"Nothing is wrong," She assured him. "I just had a few things on my mind and thought I'd come out here and try to decide what to do."

Wade nodded. He was afraid to ask her what she meant.

"Maybe talking about it will help." Cora patted the bench next to her and Wade quickly moved to sit with her. She took his hand and squeezed tightly.

"Since my husband died, I have felt a little…lost," She started in a low tone. Wade squeezed her hand in support, wanting her to stop but wanting to know what was wrong. "It's been two years now." She sighed and her eyes looked out across the pasture. "Between Wes' life insurance and Nick buying my property, I have enough money in the bank to do just about anything I want to do."

"Are you thinking about leaving?" Wade tried to keep his voice calm but he was too stunned.

"I'm not sure." She answered truthfully with another sigh. "My sister finally retired and wants me to travel with her."

"You liked the Australia trip," Wade nodded sadly, he felt his heart sinking.

"That I did," She chuckled. "But who wouldn't on a private jet and personal tour guide? I would have a hard time beating the combination. Hearing the stories from Dr. Mark's adventure around the world, I am very strongly considering her request."

Wade tightened his grip on her, as if it would keep her from leaving.

"Have you told anyone yet?"

Cora shook her head. "I wanted them to get the grand opening completed first." She sighed. "That's why I'm out here…just trying to decide what I want to do."

"Is there a hurry to make your decision?"

"She wants me to fly to Seattle next weekend so we can put together an itinerary and start our trip with a cruise to Alaska."

"How long would you be gone?" Wade was trying very hard not to cry.

"I don't know that I'll be going yet." She squeezed his hand and smiled slightly. "I'm not sure I want to be gone from everyone here."

Wade turned to look at her, "You are family here."

Tears glistened in her eyes as she nodded. "I know; I feel it every day."

"But?"

"I don't know how to answer that…which is why I'm out here." She sighed.

"Something's missing?"

"I'm still lost…"

"What can I do to help?"

Cora put an arm around him and pulled him close, Wade's head resting on her shoulder. "I just don't know."

"You'll let me know when you figure it out?"

"Yes."

###

"Aunt Dru, this is Tessa and Alex Elliot." Wade introduced them as the pair arrived at the office of The Stables.

The two women smiled at each other, shook hands, then Aunt Dru turned to Alex and shook his hand. Wade chuckled inside when he saw the look on Alex's face as he looked up at her. Her long blonde hair was down, cascading over her shoulders under a straw cowboy hat. She was wearing jeans and a blue tank top that made her eyes look even bluer. Most of his friends, and Reilly's, reacted the same way. They just stared at his aunt and could hardly talk.

"We got home yesterday and had to keep telling each other that the whole day wasn't just a dream." Tessa laughed lightly. "Alex had to keep looking at his new hat to make sure it was real."

"We were pretty surprised to hear that Wade let someone ride Rooster," Aunt Dru looked at Alex. "So you must have done a great job for him to hire you."

"I hope so," Alex nodded. "I just couldn't believe I actually rode a horse, and Mom, too!"

"And the roping!" Tessa said excitedly. "They were your brothers?"

"Scott and Grayson, yes." Aunt Dru answered. "And my ex-husband Nick."

"Your ex?" Tessa said in surprise. "You all get along?"

"Very well," Aunt Dru smiled. "My ex and my current are good friends."

"Wow…" Tessa shook her head in amazement.

"It's a long story," Aunt Dru chuckled. "But for another day. I'm sure you're anxious to get back to the horses."

"Oh, yes!" Alex grinned and followed Wade to Rooster's stall.

Aunt Dru led Tessa to Star's stall. "Do you want to stick with Star or would you like to try another horse?"

"Oh, Star, please!" Tessa nodded. "He is just wonderful and would you mind showing me how to saddle and get him ready? I was hoping to learn, not just have it done for me."

A look of approval crossed his aunt's face and he could tell she liked Tessa. Aunt Dru stood off to the side and just pointed with directions to put the tack on the horse. Tessa stood back and looked at the horse when she was done.

"All good?" She asked with a hopeful grin.

"All is good," Aunt Dru nodded with a smile.

Wade and Alex watched as his aunt showed Tessa how to get on the horse from the ground and not a mounting block. Once on top the horse, Tessa grinned down at her son.

"You look great, Mom!" Alex returned her grin then turned to Wade. "Can I lead Rooster to the mounting block?"

Wade nodded. "Just walk to his side so he doesn't step on the back of your heels. He isn't a fast walker, so you should be good."

Alex smiled nervously, took the lead rope, and limped to the mounting block.

Tessa rode to the side of her son while Wade and Aunt Dru followed.

His aunt looked down at Wade and smiled. "You have good people instincts."

Wade smiled back, he was sure that was a good thing by the look on her face.

He braced Alex as he stepped up onto the block and into the saddle then he and his aunt watched the pair laugh and giggle while enjoying their ride.

When the ride was over, Aunt Dru haltered Bodi and introduced the pair to the yearling. The little cream colored horse charmed his new friends like he did everyone else. After Alex finished brushing the horse, they let him loose in the big arena and watched him run circles, jump, buck, and kick to the delight of the group watching him.

As Bodi, Star, and Rooster were returned to their stalls, Jack joined the group.

"Tessa…Alex, this is my husband, Jack." Aunt Dru introduced them. "He'll be here to help when you ride."

"Pleasure to meet you," Jack shook their hands.

"And you," Tessa smiled. "We'll only be able to ride in the mornings since I work a late shift. Is that alright?"

"In this 100 degree weather, that's the only time you really want to ride." He answered. "I arrive at 5:00 in the morning for chores and for the early riders."

"Can I help?" Alex looked up at Jack with hopeful eyes.

"Help?" Jack looked at him confused.

"With chores," Alex explained, then reached down to touch his leg. "I won't be real fast but I'd try really, really hard. All you have to do is show me what needs to be done, and I'll do it the best I can."

Jack grinned at Alex then looked up at Tessa. "If it's alright with you, I can always use help feeding the horses in the morning."

"Oh, Mom!" Alex turned to her. "Can I please?"

"Well," Tessa hesitated. "I get off work at 5:00 in the morning and can pick him up and get here somewhere between 5:30 and 6:00."

"Whenever you get here is fine," Jack nodded.

"Where do you work?" Aunt Dru asked.

"At the convenience store on Main Street," Tessa answered in a low voice.

Aunt Dru nodded. "Those are tough hours."

"It allows me to spend more time with Alex." She smiled timidly.

"I sleep when Mom works." Alex explained.

"When do you sleep?" Wade looked at Tessa.

"Right now, anytime I can. When he starts school, then I'll sleep when he's there." She smiled.

Alex turned to Jack. "Thank you."

"Let's see if you still thank me after cleaning a few stalls." Jack grinned.

"Oh, I will." Alex nodded. "Especially since we get to ride after."

###

Wade backed Dollar against the fence and motioned for Grace to start moving. She hit the gas on the four-wheeler that was pulling the mechanical calf and he kicked Dollar after them. It took too many turns of the lariat for him to throw and he knew it. The rope came up short.

"Wade!" Uncle Grayson said from the chutes. "Where is your head?"

Wade turned to his uncle with a frown; he couldn't tell him the truth. He'd promised Cora he wouldn't say anything until she made her decision. But ever since they got home from watching Tessa and Alex ride, he couldn't think of anything else but her being gone.

"Sorry," Wade said as he trotted by his uncle.

"Maybe we should just work on Dollar rather than roping." His uncle suggested.

Wade nodded and tied his lariat to the saddle.

"Circles and figure eights then stops," Uncle Grayson said and turned to Reilly.

Wade moved to the far end of the arena and did as his uncle said and kicked Dollar into a slow gallop. He tried to clear his mind of everything but the movement of the horse; the rocking and the rhythm. He moved his hips with each stride of the horse, encouraging the forward movement.

It was these moments he loved, the connection between horse and rider. He counted how many times he went left then did the same number of circles to the right. He did big circles then little circles. The horse's hooves hitting the ground seemed to put him into a hypnotic state. He stopped at the far end of the arena, opposite everyone else and worked on leg commands.

A trickle of sweat slowly made its way down the length of his spine. He was wearing his cowboy hat to protect him from the sun but he was hot with the boots and jeans on. He looked up and Uncle Grayson wasn't in the arena anymore. Only Sadie and Nora were there.

"So, what's up with you today?" Nora asked as he joined them.

Wade shrugged, "I'm just hot."

"Me too," Sadie nodded. "I'm gonna put Scarecrow away after I hose her down first to cool her off."

The three of them walked the horses to the barn. Reilly, Grace and Kelly already had their horses put away and were walking to the house.

They walked into the barn so they could unsaddle the horses inside and away from the hot sun. Wade was graining Dollar when he heard his name called out.

He looked over the stall door and saw Grace.

"Cora wants to know if you would come in the house." She said.

Wade nodded, tears instantly pushed to his eyes. She must have made her decision. He stood in the stall and watched Dollar eat. If he didn't go in, she couldn't tell him she was leaving…then she couldn't go. It sounded good in his head…but he knew it wouldn't work. Finally, with a deep sigh, he walked out of the stall, his boots echoed throughout the barn as he made his way down the aisle.

When he opened the backdoor, he stopped and took off his boots in the open closet.

"She's in her room," Grace said and looked at him curiously.

Wade nodded, but didn't respond. He just walked past her and slowly made his way to Cora's room. He heard voices as he got closer.

As he stepped in front of her door, so they could see him, he saw Cora sitting in her chair by the window. His parents, Aunt Dru, Aunt Leah and Uncle Grayson were there.

One look at Cora, and Wade knew she was leaving. His heart sunk, shoulders dropped, throat constricted and tears instantly starting falling. She held out her arms and he ran across the room and wrapped his arms around her neck.

"I want you to be happy but I don't want you to go," Wade cried into her shoulder.

"I know," She whispered through her tears.

When he stood, everyone else had left the room so he sat in the chair next to her.

"When do you leave?"

"I fly out Friday morning."

"Are you coming back?"

"Not for a couple of months. Then I'll just be back to pack the rest of my things…then we'll be gone until spring. I'll be back for spring break and branding, it's going to be a big one this year with both ranches."

Wade wiped his tears away. He took a deep breath and let it out slowly. "I'm sad…but happy for you."

"I feel the same way."

"Where will you be going?"

"The cruise first…" She started to say when the girls and Reilly walked into the room. All the girls were crying and Reilly was trying very hard not to.

CHAPTER FIVE

"This is really exciting." Alex looked around at everyone that was joining him on his morning ride with Rooster, his T3E hat proudly on his head.

Wade was on Dollar, Sadie was riding Little Ghost, Nora on Isaiah, and Candace on Lola.

"When Mom couldn't ride, I thought I wouldn't be able to either." Alex looked at Wade. "Your Aunt Dru is the nicest lady."

Wade smiled and nodded. Tessa had to work a couple of hours longer than normal so Aunt Dru had driven into town to pick him up from the convenience store where his mother worked.

Wade didn't tell Alex that Aunt Dru was also trying to help pull him out of the depression Cora's leaving had caused.

"Let's go guys," Sadie called out and led the group away from The Stables.

"Easy trails today; it's only Alex's second ride out of the arena." Jack told them as they started their ride.

All the kids waved and nodded.

Wade had to admit that half way through the ride he was feeling better. They had laughed and joked the whole way down the gravel road.

"You look like a totally different kid than the first time we met you." Nora told Alex.

He nodded, "I feel totally different and it's only been five days."

"Is it just because of riding?" Nora asked.

Alex shrugged. "I guess so. Rooster gives me a reason to want to get up in the morning." He glanced over at her then to Wade. "I feel normal when I ride him."

"You are normal." Sadie looked confused. "Just cuz you limp doesn't mean you're not normal."

"Not everyone feels that way, Sadie." Alex said. "I get made fun of a lot and mimicked because of the limp."

"Well, that's mean." Candace frowned.

"Most kids, and adults, don't think of it as being mean…and many do it when they think I can't see them." Alex shrugged.

"Next time, tell Sadie." Wade grinned. "She's a dingo."

They all laughed and had to explain to Alex why Sadie was an Australian dog.

"Do you know any other kids that feel the way you used to?" Nora asked, her dark brown eyes narrowed and thoughtful.

"Couple of them," Alex nodded.

"I bet there are a bunch of them that could be helped by Rooster or our other horses." Nora stated.

"Probably," Alex nodded again.

Nora stopped Isaiah which made the rest of them stop. "Aunt Dru and Jack have clinics at The Stables all the time."

"Like roping, and they had a barrel riding clinic last month," Wade added.

"What if we did a clinic for all the kids that need the same thing you did?" Nora looked at Alex. "Do you think anyone would be interested? Just to come out and ride on a horse or be around them?"

Alex nodded excitedly, "I know three that would come out. Mom told them about our riding and the roping and they wanted to come out too."

"We could do the roping, too." Wade nodded.

"And let them meet Bodi." Candace added.

"And lots of kids want to meet the Tagger Herd." Sadie reminded them. "We can have them there, too."

"We need to talk to Aunt Dru and Jack." Nora decided.

"And Nikki." Candace said. "She's going to be doing rehabilitation for horses, I'm sure she'd want to help with kids, too."

"And Mom," Alex grinned excitedly. "She can help get the word out to all the parents."

They turned the horses and started walking towards The Stables.

"Nora, that was a really good idea." Alex smiled at her.

Nora stopped which caused them all to stop, again.

She looked at them in concern…her expression very serious, "I don't want anyone to know this was my idea."

"Why? It's a good one." Candace said in surprise.

"Because I've already been accused of doing things, like 4-H and the horse club, to better my chances at becoming a rodeo queen and Miss Rodeo Idaho."

"So?" Sadie asked.

"You were doing those before you decided you wanted to be Miss Rodeo Idaho." Wade reminded her.

"That doesn't seem to matter to some people. They make it seem bad that I'm doing anything now. I don't want anyone thinking we're doing the clinic for that… because we aren't…this is a good thing and I don't want them turning it bad because of me." Nora looked around at them. "This is for other kids that need a reason to get out of bed in the morning or someone that will love them unconditionally, like a horse will."

They all nodded in understanding.

"So we all swear, right now, that no one knows this was my idea…ever." Nora held up her hand.

All the other kids did the same.

"Secret forever." Sadie said seriously.

"Secret forever." Candace nodded.

"Secret forever." Wade smiled at his sister.

"Before I answer." Alex looked at Nora. "I just want to thank you for coming up with this idea. I hope we can reach a bunch of kids and make them as happy as I have been the last couple days."

Nora nodded with a smile.

"Secret forever." Alex grinned at her.

"Secret forever." Nora sighed and nudged Isaiah into a walk.

"So, what's this all about?" Jack asked as the kids stood in The Stables office. They were waiting for Nikki and Aunt Dru to arrive. Tessa was there, but she was out greeting Star while they waited.

"We want to tell everyone at the same time," Sadie answered.

"Did something happen on the ride?" He asked concerned.

"Oh, no!" Candace answered. "Everything was fun…it was a great ride."

"Is this a good thing or a bad thing?" Jack asked, looking between the five kids.

"We hope a very good thing." Nora assured him with a smile.

"Just be patient," Wade grinned.

"I'm not good at being patient." Jack leaned back in his chair with an amused look and his dimples deepening.

"Not patient?" Nora's eye brows went up in surprise. "It took you seven years to get together with Aunt Dru!"

Jack started to reply when Alex interrupted him.

"Seven years?" Alex nearly shouted; his eyes wide and jaw dropped. "She's the nicest lady ever! And she's gorgeous! What could possibly have taken you seven years?"

Jack had a surprised look as he smiled at Alex.

The kids laughed and then heard the laughter at the door behind them. Nikki, Tessa, and a blushing Aunt Dru were standing at the door.

Wade looked at Alex, who was turning different shades of red. Aunt Dru walked into the room and behind the desk to sit on her husband's knee as they looked at each other with love in their eyes.

"Mutual insanity," Aunt Dru finally turned and told Alex with a loving smile.

"So, what is it you would like to talk to us about?" Tessa asked, as she changed the subject away from her son's embarrassment.

Nikki closed the door behind her.

On the ride back, the kids had decided Wade and Candace would talk. Even though Nora was the oldest, they didn't want the adults to guess it was her idea.

Wade watched the adult's reactions as he spoke. Nikki and Tessa smiled immediately and seemed very excited. Jack had a slight smile on his face but Aunt Dru didn't have a readable expression. From Jack's lap, she just watched the kids closely as they spoke; the typical Aunt Dru poker face.

"When did you want to do this?" Aunt Dru asked the first question.

"This summer," Sadie answered.

"We're running out of weekends for the summer," Their aunt reminded them. "And you have a rodeo or show every weekend between now and when school starts. Plus harvest."

"We thought of that," Sadie nodded. "We want to give up a weekend for the kids."

Her aunt turned to her. "Jordan says you're on the way to winning your division again." Sadie nodded. "But you'll have to go to each rodeo and place to make sure of it."

"I know." Sadie answered. "I can do it if I win or get second in all the other races."

"That's a big challenge." Jack told her.

"But the kids are more important." Sadie looked at Alex. "Look how happy Alex has been the last couple days."

Aunt Dru smiled slightly, then turned to Nora and Candace. "And you're willing to give up a show?" Both girls nodded. His aunt looked at Wade next. "You've got a win under your belt and should have a couple more by then." Wade smiled at her optimism. "And you're willing to give up a rodeo?"

Wade nodded. "I agree with Sadie; the kids are more important."

"Your mother hasn't given up all the weekends and driven you all over the place to have you guys back out of your shows and rodeos now." Aunt Dru looked at them seriously.

Wade and Nora looked at each other, they knew how hard their mother worked for them.

"If you give up a weekend for your clinic," Aunt Dru continued. "Then you have to focus on the others and try even harder on them to make up for losing a weekend."

"We will." The kids answered.

"And I'll try to help them any way I can." Alex added with a serious tone, while looking up at Aunt Dru then to his mother.

"Whose idea was this?" Jack asked looking directly at Nora, who had been quiet the whole time.

Wade turned quickly to his sister to see the look of surprise and confusion on her face. He knew she didn't want to lie. She had a big issue with lying, in fact, she wouldn't lie. Their whole plan of keeping the secret was about to come to a quick end.

"It was a group idea," Wade said quickly. "Nora thought of talking to you two and Candace said Nikki, and Alex said his mom, and Sadie thought of the Tagger herd, and I thought of the roping."

Jack and Aunt Dru looked between Wade and Nora with no expression.

Wade sighed when he realized they knew it was Nora's idea. He held his breath hoping they wouldn't ask her anything more. He looked over at Nikki and Tessa; they didn't seem to realize it was Nora's idea.

Aunt Dru turned from Nora, and looked at Tessa and Nikki then down to Jack. "I like this idea," She said. "It's going to be a big family endeavor and will take an effort and input from all Tagger Enterprises...family and employees."

"We need to vote." Nikki nodded.

"Vote?" Tessa looked surprised.

"Anything that comes up, that involves all of Tagger Enterprises, has to be voted on for approval from Mom, Scott and Grayson." Nikki explained. "If it involves Circle 50 ranch, which Matt and I own, then we vote, too."

"But Matt is on a search and rescue call right now." Aunt Dru said which surprised Wade and the kids.

"Who is Matt and he does search and rescue?" Tessa asked.

"Nikki, I know your vote, so why don't you take Tessa and the kids outside to explain everything to Tessa. Jack and I will make the call to Scott and Grayson." Aunt Dru said.

As Nikki and Tessa stepped out of the office, the kids followed.

"Kids," Aunt Dru said and they all stopped at the door. "No matter which way this goes, I am very proud of all of you for coming up with this idea and being willing to give up a weekend for the clinic." She smiled proudly at them.

All the kids said thank you and smiled back at her, then left the office.

Wade and Nora walked off to the side as Candace and Alex followed Nikki and Tessa towards the stable that held Rooster and Star.

"How do you think they figured it out?" Wade turned to his sister.

Nora shook her head, "I don't know. Adults are too smart sometimes."

"Maybe you didn't talk enough."

"If I would have talked more, then they still would have figured it out…maybe even Tessa and Nikki too."

Wade shrugged, "Maybe they figured it out because they know what a good person you are, and that you would be the one to come up with helping other kids."

Nora stopped abruptly which made Wade look at her. He was shocked to see the tears that suddenly appeared and started falling down her cheeks. She quickly grabbed him and pulled him into a hug.

He didn't know what he said or what to say next, so he just hugged her back.

She let him go, but didn't say anything while she wiped the tears away. They started walking again and were about to walk into the building when they heard Jack and Aunt Dru already walking towards them.

"Good or bad?" Wade asked; he didn't expect them so soon.

Nora shrugged.

The small group inside the building petting Rooster and Bodi turned anxiously as Aunt Dru and Jack walked in the door.

Aunt Dru grinned which told them the answer.

"They didn't even hesitate," Jack informed them. "Both said yes immediately."

Aunt Dru looked at Alex, "You made quite the impression on them and all of us."

Alex grinned and took his mother's hand as he looked at her proudly.

Tears sprung to Tessa's eyes as she returned his exuberant smile.

CHAPTER SIX

Wade stood by the B&B large entry way waiting for Tessa and Alex to arrive. The clinic organization meeting was starting soon in the B&B event room. The excitement was building with everyone throwing out ideas to each other. Aunt Dru finally decided to have the meeting to get everything in order.

Between the clinic and the riding practice, Wade was keeping really busy to try from thinking about the next evening…Cora's last night. He slipped two more aspirin in his mouth thinking he should look up and see what happened if you took too many in a day.

The small white car appeared up the driveway and Wade walked out to greet them.

"Keeping your parking attendant job, I see." Tessa teased as she stepped out of the car.

Wade smiled and opened Alex's door to help him crawl out of the car.

"You need a taller car," Wade commented as he pulled Alex up and out the door.

Tessa sighed, "As soon as I can afford one. It would be so much easier if he could just step out instead of having to crawl out."

"I'm sorry," Wade said quickly. "I didn't mean to get personal."

"It's OK." She smiled; her brown eyes twinkling. She was wearing a shirt that had big pink flowers on it…it made her look cheerful. "You're thinking of what's best for Alex, I can't get angry about that."

Wade smiled, he really liked her.

"How long before you have to leave for work?" Wade asked.

"I have to be there at 9:00 tonight." She answered as they walked through the double doors.

"Plenty of time." Wade nodded.

"Are you sure? I don't want to rush anything."

"Aunt Dru keeps things moving forward at a pretty good clip." He smiled.

"She's pretty smart." Alex smiled, then blushed when they both turned and looked at him in amusement.

Footsteps could be heard coming down the hall and they looked up to see Aunt Dru and Nikki walking towards them.

"Shhh…" Alex whispered and they all three giggled.

"Glad to see you," Nikki smiled. "Are you prepared for this?"

"Well," Tessa frowned in confusion. "Prepared for what?"

Nikki laughed. "To meet the whole family at one time, plus a few of our employees."

Tessa sighed in relief. "Oh, yes. I thought you meant I had to have something prepared."

As they walked down the hall, Lucas appeared at the door of the meeting room, a phone to his ear. He smiled and nodded at the group. Wade caught a quick smile between Aunt Dru and Nikki.

Aunt Dru stopped and the small group stopped with her. "Tessa, we would like to talk to you for a minute before we go in."

"OK…" Tessa said nervously and gripped her son's hand tighter.

"Let's step in here a minute." Aunt Dru motioned to an office part way down the hall.

Wade hesitated, not knowing what to do as the women walked into the room with Tessa pulling Alex behind her.

Aunt Dru looked at Alex then to Wade, she smiled and nodded for Wade to follow them.

The office was empty except a desk and a few chairs.

"Is everything OK?" Tessa asked nervously.

"Well, we'll know in a couple of minutes." Aunt Dru said as they all took a seat.

Wade was as nervous as Tessa and Alex; they were gripping each other's hands tightly. Alex glanced nervously to Wade, who lifted his shoulders in a shrug.

"My brothers and I discussed the clinic last night and we've decided this won't be a one- time thing." Aunt Dru told them.

"Really?" Wade asked excitedly.

His aunt nodded and smiled at them.

"Which means it brings a new set of work with it," She looked up at Nikki. "And, just recently, our property doubled in size and so did our workload. Plus, we just had a friend decide to retire and her work is now on our shoulders."

Wade exhaled; he hated thinking of Cora leaving.

"Ok…" Tessa looked confused. "What does this have to do with me?"

"Nikki and I are looking for an assistant to help us with the Tagger Enterprises workload, and someone to help Jack and Paul, his assistant manager, with the clinic's planning." Aunt Dru explained.

Tessa didn't say anything, she just looked between the two women with a bewildered expression.

"We'd like to offer you that job," Nikki smiled.

Tessa inhaled sharply. Alex looked up at her excitedly and Wade grinned at his aunt and cousin.

"I'm not qualified for that job." Tessa finally said in a whisper that was barely audible.

"Why?" Aunt Dru looked at her in concern.

"I don't have any administrative skills…at all. That's why I could only find the cashier job at the convenience store." Tessa answered, she was near tears.

Aunt Dru leaned back in her chair. "Administrative skills can be taught. What you have is more important than experience in data entry or answering phones, or any other job we throw your way."

"What?" Tessa asked in surprise.

"You have experience dealing with a child that people consider to have a disability." Aunt Dru smiled gently between the mother and son. "That experience is unfortunate, but is a quality that can't be taught. You've lived it and dealt with it every day…on a very personal level. We need someone with that understanding and compassion to help with these clinics as we hold them and one-on-one appointments as they are setup."

"Plus the fact that you happen to like our horses helps." Nikki smiled.

"I love Star, Rooster and Bodi." Tessa whispered then shook her head. "I just don't think I could do it."

"Mom," Alex looked up at her. When she turned to her son, he continued. "You are always telling me that I can do whatever I put my mind too. So can you." He said earnestly.

Tessa didn't respond.

"Because you'll be doing a lot of errand runs and traveling between here and the ranch, the position comes with a company car." Aunt Dru continued which caused Tessa to gasp. "Paul, the assistant manager of The Stables, isn't convinced he really needs one, so you'll have his from the moment you start. It also includes a cell phone, of course. With horses and kids we have emergencies that you may need to be called on at any time during the day or night. Plus, you'll be assisting me and Nikki, but Scott, Grayson, Jordan and Leah will also be needing assistance now and then. Plus Jack, of course." Aunt Dru grinned.

"You may get a little overwhelmed, and we expect you to tell us if you do." Nikki smiled.

"As you'll see, we're very family oriented and usually have one or more of our kids with us when we do things." Aunt Dru looked at Alex. "Which means we expect to see a lot of Alex."

"Mom?" Alex was nearly bouncing in his seat as he looked up at Tessa.

She looked down at him, still stunned.

"And…" Nikki smiled.

"There's an 'and'?" Tessa whispered in amazement as she looked at Nikki.

Nikki lifted her arms and flipped her hands out to the side. "This is your office."

"An office?" Tessa looked around the room as if she was seeing it for the first time.

"Mom, you have to say yes." Alex turned to her pleading with his voice and eyes.

"One more thing," Aunt Dru said and reached in her shirt pocket and withdrew a slip of paper then handed it to Tessa. "This details everything we just told you plus your wage, and insurance is included."

Tessa took the paper but didn't look at it. She looked at the two women in concern.

"Insurance?" She could barely be heard.

"Yes," Aunt Dru said with a frown. "Working around animals and traveling so much, we all have insurance."

Without reading it, Tessa set the piece of paper on the desk. "I can't."

Nikki and Aunt Dru looked at her in amazement. Alex was near tears.

Wade sat up and looked at Tessa. "Why?"

She turned sad eyes to him, "The insurance…"

"Insurance?" Wade asked, nearly upset with her. "You said no because of insurance?"

"Wade." Aunt Dru said sharply.

"Mom, is this because of me?" Alex was heartbroken.

"No, Shriner's Hospital helps us with your leg." She answered firmly.

"Then is it because of…" Alex started.

"Alex." She said curtly.

"It is, isn't it?" Alex shook his head. "Mom, just tell them. You should be proud and happy."

"Alex…" Tessa started and had to wipe away a tear.

"Mom, look at them." Alex looked around the room at the three concerned but silent Taggers. "They will understand…they care. They care enough about us to let us come out and ride. They care enough to hold a riding clinic for people and kids that need extra attention and love."

Tessa's eyes were down, looking at her hands.

"Mom." Alex whispered. "Mom." He repeated when she didn't look up. "Mom." He repeated again and she finally looked up. "They care, they will understand."

She sighed as she looked desperately into her son's eyes.

"Say it loud and proud." Alex smiled and squeezed her hand tightly.

Tessa straightened her back, nodded to her son, and took a deep breath, exhaled, looked at Wade then Nikki then to Aunt Dru. "I am a breast cancer survivor."

Alex grinned proudly.

Wade was confused, he didn't understand why that was such a secret or a concern. He looked at his aunt and cousin and saw smiles of compassion and understanding.

"You have definitely had your plate full," Nikki shook her head in amazement.

"I'm very happy for you," Aunt Dru said softly. "And I understand your concern about the insurance, but the offer is still on the table and it includes the insurance…no matter the cost."

Wade still didn't really understand, but Tessa seemed to be happy with his aunt's comment.

Aunt Dru picked up the piece of paper and handed it back to Tessa. "Please accept the position, because we really need you here as soon as you can start." She reached in her pocket and placed her phone on the table. "In fact, you can use my phone to call and put in your notice right now…so we can have you as soon as possible."

Tessa reached out for the phone which made Alex bounce in his chair and grin excitedly.

When she hung up the phone, she looked at Aunt Dru. "He told me not to bother coming in tonight or again; he is going to give my shift to one of the part time workers that needed a full time job."

"So you can start in the morning?" Nikki asked excitedly.

Tessa grinned. "I can't believe this, but yes." She shook her head, her light brown curls swinging. "It might take me a couple of days to get my sleeping schedule back to normal."

"We'll understand if you need to take a nap here and there." Aunt Dru smiled. "But, one more thing."

"Oh, I can't take one more thing." Tessa exhaled.

Aunt Dru nodded in understanding, "We have a saying in our family, 'It's not my story to tell.' Which means that no one here will tell anyone your secret. It's up to you to let people know or not."

Wade was still confused. He didn't understand why surviving cancer was a secret, but he wouldn't tell anyone.

Aunt Dru stood. "Well, let's go let everyone know we have a new Tagger Enterprises employee and get out of her new office."

"Oh my gosh…" Tessa shook her head and looked around the room.

Wade sat at the big table and watched as everyone was introduced to Tessa and Alex. He was sitting between his dad and Reilly. Matt had arrived back from his search and rescue adventure and was sitting between Nick and Lucas. Even Paul and Kelly were there, everyone but Jessup and Cora. Cora wasn't there…nor would she be in the group meetings ever again.

He sighed and tried hard not to cry again at her leaving.

Wade felt his dad lean down next to him. "I miss her, too," He whispered.

Wade looked up at his dad and nodded. It was another one of those times that he had forgotten that adults had feelings too.

"Let's get this meeting going, Dru." His dad winked at Wade. "I think I'm allergic to meeting rooms."

Everyone chuckled and took their seats.

The date was set for only three weeks away which meant there was a lot of work to do. They split up all the events that would be going on at the same time during the clinic. Aunt Dru paired up an adult and a kid to work together at each one.

Paul and Kelly would have to focus on the regular business of The Stables but would help when they had time.

Wade's mom, Reilly, and Candace, would work with the Tagger Herd.

Aunt Leah would be the photographer capturing all the special moments.

Sadie and Nikki would work with Bodi and Milo, who, much to Sadie's delight, had come back into the family when the new ranch was purchased.

Nora and Tessa would work with greeting people and signing them in as they arrived. They would have Mavis and Bart with them so the kids could see the cow dogs, too.

Wade and his dad would work with Uncle Grayson, Jessup, Lucas, and Grace in the roping section.

"Can I work with Rooster?" Alex asked hopefully.

"Well, with Wade working with his dad and Grayson with roping; that means I'll be in charge of Rooster, too." Aunt Dru smiled at him, causing Alex to blush.

"I don't know about that." Jack leaned forward on the table. "Can I trust you with my wife?" He asked Alex with a grin.

Alex's blush deepened; "Maybe…maybe not." He laughed as he turned redder and smiled up at the woman in question.

She grinned and winked.

"We need more horses." Matt said as he and Nick were appointed overall horse wranglers.

"I agree," Jack nodded. "All the leased horses are unavailable which means we just have the rentals, which half of those are already spoken for that day."

"Andy's old horses might work." Uncle Grayson added. "I'll work with them between now and then to make sure they are good with kids riding them, even if just being led."

"In all reality," Nikki said. "We need more horses all around."

"Especially by next summer," Uncle Grayson nodded. "With Kit and Libby both pregnant and due in the spring, they won't be available for work."

"Grayson, put a call out to borrow a couple more ponies for the clinic." Aunt Dru told him. "Then, after the clinic, let's take a real solid look at what we need."

"Maybe it's time for a trip to Billings." Wade's dad added with a grin.

"I agree!" Matt and Nikki both grinned.

"What's Billings?" Lucas and Tessa asked in unison.

"Large horse auction…" Matt told them excitedly. "Nikki and I were too young to go last time."

"How young is too young?" Reilly asked hopefully.

"I was fourteen the last time they went." Nikki answered.

"Dad?" Reilly turned hopefully to Jack.

His dad nodded. "Let's see how big of crew is headed over before we make any promises."

Nikki turned to Lucas. "Make sure you're on this side of the ocean."

"Just make sure I have the dates and I'll be here." He smiled at her, then whispered something in her ear that made her blush.

"Lucas…" Nick frowned at him with humor in his eyes.

"Yeah, yeah, she's your daughter, Mate, but I didn't say it out loud." Lucas grinned.

"From the color of her face…you didn't need to." Aunt Dru raised a brow to him.

"You too?" Lucas shook his head.

"Hello? She's my daughter, too." Aunt Dru chuckled.

"Isn't Billings where you got Jessup?" Reilly asked.

"You got Jessup at an auction?" Tessa giggled. "What was the winning bid?"

They all laughed.

"Whatever it was, he was worth every penny." Leah declared.

"You know, Dru," Uncle Grayson said. "Between The Tagger herd and ranch horses, it may not be a bad idea to get another horse trainer to help me out." He turned and smiled at Nora. "I've got another ten years before my assistant trainer finishes college and comes on board."

Nora smiled proudly at her uncle then grinned at her mom and dad.

"I agree. Let's look at the schedule for next year and plan on the trip." She looked at Tessa and smiled. "Your first big project. But for now…back to the clinic plans."

CHAPTER SEVEN

Wade backed Dollar up against the fence and looked down at the calf in the chute. His dad and uncle had brought down calves from the ranch to use for practicing the next couple weeks. Wade was excited. It was only six in the morning but they had already gone around enough times that he had caught three calves.

"Get your head into it, Wade." Uncle Grayson yelled.

"It's there," Wade nodded. "I promised Mom I'd work hard and stay focused."

Wade swung the rope to get the feel then repositioned Dollar and nodded to his uncle.

The gate was open as Wade was kicking Dollar into action. Three twirls and a toss and the rope looped over the top of the calves head. As it dipped down, Wade cued Dollar to stop. The rope tightened then broke from the saddle.

"That was a good one!" Wade's dad yelled from the fence.

Wade grinned and nodded as he retrieved the rope. He walked over to his dad and the small group watching practice. His mom was there, holding hands with his dad. Aunt Dru, Aunt Leah, Nikki, Lucas, Matt, Nick, and Cora were all their enjoying the cool morning. It was supposed to reach over a hundred degrees that afternoon. That evening would be a big barbeque for Cora.

Wade turned and watched Grace and Reilly get their horses set. Sadie and Scarecrow, Nora and Arcturus, and Candace with Lola were at the opposite end of the arena waiting their turns.

Grace on Buttercup and Reilly on Rufio were set, their ropes ready. The chute was open and they took off. Grace let her loop fly and it floated over the head of the steer and settled around the horns. She dallied the rope around the saddle horn and turned Buttercup to make the steer turn. Reilly's loop was already flying and looping under the back legs. At just the right time, he pulled and tightened the rope. The steer straightened out and Uncle Grayson called it.

The crowd on the side erupted in cheers.

Nick leaned over to look at Aunt Dru.

"They are getting as good as Grayson and Scott were." Nick sounded impressed.

"I agree." She returned his grin...then her grin turned wicked.

As Grace and Reilly trotted by the fence, she motioned them over, climbed on the fence and whispered to them. They both started nodding excitedly.

Grace trotted to her dad and Reilly to Wade's dad. They both stepped off the horses and handed the reins and their lariats to the men.

Both men looked surprised at the kids, then turned to each other; grinned and nodded.

A cheer erupted from the group as the men adjusted the stirrups to the horses. Nick walked down to work the cattle chute.

Wade felt the anticipation run through him. This was their first time team roping together since before the accident, almost twenty years ago!

Both men trotted the horses around in circles and twirled the ropes. They smiled at each other then turned to their sister who still had the wicked grin on her face.

They trotted down to the boxes next to the chutes and prepared the horses.

"You two sure you can still pull this off?" Nick teased them. "You don't want to embarrass yourselves in front of the kids."

"Just pull the lever, Bull Rider." Uncle Grayson called out to him with a grin, and made everyone laugh.

Nick chuckled; "Here we go."

Wade's dad nodded and Nick pulled the latch releasing the calf. Men and horses bolted from the box with ropes twirling. Grayson's lariat floated over the horns of the steer and he pulled the rope and dallied around the saddle horn and turned Buttercup. His dad twirled the rope then he let it fly, perfectly under the steer's back hooves. The steer stretched and Matt made the call for a good catch.

The entire crowd erupted so loud they were sure they woke the neighbors.

The two brother's grinned then trotted to each other for a high-five. They turned and looked at their sister, then up to Sadie and Scarecrow, then back to Aunt Dru. Her smile disappeared, she shook her head, and stepped away from the fence. They nodded and trotted back to Reilly and Grace.

Wade trotted over to his dad, "Why didn't she want to ride?" He whispered.

His dad sighed and glanced over at her. "She hasn't run a barrel since the day our parents and grandparents died."

"But you two rode." Wade frowned while thinking how sad it was for Aunt Dru.

"We had already stopped roping to go to school that year." He shrugged. "The connection isn't there; from our roping to the accident, like it is for her. She had just finished the best ride ever on Jet, minutes later the sheriff showed up and told her about the accident."

"Do you think she'll ever do it?" Wade asked.

"I don't think so." His dad shook his head. "Honestly, even after all these years, there are people I connect to my parents. I can't be around them because they remind me so much of Mom and Dad."

"What do you mean?"

"Mom and Dad's best friends live in Grangeville. Growing up, I never saw them unless they were with my parents." He sighed. "Now, when I see them, I expect my parents to be there…it's hard when they aren't." He shrugged. "It's like losing them all over again."

He could see the flash of sadness in his dad's eyes before he turned away.

Wade trotted to the box next to the chute and made his mind think of his arm, the rope, the horse, the calf, and then he nodded. The calf was caught faster than he had caught any other calf.

Cheers erupted from the crowd. Wade turned to his dad and saw the light of laughter and pride shine in his eyes. A contented happiness spread through Wade. He wished the laughter would always be there instead of the sadness.

"So, Jordan, where is the rodeo and show at this weekend?" Cora asked as they enjoyed the barbeque prepared by Uncle Grayson and Jessup.

"Moses Lake for the rodeo," She answered. "And Paige will be taking the girls up to Grangeville for the 4-H horse show."

"How is it going between Paige and Candace?" Cora asked.

Wade looked at his mom, he was curious about it too.

"It was a rough start. Candace had a panic attack when she thought she was being taken from Nikki." His mom answered. "But each week is easier. Last Sunday, they had a great time. Paige took her to Wallowa Lake and they had a wonderful time together, just the two of them. This weekend, Nikki is going to go for the day and watch the show but head back to the ranch for the night. Paige and the girls will stay in the trailer together in Grangeville."

"I imagine Nikki will be staying at the ranch with Lucas every night while he is here." Cora nodded.

"He's headed back to Australia for a week, but will be back before the kid's clinic." His mom answered.

Wade looked over at Nikki and Lucas, a smiling Candace was sitting between them. Paige was sitting across from them and Nick was sitting next to her. From where Wade was sitting he could see Paige reach under the table and lay her hand on Nick's leg.

Wade's eyebrows shot up in surprise. He didn't know there was something going on between the two of them. He was even more surprised when he saw Nick reach down and take her hand and place it back on her own lap. Paige turned and looked up at him, but he was talking to Lucas and didn't look back at her.

Paige looked across at Lucas and Nikki then smiled. A few minutes later, she excused herself and walked into the kitchen.

Curious, Wade followed her. She had made it in the kitchen by the time he walked in the door. He could hear her whispering to someone.

"Well, that didn't last long." Paige said.

"What happened?" It was Aunt Leah.

"I don't know. We went on a couple of dates; I thought everything was going well. Then he postponed Saturday's date to Monday. We went out to dinner and he said it wasn't going to work out."

"No reason?"

"He just said he didn't want to keep things going when he didn't have the feelings he should have. He didn't want to hurt me and give me any idea or hope there would be a future." Paige sighed.

"That sounds honorable to me," Aunt Leah responded. "He met you in person instead of a phone call, that's pretty good now days."

"I know, but it just made me like him more. He was such a gentleman the whole time we were together, you don't see that as much now days either."

"It was just a couple of dates, Paige. You make it sound like you were together a long time."

Wade heard them giggle softly.

"Did you have the feeling it was going any farther?" Aunt Leah whispered.

"It would have wrapped things up so nicely with Candace and Nikki, we could have been one happy family."

"And your feelings?"

"Nick's gorgeous, sexy, a cowboy and a gentleman…how could I not fall for him?"

"That didn't exactly answer my question."

"I know, if I admitted it to myself? No, he's a bit of an introvert and doesn't talk too much. I like debates and in-depth conversations."

Aunt Leah giggled. "Well, you wouldn't have gotten that with Nick."

"I know, but I sure wish I could have had one good night with him."

"You didn't?"

"No."

Wade turned quickly and headed back out the door. He didn't want to hear that part!

He sat back in his chair and smiled at Cora who was talking to Aunt Dru.

His eyes went to Nick. Paige had called him gorgeous, sexy, a cowboy and a gentleman. Wade chuckled to himself, he agreed with the cowboy and gentleman but had no clue about the other two.

"What's so funny?" Cora asked him.

Wade chuckled again. Wouldn't she have been shocked if he told her?

He shook his head. "Nothin'."

Wade smiled as Jessup came up and started talking to Cora.

Wade and Cora had spent a couple hours together watching '*The Cowboys*' one more time, just the two of them. They had barely spoken; but just enjoyed being together. They promised each other that when she came back, they would watch it again. When he saw Aunt Dru was walking towards her truck, he quickly stood and followed her.

She reached in the truck and reemerged with her phone in her hand.

"Aunt Dru?"

She smiled as she walked towards him. "What?"

"I was just curious, how was Tessa's first day?"

His aunt's smile widened. "She was a bit overwhelmed and very tired. I think she'll need the weekend to get her sleep pattern adjusted."

"I'm really glad you hired her."

"I'm really glad you found them."

Wade chuckled. "They must have been in the lost and found."

"You should have seen the look on her face when I handed her keys to the SUV and a cell phone."

Wade stopped, making her stop and look down at him. He looked at her trying to decide if he should ask her...

"Just spit it out." She smiled at him.

"Well," Wade hesitated, looked around them to see if anyone was near then did as she said. "I was wondering why Tessa didn't want to admit she was a survivor of breast cancer. It seems that's a good thing…like Alex said."

Aunt Dru nodded, "That was pretty tough…almost enough to turn down the job she wanted and needed so badly. It's a good thing Alex was there, I don't think she would have taken it without his encouragement."

"But, I don't understand why."

"Cancer is a terrible thing," She started. "It does awful things to the body and handling it is tough on the mind. No two people will deal with it the same way. Tessa not only had her battle to go through, but also dealing with Alex's leg. She's only 32, and I haven't seen nor heard about family or a support system being there for her."

Wade shook his head. "Alex said his dad left when he was five, they only hear from him at Christmas and on his birthday. Evidently, he has a wife and two other kids."

"So she's dealt with that, too." Aunt Dru sighed sadly.

"Why was the insurance going to make her turn it down?"

"Getting insurance when you've had a prior condition, like breast cancer, can be hard…and expensive."

"But you were going to pay for it…so why was she going to turn it down?"

"I'm sure it's because of the additional cost she didn't want us to incur. If it wasn't for the insurance part, she wouldn't have had to tell us about the cancer."

"She sure has had a tough time."

She smiled down at him. "Well, I guess you found them for a reason. We'll just have to become the support system she and Alex need."

Wade smiled back. "You hiring her sure helps, and Alex has all of us kids, too."

"You can't ask for anything better than that."

They started walking back to the group.

"It still doesn't answer why she didn't want to tell anyone." Wade frowned.

"No, we may never know, but we'll be there for her if she needs us."

CHAPTER EIGHT

Wade heard the truck engine start. It was early in the morning so he knew someone was taking Cora to the airport. He slowly rolled out of bed and walked to the window. The sun was already rising. He watched the truck drive all the way to the end and turn right…towards Lewiston and the airport. A sadness covered his heart as the truck disappeared into the twinkling lights of town.

Cora told him not to be sad, this was a good thing, and she would be back for visits. She was flying to Seattle today, then Sunday, she and her sister would be taking a cruise and traveling up to Alaska for a week. She promised to send him pictures every chance she could.

Wade turned from the window and looked at his bed…he was too awake now to go back to sleep. The whole house was quiet. Reilly was sprawled out sound asleep on his own bed.

Wade sighed…he knew what he needed…Rooster and Dollar, but Rooster was still at The Stables. He changed clothes and made it out the door without waking Reilly. The only light on was in the kitchen, so after taking more aspirin he headed out the door.

He stepped out into the cool morning and jogged towards the barn. They were leaving late in the morning for Moses Lake and the rodeo, so he could sleep on the ride there. Right now he needed horse love, so he stepped into the barn. The morning light was already filtering into the barn through the windows and doors illuminating the aisle of the barn. He made his way to Dollar and found the horse lying down; so he joined him. Wade curled up in the corner next to the horse and quickly fell back to sleep.

Someone was laughing, which made Wade open his eyes. Dollar had stood up and was eating hay from the feeder. Wade had to look under the horse's belly to see who was at the door laughing at him. He grinned when Alex waved.

"How did you get here?" Wade asked as he stood.

"Mom dropped me off on her way to work." Alex said excitedly. "She said I can stay here until you guys leave."

"I wish you were coming with us."

"Me too, it would be so fun, but I don't think she's ready for it. She had to keep reminding me we've only known you guys for a week." Alex chuckled. "I have a list of rules of what I can say and what I can't, and how I'm supposed to act."

"Just act like an eleven-year-old." Wade shook his head with a smile.

"Show me the horses!" Alex yelled.

Wade laughed and they spent the next hour with the horses.

"I'm hungry," Wade looked over at Alex, who nodded in agreement. They stepped out of the barn just as Nick stopped his black truck.

"Nick!" Alex yelled with a grin and he limped faster towards the truck.

Nick stepped out of the truck and watched them approach. "Well, you're a surprise. I wasn't expecting you here."

"Mom dropped me off to spend the morning with Wade before they left."

"Well, I came to steal Wade for the morning." Nick placed his hands on his hips and looked between the two boys. "So, now what?"

"You're stealing me?" Wade felt the excitement start to build. Man work! Then he looked at Alex.

"I guess you can take me to Mom." Alex said dejectedly.

"You don't want to go?" Nick asked.

"Yes!" Alex nodded. "But I don't think she'll let me."

"Why?" Nick asked.

"I'm not supposed to ask for anything special." Alex answered.

Nick laughed, "Well, you're not…going with me isn't anything special."

"Yes it is!" Wade argued with a grin.

Nick shook his head at Wade then looked at Alex. "Let's at least give it a try." He handed Alex his cell phone. "Give her a call."

"Do you know her new number?" Wade asked.

"Yep, I memorized it." Alex said as he pushed the buttons.

"Hi, Mom…what? No, it's Nick's phone. He's here at the Tagger house too." Alex nodded as he listened. "He came to steal Wade for the morning and wants to know if I can go, too." A pause. "No, I didn't ask him to go, he asked me." Alex's face fell.

Wade and Nick looked at each other then back to the disappointed Alex.

Nick reached for the phone.

"Nick wants to talk to you." Alex handed over the phone.

"Hi Tessa." Nick spoke. "No, he didn't ask. I caught the boys as they were coming out of the barn. I came to get Wade to help me get fencing and farrier supplies for the weekend." He paused and smiled. "No, I hate shopping, can't stand it, so I always take one of the kids with me to make it more of an adventure." He paused. "You would really be doing me a favor if you would let him go with me. I promise to take care of him, not leave him behind or lose him anywhere." A pause. "I was just kidding. I haven't done that to any of the kids…yet." He smiled. "You can call Jordan; I take Nora or Wade all the time." He paused. "What if I said pretty please with whiskey on top?" He winked at the boys. "No, it sounds more believable with whiskey."

A pause, a nod, a smile. "Thanks, Wade has to be back by noon so I'll just bring Alex over there after dropping off Wade." Nick smiled as the boys silently cheered. "It's no problem, I need to talk to Jack so I'll be coming over there anyway." A pause, Nick pointed to the truck and the boys ran for the door. "I appreciate it, OK, yep." He ended the call.

"Thanks Nick!" Alex grinned as Wade helped him into the truck.

Their first stop was for breakfast at Waffles and More, then they headed to the ranch store for the supplies.

As they walked through the store, Wade noticed the people that would watch Alex limp down the aisles. This was the first time that Wade was around Alex outside of the Tagger property. As excited as he was, his new friend was moving fast, so his limp was even more pronounced.

Most people would just glance over then turn away. Other's smiled compassionately.

Alex limped over to the boots section and stared. He looked at Wade. "Mom said she'd buy me a pair of boots in a couple of weeks; after a couple paychecks."

"Would she be mad if I bought you a pair today?" Nick walked up behind them.

Alex's eyes grew wide and he looked around at all the boots. "Probably," He sighed.

"What if I buy you a pair today and if she insists on paying me back, she can do it when she's ready?" Nick suggested.

Alex shook his head.

"You need a pair for the kid's clinic." Wade told him.

Alex's shoulders drooped and he shook his head.

"What if you come help me fix my fence and earn the boots?"

Alex looked at him hopefully and shrugged.

"Alright, how about this," Nick said. "I'll buy them now, and if Tessa doesn't agree then I'll just bring them back."

Alex looked up at Nick. "You did talk her in to letting me come today."

"And I'll do everything I can to talk her into letting you keep the boots," Nick assured him.

"OK, but not a very expensive pair." Alex smiled nervously and walked to the boots.

Wade looked out the truck window at the farmer's fields passing by. They were an hour into a three hour drive. There was still no word from Nick on whether Tessa let Alex keep the boots. They looked just like Nick's, except Nick insisted he have a good tread on the bottom of the boots so his limping stride wouldn't slip on slick floors.

Wade sighed and stretched his shoulders and tried to roll his hips, they really ached on the long trips. He and Sadie were riding in the back seat and Grace and Reilly were in the front seat with his mom driving. Rufio, Buttercup, Dollar, and Scarecrow were in the horse trailer.

"What are you doing at this rodeo?" Sadie asked him.

"Breakaway and Steer Daubing." Wade answered. "Are you doing more than barrels?"

Sadie nodded. "I'm doing poles, barrels, and I'm doing breakaway too!"

Wade looked at her in surprise. "You haven't done breakaway before."

"I know, but I figured since we're here…might as well do as much as possible." She grinned. "I practice it at home all the time."

"There isn't team roping at this rodeo." Grace frowned then looked at their driver. "Why are we going to this rodeo this year, we haven't before?"

"Just trying to mix it up, but I agree, we should be sticking to ones that have team roping for you two." Wade's mom answered. "Sorry guys."

"Gives us a chance to try something else," Reilly shrugged. "I'm doing chute doggin and calf roping, Dad said no on the bull riding unless I do training first."

"What are you doing Grace?" Wade asked.

"Steer daubing, breakaway, poles, and barrels." Grace answered. "Nora wants me and Sadie to go for the club's royalty this year with her. If she's appointed, she'll be doing more rodeos with us next year and not just horse shows."

"That would be a relief!" His mom laughed.

A phone message alert went off and Wade sat up looking up at his mom.

"Grace, would you check that for me?" His mom asked.

There was a pause… "That's an odd message…it's for Wade from Nick." Grace told them.

"What's it say? Give me the phone!" Wade reached forward.

"All it says is 'He keeps them, took 30 minutes of talking' and that's all it says." Grace said and didn't hand the phone to him.

Wade grinned. Alex must be jumping for joy!

"If she wins this, she'll probably win all-round." Wade smiled at his mom.

"She won't be complaining about coming to this rodeo again." She grinned. "This has been one of the best weekends we've ever had."

"I won both my events…so I agree." Wade chuckled.

"I got third in breakaway!" Sadie excitedly. "Dad is going to be surprised!"

"He'll be thrilled." Her aunt nodded. "And that goes with your win in the barrels and second in poles."

"Scarecrow's awesome!" Sadie grinned. "I wish I could bring Little Ghost for roping."

"Me too!" His mom laughed. "We'll have to get a bigger horse trailer."

"Where's Reilly?" Wade asked.

"Over talking with Grace to keep her calm for her steer daubing," His mom answered.

"With his win in chute doggin and Grace's win in breakaway and poles, we're all four going home with buckles!" Sadie told them with a grin.

"Here comes Grace!" Wade announced.

Grace and Buttercup pranced toward the box, the long daubing stick in Grace's hand. Reilly ran up to the bleachers just in time for the announcer to call her name.

Grace nodded and the calf was released as she and Buttercup bolted out of the box, 1.6 seconds later, Grace tapped the stick in the circle on the calf's side leaving behind a yellow spot of paint. She had her win!

"Man that was fast!" Wade shouted over the cheering crowd.

"She's going to get one of the big buckles!" Sadie cheered.

Reilly turned to Wade with a huge smile. "I want to be home now! To show everyone!"

"Me too!" Wade nodded.

"Well, let's go get the horse's in the trailer so we can as soon as possible." His mom said excitedly.

Very reluctantly, Wade had taken off his belt buckle for the win at Winchester and put on the new buckle for a group picture. It was a team win, which meant a lot to the whole group in the truck that was pulling into The Homestead driveway.

As soon as the truck stopped, Grace and Sadie burst out of the truck and ran for their dad. Wade laughed and followed. He looked up and watched everyone step out the back door…everyone but Cora. He sighed. How long was it going to take for him not to expect her to be there? She always greeted them with a proud smile when they arrived from a trip.

Nick was sitting in the chairs on the back deck with Jack. Reilly was talking excitedly with them. Wade ran back to the horse trailer to get Dollar to the barn so he could find out from Nick about Alex and his boots. He had made sure the horse was last in the trailer so he was first out.

Wade lifted the latch of the trailer and swung the door open. He was greeted by a pool of blood on the floor.

CHAPTER NINE

"DAD!" Wade yelled as loud as he could, panic in his voice.

Within seconds his dad and everyone else were at the back door with him. Wade stepped into the trailer and reached for Dollar's lead rope.

"Wait, Wade." His dad reached for him.

"The blood starts up farther in than Dollar, I gotta get him out." Wade panicked.

"It could have gone back and forth during the trip." His dad told him.

Wade tossed off his hat then squatted down to look under Dollar's stomach. He didn't see anything so he maneuvered himself under the horse and looked at his legs.

"He's OK." Wade told them and untied him quickly.

As Dollar stepped out, Wade's dad and uncle stepped in.

He walked the horse away from the trailer and turned to watch. His heart was racing; either Rufio, Scarecrow, or Buttercup were hurt.

Next in the trailer was Buttercup. Uncle Grayson checked the horse as best he could and didn't see any injuries. He untied her and threw the rope to Grace who quickly walked the horse to stand next to Wade.

Sadie was crying at the end of the trailer with Reilly next to her. Their hands entwined and squeezed for support.

Everyone was silent as the men checked on Scarecrow, who was next in the trailer.

"There's blood on her leg." Uncle Grayson said quietly which made Sadie sob. Reilly held her tighter and her mother was right behind her with a hand on her daughter's and Reilly's shoulders.

"It's not hers, it splashed up somehow." Uncle Grayson informed them and untied the horse and tossed the lead rope to Aunt Dru who walked her out and handed the rope to Nick. He turned and walked to stand with Wade and Grace.

Sadie watched Scarecrow walk away but stood holding hands with Reilly as Rufio was examined.

"How in the heck did he do that?" Uncle Grayson muttered.

"What?!" Reilly cried out.

"He has a cut up high on his front leg, in the back." Wade's dad answered. "He'll need stitches."

"I've already called the vet clinic and left an emergency message." Aunt Dru assured Reilly. "Everyone back up. Give him room to come out."

Everyone stepped backwards but Sadie and Reilly.

Uncle Grayson turned Rufio and slowly led the limping horse to the end of the trailer.

As Wade's dad stepped out of the trailer he looked over and frowned. "It's not your fault Jordan." He said quickly and walked to her.

Wade turned quickly. His mom was crying; her eyes wide in shock.

He watched his dad engulf his crying wife in his arms.

"We didn't stop short or have any hard turns." She mumbled against his chest.

"None at all." Grace confirmed.

"It's not your fault, Tink." His dad repeated. "These weird mishaps just happen."

Rufio stepped out of the trailer and groaned when his leg hit the ground. Uncle Grayson stopped the horse once his back legs were on the ground and the horse lifted his front left leg off the ground.

Aunt Dru was there with a large pad of gauze to help stop the bleeding.

"Reilly, come on over." Uncle Grayson nodded.

Reilly quickly walked over, pulling Sadie with him. They both bent down and looked at the cut.

"It didn't happen very long ago." Reilly sighed.

"How did that happen, Dad?" Sadie whispered as she wrinkled her face at the cut.

He shook his head. "It had to be the back hoof reached it somehow. There isn't anything sharp on the wall of the trailer." He looked over at his sister-in-law. "Scott's right, Jordan, this isn't your fault. There's nothing you did to make him do this."

Wade looked at his mom, she nodded sadly.

"I'm sorry, Reilly," She whispered.

"It's not your fault," Reilly stood and turned to her with sincere eyes. "I was with you, you did nothing different…come look."

As Wade's mother made her way to the horse, Aunt Dru's phone rang.

"Grace," Nick said. "Give me Buttercup, I'll take these two and put them in their stalls."

"The vet will be here in about 30 minutes." Aunt Dru announced. "Let's get the trailer pulled over to the pasture and washed out."

"I got it." Leah said and hurried to the truck.

"I'll get the gate." Jack turned.

They all turned when they heard a truck coming up the driveway. It was Paige bringing Nora and her horse's home from the horse show. Candace would have been dropped off with Nikki at Circle 50.

"The bleeding stopped," Uncle Grayson said as he started leading the horse. "Let's get him into the barn."

Reilly, still holding Sadie's hand, walked behind his horse as they made their way to the barn. Wade followed behind them with Dollar.

As they waited for Kate, the veterinarian that purchased Dr. Mark's clinic, all the horses were put away and fed. Straw bales were placed outside of Rufio's stall. Reilly and Sadie, hand-in-hand, stood in the stall with his horse. Uncle Grayson's bandage wrap was keeping the wound from bleeding.

Before taking his seat on a bale, Wade checked on Rufio's cut. It was about nine inches long. It reminded him of the cuts Monty had on his chest when he rammed the fence to save him.

Wade stroked the horse's neck, his hand sliding under the long mane. Then he stopped and went backwards...there were bumps under the mane. He pulled the hair back and exhaled.

"Reilly, come look." Wade stared at the marks.

Dragging Sadie, Reilly stepped up next to him.

"Dang!" The two said in unison.

"What's wrong?" Wade turned to see his mother had joined them.

"Come look, Jordan," Reilly told her. "We told you it wasn't your fault."

She stepped into the stall with them and ran her hand lightly over the bumps. "These look like bee stings or hornets," She frowned and released the mane to look through the hair.

"There are three hornets caught up in his mane," She pointed out to them. "They're dead now, but they sure did a number on him."

"That's why he cut himself; he was trying to use his back hoof to get them away from him." Sadie nodded with wide eyes.

Kate and Uncle Grayson appeared at the stall door and looked in with amused, curious expressions.

"Come look," Reilly told them and pointed to the horse.

"I'm not sure it's practical for all of us to be in there," Kate chuckled. She was a tall woman with brown hair that she always had pulled back when she worked. Wade liked her, but really didn't like her sister, Helen, the other new owner of the clinic. The two women looked alike but Helen had darker, almost black hair.

"There are three hornets in his mane and a ton of bumps on his neck." Sadie told them as Reilly led her out of the stall. Wade followed and they turned at the door and watched.

Uncle Grayson looked at the bumps then over at his sister-in-law. "Now, do you believe us? It wasn't your fault."

"Yes," She smiled sadly, "As much as it must have hurt him, it makes me feel better to see them, which is a terrible thing to say."

"Well, I'll give him something to help with those but let's take a look at the leg." Kate said as she knelt down next to Rufio.

Wade, Sadie, and Reilly sat on the bales next to Grace and Nora.

As his mother stepped out of the stall, Wade patted the bale next to him. She smiled and sat between him and Nora. They all held hands in support of each other and Rufio.

"No riding for at least a month," Kate told them, as she finally walked out of the stall. "I'm sure you're all aware of that."

Reilly nodded, "We'll do whatever's needed. I'll use Cooper for the rest of the summer."

Kate smiled. "For now, let's exit the building, he'll be fine. I have no doubt that you'll take good care of him. Jessup speaks highly of you. If Jessup isn't down in the next week to take a look at it, let me know and I'll swing by."

Wade's eyebrows shot up in surprise. Another secret romance?

"Jessup's the best," Reilly smiled. "And thank you for coming tonight."

As they walked out of the barn, Reilly turned to Sadie and looked down at the hand he was still grasping. "Thank you, Sadie."

"You're welcome, Reilly." She smiled matter-of-factly. "You were there for me when Angel died, I'm just glad it wasn't as bad."

"Me, too," Reilly sighed as he took one more look at Rufio before the lights were turned off.

###

Wade scrolled through the websites again, looking for a reason for his pain and now the sudden weight loss he noticed when putting his jeans on that morning. Maybe he should talk to Sadie, she would be able to figure it out. She was good with details, but would she keep it quiet? He nodded…she would, Sadie was a vault when it came to secrets.

They were the only two at The Homestead; Nora didn't ride the bus home; she had a 4H leaders meeting. Wade turned off the computer and headed outside to the barn where he knew Sadie was. He hesitated in the hallway and looked down to Cora's door. His heart ached, he missed seeing her when they got home from school…at breakfast…dinner…all the time.

He made his way down to her room and slowly opened the door. Everything looked normal, like she was just gone to the store. It was going to be a terrible day when she packed all her belongings and left for good.

Wade shut the door and walked outside to find Sadie before anyone else got there. He was surprised to see the veterinarian truck parked outside the barn. He must have been staring so hard at the scary websites that he didn't hear them come in.

Wade hoped it was Kate and not Helen checking in on Rufio…but his hopes were dashed when he heard Sadie's voice coming from the barn.

"You're NOT going to do that," Sadie was saying loudly. Dingo!

"Just leave then," Helen's voice was gruff.

"I have NO intention of leaving you with this horse by yourself." Sadie's voice was rising in volume.

"Listen, I've been around and worked on horses three times as long as you've been alive."

"That doesn't make you right! It just makes it sad that you won't listen to me!"

"Like I said," Helen's voice was rising with irritation and volume. "Leave."

"Not gonna happen," Sadie's voice was as loud as Wade had ever heard it and she was pissed.

He looked around and didn't see anyone else; confirming it was just him and Sadie. He moved from a fast walk to a jog to get into the barn faster.

"Listen, you little blonde headed pip-squeak, just let me get my job done so I can get the heck out of here."

"WHAT DID YOU CALL ME?" Sadie yelled as Wade walked into the barn. Her eyes were blazing at the veterinarian who had her hands on hips glaring back at Sadie.

Sadie had Rufio in the aisle and was standing between the agitated horse and the irritated older lady.

"A pip-squeak," The lady said it like a curse word. "You may think you can get your way because of your looks, but I don't care about them. So give me back the horse, so I can get his leg taken care of and get away from here."

"YOU'RE NOT TOUCHING THIS HORSE OR INSULTING ME AGAIN!" Sadie screamed and turned Rufio and started to walk away.

Helen reached for Sadie's arm that was holding the lead rope, making Rufio jump sideways.

"HEY!" Wade yelled and made them both jump.

Helen had gotten a hold of the rope, but when Wade yelled she dropped it and turned towards him.

Sadie stopped walking away and turned to Wade; a little relief flickered in her eyes.

"Tell this girl to give me back the horse." The woman ordered him.

"Why in the world would you think she would listen to me? We're the same age." Wade said tartly. "And I wouldn't do it unless I knew what was wrong."

"She didn't agree with how I was doing my job!" Helen's eyes were glaring.

"She was going to use a TWITCH on RUFIO! And she wanted ME to help!" Sadie hollered, pointing to the woman. "So I got Rufio away from her."

"A twitch?" Wade turned and looked at the veterinarian like she had three heads. "On Rufio?" His voice went up two octaves on the horse's name.

The woman exhaled loudly. "It's used all the time for unruly horses."

"He wasn't unruly!" Sadie argued, her dingo expression nearly making Wade nervous. "He was just scared at your rough handling."

Helen leaned her head back and looked at the ceiling. "I can't believe I have to stand here and argue with you two pip-squeaks so I can get my work done."

"I TOLD YOU TO QUIT INSULTING ME!" Sadie screamed, her face turning redder.

Wade stepped between his cousin and the veterinarian. He needed to be the cooler head here even though he had become quite irritated, too.

He turned to Helen, who was now glaring at him. "Lady, neither one of us is going to let you near that horse again." He tried to sound like his dad when he was mad but maintaining his composure. "So…you can either stand there and wait for someone else to get here, that MAY let you touch the horse, OR you can just leave now."

Helen's face turned red and without another word she walked into Rufio's stall.

Wade looked over at Sadie who was still red and glaring. Rufio stood calmly behind her. The other horse's heads were all sticking out of the stalls and into the aisle watching the commotion.

Within minutes, Helen walked out of the stall with her supply box in her hand and, without looking at the cousins again, walked out of the barn.

Sadie and Wade looked at each other when they heard her truck start and gravel fly. They could hear the tings ring out from rock hitting the metal side of the barn.

"Now what?" Sadie asked as her skin color returning to normal.

"We can't call Kate, I'm sure Helen is already talking to her or busy at the clinic." Wade looked down at Rufio's uncovered wound.

"Aunt Dru told me that we should come up with a solution for a problem before offering up the problem."

"I know…" He walked to the barn office and picked up the phone. It had speed dial numbers programmed so he pushed the top button.

"Dr. Mark?"

CHAPTER TEN

Wade smiled at Sadie when he heard the familiar voice. Sadie sighed in relief.

Wade quickly told the older veterinarian what happened, nodded, and hung up.

"He'll be here in ten minutes," Wade told Sadie as they walked Rufio back to his stall.

"That quick?"

"He only lives that far away. Said he'd be right over."

"Should we call our parents?"

Wade shrugged, "I'm sure she already has."

"Think we're in trouble?"

"Sadie, I don't think any of the parents in our family would let her use a twitch on any of the Tagger Herd."

"What's a pip-squeak?" She sat on the stool, still holding Rufio's lead rope. "I wasn't sure whether I should be mad or not…except for the way she said it."

"I don't know, but I don't think it's really bad…but I agree, the way she said it sounded insulting."

"She shouldn't have called me it anyway…plus me using my looks to get my way…that IS insulting." She looked at Wade in concern. "I don't do that…do I?"

Wade frowned and lifted a brow at her while he thought. "No…I thinks it's more your temper that makes you get what you want…not your looks. Except with our parents, most people will let have what you want so they don't have to face The Dingo."

Sadie frowned, "I didn't think so…but I don't know." She looked depressed, "I don't get mad because people won't give me my way. I get mad when they try to take something from me or they won't listen to me because I'm only eleven."

Wade shrugged then walked to the doors of the barn to watch for Dr. Mark.

"If the parents are mad at us, there isn't much we can do about it now." She leaned against the stall wall and stroked Rufio's long nose.

"It's just the way it is." Wade muttered and saw the older veterinarian's truck turn down the driveway.

Wade waved excitedly, he'd known the doctor his entire life but hadn't seen him for months. Dr. Mark's grin was hidden behind his large mustache, which was greyer now, but his eye's sparkled letting Wade know that he was glad to see him, too.

"Look at you, Mr. Tagger." The doctor shook Wade's hand making him feel grown and mature.

Dr. Mark turned into the barn. "And there is my little Tagger." Sadie jumped up and gave him a big hug.

"I love seeing you! I've missed you so much!" Sadie grinned then it started to fade. "Even if we get in trouble."

"For calling me?" He raised a brow.

"No, for kinda running Helen off." Wade answered.

Dr. Mark lifted a shoulder in disinterest. "Let's just check on Rufio and see how he's doing."

The doctor knelt down and worked on the horse while Sadie and Wade watched silently. Wade wondered what his parents were going to say and how he could sneak in a couple aspirin without anyone seeing.

When the doctor finished with Rufio, they took a tour of the rest of the horses. He played and gave treats to each one.

"I can't believe how different they are since the first time we saw them." He stroked Buttercup's jaw. "Where's Rooster?"

"He's at The Stables for the summer," Wade answered.

"So, what's this I hear about a clinic at The Stables for kids?" Dr. Mark asked.

Wade and Sadie excitedly told him about Alex and the kid's clinic while they wandered through the barn.

"That just sounds like a great deal." Dr. Mark nodded. "How do I get in on it?"

"Really?" Wade asked eagerly.

"You bet. I've got all kinds of time to help with preparation and during the event." He nodded as they walked out of the barn.

"Want some lemonade?" Sadie asked, her blue eyes shining in excitement. "I'll get some and we can sit on the deck and talk."

"Let's hit the kitchen." He smiled, which was only seen in his eyes. "This hot temperature doesn't like me...or vice-versa."

"OK!" Sadie ran into the house while Wade walked with the veterinarian to his truck to put the supplies away.

Three glasses of lemonade were sitting on the table but Sadie wasn't with them.

"Where do you think my little Tagger ran off too?" Dr. Mark slid into a chair at the table. "Course as tall as she's gotten, can't say she's too little anymore."

"What's a pip-squeak?" Sadie asked as she descended the stairs with a horse statue in her arms.

"A what?" He asked watching her.

"A pip-squeak...that's what Helen called me, a blonde headed pip-squeak." Sadie put the clear statue on the table. "Well, she called us both pip-squeaks."

"It's not the worst thing to be called…but she still shouldn't have called you anything." He frowned.

"What's it mean?" Wade asked.

"It's means small or insignificant." He answered looking between the two eleven-year-olds who were quickly irritated again.

"I KNEW she insulted me," Sadie exhaled sharply.

"Well, don't get all worked up about it." Dr. Mark patted her hand. "She isn't worth your emotions or thoughts if she's going to start calling you names."

Wade nodded, "What's the statue for?" He asked trying to shift Sadie's thoughts.

"Oh, yeah," Sadie smiled. "I thought we'd have a small education area for you to teach the kids about horses. You can use this to help. You can see all the bones and stuff on this one. It's what I used to learn with."

Dr. Mark's eye brows shot up. "I can do that. In fact, I have lots of posters and props we can use."

"Posters…" Wade smiled. "We should give the kids something to take home with them so they remember their day."

"How many do you have coming?" He asked.

Both kids shrugged.

"Well, let's find out, then I'll order some posters in for the kids, my contribution to the clinic." Dr. Mark looked between the two. "What kind should we order?"

"Let's go look on the computer." Wade suggested.

They were still in the library looking through posters on the internet sites when they heard the back door open and close.

"Sadie…Wade…why is there a truck in the driveway?" Aunt Dru asked as she walked through the house.

"Because I didn't want to walk," The older man laughed at their aunt as she turned the corner into the library.

"Ah!" Aunt Dru's face lit up and she grinned from ear to ear when she saw him. She quickly wrapped him into an embrace. "I just love that you're back."

"Me, too." He stepped back and smiled at her, with love shining in his eyes, matching hers.

"Dr. Mark is going to help with the clinic!" Wade announced.

Aunt Dru was ecstatic and they sat for another hour and discussed the details until the door opened again and Grace and Reilly came in. Slowly the whole family joined the group in the library, welcoming the doctor and talking about the clinic.

"I need to head out; the wife will have dinner on the table soon." Dr. Mark stood. "But before I do, I'd like to discuss this afternoon's events that brought me here."

Sadie and Wade quickly glanced at each other, eyes wide, and leaned back in their chairs.

"What happened?" Uncle Grayson looked between the doctor and the kids. From the look on his face, Wade knew that he and Sadie looked guilty.

"You haven't received a call? Any of you?" Dr. Mark looked between the adults. They all shook their heads no. The doctor looked at Wade then Sadie, "Well, these two pip-squeaks seemed to have had a run-in with Helen."

"What?" Aunt Leah gasped.

"Pip-squeaks?" Grayson frowned. "I've never heard that out of you before."

Dr. Mark turned to Sadie.

"That's what Helen called me," Sadie glanced around at the adults. "But not so nicely…then she called Wade one, too."

"What happened?" Wade's dad asked with a look of concern.

Sadie explained the incident, down playing how mad she had gotten.

"A twitch?" Jack said gruffly.

"On Rufio?" Reilly gasped, looking incredulously at his dad.

Dr. Mark winked at Wade, "Well, I'm glad the kids called me. I really enjoyed seeing the horses again. I followed their Facebook page during our travels but it just wasn't the same as visiting with them."

"You have an open invitation to come visit them any time." Aunt Dru smiled.

"Well, I'll take you up on that." He nodded.

"And Nikki wants to talk with you about helping with her rehabilitation program." Aunt Dru continued.

"And you have free access at The Stables too." Jack stated.

Dr. Mark shook his head in amusement. He turned to Sadie and Wade. "See what you two started?"

They both smiled at him.

"At least my temper finally did something good…" Sadie stopped talking and the look on her face indicated she had realize what she had said. Her worried eyes slowly moved to her parents to see if they heard her.

"Your temper?" Her dad frowned at her. "How bad was it?"

Sadie pursed her lips, scrunched her face, and looked over at Wade.

Wade looked at his parents, then over at Uncle Grayson. He rolled his lips closed.

"That bad?" Aunt Leah sighed heavily while looking between him and Sadie.

Grace, Reilly, and Nora quickly left the room without being told.

Uncle Grayson's phone rang. He frowned while looking between the two then walked out of the library as he answered it.

Sadie's eyes rolled to Wade.

Dr. Mark smiled between the two, "You did fine in my book." He winked again, said his goodbyes, and headed for the door with Aunt Dru and Jack following.

Wade stared at the computers. He wanted to talk with Sadie and search the web for achy body and weight loss, just not going to happen now. Looking around at the family, he was surprised no one had noticed the weight loss…they must all be too busy.

"Well, your temper really did the trick this time, Sadie." Her dad walked in and sat across from them while glaring at his daughter.

Sadie's shoulders drooped, she slid down into the chair, and her eyes went to the table.

"What happened?" Her mom sat next to him. Wade's parents sat down too.

"That was Jessup, Kate called him." He glared at Wade and Sadie. "Helen and Kate are going to be splitting the clinic. Kate will do large animals and Helen small animals. Helen refuses to come here again, even in an emergency."

Wade and Sadie glanced at each other nervously.

"Dr. Mark will handle the calls Kate can't. He just said we could call anytime." Aunt Dru said from the door. She was frowning at Wade and Sadie though.

"Either of you have anything to say?" Wade's dad frowned at them.

The cousins looked at each other again.

Wade took a deep breath and hoped he wouldn't get in trouble for actually saying something.

"She really wasn't very nice to Sadie." Wade started looking around at them. "It only took ME seconds to get upset with Helen."

"Her temper…" Aunt Leah started but Wade interrupted.

"After she called Sadie a blonde headed pip-squeak, she told Sadie that…I'm not sure exactly the words, but she said Sadie thought her looks would get her anything she wanted but Helen didn't care about her looks, she just wanted to get the horse back so she could get the heck out of here." He looked at everyone in the room. "Sadie was just protecting Rufio and only lost it after the "looks" thing…that and the "pip-squeak" thing." Taking another deep breath he continued. "Sadie tried to leave, but Helen wouldn't let her. And I'm the one that told Helen to go…not Sadie."

Aunt Leah's hand covered her eyes and massaged her temples.

"I don't have any idea what to say to this." Wade's mom exhaled.

"Well, since she didn't bother calling any of us, Helen knew her actions were wrong." Aunt Dru leaned against the door.

"A screaming eleven-year-old will do that to you." Uncle Grayson stopped glaring at Wade and Sadie and looked out the window. He looked upset and concerned at the same time.

Wade wished Sadie was close enough he could hold her hand.

"That doesn't excuse what she said OR trying to use a twitch on one of the gentlest horses around." Jack argued.

Uncle Grayson nodded. "Go upstairs, Sadie."

"You too, Wade." His mother said and they both nearly knocked over their chairs trying to get out of the room and ran up the stairs.

Both just had socks on so when they reached the top, they ran half way down the hall then jumped into a slide. They both giggled in relief as they stopped in front of their bedroom doors.

###

Sadie held Scarecrow's reins back tightly to keep the horse from running down the arena entry aisle. The horse bounced her excitedly, waiting for her to release her grip. The second she did, the palomino took off running down the ally, into the arena and around the first barrel. Wade shouted out to them from on top of Dollar. The pair turned sharply around the second barrel and headed for the third. He yelled out Scarecrow's name as they made the turn.

The two blondes flew down the arena, Sadie's legs kicking and Scarecrows thundering.

They won by a half second!

Wade turned and looked up in the stands. Grace, Reilly, and his mother were yelling and clapping. Nora was beside them…she'd joined the rodeo and ran poles with Cooper. She came in second and was thrilled…it was only her third time competing in the event. Cooper's speed going up and down the poles, made up for Nora's inexperience.

It was good to get back to the rodeo after such a long week. This was their last rodeo before the clinic; Sadie won a buckle, Grace and Reilly placed third in team roping. It was Cooper's first competition in months and he was too excited and nearly ran past the steer. Both riders were pleased with third place; they were just having fun like Uncle Grayson told them to.

Wade made his way into the arena to stand next to the other competitors to wait his turn. He was last this time…he didn't like running last, it was too stressful…hard to stay focused. Wade slowly traced the Rooster imprint on his saddle and waited…through eight riders.

First rider missed the calf.

Second rider was nearly at the far end of the arena before he caught the calf and the rope went flying in the air. His time 29.5…another half-second and they would have been disqualified.

Third rider missed.

Fourth rider's loop went gently over the calves head and floated down around the neck…the calf jumped through it before the rider had a chance to stop and close the loop.

Fifth rider was half way across when his calf was caught and rope released. Time 21.2.

Sixth rider was only a few strides from the chute. Time 9.82

Wade sucked in lungs full of air and let it out slowly. His finger continued to circle Rooster.

Seventh rider nodded, bolted, ran…rope flew in the air and nestled around the calf's neck, horse skidded to a stop…8.67.

Crikey…

Wade nudged Dollar towards the box. He took another deep breath, swung his rope around his head then to his side; everything felt good. Deep breathe, he was relaxed. He concentrated on the rope, his arm, the horse, the calf.

He backed Dollar into the fence and nodded. Rope was good…arm felt good… the calf bolting…Dollar was flying… the arm throwing…the rope floating…around the head…Dollar stopping…rope flying...all in 8.4 seconds.

Wade grinned as he stared at the timer…three in a row.

He heard the group on the bleachers screaming his name and Dollar's. Wade patted his horse's neck and watched the tassel hanging from the bridle bounce. His hand went to the imprint. Rooster was there, the three of them had won together.

After loading the horses in the trailer, and with the excuse of checking the latch one more time, Wade got out of view of his family and took his last three aspirin. The roping and riding was getting tough on the achy joints. He'd had to take in his belt a full notch that morning. Pretty soon, he was going to have to tell someone, two months of pain with no sign of it stopping.

He jogged back to the truck and climbed in to the applause of the family. Nora handed him the belt buckle and he grabbed it tightly. It had been a long road to finally winning…but would he be able to continue roping if the pain didn't stop?

CHAPTER ELEVEN

"Anyone want to stop for dinner or just go home?" His mom asked the group in the truck.

"Can we just grab and go this time?" Grace asked.

"Scott's not too fond of eating in this truck." She answered. "…but if you won't tell him, neither will I…I'm tired, hungry and want to be home!" His mom laughed.

They all agreed and stopped at two different fast food restaurants in Couer D' Alene before the two and a half hour drive home.

Wade glanced at Sadie. She was already starting to fall asleep after finishing her dinner. He now regretted not cornering her to help him search the internet for his aches and weight loss. After the parents got done with their discussion about Helen, they didn't say anything to Sadie or Wade. Neither of them were punished either.

Maybe in the morning they would have time to get on the computers. Probably not since Alex was coming over to spend the night for the first time at The Homestead. He didn't know how Alex was with secrets…he was good with his mother's cancer secret…maybe Wade had cancer…his heart skipped a beat. Would he want Alex to have to go through another person in his life battling the terrible disease?

Inside his mind, Wade shook his head. He wouldn't put his friend through that. What could he do? Inside again, so no one could see the turmoil, Wade sighed. He would break the new friendship to save his friend from that terrible emotional trauma.

"Wade?" Nora nudged him in the ribs.

"What?" He jumped.

"We're coming to the top of the grade," She answered and pointed out the window.

It didn't matter how many times they drove into the valley, they never got tired of seeing the beauty and lights of Lewiston and Clarkston. The Snake River crossing South to North; the Clearwater river crossing East to West. The sun shone on both rivers making them look like liquid silver. The two rivers met with the Clearwater's lonesome flow ending as it combined into the Snake. This view always said home.

"It's so pretty," Nora whispered next to Wade's head.

He playfully pushed her back into her seat. "You know; your joining us has really cramped this truck." He chuckled.

She playfully punched him in the shoulder.

"I enjoyed having all of you together and competing." His mom told them.

"I liked it too." Nora admitted. "But I still like doing horse shows better."

"Why rodeo then?" Sadie asked behind half closed eyes.

Nora sighed with a grin. "After hearing all your stories, I wanted to do it too…and I like being with the family too…this is fun…I don't know why everyone doesn't do it"

"Where's Candace?" Grace turned in her seat.

"With her Aunt Paige doing a horse show in Walla Walla." Their mom answered. "They have a court hearing pretty soon to decide where she's going to be living so they can get her in school."

They drove across the bridge over the Clearwater River. The water seemed to shimmer and sparkle in the late afternoon light.

"It's hotter here in the valley." Reilly commented.

"Always seems that way, the truck thermometer says its 101 degrees." Grace answered. "I hope the horses are alright."

Wade chuckled. "They have air conditioning through the windows."

"As long as they don't have hornets," His mom said loudly and everyone nodded.

"Dad put the screens back on the windows. That should keep that from happening again." Grace added.

His mom had driven the back way to The Homestead so they didn't have to drive through town with the big horse trailer. She took the final turn that led down the road to the steep hill that ended near the driveway of The Homestead.

"Five minutes!" Nora announced happily.

"It seems like it's been a long weekend." Wade mumbled looking out the window.

"Lots of work this week too, getting ready for Saturday's clinic." Grace grinned.

"How many people are signed up?" Sadie asked with her eyes closed. Wade smiled, he thought she was asleep.

"Twenty officially signed up but they are expecting twice that many by the end of the day." His mom answered. "We'd be happy with the twenty for the first clinic, but whether it's ten or a hundred, as long as they walk away happy, you kids should be very proud."

The truck slowed down for the steep hill.

"We are." Sadie yawned, which made everyone smile.

Wade stared at The Homestead. Home...and much needed aspirin when he got there.

"Grayson is going to be so happy to see your win, Wade." His mom glanced back at him.

Wade nodded. "I'm glad we decided not to tell them before we get home. I like to see the looks on everyone's faces…now that I'm winning." He grinned.

"He'll be proud of ME too!" Sadie sat up.

"Everyone is always proud of all of you whether you win or not." His mom laughed at Sadie.

Wade looked out the window…how long would it take, how many rodeos did he have to return from, to stop missing Cora when they arrived back home?

They turned down the driveway and could see the remaining Tagger Herd trotting across the pasture. Except Rooster…Wade sighed in depression. He forgot Rooster wasn't there either and wouldn't be able to tell him about the win…probably not until Monday. He suddenly felt tired.

He looked over at Sadie who was stretching her neck high to see over his mom and down the driveway. He needed to get her at the computer tonight so they could find out what would help decrease his aches and pains.

The truck stopped and Wade slid out of the door and walked to the back of the trailer. He'd help get the horses put away then run in and take the aspirin before anyone saw him.

"Hopefully there isn't any blood this time." Wade smiled at his mom as they met at the back of the trailer.

She nodded, then looked around him and smiled. It was probably his dad she was looking at. They always looked at each other with love and light in their eyes after being separated all weekend.

Wade turned and saw everyone on the back deck or walking towards the trailer to help. Everyone was there including Nikki and Matt who had been at their ranch all week. Nick, Cora, and even Jessup were there too.

Wade turned to the trailer and lifted the handle to the door…then he froze, was he just imagining that? Did he just WANT her to be there so he saw her?

He turned his head and looked back at the deck…she was standing at the top of the steps, wearing her Tagger Drive Team T-shirt and smiling at him. Cora was there!

Sadie and Nora yelled her name and ran for the woman who wrapped them into a welcoming embrace. Grace and Reilly were right behind them to welcome her home.

Wade just stared at her, his hand still in the air holding the handle. His heart hurt…his muscles constricted, why was she there? She wasn't supposed to be back for weeks, then to just pack and leave again. So now…he had to face her packing all her stuff and leaving again. He didn't want to see that!

He rolled his lips tight to keep the disappointed tears in check. He lowered his arms and turned to his mom. She was still standing next to him.

"Go greet her first, then we can let the horses out."

"Did you know?"

"No, no one said a thing."

"How long is she here for?"

"I don't know, I didn't know she was coming." She repeated with a bewildered smile.

"It's OK," Wade finished lifting the handle. "She'll understand the horses come first."

"Wade…" She exhaled in surprise.

"She'll understand." He repeated and swung the door open, blocking out the group on the deck…and blocking out Cora.

Scarecrow was first and Uncle Grayson was there to take her. Wade showed no emotion, didn't even look at him. Why did Cora have to be there? Five minutes ago, he missed her…but not as much as last week…in the future it would hurt less. Why did she have to be there and start it up all over again?

He unhooked Cooper and handed him to his dad…again without looking. Buttercup was next and was stepping back and forth, anxious to be out of the trailer. Wade talked to her soothingly, not sure if the tone was for him to calm himself down or for Buttercup. He handed her to Jack, without looking at him.

Wade turned to Dollar, he just wanted to grab the horse and keep walking all the way to The Stables and to Rooster. He didn't want to hurt anymore; physically or mentally. He turned and led the horse out of the trailer himself, no one would expect him to hand off his own horse. Jessup was there to shut the trailer door.

Wade glanced up at him and nodded 'thanks'. Jessup had a slight smile and nodded 'you're welcome'.

Wade turned quickly and walked to the barn. He ached…inside and out…and the closer he got to the barn, the closer he got to having to go to the house and see her. Everyone would expect him to be happy and excited. How can he deal with trying to mask his true feelings…the disappointment that he was going to have to see her leave again? And do it in front of everyone?

Wade made it to Dollar's stall without having to talk to anyone but when he turned, Cora was standing at the door.

She smiled, a bit nervously. "Hi."

"Hi, how was your cruise?" He asked as he unhooked the horse's halter. There was already hay in the feeder and Dollar impatiently bounced his head so he could eat.

She stepped back as he walked to the door. "It was OK, not what I expected."

"What do you mean?" He asked, he tried to remain calm, he missed her…but he was also mad at her for coming back. It was tough to be eleven and have to handle all the confusing emotions.

He hung the halter on the hook on the wall outside the stall. Hoping his inner turmoil didn't show, he calmly turned to face her. They were the only two remaining in the barn.

"I expected to find something, and I didn't." Cora shrugged, her eyes soft and the smile that always warmed his heart was there, almost but not quite breaking his guard.

"You were lost," Wade nodded; remembering their conversation.

"And I still am."

"I don't understand," He pulled the stool over for her to sit down and he sat on the bale of straw across from her. He wanted to talk out here, not at the house with everyone else around. He needed to get his emotions in control.

"I miss Wes," Her eyes glimmered from the gathering tears and her words shook. "But no matter where I am, I'll miss him. Everywhere we went, we enjoyed ourselves and the scenery was magnificent," She paused and sniffed daintily. "But I still missed Wes." Cora looked around the barn. "This is the original part of the barn...here by the doors."

Wade nodded.

"I remember the first time I walked through those doors," She glanced down at them, a tear quickly wiped away. "I don't think I was even in the door yet when you were at my side."

Wade didn't speak, his throat constricted, lungs not working, and heart pounding. Why did she have to bring that up? He remembered like it was the day before. The fear in her eyes of what she was about to see is what drew him to her. It was going to be hard on her, he knew it...it was hard on all of them but they had each other to lean on. She didn't have anyone...so he was there to help, to hopefully make it a little better for her...to let her know she wasn't alone.

Without looking at him she continued, "I truly appreciated you at that moment, leaned on you…needed you." She wiped away more tears. "It was the first time in 50 years that I faced a truly horrible situation and didn't have Wes by my side. It was so hard."

Wade couldn't look at her anymore; he turned his head and looked down the barn aisle.

"The night Angel died…you leaned on my shoulder and comforted me."

"Cora…" His whisper was barely audible. She was killing his resolve…he was fighting hard not to cry. She needed to stop.

She sniffed and wiped away the tears. "Didn't think I'd bring that up," She exhaled. "But, I want you to know." She swallowed hard trying to keep the emotions down. "From that moment, I have looked at you as a grandson."

Wade felt the first tear fall as he looked back at her. Then why did she leave?

"I thought I was lost," She finally continued. "But when we left here, I realized I wasn't."

Wade cleared his throat of the emotions constricting the muscles. "I don't understand."

"I wasn't lost, Wade." She looked at him with tear filled eyes, her chin quivered slightly. "I just missed my husband."

He reached out and took her hand and squeezed. As much as he had missed her over the last couple of weeks; he couldn't imagine what it was like to miss your husband of 48 years.

"No matter where we were, I still missed him, but it was even worse."

"Why?"

"When I went to Australia with Nick, I knew I was coming home, plus he was there…the connection to here."

Wade nodded, he understood that.

"When I left here…as in LEFT." Her eyes widened and she shook her head slightly. "It was the hardest thing…I cried the whole way on the plane from here to Seattle…I just wasn't sure I was doing the right thing. When we got on the cruise and every day out there, I was miserable, until half way."

"What happened?" He sniffed and wiped the tears away with his free hand.

"I received the emails and photos of you, Sadie, Grace and Reilly grinning from your weekend wins! Buckles for all four of you and all-around for Grace!" She shook her head. "I just about threw a fit that I wasn't here to greet you on such a wonderful weekend." She squeezed his hand. "And the story and pictures of poor Rufio's leg…my goodness, one of my horses was hurt and I wasn't here. My heart just ached for him and Reilly."

She took a deep breath and let it go. "My sister and I called them my roses the whole trip." She chuckled. "All I did was talk about you kids and my dozen roses." She grinned at Wade which made his heart melt from the pride in her eyes. "I talked so much about you all, people started avoiding me." She giggled.

Suddenly Wade realized that she wasn't talking about leaving again.

"What does that mean?"

She looked at him with sincerity. "Half way out on the cruise I realized what I wanted. I will miss my husband, and feel that loss for the rest of my life, no matter where I am." She took a deep breath and exhaled quickly. "But I have talked to the Trio and convinced them that the last two weeks was just a vacation and I was ready to come back to work."

"You're not leaving again?" His voice rose, his heart hoped.

"Like you said when the Trio hired me, Wes would be very happy that I had a new family. And, I know, that he would be very upset that I left them."

"You're really not leaving?"

"Never again, you are my family; human and horse." She turned and looked at Cooper and Dollar who had their heads over their doors watching the two of them. "I couldn't imagine being away from here again."

"I've missed you so much," His voice quivered, his insides relaxing in relief. "I don't know what it's like to have a grandmother…but I always imagined it's the way I've always felt about you."

They stood and embraced, both letting the tears fall.

"Well," She wiped away her tears and smiled at him. "I heard you won at the rodeo I missed. How did this week go?"

Wade grinned, the answer in his eyes.

"Oh, you won! Three in a row!" She beamed in pride. "Well, next time, in two weeks I've been told, I'm going to be there in person to see you win the fourth."

"You're going with us?" Wade asked in surprise. She had only gone to the Winchester rodeo which was close to home.

She slid her arm through his and they walked out of the barn.

"I've decided that I will miss Wes anywhere, so I might as well get out in the world and enjoy my new family…horse and human." She laughed, making Wade sigh. She was home and happier than ever.

CHAPTER TWELVE

Friday night, Cora placed more biscuits on the table for the very happy family as well as Tessa and Alex.

"You may be a dingo, but I'm still going to call you and Scarecrow my golden girls." She told Sadie.

"As long as you don't call me a blonde headed pip-squeak, I'm OK with that." Sadie grinned then looked nervously to her parents.

Neither said a word or acknowledged the statement as Cora burst out in laughter.

Wade's heart warmed at the happiness that radiated from her…it was a different kind of happy…a contented happiness. He glanced around and saw that everyone else felt it, too.

"Well, tomorrow's the big day." Aunt Dru smiled around the dinner table. "Everyone ready?"

The dinner chatter began; everyone was excited for the clinic. Cora took her seat next to Wade and looked around at the family talking happily.

"You're home," Wade whispered, his heart ready to burst.

"I am," Her eyes twinkled of love.

###

Wade stepped out of the truck and looked at the sea of grey western shirts with the T3E logo and straw cowboy hats walking towards The Stables. It was 7:30 in the morning and the clinic opened at 9:00. First thing on the agenda was a group picture in front of the buildings, but they had to wait for Jessup to arrive from the ranch.

Wade felt like bouncing like Reilly, as they waited for the foreman. It was the first time that Alex and Jessup would meet. He turned and grinned at Alex.

"What?" Alex asked excited and confused.

Wade shook his head then bounced when he saw the familiar ranch truck pull into the driveway with a trailer loaded with a couple of Andy's old horses, Harvey, Trooper, and Milo.

"Come on, Alex." Wade motioned for him then walked as fast as Alex's limp would allow them towards the truck and trailer.

Jessup turned and watched the two of them approach. He looked at Wade, then to Alex then back to Wade. Wade smiled and Jessup nodded. He understood, which made Wade relax.

As Jessup opened his door and stepped out of the truck, Wade turned to Alex.

"Remember when we first met and I said two of my best friends limp?"

Alex nodded and looked quizzically at Jessup.

"Well, one was Rooster and this is Jessup." Wade motioned to the older man then turned to him. "And this is my new friend Alex Elliot."

The two shook hands and nodded to each other.

"Skiing accident," Jessup informed Alex.

Alex's eyes grew wide as he looked up at the man. "You ski?"

"I did…once." Jessup grinned with a wink and Alex burst out laughing.

"Mine isn't as cool as a skiing accident, it's just growing issues." Alex told him as they limped to the back of the trailer together.

Wade caught himself smiling at two of his best friends as they got to know each other.

The horses were quickly taken to their respective corrals so the pictures could be taken. Wade lined up between Alex and Cora, Jessup stood right behind him. He stood proudly for the picture.

Next were individual pictures of everyone with horses. Wade had his picture taken with Dollar and Rooster, then Alex was taken with Rooster, then both boys and red horses were taken together.

By the time pictures were done, the first car drove in the parking lot.

They were friends of Tessa and Alex so the mother and son walked the young couple and their son around the horses. Wade watched as the boy, he guessed around six-years-old, stood with his arms tightly around himself, his hand clutched his shirt and his eyes were staring at the ground. Alex used his hands low and in front of the boy's face to encourage him to follow as he led him right to Rooster.

The boy's head slowly rose and he stared at the horse. Rooster turned his nose to the boy and stretched it towards him. The boy's hand reached out and touched the tip of the horse's nose. He wiggled his fingers then touched Rooster again.

Alex turned excited eyes at the boy's family, they were staring in amazement.

Wade didn't know what the boy's story was, but from the look of the boy's face and the parent's reaction… Rooster made a difference, for the good. There was something special about that red horse.

Wade grinned and turned to see more cars arrive. Soon, The Stables were buzzing with kids and families coming to enjoy the horses.

Uncle Grayson was helping a young boy in a wheelchair throw a rope at the calf head. Grace was showing a young girl how to hold the rope and swing it. Lucas was kneeling down in front of a young boy, who wore a neck brace. He was talking in an exaggerated Australian accent making the boy laugh. Jessup was getting a girl lined up in front of a bale to throw. Wade's dad waved to him.

"Run and get some water bottles to refill the cooler." He yelled out to Wade.

Wade turned and headed towards the first stable building that held the supplies. He passed a teenager, about Reilly's age, that was leaning against the building staring into the distance. Wade quickly glanced at the direction the he was looking and only saw The Tagger Herd. Reilly, Candace and his mom had Scarecrow, Arcturus, and Little Ghost haltered and held them so the kids could pet them. The rest of the horses were hanging over the fence watching all the commotion.

He looked back to the teenager. There was something about the way he was looking at the horses that made Wade watch him carefully. After he dropped off the water with his dad, Wade stood to the side and just watched the teenager. The boy didn't move…he just stared at the horses.

Wade needed to do something; the boy looked lonely and a little lost. He turned and looked at the roping area. He wasn't needed yet, so, taking a deep breath to calm his nerves and strengthen his courage he walked toward the teenager.

"Hi," Wade said as he got closer.

The teenager's eyes flickered to Wade and widened worriedly, then shifted looking for a direction to move.

"It's OK." Wade smiled, trying to keep his stomach from shaking nervously. "I'm Wade Tagger. I saw you looking at the horses, would you like to meet them?"

The boy had taken a step away but hesitated, looking apprehensively between Wade and the horses.

"It's OK," Wade repeated. "Which one do you like the most? Lots of people go off of color, but others might like a long mane or a gentle eye."

"A gentle eye?" The boy looked confused.

Wade smiled and his insides relaxed. "Yeah, come look." They walked to the fence together. It was then that Wade noticed the boy was missing his entire left arm. Wade's throat constricted, but he just smiled and introduced the teenager to the horses.

Cooper, Buttercup, and Eli stuck their noses in the two boy's faces as soon as they got close enough. The teenager started laughing as he gently pushed them away.

"Do they always do that?" The loneliness in his eyes was replaced by enjoyment.

"This group and the red one over there," Wade pointed to Rooster who was giving a little girl a ride with Alex leading him. "They are known as the Tagger Herd. We rescued them from starvation a couple years ago, so they've basically been hand raised. They are pretty friendly."

"They look really good." The boy continued to pet the three horses like he'd never seen one before.

"My cousin Nikki, she's got the long dark hair over there, with the little cream colt and red pony, she is an equine nutritionist...or something like that." Wade chuckled. "She does all the feeding programs plus we do rodeos and horse shows with them so they get a lot of exercise. Then there's the ranch."

"You do a lot with them. Is that where you got that buckle?"

Wade grinned proudly, "I won it a couple weeks ago, I'm up to three now. Have you ever been around horses?"

"Just when I was little. I saw the article in the paper and thought I'd come out and see them." He looked around at all the people and kids. "Am I too old?"

"No age limit here and you can never be too old for horses." Wade chuckled; he could see the boy relax. "I'm Wade."

"I'm Vic."

"You want to ride one?"

Vic's eye got wide and he shook his head. "I can't."

"Why?"

"My arm."

"What about it? You don't need two arms to ride, you just have to make sure you have the right horse."

Vic stared at him then looked longingly toward the horses. Cooper and Eli had walked off but Buttercup had come over to check for treats.

"Here," Wade pulled a few treats from his shirt pocket and showed him how to hold them and feed Buttercup.

Vic grinned as the horse's soft muzzle tickled his hand as she took the treat.

"Want to ride?" Wade repeated. He could see the boy wanted to.

Vic's nod was so slight that Wade nearly missed it.

"Which one? I'd say the only one that wouldn't work with one arm is Buttercup…the one you just gave the treat to."

"How about that tan one?" Vic pointed towards Eli.

"Good eye!" Wade grinned and received a genuine excited smile in return. "That's Eli. He's been trained by my uncle who is also my roping coach and THE best horse trainer ever."

Wade looked over at the roping area. They were packed with kids.

"I have to get back to the roping, but follow me."

Vic followed him to Matt and Nick. Both men agreed to help Vic ride.

"Thanks, Wade." Vic smiled…his whole demeanor was completely changed from when Wade first saw him. Horses will do that to you.

"They'll take care of you." Wade nodded and jogged back to the roping section.

An hour later, Wade looked down to the Tagger Herd and saw Vic still riding Eli. Nick was giving him riding lessons.

It reminded him of the first time he met Alex just over a month before. Wade turned to look at his friend who was leading a small girl riding on Milo. Alex was grinning and nodding at the girl, who started giggling and threw her arms in the air then started patting the riding helmet she was wearing. Her mother laughed as she held her daughter on the horse. The young girl's wheelchair was sitting by the gate.

Wade did a quick look around; there were smiles and laughter everywhere.

"What are you doing?" His dad's voice pulled him out of his haze.

"Just looking at how it's going." Wade smiled up at him.

"It's going better than we ever hoped."

"I agree."

"Look at your mother." He pointed.

His mom had Little Ghost in a halter standing next to a makeshift shelf that held the multitude of trophies that the horse had won in cow cutting. A young girl smiled shyly as she traced the scars on the horse's side as his mom spoke to her. The girl had a burn scar down the side of her face and neck that disappeared into her shirt just to reappear on the arm just under the shirt sleeve.

"Who would have ever thought the little injured and starving grey horse we carried on a canvas would survive to give a little girl hope and inspiration like that?" His dad whispered with a sense of wonder in his eyes.

Wade and his dad looked at each other, smiled, and walked back to the roping session.

He spent the next couple hours showing kids how to throw ropes and talking about his belt buckle, which seemed to fascinate the kids.

He was relieved when they started taking turns for lunch, his body was aching and he needed aspirin.

Cora handed Wade a bottle of water to drink, "This is just fantastic, I am so glad I got back for this."

He nodded as he drank the entire bottle like Nick always did.

He turned and looked down at the horses where Nick and Matt were still being kept company by Vic. Wade chuckled. He sure hoped it was a good thing or his ex-uncle and cousin would never let him hear the end of it.

"I gotta check on something," Wade hugged her quickly as Candace and Aunt Leah arrived in the lunch area. "I'll be right back."

All three were smiling when he arrived.

"Having a good day?" Wade turned to Vic.

"Yes!" Vic grinned, all sign of the loneliness gone. "Do you know who The One Arm Bandit is?"

Wade was surprised by his question, he sure didn't expect that. "He's a rodeo entertainer."

"Yeah! Nick showed me videos of him riding horses onto trucks and trailers and he had buffalo! Nick said he met him at the rodeos when he was riding bulls."

Wade glanced at Nick who just nodded with a slight smile.

"See, I told you. You didn't need both arms to ride." Wade looked thankful at his cousin and ex-uncle.

"Boy were you right!" Vic looked at Eli out in the pasture. "He's the best horse ever. Nick and Matt showed me how to tell him what I wanted with my legs instead of the reins, I was even trotting on him."

"You'll gallop next time." Matt encouraged.

"I was just nervous." Vic admitted shyly. "I didn't really expect to ride today."

"That's Wade's specialty." Nick grinned.

Wade just smiled and shrugged.

"Paige looks like she's having fun," Wade said to Candace as they sat alone at a small table in the supply barn eating their lunch. Paige and Aunt Leah were chatting and smiling as they served lunch to those workers taking a break.

"She is," Candace's blond curls bounced as she nodded, her brown eyes shining. "She was really excited about coming here today to help."

"So what's the deal?" Wade asked, being more direct than normal, but he was tired of not knowing.

Candace's head started to drop.

"Chin up." They said in unison, then chuckled at each other.

"My parents are in jail." Candace whispered.

Wade's jaw dropped in shock. "Why?"

Candace frowned, "Secret?"

"Of course." He nodded and looked around them to make sure they wouldn't be overheard.

"They abandoned me and Lola at the rodeo grounds. Nora, Nikki, and Lucas came and rescued me."

"Dang, Candace." Wade shook his head in amazement. "Why are you telling me now?"

Candace shrugged. "You never asked me before."

Wade smiled at her, geez if that was all it took, he would have asked a long time ago.

"I can see why you like Nikki. Are you going to live with her?"

"I don't know. We go to court next week."

"What do you want? Do you want to go with Paige?"

"I'm just not sure what to ask for." She sighed. "The child protective lady said they would consider what I wanted."

"How are you going to decide?"

She shook her head making the curls sway. "Aunt Paige has done so much. She even moved from an apartment to a house with a horse pasture for Lola."

"Wow. She must really love you. She MUST want you to go live with her if she did that."

She nodded. "She said that even if I go live with Nikki, full time, she would keep the place so I can bring Lola on visits. Plus, she'll still do shows with me."

"Why wouldn't you go live with her then, if she's willing to do all that for you?"

Candace sighed. "But Nikki wants me too, and Nora…"

"But Paige is your family."

"I know."

"Does she have any other family?"

She shook her head. "Two sisters, she was married once a long time ago, but she traveled with her work and never found anyone again. No kids."

Like Paige said, when he was eaves dropping at Cora's party, it would have wrapped the whole family thing together if she and Nick had gotten together.

"Candace?" He turned and looked at her seriously. "Why would you choose Nikki over your aunt? Your own family…that obviously wants you?"

Tears sprung to her eyes, making Wade feel bad. "Nikki's done so much. I would have died out there!"

"That's not the reason to choose her…for the rest of your life." Wade argued. "What did Nikki say?"

"She said that she wouldn't let me go anywhere unless she knew I was going to be loved and taken care of." Candace wiped away a tear.

"Paige is obviously doing that. She changed her whole life for you…to take care of you…and Lola."

She nodded and sighed. "I don't want to upset Nikki."

"So you really want to go with your aunt?"

Candace stared at him, her eyes wide. "I think I do. I didn't realize that."

Wade smiled, "Sometimes you just have to talk it out."

He looked up to see his mother motioning for him.

"I have to go," He stood. "Nikki loves you and only wants what's best for you. Your aunt loves you…and wants you."

Candace stood with a smile. "Thank you, Wade." And before he knew what was happening she leaned in and gave him a kiss on the cheek.

"Geez, Candace." He giggled and blushed.

"You'll be my friend for life!" She laughed and nearly skipped out of the building.

Wade watched her leave, then looked around to see if anyone saw the kiss. His mother was watching him with an amused look.

"Don't tell anyone!" He blushed again.

She shook her head with a laugh. "Go relieve Grace so she can come eat."

Heading back to the roping area, Wade stopped at the registration desk. "How's it going?"

"Just fantastic," Tessa answered, she looked tired and exhilarated at the same time. "The kids are all leaving either sound asleep from exhaustion or with grins on their faces." Tessa sighed.

"Except the ones that are crying because they didn't want to leave the horses." Nora sighed. "But they all clutch the posters and gift bags with a death grip. Next year we should do T-shirts!"

Wade stared at his sister as she spoke, pride rose in him as he remembered that this was her idea. He wished he hadn't made the promise to keep it secret. She deserved to be recognized for this. It was a shame some kids could be so mean that she would want to keep it a secret.

"Wade, why are you staring?" Nora tilted her head slightly.

"Just looking at my sister, who looks like she's having a great time." He smiled, trying to tell her with his eyes how proud he was.

Her eyes glistened and she nodded slightly. She knew.

"I gotta get back." He smiled at the guests that were talking with Tessa and playing with Mavis and Bart.

"Have fun!" Nora called out as he walked away.

Halfway to the roping area, a sharp pain shot through his hip instantly bringing tears to his eyes. He stopped and took a deep breath. Another step, another shot of pain ran down is entire leg making his toes tingle. What was he supposed to do now?

CHAPTER THIRTEEN

Taking a deep breath he took another step, no pain. He gently took step after step after step. He made it to Dr. Mark and Cora who were busy at the educational area. They had four kids with families standing around listening to the veterinarian and accepting the posters from Cora.

Wade kept walking, with each step he was expecting the pain to return.

He made it to the roping area and took over for Grace. There was no more pain as he helped his dad, uncle, Jessup and Lucas with the kids until Grace returned.

"Wade, head over to Bodi and Milo. Give Sadie a break." Uncle Grayson told him.

He nodded and jogged over to the little horses.

"How's it going here?" He asked Nikki after Sadie left.

"The kids love Bodi, he's so adorable." Nikki answered her brown eyes glistening with pride. "Then there's Milo, who's barely had a break today."

"Say the word."

Wade looked quizzically at Nikki then turned to see who said it.

There was a man with a small boy in his arms. The boy had a mass of blonde curls framing his face and highlighting a large pair of happy blue eyes.

"Say the word," The man repeated to the boy.

The boy closed his eyes. His lips formed a circle that wiggled from side to side as he said the word. "Ho..r..se."

"Very good!" The man cheered animatedly.

The little boy smiled and looked proudly at Nikki and Wade. They grinned in return, even though they didn't know what was going on.

The man turned to Nikki and Wade. "Hi, this is Jeremy and I'm…" He turned back to the boy. "What is my name?"

The boy stared at him. Wade could tell he was thinking really hard.

"G..a...r...y." The boy grinned at his accomplishment.

"Yes!" Gary gave the boy a high five then turned happily to Wade and Nikki. "Jeremy would like to pet the…" He looked at the boy.

Jeremy closed his eyes, "Ho..r..se." When he opened his eyes, he smiled at Wade. Wade's heart melted as he looked into the blue cheerful eyes.

"Absolutely," Nikki smiled, her voice soft and soothing. She had melted too.

Wade pulled his eyes from the boy and untied Milo from the fence and walked him to the man and boy.

Jeremy's eyes widen as he got closer and his head started bobbing. Wade was confused until he realized the boy was bobbing his head to Milo's hoof beats.

"We use music to help with his speech cadence." Gary explained. "I'm a speech therapist."

"That's fantastic." Nikki smiled. "I've read you can use the horse's hoof beats to help with the cadence. Can he sit on Milo while Wade walks him around?"

Gary's eyebrows rose. "Yes! I was hoping to try that out. I'm pleased you've heard of it so I didn't have to explain."

"I'm starting a horse rehabilitation business, so I've read a lot about equine and equine-assisted human therapy. Hippotherapy is very interesting." Nikki explained.

Wade looked at his cousin, completely impressed with her.

Nikki knelt before him and carefully put the riding helmet on the boy.

"How old are you?" She asked the excited child.

Jeremy looked up at Gary with a devious smile then looked at Nikki and held up three fingers.

Gary chuckled, "Use your words, Jeremy."

The boy rolled his eyes with a smile. "Th…r…ee."

"Very good," Nikki smiled at him. The boy reached up with both hands and lightly touched the sides of her face.

Wade could see his cousins' eyes shine. She was thoroughly enthralled with the boy.

"My name is Nikki." Her voice was light and airy.

Leaving his hands on her cheeks, "N…i…kk..i" He said matching her gentle tone.

She grinned and received a happy giggle in return.

Jeremy's whole body was shaking in excitement as Gary placed him on Milo's saddle. Wade beamed at him.

"My name is Wade." He said, pronouncing every syllable carefully like Gary did.

The boy squinted his eyes as he stared at him, "Wa…de." The boy smiled sweetly.

Wade returned his smile, his body seemed to relax just looking at the cheerful boy and his twinkling eyes.

"This is Milo." Wade pointed to the red pony.

Jeremy leaned forward, petting the horse just in front of the saddle. His grin lit up the world when he looked at Wade then to

Gary and Nikki. Gary positioned himself next to the horse to hold onto Jeremy, then nodded to Wade.

Wade carefully pulled Milo into a walk and moved into the round pen away from all other riders. He looked back to see one of the happiest expressions he'd ever seen. Jeremy was moving his body with the cadence of the horse's hoof beats.

"Stop for a minute, Wade." Gary instructed.

Wade stopped and turned.

"Jeremy, say Milo." Gary instructed.

Jeremy stared at Gary, "Mi…Lo."

"Say it again." He said softly.

"Mi…Lo." Jeremy nodded still staring at Gary. He seemed to understand this was a therapy session.

Gary nodded at Wade so he started Milo walking.

"Say Milo and repeat to the rhythm." Gary started bouncing his body to Milo's cadence.

Jeremy rocked his body in the saddle.

"Mi…Lo." Jeremy said a syllable to every other hoof beat. Wade found himself repeating it silently with the boy.

Mi…pause…Lo…pause…Mi…pause…Lo …pause.

Two circles around with Jeremy repeating the word, he was saying a syllable with the first two hoof beats in the cadence and a pause with the third and fourth beat in the cadence.

Mi…Lo…pause…pause…Mi…Lo…pause…pause.

"I think that's good for today." Gary said with pride. "You did very good." They high fived.

Jeremy clapped his hands excitedly and grinned at Wade then over to Nikki as they approached her.

"You did so good." Nikki clapped as they reached her.

Jeremy nodded, to the rhythm of the horse, his smile jubilant.

Gary lifted the boy off the saddle and set him on the ground.

Nikki smiled at the boy as she knelt down and took off the helmet and releasing the mass of blonde curls. "You are adorable."

Jeremy's eyes twinkled as he nodded at her, which made them all laugh.

Milo lowered his head down next to Jeremy. The boy turned and placed a hand on each side of the horse's face and kissed his nose, then lay his cheek on top of it, resting peacefully. Milo didn't move.

"You just slay me." Gary shook his head in wonder and lifted the boy into his arms.

Jeremy laughed and wrapped his arms around the man's neck.

Gary sighed and smiled at Wade and Nikki. "Thank you."

"It was totally our pleasure!" Wade said excitedly, finally breaking out of the trance the boy had put him in. The sound of the clinic assaulted his ears.

"Please call me," Nikki handed Gary her business card. "Let's do this again."

"I would love to," Gary stuck the card in his pocket and retrieved one of his own and handed it to her. "I have a couple other clients that could use this therapy too."

Sadie had returned and was showing Bodi to the line of kids waiting to ride Milo.

"I'll let you get back to your clinic." Gary looked at the line. "Jeremy, tell Wade goodbye."

Jeremy smiled at Wade and closed his shining blue eyes; "Goo...d...bye." He opened his eyes and looked at Nikki, then closed his eyes. "Ni...kk..i. Goo...d...bye." He opened his eyes wide and happy.

"Goodbye, Jeremy." Wade and Nikki said in unison and waved as they walked away.

"Mi...lo." Jeremy waved at the horse, his blonde curls swaying and blue eyes sparkling.

They watched the man and boy disappear into the crowd then turned to each other.

"Wow," Nikki shook her head in amazement; a hand on her chest.

"I agree," Wade grinned. "That was awesome."

A hand rested on his shoulder and he looked up to see Aunt Leah. Without a word she held out the camera she was holding and turned the viewer to them.

She had captured the moment Jeremy had kissed Milo's nose and when he had laid his cheek on top of the kiss. His eyes shone and his gentle smile said it all. Heaven!

"How's it going?" Jack asked as Wade was walking to Alex and Aunt Dru.

"Long day." Wade smiled happily.

"I think I've just about talked myself out today." Jack nodded in agreement. "This was a whole lot more than we expected. I'm glad we stocked up more water than what we thought we needed."

"Seems like it's winding down though."

"It's 5:30, we were supposed to be done at 5:00. We probably won't be done until 6:30, then there's the cleanup."

"I'm hungry." Wade admitted. "I could go for some pizza and a beer."

Jack laughed. "I'll go for the pizza and beer too, but a root beer for you."

"Sounds good." Wade shrugged with a smirk.

"I'll go order the pizzas and have them delivered. You tell Dru."

"Happy to," Wade answered.

There were still two kids in line to ride Rooster when Wade joined his aunt and Alex.

Aunt Dru was walking a boy around the arena on Rooster. Alex was sitting on a bale of straw talking with the parents of the three kids.

"This is Wade!" Alex's eyes brightened when he saw him.

The parents turned and greeted Wade with a surprised expression.

"They follow the Tagger Herd on Facebook." Alex explained. "They've been following Rooster since before his surgery!"

The parents nodded.

The mother shocked Wade as she gave him a big hug. "Bless you and your family for everything you did for these horses." She released him with a grin. "I saw they were going to be here today and just had to come see them in person."

"Thank you, ma'am." Wade said, a little in shock.

"We spent the last hour over with the rest of the herd…the line for Rooster was just tremendous!" The husband said in amazement.

"Our son, who's riding Rooster now, is deaf." The mother looked out at the smiling boy. "Dru was so nice, she said the other two kids could ride him, too."

"Well, of course, ma'am." Wade smiled out at his aunt. The boy looked around eight-years-old and he was smiling at Aunt Dru like she was a queen.

"You wouldn't happen to have any pictures or posters of Rooster that you're giving away do you? We'll buy one! They would love to have one to take home." The mother asked with hopeful eyes.

Wade looked at her in surprise, he'd never thought anyone would want a picture of his horse.

"Well, we don't, but we could have one taken with him and your family and send to you." Wade offered and was surprised at her overjoyed reaction.

"Oh yes, please!" She said happily. "We've watched him grow on Facebook. The pictures of you riding and roping on him…he is such an inspiration."

When the kids were done riding, Aunt Leah took their picture with Rooster who posed proudly, head held high. The whole family got in the picture then drug Wade in with them. He was sure his face was red with embarrassment in the final photo.

As the family left, which officially closed the clinic, Wade looked up at his aunt.

"It was like that all day." She sighed, exhausted but happy.

"They all loved Rooster." Alex agreed, still sitting on the bale. "You need to do posters of him next year."

"I never thought of that." Wade shook his head, still amazed.

"Me either, but his imperfection just made the kids, and parents, love him. They just couldn't get enough of him." Aunt Dru said with a big sigh as she looked over at the stable. "Pizza?"

"Oh, I forgot to tell you Jack was ordering a bunch for everyone." Wade told her.

"That's why I love that man." She grinned at him.

"I'll let you love him…but it was my idea." Wade teased.

"That's why I love you." She hugged him and looked down at Alex. "And after today? I'm lovin' on you a bit, too."

Alex blushed and chuckled, "Don't tell Jack."

They all three laughed until Alex leaned sideways to stretch his back.

"Are you OK?" Wade asked Alex. His friend had sat on the bale since he got there.

"My back is tired," Alex admitted. "We did a lot of walking."

"That we did," Aunt Dru nodded. "I'll get some hay to Rooster. We can clean up tomorrow."

"Stay there Alex, I'll be right back." Wade told him and headed for the barn.

Wade pushed the wheelbarrow towards his friend who laughed.

"Seriously?" Alex snorted.

"Why not?" Wade helped him get in.

"Perfect!" Aunt Dru nodded.

She took one handle and Wade took the other and they rolled the laughing Alex into the building.

Tessa's expression was of humor and concern at the same time. "Are you OK? Back sore?" She asked as she handed him pizza and a bottle of root beer.

Alex nodded. "It just needs rest."

"Mine, too." Jessup took a seat next to the very pleased Alex. "I'm going to have to go to the chiropractor Monday."

"Therapist for me. Mom figured I'd need it and already booked the appointment." Alex nodded with a grin. "But it was worth it."

"I agree with you on that one." Jessup said as they clinked their beer and root beer bottles together.

Wade looked around the building full of tired but happy friends and family.

He thought of the first guest, the boy Alex introduced to Rooster...to the last guest, the family that had followed Rooster on Facebook for years. There were so many faces...Vic and Jeremy included.

This family and friends around him, volunteering their time and effort to do this...

"Wade?" His mother sat down next to him. Nora and his dad sat opposite of him. "Are you OK?

"It was such a great day." Wade nodded, his voice constricting from emotion.

"It was one of the best days I've ever had." His mom smiled.

"Absolutely." His dad nodded.

Wade looked at Nora. It just wasn't fair…everyone should know this was because of her. The lives they had touched that day…everyone should know. She turned and looked at him, smiled happily, and shook her head slowly. She knew what he was thinking and still wouldn't let him tell everyone. He wouldn't…he'd promised…a secret forever…it just wasn't fair.

CHAPTER FOURTEEN

"Why not?"

"Because I don't need it, Wade." Nora explained. "We know…that's all that matters."

Wade looked up at the ceiling. He returned to his bedroom after breakfast and splayed his body across the bed, letting it rest.

Nora was lounging in the chair with her feet resting on his bed. She still had bed head with her long tangled hair hanging down past her shoulders.

"It was a group thing."

"No it wasn't"

Nora rolled her eyes in humor, "It was a group effort to put it on, especially as fast as we did. Everyone involved with Tagger Enterprises and the clinic deserves the credit."

Wade agreed with that, so he just sighed and stared at the unchanging ceiling.

"Why are you just lying there?"

"My body hurts." He finally said it out loud.

"I'm sure everyone's does after yesterday. I'm exhausted. I don't ever remember talking so much…or smiling."

"No, Nora." He turned his head and looked at her intently, it was time to get it out…to stop the pain. "Mine has hurt for months."

She tilted her head and frowned at him. "What do you mean?"

"It means, I HURT. All the time, everyday… sometimes it feels like every minute."

She leaned forward, her feet hitting the floor with a thud.

"Are you sick?"

"I don't know."

"Have you talked to Mom and Dad?" Her voice was low and dark brown eyes concerned.

"No. I haven't talked to anyone about it."

"Why not?"

He turned and looked back at the ceiling. "I don't know…just too scared I guess."

She was out the door before he could turn his head to look at her.

He stared at the door and waited…he knew she was headed for their parents. A nervous sinking feeling settled in his stomach. No matter how bad it was…it couldn't be worse than anything the kids he met and saw yesterday had gone through. If they could brave through it, he would too.

It didn't take long before all three walked in the door looking concerned.

"Nora said you hurt." His mother sat on the edge of the bed and lay her head on his forehead.

Wade chuckled, "I don't have a fever, Mom."

"Then what is it, Buddy." His dad pulled the chair closer to the bed, sat and leaned towards him. His blue eyes looked darker when he was worried.

"I don't know. I just hurt all the time." Wade looked between his parents.

"Muscles, bones, joints…?" His dad asked.

"It could be one…or all." Wade shrugged. "Most of the time it's after roping or when we've been doing a lot…like yesterday."

"Did you have problems yesterday?" His mom was gripping his hand tightly.

Wade told them about the previous day and all the days before. They listened quietly, their expressions showing their worry.

"I've been living off of aspirin," He admitted. "Probably more than I should."

"Why didn't you tell us?" Nora asked.

Wade sighed, "I just didn't want to worry everyone but it's lasted so long. Then I got nervous about it so I started looking up the symptoms on the medical websites." He rolled his eyes, "That REALLY scared me."

"Why didn't you just tell us?" His mother asked, a bit of irritation in her voice.

"I honestly was too scared to know." He tried to say he was sorry with his eyes.

His dad shook his head. "So you decided to just let it build up…the hurt and terror?"

"Yeah…I guess so." Wade started to feel a mixture of stupidity against himself and guilt for what he was doing to his family.

"What made you finally decide to tell us?" His mom asked.

"Yesterday…all the kids and what they've gone through." He felt the emotion swelling. "There was this little boy named Jeremy. He has some sort of speech problem, I don't know why, but he was just the happiest boy even though he had that problem." Wade swallowed hard. "Then this kid named Vic, he was missing his left arm. I left him with Matt, Nick and Eli for just a couple hours, and he went from frightened and lonely to…just happy and ready to ride even if he was missing an arm."

His dad nodded, "Nick and Matt told us about him…said he was headed home to ask his parents for a horse. Grayson got the call this morning. They want to hire him to find and train a horse for their son…a horse like Eli."

Wade nodded, "And all those kids had gone through so much…but I was scared just to find out what was wrong." He glanced between his parents and sister. "I kinda feel like a coward now."

His mom shook her head and sighed, "You're not a coward, Wade. You'd be surprised at how common that is."

"But, delaying the diagnosis, delays the medical attention and could make things worse if not fatal." His dad frowned.

Wade's eyes grew wide…fatal!

"Sorry," His dad said quickly. "I don't believe it's fatal." He sat back in the chair and stared at Wade, thinking. He turned to Nora; "Go get Grayson."

She turned and ran out the door.

"What can Grayson do?" His mom asked.

"I have an idea of what it might be." He tried to assure them. "Have you taken any aspirin today?"

"Not yet. There's a bottle under my mattress next to the table." He admitted; drowning in embarrassment.

"To the point you're hiding it?" Her eyes opened wide. "Don't do that! You have to come talk to us when you have problems, don't rely on websites."

His uncle walked in the room, followed by Aunt Leah, Aunt Dru, and Jack.

"You can't expect something like this to be going on with one of our kids and not have all of us here." Aunt Leah smiled gently.

Wade chuckled. Just having them all there made him feel better. "We can go down in the library." He started to rise.

"No, you just lay there and let us hover over you." His uncle chuckled but with concerned eyes.

"OK." Wade settled back on the bed and looked around the group of them.

His dad told the group what Wade's symptoms were. "Didn't you deal with something like this?" He asked Uncle Grayson.

His uncle nodded; "Nearly identical; have one that numbed your toes?"

"Yesterday." Wade nodded in amazement that he would know.

His uncle smiled. "I dealt with them for three or four months at a stretch, twice. Once when I was around eight and the other in junior high…your age."

"What was it?" Wade's mom asked.

Uncle Grayson shrugged with one shoulder. "They called them growing pains but said that didn't mean it was caused by my actual growing. But I grew four inches that summer just before 7th grade and another three over the winter."

"Seven inches in a year?" Wade's jaw dropped. "That does sound painful."

"And he was a bean pole." Aunt Dru chuckled.

"I've lost a lot of weight." Wade nodded.

"We noticed that." His mom said.

"Really? I didn't think anyone noticed." Wade turned to her.

"We noticed that and the fact that you've grown a few inches this summer." His dad told him. "You've just been so height conscience that we just decided not to say anything."

"I just figured you were all too busy." Wade relaxed back into his pillow.

"Too busy to notice that I am now, officially, the shortest person in this entire family?" His mom laughed. "You've caught up with Nora."

Wade was shocked, he hadn't noticed.

"Pretty soon, you'll catch back up with Sadie." Aunt Leah informed him. "And probably Grace. Sadie may end up taller than her, too."

Wade looked at his mom and smiled. "It works for you, Mom, but I don't want to be short." They all laughed.

"It works perfect for you, Tink." His dad winked at his smiling wife.

Wade looked at Uncle Grayson. "You mean I won't be short forever?"

He shook his head. "No, you've got a few years yet to grow and in between the growing spurts, you'll put the weight back on."

"Spurts…" Wade looked at Jack. "You told me about those before."

Jack nodded. "I believe that was the night before Rooster's surgery."

Wade exhaled loudly, his heart suddenly hurt, and his hand came up to rest over the top. He felt the tears rising.

"Wade?" His parents said in concern.

"Rooster," Wade looked at them with sad eyes. "If I grow and put weight on…I can't ride him anymore."

His mother gripped his hand tightly, understanding his emotions. "It may only be a couple more months…"

Wade nodded and exhaled a shaky breath. "I knew this day would come… I didn't want to be short…but I didn't want to have to stop riding Rooster."

"Be thankful for the time you've had and the next couple months." Aunt Dru said softly. "He was a huge hit yesterday."

Wade nodded. "He'll still have purpose."

"Of course, he will." Aunt Dru agreed. "Alex will be able to ride him for a while, and there's Sadie and Nora."

Nora nodded encouragingly. "The doctor said I was done growing in height, so as long as I stay skinny I can ride him."

Wade grinned; "You have Isaiah and Arcturus and now Cooper to work with, Rooster would make four."

She sighed, "I'll try, Wade."

"I know, but I got a couple months…maybe." He looked at Uncle Grayson. "How did you stop hurting?"

"They eventually just stopped, but I took a lot of hot baths after we did anything strenuous, like roping or football." He answered.

Wade smiled and looked at his Aunt Dru.

He didn't even have to say anything, she just laughed. "Of course you can use my Jacuzzi tub."

"How come you guys don't have one?" Nora looked at their dad and uncle.

"Because they didn't listen to their sister!" Aunt Leah and their mom said loudly.

"Huh?" Nora frowned.

"When they were designing the plumbing on the house, she said she wanted one and suggested they get one. But THEY didn't see the need for one, THEY just wanted them to be big, not necessarily have the water jets." Aunt Leah pouted at her husband.

Uncle Grayson smiled at Nora then Wade, "Probably the only time I regret NOT listening to her."

They all laughed.

"There's been more." Aunt Dru pointed out playfully.

"We would NEVER admit that." His dad grinned up at her from his chair.

Wade's mom squeezed his hand again. "We'll get you into the doctor tomorrow to make sure they are just growing pains, and see if they have anything to help. It's been thirty years since your uncle was your age, they might have come up with something by now." She chuckled.

"Hey!" Uncle Grayson glared at his sister-in-law with a glint in his eyes.

"Thanks, Mom." Wade smiled at the group, thankful he'd finally spoke up, but kicking himself that he didn't do it a long time before. He'd scared himself for no reason.

"Well, we're headed to The Stables at noon to start the cleanup and fetch the horses." His dad told him. "You want to just hang out here?"

"Oh, no." Wade sat up, his body feeling better already from the reduced stress he had been putting it under. "I'll go, I want to see Rooster."

"Soak in the tub first." His mom stood and his aunts and uncles walked out his bedroom door.

He heard running then laughter.

Wade's eyes opened wide and he looked at his dad, "They didn't!"

His dad just grinned, "I'm betting all four of them did. We're going to have to strengthen that banister."

"Well, let's do a family one then." His mom's eyes twinkled in mischief.

Wade quickly slid out of bed and joined his parents and Nora just outside his bedroom door. They took off at a run, then at the same time, jumped into a slide.

Wade raised the hose over the top of Rooster and let the water run down his back and haunches. Rooster shook, sending water flying back at him.

"Hey! I thought you liked this!" He wiped the water droplets from his grinning face.

Rooster just bounced his head.

He ran the water up the horse's neck then around to his chest. Then down to his front legs, under his belly and down his back legs.

Before Wade had a chance to move, the horse shook again, sprinkling him with water again.

"Rooster!" Wade chuckled. "I'd swear you're a dog most of the time."

The horse swung his head back and looked at him then swung it back in front.

"Is that your way of laughing?"

Rooster bounced his head.

"Yeah, that's what I thought." Wade chuckled.

"You're wetter than Rooster!" Sadie giggled as she ran the hose over Bodi's back.

"I know," Wade turned the water off to his hose. "He keeps shaking."

"He's a dog horse." Nora walked over and leaned against the building next to Alex who was watching them hose down the horses.

"That's what I told him." Wade ran the water squeegee down the horses back. Rooster leaned into him.

"Their stall is ready for them." Alex informed them.

Nora looked curiously toward Wade. "Didn't you go to the doctor today?"

He nodded.

"What'd he say?" Grace and Reilly asked in unison as they walked up to them.

"Just what Uncle Grayson said…growing pains." Wade answered and unhooked Rooster from the post. "Ready?" He asked Sadie.

She finished scraping the excess water off the little creamelo colt who had been standing patiently until his stable mate Rooster was walked away.

"Stay there." Sadie told Wade as the colt danced from side to side.

"Well, hurry up." Wade ran his hand down the horse' long nose. The horse's eyes half way closed as he warmed himself in the hot August sun.

Sadie quickly trotted Bodi to catch up with them while Reilly, Grace, Alex and Nora followed next to them.

They walked by the round corral and Wade looked in, Jack was training a horse. They walked past the smaller arena. There were a couple young girls on ponies getting riding lessons from Paul, the assistant manager.

The two large stables were on their left, Rooster's and Bodi's stalls were in the second building, across from the large arena…which was empty.

Wade smiled and headed for the open gate.

"What are you doing?" Nora turned confused eyes to him.

"You just washed him!" Grace laughed.

Wade shrugged, walked his wet horse into the arena and unhooked the halter. Rooster leaned over and rubbed his head on Wade's arm. They all laughed as Wade nearly fell over.

Rooster shook again and wandered out to the middle of the arena with his nose down, sniffing the ground.

The kids started counting…ten, nine, eight, seven, six, five, four, three, two, one… Rooster lay down and rolled…onto his side then all the way over, the dirt quickly turning to mud on his sides. The red horse slowly got up and turned to Wade and the kids then shook.

"I think he just said thank you." Alex giggled.

Wade grinned at Rooster. Ever since he could remember, he wanted to grow and be tall. Now…he'd give anything not to grow so he could ride his horse forever.

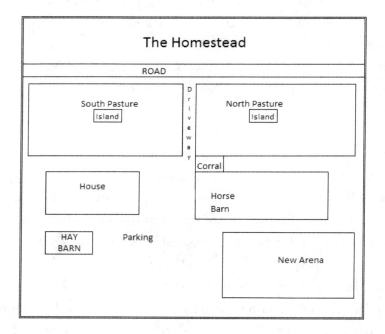

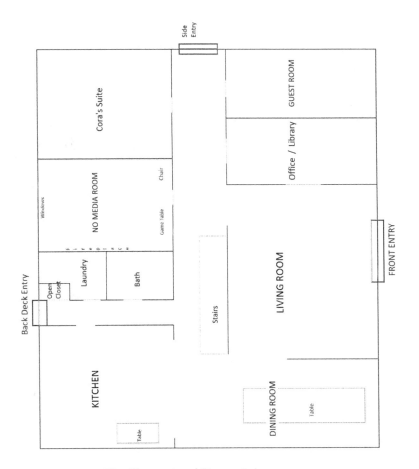

The Homestead Downstairs

The Homestead Upstairs

The Tagger Family

Drucilla
Nikki
Matt —— Nick

Grayson
Leah
Grace
Sadie

Scott
Jordan
Nora
Wade

Jessup: Tagger Ranch

Jack Morgan: The Stables
Reilly

Cora Smith: The Homestead

Tagger Property History:
Mathew and Grace
Anderson and Nora
Mathew and Anne
Grayson Mathew, Scott Anderson, Drucilla Anne

ABOUT THE AUTHOR

I was raised with Shetlands and ponies and have loved horses since I watched a Shetland colt born when I was four.

Growing up, the TV show Bonanza was my favorite. I loved that western life and wanted to be Little Joe and Hoss' little sister. I wanted to live at the Ponderosa. Watching rodeos on television and attending when I could, was the closest I could get to the cowboy way of life.

That changed when I purchased my first 'big horse' when I was twenty-one and living in Alaska. I now have the great-granddaughter of that horse in my pasture.

I am also a photographer specializing in the equine industry; shows, races, jackpots, and rodeos. With my photography, I create my own covers.

The Tagger Herd Series was my first venture into fictional writing and I love the family and horses in the series.

My first 'stand-alone' novel was Hoofbeats in the Wind which ventured into rodeo.

My next book, Coffee With Cowboys delved deeper into the rodeo world and researching for the book was an adventure. I have met wonderful people from fans, stock contractors, and competitors. I thank every one of them that have helped make that book a possibility. It will always be special to me because of the people I met.

Bijou Bay was inspired by Idaho's Black Rock Ranch and the a true story I was fortunate enough to be told.

Writing, researching, photography, my two dogs, Morgan and Tagger, and Kit in the pasture, fill my world and keep me busy.

CPSIA information can be obtained
at www.ICGtesting.com
Printed in the USA
BVHW031953230922
647846BV00011B/407

9 781733 952842